# The Moon Sister

## Tiggy's Story

Lucinda Riley was born in Ireland, and after an early career as an actress in film, theatre and television, wrote her first book aged twenty-four. Her books have been translated into over thirty languages and sold over fifteen million copies worldwide. She is a *Sunday Times* and *New York Times* best-selling author.

Lucinda is currently writing the Seven Sisters series, which tells the story of adopted sisters and is based allegorically on the mythology of the famous star constellation. The first three books, *The Seven Sisters*, *The Storm Sister* and *The Shadow Sister*, have all been No. 1 bestsellers across Europe, and the rights to a multi-season TV series have already been optioned by a Hollywood production company.

# The Moon Sister

## Tiggy's Story

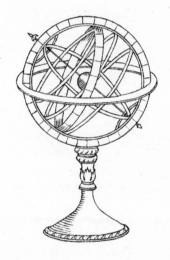

# LUCINDA RILEY

MACMILLAN

First published 2018 by Macmillan
an imprint of Pan Macmillan
20 New Wharf Road, London N1 9RR
Associated companies throughout the world
www.panmacmillan.com

ISBN 978-1-5098-4010-6

3 5 7 9 8 6 4 2

A CIP catalogue record for this book is available from the British Library.

Typeset by Palimpsest Book Production Ltd, Falkirk, Stirlingshire
Printed and bound by CPI Group (UK) Ltd, Croydon, CR0 4YY

Visit **www.panmacmillan.com** to read more about all our books
and to buy them. You will also find features, author interviews and
news of any author events, and you can sign up for e-newsletters
so that you're always first to hear about our new releases.

For Jacquelyn

Friend, helpmeet and sister in another life

*Be the change that you wish to see in the world.*
Mahatma Gandhi

# Cast of characters

## ATLANTIS

Pa Salt – *the sisters' adoptive father (deceased)*
Marina (Ma) – *the sisters' guardian*
Claudia – *housekeeper at Atlantis*
Georg Hoffman – *Pa Salt's lawyer*
Christian – *the skipper*

## THE D'APLIÈSE SISTERS

Maia
Ally (Alcyone)
Star (Asterope)
CeCe (Celaeno)
Tiggy (Taygete)
Electra
Merope (missing)

# Tiggy
## Inverness, Scotland
### November 2007

*European hedgehog*
*(Erinaceus europaeus)*
*'Hotchiwitchi' in the*
*British Romani language.*

*1*

'I remember exactly where I was and what I was doing when I heard my father had died.'

'I remember where I was too, when it happened to me.'

Charlie Kinnaird's penetrating blue gaze fell upon me.

'So, where were you?'

'At Margaret's wildlife sanctuary, shovelling up deer poo. I really wish it had been a better setting, but it wasn't. It's okay, really. Although . . .' I swallowed hard, wondering how on earth this conversation – or, more accurately, *interview* – had veered on to Pa Salt's death. I was currently sitting in a stuffy hospital canteen opposite Dr Charlie Kinnaird. Even as he'd entered, I'd noticed how his presence commanded attention. It wasn't just that he was strikingly handsome, with his slim, elegant physique clad in a well-tailored grey suit, and a head of wavy dark-auburn hair; he was simply someone who possessed a natural air of authority. Several of the hospital staff seated nearby had paused over their coffees to glance up and nod respectfully at him as he'd passed. When he'd reached me and held out his hand in greeting, a tiny electric shock had shot through my body. Now, as he sat opposite me, I watched those long fingers playing incessantly with the pager that lay between them, revealing an underlying level of nervous energy.

'"Although" what, Miss D'Aplièse?' Charlie prompted, his voice exhibiting a soft Scottish burr. I realised he was obviously not prepared to let me off the hook I was currently hanging myself on.

'Umm . . . I'm just not sure Pa's dead. I mean, of course he *is*, because he's gone and he'd never fake his death or anything – he'd know how much pain it would cause all his girls – but I just feel him around me all the time.'

'If it's any comfort, I think that reaction is perfectly normal,' Charlie responded. 'A lot of the bereaved relatives I speak to say they feel the presence of their loved ones around them after they've died.'

'Of course,' I said, feeling slightly patronised, although I had to remember it was a doctor I was talking to – someone who dealt with death and the loved ones it left behind every day.

'Funny, really,' he sighed as he picked up the pager from the melamine tabletop and began to turn it over and over in his hands. 'As I just mentioned, my own father died recently, and I'm plagued by what I can only describe as nightmare visions of him actually *rising* from the grave!'

'You weren't close then?'

'No. He may have been my biological father, but that's where our relationship began and ended. We had nothing else in common. You obviously did with yours.'

'Yes, although ironically my sisters and I were all adopted by him as babies, so there's no biological connection at all. But I couldn't have loved him more. Really, he was amazing.'

Charlie smiled at this. 'Well then, surely that just goes to prove that biology doesn't play a major part in whether we get on with our parents. It's a lottery, isn't it?'

'I don't think it is actually,' I said, deciding there was only one 'me' I could ever be, even in a job interview. 'I think we're given to each other for a reason, whether we're blood relatives or not.'

'You mean it's all predestined?' He raised a cynical eyebrow.

'Yes, but I know most people wouldn't agree.'

'Me included, I'm afraid. In my role as a cardiac surgeon, I have to deal on a daily basis with the heart, which we all equate with emotions and the soul. Sadly, I've been forced to view it as a lump of muscle – and an often malfunctioning one at that. I've been trained to see the world in a purely scientific way.'

'I think there's room for spirituality in science,' I countered. 'I had a rigorous scientific training too, but there are so many things that science hasn't yet explained.'

'You're right, but . . .' Charlie checked his watch. 'We seem to have wandered completely off track and I'm due in clinic in fifteen minutes. So, excuse me for getting back to business, but how much has Margaret told you about the Kinnaird estate?'

'That it's over forty thousand acres of wilderness, and you're looking for someone who knows about the indigenous animals who could inhabit it, wildcats in particular.'

'Yes. Due to my father's death, the Kinnaird estate will pass to me. Dad used it as his personal playground for years; hunting, shooting, fishing and drinking the local distilleries dry with not a thought for the estate's ecology. To be fair, it's not entirely his fault – his father and numerous male relatives before him were happy to take money from the loggers for shipbuilding in the last century. They stood back and watched as vast tracts of Caledonian pine forests were stripped bare. They didn't know any better in those days, but in these enlightened times, *we* do. I'm aware that it will be impossible to turn back the clock completely, certainly in my lifetime, but I'm keen to make a start. I've got the best estate manager in the Highlands to lead the way with the reforestation project. We've also spruced up the hunting lodge where Dad lived, so we can let it to paying guests who want a breath of fresh Highland air and some organised shoots.'

'Right,' I said, trying to suppress a shudder.

'You obviously don't approve of culling?'

'I can't approve of any innocent animal being killed, no. But I do understand why it has to happen,' I added hurriedly. After all, I told myself, I was applying for a job on a Highland estate, where the culling of deer was not only standard practice, but the law.

'With your background, I'm sure you know how the whole balance of nature in Scotland has been destroyed by mankind. There are no natural predators, such as wolves and bears, left to keep the deer population under control. Nowadays, that task is down to us. At least we can perform it as humanely as possible.'

'I know, although I have to be totally honest and tell you that I'd never be able to help out at a shoot. I'm used to protecting animals, not murdering them.'

'I understand your sentiments. I've had a look at your CV and it's very impressive. As well as gaining a first-class degree in zoology, you specialised in conservation?'

'Yes, the technical side of my degree – anatomy, biology,

genetics, indigenous animals' behavioural patterns and so on
– was invaluable. I worked in the research department at Servion Zoo for a while, but I soon realised I was more interested
in doing something hands-on to help animals, rather than just
studying them from a distance and analysing their DNA in a
Petri dish. I . . . just have a natural empathy with them in the
flesh, and although I have no veterinary training, I seem to
have a knack for healing them when they're sick.' I shrugged
lamely, embarrassed to be blowing my own trumpet.

'Margaret was certainly very complimentary about your
skills. She told me you've been caring for the wildcats at her
sanctuary.'

'I've done the day-to-day stuff, yes, but it's Margaret who's
the real expert. We were hoping the cats would mate this season
as part of the re-wilding programme, but now the sanctuary is
closing and the animals are being rehomed, it probably won't
happen. Wildcats are incredibly temperamental.'

'So Cal MacKenzie, my estate manager, tells me. He's not
at all happy about adopting the cats, but they're indigenous
to Scotland and so rare, I feel it's our duty to do what we can
to save the breed. And Margaret thinks that if anyone can help
the cats adjust to their change of habitat, it's you. So, are you
interested in coming up with them for a few weeks and settling them in?'

'I am, although the wildcats alone wouldn't really be a
full-time job once they're in situ. Is there anything else I could
do?'

'To be honest, Tiggy, so far I haven't had much chance to
think through future plans for the estate in detail. What with
my job here and trying to sort out probate since my father
passed away, I've been up to my eyes. But whilst you're with

us, I'd love it if you could study the terrain and assess its suitability for other indigenous breeds. I've been thinking about
introducing red squirrels and native mountain hares. I'm also
investigating the suitability of wild boar and elk, plus restocking the wild salmon in the streams and lochs, building salmon
leaps and so forth to encourage spawning. There's a lot of
potential, given the right resources.'

'Okay, that all sounds interesting,' I agreed. 'Although I
should warn you, fish aren't a speciality of mine.'

'Of course. And I should warn *you* that financial realities
mean I can only offer a basic wage, plus board, but I'd be very
grateful for any help you can give me. As much as I love the
place, Kinnaird is proving a time-consuming and difficult
proposition.'

'You must have known the estate would come to you one
day?' I ventured.

'I did, but I also thought Dad was one of those characters
who would creak on forever. So much so that he didn't even
bother to make a will, so he died intestate. Even though I'm
his only heir and it's a formality, it means another pile of
paperwork I didn't need. Anyway, it'll all be sorted by January,
so my solicitor tells me.'

'How did he die?' I asked.

'Ironically, he dropped dead of a heart attack and was
helicoptered in to me here,' Charlie sighed. 'He'd already left
us by then, borne upwards on a cloud of whisky fumes, so the
post mortem indicated later.'

'That must have been tough for you,' I said, wincing at the
thought.

'It was a shock, yes.'

I watched his fingers grab the pager once more, betraying his inner angst.

'Can't you sell the estate if you don't want it?'

'Sell up after three hundred years of Kinnaird ownership?' He rolled his eyes and gave a chuckle. 'I'd have every ghost in the family haunting me for life! And if for no other reason, I have to try and at least caretake it for Zara, my daughter. She's absolutely passionate about the place. She's sixteen and if she could, she'd leave school tomorrow and come up and work at Kinnaird full-time. I've told her she has to finish her education first.'

'Right.' I looked at Charlie in surprise and immediately adjusted my view of him. This man seriously didn't look old enough to have kids, let alone one who was sixteen.

'She'll make a great laird when she's older,' Charlie continued, 'but I want her to live a little first – go to university, travel the world and make sure committing herself to the family estate is really what she wants.'

'I knew what I wanted to do from the age of four, when I saw a documentary on how elephants were being killed for ivory. I didn't take a gap year – just went straight to university. I've hardly travelled at all,' I said with a shrug, 'but there's nothing like learning on the job.'

'That's what Zara keeps telling me.' Charlie gave me a faint smile. 'I have a feeling the two of you will get on very well. Of course what I should do is give this up' – he indicated our surroundings – 'and devote my life to the estate until Zara can take over. The problem is, that until the estate's in better shape, it doesn't make financial sense to pack in my day job. And between you and me, I'm not even sure yet if I'm cut out for life as a country laird.' He checked his watch again. 'Right,

I must go, but if you are interested, it's best you visit Kinnaird and see it for yourself. It hasn't snowed up there yet, but it's expected soon. You need to be aware that it's as remote as it gets.'

'I live with Margaret in her cottage in the middle of nowhere,' I pointed out.

'Margaret's cottage is Times Square compared to Kinnaird,' Charlie replied. 'I'll text you the mobile number for Cal and also the landline at the Lodge. If you leave messages on both, he'll get one or the other eventually and call you back.'

'Okay. I—'

The beeping of Charlie's pager interrupted my train of thought.

'Right, I really must go.' He stood up. 'Email me with any more questions you have and if you let me know when you're going up to Kinnaird, I'll try to join you there. And please, think about it seriously. I really need you. Thanks for coming, Tiggy. Bye now.'

'Bye,' I said, then watched as he turned away and weaved through the tables towards the exit. I felt weirdly elated, because I'd experienced a real connection with him. Charlie seemed familiar, as though I'd known him forever. And since I believed in reincarnation, I probably *had*. I closed my eyes for a second and cleared my mind to try to focus on which emotion stirred first in me when I thought of him, and was shocked at the result. Rather than being filled with a warm glow about someone who might represent a paternal employer-like figure, another part of me altogether reacted.

*No!* I opened my eyes and stood up to leave. *He's got a teenage daughter, which means he's far older than he looks and probably married*, I chided myself as I walked through the brightly lit hospital corridors and out of the entrance into the foggy November afternoon. Dusk had already begun to fall over Inverness, even though it was only just past three o'clock.

Standing in the queue for the bus that would take me to the train station, I shivered – from cold or the tingle of excitement, I didn't know. All I *did* know was that I was instinctively interested in the job, however temporary. So I found the number Charlie had given me for Cal MacKenzie, pulled out my mobile and dialled it.

'So,' Margaret asked me that evening as we settled down for our customary cup of cocoa in front of the fire. 'How did it go?'

'I'm going up to see the Kinnaird estate on Thursday.'

'Good.' Margaret's bright blue eyes shone like laser beams in her wrinkled face. 'What did you think of the Laird, or Lord as he'd be called in English?'

'He was very . . . nice. Yes, he was,' I managed. 'Not at all what I was expecting,' I added, hoping I wasn't blushing. 'I thought he'd be a much older man. Possibly with no hair and a huge belly from too much whisky.'

'Aye,' she cackled, reading my mind. 'He's easy on the eye and that's for sure. I've known Charlie since he was a bairn; my father worked for his grandfather at Kinnaird. A lovely young man he was, though we all knew he was making a mistake when he married that wife of his. So young he was too.' Margaret rolled her eyes. 'Their girl Zara's sweet enough, mind you, if a little wild, but her childhood's nae bin an easy one. So, tell me more about what Charlie said.'

'Apart from looking after the cats, he wants me to research indigenous breeds to introduce to the estate. To be honest, he didn't seem very . . . organised. I think it would only be a temporary job whilst the cats settle in.'

'Well, even if it's only a short wee while, living and work-ing up on an estate like Kinnaird'll teach you a lot. Mebbe there you'll start to learn that you cannae save every creature that comes into your care. And that goes for lame ducks of the human variety too,' she added with a wry smile. 'You have tae learn tae accept that animals and humans have their own destinies to follow. You can only do your best, an' no more.'

'I'll never toughen up to the plight of a suffering animal, Margaret. You know I won't.'

'I do know, dear, and that's what makes you special. You're a wee slip o' a thing, with a great big heart, but watch you don't wear it out wi' all that emotion.'

'So, what's this Cal MacKenzie like?'

'Och, he comes across a bit gruff, but he's a poppet under-neath, is Cal. The place is in his blood an' you'd learn a lot from him. Besides, if you don't take this, where else will you go? You know me and the animals are gone from here by Christmas.'

Due to her crippling arthritis, Margaret was finally moving into the town of Tain, forty-five minutes' drive from the damp, crumbling cottage we were currently sitting in. On the shores of Dornoch Firth, its twenty acres of hillside land had housed Margaret and her motley crew of assorted animals for the past forty years.

'Aren't you sad about leaving?' I asked her yet again. 'If it was me, I'd be crying my eyes out day and night.'

'Course I am, Tiggy, but as I've tried to teach yae, all good things must come tae an end. And with the will o' God, new and better things will begin. No point in regretting what was, you just have tae embrace what will be. I've known this was coming for a long time now, and thanks tae you helping me I've managed an extra year here. And besides, my new bunga-low has radiators yae can turn up when they're wanted, and a television signal that works all o' the time!'

She gave me a chuckle and a big smile, although I – who prided myself on being naturally intuitive – didn't know if she really *was* happy about the future, or just being brave. Which-ever it was, I stood up and went to hug her.

'I think you're amazing, Margaret. You and the animals have taught me so much. I'm going to miss you all terribly.'

'Aye, well you won't be missing me if yae take the job at Kinnaird. I'm a blow o' wind down the valley and on hand to give you advice about the cats if you need it. And you'll have tae visit Dennis, Guinness and Button, or they'll be missing you too.'

I looked down at the three scrawny creatures lying in front of the fire: an ancient three-legged ginger cat and two old dogs. All of them had been nursed back to health as young-sters by Margaret.

'I'll go up and see Kinnaird and then make a decision. Otherwise, it's home to Atlantis for Christmas and a rethink. Now, can I help you to bed before I go up?'

It was a question I asked Margaret every night and she responded with her usual proud reply.

'No, I'll sit awhile here by the fire, Tiggy.'

'Sweet dreams, darling Margaret.'

I kissed her parchment-like cheek, then walked up the uneven narrow staircase to my bedroom. It had once been Margaret's, until even she had realised that mounting the stairs every night was a number of steps too far. We had subsequently moved her bed downstairs into the dining room, and perhaps it was a blessing that there had never been funds to move the bathroom upstairs, because it still lay in the toe-bitingly cold outhouse only a few metres from the room she now used as her bedroom.

As I went through my usual routine of stripping off my day clothes then putting on layers of night clothes before I climbed between the freezing cold sheets, I was comforted that my decision to come here to the sanctuary had been the right one. As I'd told Charlie Kinnaird, after six months in the research department of Servion Zoo in Lausanne, I'd realised I wanted to take care of and protect the animals themselves. So I'd answered an ad I'd seen online and come to a crumbling cottage beside a loch to help an arthritic old lady in her wildlife sanctuary.

*Trust to your instincts, Tiggy, they will never let you down.*

That's what Pa Salt had said to me many times. 'Life is about intuition, with a splash of logic. If you learn to use the two in the right balance, any decision you take will normally be right,' he'd added, when we'd stood together in his private garden at Atlantis and watched the full moon rise above Lake Geneva.

I remembered I'd been telling him that my dream was to one day go to Africa, to work with the incredible creatures in their natural habitat, rather than behind bars.

Tonight, as I curled my toes into a patch of bed I'd warmed

up with my knees, I realised how far I felt from achieving my dream. Looking after four Scottish wildcats was not really in the Big Game league.

I switched off the light, and lay there thinking how all my sisters teased me about being the spiritual snowflake of the family. I couldn't really blame them, because when I was young I didn't understand that I was 'different', so I'd just speak about the things that I saw or felt. Once, when I was very small, I'd told my sister CeCe that she shouldn't climb her favourite tree because I'd seen her fall out of it. She'd laughed at me, not unkindly, and told me she'd climbed it hundreds of times and I was being silly. Then, when she *had* fallen out half an hour later, she had glanced away from me, embarrassed by the fact that my prophecy had come true. I'd since learnt it was best to keep my mouth shut when I 'knew' things. Just like I knew that Pa Salt wasn't dead . . .

If he was, I would have known when his soul had left the earth. Yet I'd felt nothing, only the utter shock of the news when I'd received the call from my sister Maia. I'd been totally unprepared; no 'warning' of the fact that something bad was coming. So, either my spiritual wiring was faulty, or I was in denial because I couldn't bear to accept the truth.

My thoughts spun back to Charlie Kinnaird and the bizarre job interview I'd had earlier today. My stomach resumed its inappropriate lurches as my imagination conjured up those startling blue eyes and the slim hands with the long, sensitive fingers that had saved so many lives . . .

'God, Tiggy! Get a grip,' I muttered to myself. Maybe it was simply that – living such an isolated life – attractive, intelligent men were not exactly streaming through the door.

Besides, Charlie Kinnaird must be ten years my senior at least . . .

Still, I thought, as I closed my eyes, I was really looking forward to visiting the Kinnaird estate.

Three days later, I stepped off the little two-carriage train at Tain and walked towards a battered Land Rover – the only vehicle I could see outside the front entrance to the tiny station. A man in the driver's seat rolled down the window.

'You Tiggy?' he asked me in a broad Scottish accent.

'Yes. Are you Cal MacKenzie?'

'I am that. Climb aboard.'

I did so, but struggled to close the heavy passenger door behind me.

'Lift it up, then slam it,' Cal advised me. 'This tin can has seen better days, like most things at Kinnaird.'

There was a sudden bark from behind me, and I twisted round to see a gigantic Scottish deerhound sitting in the back seat. The dog edged forward to sniff my hair before giving my face a rough-tongued lick.

'Och, Thistle, down with you, boy!' Cal ordered.

'I don't mind,' I said, reaching back to scratch Thistle behind the ears, 'I love dogs.'

'Aye, but don't start pampering him, he's a workin' dog. Right, we're off.'

After a few false starts, Cal got the engine going and we drove through Tain – a small town fashioned out of dour grey slate – which served a large rural community and housed the only decent supermarket in the area. The urban sprawl soon disappeared and we drove along a winding road with gentle, sloping hills covered in clumps of heather and dotted with Caledonian pines. The tops of the hills were shrouded in thick grey mist, and on turning a corner, a loch appeared to our right. In the drizzle, it reminded me of a vast grey puddle.

I shivered, despite Thistle – who had decided to rest his shaggy grey head on my shoulder – warming my cheek with his hot breath, and remembered the first day I'd arrived at Inverness airport almost a year ago. I'd left a clear blue Swiss sky and a light dusting of the first snow of the season on top of the mountains opposite Atlantis, only to find myself in a dreary facsimile of it. As the taxi had driven me to Margaret's cottage, I'd truly wondered what on earth I had done. A year on, having lived in the Highlands throughout all four seasons, I knew that when the spring came, the heather would bring the hillsides alive with the softest purple, and the loch would shine a tranquil blue under a benevolent Scottish sun.

I glanced surreptitiously at my driver: a stocky, well-built man with ruddy cheeks and a head of thinning red hair. The large hands that clutched the wheel were those of a man who used them as his tools: fingernails engrained with dirt, skin covered in scratches and the knuckles red from exposure. Given the physically punishing job that Cal did, I decided he must be younger than he looked and put him somewhere between thirty and thirty-five.

Like most people I'd met around here, who were used to living and working on the land and being isolated from the rest of the world, Cal didn't speak much.

*But he is a kind man . . .* my inner voice told me.

'How long have you worked at Kinnaird?' I broke the silence.

'Since I was a wee one. My father, grandfather, great-grandfather and great-great-grandfather afore me did the same. I was out with my pa as soon as I could walk. Times have changed since then and that's for sure. Changes bring their own set o' problems, mind. Beryl isnae pleased tae have her territory invaded by a bunch o' Sassenachs.'

'Beryl?' I questioned.

'The housekeeper at Kinnaird Lodge. She's been workin' there o'er forty years.'

'And "Sassenachs"?'

'The English; we have a load of poncey rich folk from across the border arriving tae spend Hogmanay at the Lodge. An' Beryl's nae happy. You're the first guest since it's been renovated. The Laird's wife was put in charge and she didnae skimp on anything. The curtain bill alone must ha' run intae thousands.'

'Well, I hope she hasn't gone to any trouble for me. I'm used to roughing it,' I said, not wanting Cal to think I was in any way a spoilt princess. 'You should see Margaret's cottage.'

'Aye, I have, many a time. She's the cousin o' my cousin, so we're distantly related. Most folk are around these parts.'

We lapsed into silence again as Cal turned a sharp left by a tiny run-down chapel with a weathered 'For Sale' sign nailed lopsidedly to one of its walls. The road had narrowed and we were now driving through open countryside, with drystone walls on either side keeping the sheep and cattle safely corralled behind them.

In the distance, I could see grey clouds hanging atop further mountainous terrain. The odd stone homestead appeared sporadically on either side of us, plumes of smoke belching from the chimneys. Dusk was fast descending as we drove on and the road became pitted with potholes. The old Land Rover's suspension was seemingly non-existent as Cal navigated a number of narrow hump-back bridges that straddled swirling streams, the tumble of rocks producing a froth of white bubbles as the water roared downwards over them, indicative of the fact that we were climbing upwards.

'How much further?' I asked, glancing at my watch and realising it was an hour since we had left Tain.

'No' far now,' Cal said as we took a sharp right and the road became little more than a gravel track, the treacherous potholes so deep that the mud within them splashed upwards and splattered the windows. 'You can see the entrance tae the estate just ahead.'

As a pair of stone pillars flashed past in the beam of the headlights, I wished I'd arrived earlier in the day so I could orientate myself.

'Almost there,' Cal reassured me as we twisted and turned and bumped along the drive. As the Land Rover proceeded up a steep slope, the wheels spun as they struggled for a grip on the loose water-logged gravel. Cal finally brought the car to a halt, the engine shuddering to a relieved standstill.

'Welcome tae Kinnaird,' he announced as he pushed open the door and climbed out. I noticed he was light on his feet, considering his physical bulk. He walked round and opened the passenger door for me, then offered his hand to help me.

'I can manage,' I insisted as I jumped down and promptly landed in a puddle. Thistle leapt out beside me and gave me a friendly lick, before ambling off to sniff around the driveway, obviously pleased to be back on familiar territory.

I looked up and in the moonlight, made out the sharp clean lines of Kinnaird Lodge, its steeply pitched roofs and lofty chimneys casting shadows into the night, warm lights glimmering behind the tall sash windows that peered out from the sturdy shale-rock walls.

Cal collected my holdall from the back of the Land Rover, then led me round the side of the Lodge towards a back door.

'Servants' entrance,' he muttered, cleaning his boots on the scraper placed outside. 'Only the Laird, his family and invited guests use the front door.'

'Right,' I said as we stepped inside and a welcome blast of hot air hit me.

'Like a furnace in here,' Cal complained as we made our way along a passageway that smelt strongly of fresh paint. 'The Laird's wife has put in some fancy heating system and Beryl hasn't learnt how tae control it yet. Beryl!' he shouted as he led me into a large ultra-modern kitchen, illuminated by numerous spotlights. I blinked to let my eyes adjust as I took in the vast, gleaming centre unit, the rows of shiny wall cupboards, and what looked like two state-of-the-art ovens.

'This is very stylish,' I said to Cal.

'Aye, that it is. You should have seen this room afore the old Laird died; I'd reckon there was a hundred years o' grime hidden behind the old cabinets, as well as a large family o' mice. It'll all fall down, mind, if Beryl cannae learn tae work those newfangled ovens. She's cooked on the old range for the whole o' her time here, and you need a degree in computer science tae use those two.'

As Cal spoke, an elegant, slim woman with snow-white hair scraped back into a bun at the base of her neck walked in. I felt her blue eyes – set on either side of a hawk-like nose in a long angular face – assess me.

'Miss D'Aplièse, I presume?' she said, her modulated voice holding just a hint of a Scottish accent.

'Yes, but please call me Tiggy.'

'Likewise, everyone here calls me Beryl.'

I thought how her name belied her. I'd imagined a motherly type with an over-ripe bosom, reddened cheeks and hands as rough and large as the pans she juggled with every day. Not this handsome, rather stern woman in her immaculate black housekeeper's dress.

'Thank you for having me to stay tonight. I hope it's not too much trouble whilst you're so busy,' I said, feeling tongue-tied, like a child addressing a headmistress. Beryl had an air of authority about her that simply demanded respect.

'Are you hungry? I've made soup – about all I can manage safely until I've worked out the programmes on the new ovens.' She gave Cal a grim smile. 'The Laird tells me you're a vegan. Will carrot and coriander suffice?'

'It will be perfect, thank you.'

'Well now, I'll be leavin' you both,' said Cal. 'I've some stag heads tae boil in the shed from yesterday's shoot. Night, Tiggy, sleep well.'

'Thanks, Cal, you too,' I said, stifling an urge to retch at his parting words.

'Right then, I'll take you upstairs to your bedroom,' said Beryl brusquely, indicating I should follow her. At the end of the corridor, we turned into a grand flagstone-floored entrance hall, containing an impressive stone fireplace, over which hung a stag's head, complete with a magnificent set of antlers. She led me up the freshly carpeted stairs, the walls lined with portraits of Kinnaird ancestors, and along the wide landing above, then opened a door to a large bedroom, decorated in soft beige hues. An enormous four-poster bed draped with red tartan took pride of place; leather chairs with plump cushions sat next to the fireplace and two antique brass lamps standing on highly polished mahogany side tables gave off a soft glow.

'This is beautiful,' I murmured. 'I feel as if I'm in a five-star hotel.'

'The old Laird slept in here until the day he died. He'd hardly recognise it now, mind, especially the bathroom.' Beryl indicated a door to our left. 'He used it as his dressing room. I put a commode in there towards the end. The facilities were at the other end of the corridor, you see.'

Beryl sighed heavily, her expression telling me her thoughts were in the past – perhaps a past she yearned for.

'I rather thought I could use you as a guinea pig; test the suite for problems, if you like,' Beryl continued. 'I'd be grateful if you'd take a shower and let me know how long it takes for the hot water to come through.'

'My pleasure. Where I live at the moment, hot water's a rare thing.'

'Right then, we're still waiting for the dining room table to return from the restorer, so the best thing is that I bring a tray up to you here.'

'Whatever's easiest really, Beryl.'

She nodded and left the room. I sat down on the edge of what felt like a very comfortable mattress and mused that I couldn't quite work Beryl out. And this lodge . . . the luxury surrounding me was the last thing I'd expected to find. Eventually, I raised myself from the bed and went to open the door to the bathroom. Inside I found a double marble-topped sink, a freestanding bath and a shower cubicle with one of those huge circular shower heads that I just couldn't wait to stand under, after months of bathing in Margaret's chipped enamel tub.

'Heaven,' I breathed as I stripped off and turned on the shower, then spent an indecently long time beneath it. Stepping out, I dried myself, before putting on the gloriously fluffy robe that hung on the back of the door. Towel-drying my unruly curls, I went back into the bedroom to find Beryl placing a tray onto a table next to one of the leather chairs.

'I brought you some homemade elderflower cordial to accompany the soup.'

'Thank you. The water came straight through and was piping hot, by the way.'

'Good,' Beryl replied. 'Right, then I shall leave you to eat. Sleep well, Tiggy.'

And with that, she swept out of the room.

## 2

Not a glint of daylight appeared through the heavy lining of the curtains as I fumbled for the light switch to see what time it was. Surprisingly, it was almost eight o'clock – a real lie-in for someone who normally rose at six to feed her animals. I clambered out of the enormous bed and walked across to open the curtains, letting out a gasp of delight at the beautiful vista beyond the window.

The Lodge was set on a hill overlooking a glen, the terrain falling gently down to a narrow, winding river in the flat valley bottom, then rising again on the other side to a range of mountains with an icing-sugar dusting of snow atop them. The whole landscape shimmered with frost under the newly risen sun and I opened the freshly painted window to breathe in a lungful of Highland air. It smelt pure – scented by the merest hint of peaty autumnal earth as grass and foliage decomposed in order to fertilise the new growth next spring.

All I wanted to do was run outside and lose myself in the miracle of nature at its finest. I threw on my jeans and jumper, added my ski jacket, beanie and my pair of sturdy boots, then made my way downstairs to the front door. It was unlocked and as I stepped outside, I revelled in the ethereal earthly paradise spread in front of me, miraculously untouched by either humans or their habitations.

'This is all mine,' I whispered as I walked across the coarse, frost-crisp grass of the front lawn. I heard a rustle from the trees to my left and saw a young roe deer with its large pointed ears, long eyelashes and auburn spotted coat leaping lightly between them. Even though Margaret's deer enclosure was large and fashioned as best she could to mimic their habitat while the deer were rehabilitated, it was closely fenced in. Here, at Kinnaird, the deer had thousands of acres in which to roam wild and free, even though they still faced peril from human predators, rather than their natural enemies of yesteryear.

Nothing in nature was safe, I mused, not even humans – the self-fashioned masters of the earth: with all our arrogance, we believed ourselves to be invincible. Yet I'd seen countless times how one mighty puff of wind from the gods in their heavens could wipe out thousands of us at a blow during tornados and hurricanes.

Halfway down the hill, I stopped beside a rushing stream, swollen with last night's fresh rainfall. I breathed in the air and looked around me.

*Could I live here for a while?*

*Yes, yes, yes!* came my soul's reply.

Yet even for *me* the total isolation was extreme: Kinnaird truly *was* another world. I knew my sisters would tell me I was mad to cut myself off here, that I should spend more time with people – preferably some suitable males – but that wasn't what made my heart sing. Being in nature made me feel alive, made my senses sharpen and soar, as if I was rising above the earth and becoming part of the universe. Here at Kinnaird, I knew that the inner part of me that I hid from the world could blossom and grow as I woke each morning to the gift of this magical glen.

'What do you think of me coming to Kinnaird, Pa?' I asked the skies above me, fervently wishing I could make that vital, invisible connection with the person I loved most in the world. Yet again, I was talking to thin air, both physically and spiritually, and it was deeply upsetting.

A few hundred metres from the Lodge, I found myself staring down from a rocky crag into a sloping, heavily wooded area. It was a private spot, yet as I scrambled down the slope to investigate, it proved easily accessible. This was the perfect place for Molly, Igor, Posy and Polson – aka the four wildcats – to have their enclosures.

I spent some time walking the area, knowing that the wooded back slope would provide the feeling of security that the wildcats needed if they were to become comfortable enough to venture out and, eventually, to breed. It was only ten minutes from the Lodge and surrounding cottages – close enough for me to provide their daily rations, even in the depths of winter. Feeling pleased with my choice, I made my way back up the slope to the uneven, narrow path that obviously served as an access road through the glen.

Then I heard the sound of an engine chugging towards me and I turned to see Cal hanging out of the Land Rover window, relief on his face.

'There yae are! Where've you been? Beryl had breakfast ready ages ago, but when she went tae call you in your room, she found it empty. She was convinced you'd been taken in the night by MacTavish the Reckless, the Lodge's resident ghost.'

'Oh gosh, I'm really sorry, Cal. It's such a beautiful

morning, I came out to explore. I also found the perfect spot to build the wildcat enclosure. It's just down there.' I pointed to the slope.

'Then it was worth getting Beryl and her breakfast in a fuddle. Besides, it does her nae harm tae get her senses going, give her some excitement, if you know what I mean.' Cal winked at me as I heaved the passenger door closed. 'O' course, the problem is that she believes she's the *real* lady o' the Lodge, and I cannae deny that, in many ways, she is. Climb in an' I'll give yae a lift back.'

I did so and we lurched off.

'These roads get treacherous when it snows,' Cal commented.

'I've lived in Geneva all my life, so at least I'm used to driving in snow.'

'That's good then, as you'll be seein' a lot o' it for months on end. Look.' Cal pointed. 'Just beyond the burn in that birch copse is where the stags like tae take shelter at night.'

'That doesn't look like it gives much protection,' I said, looking at the sparse cluster of trees.

'Aye, and that's the trouble. Most of the natural woodland has gone from the glen. We're startin' tae reforest, but it'll all need to be fenced off or the deer will nibble away the seedlings. It's a huge job the new Laird's undertaken. Och, Beryl, don't do this.' There was a grinding noise as Cal tried to shift the Land Rover into gear. The car juddered for a few seconds, then ran smoothly again.

'"Beryl"?' I repeated.

'Aye,' he chuckled, 'named after our housekeeper herself; this Landy's as tough as old boots, an' mostly reliable, despite its hiccups.'

When Cal and I returned to the Lodge, I apologised profusely to the human Beryl for disappearing before breakfast, then felt obliged to work my way through the Marmite sandwiches she'd made for me – 'in lieu of the breakfast you didn't eat'. And I really wasn't a Marmite fan.

'I don't think she likes me,' I mumbled to Cal, as she left the kitchen and he helped me out by eating a couple of the doorstoppers.

'Ah, Tig, the poor woman's just stressed,' Cal said sagely as his huge jaws demolished the sandwiches. 'So now, what time train are yae thinkin' o' getting? There's a 3.29, but it's up to you.'

The ring of a telephone broke into the conversation, then stopped. Before I could answer Cal, Beryl arrived back in the kitchen.

'The Laird wishes to speak to you, Tiggy. Is it a suitable time?' she asked me.

'Of course.' I shrugged at Cal, then followed Beryl along the back corridor and into a small room that obviously served as an office.

'I'll leave you alone,' she said, indicating the handset that lay on the desk. The door closed behind her.

'Hello?' I said into the receiver.

'Hello, Tiggy. Apologies for not being able to join you up at Kinnaird. A couple of emergencies came up at the hospital.'

'No problem, Charlie,' I lied as I *was* disappointed.

'So, what do you think of Kinnaird?'

'I think . . . that it's one of the most incredible places I've ever seen. It's breathtaking, really, Charlie. Oh, and by the way, I think I've found the perfect place for the wildcats.'

'Really?'

'Yes.' I explained where it was on the estate and the reasons behind my choice.

'If you think it's right, Tiggy, then I'm sure it is. So, what about you? Would you be happy to come with them?'

'Well . . . I love it here,' I said, smiling into the receiver. 'In fact, I don't just love it, I adore it.'

'So, could you live there for a while?'

'Yes,' I replied without a pause. 'Definitely.'

'Then, well, that's . . . fantastic! Cal in particular will be thrilled. I realise we haven't talked money or terms yet – but are you happy for me to email you over something? Shall we say an initial period of three months?'

'Yes, that's fine, Charlie. I'll read the email and reply.'

'Great. I look forward to showing you round myself next time, but I hope Beryl made you feel comfortable in the Lodge.'

'Oh, she did.'

'Good. Well then, I'll send that email and if you agree to come and work at Kinnaird, perhaps you could travel up with the wildcats at the beginning of December?'

'That sounds perfect.'

After a polite goodbye, I ended the call, wondering whether I'd just made the best or worst decision of my life.

After I'd offered profuse 'thank yous' to Beryl for her hospitality, Cal gave me a quick glance at the rustic but charming cottage I'd share with him if I took the position. Then we climbed into Beryl the Land Rover and set off for Tain station.

'So now, are yae comin' up wi' the cats or no?' Cal asked me bluntly.

'I am, yes.'

'Thank the heavens for that!' Cal thumped the wheel. 'The

cats are the last thing I needed on my plate, along wi' everything else I have tae do.'

'I'll be arriving with them in December, which means you need to start organising the building of their enclosure.'

'Aye, and I'll need serious advice from you on that, Tig, but it's great news you're comin'. Are you sure you can cope with the isolation?' he said as we bumped along the road that led out of the estate. 'It's no' for everyone.'

At that moment, the sun chose to emerge from behind a cloud, lighting up the glen below us, which was swathed in an ethereal mist.

'Oh yes, Cal.' I smiled, feeling a bubble of excitement rise up inside me. 'I know I can.'

## 3

The following month passed in a flash; a month that contained a lot of sad farewells as Margaret and I said painful goodbyes to our beloved animals. The deer, two red squirrels, hedgehogs, owls and our one remaining donkey were all seen off to their new homes. Margaret was far calmer about it than I was – I wept buckets after each one left.

''Tis the circle of life, Tiggy, it's full of hellos and goodbyes and yae'd do well to understand that as soon as you can,' she'd advised me.

Numerous emails and phone consultations concerning the wildcat enclosure ensued with Cal, who then engaged a company to construct it.

'I'm tae spare no expense, apparently,' Cal told me. 'The Laird's applied for a grant and is determined the cats should breed.'

From the photos he sent me, I could see it was state-of-the-art – a series of pavilion-like cages linked by narrow tunnels and surrounded by trees, vegetation and man-made hidey-holes for the cats to explore. There would be four pavilions in total so they could all claim their own territory and the females could be kept away from the males if and when they became pregnant.

I showed Margaret the photos as we had a glass of sherry on our final evening together. 'Lord! They could house a couple o' giraffes comfortably in there, let alone a few scrawny cats,' she chuckled.

'Charlie's obviously dead serious about his breeding programme.'

'Aye, well, he's a perfectionist, our Charlie. Shame he had his dream snatched away when he was so young. I don't think he's fully recovered since.'

My ears pricked up. 'From what?'

'I shouldn't ha' mentioned it, but that sherry loosened my tongue. Let's just say, he's been unlucky in love. Lost a girl to another, then married that wife o' his on the rebound.'

'Have you met his wife?'

'Only once in person, which was at their wedding over sixteen years back now. We exchanged a few words but I didn't like the cut of her. She's very beautiful, mind, but just like in the fairy tales, physical beauty doesn't always translate intae inner beauty and Charlie always was naive when it came tae women. He was wed at twenty-one, in the third year of his medical degree at Edinburgh,' Margaret sighed. 'She was already pregnant with Zara, their daughter, y'see. I'd reckon Charlie's whole life before that had been a reaction to his father's behaviour. Medicine and marriage gave him an escape. Mebbe this is Charlie's time now,' said Margaret, taking a final swig of her sherry. 'He's certainly due it.'

The following morning, I fussed around in the back of Beryl the Land Rover, which currently contained Molly, Igor, Posy and Polson, who were yowling and screeching in protest from within their cat boxes. It had been a job and a half to get them loaded, and despite my thick jumper and heavy-duty gloves, my wrists and arms sported several deep scratches. Although Scottish wildcats are roughly the same size and colouring as domestic tabby cats, that is where the similarity ended. They weren't known as 'Highland tigers' for nothing. Polson, in particular, had a tendency to bite first and ask questions later.

Yet despite their grumpy and often vicious natures, I loved them all. They were a small flicker of hope in a world where so many native species had given up the ghost. Margaret had told me that to prevent them from mating with domestic cats, several breeding programmes around Scotland aimed to produce purebred kittens in order to re-wild them at a later date. As I closed the doors on the cats' growls of indignation, I felt the weight of responsibility as one of the guardians of their future.

Alice, my pet hedgehog – named so because she had fallen down a rabbit hole as a baby and I'd rescued her from Guinness the dog's jaws as he pulled her out – was in her cardboard box on the front seat, along with my rucksack containing the few clothes I owned.

'Ready to go?' asked Cal, who was already sitting behind the wheel, eager to get off.

'Yes,' I gulped, knowing that I had to walk back into the house and say goodbye to Margaret, which would be the most heartbreaking moment of all. 'Can you give me five minutes?'

Cal nodded in silent understanding as I ran back into the cottage.

'Margaret? Where are you? Hello?'

She was nowhere to be seen, so I went in search of her outside and found her sitting on the ground in the centre of the empty wildcat enclosure, with Guinness and Button standing guard on either side of her. Her head was in her hands and her shoulders were shaking.

'Margaret?' I walked over to her, knelt down and put my arms around her. 'Please don't cry, or I know I will.'

'I cannae help it, lassie. I've tried tae be brave, but today . . .' She took her hands from her face and I saw her eyes were red-rimmed. 'Well, today really is the end o' an era, what with the cats and you leavin'.'

She reached out a gnarled, arthritic hand, the type one associates with evil witches in fairy tales, yet it conveyed the opposite: kindness itself.

'You've been like a granddaughter tae me, Tiggy. I can never repay you for keeping my animals alive and well when I didn't have the physical strength tae do it alone.'

'I'll come and see you in your new bungalow soon, promise. We're not that far apart, after all.' I took her in my arms and gave her a last hug. 'It's been a pleasure and I've learnt so much. Thank you, Margaret.'

'The pleasure was all mine. And talkin' o' learning, you be sure to visit Chilly while you're there. He's an old gypsy who lives on the estate, and a regular goldmine about herbal remedies for animals an' humans.'

'I will. Goodbye for now, darling Margaret.' I stood up and, knowing I was about to cry too, walked swiftly towards the gate. Cal appeared by my side.

'You just make sure those cats o' ours beget a few bonnie kittens, won't you?' Margaret called out as, with one last wave, I climbed up into Beryl and headed into the next chapter of my life.

'This is your bedroom, Tig,' said Cal, dumping my rucksack on the floor.

I looked around the small room, its low ceiling threaded with veiny cracks and bulges in the plaster, as if it was exhausted from holding up the roof above it. It was a) freezing cold and b) spartan, even in terms of what I was used to, but at least it contained a bed. And a chest of drawers, on top of which I placed Alice the hedgehog, still in her travelling box.

'Can I bring her cage in here too?' Cal offered. 'I can't cope wi' her in the sitting room. If she escapes in the night, I might step on her an' squash her by mistake on the way to the lavvy! Isn't she meant tae be hibernatin'?'

'She would be in the wild, but I can't risk it,' I explained. 'She's not put on enough weight since I rescued her and she'd never make it through the winter. I've got to keep her nice and warm, make sure she keeps feeding.'

Cal brought in her cage, and having settled Alice back into her home and given her a sachet of her favourite cat food, I felt so tired that I sat heavily on my bed, wishing I could lie down on it.

'Thanks so much for your help today, Cal. I couldn't have got those cats down the slope to the enclosures by myself.'

'Aye.' Cal's eyes swept over me. 'You're a wee fairy, aren't you? Doubt I'll be askin' you tae help me mend fences or chop the wood for the fires this winter.'

'I'm stronger than I look,' I lied defensively, because I really wasn't. Physically anyway.

'Aye, well, I'm sure yae have other strengths, Tig.' Cal indicated the cold, bare room. 'This cottage needs a woman's touch,' he hinted. 'I haven't a clue.'

'I'm sure we can make it more cosy.'

'You want something tae eat? There's some venison stew in the fridge.'

'Er, no thank you, I'm a vegan actually, if you remember—'

''O' course. Well.' He shrugged as I gave an enormous yawn. 'Mebbe you need some sleep.'

'I think I do.'

'There's a tub in the bathroom if you want a soak. I'll wait until you've had the first hot water.'

'Really, don't worry. I'm for my bed now,' I replied. 'Night, Cal.'

'Night, Tig.'

Finally the door closed behind him and I sank backwards onto what was a deceivingly comfortable and well-broken-in mattress, pulled the duvet over myself and fell asleep instantly.

I woke up at six o'clock – heeding both the freezing temperature and the call of my internal alarm. Turning on the light, I saw it was still pitch black outside and the inside of the windowpanes had frozen over.

Not needing to dress, because I was still in my jumper and filthy jeans, I pulled on an extra cardigan, my boots, beanie and ski jacket. I walked into the heavily beamed sitting room, which also housed a generous inglenook fireplace. Grabbing the torch that Cal had shown me hung on a hook by the front door, I switched it on and braced myself to venture outside. Navigating my way by torchlight and memory, I went to the large barn that contained a cold room, to fetch the pigeon and rabbit carcasses to feed the cats. As I entered, I noticed Thistle, asleep on a bale of straw in one corner. At my approach, he roused himself and stretched sleepily before ambling across to greet me on his impossibly long legs and shoving his pointed nose into the palm of my outstretched hand. As I looked into his intelligent brown eyes, fringed with grey fur that gave the almost comical impression of shaggy overgrown eyebrows, my heart melted.

'Come on, boy. Let's see if we can find you something to eat too.'

After retrieving the cats' food and selecting a juicy bone from the slab for Thistle, I made my way outside again. Thistle attempted to follow me, but I reluctantly pushed him back into the barn.

'Maybe another day, darling,' I told him. I couldn't risk spooking the cats when they'd only just arrived.

I walked across the frosted lawn and down the slope towards the enclosures. The inky blackness of the sky was the most intense I'd ever seen – without a chink of human-made light. Using the torch to guide me down the slope, I reached the entrance to the enclosures.

'Molly?' I whispered into the darkness. 'Igor? Posy? Polson?' I turned the handle out of habit, then I remembered that here, where visitors might come in the future, there was a keypad above the lock to prevent people entering the enclosures at random and disturbing the cats. Forcing my brain to remember the code that Cal had told me, I pressed what I thought was the right combination, and on the third try there was a small click and the gate finally slid open. I closed it behind me.

I called the cats' names again, but there was nothing; not the faintest sound of a paw on a crackling leaf. With four huge pavilions, the cats could be anywhere and they were all obviously in hiding, probably sulking.

'Hey, guys, it's me, Tiggy,' I whispered into the utterly silent air, my breath appearing in misty waves in front of me. 'I'm here, and there's no need to be afraid. You're safe, I promise you. I'm here with you,' I reiterated, then waited again to see if they'd respond to my voice. They didn't, and after investigating each pavilion and listening for as long as I could without dying of exposure, I distributed the kill, exited through the gate, and walked back up the slope.

'Where ha' you been so bright and early?' Cal asked me as he emerged from the tiny kitchen with steaming cups of tea for us both.

'I went to check on the cats, but they didn't come out. The poor things are probably terrified, but at least they heard my voice.'

'As you know, I'm not a fan o' cats in general. Selfish, scratchy, antisocial buggers whose loyalty lies with whoever feeds 'em. Give me a dog like Thistle any day,' Cal commented.

'I saw him in the barn this morning, I gave him a bone from the cold room,' I admitted, sipping the strong brew. 'Does he always sleep there?'

'Aye, he's a working dog, like I said, not some pampered townie pooch.'

'Couldn't he sleep in the cottage sometimes? It's awfully cold out there.'

'Och, Tig, you're too much of a softie. He's used to it,' Cal admonished me mildly as he walked back towards the kitchen. 'Want some toast and jam?'

'I'd love some, thanks,' I called, as I entered my bedroom and knelt down in front of Alice's cage to open the gate. I saw two bright eyes peering out of the little wooden hut she liked to burrow in. One of her tiny legs had been badly broken in her fall down the rabbit hole and had never fully recovered. She limped around her cage like a pensioner, even though she was less than a few months old.

'Good morning, Alice,' I whispered. 'How did you sleep? How about some cucumber?'

I went back into the kitchen to retrieve the cucumber from the fridge – which I saw needed a thorough clean to remove the green tinge of mould from the back and the shelves. I also noticed the sink was full of dirty pots and pans. I pulled the toast out of the grill and spread it with margarine on the cramped work surface, which was littered with what must have been a good week's worth of breadcrumbs.

*Typical man*, I thought to myself. Even though I wasn't anal about cleanliness, this was beyond my tolerance levels and my fingers itched to set to work. After feeding Alice, I sat with Cal at the small table in the corner of the sitting room and ate my toast.

'So what do yae usually give the cats o' a morning?' he enquired.

'Today, I threw in the pigeons and a couple of the rabbits I brought with me.'

'Well, I've got a mound o' deer hearts for yae stored away in the freezer. I'll show yae – it's in a shed in the courtyard at the back o' the Lodge.'

'They'll love those, Cal, thanks.'

'I don't get it, Tig. You say you're a vegan, so how can yae cope with handlin' dead meat every day?'

'Because it's nature, Cal. Humans are evolved enough to make conscious decisions about our diet and we have plenty of alternative food sources to keep us alive, whereas animals don't. Alice eats meat because that's what her species does, and likewise the cats. It's just the way it is, though I admit I'm not a fan of handling deer hearts. The heart is the essence of us all, really, isn't it?'

'I cannae comment; I'm a man and I like the taste of red meat between my teeth, be it offal or the best cut o' steak.' Cal wagged his finger at me. 'And I'm warning you, Tig, I'll never evolve, I'm a carnivore through an' through.'

'I promise that I won't try to convert you, though I will draw the line at cooking you lamb chops and stuff.'

'Besides, I thought all you Frenchies loved your red meat?'

'I'm Swiss, not French, so maybe that explains it,' I countered with a grin.

'Margaret told me you're also a bit o' a boffin, aren't yae, Tig, with your degree an' all? I'm sure you could be getting a well-paid, high-flyin' job in some lab, instead of nurse-maiding a few mangy cats. Why Kinnaird?'

'Actually I did work in a zoo lab analysing data for a few months. The money was good but I was miserable. It's the quality of your life that counts, isn't it?'

'Aye, given what I'm paid for all the back-breaking hours I work, I need tae believe that!' Cal gave a deep chuckle. 'Well, it's good you're here, I'll be glad o' the company.'

'I thought I'd give the cottage a spring-clean today, if that's okay.'

'It could do with it an' that's for sure. Thanks, Tig. I'll be seeing yae later.'

With that, he shrugged on his old Barbour and stomped towards the door.

I spent the rest of the morning down with the cats – or, in reality, without them, because no matter how much I looked for them in the dens carefully concealed in the foliage, I couldn't spot them.

'What a disaster it would be if my charges died in the first week,' I said to Cal when he popped into the cottage at lunchtime for one of his mega sandwiches. 'They're not touching their food.'

'Aye, that it would be,' he grunted, 'but they looked like they had enough fat on them tae sustain them for a few days at least. They'll settle down, Tig.'

'I hope so, I really do. Anyway, I need to do some shopping for food and cleaning supplies,' I said. 'Where's the nearest place for that?'

'I'll come with you tae the local shop now. Give you a driving lesson – Beryl takes some getting used tae.'

I spent the next hour navigating Beryl and learning her eccentricities as we drove to the local shop and back. The shop proved a disappointment, selling goodness knows how many varieties of shortbread for passing tourists, but not much else. At least I was able to get potatoes, cabbage and carrots, some salted peanuts and lots of baked beans for protein.

Back at the cottage, Cal left me to it, but having searched for a mop and a broom with no success, I decided there was nothing for it but to go up and ask Beryl if she had some equipment I could borrow. I walked across the courtyard towards the back door of the Lodge. Knocking brought no response, so I opened the door and stepped inside.

'Beryl? It's Tiggy from the cottage! Are you here?' I called as I walked along the passage towards the kitchen.

'I'm upstairs, dear, sorting out the new daily,' came a voice from above. 'I'll be down in a few seconds. Go and put the kettle on in the kitchen, will you?'

I followed Beryl's instructions and was just searching for a teapot when she walked in with a whey-faced young woman, who was wearing an apron and a pair of rubber gloves.

'This is Alison, who'll be keeping the Lodge spick and span when the guests arrive at Christmas. Won't you, Alison?' Beryl spoke slowly, enunciating her words, as if the girl was hard of hearing.

'Yes, Mrs McGurk, tha' I will.'

'Right, Alison, I'll see you tomorrow morning at eight sharp. There's a lot to be done before the Laird arrives.'

'Yes, Mrs McGurk,' the girl repeated, looking positively terrified of her new boss. She nodded a goodbye then scurried out of the kitchen.

'Dearie me,' commented Beryl as she opened a cupboard and pulled out a teapot. 'Not blessed with brains is our Alison, but neither am I blessed with a wide choice of staff round these parts. At least she can walk to work from her parents' croft, which – during the winter – means everything.'

'Do you live close by?' I asked Beryl as she spooned tea leaves into the pot.

'In a cottage just across the glen. I presume you don't take milk with your tea?'

'No.'

'Is a piece of my homemade Millionaire's Shortbread allowed? It does have butter in it.' Beryl indicated a tempting rack of biscuits covered in thick layers of caramel and chocolate. 'After all, the local dairy is on the doorstep and I can personally vouch for the fact that the cows are very well cared for.'

'Then thanks, I'd love a piece,' I said, deciding now was not the time to try to explain it was the fact that newborn calves were torn from their mothers, who were continually kept pregnant to provide unnatural levels of milk for humans, that I objected to. 'It's mainly meat and fish I absolutely won't eat. I do have the occasional lapse when it comes to dairy; I love milk chocolate,' I admitted.

'Don't we all?' Beryl handed me a slice on a plate with a glimmer of a smile and I felt we had taken a tiny step towards bonding, even if it was at the expense of my principles. 'So, how are you coping at the cottage?'

'Well,' I said, savouring every bite of the fabulously buttery shortbread, 'I've come to ask if you had a mop and broom and possibly a vacuum cleaner I could borrow so I could give it a good clean?'

'I have indeed. Men do seem to enjoy living like pigs in their own muck, don't they?'

'Some men, yes, though my father was one of the most

fastidious people I've ever known. Nothing was ever out of place, and he made his own bed every morning, even though he had – *we* had – a housekeeper to do it for us.'

Beryl eyed me as though she was reassessing my status. 'So you're from gentry, are you?'

It was a word I wasn't familiar with. 'What does that mean?'

'Sorry, Tiggy, your English is so good that I forget you must be French, from that accent I hear.'

'I'm Swiss actually, but my native language is French, yes.'

'I meant that I was wondering if you come from nobility,' said Beryl. 'Given the fact that you say you had a housekeeper.'

'No, or at least, I don't think so. Me and my five sisters were adopted by my father as babies, you see.'

'Is that so? How fascinating. Has your father told you where you were originally from?'

'Sadly he died just over five months ago, but he left each of us a letter. Mine tells me exactly where he found me.'

'And will you go to this place?'

'I'm not sure. I'm just happy being me – I mean, the "me" I've always been, and having wonderful memories of my sisters and adoptive father.'

'And you don't want anything to disrupt those?' said Beryl.

'No, I don't think I do.'

'Who knows? One day you may wish to, but for now, I'm sorry for your loss. Now, the mops and brooms are in the cupboard down the passageway on your left. You can take what you need, as long as you bring them back when you're finished with them.'

'Thank you, Beryl,' I said, touched by her words of comfort about Pa.

'Anything else you require to make that cottage of yours more habitable, let me know. Now, I must radio Ben, our handyman, and get him to top up Chilly's firewood.'

'He's the old gypsy who lives on the estate?'

'That's him.'

'Margaret said I should meet him.'

'Well, he's always in, dear. He's doubled up with arthritis, and how he survives the winters out there in the glen, I'll never know. At least he has his log cabin that the new Laird built him in the summer. It's insulated, so he's warm.'

'That was kind of Ch—the Laird.'

'Well, I've already said to him that for Chilly's own safety, he really should be moved into the village by the social services. The problem is, every time they've made the trek out to assess him, he's gone into hiding and no one can find him. Next time they come, I'm not going to give him any warning,' Beryl sniffed. 'It also means that one of us has to check on him every day, take him food and fill up his log basket. As if we don't have enough to do. Anyway' – Beryl reached for the radio pack – 'I must get on.'

After collecting a mop, broom and vacuum cleaner, I manhandled them across the yard, not helped by Thistle crisscrossing excitedly in front of me.

'Hey, Tig,' came a voice from the bowels of the shed in the courtyard. 'I'm in here, boiling a couple of stag heads. You putting a brew on any time soon?'

'Yup, but you'll have to come out of there and get it – there's no way I'm setting foot inside while you're doing that,' I called back.

'Cheers, Tig, two sugars, please.'

'Yes, your Lordship,' I replied. 'I'll just put my bucket and mop down, if you don't mind.' I bobbed a curtsey before opening the door to the cottage.

# 4

It was only two weeks until Christmas and the days had further shortened ahead of the winter solstice. Despite the frost at the windows, it had not yet snowed, and I was pleased I had managed to make the cottage far more cosy than it had been. Beryl had appeared with armfuls of pretty floral curtains the day after I'd borrowed her mop, vacuum and broom.

'Take your pick,' she'd told me. 'These used to hang in the Lodge before it was refurbished, and they were too good to throw out. There's some rugs going spare as well – a bit moth-eaten, but they'd add some warmth to those flagstone floors. Tell Cal there's an old leather chair in the barn that would go nicely by that fire.'

'Quite the little homemaker, aren't you?' Cal had chuckled when he'd seen the newly redecorated sitting room.

Despite myself, I'd enjoyed the process, because I'd never had a proper home of my own. Now, sitting in front of the huge fire in the evening in the worn leather chair with Cal lying on the sofa, was a pleasure. Although he'd initially ignored Alice, Cal had now fallen under her spell, and often he'd take her from the cage and have her curl up contentedly in his large palm. It upset me slightly that he was happy to have Alice as a house guest, but continued to draw the line at Thistle.

'Are yae goin' back to your family for Christmas?' he asked me as we ate breakfast together, the frost around the windowpane framing the spectacular glen beneath us.

'I was originally thinking I might go home to Switzerland for a couple of days, but with the cats still so unsettled, I don't think I can. All I'd do is fret, and besides, none of my sisters are going home this year either, so it would be really weird to be there without them and Pa.'

'Where do they all live?'

'Maia, the eldest, is in Brazil, Ally is in Norway, Star is down in the south of England, CeCe has apparently taken off on one of her adventures, and Electra, my little sister . . . well, she could be anywhere. She's a model. You might have heard of her. Most people have.'

'You don't mean *the* Electra? Like, the one who's even taller than me and is always on the front of the papers half-naked and hangin' on to a rock-star?'

'Yup, that's the one,' I confirmed.

'Wow, Tig! You're a wee bundle o' surprises, aren't you?' He studied me closely. 'Nope, you don't look anything like her.'

'We were all adopted, if you remember, Cal,' I giggled. 'We don't share an ounce of blood between us.'

'Aye, o' course,' he said. 'Well, tell Electra that if she ever fancies visiting her sis, I'd be happy to escort her down tae the local for a few drams o' whisky.'

'I'll tell her next time I speak to her,' I replied, and seeing the stars in his eyes, I briskly changed the subject. 'So, what are you doing at Christmas?'

'What I do every year. I'll be with my family in Dornoch. You'd be welcome at ours, Tiggy. You're hardly going tae hog all the turkey, are you?' he chuckled.

'That's really kind of you, Cal, but I still haven't made a final decision. I feel bad that none of us will be there for Ma, the lady who's taken care of us since we were small. Maybe I should invite her over here,' I mused.

'Was your "Ma" married tae your daddy?'

'No, though she might as well have been. Not in an intimate sense,' I explained hurriedly. 'She was employed by him as a nanny for us all when we were growing up and she's never left.'

'You have an odd family set-up, if you don't mind me sayin', Tig. At least, compared tae me.'

'I know I do, but I love Ma and Claudia, our housekeeper, and my sisters just as much as you love your family. I really don't want Pa's death to break us all up. He was the glue that held all of us together,' I sighed. 'We always tried to get home for Christmas.'

'Aye, family is everything,' Cal agreed. 'We might hate their guts, but if an outsider hurts them, we'll defend them tae the hilt. If you want tae ask your ma tae come here, that's fine, and we'll do our best to make Christmas as . . . Christmassy as we can. Now, I'd better be off back tae my fences.' He stood up and patted my shoulder as he passed me.

I called Ma later that morning and made the offer of a Scottish Christmas, but she declined.

'Tiggy, *chérie*, it's so sweet of you to think of me, but I feel I can't leave Claudia by herself.'

'She's very welcome here too,' I offered, 'although it might be a bit of a tight squeeze.'

'As a matter of fact, we've already invited Georg Hoffman over. And of course, Christian will be with us too.'

'Right. Well, if you're sure,' I said, thinking how sad it was that Christmas at Atlantis would only comprise the staff, rather than any family members.

'I am, *chérie*. Now, how are you? And how is that chest of yours?'

'It's fine. I'm getting buckets of fresh mountain air, Ma.'

'Make sure you keep wrapped up warm. You know your chest does not take well to the cold weather.'

'I will, Ma, I promise. Bye now.'

A few days later, I called Margaret to see how she was, and she invited me to have Christmas lunch with her, an offer which I gratefully accepted. Relieved that I wouldn't have to disturb Cal's family Christmas, or to be more truthful, deal with the mound of dead roasted bird that would be their lunch, I took Thistle for a walk around the estate. He seemed to have attached himself to me, much to Cal's amusement, following me around like a witch's familiar whenever he wasn't needed for a shoot. I'd even occasionally smuggled him into the cottage when I knew Cal wasn't there. He'd toast himself by the fire while I brushed burrs and knots out of his rough coat, hoping his master wouldn't notice. I'd always longed for a dog of my own.

When I got back home, I opened the door to find Cal positioning a small Christmas tree in the corner of the sitting room.

He looked up and frowned at Thistle, who had followed

me to the door and was now sitting at the threshold with a pleading look in his eyes.

'Now, Tig, I've told you time and again, he's not supposed tae come in. It'll make him nesh.'

'"Nesh"?' I queried, wondering guiltily if Cal already knew I'd been disobeying his orders.

'Aye. You'll turn him soft. You leave him outside.'

Reluctantly, I scooted Thistle out into the courtyard, whispering that I'd see him later, then closed the door.

'Thought this tree would cheer you and the old place up,' Cal commented. 'I dug it up from the forest, roots an' all, so we can replant it afterwards. Maybe yae could go tae Tain tomorrow and buy some lights and decorations for it?'

Tears pricked my eyes at the sight of the little tree, currently standing at a lopsided angle in its bucket of earth.

'Oh Cal, that's so sweet of you, thank you.' I went over to him and gave him a hug. 'I'll go after I've fed the cats tomorrow.'

'Well, make it early, the snow is coming in tomorrow for sure. Them Sassenachs down south are always dreaming o' a white Christmas, but I cannae remember one Yuletide up here without the stuff.'

'And I can't wait,' I said with a smile.

As Cal had predicted, I woke the next morning to the first snowfall of the season. I took the spare Land Rover, which was even clunkier and older than Beryl, and drove carefully into Tain.

With only a few days to go, the small town was bustling

with Christmas shoppers and after I'd bought my tree lights and decorations, I chose a soft tartan scarf for Cal and a pink woollen jumper for Margaret. When I arrived home, I noticed there was a beaten-up Range Rover parked in front of Kinnaird Lodge. Beryl had been in a flap for days because Charlie and his family were coming up from Inverness to spend Christmas at the Lodge, before giving it over to the first paying guests for Hogmanay.

By the time Cal arrived home, our own little tree was decorated and lit, and a fire was burning merrily in the hearth. A CD of Christmas carols that I'd bought in Tain was playing on Cal's ancient portable system.

'I'm expecting Old Saint Nick himself to fall down the chimney any second,' Cal chuckled as he hung his jacket, hat and scarf on the coat hooks I'd had him screw in by the front door. 'We even have the reindeer outside, Tig, look.'

I peered out of the window and saw that the six deer that usually hung around on the lawn by the Lodge had ventured across to see us. All stags, they were tame enough to feed, and Cal had told me that they'd been hand-reared on the estate.

'Are you feelin' the spirit o' Christmas yet, Tig? You wait until you've had a taste of my mulled wine. You'll certainly feel it then. What's fer supper?'

'Bean casserole, or you can cook your own kill,' I retorted as I left the sitting room to go to the kitchen.

'Aye, go on then. The last one you made was really tasty.'

Over the casserole and a bottle of cheap wine, Cal and I discussed the cats' progress.

'At least the pigeons and deer hearts are now disappearing from where I leave them every day, but apart from Posy, the other three are still refusing to come anywhere close to me. I'll have to get them all checked by a vet soon and I don't know how I'm going to get near them.'

'Tig, you cannae force animals to adjust to their new habitat on a timetable.'

'I know,' I sighed, 'but I feel under such pressure, Cal. The mating season starts in January, but they've been so unsettled that they're barely stirring from their separate boxes, let alone spending time getting friendly. And to be honest, I'm not sure they ever fancied each other in the first place. There was no chemistry that I ever saw.'

'I'm not sure that mating has anything tae do with chemistry. In rutting season, I've seen stags mount six hinds one after the other. It's called nature, an' you just have tae hope that those boys o' yours feel the urge.'

'Some wildlife consultant I'm turning out to be,' I said. 'If no kittens arrive by the spring, I'll feel I've totally failed Charlie.'

'Och, the Laird's no' a monster, Tig. I saw him earlier up at the Lodge, and he says he'll be down tae see you and the cats sometime over Christmas.'

'Oh my God,' I groaned. 'What if they won't come out when he comes to visit them?'

'He'll understand. By the way, I was wanting tae ask your advice, given you're a girl and Missus Christmas tae boot. I have tae buy something for Caitlin. And I haven't a clue in my head what.'

'Caitlin?'

'My girl. She lives in Dornoch, but she won't be my girl for much longer if I don't come up with something decent as a Christmas present.'

I looked at Cal in barely concealed surprise. 'You have a

girlfriend? Wow, Cal, why have you never mentioned her to me before?'

'Personal stuff, isn't it? Besides, the subject's nae come up before.'

'But you're always here on the estate. Doesn't Caitlin get . . . irritated by the fact she barely sees you?'

'No' really, because it's always been like this. I see her fer a weekend once a month and every first Thursday.'

'How long have you been together?'

'Twelve years or so,' he said as he shovelled more casserole into his mouth. 'I popped the question a couple o' years ago.'

'Goodness! Then why isn't she living up here in the cottage with you?'

'Tae begin with, she's a building society branch manager in Tain, which as you know, is an hour's drive away. What with the weather being as it is, she can't risk getting snowed up here on the estate. And she doesnae want to be living in a damp dump like this. Mind you, if she saw it since you arrived, she might change her mind.' He gave his growling chuckle. 'Now we're about it, what about you? D'you have someone special in your life, Tig?'

'There was a guy I met in the lab at Servion Zoo and we had a thing for a while, but it wasn't serious. I've not met "the one" yet,' I said, taking a slurp of my wine. 'You're lucky you have. I'd love to meet Caitlin, Cal. Why don't you invite her here one evening over Christmas?'

'The thing is, Tig,' Cal said with a frown, 'I may ha' mentioned that I'm sharing my digs with a prize-fighting bearded woman, not a pretty lassie like you. Yae know what women are like, I'd never hear the last of it.'

'That's all the more reason to have her here: I can reassure her that I'm no threat. Anyway, I would like to meet her at some point because she's your "person". Oh, and I suggest you buy her jewellery.'

'She's a practical sort of a girl, Tig,' Cal said doubtfully. 'Last year I bought her a pair o' thermal bedsocks and some waterproof gloves. She seemed pleased enough.'

'I promise you, Cal,' I replied, stifling a giggle, 'women, no matter how practical they may be – or pretend to be – are suckers for jewellery.'

An hour later, we said goodnight and went to our beds. I felt happy about Cal's revelation – in my experience, however modern society was these days, the relationship between any male and female who lived together always had an edge to it until the ground rules had been established. Which they just had been by our conversation. Not that there was any part of me that was sexually attracted to Cal, but I definitely felt close to him. The good news was that having grown up with five sisters, Cal could now become what I'd always longed for – a big brother.

I looked up at Polson, who was sitting out on one of the wooden platforms above me. He was preening himself in the sun, his rear end pointed in my direction, blatantly ignoring me. I didn't care. At least he was out of his box and in the open, which gave me hope he was finally recovering from his trauma.

I took a quick photo on my camera, just in case the Laird – as I'd come to call Charlie Kinnaird along with everyone else here – wanted proof that the cats were alive.

'Happy Christmas Eve,' I said to Polson, 'and maybe tomorrow morning you'll actually deign to look at me so I can wish you a Merry Christmas eye to eye.'

I scrambled back up the slope, thinking that if cats had a reputation for being as haughty and capricious as royalty, then Polson was king. As I looked up, I saw a very slim woman standing at the top of the slope staring down at me. She had long legs like a giraffe, and was dressed in what Cal would call a 'townie' ski jacket with a glamorous fur collar. Her thick hair shone white-blonde like a halo in the sunlight, framing a pair of big blue eyes, and lips that looked like they could double as pillows. Whoever she was, she was very beautiful. She began to crunch noisily towards me. At the sight of her, Polson retreated immediately.

'Er, hi,' I said as I doubled my pace upwards. Having reached her, we were face to face, or, rather, my eye-line was on a level with her stomach as she towered above me on the slope. 'I'm so sorry, madam, but this area is out of bounds.'

'Really?' she drawled, looking down at me disdainfully. 'I don't think so.'

'It actually is for the moment, because we have wildcats just arrived, you see. I'm trying to settle them in, and they're very temperamental and don't like strangers and I've just encouraged them to start coming out into the open and—'

'Who might you be?'

'My name's Tiggy, I work here.'

'Do you now?'

'Yes. It's fine if you stay up there. I mean, I know you can't see much, but the Laird is trying to breed the cats, because there are only three hundred of them left in Scotland.'

'I know all that,' she said, and I heard the timbre of a foreign accent, plus the barely concealed antipathy in her words. 'Well, far be it from me to disturb your little project.' She gave a tight smile. 'I'll do as I'm told and beat a retreat. Goodbye.'

'Goodbye,' I called to the Claudia Schiffer lookalike as I watched her stalk back up the hill. Instinctively, I knew that I'd just made a mistake.

'I met a woman down by the cats today,' I said to Cal when he came in at lunchtime. 'She was blonde with Disney princess lips and really tall.'

'That'll be the mistress, then,' Cal replied as he slurped his soup. 'The Laird's wife, Ulrika.'

'Shit,' I whispered.

'Not like you to swear, Tig. What's up?'

'I may have been really rude to her, Cal. I'd just managed to get Polson out of his lair when she arrived and made him scarper back inside. So I basically told her to go away.' I bit my lip and waited for Cal's reaction.

'That'll have gone down like a cup o' cold sick,' he said as he wiped a chunk of bread around his bowl then stuffed it in his mouth. 'That's probably the first time she's ever been told tae bugger off by anyone.'

'Christ, Cal, I was only trying to protect the cats; surely she'll understand, if she knows anything about wild animals?'

'All she knows about are the ones she wears on her body, Tig. Right fashion plate, she is. She did some modelling when she was younger.'

'I should have realised who she was when I saw her,' I groaned.

'Whoever she was, yae didnae want the cats disturbed. Never mind, Tig, I'm sure she'll get over it. I'd reckon she wasn't coming tae visit the cats anyway, but to take a look at their keeper. Charlie's probably told her about yae, and knowing what I do about her, she wouldn't be keen on a young woman invading her territory. Especially one as pretty as you are.'

'Hah! Well, thanks for the compliment, Cal, but I doubt she'd be threatened by me.' I indicated my little body that had never sprung the womanly curves it was meant to, covered in my old Aran jumper, with as many holes as it had knitting due to the moths in Margaret's cottage.

'I'll bet you scrub up pretty well all the same. And that's what you'll be doing at tonight's little shindig up at the Lodge. I forgot tae mention that the Laird's continuing his father's tradition of holding drinks and a ceilidh on Christmas Eve in the main hall, so you'll need tae be getting out your glad rags.'

'What?!' I looked at Cal in horror. 'I don't have any nice clothes with me.'

'Well, mebbe you can at least have a bath so you don't go smellin' of wildcat.'

That night, I realised all I had that was not a moth-eaten jumper was a red-checked shirt and my pair of 'best' black jeans. I left my chestnut hair loose instead of scraped back in a ponytail, and added a lick of mascara and a dab of red lipstick.

I gasped in surprise when I joined Cal in the sitting room. He was dressed in a dark-blue-and-green kilt, a sporran hanging from his belt buckle, and a knife tucked into his sock.

'Wow, Cal, you look incredible!'

'You've spruced up quite well too,' he said approvingly. 'Right, let's go.'

We walked across to the front entrance to the Lodge, where I could already hear the murmur of voices from within.

'This is the only occasion o' the year when we peasants are allowed tae cross the main threshold,' he murmured to me as we stepped inside and I looked up to the lights of the gorgeous Christmas tree that sat in the stairwell. A huge fire was burning in the grate and arriving guests – the men dressed in kilts like Cal, the women sporting tartan sashes – were being offered mulled wine and mince pies by Beryl and Alison.

'You look very nice, Tiggy,' Beryl said. 'Merry Christmas to you.'

'Merry Christmas,' I toasted her and took a gulp of my mulled wine as I surreptitiously searched the room for a glimpse of Charlie Kinnaird and his wife.

'They're both still upstairs.' Beryl read my mind. 'The new mistress always does take a long time to get ready. And she's preparing to greet her subjects after all,' she added through pursed lips.

Beryl moved on to serve other recent arrivals, and I wandered across the hall, musing that the majority of guests seemed to be of pensionable age. Then I saw a teenage girl, who stuck out like a sore thumb amongst the greying heads. She was standing alone with her glass of mulled wine and looking as bored as anyone her age would at such a gathering. As I approached her, I saw she looked familiar – the same bright blue eyes and unblemished skin as the woman I'd met at the wildcat enclosure this morning, but with a head of wavy mahogany hair cut very short. It was obvious from her

59

sweatshirt and ripped jeans that she'd made no effort to dress up for tonight's festivities.

'Hello.' I smiled as I approached her. 'I'm Tiggy. I've just started to work here on the estate. I'm looking after the wild-cats while they settle in.'

'Yeah, Dad's mentioned you. I'm Zara Kinnaird.' Zara's blue eyes appraised me, just as her mother's had earlier in the day. 'You look too young to be Dad's wildlife consultant. How old are you?'

'Twenty-six. You?'

'Sixteen. How are the cats settling in?' she asked me, seeming genuinely interested.

'It's taking time, but we're getting there.'

'I wish I could be you, out in the open air all day working on the estate with the animals, rather than being stuck in a classroom doing boring maths and stuff. Mum and Dad won't let me come and work here until I've finished my education.'

'You don't have long left, do you?'

'A whole eighteen months. And even after that, Mum probably expects me to become editor of *Vogue* or something. I don't think so,' she snorted. 'Do you smoke?' she whispered to me.

'No, I don't. Do you?'

'Yeah, when Mum and Dad aren't looking. Everyone does at school. Will you come outside with me so I can have one, and then say you took me off to look at the stag heads in the shed or something? It's sooo boring in here.'

The last thing I needed was to be caught behind the metaphorical bike sheds encouraging the Laird's daughter to smoke. But I liked this girl, so I said yes, and we slipped out of the front door. Zara promptly burrowed in her hoodie pocket for a battered rollie and lighter and lit up. I noticed the heavy silver rings on her fingers and the black nail polish, which reminded me of my sister CeCe at Zara's age.

'Dad said I should talk to you whilst I'm up here and find out what you did at Margaret's sanctuary,' she said, blowing out a stream of smoke into the freezing air. 'Are you named after the hedgehog in the Beatrix Potter stories?' she continued before I'd had a chance to reply.

'That's where my nickname comes from, yes. Apparently my hair stood up in spikes like a hedgehog when I was a baby. My real name's Taygete.'

'That's unusual. Where's it from?'

'My sisters and I are all named after the Seven Sisters star cluster. Look.' I pointed up to the perfectly clear night sky. 'There they are, just above those three stars all in a line that look like an arrow. That's called Orion's Belt. Legend has it that Orion chased the sisters across the skies. Can you see them?'

'I can!' Zara said with childlike excitement. 'They're tiny, but if I look really closely I can see them all twinkling. I've always been interested in the stars, but they don't really teach that kind of stuff at school, do they? So, did you enjoy your zoology degree? If I'm forced to go to uni, I want to do something like that.'

'I did, and I'm happy to tell you about it, but don't you think we should be getting back inside? Your parents might be looking for you.'

'No, they won't be. They've had a massive argument. Mum is refusing to come down and Dad's trying to persuade her. As usual.' Zara rolled her eyes. 'She gets hysterical, you see, if

Dad doesn't agree with her, then he has to spend ages pleading with her to calm down.'

From what I'd seen of Zara's father so far, I found it hard to equate such a scene with a man who'd seemed so in command of his environment. But it wasn't my place to probe further, so I proceeded to tell Zara as much as I could about my degree, then my work at Margaret's sanctuary, and her eyes shone in the moonlight.

'Wow, that sounds amazing! Now that Dad's finally in charge, I've told him that he should put aside a few acres to open an animal sanctuary like Margaret's. And maybe a petting zoo too, which would mean local parents could bring their little ones, and encourage them to enjoy the estate.'

'That's a great idea, Zara. What did he say?'

'That there's no money at the moment to do anything,' Zara sighed. 'I told him I'd leave school and come up here full-time to help him, but he just went on about me finishing school then going to uni. Margaret didn't have a degree, did she? All you need is a love for animals.'

'True, but a degree does help you get onto a career path, Zara.'

'I have a career path!' The blue eyes blazed with passion as she opened her arms as if to embrace the estate. 'I'm intending to spend the rest of my life up here. Did you know you wanted to work with animals when you were my age?'

'Yes.'

'Animals are so much better than humans, aren't they?'

'Some humans, yes, but then, one of the wildcats – Polson – is a real prima donna. I honestly don't think I'd like him much if he *was* human.'

'Sounds like my mum . . .' Zara giggled. 'C'mon, I suppose we'd better get back inside and see if my 'rents have managed to make it downstairs yet.'

As we walked back to the Lodge, I thought how Zara was the epitome of a teenager: stuck uncomfortably between child and womanhood.

The entrance hall was now crowded and I watched as Zara simultaneously waved and blew kisses to various faithful retainers in the crowd, who, judging by their age, had undoubtedly known her since a tiny baby. She was their 'princess' after all – the future heiress to the Kinnaird estate. Part of me couldn't help being envious that one day all this beauty would pass to her, but at least she displayed a genuine passion for Kinnaird.

My musing was interrupted by the arrival beside us of a petite woman with wary blue eyes, and a mane of bright red hair.

'Zara, will you no' introduce us?' the woman asked.

Zara turned to kiss the woman on both cheeks. 'Caitlin! How lovely to see you. Tiggy, this is Caitlin, Cal's better half. Caitlin, this is Tiggy, she's come to work on the estate for a few months.'

'Aye, Cal's told me about you. So, how are you getting on in the cottage with him? It's nae the most comfortable place to rest your head, is it?'

'Oh, it's fine really, and your Cal's made me feel really welcome. The cottage is looking a lot better than it did, I've made a real effort to make it cosy for the two of us . . .'

*Tiggy, just shut up!* I told myself, as I saw the look on Caitlin's face.

Zara came to my rescue and started to ask Caitlin about

her job at the building society, then a few seconds later we were joined by Cal himself, a dram of whisky in each hand, accompanied by a slim attractive woman who I guessed was in her early forties. I could see how uncomfortable he was at the sight of his fiancée and housemate standing together.

'I see you two've met already. I was, er, planning tae get the pair o' you together earlier but I couldn't find Tiggy.' He smiled affectionately at Caitlin, throwing his brawny arm around her delicate shoulders, the whisky sloshing perilously in his hands as he did so.

'Yes, we've met.' Caitlin returned his smile, but it didn't quite reach her eyes.

'Aye, anyway,' he continued, clearly wanting to move the conversation along. 'I just brought Fiona here over to introduce her tae Tiggy. Tiggy, this is our local vet, Fiona McDougal. You said you'd be needin' someone to look over the cats an' this is your woman.'

'Hi, Tiggy, it's a pleasure to make your acquaintance.' Fiona's voice was soft and warm, with a refined Scottish accent.

'Likewise,' I replied, grateful for the diversion from Caitlin.

Before anyone could say anything further, we were interrupted by a sudden flash of colour on the staircase above us. Like the rest of the occupants of the hall, we looked up. Applause broke out as the woman I'd seen at the wildcat enclosure earlier – now wearing a skin-tight red dress with a tartan sash pinned across her shoulder – walked down the stairs on the arm of her husband, Charlie Kinnaird. Now, rather than the hospital scrubs I had last seen him in, he was wearing a dinner jacket, bow tie and kilt, the very image of the centuries of lairds that graced the paintings in the Lodge.

As they turned the corner on the dog-leg stairs to descend

the final few steps, I drew in a breath. Not because of her, even though she looked stunning, but because of *him*. I blushed with embarrassment as I experienced the same sharp dig in my lower gut that I'd felt the last time I'd met him.

Husband and wife paused halfway down the stairs and I watched as the woman waved at the crowd below her, as if she'd been taking lessons from the elderly British sovereign. Charlie stood next to her, the set of his shoulders betraying that inner tension I'd noticed at the interview. Despite the smile pasted onto his lips, I knew he was uncomfortable.

'Ladies and gentlemen.' Charlie raised a hand for silence. 'First of all I'd like to welcome you to our annual Christmas Eve gathering. This is the first that I've hosted, even though I've attended every single one of them for the past thirty-seven years. As you all know, my father Angus died suddenly in his sleep last February and before I say anything else, I wish you to raise the drams of whisky that Beryl has kindly been handing out and make a toast to him.' Charlie took a glass from Beryl's proffered tray and lifted it to his lips. 'To Angus.'

'Tae Angus,' chorused the room.

'I'd also like to say thank you to each one of you for helping to steer the estate over the years. Many of you already know that despite the months of uncertainty following my father's death, I have a vision for the future, to bring the Kinnaird estate into the twenty-first century, yet at the same time do my best to restore it to its former natural glory. It's a hard task, but I know that with support from the local community I can do it.'

'Aye, that yae will,' shouted the man next to me as he took a hip flask out of his jacket pocket, opened it and took a deep slurp.

'And lastly, I'd like to thank my wife, Ulrika, for standing by me during this difficult year. Without her support, I couldn't have done it. To you, darling.'

Everyone raised a glass again although they were all empty, so Charlie hurried on.

'And of course, my daughter Zara. Zara?' He looked around the room and so did I, but she'd vanished. 'Well, we all know of old how she likes to disappear at inopportune moments.'

There was a general murmur of amusement at the Laird's comment.

'So, all that remains to be said now is Merry Christmas to each and every one of you.'

'Merry Christmas,' we all chorused back.

'Now please, top up your glasses, and we'll be rolling back the carpets ready for the ceilidh in a few minutes' time.'

'Well, wasn't that a rousing speech?' said Cal, before grabbing Caitlin's hand in his bear-like paw and muttering something about the two of them fetching more drinks.

'He's a good man, that one,' Fiona said as Cal pulled Caitlin away. 'So, how are you getting on here?' She turned her full attention to me, and I was struck by the intelligent gaze in her lovely green eyes.

'I'm adjusting to it,' I said. 'It's so beautiful that I sometimes feel as though I could lose myself in it. I'm finding it strange to be with so many people this evening, after the last three weeks of isolation.'

'I know what you mean. I experienced something similar when I first moved here from Edinburgh.'

'Oh, what brought you from the big city to the Highlands, if you don't mind me asking?'

'I fell in love with a local man,' she replied simply. 'I'd almost completed my veterinary training at Edinburgh University and was doing some work experience at the local practice near Kinnaird when I met Hamish. He farmed a small croft nearby. After I'd finished my degree, I was offered a job with a big practice in Edinburgh, but my heart won and I married Hamish and moved here. I joined the local practice, then took over when Ian, my partner, retired a couple of years ago.'

'Right. Are you kept busy?'

'Very, though it's a different kind of patient I treat up here. Few domestic pets like I'd have had in Edinburgh, and endless sheep and cows.'

'Do you enjoy it?'

'Oh, I love it, although getting a call-out at three in the morning to help a struggling pregnant heifer in a foot of snow can be a challenge,' she chuckled.

A tall, broad-shouldered blond youth appeared beside her.

'Hello, Mum, I was wondering where you'd got to.' His clear grey-green eyes – so like Fiona's that anyone could see he was her son – shone under the lights.

'Hello, Lochie,' said Fiona with a warm smile. 'This is Tiggy, the lass who's looking after the new wildcats on the estate.'

'Pleasure tae meet you, Tiggy.' Lochie extended his hand to me, then, as Zara rejoined us, I saw him blush scarlet.

'Hi, Lochie,' Zara said. 'Haven't seen you for ages. Where've you been hiding?'

'Hi, Zara.' His blush deepened. 'I've been at college in Dornoch.'

'Right. What are you doing now?'

'Looking for a job as an apprentice. There's not much around, so I've been helping my dad on our croft.'

'I've told him he should catch Cal tonight and ask him if there's anything going here at Kinnaird,' Fiona added pointedly.

'Cal's desperate for help,' I butted in.

'But Dad doesn't have any money,' Zara sighed.

'I'd work for nothing, just for the experience,' Lochie said and I felt his desperation.

'Maybe not nothing, Lochie,' his mother interjected.

'Well, put in a word for me, won't you, Zara?'

'Course I will. Fancy grabbing me a drink?' she asked him.

'Blimey, he's grown up!' Zara whispered to me as Lochie nodded eagerly and wandered off towards the laden table at the back of the hall. 'He used to be short and fat and covered in acne! I think I should go and give him a hand.'

'You do that,' I said to her departing back.

'Teenagers, eh?' Fiona rolled her eyes at me and we both chuckled.

Cal returned bearing yet more glasses of whisky, but I refused mine, feeling suddenly light-headed. I noticed Charlie and Ulrika glad-handing the guests and drawing ever closer to us. 'Actually, I'm feeling a bit queasy. It must be the alcohol. I think I'm going to disappear off home.'

'But, Tig, you have tae stay for the ceilidh. It's the big moment of the year! And I know Charlie wants tae say hello.'

'He's got a lot of people to see and I'm sure there'll be another chance for us to talk over Christmas. You stay here, Cal, and enjoy yourself. I'll see you at home. Fiona, it was lovely to meet you.'

'You too, Tiggy, and let me know when you want me to visit your cats. Cal's got my number.'

'I will, thanks, Fiona.' I turned away before Cal could stop me then stepped outside to see a heavy fog had descended, the twinkling lights of the Christmas tree on the lawn shrouded by the cobweb-like mist that swirled around it. Another flicker of light appeared a few metres from the tree and I realised someone close by was smoking a cigarette.

'Merry Christmas,' I said as I passed the figure.

'And you. Er . . .' The figure walked towards me and as he emerged from the fog I saw he was very tall, but in the darkness I couldn't make out much else about him.

'Nice party?' he asked me, his voice betraying a hint of an accent that I couldn't place.

'Very nice, yes.'

'Is Char— the Laird in attendance?'

'Yes. He's hosting the party with his wife. Haven't you been in yet?'

'No.'

'Is that you, Tiggy?' A torch beam shone in our direction. 'I've been hunting high and low for you inside.'

Charlie Kinnaird walked towards me, then halted abruptly as he angled his torch on my companion.

The seconds ticked by before he said, 'What are *you* doing here?'

'I've come home to visit my old mum for Christmas. Thought I'd surprise her. No law against that, is there?'

Charlie opened his mouth to reply, then closed it again. The antipathy emanating from him was palpable.

'Well then,' I said with all the false cheer I could muster, 'I'll say goodnight. Merry Christmas,' I added as I turned tail and walked as quickly as I could towards the cottage. I could hear the two men talking . . . or in fact growling at each other as I opened the door. Charlie's normally soft tones were edged with a harshness that spoke of . . .

*What, Tiggy?*

'Hatred,' I whispered with a shudder.

I closed the door to block out the sound of the raised voices and what was obviously a developing altercation. The cottage was freezing because the fire had almost died and the storage heaters had gone off. I rekindled the fire and huddled in front of it, suddenly feeling very alone, and realising afresh that it was the first Christmas I'd ever spent away from Atlantis, my sisters and Pa.

I took my mobile off charge and, still in my ski jacket, walked into the bathroom to see if the phone fairies with their meagre two bars of signal were visiting. They were, and I was able to read various messages from my sisters, and retrieve a voicemail from Ma, which made me feel much better.

I tapped some letters into the phone.

May the grace and joy of the Christmas spirit be with you darling, love Tiggy . . .

I sent the same text off five times to all my sisters, and left a voicemail in return for Ma. Then, as I sat in front of the fire with Alice on my knee for company, I heard the chapel bell across the glen herald the arrival of Christmas Day.

I heard a whine at the door, and stood up to let Thistle in, knowing Cal wouldn't be home for hours. He bounded in happily and proceeded to try to climb onto my knee as I curled up in front of the fire.

'Thistle,' I said as I was swamped in smelly grey fur, 'you're just too big.'

Still, I was glad of his warmth and company.

'Two lonely creatures together. Merry Christmas, darling,' I whispered as I stroked his soft ears then kissed them. 'And to you, Pa, wherever you are.'

# 5

I woke up on Christmas morning feeling far more cheerful. There had been a further snowfall overnight and the first hint of a pink dawn on the horizon promised a spectacular sunrise.

I'd heard Cal and Caitlin arrive back at three in the morning. Not wanting to disturb them, after wrapping myself up warmly, I tiptoed out of the cottage and made my way to feed the cats. Although it was supposedly a holiday for humans, nature did not pause for an arbitrary date on the calendar. As I reached the top of the slope, I made out a tall figure down by the enclosure, dressed in a Barbour jacket and woolly hat, collar turned up against the cold. My heart beat just a little faster as I realised it was Charlie Kinnaird.

'Merry Christmas,' I called to him softly as I approached.

He turned to me, startled. 'Tiggy! I didn't hear you, you're so light on your feet. Merry Christmas to you too,' he added with a smile.

Up close, I could see dark smudges under his blue eyes, and the shadow of a beard beneath his sharp cheekbones.

'I came down to see the cats, but then I realised I don't know the combination to get in,' he continued.

'It's four sevens, for future reference,' I said. 'I really don't want to be negative, but the cats rarely come out, even for me. They'll already have smelt your new scent and you might have to come a few times before they'll deign to appear.'

'I understand. Cal told me you've had to work very hard to encourage them out. I don't want to disturb them, Tiggy. Would you prefer me to leave?'

'Of course not! You're the one who has offered them their lovely new home. They are incredibly temperamental, but it'll be worth it if we can get them to breed.'

'Even if they're hardly cuddly giant pandas,' Charlie said ruefully.

'Now they *would* pull in the crowds.' I smiled.

'Well, rather than me disturbing them further, shall we walk for a while instead?' he suggested as I tipped the cats' daily dose of meat into the enclosure.

'Okay,' I agreed.

After making our way back up the slope, we meandered in silence until we reached a rocky outcrop, which we climbed to give us the best vantage point for the sunrise. As the lucent, peachy rays began to emerge from behind the mountains, I turned to him.

'How does it feel to know that all of this is yours?' I asked.

'Honestly?' He looked down at me.

'Honestly.'

'Terrifying. Give me the responsibility of saving a human life over sorting out Kinnaird any day. At least I know what I'm doing in a hospital – there's a methodical approach that will either fix the problem or won't. Whereas this . . .' Charlie indicated the wild terrain, 'is largely beyond my control. Even though I want to do my best for Zara and future Kinnairds, I wonder if it's just too much for me to take on. Everything I'd like to accomplish seems to involve yet more expense and a long timescale.'

'But it's all so worthwhile,' I breathed, unable to prevent my arms gesturing expansively at the incredible landscape that lay all around us, glistening with a life of its own in the emerging sunlight. He stared at me for a second, then followed my lead and gazed out across the glen, inhaling deeply as he surveyed what was effectively his kingdom.

'You know what?' he said after a pause, during which his shoulders seemed to relax and release some of their tension. 'You're right. I have to remain positive about it, realise how lucky I am.'

'You are lucky, yes, but I totally understand how it must feel overwhelming. We're all behind you though, Charlie, really we are.'

'Thanks, Tiggy.'

Spontaneously, he reached out to briefly touch the sleeve of my ski jacket, and our eyes locked for a moment. I pulled mine away first and the moment was gone as swiftly as it had arrived.

Charlie cleared his throat. 'Listen, I want to apologise for that unfortunate scene you witnessed last night.'

'Don't worry about it. I hope it got sorted anyway.'

'No it didn't, and it never will be,' he said abruptly. 'I didn't sleep a wink last night, which is why I got up early and came down here. I thought some fresh air might clear my head.'

'I'm sorry, Charlie, for whatever it was. My father used to tell me that there were some problems you could sort out, and the ones that you couldn't, you just had to accept, close the door and move on.'

'Your father sounds like a very wise man. Unlike me,' he

74

said with a shrug. 'But he's right. Fraser's back at Kinnaird for reasons unknown and there's nothing I can do. Right, I'd better go back or Beryl's full Scottish breakfast will be getting cold.'

'She won't like that,' I smiled.

'She certainly won't,' he agreed as we turned to make our way back towards our respective dwellings. 'Where are you spending today?'

'Margaret's invited me to her new bungalow for lunch.'

'Send her my best, won't you? I've always been very fond of her,' Charlie said as we paused in front of the Lodge. 'Merry Christmas once again, Tiggy. Thanks for your company this morning. And I hope we'll get a chance to talk some more.'

'I hope so too. Merry Christmas, Charlie.'

Margaret's bungalow was everything a new bungalow should be and we both made appreciative noises as she demonstrated how the taps produced immediate hot water, and we touched all the radiators and flipped the channels on the television.

'This is so cosy, Margaret,' I said as she guided me to a new pink Dralon sofa and handed me a whisky. She looked well and rested, and her two dogs and the cat were sleeping peacefully in front of the fire.

'I must say, I don't miss gettin' up at the crack o' dawn. After all those years, it's a true luxury to have a lie-in until seven! Now yae relax, Tiggy, and I'll be seein' to our lunch.'

I sipped my whisky slowly, the heat trickling pleasantly down my throat, and I eventually followed her to the small table that she'd dressed with a ruby-red poinsettia and candles.

While I enjoyed my nut roast, made the way only she knew how, Margaret tucked into a turkey breast.

'How was the Christmas Eve ceilidh at the Lodge last night?' she asked me. 'Was Zara there?'

'I was really tired so I didn't stay for the dancing, but yes I did meet Zara. She's quite a character,' I said, suppressing a smile. 'Actually, when I left the Lodge, there was this really tall man hanging around outside. Then Charlie came out and . . . well,' I shrugged, 'he didn't seem very pleased to see him.'

'Yae say he was tall?'

'Very,' I confirmed. 'And he had what I think was an American accent.'

'Canadian, more like. No . . . it couldn't be.' Margaret set her fork down and stared into the candlelight.

'His name was Fraser,' I prompted. 'Charlie said so this morning.'

'Then it was him! What on earth is that lowlife doin' back here? Hah!' Margaret took a deep swig of her whisky then thumped the table. 'I'd bet I know.'

'Know what?'

'Nothin', Tiggy, but yae stay clear o' him. He's trouble in a teapot, that one. Poor Charlie – that's all he needs just now. I wonder if *he* knows?' Margaret mused to herself, obviously not inclined to share. 'Anyway, we'll be forgettin' about him. It's Christmas Day after all.'

I nodded compliantly, not wishing to upset her. After lunch, we sat down and I enjoyed one of her homemade mince pies. We watched the Queen's traditional Christmas Day speech and after that, Margaret dozed whilst I did the washing-up. I did my best not to think about Pa and the fact I really missed all my sisters and the sense of belonging they gave me. Even if we were a disparate bunch, with zero blood links between any of us, our Christmas gatherings had always been warm and massively comforting, glued together by our traditions. We all used to decorate the tree together on Christmas Eve, then Pa would lift Star up to put 'herself' on the very top of the tree. Claudia, our housekeeper, always prepared the most amazing food, and while everyone else tucked into meat fondue or goose, I'd have little vegan treats made just for me. Then, feeling deliciously full and warm, we'd open our presents together in the sitting room, the windows glazed with snow and the stars in the night sky winking through. On Christmas morning, we'd run into Pa's bedroom to wake him up, then go downstairs for one of Claudia's traditional sweet crêpe breakfasts, followed by a brisk walk, warmed afterwards by a mug of her mulled wine.

When Margaret woke up, we had a cup of tea and a slice of her fantastic Christmas cake, the remainder of which she insisted I take with me to share with Cal. I indicated the already darkening sky and the few flakes of snow beginning to fall beyond the window.

'I think I should get going.'

'O' course, Tiggy, yae be careful driving home now, and drop by any time you're in town.'

'I will, Margaret,' I promised as I kissed her goodbye. 'Thank you for today. It was lovely.'

'Have yae met Chilly yet by the way?' she called to me as I climbed into Beryl.

I realised that in the build-up to Christmas, I'd forgotten all about him.

'No, but I promise I will soon.'

'Yae make sure you do that, dear. Goodbye now.'

I woke at my usual early hour on Boxing Day and went to feed the cats. The snow was thick this morning, and as I threw in their meat rations, I couldn't blame them for staying snug in their beds. I was surprised but gratified to find Charlie waiting for me when I emerged from the enclosure.

'Good morning, Tiggy, I hope you don't mind me coming down again. I woke up early and couldn't seem to get back to sleep.'

'It's no problem, Charlie,' I assured him.

'Shall we walk again for a while? Unless you've somewhere else you have to be,' he added.

'I've nothing waiting for me at the cottage except a smelly old deerhound and a lame hedgehog. Even Cal has abandoned me. He's with his family in Dornoch.'

Charlie laughed. 'I see.'

As we set off, he seemed much more positive about the estate, pointing out favourite spots, and telling me more of its history.

'There used to be an amazing house that looked like a medieval castle and stood just to the right of the Lodge,' he explained. 'That's where all the lairds and their families lived until the 1850s, when my great-great-grandfather managed to burn it down by falling asleep with a big fat cigar. He went up with the place – he was well into his eighties by then – and the whole lot was razed to the ground. You can still see the foundations in the copse next to the Lodge.'

'Wow, you have so much family history, whereas I have none.'

'Is that a blessing or a curse, I wonder? It's certainly weighed me down recently, that's for sure. Although it really helped me talking to you yesterday, Tiggy. I think I'd almost become immune to the beauty of Kinnaird in recent months, viewing it more as a liability than an asset.'

'Well, that's understandable, Charlie. It's a huge responsibility.'

'It's not just that,' he admitted. 'It's also the fact that it somewhat threw my vision of my own future off course.'

'What was your vision?'

There was a long pause, as if he was debating whether or not to confide in me.

'Well, I'd been thinking about going abroad to work as a doctor with Médecins Sans Frontières once Zara has finished school. The NHS is a wonderful institution, but its staff are weighed down by paperwork and government budgets. I just want to be free to use my skills where they're really needed, somewhere I could really make a difference.'

'I know exactly what you mean. I've always dreamt of working with endangered species in Africa. Not that I don't adore the wildcats, of course, but—'

'I understand,' Charlie cut me short, but smiled sympathetically. 'This is hardly the African savannah. It sounds as though we share a similar dream.'

'Well, dreams take time to come true and even then, they're not always in the places we expect to find them. I suppose we have to be patient and concentrate on what we have today.'

'Yes, you're right, and talking of that, have you had a chance to think of any other breeds we could introduce here?'

'I reckon red squirrels are definitely one for the future,

when the reforestation is more advanced. I've been researching the wild salmon you mentioned, but restocking sounds
quite complicated, and as I told you, I'm not a fish expert, so
I'll need to pick an expert's brain. In the meantime, I think
European elks could be the next step – I might know someone
at Servion Zoo who could advise us. Although obviously we'd
need a budget; I was thinking you might be able to apply for
some grants.'

'Tell me about it,' Charlie sighed. 'I've been trying to fill in
a grant application to the Rural Development Programme
here in Scotland, as well as a couple to the EU, but they're a
nightmare. I simply don't have enough time to gather the
information in the detail they want.'

'I could help you, I've got plenty of time on my hands.'

'Could you? Have you any experience in that area?'

'Yes, at uni and at Servion Zoo I had to apply for funding
for research projects. I've only done a few, but I vaguely know
my way around the bureaucracy of it all.'

'Well, that would be incredible. I've been tearing my hair
out over the applications. I've been either at the hospital or
had my head bent over legal paperwork ever since my father
died. My wife keeps trying to convince me to either sell up or
convert the place into a golf course, and I don't blame her.'

'I hear she took over the renovations of the Lodge. She did
a great job, it's stunning.'

'Yes, even though the project came in at way over the
original budget. But it's unfair of me to criticise her. It's not
been easy for her and she was only trying to help.'

'And I'm sure the Lodge will attract discerning clients in
future,' I said firmly as Charlie glanced at his watch.

'Yes, right, I need to get back. Perhaps I can bring over the application forms to the cottage – as far as I've got with them – for you to have a look through at some point?'

'Any time, Charlie.'

By the time I got back to the cottage, a bitter wind was howling along the glen, so after I'd eaten breakfast, I lit a fire and curled up on the sofa with a book. Last night, knowing Cal was away, I'd let Thistle into the cottage and this morning he was back on my doorstep. He promptly attempted to climb onto my lap, and, eventually, I turfed him off and he curled up at my feet, his wheezing snores and the gentle crackling of the fire comforting me as I read.

I jumped as I heard feet stamping on the mat outside. If it was Cal, I knew I was in for a mouthful about Thistle, but instead, a pair of bright blue eyes appeared round the door.

'Hi, Tiggy, am I disturbing you?' said Zara.

'Not at all, I was just reading,' I said as I sat upright. 'Are you having a nice Christmas?'

'Any day is nice when I'm at Kinnaird,' she said as she sat down next to me on the sofa. Thistle immediately bounded over to her and put his head in her lap. 'I drove to Deanich Glen this morning – Mum and Dad were having another of their rows – so I went for some peace and quiet. It's fantastic down there, have you been?'

'No, but Zara, should you really be driving out there alone? The roads are treacherous in this snow . . .'

'I've been driving around the estate since I was ten, Tiggy! This is our land, remember? I don't need a licence or anything here. I take a radio and a hot flask and stuff in case anything goes wrong – I know the rules, okay? I went to give Chilly his Christmas box. I stole a bottle of Dad's whisky to perk it up.' Zara gave me a conspiratorial wink. 'We shared a dram and a few rollies. Even though he's mad and he smells terrible, he's more fun than anyone else round here. Except you, of course.'

'My friend Margaret was talking about him yesterday. I'd love to go and meet him.'

'I can take you down whenever, if you want. It's probably best if I introduce you to him first and explain who you are, because he doesn't take well to strangers.'

'A bit like my wildcats.' I smiled at her.

'Yeah, exactly. So, how about – in return for taking you to meet Chilly – I get to say hello to them? I'm very quiet on my feet like you are, Tiggy, promise, and I really would love to meet them. What are their names?'

I told her, thinking that if I *did* take Zara to see them, how could I explain it to her mother after I'd shooed *her* away?

'Why don't I see how sociable they're feeling tomorrow? I'm just paranoid about them scenting strangers and going back into hiding.'

'I understand, Tiggy. I'm here until just before Hogmanay, so I have a few days yet. And while I'm here, I was wondering if I could . . . be your assistant, or something? Follow you round and see what you actually do?'

'I'm afraid at the moment, until we've arranged to bring other animals onto the estate, the cats are the highlight of my working day.'

Zara checked the time on her mobile. 'I'd better be off. We've got a load of neighbours coming for dinner and Mum's forcing me to wear a dress!' She rolled her eyes, stood up and walked to the door. 'If it's okay with you, I'll swing by tomorrow around noon.'

'You're welcome here any time. Bye, Zara.'

'See you, Tiggy.'

Zara appeared the following lunchtime, and I was glad to have her. Cal had been out on a shoot all morning and I really was feeling like a lonely old spinster.

'Hi, Tiggy.' She smiled as she stepped through the front door. 'I'm going down to Deanich Glen to take Chilly his lunch, so how about I introduce you to him?'

'That would be great.' I grabbed my outerwear. 'Lead the way.'

Once Zara was strapped into the passenger seat next to me, we set off. The bitter wind of yesterday had died overnight and it was a pure, fresh sunny day. The snow glittered all around us as I steered the car down the slope, innocently blanketing the treacherous ice that lay beneath it. Zara gave me directions then chattered away about how boring last night's dinner had been and how she was dreading going back to her school on the North Yorkshire moors after New Year.

'Just 'cos generations of Kinnaird ancestors went there, doesn't make it right for me. Isn't it ridiculous that at sixteen you can legally get married, have sex and smoke, but at boarding school you still get treated like a ten-year-old, with lights out at nine thirty!'

'It's only eighteen months, Zara. It'll pass in a flash, really.'

'We're not around that long on this earth, so why waste

all that time – like, over five hundred and forty days, 'cos I counted – being somewhere I hate?'

I secretly agreed, but the sensible adult I'd become knew better than to say so. 'Life is full of ridiculous rules, but there are also some good ones put in place to protect us all.'

'Do you have a boyfriend, Tiggy?' Zara asked me as she directed me across the little river and along a narrow wooden bridge, the water on the rocks below us frozen into incredible ice sculptures.

'No. Do you?'

'Sort of. I mean, there's someone I really like at school.'

'What's his name?'

'Johnnie North. He's really fit and all the girls in my year are in love with him. We've met each other a couple of times in the woods, shared some rollies. But . . . he's a bad boy, you know?'

'I do know, yes,' I murmured, wondering why so many women were eternally drawn to the type of male who would use and abuse them, when the nice ones – and there were a lot of nice ones – sat on the sidelines watching and wondering why they couldn't get a girl.

'Actually, I don't think he really *is* bad, he just likes to pretend he is so he looks cool in front of his mates. When we've been alone, we talk about really deep stuff,' Zara continued. 'He had a difficult childhood, y'know? Underneath, he's really vulnerable and sensitive.'

I glanced at Zara's dreamy expression and realised she'd just answered my question: every woman who fell for a bad guy thought that he wasn't really bad at all, just misunderstood. Worst of all, they believed they were the only one who understood and, therefore, could save him . . .

'We got really close last term, but all my mates say he's just interested in getting into my pa—' Zara stopped herself and had the grace to blush. 'You know what I mean, Tiggy.'

'Well, your mates might be right,' I replied, amazed at Zara's openness. At her age, I'd never have dreamt of talking about sex to a 'grown-up' – especially one I hardly knew. I drew Beryl to a careful halt and felt the tyres skid slightly on the frozen snow a few metres away from a log cabin tucked into a crevice. The mountains rose in an elegant arc around us, the isolation both eerie and spectacular. We climbed out and walked towards the cabin, the freezing air biting at every centimetre of my exposed flesh. I pulled my scarf up over my nose because it actually hurt my lungs to breathe the air.

'Wow, it must be minus ten out here. How does Chilly survive?'

'I s'pose he's used to it. And now he's got his cabin, he's okay. You wait here,' Zara said as she paused outside the door. 'I'll go in and tell him he has a visitor but that you're not from the social services.' She winked at me, then walked across the snow and disappeared through the front door of the cabin.

I studied it and saw that it was well constructed from sturdy pine logs, one piled up on the other like the older skiing lodges on the mountain slopes in Switzerland.

The door opened and Zara peered round it. 'You can come in now,' she called to me.

I walked across to Zara. Stepping inside, I was relieved at the blissful blast of warm, smoky air. My eyes adjusted to the dimness of the room – the only light came from a couple of oil lamps and the flickering of the flames in the woodburner.

Zara grabbed my hand and led me a couple of steps towards a worn leather armchair set in front of the fire.

'Chilly, this is my friend Tiggy.'

A pair of bright, nut-brown eyes peered at me from a face so wrinkled it resembled a road map of a sprawling capital city. I realised the strong smell of smoke wasn't coming from the woodburner, but in fact from a long wooden pipe that hung from the diminutive man's mouth. With not a hair on his head and his deeply leathery skin, he reminded me of an ancient monk.

'Hello, Chilly,' I said as I took another step towards him and offered out my hand. He didn't offer his in return, only continued to stare at me. As he did so, my heart began to beat faster. I closed my eyes to steady myself and an image appeared in my mind's eye; I was in a cave staring up into the eyes of a woman. She was whispering softly to me as smoke drifted across her face from somewhere nearby and I was coughing and coughing . . .

Then I realised I *was* coughing. I opened my eyes and staggered slightly, bringing myself back to reality. Zara caught my arm.

'Are you okay, Tiggy? The air's pretty rancid in here, I'm afraid.'

'I'm fine,' I said, my watering eyes fixed on Chilly's. I couldn't seem to drag them away, even though I wanted to.

*Who are you to me . . . ?*

I watched his lips move as he muttered something to me in a language I didn't understand, then beckoned me forward with his bony finger until I stood only a few centimetres away from him.

'Sit down,' he said in heavily accented English, pointing to the only other seat in the room, which was a roughly fashioned stool set near the woodburner.

'Go ahead. I'm happy on the floor,' Zara said as she grabbed a pillow from the brass bed to soften what was just bare concrete below us.

'Hotchiwitchi!' Chilly exclaimed suddenly, his bent claw-like forefinger wagging at me. Then he threw back his head and laughed as if he was delighted. '*Pequeña bruja!*'

'Don't worry, he's always talking gibberish in English and Spanish,' muttered Zara. 'Dad says he speaks some of the old Romani language too.'

'Right,' I said, though I was pretty sure Chilly had just called me a witch.

Chilly had finally disengaged his eyes from me and was refilling his pipe with what looked like moss. Once it was lit again, he smiled at me.

'Speak English or Spanish?'

'English and French, but only a little Spanish.'

Chilly clucked in disapproval and sucked on his pipe.

'Have you been taking the pills the doctor gave you?' enquired Zara from her pillow.

Chilly turned to look at her with a mixture of mirth and derision in his eyes. 'Poison! They do try to kill me with that modern medicine.'

'Chilly, they're painkillers and anti-inflammatories for your arthritis. They help you.'

'Use my own ways,' he stated as he raised his chin to the wood-cladded ceiling. 'And you will too . . .' He pointed to me. 'Give me your hands,' he ordered.

I held them out as asked, palms up, and Chilly took them in his own, his touch surprisingly soft. I felt a tingle in my fingertips that grew stronger and stronger as he traced the lines on my palm and gently squeezed each finger in turn. Finally he looked up at me.

'So, your magic is in these,' he declared, indicating my hands. 'You help the small creatures of the earth . . . *los animales*. This your gift.'

'Right,' I said, casting a puzzled glance at Zara, who merely shrugged.

'*Bruja* power. But not complete, because your blood not pure, see? What is it you do, Hotchiwitchi?'

'You mean my job?'

He nodded and I explained. When I'd finished, he looked at me and clucked.

'Wasted. Your power here.' He gestured towards my hands and my heart. 'Not there.' He pointed to my head.

'Oh,' I said, offended. 'Well, at least my zoology degree helps me understand animal behaviour.'

'What use the statistics and the paperwork and the computer machines?' He waggled his bony finger at me again. 'You choose wrong path.'

'Did you eat that turkey I brought down yesterday?' Zara butted in, seeing my obvious distress. She stood up and walked to a corner of the cabin to open an old dresser, which contained a number of dented tins and a mish-mash of crockery.

'*Sí. Bleurgh!*' Chilly made sick noises. 'Old bird.'

'Oh well, today it's turkey soup.' Zara shrugged as she took a tin bowl from the dresser, filled it with soup from the flask she'd brought with her, added bread and a spoon and took it over to him. 'Right, you eat that and I'll go and get you some more wood.' Picking up a log basket, Zara left the hut.

I watched Chilly slurp up the soup mouthful after mouthful as if he wasn't even tasting it. When he had emptied the bowl, he put it down beside him, wiped his mouth with his forearm and lit up his pipe again.

'You feel the Spirit of the Earth, sister?'

'Yes, I do,' I whispered, surprised that, for the first time, I understood exactly what he meant.

'"Is it real?" you ask.'

'Yes, I do.'

'I will help you trust it before you leave here.'

'I'm not thinking of leaving Kinnaird yet, Chilly, I've only just arrived!'

'That's what you think,' he cackled.

Zara appeared with the basket of logs and dumped them next to the woodburner. Then she took some Christmas cake out of a tin and the whisky bottle she'd stolen from her father, which was already a third empty, and poured some into a tin mug. 'There you go, Chilly,' she said, setting the whisky and cake on the small table next to his chair. 'We've got to go now.'

'You,' he said, pointing at me. 'You come back soon, okay?'

It wasn't a request, it was an order, so I shrugged noncommittally. We said our goodbyes and walked back to Beryl across the freezing earth. I felt very strange – floaty – as if I'd had some kind of out of body experience. Whatever and whoever Chilly was, he'd seemed to know me, and despite his rudeness, I felt a weird synergy with him too.

'The problem is that he's very proud,' Zara chattered away as we drove back. 'He spent all of his life taking care of himself and now he can't. Dad's even offered to put in a generator

89

down there for him, but he refuses. Beryl says he's becoming a liability and taking up too much of our time, that for his own sake he ought to be in a care home.'

'She told me,' I answered, 'but the trouble is, Zara, now that I've met him, I understand why he wants to stay where he is. It would be like taking an animal out of its natural habitat after a lifetime of living in the wild. If he was carted off to a town, he'd probably be dead within a few days. And even if he did set the cabin on fire by mistake or have a heart attack, I'm sure he'd prefer to go like that rather than be stuck in a centrally heated nursing home. I certainly would.'

'Yeah, you're probably right. Anyway, he seemed to take to you, Tiggy. He invited you to go back and see him. Will you go?'

'Oh yes,' I said, 'I certainly will.'

# 6

Early the next morning, keeping to my side of the bargain, I met Zara in the courtyard and we walked down with a basket of meat to see the cats. I didn't think it would do any harm – there had been further snowfall overnight and any sensible animal would be buried deep inside its cosy nest anyway.

'Right,' I said as we stood on the path above the enclosures. 'From now on, as quiet as you can, okay?'

'Roger, boss,' Zara whispered, saluting me. We slithered down the icy slope to the first enclosure, where I unlocked the gate and threw the kill inside.

'Molly? Polson? Posy? Igor . . . ?' I called them, and with Zara tailing me, we walked around the other enclosures throwing food into each one and chatting to my invisible friends. When I indicated with a shake of my head that they weren't coming out to play, Zara refused to leave.

'Five more minutes, please? Can I try calling them?' she begged me in a whisper.

'Okay, why not?' I shrugged.

She stood up and walked toward the nearest enclosure. Lacing her gloved fingers around the wire fencing, she pressed her face against it and called the cats' names. I followed her around the enclosures as she spoke to them and waited, then suddenly I saw a movement in the box that Posy favoured.

'Look, it's Posy,' I hissed, pointing to the box shrouded in undergrowth.

Sure enough, a pair of amber eyes glinted at us from the gloom.

'Oh. My. God!' Zara whispered in excitement. I watched as she fixed her eyes on those of the cat and blinked very slowly. 'Hi, Posy, I'm Zara,' she said softly, and to my utter surprise and delight, Posy mimicked her and blinked back. Then there was a sudden sound of feet crunching on snow and the cat immediately retreated.

'Damn!' swore Zara. 'I thought she was about to come out.'

'Maybe she was,' I said as we retraced our footsteps up the hill to see who had scared the cat off. There, at the top of the slope, was Charlie Kinnaird.

'Dad!' Zara scrambled up towards him. 'I just managed to coax one of the cats out and then she heard your footsteps and disappeared,' she said in an exaggerated whisper.

'Sorry, darling. I came to see the cats too,' Charlie whispered back. 'And to see you, Tiggy. Maybe we should go up to the house where it's warmer and we're actually allowed to speak?'

Charlie smiled at me and I felt my insides melt like snow in the sun.

'Well, here you all are!' A loud voice came from up above. I looked up and saw Ulrika walking along the path towards us. 'I thought these animals were out of bounds to everyone except you?' Ulrika pointed to me. 'You *are* honoured,' she remarked as Charlie and Zara scrambled up the rest of the slope ahead of me. 'I was shooed away a few days ago.'

With her hands on her hips, her height and her vantage point above me, Ulrika reminded me of an angry Valkyrie.

'She only brought me because I begged and begged and wore her down, Mum,' Zara said, trying to placate her.

'So, I must go on my hands and knees and also beg you next time?' Ulrika spoke lightly, but as she looked down at me, her eyes were hard and cold.

'Come up to the house with us, Tiggy, and have a coffee and a chat,' Charlie suggested as we all headed back towards the Lodge.

'Sorry, darling, but I'll need you to drive me to Dornoch to visit Lady Murray. She's expecting me for coffee at eleven. Maybe another time, Tiggy?' Ulrika suggested coldly.

'Of course.'

'I'll pop across to the cottage when I'm back later,' Charlie said. 'I want to give you those grant application papers and also talk to you about bringing European elk onto the estate in the spring.'

'Okay. Well then, bye Zara, bye Ulrika,' I said, and beat a hasty retreat to the safety of the cottage.

'Wow!' I breathed as I slumped onto the sofa.

'What's "wow"?' Cal asked me as he came into the sitting room with a slice of toast.

'Ulrika Kinnaird,' I sighed. 'I get the feeling she doesn't like me very much.'

'I don't think she likes anyone very much, Tig. Don't take it personally. What's she said tae you?'

I explained what had happened and Cal laughed.

'Whoops,' he said, 'I think you're off her Christmas card

list for the next few years. Ulrika doesn't like tae be left out of anything, especially when it's tae do with her husband. Mebbe she's just really insecure, y' know?'

'Maybe she'll tell her husband to fire me.'

'The Laird really rates you, Tig, don't worry. Now, I've got tae go. Her Majesty has requested I shovel the drive o' snow and lay down some salt so she won't fall flat on her precious wee arse.' Cal winked at me and left the cottage.

'So did the Laird make it round for a cuppa and a chat?' Cal asked me when he arrived through the door at eight that night.

'No, he didn't,' I said, pouring Cal a glass of whisky and handing it to him.

'Right, mebbe he got caught up with other things.'

'Perhaps, but it's not a million miles to walk over from the Lodge to tell me. I sat in here all day waiting for him.'

'Aye, and they were in at the Lodge all right; I saw their car come back around three. C'mon, Tig, don't look so down.'

'Well, as he's definitely not coming now, I'm going for a bath.'

There was only lukewarm water, and I lay there pondering whether Chilly saying I'd be leaving soon had anything to do with the blonde Valkyrie appearing this morning.

There was a sudden rapping on the bathroom door. 'Tig? Are you out yet? We have a visitor.'

'Er, nearly,' I said, pulling the plug and stepping out. 'Who is it?'

I held my breath for Cal's reply, only hoping it wasn't

Charlie Kinnaird. I really didn't want to emerge into the sitting room in my ancient blue woolly dressing gown, and have to dash to my bedroom to retrieve my clothes.

'It's Zara an' she's in a bit o' a state,' he hissed.

'Okay, coming,' I called through the door.

When I opened it and walked into the sitting room, I saw Zara sitting on the sofa, head in her hands. She was sobbing loudly.

'I'll leave you ladies to it.' Cal raised an eyebrow and left.

'Zara, what's wrong?' I said, sitting down on the sofa next to her.

'Dad promised we could stay until the day before Hogmanay, but now he's saying we're leaving! Two whole days more that I could have spent here, and now I have to go back to Inverness!'

'Why?'

'I don't know. A man came to the house this morning and had some kind of big argument with Dad. I didn't dare go downstairs, but I could hear them yelling at each other. Then Dad came upstairs and told me we were going home. And I don't want to go!'

'Do you know what the argument was about? Or who the man was?'

'No, he wouldn't say.'

'Zara, darling,' I said as I circled her in my arms. 'I'm so sorry. You just have to remember that it's really not long until you're eighteen, and then if being at Kinnaird is what you want, no one can stop you.'

'Dad said I could spend my whole Christmas holiday up here if I wanted to, but Mum won't let me stay on. She hates it here.'

'Maybe the estate's just not her kind of life.'

'Nothing is her kind of life, Tiggy.' Zara sighed, her expression a picture of weariness and despair. 'She's always saying she'll be happy if Dad does this or that, like take her on swanky holidays with money he hasn't got, or buy her a new car or a picture she likes because that'll make it better. But it doesn't ever. She's just a really unhappy person, you know?'

As I sat and stroked Zara's silken hair, I knew that even though she might be exaggerating due to dramatic teenage hormones, I'd seen enough of Ulrika to understand that she was a difficult character. And it suddenly struck me that even though I'd been adopted and had lived under the care of a woman employed by my adoptive father, and had often secretly dreamt of being the beloved child of two married, biological parents, I'd idealised the thought. I had no experience of warring parents. Never once at Atlantis had I heard Pa Salt and Ma have an argument – we had been brought up in total tranquillity, and for the first time I acknowledged how rare that actually was. What Zara was experiencing was what lots of other friends of mine at school had said they had gone through too. We sisters had lived in a fantasy of perfection in our fairy-tale castle, certainly in terms of our two 'parents'. Of course, the saving grace of our childhood had been that there were six of us. Harmony had certainly not reigned supreme between us. Someone was always falling out with someone else, and normally that 'someone else' would be my baby sister, Electra . . .

Silence ensued as I continued to stroke Zara's hair. It lasted so long that I actually wondered if she had fallen asleep, but her head suddenly bobbed up.

'I know! I could ask Dad if I can stay here with you and

Cal at the cottage! I could say you needed me to help you out until the end of the holidays!' Her face lit up with excitement at her new idea. 'Could I, Tiggy? I promise I wouldn't be any trouble. I can sleep here on the sofa, as long as Cal wouldn't mind, which I'm sure he wouldn't because we get on really well and he likes me and—'

'I'd love to have you here, Zara, but your mum hardly knows me and I doubt she'd trust her precious girl to a stranger.'

'Well, Beryl's at the Lodge and Mum trusts her and Dad's known Cal since he was born and—'

'Zara, all you can do is speak to your parents. If they're happy for you to stay here with me and Cal, then yes, we'd be happy to have you.'

'I will,' she said, 'and if they don't let me, maybe I'll just run away.'

'Don't say that, Zara, it's a threat, and if you want everyone to believe that you're grown up enough to make your own decisions, that isn't the way to handle it. Why don't you go back to the Lodge and ask them? If they agree, you need to give them time to come down and see me before they leave,' I encouraged her.

'Okay, I will. Thanks, Tiggy.' She stood up and walked to the door. 'One day, I swear I will come and live here at Kinnaird. Permanently. And even Mum won't be able to stop me. Night, Tiggy.'

As I'd expected, there'd been no visit that night from either Charlie or Ulrika, and the missing Range Rover the next morning confirmed that the three of them had left for Inverness.

'Poor wee kiddie, caught in the middle o' all that,' Cal said as he sipped his coffee. 'Dysfunctional families, eh? Mine isn't perfect, but at least I'd say we're fairly normal. Right, that's me off.'

Cal walked to the front door, then bent down to pick up an envelope from the mat. 'You've got mail, Tig,' he said handing it to me as Thistle's head appeared longingly round the open door. 'An' you're comin' with me, Thistle,' he said, shooing the dog out.

I opened the envelope and read the short note inside.

*Dear Tiggy – in haste – I apologise for my abrupt
departure and for not coming to see you. A legal issue
has cropped up. I'll be in contact soon.
Many apologies,
Charlie*

I had no idea what he meant but I had to presume it was something to do with the big argument Zara had mentioned.

I went to my bedroom; all this talk of families making me miss mine. I opened my bedside drawer and pulled out the letter Pa Salt had written me. I'd read it so many times, it was starting to look grubby. Unfolding it, I started to reread it, comforted just by the sight of Pa's looping, elegant handwriting.

*Atlantis
Lake Geneva
Switzerland*

*My darling Tiggy,
    Well now, there is little point in spending time
writing the usual platitudes about my sudden*

*disappearance from your life – I know you will refuse to believe that I have gone. But gone I have. Even though I know you will feel me still all around you, you must accept that I am never coming back.*

*Of course, I write this letter at my desk in Atlantis, still here on this earth, so I cannot yet tell you what the beyond is like, but the one thing I am not is afraid. You and I have talked many times about the miraculous hand of fate, of destiny and a higher power – God to some – touching our lives. It saved me when I was a child, and my belief in it – even through the harder times I have had in my life – has never wavered. Neither must yours.*

*With your other sisters, I have been careful to make sure that I only gave them limited information about where I originally found them, because I didn't want to disturb their lives. However, you are different. When your family gave you to me, it was on the condition I promised that one day, when I felt the time was right, I would send you back to them.*

*You are part of an ancient culture, Tiggy, one that these days is derided by some. I believe it is because many of us humans have forgotten our roots in nature and where our heart and soul lies. You, I was told, come from a special line of gifted seers, although the woman who handed you over to me made it clear that the gift often misses a generation, or does not grow to its fruition.*

*I was told to watch you as you grew, and I did so. From a fretful sick baby, you became an inquisitive child who loved nothing more than surrounding herself with nature and animals. Even though you were unable to have your own pet due to Ma's allergy, you still dedicated yourself to every wounded sparrow you found, and the hedgehogs in the garden that you fed.*

*Perhaps you don't remember the moment you came to me when you were five or six, and whispered in my ear that you'd just spoken to a fairy in the woods. She had told you that her name was Lucía, and that the two of you had danced together, barefoot in the forest.*

*Well, it's hardly uncommon for a child so young to believe in fairies, but in this case, it was then I knew that you had inherited the gift. Darling Tiggy, Lucía was the name of your grandmother.*

*So now, I fulfil the promise I made by telling you that at some point in your life, you should travel to Spain, to a city named Granada. On a hill opposite the magnificent Alhambra, in an area called Sacromonte, you must knock on a blue door situated on a narrow path called the Cortijo del Aire and ask for Angelina. There you will find the truth of your birth family. And perhaps your own destiny too . . .*

*Before I close, I must also reveal to you that if it hadn't been for one sentence offered by a relation of yours many years ago, I would not have been given the gift of all my beloved daughters. She saved me from despair and I can never repay my debt to her.*

*All my love to you, my darling, gifted girl. I am so very proud of you.*

*Pa x*

I then drew out the paper that contained the information that had been engraved on the armillary sphere, which had suddenly appeared a few days after Pa's death in his special garden. Each of the bands upon it bore our names, a quotation in Greek and a set of coordinates, which indicated where in the world Pa had found us.

Pa's quotation for me, translated by my eldest sister Maia, had brought tears to my eyes, because it suited me so perfectly:

*Keep your feet on the fresh carpet of the earth, but raise your mind to the windows of the universe.*

As for the coordinates, Ally, who was a sailor and used to that kind of thing, had worked them all out for us. Mine had corresponded exactly with what Pa had told me in his letter. Until today, I hadn't really dared to understand what Pa had meant about coming from a special and 'gifted' line. Yet Chilly had seemed to know who I was, and had even told me I had 'power' in my hands. I stood up and walked to the small mirror that hung on the wall above the chest of drawers. I studied my features – my tawny-brown eyes, dark eyebrows and olive skin. Yes, if I dragged my hair back, I probably could be taken for someone with Mediterranean blood. Yet my hair, even though it was dark, had a rich chestnut tinge to it. All the gypsies – if that was what I was – I'd ever seen on TV or in pictures had jet-black hair, so even if I did have some Romani in me, Chilly himself had told me I was not pure-blood. But then, who was these days? Two thousand years of interbreeding meant we were all mongrels.

I knew nothing about gypsies, except that many tended to live on the outskirts of society. I was aware that they didn't have the best reputation, but as Pa had often said to me and my sisters, '*Never judge a book by its cover. A dull clump of earth can hide the most precious jewel . . .*'

And I had always prided myself on believing the best about everyone until proven wrong. In fact, perhaps my greatest weakness was my naivety about others, ironically engendered by my best quality: my unerring faith in the goodness of human nature. Other people rolled their eyes when I stated that good always triumphed over evil. After all – in simplistic terms – if it didn't, then all the evil souls would have murdered the good ones, and then murdered each other, so the human race would no longer exist.

Whatever race Chilly came from, I knew he had a good soul. He was the first gypsy I'd ever knowingly met and I definitely wanted to learn more, I thought, as I replaced the precious letter in my bedside drawer.

# 7

On New Year's Eve, I woke up, looking forward to the Hogmanay celebration that Cal was taking me to in the local village hall, so I could see in the New Year in traditional Scottish fashion. Arriving back at the cottage after feeding the cats, I found Beryl pacing our sitting room, anxiety painted on her features like a mask.

'Tiggy, how are you?' she said.

'I'm fine, thank you, Beryl. You?' I could see she was uncharacteristically flustered.

'Some . . . unfortunate circumstances have cropped up, but they're not for bothering you with just now.'

'Right.'

I wondered if the 'circumstances' were anything to do with the sudden departure of the Kinnaird family, but I knew Beryl well enough by now not to press her on the subject.

She gathered herself together with considerable effort and continued. 'However, my most immediate problem is that Alison has called in sick this morning. Apparently, so her mother told me, she has a terrible cold, but it's left me high and dry. The New Year guests are arriving at four o'clock today – eight of them – expecting a full high tea! I have a mountain of unironed sheets – I had to strip all the beds because the dust from the renovations had fallen again, so each room needs to be hoovered, the furniture polished, the dining table and all the fires to be laid, and that's on top of the dinner to be cooked and I haven't even plucked the pheasants yet—'

'Can I help?' I offered, registering Beryl's barely disguised need for assistance.

'Would you, Tiggy? The gentleman who's booked the Lodge for the week is a billionaire apparently, and very influential. The Laird is counting on him to spread the word about Kinnaird amongst his rich friends, and what with everything else that's happened recently, I can't let him down.'

'Of course you can't. I'll come up to the Lodge with you now.'

Cal, who'd been listening from the kitchen, offered his services too, and for the rest of the day we ironed sheets, made beds, hoovered floors and laid fires as Beryl slaved away in the kitchen. By three o'clock we joined her for a cup of tea, all of us worn out.

'I can't thank you both enough for today,' Beryl said as we all enjoyed a piece of warm shortbread. 'I don't know what I'd have done without you. At least everything's prepared for tonight.'

I glanced at all the food laid out on the kitchen centre unit and in a plethora of covered dishes and pans on the worktops.

'Have you got someone coming to help you serve it tonight?' I asked.

'No, Alison was going to be my waitress too, but I'm sure I can manage.'

'Listen, I'll stay and help you, Beryl. You can't do all this by yourself, certainly not properly as the Laird would want it.'

'Oh no, Tiggy, I won't ask that of you. It's Hogmanay and Cal's taking you down to the ceilidh.'

'He was, but I can go another time. Beryl, you need me.'

'Yes, I do,' she admitted, 'although the Laird has asked that the help serve in uniform.'

'Och, Tig, I cannae wait tae see you dressed up as a French maid!' Cal winked at me.

'I feel terrible about this,' Beryl sighed. 'You're a wildlife consultant with a degree, not a serving girl.'

'As a matter of fact, I worked an entire summer in a silver service restaurant in Geneva once.'

'Then that seals it, but I'm going to call the Laird tomorrow and tell him that if we are opening what he wants to be a five-star hotel, then he has to allow me to employ some proper staff. It's not fair on you – or me.'

'Really, it's no problem. Do you want some help with afternoon tea? I'd better get my maid's uniform on pretty fast.' I grinned as I saw it was half past three.

'No, you go home, have a bath and get some rest. Dinner's at eight, but I'll need you from six to serve drinks, if that's all right by you?'

'It's fine, Beryl.'

'Could you possibly take this down to Chilly before you leave?' I asked Cal as we walked across the courtyard to our cottage and handed him a container of pheasant stew I'd spooned out of one of Beryl's dishes. 'Wish him Happy New Year from me and tell him I'll be down to see him soon.'

'O' course. Shame you cannae come with me tonight, but you've won a place in Beryl's heart forever now.'

I was back up at the Lodge at six, and Beryl gave me my uniform for the night, complete with white apron.

'Alison's would have drowned you, so I dug this out of an old chest in the attic. It smells of mothballs, but it should fit,' she said. 'Put it on in the laundry room, and I'm afraid you'll have to tie your hair back too.'

I did as she'd asked and when I was ready, I walked back to the kitchen. 'How do I look?'

'Lovely,' Beryl said, hardly glancing at me.

'Do I really have to wear this as well?' I asked her, holding up the white headband with a black stripe that I was meant to tie across my forehead.

'I don't think that'll be necessary. Now, they'll all be down in a few minutes, so you'll need to open the champagne. There's sparkling water and elderflower cordial for any tee-totallers in the fridge over there. The spirits are laid out on top of the drinks cabinet in the Great Room. You just need to add a bucket of ice.'

'Right.' I scurried off to go about my duties.

I'd always enjoyed acting in school plays, and I really got into character whilst I was handing round the champagne in the Great Room, almost wanting to add, 'Yes, m'Lord', 'thank you, m'um,' and perform a quick bob before I moved on to the next guest. From my vantage point near the drinks cabinet, I could see the guests were a well-heeled bunch; five men dressed in black tie, three women in cocktail dresses and expensive-looking jewellery. Even though they spoke English as a group, I could also hear a variety of accents, ranging from German to French.

'How's it going in there?' Beryl asked as I appeared in the kitchen and ran to the fridge.

'Fine, although we've finished the first six bottles of champagne already.'

'I'll call them in for dinner in about twenty minutes or so. I just hope that Jimmy the Bagpipes remembers he's meant to arrive at the front door to play in the New Year.'

I returned to the Great Room with the fresh tray of champagne, and all eyes turned to me.

'Ah! Here she is! For a moment, I wondered if the staff had drunk all the cases I had sent up!'

The entire party laughed and I presumed that the man walking towards me was the host. As he drew closer, I saw he was shorter than average, broad shouldered, with dark blond hair, aquiline features and unusual deep-set green eyes.

'Thank you.' His eyes swept over me in appraisal. 'What is your name?'

'Tiggy.'

'That is unusual, is it Scottish?' he asked as he held out his champagne flute for me to fill.

'No, it's a nickname. My real name is Taygete. It's Greek.'

I was surprised to see a fleeting glimpse of recognition cross his features.

'Right. Is that a French accent I can hear?'

'It is, although I'm Swiss.'

'Are you indeed?' he said thoughtfully, studying me again. 'Well, well. Do you work here?'

In any other circumstance – for example if we'd met in a bar – I could understand why he was asking me all this, but here, where he was the host and I was ostensibly the 'help', it felt distinctly odd.

'Yes, but not normally in this capacity. I'm just helping out

for the night because the maid is off sick. I'm a wildlife consultant on the estate.'

'I see. Are you sure we have not met before?'

'Quite sure,' I said. 'I never forget a face.'

'Where's that champagne?' one of the guests called from
across the room.

'I'd better go,' I said with a polite smile.

'Of course. By the way, my name is Zed. Good to meet
you, Tiggy.'

I arrived home at two in the morning, hardly able to put one
foot in front of the other, and decided that all waitresses were
totally undervalued.

'Give me lions and tigers to care for any day,' I groaned as
I stripped off my clothes, put on the thermal pyjamas Cal had
bought me for Christmas and fell into bed.

The good news was that the dinner had gone like clockwork. Between us, Beryl and I had pulled off a successful
evening that had flowed seamlessly from one event to the next.
I closed my eyes gratefully as my pulse slowed down, but sleep
wouldn't come. Instead, I kept seeing Zed's green eyes, which
– although maybe I had imagined it – I'd felt had followed me
around the room all evening. Just before midnight, when I'd
arrived with further champagne and whisky, Beryl had pressed
a piece of coal into my hand.

'Get round to the front door, Tiggy. Here's an egg timer
and it's set for eleven fifty-nine and fifty seconds. When it
buzzes, knock as hard as you can on the front door. Three

times,' she'd added. 'Jimmy the Bagpipes is positioned there already.'

'What do I do with this?' I'd asked her, studying the coal.

'When the door is opened, Jimmy will start playing and you hand the coal over to the person who's opened the door. Got that?'

'I think so, yes. But—'

'I'll explain later. Now shoo!'

So I'd joined Jimmy the Bagpipes outside; he was swaying slightly after one too many drams, and waited until my timer had gone off, then knocked loudly on the door. The bagpipes had rung out into the frosty air as the door opened and I saw Zed standing behind it.

'Happy New Year,' I said as I handed him the piece of coal.

'Thank you, Tiggy,' he smiled at me, then reached forward and kissed me gently on the cheek. 'Happy New Year to you too.'

I hadn't seen him after that, because I'd been busy in the kitchen clearing up with Beryl, but now I thought about the kiss, it felt like an oddly intimate gesture to make to a complete stranger, especially one masquerading as a maid . . .

I woke at seven to a silent cottage and immediately jumped out of bed. Beryl had assured me she could manage the brunch she would serve at noon but still, I went to the Lodge after feeding the cats to see if she needed a helping hand.

'Only the host is up. I've served him coffee in the Great Room,' Beryl said.

'Right. Are you sure you don't want me to stay?'

'No. Alison's managed to rouse herself from her sickbed and is laying the table in the dining room. She'll be a bit of a come-down for the guests after your professional service last night,' she added. 'You know what they say, you pay peanuts, you get – well – Alison!'

'Beryl, honestly, the poor girl had a terrible cold. So, if you're sure there's nothing else I can do, I'll take Chilly's lunch to him.'

'Is there any more coffee available, Beryl?' Zed appeared in the kitchen proffering a cup. He was attired in a jade-green turtleneck jumper and jeans and looked as fresh as a daisy.

'Of course.' Beryl took the cup and while she poured a fresh coffee, his glance turned to me.

'Good morning, Tiggy. How are you?'

'I'm well, thank you.' It was ridiculous, but I could feel the heat rising to my cheeks.

'Beautiful day, isn't it?'

'Yes. It's always beautiful up here when the sun shines.'

'I have never been to Scotland before, but I think I have fallen in love,' he said, his gaze still upon me.

'Here's your coffee, sir.'

Beryl came to the rescue with her usual impeccable timing. Zed averted his eyes from mine in order to take the cup.

'So,' he said to her, 'brunch at noon – then perhaps a tour of the estate? I think my guests could all do with a breath of fresh air.'

'Of course. Cal will be happy to take you all out in the Land Rover,' Beryl replied.

'Excellent,' he said, and I heard the definite tinge of a German accent. 'If my guests are not up in the next thirty minutes, I give you full permission to throw a glass of iced water in each of their faces.' He nodded formally at both of us and left the kitchen.

'Is Cal back from Dornoch yet?' Beryl asked me tensely.

'He wasn't when I left to come here, no.'

'Then can you use the Lodge telephone to call his parents' number and make sure he's here by two? And sober enough to drive our guests around without hurling them to their deaths in the glen.' Beryl indicated the number on the list above the receiver. 'I'm off to deal with Alison.'

As I dialled the number, I was reminded of an English programme about an eccentric man running a hotel with only two members of staff at his disposal. I couldn't help feeling that Cal and I had become reluctant members of the cast.

Having spoken to Cal's mother, who promised she'd rouse Cal from his bed immediately, but that it'd been quite a 'hoolie', I went into the office and checked my emails on the computer.

There was a lovely one from my eldest sister, Maia, in Rio, wishing me a Happy New Year, and hoping that 'all my dreams came true'. In many ways, she was the sister I felt I had most in common with – she too was a dreamer and out of all of us, had probably taken Pa's death the hardest. But now, six months on, she was living a new life in Brazil and every word she wrote felt as if it had a spring in its step.

I wrote a quick note back to her, wishing her the same and telling her that we must organise a plan to bring all of us sisters together to lay a wreath in the spot off the Greek island where our sister Ally believed she'd witnessed Pa's burial at sea. Just as I'd sent the email off, there was a ping as a new one came through.

1st January 2008

Dear Tiggy,

First of all, Happy New Year! Once again, I'm very sorry I wasn't able to come and see you for a chat as I'd promised. I'm hoping that I will be able to find the time in the next two or three weeks to come up there. Meanwhile, I've posted the grant application forms to you with what I've already managed to fill in.

Also, I'd like to thank you for your kindness to Zara over the time she was staying up at Kinnaird. I know she's tricky – all teenagers are, so I appreciate your patience. She sends love and says she hopes to see you very soon. As do I.

With very best wishes,

Charlie

While I was in front of the computer, I wrote a short email to my contact at Servion Zoo about the European elks and asked him for a convenient time to book a telephone call, then I went into the kitchen to find it deserted. Presuming that Beryl was busy serving the guests, I spooned some kedgeree into a Tupperware box and set off to see Chilly.

'Where you bin hidin' yourself, Hotchiwitchi?' a voice from the leather chair demanded as I opened the door.

'Happy New Year, Chilly,' I said as I decanted the kedgeree into his bowl. 'I've been helping Beryl up at the Lodge.'

'Have you now?' He eyed me as I handed him a spoon and the bowl. 'That place holds things you like, don't it?'

He cackled then, like the old witch he was.

'Which year is it now?' he asked as he guzzled the food down.

'2008.'

His spoon paused below his mouth as he looked into the woodburner.

'Those rich fellas are in for a reckoning this year,' he said then carried on eating.

'Which rich fellas?'

'Never you mind, you're poor like me, but them has been greedy . . . they all get found out in the end. You heard from the Laird?'

'I got an email from him today.'

'He got big problems. You take care around him.'

'I will,' I said.

'Around all of them up at that house. Winter comes before spring . . . You remember that, Hotchiwitchi.'

'What is a "hotchiwitchi", Chilly?' I asked him.

'You a hedgehog, is your name in Roma language.' He shrugged as I stared at him in shock, wondering how he could have known . . .

'You come from long way away. *España* . . .' My ears pricked up at this. Again, how could he know?

'My father said that too, in a letter he wrote me before he died. He told me I should go back there and . . .'

I looked at Chilly, but he had nodded off, so I took the opportunity to go to the cave next door and bring in some firewood. The sun had climbed above the mountains, its delicate fingers of light reaching down to illuminate the pure whiteness of the glen. It was a mystical sight, a place in which it was very easy to become disconnected from reality. As I stood with the basket of logs looped over my arm, I was thrown back again to an image of a rough whitewashed ceiling above me, and the sound of a voice I was sure I recognised.

'*Come, little one, I will take care of you until you're grown.*'

'*Bring her back home to us . . .*'

I was being lifted up towards the ceiling, but I wasn't frightened because I knew the pair of arms that held me was safe.

I staggered slightly as I came to and realised my feet were planted firmly on the ground and I was standing alone in the icy-cold cave.

As I walked back into the cabin, I knew for certain that one of the voices I'd heard had been Pa Salt's.

'I have some news for you, in fact two bits of news,' Cal said over supper that night.

'What?'

'Well, the first is that last night, me and Caitlin named the date. It's to be in June.'

'Wow, Cal!' I smiled at him. 'That's fantastic. It doesn't give you a long time to plan though.'

'Aye, well, Caitlin has been planning the wedding for twelve years, so she's had long enough.'

'Congratulations, Cal, I'm really happy for you. And, really, you must invite her for supper at the cottage very soon. I only met her briefly on Christmas Eve, and I'd love to see her again.'

'I will, Tig. Thing is, now that we'll be wed in a few months, she's given me a lecture, told me I must ask the Laird for a pay rise and an assistant tae boot. This job'll be the death of me – or certainly my back – if I carry on alone.'

'How about the vet's son, Lochie? He seemed like a nice young man.'

'Aye, he is, an' he knows what he's doin' on the land too. I'll give the Laird a buzz, get the okay, and then speak tae him.'

'Don't take no for an answer, will you, Cal?'

'That I won't. Tomorrow I'll be up at dawn tae take the men out on a shoot an' I spent this afternoon sussing out where the stags were hiding on the estate. Nothing shags the client off more than spending hours tramping through the glen tae not even get a sight o' a deer.'

'Serves them right for being so bloodthirsty,' I said primly. 'I shall use all my powers to make sure the stags hide themselves away.'

'Don't you be doing that, Tig, or I'll just get earache from all o' them. They want tae go home with their trophies and show them off tae their women like the cavemen they are, underneath all their fine clothes. Aye, with any luck, I'll be blooding then boiling a few stag heads tomorrow night.' He winked at me.

'Enough, Cal. I know it's the way of things and that the deer have to be culled, but there's no need to ram it down my throat.'

'Tae make you feel a little better, here's my second piece o' news for you.'

'Which is . . . ?' I was still cross with him.

'Well, lassie, it turns out that the host o' this house party – one Zed – wasn't able tae make the tour o' the estate with the others today, so he's suggested that whilst I'm taking the rest o' the party out with their guns tomorrow, you'd escort him on his own private tour.'

'Surely he'd be better to wait a day and have you take him?' I frowned. 'You know the estate far better than me.'

'I don't think it's the flora and fauna he's interested in, Tig, more the guide. He insisted it should be you that drove him.'

'And what if I don't want to take him?'

'Tig, you're being obtuse. It's only a couple o' hours and as we both know, the Laird wants tae establish a reputation for pleasing his guests. There's no doubt that the guy has got bags o' money. The cost o' renting this place for all his friends for a week was more than you and I earn in a year put together. Look on the bright side; yae might have bagged yourself a billionaire.'

'Oh very funny.' I grabbed his plate before he could see the heat that was rising to my cheeks.

'So, will you do it? Beryl wants tae know.'

'Yes,' I sighed from the kitchen as I turned the tap on.

'Perhaps you should wear your maid's uniform from last night,' he cackled.

'Enough, Cal, please!'

# 8

As requested, I appeared up at the Lodge at ten o'clock the following morning. Beryl was in the kitchen, seasoning two enormous salmon, presumably for dinner that evening.

'Morning, Tiggy.' She gave me a tense smile. 'Ready to play tour guide? He's waiting in the Great Room.'

'I just hope I don't get lost, Beryl. I've never driven around the whole estate without Cal.'

'I'm sure you won't, and you'll have your radio pack with you, just in case. There's a flask of hot coffee and a tin of shortbread too in that basket over there.'

'Thanks.'

'Well now, you'd better be off. If it starts to snow heavily, come back immediately.'

'I will.'

I walked out of the kitchen and made my way along the corridor to the Great Room. Zed was sitting in front of the fire, a laptop on the coffee table in front of him. The air smelt heavily of stale cigar smoke and alcohol.

'Ah, I see my chauffeur has arrived,' he said, smiling up at me. 'Which is good, as I was just about to throw my laptop out of the window. The only reliable internet connection is in Beryl's office and I do not like to invade her territory.'

'I'm sure she wouldn't mind.'

'She is an interesting woman; not to be challenged, I'd say,' Zed commented as he stood up and walked towards me. 'I am not sure she approves of me.'

'Oh, I'm sure she does, really, she told me on New Year's Eve that she thought you were a gentleman.'

'Then she does not know me at all.' He chuckled as he saw the expression on my face. 'I am only joking, Tiggy. Right, shall we go?'

Outside, I loaded the radio pack and the basket of coffee and biscuits onto the back seat of Beryl, then climbed up behind the wheel. I showed Zed how to heave the passenger door closed, once he'd installed himself on the seat next to me.

'I think it is time the owner invested in some new transportation for his guests,' he said as we rattled off. 'The ladies came back from their tour yesterday with very sore backsides.'

'I'm sure it's on his list, but as you know, he's only just opened the Lodge to guests. Have you found everything comfortable so far?'

'Extremely, yes, apart from this car.' He glanced at me while I navigated a steep bend. 'You are tougher than you look, aren't you?'

'I'm certainly used to the outdoor life, yes.'

'So what is a girl from Switzerland doing up in the wilds of Scotland?'

I explained as briefly as I could as I drove us carefully downhill into the main glen. 'Look,' I said, bringing the car to a slithery halt, grabbing the binoculars from the back seat and handing them to him. 'Up there, on the hillside beneath that clump of trees, there's a small herd of hinds.'

Zed took the binoculars and, following my finger, focused them on the snow-covered cluster of trees.

'Yes, I see them.'

'A lot of them are pregnant at the moment, so they stay away from the males, who we'll see on the south side of the glen. They bask in the sun whilst the females shiver in the shadows,' I added.

'Typical males, choosing the warmest spot for themselves,' Zed chuckled, handing back the binoculars.

'I'm afraid there's not much to see here at this time of year, given all the snow. You should come back in the summer when the glens come alive. It's truly beautiful.'

'I can imagine, but I am more of a city person myself.'

'Where do you live?'

'I have places in New York, London and Zurich, and a boat I keep in Saint-Tropez for the summers. I travel a lot.'

'Sounds like you're a very busy man.'

'Yes, the last few months in particular have been hectic.' He let out a deep sigh. 'Is this all there is?' he said as we drove deeper into the estate, which, covered by ice and snow as it was, did not give me much to show him.

'There's the Highland cattle just ahead in the glen. They're very cute. And if you're really lucky, you might see a golden eagle.'

'Or in fact I may not. I think I have seen enough, Tiggy. What I want is a quiet lunch and a glass of wine by a roaring fire. Do you know of a pub or a restaurant close by?'

'I'm afraid not. I haven't been out to eat or drink since I arrived and there's nothing "close by" to Kinnaird.'

'Then it's back to base camp, please. I am freezing. If I had known the car did not have heating, I would have worn my ski suit.'

'Okay,' I said with a shrug and did a slippery three-point turn. 'I'm sure Beryl can rustle up something for you back at the Lodge.'

'I will be honest with you, Tiggy: it was not the country-side I wanted to see today.'

I could feel his eyes boring into me as I concentrated on navigating the icy track back. I felt a blush rise to my cheeks and I hated myself for it.

Back at the Lodge, I trooped in behind Zed, who marched into the kitchen to speak to a surprised Beryl. She'd obviously been giving Alison a lesson in pie-making and the girl was covered in flour as she rolled the pastry into the shape Beryl required.

'It is simply too cold out there, Beryl,' said Zed. 'And there is no heating in that Land Rover. In retrospect, we should have taken my car, but it is too late now. I would like the fire lit and some sandwiches for both of us in the Great Room. Oh, and two glasses of that white Cabernet Sauvignon I brought with me.'

'I should really get on with my work . . .' I murmured.

'Surely you can take a short break for lunch, Tiggy? Besides, I do not want to eat alone.'

I threw a despairing glance at Beryl, which she blatantly ignored.

'Right you are, sir. You go into the Great Room and I'll bring the sandwiches and wine. Take him through, Tiggy, and light the fire if you would. I'll be along in a few minutes.'

This wasn't a request, it was an order, so I led Zed to the Great Room and did as Beryl had asked.

'This is more like it,' Zed said as he sat down in a chair and warmed his hands against the fire. 'A shame we don't have any mulled wine. I like a glass at lunchtime to warm myself up on the slopes. Do you ski, Tiggy?'

'I'm Swiss. Of course I do.'

'I would love to take you to a chalet I know in Klosters. It is the ultimate for me; ski in, ski out, so you can be home at lunchtime and have the Michelin-starred chef provide you with the most superb veal scallopini. Where did you go to school by the way?' he asked me suddenly.

I named the establishment and Zed nodded smugly. 'The best there is. I imagine your French is fluent.'

'It's my native language, although all my sisters and I were brought up to speak English as well. What about you?'

'German, but I too was taught English from the cradle, as well as Russian and French. Like my houses, I belong to everywhere and nowhere. In other words, I am a typical twenty-first-century citizen of a global world,' he said as Alison walked in with a tray containing a bottle of white wine and two glasses.

'Leave it there,' said Zed imperiously. 'We will pour it ourselves.'

The girl said nothing, just gave an odd movement that could have possibly been a curtsey, and scuttled out of the room.

I watched Zed check the label on the bottle, pour a little of the wine into his own glass then sniff, swirl, and drink, before nodding and filling mine.

'Perfect for lunch. Fresh, crisp, with a good nose, but a tasty afterbite to follow. *Santé*.'

'*Santé*.'

We chinked glasses, and whereas Zed took a serious slug, I took a tiny sip to be polite because I wasn't used to drinking at lunchtime. As I stared into the fire, I felt his eyes on me again.

'You do not look particularly Swiss, Tiggy.'

'That's because I'm adopted. As are all my sisters.'

Again, he gave me that strange knowing nod. 'So, where are you originally from?'

'Spain, or so I believe. My father died last year and in the letter I was given by his lawyer afterwards, that's where he said he found me.'

'You are a very unusual woman, Tiggy.' His green eyes glinted in the firelight. 'Many of the girls at your expensive Swiss boarding school must have been rich little princesses, but you . . . you are certainly not that.'

'I don't think any of us sisters were brought up to be so.'

'Even though you have had the best of everything?'

'We've had a very privileged lifestyle, yes, but we were taught to know the value of things, and also what really matters in life.'

'Which is?' he asked me as he refilled his own wine glass, then topped up mine, which didn't really need it.

'In essence, to be a good person. To never judge others by their position in life, because as Pa always said, life's a lottery, and some people win and some people lose.'

'I agree in principle of course,' Zed nodded, his searing gaze still upon me. 'But then again, what would either you or I know about struggling? I have had money all my life, and so have you. Whether we like it or not, we have always known the safety net is there, ready to catch us if we fall. So even though we can live like we have nothing, we can never really know the fear that real poverty brings.'

'True, but at least we can empathise, and be grateful, and try to use our privilege to do some good in the world,' I countered.

'I admire your altruism. You are living it too, by working up here and caring for the animals, probably for next to nothing.'

'Yup,' I agreed.

'I warn you, Tiggy, that your good intentions may get lost somewhere along the way.'

'Never.' I shook my head firmly.

'So,' he took a sip of his wine as he assessed me, 'are you wearing a metaphorical hair shirt?'

'Not at all! I'm doing what I love in a place that I love, and there's no other motive, certainly not guilt. I live on what I earn, and that's the end of the story.' I felt he was trying to make me admit to something that simply wasn't inside me. 'I'm just . . .' I shrugged, 'who I am.'

'Maybe that is why I find you fascinating.'

I watched him snake his hand towards mine and thank God, there was a sharp tap at the door. I stood up to open it.

'Your luncheon,' said Beryl as she came in carrying a tray.

'Thank you so much,' I said as she marched towards the low table in front of the fire and placed the tray upon it.

'Yes, thank you, Beryl.' Zed smiled at her. 'You are most kind and I am very sorry if I have disrupted your day.'

'Not at all, sir, that's what I'm here for. Do you wish me to serve the sandwiches?' Beryl asked.

'No, I am sure that Tiggy and I can manage. I must compliment you – and the Laird – on your superior choice of staff,' he said, indicating me with a nod of his head. 'Tiggy and I have much in common.'

'I'm happy you're happy, sir,' Beryl said diplomatically. 'Enjoy your meal.'

She left the room and Zed smiled.

'She is not what she seems either.'

'Sandwich?' I asked him, as I transferred one onto a plate and offered it to him.

'Thank you.'

'So, what is it that *you* do?' I asked him.

'I run a large communications company.'

'Right, I have no idea what that actually means.'

'Sometimes, neither do I,' Zed chuckled. 'Just think of it as an umbrella under which television, the internet, mobile phones and satellites, i.e., anything that allows the human race to communicate, sit.'

'You're a businessman?'

'I am.' He took a large bite of his open prawn sandwich and nodded in approval. 'I must admit, being up here for the last couple of days has made me realise how much I needed a break. I spend most of my life in transit, racing across the world to meetings.'

'That sounds very glamorous.'

'Anything can look glamorous from the outside until you are living in it. Fast cars, first-class travel, the best hotels, wine and food . . . but it all becomes normal after a while. Being up here in this . . .' Zed gestured towards the view of the mountains, 'puts things into perspective, doesn't it?'

'Nature tends to do that, yes. Living here all the time, I

have quite a lot of perspective.' I smiled. 'I take the day for what it is, try to live in the moment and enjoy it.'

'Mindfulness,' Zed muttered. 'A life coach once gave me a book to read on the subject. It is definitely not something that comes naturally to me. But then, how can it, when I am always leaving on a plane one day and arriving in a different country the next? I have to prepare for it, look to the future, not just drift along in a haze of good intentions.'

'Your lifestyle's your choice though, isn't it?'

'Yes, it is.' He looked at me as though I had suddenly given him the key to life itself. 'I mean, I have enough money – I could sell the business and just . . . stop.'

'You could. Now.' I looked at my watch. 'I'm really going to have to leave you. I have work to do.'

'Really? You have hardly touched your wine.'

'I don't want to fall asleep at the wheel. I hope the tour this morning wasn't too disappointing for you.'

'Oh no, it was not disappointing in the slightest.' He eyed me as I stood up and walked towards the door.

'Tiggy?'

'Yes?'

'I am leaving tomorrow, but may I say, it has been a pleasure to meet you.'

'And you,' I said. 'Goodbye then.'

'Goodbye.'

'You have been busy, little Hotchiwitchi. I smell a man,' said Chilly later that day as I doled out his lunch into his tin bowl.

'There you are,' I said, ignoring his comment and placing the bowl on the small table next to him.

'You take care. He ain't what he seems.' Chilly paused then, with his head cocked on one side, scrutinising me. 'Or maybe he *is*!' he cackled. 'You smell danger, Hotchiwitchi? You should.'

'Really? I'm not sure I smell anything at all. I hardly know him,' I said. I was getting used to Chilly's dramatic sweeping statements, but I was interested that he'd picked up on a man being around. And also, if I was truthful, the sense of discomfort I felt around Zed.

'Now, sit down there and tell me what your daddy say 'bout where you did come from,' he said as I placed a cup of the revoltingly strong coffee he liked to drink next to him.

'Well, he said that I had to go to a city called Granada, and that opposite the Alhambra was a place called Sacromonte. I have to knock on a blue door and ask for someone called Angelina.'

At first I thought that Chilly was having some kind of fit, because he was doubled up and making strange guttural sounds. But when he lifted his head, his expression showed he was either laughing or crying, because there were tears streaming down his cheeks.

'What? What is it?'

He mumbled under his breath in Spanish, and fiercely wiped his cheeks with his fists.

'What? What is it?'

'The wind did blow you here to me. After all these years, you came as was told.'

'What was "told"?' I frowned.

'That you would come and I do guide you home. Yes, you were born in a cave in Sacromonte, little Hotchiwitchi, and I did already know it,' he nodded vehemently. 'The seven caves of Sacromonte . . . Sacromonte . . .'

He then repeated the word over and over, continuing to cradle his emaciated frame, arms clasped around his chest. I felt strange and shivery as I suddenly remembered those visions I'd had of being lifted towards the roof of a cave . . .

'It is . . . your home,' he whispered. 'Why be afraid? Kin knows kin, you were sent here to me. I do help you, Hotchi-witchi.'

'This place . . . Sacromonte, why is it so special?'

'Because it is *ours*. A place that do belong to us. And also because . . .' his finger pointed to the brass bed, 'of that.'

I looked at the bed but could see nothing, except a brightly crocheted blanket.

'That, girl.' Chilly realigned his finger, and I saw he was now pointing to a guitar that stood against the wall. 'Bring it here,' he ordered me. 'I show you.'

I stood up, took the instrument across to him and laid it into his outstretched hands. I watched as he caressed it, almost like a mother would her child. It was an old guitar, with different proportions to ones I'd seen before, the dark wood polished to a high shine, the area around the sound hole inlaid with gleaming mother-of-pearl.

Chilly's gnarled fingers clasped the guitar's neck and pulled it across his chest. He swiped his fingers downwards and a hollow, discordant sound filled the smoky room. He swiped again, then I watched as he fiddled with each string, one hand testing the sound, as the other struggled to manipulate the tension.

'*¡Ahora!*' he said, having given one last strum. His booted foot began to beat time on the floor in a steady rhythm and his fingers moved across the strings as his foot pounded faster and faster. Then his fingers – that seemed as if they were released from their arthritic state simply by the joyous sound they were making – strummed at speed until the little cabin was filled with the pulsating cadences of what could only be associated with one unique sound:

Flamenco.

Then Chilly began to sing, his voice breaking at first, as tired and worn as the strings his fingers were manipulating so deftly. Slowly, the growl of years of phlegm collected from his pipe smoking dissipated and a deep resonant sound replaced it.

I closed my eyes, my feet pounding too, the entire cabin vibrating with the pulse of the music. I knew this rhythm as I knew myself, the incessant beat of the music making me desperate simply to get up and dance . . .

My arms rose above my head of their own accord, and I stood up, my body and soul responding naturally to the incredible music Chilly was playing. And I *danced* – by some alchemy, my feet and hands knowing exactly what to do . . .

One last strum of the strings, an '*¡Olé!*' from Chilly, then there was silence.

I opened my eyes, feeling breathless from exertion, and saw Chilly was collapsed over the guitar, panting heavily.

'Chilly, are you okay?'

I went to him, feeling for his pulse, and there it was, beating fast but steadily.

'Can I get you some water?'

Eventually, he raised his head a little and turned it towards me, his eyes bright.

'No, Hotchiwitchi, but you can get me some whisky.' He grinned.

# 9

I woke up the following morning and thought what an extraordinary day yesterday had been. With Chilly, it felt that every time I went to visit him, the entire experience had a dreamlike quality. As for Zed, I'd never had a man pay me that amount of attention or compliments and I didn't really know how to react. Yes, he was physically attractive, but there was also something about him – about his strange . . . familiarity with me, that I couldn't work out.

'As if he knows me,' I whispered to myself. One of my big problems was that I was pretty innocent when it came to men. I'd had very few relationships and I'd taken each one at face value and trusted them. I'd been burnt more than once because of that, and these days, I felt I must give any prospective suitor a number of in-depth interviews before we even reached the holding hands stage. I'd been called 'frigid' for my refusal to jump into bed two seconds after I'd met someone, but I didn't care – rather that than end up loathing myself the next morning. Me and my psyche just weren't built for one-night stands; we were more 'forever' love, and that was just the way it was.

I walked down to the cats and entered the enclosure,

enjoying the warmth on my face as I looked up at three of them sitting outside in the sun. I chatted to them for a while as I threw in their breakfast, then walked back up the slope towards the house, opened the back door of the Lodge and went inside.

'Beryl?' I called as I walked along the corridor.

She wasn't at her usual station in the kitchen, but I could tell a fried breakfast had been on the go by the pans in the sink and the smell of bacon. I went to the fridge and took out Chilly's lunch to take to him later, then went back out to the corridor. Beryl was probably upstairs changing the beds, and I decided I'd come back this afternoon to beg access to the computer in her office so I could look up the seven caves of Sacromonte in Granada.

'Tiggy,' said a voice behind me just as I made to leave.

'Hi, Beryl.' I turned round and smiled at her. 'I bet you're relieved everyone's gone and peace is restored?'

'Well, that was how things were last night, but,' she lowered her voice, 'then I woke up to an email from the Laird this morning, telling me that Zed has apparently decided to stay on here for the foreseeable future. The other guests have left, but he's still here and currently hogging my office. This huge Lodge just to accommodate one person!'

'Zed's decided to stay on?' I repeated dully.

'Yes, it seems he wishes to take a sabbatical, get away from it all for a little longer, so the Laird said.'

'Oh God,' I whispered more to myself than Beryl. 'Well then, I'll come back and beg the internet another time.'

'By the way,' Beryl said as I headed for the door, 'he told me this morning that his decision to extend his stay was to do with something you'd said to him yesterday.'

'Really? Well, I can't think what. I'm off to see Chilly, Beryl. Bye.'

As I drove towards Chilly's cabin, I pondered how I felt about Zed's continuing presence, and felt a tingle of trepidation in my stomach.

'You early,' Chilly muttered when I knocked and let myself in. Although how he knew I was, given there wasn't a clock in the place, I didn't know.

'I was worried about you after yesterday, so I came to check you were okay.'

'No need to worry, girl. Yesterday the best time I did have in years.'

'Chilly, this Sacromonte place, the caves . . . is that where you were born too?'

'No, I'm a Catalan, born on the beach in Barcelona, under a wagon.'

'So how come you know about Sacromonte?'

'My great-grandmother was born there. She was a powerful *bruja*. Cousins, aunties, uncles . . . many family were from there.'

'What's a *bruja*?'

'A wise woman, someone who see things. Micaela, she deliver your grandmother into the world. She was one who tell me you would come. And that I would send you home. I was itty-bitty boy, an' I did play guitar for your grandmother. She become very famous.'

'Doing what?'

'Dancing, of course! Flamenco!' Chilly put his hands together and beat out a rhythm. 'It be in our blood.' He picked up his pipe and relit it. 'We were in Sacromonte at the great festival held at the Alhambra. She a kid like me.' Chilly chuckled in delight. 'I think after eighty-five years of waitin', Micaela make mistake, that you would not come, but here you be.'

'How do you know it *is* . . . me?'

'Even if your papá not leave you letter, I would know.'

'How?'

'Ha ha ha!' Chilly clapped his hands together, then slammed his fist down on the side of his chair. He reminded me of Rumpelstiltskin, and if he was upright I was sure that he would be doing a strange dance and chanting around a cooking pot.

'What?'

'You have her eyes, her grace, though you be pretty! She was ugly, until she dance. Then she beautiful.' He pointed to the old brass bed. 'Underneath, please. You get the tin and I be showing you your grandmother.'

I stood up to do as he asked, wondering at the ridiculousness of being in an icy Scottish wilderness with a crazy ancient gypsy, who was telling me that my arrival here had already been foretold. I knelt down and drew out a rusting shortbread tin.

'I show you.'

I placed the tin on his lap and his arthritic fingers struggled to open it. When he did, black and white photos spilled onto his knees and the floor. I picked up the ones that had fallen and handed them to him.

'Now, this be me. I did play at La Estampa in Barcelona . . . I was handsome, *sí*?'

I studied the black and white photo and saw a Chilly of perhaps seventy years ago; dark-haired and lithe-limbed beneath the traditional ruffled shirt, his guitar clutched to his chest. His eyes were on a woman who stood in front of him, arms held above her head, wearing a flamenco gown and a large flower in her gleaming hair.

'Goodness, she's beautiful. Is that my grandmother?'

'No, it was my wife, Rosalba. Yes, she was *muy linda* . . . so beautiful. We married at twenty-one . . . the other half of my heart.' Chilly clutched his chest.

'Where is she now?'

Chilly's expression darkened and he looked down. 'She gone. Lost in Civil War. Bad time, Hotchiwitchi. The devil entered hearts and minds of our countrymen.'

'Chilly, I am so sorry.'

'It's life,' he whispered, as he caressed the face of his poor wife with his filthy thumb. 'She do speak to me still, but her voice is fainter because she be travelling further away.'

'Was that why you left Spain? I mean, after you lost your family?'

'*Sí*. Nothing left there for me, so I did move on, best leave the past behind.'

'And ended up here?'

'After many travels in England before, yes. Now . . .' Chilly went back to the pile of photographs, the ones he discarded flying to the floor yet again. As I collected them, I saw they were all of guitarists and dancers in different bars and clubs, yet the look of ecstasy on each artist's face – caught on camera for eternity – was identical.

'*¡Aquí!* Here she is.'

Chilly beckoned me towards him and I looked down at another photograph of a flamenco scene. At the forefront was a diminutive dancer, her hands raised above her head, but instead of the flowing traditional dress, she was wearing a pair of fitted trousers and a waistcoat. Her skin was pale, her hair black and slick with oil, a single curl in the centre of her forehead.

'La Candela! The flame that burns in the heart of all our people. Can you see, my Hotchiwitchi? Look at her eyes . . . they are your eyes.'

I stared hard at the eyes of the tiny woman in the photograph, but it was black and white and for all I knew, the tiny dots could be blue or green.

'That is her! Lucía Amaya Albaycín, your *abuela*, La Candela, the most famous dancer of her day! She be born in Sacromonte and delivered by Micaela's hands . . .'

Yet again my mind conjured a fleeting glimpse of candlelight flickering on a whitewashed oval ceiling above me as I was lifted up towards it . . .

'Now, Hotchiwitchi, I do tell you the story of your family. We do begin in 1912, the year of your grandmother, Lucía's, birth . . .'

# María
## Sacromonte, Granada, Spain
### May 1912

*Spanish castanets (castañuelas)*
*A percussion instrument used when dancing a*
*zambra, siguiriyas or Sevillanas in the flamenco*
*tradition.*

# 10

The air was eerily still, as if even the birds were holding their breath in the olive groves that fell below the steep winding paths that wove between the caves of Sacromonte. María's groans echoed around the walls of the cave, the abnormal silence amplifying her own guttural sounds.

'Where is everybody?' she asked Micaela.

'At Paco and Felicia's wedding, remember?' Micaela answered. The *bruja*'s long black hair had been pulled back into a practical knot on her head, at odds with the elegant ruffled dress she was wearing.

'Of course, of course . . .' María murmured as a cool cloth was placed on her sweating brow.

'Not long now, *querida*, but you must push again. The baby needs your help.'

'I can't,' María groaned as another contraction ripped through her body. 'I am spent.'

'Listen, María,' said Micaela, one ear cocked. 'Can you hear it? They are beginning the *alboreas*. Listen to the rhythm and *push*!'

María heard the slow, steady beat of hands on the *cajón* drum, a pulse that she knew would soon build into a joyful explosion. The guitars joined in, and the ground beneath them began to vibrate from the stamping of a hundred feet as the dance began.

'¡*Dios mío!*' she screamed. 'This baby will kill me!' She moaned as the child surged further down through her body.

'It wants to come out and dance, like its mamá. Listen, they are singing for you both. It is the *alba*, the dawning of new life!'

Minutes later, as the air filled with the glorious sound of flamenco guitar and voices as the *alboreas* reached its climax, the baby made its entrance into the world.

'It's a girl,' said Micaela as she cut the cord with a knife then dealt swiftly with the afterbirth. 'She is very small, but she seems healthy enough.' She turned the baby over and patted its tiny behind. With a small cough, the baby opened its mouth and began to scream.

'Here,' Micaela said as she expertly swaddled the infant as though wrapping up a piece of meat. 'She is all yours. May the Virgin bless her with health and happiness.'

'Amen.' María looked down at the tiny face – the large eyes, bulbous nose and plump lips seeming too big for their setting. Little hands were balled into fists and punched the air angrily as the baby gave full voice to her lungs. Two deter-mined feet unlocked themselves from the sheet and joined the two arms in exploring their first taste of freedom after release from the womb.

'She is a fiery one. She has the power, the *duende*, in her, I can feel it.' Micaela nodded at the baby as she offered María some rags to stem the bleeding, then washed her hands in the already bloody basin. 'I will leave you together to get to know each other. I will tell José he has a daughter and I am sure he will return from the fiesta to see her soon.'

Micaela left the cave and María sighed as she latched the baby onto her breast to quell the squawking. No wonder the *bruja* had been so eager for the birth to come quickly; the entire village of Sacromonte was at the wedding – anticipated for months as the bride was the granddaughter of Chorrojumo, the late gypsy king. The brandy would be flowing and there would be a feast fit for royalty. María knew her husband would no more leave the ensuing fiesta to visit his wife and new daughter than he would ride through the streets of Granada naked on his mule.

'It is you and me, little one,' she whispered as the baby finally suckled and silence descended once more in the cave. 'You are born a girl, and that is your bad luck.'

María staggered out of bed, the baby still clasped to her, desperate to take a drink of water. Micaela had left in such a rush she had not filled her patient's mug. She walked from her bedroom to the kitchen at the front of the cave feeling dizzy from thirst and exertion. Grabbing the water jug, she put it to her lips and drank. Looking out of the tiny window hewn into the rock at the front of the cave, she saw it was a beautiful clear night and the stars shone brightly, framing a perfect crescent moon.

'Light.' She whispered and kissed the top of her baby's downy head. 'I shall call you Lucía, little one.'

After making her way back to bed, still clutching the baby in one arm and the jug in her other, María finally fell into an exhausted sleep, lulled by the distant rhythm of the flamenco guitars.

### 1922, ten years later

'Where have you been, you naughty girl?' María stood with her hands on her hips at the mouth of the Albaycín cave. 'Alicia told her mamá you were not in school again today.'

'Alicia is a sneaky she-devil who should mind her own business.' Lucía's eyes flashed in anger.

María saw her daughter had mimicked her stance and was also standing with her own hands on her tiny hips.

'Enough of your cheek, *pequeña*! I know where you were, because Tomás saw you by the fountain, dancing for coins.'

'So what if I was? Someone has to earn some money around here, don't they?' Lucía pressed some pesetas into her mother's hand, then with a toss of her long black hair, she marched past her and into the cave.

María looked down at the coins, which were enough to buy vegetables from the market and even a blood sausage or two for José's supper. Still, it did not excuse the child's insolence. Her ten-year-old daughter was a law unto herself; she could be taken for a child of six due to her tiny stature, but that fragile outer packaging contained a volcanic and passionate temperament, which her father said only added to her exceptional flamenco skills.

'She was born to the sound of the *alboreas*! The spirit of the *duende* lives inside her,' José said that evening, as he hoisted his daughter onto the mule to take her off to dance in the city's main plaza to the sound of his guitar. José knew the money he'd earn with Lucía's tiny form stamping and whirling

would triple his usual tips from those drinking at the surrounding bars.

'Don't bring her back too late!' María called to her husband as the mule clopped off down the winding path.

Then she squatted back down on the hard dusty earth
outside the cave to continue weaving her basket out of the
esparto grass that had dried since harvest. Leaning her head
back against the wall for a moment, she enjoyed the mellow
warmth of the sun on her face. Opening her eyes, she glanced
down into the valley beneath her, the River Darro running
through it, swollen with springtime thaw from the Sierra
Nevada mountains. The setting sun cast a rich orange glow on
the Alhambra, which sat above her on the opposite side of the
valley, its ancient towers rising up out of the dark green forest.

'Even though we live little better than mules, at least we
have beauty,' she murmured. As she worked, a sense of calm
flowed through her, despite the ever-lingering anxiety that José
was using Lucía to earn the family a living. He was too lazy
to take a normal job, preferring to rely on his precious guitar
and his daughter's talent. Sometimes, they would receive an
offer from a rich *payo* – a non-gypsy – to perform at a party
in one of their grand houses in Granada. This had only added
to Lucía's delusions of grandeur – she didn't understand that
the *payos* came from another world that she could never hope
to aspire to.

Yet Lucía seemed to thrive on it. It was hard to remember
a time when she had not been tapping out a rhythm – even as
a baby sitting in her highchair eating with her iron spoon, her
feet would be continually beating. The child was never still.
María remembered the moment when, at only nine months
old, Lucía had hauled herself to her feet by grabbing the table

leg and determinedly taken her first few teetering steps unaided. It had been reminiscent of watching a fragile china doll getting up to walk. The residents of Sacromonte had backed away in fear at the sight of her when María had taken her out and about.

'Devil child,' she'd heard one neighbour whisper to her husband, and indeed, as Lucía's toddler rages had made her ears ring, María had thought the same. Desperate for some peace, she had eventually discovered her daughter would only quieten to the sound of her father's flamenco guitar, tapping her little hands and feet along to it. Then, as María had practised her *alegrías* in the kitchen in preparation for a fiesta, she'd looked down and seen two-year-old Lucía's diminutive form copying her movements. From the proud tilt of her chin, to the way her hands swept gracefully about her little body and the fierce stamping of her feet, Lucía had managed to capture the very essence of the dance.

'*¡Dios mío!*' José had whispered, glancing at his wife in amazement. 'You want to learn to dance like your mamá, *querida*?' he'd asked the child.

Lucía had fixed her father with her intense gaze. '*Sí*, Papá. I dance!'

Eight years on from that moment, there was no doubt that María's own ability as a flamenco artist – she was considered one of the best in Sacromonte – had been surpassed by her daughter's prodigious talent. Lucía's feet could tap out so many beats to the minute, that even though Lucía begged her to count them, María could not count fast enough. Her *braceo* – the use of her arms in the correct position – was almost faultless, and above all, there was a light in her eyes, which came from an invisible flame inside her and elevated her performance to another level.

Most evenings, as white wisps of smoke rose from the chimneys of the many caves, the mountain of Sacromonte was alive with the strumming of guitars, the deep male voices of the *cantaors*, and the clapping and stamping of the dancers. No matter that its gypsy residents were poor and hungry, they knew the spirit of flamenco could lift them up.

And Lucía embodied that spirit more than anyone. As she danced with the rest of the village at fiestas in one of the large communal caves used to celebrate such events, others would stop to marvel at the *duende* inside her; a power that could not be explained, that soared out of one's soul and held the onlooker hypnotised, because it contained the gamut of human emotion.

'She's too young to know she has it,' José had said one night after Lucía had performed for a crowd that had gathered outside their cave, drawn by the pounding feet and the flashing eyes of a small child who did indeed seem possessed. 'And that is what makes her even more special.'

'Mamá? Can I help you with the baskets?' Lucía asked her a few days later.

'If you have time in your busy schedule, yes.' María smiled, patted the step next to her and handed her daughter some esparto grass. They worked together for a while, María's fingers slowing down as weariness overcame her. She'd been up at five to feed the mule, the chickens and the goats that lived in the cave which served as a stable next door, then she had lit the fire under the pot to provide her four children and husband with a meagre breakfast of maize porridge. Her lower back ached after carrying water from the large cisterns at the base of Sacromonte mountain up through the steep cobbled alleyways of the village.

At least she now felt a rare moment of peace, sitting here with her daughter working quietly beside her. Even though on so many occasions, she'd looked up at the great Alhambra, its position and grandness signifying everything that was so unfair in her life, and had railed at it – at her life of constant struggle. Yet she had the comfort of being surrounded by her own people, tucked away in their small hillside community. They were *gitanos*, Spanish gypsies, whose ancestors had been forced outside Granada's city walls to carve out their homes in the unforgiving rock of the mountain. They were the poorest of the poor, the lowest of the low, those who the *payos* looked down upon with disdain and mistrust. They only came to the *gitanos* for their dancing, their ironmongery, or their *brujas*, like Micaela, the medicine woman, whom the *payos* would consult in secret when in desperate need of help.

'Mamá?'

'Yes, Lucía?' María watched her daughter point to the Alhambra.

'One day, I will dance up there in front of thousands.'

María sighed. Had any other of her children uttered such a thought, María would have boxed them round the ears. Instead, she nodded slowly.

'I don't doubt you will, *querida*, I have no doubt at all.'

Later that evening, when Lucía had finally subsided onto the pallet that lay wedged next to her parents' bed in the small hollow built deeper into the rock behind the kitchen, María sat outside the cave with her husband.

'I worry about the girl. Her head is full of ridiculous dreams, inspired by what she has seen at the *payo* houses you have danced in,' María said.

'What's wrong with dreaming, *mi amor*?' José ground out the cheroot he'd been smoking with his boot heel. 'In this miserable existence of ours, it is all that gets us through.'

'José, she does not understand who she is, where she's come from and what it means. And you taking her so young to see the other side' – María pointed to where the city wall of Granada began along the hillside, half a mile away – 'is turning her head. It's a life she can never have.'

'Who says so?' His eyes, so like his daughter's, flashed angrily within the dark skin inherited from his pureblood *gitano* forefathers. 'Many of our people have risen to fame and fortune through their talents, María. Why can that not happen to Lucía? She certainly has enough spirit. When I was a guitarist in Las Ramblas in Barcelona, I met the great dancers Pastora Imperio and La Macarrona. They lived in grand houses like *payos*.'

'That is two out of tens of thousands, José! The rest of us must simply sing and dance and struggle any way we can to earn enough to put food in the pot. I worry that Lucía will be disappointed when her big dreams come to nothing. The child cannot even read or write! She refuses to go to school, not helped by you encouraging her, José.'

'What does she need with words and numbers when she has her gift? Wife, you are turning into a miserable old woman who has forgotten how to dream. I'm going to find some better company. *Buenas noches.*'

María watched her husband stand and saunter off along the dark, dusty path. She knew he would head for one of the drinking dens, housed in one of the many hidden caves, where he and his friends would carouse until the early hours. He'd been out all night more often recently and she wondered if he had a new mistress. Even though his once taut body was ageing fast with the passing of years, brandy and the harshness of the life they led, he was still a handsome man.

She vividly remembered her first sighting of him; she only about the same age as Lucía was now, he a strapping sixteen-year-old, standing outside the mouth of his family cave, strumming his guitar. His dark curly hair had shone mahogany in the sun, his full lips curved into a lazy smile as she'd passed. She'd fallen in love with him then and there, even though she had heard bad things about 'El Liso' – 'The Smooth One' – his nickname due to his skill on the guitar. *And* – as she would sadly discover later – for his reputation with women. At seventeen, he'd gone off to Barcelona in a haze of glory, having been contracted to play in Las Ramblas, a district packed with famous flamenco bars.

María had been convinced she would never see him again, yet five years later, he'd returned, sporting a broken arm and a number of yellowing bruises on his handsome face. Local gossip told her he'd got into a fight over a woman, others that his contract at the flamenco bar had been cancelled due to his drinking, and that he'd had to turn to bare-knuckle fighting to earn a crust. Whichever it was, María's heart had beaten faster as she had walked past his family cave on her way down to the Alcaicería, to buy vegetables from the market stalls in the town. And there he'd been, smoking on his parents' door-step.

'*Hola*, little beauty,' he'd called as she'd walked past him. 'Are you the girl I hear dances the *alegrías* better than any other in the village? Come and talk a while. Keep a sick man company.'

Shyly, she had joined him, and he'd played his guitar for her, and then insisted she go and dance with him in the olive grove beyond his cave. After his hands had clapped out a *palmas* then encircled her waist to draw her closer, and their bodies had swayed to the sensuous invisible beats of their hearts, she'd arrived home that night breathless and dreamy, having been kissed for the first time in her life.

'Where have you been?' Paola, her mother, had been wait-ing for her.

'Nowhere, Mamá,' she'd said as she'd passed her, not wish-ing Paola to see her blushes.

'I'll find out, miss!' Paola had wagged a finger at her. 'And I know it's to do with a man.'

María had been aware that Paola and Pedro, her father, would heavily disapprove of any relationship between her and José. His family, the Albaycíns, lived in poverty, whereas she, as an Amaya, came from a rich family – at least by *gitano* standards. Her parents already had an eye on the son of a cousin; Paola had produced only one live baby girl from her seven pregnancies, and an heir to the successful blacksmith's forge that Pedro ran was urgently needed.

Even though María knew all this – and up to now had been a caring and dutiful daughter – all her good intentions had flown like trapped butterflies released from her senses as José had relentlessly pursued her.

Falling further under the spell of his charm, as his fingers caressed both his guitar and her body, she'd finally let him convince her to sneak out of her family's cave at night, and had lain with him in the olive grove at the foot of the Valparaiso mountain. All through the unusually hot summer, as her father's forge billowed a fierce unbearable heat, María had felt as if her mind and body were on fire too. All she could think of was the long, cool night ahead, when José's body would wrap around hers.

Their night-time trysts had been cut short by the wrath of her father. Even though they had been careful, someone in Sacromonte had seen them and gossiped.

'You have brought shame upon this family, María,' Pedro had roared after he'd dragged both his daughter and her lover to the cave to face their disgrace.

'I am sorry, Papá,' María had wept, 'but I love him.'

José had gone down on his knees to beg forgiveness, and immediately asked Pedro for her hand in marriage.

'I love your daughter, señor. I will take every care of her, believe me.'

'I do not, boy. Your reputation goes before you, and now you have ruined my daughter's too! She is only fifteen years of age!'

María had sat outside the cave as her father and José had discussed her future. Her mother's face, taut with disappointment and humiliation, was perhaps the worst punishment of all. A *gitano* woman's purity was sacrosanct – the only currency she had to offer.

A week later, the village of Sacromonte had celebrated a hastily arranged engagement party for the couple, then, a month afterwards, a large wedding. The traditional celebration lasted three days. On the last evening, María – bedecked in a dress of blue and fuchsia with a long train, her hair adorned with red pomegranate flowers – had climbed onto a mule behind her new husband, and the entire village had formed a procession, following them down to her family cave for the final ceremony of the night.

María still remembered how she had shaken with fear at the prospect of the *Tres Rosas* ceremony. José's face was above her in the dark cave, the smell of alcohol on his breath as he kissed her, then mounted her. Outside, María could hear raucous laughter and her heartbeat was as fast as the hands beating on the *cajón* drums.

'It is done!' roared José as he'd rolled off her and summoned her mother. María had lain there, waiting for Paola to press a white handkerchief against the most intimate part of her, knowing that the three blooms of her virginity would not appear.

'Don't make a sound, daughter,' Paola had warned her in an urgent whisper.

In the flickering candlelight, María had watched as her mother pulled a small blade from a pocket and pressed it into the tender flesh of her daughter's thigh. María had stifled a cry as she saw blood from the wound drop onto the cloth her mother held.

'You have made your bed, *querida*, and now you will lie in it for the rest of your days,' Paola had whispered fiercely, before leaving the cave with the handkerchief held out in front of her.

Outside, the village had erupted with cheers and applause as Paola had waved it to all for their inspection.

'So, wife.' José had reappeared beside her soon after, a

flask of brandy in one hand, a cheroot in the other. 'Shall we drink to our union?'

'No, José. I do not like the taste.'

'But you like the taste of this, don't you?' He'd grinned at her, as he dropped his breeches to the floor and joined her again beneath the colourful blanket it had taken her a month to crochet.

An hour later, as María had dozed from the strain of the past few days, she'd heard José leave the bed and pull on his clothes.

'Where are you going?'

'I left something behind. You sleep now, *mi amor*, and I will be back soon.'

Yet when María had opened her eyes to the dawn the following morning, José had still not returned.

María sighed as she made her way to the smelly public latrine used by the cave dwellers. If she had believed then – eighteen years ago now – that José loved her as much as she loved him, any such romantic thought was now long dead. Perhaps, she thought bitterly, José had known the marriage was to his advantage. Her parents had been wealthy enough to pay for a new cave – albeit far further up the mountain – as a wedding gift, plus an exceptional set of iron kitchenware.

Their first child had been born prematurely at eight months – or so she had been told to say by her mother – but had survived no longer than six weeks. The second and third babies she'd miscarried in the second month. Then finally, Eduardo had arrived and María had buried herself in motherhood. At last she was able to sit with the other women to talk over remedies for colic, fever and the diarrhoea that hit the young and old of Sacromonte like a plague as the rain fell in the winter, the mud running down the dusty narrow pathways and the cesspits overflowing. No matter that her husband was rarely at home, or that there were no pesetas in the tin they kept hidden in a locked wooden cupboard behind a painting of the Blessed Virgin. At least her father had already promised that baby Eduardo would have a future in his forge, and Paola slipped her enough vegetables to keep mother and son alive.

'No more than this will I give,' her mother would say. 'That river rat of a husband would spend any money I gave you on brandy.'

Emerging from the latrine, María smiled as an image of Eduardo rose in her mind. He was such a good boy – now sixteen and working alongside his grandfather. As for her other two sons . . . there was no doubt they took after their father. Both of them had the same wild streak that seemed to be inherent in pureblood *gitanos*. Carlos was almost fifteen and earned his living bare-knuckle fighting – a fact he would never admit to, but was obvious to his mother when he began to appear in the cave in the mornings, his face swollen and his young body covered in bruises. Felipe, now thirteen, had been sickly as a baby and was more sweet-natured, but easily swayed by the older brother he adored. Felipe was a talented guitarist, for whom his father had great hopes, but instead of developing his talent, he followed Carlos around like a lamb, eager to gain his approval in any way he could. As she reached her cave, to comfort herself, María turned her thoughts to little Lucía, in whom she'd placed so much hope when she'd found herself pregnant after three fallow years.

'It will be a girl,' Micaela had told her when María had gone to see her in her third month. 'She will be possessed of many talents. She will be special.'

María knew now that every word Micaela had spoken was true. As a *bruja* – or 'witch', as the ignorant *payos* would call her – she had the third eye and had never been wrong. Everyone in Sacromonte counted on Micaela to give them the prophecies they desired, and they were none too pleased if she told them something they did not want to hear.

And it was María's own mistake for interpreting Micaela's words in the way that she'd wished to. 'Special' and 'talented' had meant to her what she had wanted them to mean: another woman in the house, talented at home-making and rearing children, a daughter who was kind, gentle, who would help and support her through the latter years of her life.

'That is the problem with seers and their prophecies,' María muttered as she undressed by the light of the flickering candle, then carefully folded her embroidered bolero, apron, blue skirt and petticoat before donning her nightgown. It was not that they gave the wrong message, but simply that the person who received it could mould it into what they wanted and needed it to be.

She had hoped that one of her children would have inherited her great-grandmother's gift. She had been the village *bruja* before Micaela and the gift ran in her family. She'd dreamed that Micaela would inspect the new baby and tell her that yes, *this* was the child who would one day become the next *bruja*. Then everyone would have come to their cave to visit, knowing that her baby possessed the gift of seeing and would grow to be the most powerful woman or man in their community.

Returning to the kitchen, María scooped some water out of the barrel to wash her face. Then she tiptoed across the room; to her left lay the boys' sleeping quarters, separated from the kitchen by a curtain. Twitching the fabric aside and holding the flickering candle in front of her, she could just make out Felipe's slight form under his thin blanket, his breathing still heavy from a recent chest ailment. Beside him on the straw pallet was Eduardo, his hand flung carelessly across his face as he slept. María suppressed an irritated sigh as she noted that Carlos was not yet home.

She made her way across the earthen floor to her own room right at the back, and saw Lucía sleeping peacefully on her pallet. Using the last of the candlelight, she navigated her way beneath her own blanket. Snuffing out the remnants of the flame with her fingers, she lay her head on the hard straw-filled pillow and stared into the blackness. Even though the evening was warm, María shivered in the stale, fetid air of the cave. She wished that José's arms were there to embrace her, to take away the fear she felt for the future. But those strong arms did not want a woman whose body was turning flaccid from birthing five children and lack of nourishment. At thirty-three, María felt she looked far older than her age.

*What is it all for?* she asked the heavens and the Blessed Virgin. Then, receiving no answer, María closed her eyes and slept.

## *11*

'Why do I always have to help with the cooking?' Lucía
pouted as María dragged her into the kitchen. 'Papá and
Carlos and Felipe – they sit outside, playing guitar and smoking whilst we do all the work!'

It was another morning, and María already felt weary to
her bones at the thought of all that lay ahead of her that day.

'Cooking is women's work, Lucía. You know very well
that is the way it is.' María handed her a heavy iron pot. 'The
men go out to earn the money, we take care of the house.
Now, stop your complaining and peel those vegetables!'

'But I earn money too! When I dance with Papá in the
cafés, he takes people's coins and drinks brandy with them, yet
I still have to peel vegetables. Why should I do both? One day
I will no longer live in a cave like an animal, but in a great big
house with a floor that isn't made of earth, and a bedroom all
of my own,' Lucía declared as she looked round in disgust at
the Albaycín cave. 'Why can't we get a machine that cooks
things? I saw one in the kitchen of the rich *señorito* when Papá
and I performed at his house. They had a woman who did all
their cooking. I will have one of those too.' Lucía threw the
vegetables into the pot that bubbled over the fire. 'And it had

a tap of water all for one family. Imagine that,' she said in wonder, grasping the last carrot to her chest before she threw it in with the rest. 'What it must be to be rich.'

'Get along with you now,' María cut her short by handing her a pitcher, 'and fetch the water.'

'One of the boys can do that, can't they? It is such a long walk and I am tired.'

'Not too tired to carry on with your chatter,' María scolded her. 'Off you go!'

'One day, *I'll* have a water tap all to myself!' came Lucía's parting shot.

'And one day, I will be dead from exhaustion,' muttered her mother.

A rattling cough emanated from the boys' bedroom and a few seconds later, Felipe shuffled out, rubbing the sleep from his eyes.

'What's for breakfast, Mamá?' he mumbled. 'Porridge again?'

'Yes, and I've made another mint tonic for your chest, *querido*.'

Felipe grimaced as he sat down at the table and began to spoon up the watery maize. 'I hate mint tonic.'

'But it helps you breathe, so drink, or we will have to get Micaela to come and give you another even stronger remedy.'

Felipe's eyes widened in alarm and he reluctantly gulped down the liquid in the mug in front of him.

'Where has your brother Carlos got to?' she asked him. 'Eduardo told me he had planned to take him to the forge today. He is old enough to start learning his trade alongside his brother.'

Felipe shrugged, and continued eating his breakfast,

refusing to meet her eyes. María knew that he would never betray his brother's secrets.

As if on cue, Carlos sauntered into the cave, a black eye blooming on his face. '*Hola*, Mamá,' he said nonchalantly and dropped onto a stool beside his brother.

Rather than handing him his bowl of porridge, she crouched down and tentatively prodded the tender skin around his eye.

'What's this, Carlos?! Who have you been fighting?' she demanded.

He ducked out of her reach. 'It's nothing, Mamá, stop fussing—'

'Was it for money again? I'm not stupid, Carlos. I hear what is happening in the abandoned caves at the top of the mountain.'

'Just a scrap with Juan about a girl, I promise.'

María narrowed her eyes as she handed him his breakfast. Sometimes she despaired at the fact that nothing she said or did had any impact on the men in her family, except for her beloved Eduardo.

'Have you heard the news, *mi amor*?'

María looked up to see her husband had entered the cave. He took off his black *calañes* hat that shielded his eyes from the bright morning sun.

'What news?' she asked.

'There is to be a flamenco competition held at the Alhambra in June.' He sat down opposite his sons and barely cast a glance at Carlos's black eye.

'And what of it?' she said, as she put a bowl in front of him.

'It is open to amateurs! It is the *Concurso de Cante Jondo*, organised by the great composer Manuel de Falla, and there are to be no professionals over twenty-one. As I retired many years ago, I am eligible to enter.'

'And I am too,' María murmured.

'Yes, of course you are, but don't you see, this is Lucía's chance! Everyone will be there – Antonio Chacón himself is on the judging panel, and it is rumoured that La Macarrona will be dancing, even though she is not eligible to win.'

'You are saying you should enter Lucía?'

'Of course!'

'But, José, she is just ten years old!'

'And dances like a queen already.' He executed a short *palmas*, his hands beating lightly together to demonstrate his excitement.

'I am sure there will be a rule about children performing, José, or else every proud parent would be bringing their own little Macarrona to show off in front of the judges,' María sighed.

'Maybe, yes, but I will find a way to show her talent to the world. You must sew her a dress with a train that will catch the eye,' José said as he lit one of his endless cheroots. The smoke curled above the kitchen table as the boys quickly gulped down the rest of their breakfast, sensing an argument brewing between their parents. They got up and left the cave immediately after they'd finished.

'We barely have the money to feed our family,' María said, rounding on José, 'let alone for a new dress for Lucía!'

'Then I will find it, I swear,' he said. 'This may be our only chance.'

'Promise you won't go stealing, José. Swear to me,' she begged him.

'Of course, I swear it on my father's name. And don't I always keep my promises?' He smiled and wound an arm around her waist, but she escaped his grasp and went to collect her half-finished basket, then walked wearily to the stable next door where she stored her materials with their skinny mule and the goat. There was only one rule she had ever laid down to José and her sons throughout the difficult life they led, and that was never to steal. She knew many other families in Sacromonte resorted to pilfering pockets in the marketplace when they were desperate. Then they became foolhardy, got caught and ended up being slung into the local jail or given a sentence by an unforgiving *payo* judge that far exceeded the crime committed. There was little mercy or justice for *gitanos*.

So far, she believed that her husband and three sons had kept their word, but the excitement in José's eyes told her he would stop at nothing to find the money to buy Lucía a dress.

Walking outside, she looked up at the Alhambra, remembering how only recently her daughter had told her she would dance there one day. A thought came to her and she sighed, knowing what she had to do. It brought tears to her eyes, but she steeled herself as she re-entered the cave and found José helping himself to seconds from the pot.

'I will cut down my own flamenco dress to her size,' she said.

'Really? You would do that for your daughter?'

'If it will keep you out of jail, José, then yes, I will.'

'Mamá, have you heard? I am to dance at the Alhambra, just as I said I would!'

Lucía dug her small feet into the earth and executed a quick *zapateado*, her tiny feet beating fast against the ground. 'Papá says there will be thousands watching me and I will be discovered and taken off to Madrid or Barcelona to be a star!'

'I have heard, yes, and it is very exciting news.'

'Will you be dancing, Mamá? Papá is entering and says I must sneak onto the stage when he starts to play, because I am too young to enter properly. It is a good plan, *sí*?'

'Yes, but, Lucía,' María put her finger to her lips, 'it must be a secret. If anyone finds out what your father is planning, they will try and stop you. Do you understand?'

'*Sí*, Mamá. I say nothing,' she whispered. 'Now, I must go and practise.'

Two days later, María took the scissors to her beautiful flamenco dress. It was a deep red, with black and white ruffles – each one of which she had sewn on herself. She remembered the joy with which she had worn it in her younger years, how her body had felt transformed as it was hugged by the corset, the delicate cotton sleeves dusting her shoulders. It was as if she was cutting out her heart, saying goodbye to all the dreams she'd once had in her youth: of a happy loving marriage, contented children, and dancing into a gilded future with her handsome husband.

*Snip, snip, snip* went the scissors as row after row of ruffles on the train fluttered to the ground until only a short length of them – specified by José – was left.

When she had finished, María gathered the entrails of her dress together. And despite knowing that each intricately sewn band could be reused on a future dress, or to liven up the hem or waistband of one of her skirts, María took the scissors to them again and snipped away until nothing remained but a pile of fragments. She swept them into her basket, then took them over to the fire and threw them onto the flames.

By the boiling June morning of the first *Concurso de Cante Jondo* – the Contest of the Deep Song – the village of Sacromonte had increased its population by twenty-fold and more. Those *gitanos* who had arrived from all over Spain and could not fit into their friends' and relatives' caves were camping out along the narrow paths that wound through the maze of caves on the hillside, and in the olive groves beneath it.

Some of José's Barcelona cousins had come to stay, their Catalan accents as strong as their appetites; María had made a large vat of her famous *puchero a la gitanilla* – a thick stew of meat, vegetables and garbanzo beans – for which she had reluctantly snapped the neck of her oldest chicken.

The Barcelona cousins left early in the afternoon with Felipe in tow, eager to take the long walk down the valley across the River Darro and up the steep mountainside to the Alhambra.

'Felipe, you must take care of yourself and not come home too late,' María had said as she had helped him tie his bright blue sash around his waist. He twitched out of her reach as she tried to brush dirt from his vest.

'Enough, Mamá,' he'd muttered, his thin face reddening in embarrassment as two young girl cousins looked on in amusement.

María watched them saunter down the path with several other young men and women from the village, all dressed in their finest, their boots polished to a shine, their dark hair gleaming with oil.

'Our village has never been so popular,' José commented as he manoeuvred round a family of six who were making camp on the dusty path just outside their cave. 'And to think most of them left here, vowing never to return. They spat on us then, but now they all clamour to come back,' he said with satisfaction as he passed her to step inside.

*You left once and came back too . . .*

Still, this was indeed a moment to be savoured: this week Sacromonte would be the centre of the flamenco universe. And because flamenco *was* the *gitanos*' universe, it seemed every member of their clan had travelled here from far and wide to be part of it. Smoke continually billowed out of every cave as the women tried to cook enough food to keep their guests' stomachs full. The air was filled with the smell of unwashed bodies and the stench of the dozens of extra mules that stood in the shade of the olive groves, their eyelids drooping in the heat, their large ears flicking away the flies. On each of her many trips to fetch more water, María was hailed by a raft of faces she hadn't seen for years. The question they asked her was always the same: 'When can we see you dance?'

When she told them she had not entered the competition, they were aghast.

'But you must enter, María. You are one of the best!'

Having offered the first few enquirers a feeble explanation – that she'd given up, was too busy with her family, to cries of 'But no one is too busy to dance! It's in your blood forever!' – María learnt to offer none. Even her mother, as one of the wealthier residents of Sacromonte – a woman who usually turned up her nose at flamenco because she saw it as another way that *gitanos* sold their bodies to the *payos* – had looked surprised when María told her she wasn't entering.

'It is a pity you have lost your passion for dancing. Along with much else,' she'd sniffed.

The hubbub of guitars and stamping feet slowly subsided as the village of Sacromonte made its way down the snaking pathways. María watched the colourful, noisy line for a while, trying to capture a little of their exuberance for herself, but her soul was closed to it. Last night, José had rolled into bed at dawn, stinking of cheap perfume. She hadn't seen Carlos since yesterday lunchtime, but at least Eduardo had been by her side to help fetch and carry this morning.

'I must go too,' said José, emerging from the cave, looking handsome in his white ruffled shirt, black trousers and sash. 'You know what to do with Lucía. Don't be late,' he said as he slung his guitar over his shoulder and hurried off to join the rest.

'*¡Buena suerte!*' she called to him, but he did not turn back to acknowledge her.

'Are you well, Mamá?' Eduardo asked her. 'Here, take some water, you look so tired.'

'Thank you.' She smiled gratefully at her son, took the mug and drained it. 'Have you seen Carlos?'

'Earlier, yes. He was down at the bar with some of his friends.'

'Is he coming tonight?'

'Who knows?' Eduardo shrugged his shoulders. 'He was too drunk to talk.'

'He is only fifteen,' María sighed. 'You should catch up with your father, Eduardo. I must stay here and help Lucía dress.'

'She is waiting for you in your bedroom.'

'Good.'

'Mamá . . .' Eduardo hesitated for a moment. 'Do you think that this plan of Papá's is right? My sister is barely ten years old. It is said there are to be crowds of over four thousand people there tonight. Will she not make a fool of herself? Of Papá? Of us all?'

'Eduardo, there is nothing about your sister that is foolish and we must both believe your papá knows what he is doing. Now, I will see you up at the Alhambra when I have dressed Lucía.'

'*Sí*, Mamá.'

Eduardo left the cave and María made her way back inside – even in the bright afternoon sunlight, the kitchen was dim.

'Lucía? It is time to get ready,' she called as she opened the curtain and entered the blackness of their bedroom.

'Yes, Mamá.'

María fumbled for the matches and candle beside the bed, thinking that Lucía did not sound like herself at all.

'Are you ill?' she asked as she looked down at her little daughter curled up in a ball on her pallet.

'No . . .'

'Then what is wrong?'

'I . . . feel frightened, Mamá. So many people . . . maybe we could stay here together instead? You could make those little cakes I like and we can eat a whole plate of them, and then when Papá comes back, we can tell him that we got lost on our way?'

In the candlelight, Lucía's eyes were huge and bright with fear as María pulled her up into her arms and sat her on her knee.

'*Querida*, there is no need to be frightened,' she said gently as she undressed her daughter. 'It is the same, however many people you are dancing in front of. Just close your eyes and pretend that you are at home here, dancing in the kitchen for me and Papá and your brothers.'

'What if the *duende* doesn't come, Mamá? What if I can't feel it?'

María reached for the miniature dress she had fashioned for Lucía and put it over her head. 'It will happen, *querida*, once you hear the beat of the *cajón* and your father's guitar, you will forget everything. There.' María put the last hook in place on Lucía's slender back. 'Stand up and let's have a look at you.'

She lifted her daughter off her knee and Lucía twirled, the train swishing behind her like a hungry shark. In the past two weeks, she had taught Lucía how to handle it, afraid of the ignominy of her daughter tripping over it in front of thousands of people. Yet, like everything else to do with dancing, Lucía had taken the train in her stride. María watched now as she flicked it expertly out of her way and turned towards her mother.

'How do I look, Mamá?'

'Like the princess you are. Now come, we must go. You must wear your train hitched up under your cloak so that nobody sees.' María leant down and nuzzled her daughter's nose with her own. 'Ready?' she said, as she offered her hand.

'Ready.'

María saddled Paca, the mule, and lifted Lucía onto her back, making sure the train of the dress was hidden. They joined the stragglers at the rear of the procession that was still winding its way down the mountain, and the closer they got to the Alhambra, Paca panting from the effort of climbing the steep hill, the more elated Lucía appeared as she waved down at friends and neighbours. An elderly woman broke into song, her hoarse voice lifting into the light June breeze, and María and Lucía clapped along, joining in the chorus with the other villagers.

Two hours after they'd set off, they arrived at the Gate of Justice, where people were streaming through the keyhole-shaped entrance to the Alhambra's main square. María helped Lucía off Paca's back and tied the mule beneath a cypress tree, where she happily grazed on a small patch of grass.

Although it was almost six o'clock, the sun was still strong and illuminated the intricate ancient carvings on the walls. Everywhere people were touting their wares, selling water, oranges and roasted almonds. María held tightly onto her daughter's hand as they followed the noise of hundreds of guitars and stamping feet. Behind the Plaza de los Aljibes, where the competition was being held, the great red walls of the Alhambra were lit up, forming a breathtaking backdrop. She pulled Lucía towards the Gate of Wine, where they were to meet José. She looked down and saw that the tiled floor had been covered in lavender buds, perhaps to mask the stench of so many sweating bodies packed closely together.

'I am thirsty, Mamá, can we sit down and take a drink?' Lucía sank to the ground as María hurriedly searched in her basket for the tin flask she'd brought with her. She crouched next to her daughter as a wave of cheering broke out, signalling that the next contestant had just walked onto the stage.

'Look at him! Surely, he should be dead?!' María heard someone comment. And indeed, as the crowd surged forward and she pulled up her daughter before she was trampled on, she could see that the small figure standing with his guitar was a very old man.

'El Tío Tenazas!' announced a disembodied voice from somewhere in front of them. A hush fell as the man tuned his guitar. Even from this distance, María could see that his hands were shaking violently.

'He used to be famous,' her neighbour whispered.

'Someone said he walked for two days to get here,' said another.

'Mamá, I can't see!' said Lucía, tugging at her mother's skirt. A man next to them lifted Lucía up in his arms.

The old man on stage strummed his guitar slowly and then began to sing in a surprisingly strong voice. Those who had been whispering and giggling fell silent as he performed. It was a song that immediately took María spinning back to when she'd heard her grandfather sing – a poignant *cante grande* that she'd listened to many times. Like the rest of the crowd, she felt every painful word cut into her soul as El Tenazas mourned the loss of the love of his life.

The whooping cries of '*¡Otra! ¡Otra!*' showed that he'd been a great success amongst the most demanding crowd imaginable.

'He has the *duende*, Mamá,' Lucía whispered as she was lowered to the ground. Then a hand grasped María's shoulder and she turned to see José.

'Where have you been? I told you to meet me near the Gate of Wine. Come, we are on after the next *cantaor*.'

'We got swept up in the crowd,' María explained, struggling to keep hold of Lucía's hand amidst the mass of people as her husband led them towards the stage.

'Well, thank the gods you are here now, or all this would

have been for nothing. Hide behind this cypress tree and fix her hair,' he ordered as the crowd roared to welcome the next performer. 'I must go. Now, my Lucía.' José bent down and took his daughter's small hands in his. 'Wait until the fourth bar like we practised. When I shout "*¡Olé!*" you run from here straight onto the stage.'

'Do I look well, Papá?' Lucía asked him as María removed the cloak from her shoulders and unhitched the train from the back of her dress.

But José was already heading towards the side of the stage.

María's heart beat in rhythm to the music as she decided that her husband must have been afflicted by some mental derangement to even think this plan could work. She gazed down at her little girl, knowing that if Lucía's nerve failed her and she ran from the stage in fright, they would be the laughing stock not only of Sacromonte, but of the whole *gitano* world.

*Blessed Virgin, protect my beloved daughter . . .*

All too soon, the *cantaor* took his bow to a mixed reception and a few seconds later, José strode onto the stage.

'I wish I had some shoes, Mamá, the beats would be so much clearer,' Lucía sighed.

'You do not need shoes, *querida*, you have the *duende* in your feet.' As José began to play, María pushed her daughter forward. 'Run, Lucía!' she shouted, then watched her darting through the crowd, her train held over her small arm.

'*¡Olé!*' shouted José, pausing after the fourth bar.

'*¡Olé!*' repeated the crowd as Lucía leapt onto the stage then sashayed over to the centre of it. Immediately, there were shouts of disapproval, and 'Get the baby off and back to her cradle!'

In horror, María saw a large man climbing up the steps towards her daughter, who had taken up her opening position, her arms raised above her head. Then the sound of those extraordinary tiny feet began to beat the ground, Lucía holding her position as she stamped out a mesmeric pulsating rhythm. The large man attempted to walk onto the stage and grab her, but another man stopped him as Lucía turned in a circle, her feet still beating, maintaining her opening position. By the time she was back facing the audience, her hands were clapping in a *palmas* in tandem with her feet. Her chin was raised and her eyes looked heavenward.

'*¡Olé!*' she shouted as her father resumed his playing.

'*¡Olé!*' rejoined the audience as her feet continued to beat out the rhythm. José watched his daughter take centre stage, the turn of her head majestic as the audience quietened in awe. María looked at her daughter's eyes, bright under the spotlight that was now trained on her, and knew she had travelled to a faraway place where she could not be reached until her dance was over.

José's voice – never usually his strong point – soared out from the mountain as he accompanied her.

With a sigh of exhaustion, María looked beyond her husband and daughter to the great fortress of the Alhambra, then sank to her knees, dizziness overwhelming her.

Tonight, she knew she had lost both of them.

She came to minutes later, to the sound of cheering that seemed to go on and on.

'Are you well, señora? Here.' A flask of water was thrust at her by a neighbour. 'Drink some, it is very hot.'

María did so, her senses slowly returning to her. She thanked the woman and rose unsteadily to her feet.

'What has happened?' she asked, still dazed.

'The little girl has caused a riot!' the woman said. 'They are calling her "*La Candela*", for she burns so bright.'

'Her name is Lucía,' María whispered as she regained her bearings and stood on the tips of her toes to see her daughter standing on stage with a woman in an ornate white flamenco dress. The woman was on her knees in front of her daughter.

'Who is that?' María asked her neighbour.

'Why, it is La Macarrona herself! She is bowing to the new little queen.'

María saw La Macarrona rise, take Lucía's hand in hers and kiss it. More cheering from the audience followed as woman and child took a further bow, then La Macarrona swept Lucía off the stage.

'Who is she?' was the chat amongst the crowd as María made her way towards the stage to collect her daughter.

'She's from Seville . . . Madrid . . . Barcelona . . .'

'No, I have seen her dancing by the fountain here in Granada . . .'

There was a crowd of bodies twenty deep at the side of the stage. María could not see her daughter in the centre of them, only José smiling beneficently. Just as she was about to kill to find her daughter, José bent down and hoisted Lucía onto his shoulders.

'She is safe, she is safe,' María panted as she stared with the rest of the crowd at the jubilant child.

'Mamá?'

'Eduardo! *Gracias a Dios*,' she said, tears of relief falling down her cheeks as her eldest son embraced her.

'It was a triumph!' Eduardo murmured. 'Everyone here is

talking about Lucía. We must go and congratulate both her and Papá.'

'Yes, of course we must.' María scraped her knuckles across her wet eyes and pulled away from her son's chest. 'She must come home now; she will be exhausted.'

It took another few minutes to push through the crowd surrounding José and Lucía. Even though the next performer was on stage, they had created a court of their own at the side of it.

'Congratulations, *querida*. I am very proud.'

Lucía, her train trailing down the side of her father's body, glanced down at her mother.

'*Gracias*, Mamá. The *duende*, it came,' she whispered as María reached up to hear her.

'Didn't I tell you it would?' María grasped her daughter's hand as José ignored her and talked to the clamour of people around them.

'You did, Mamá.'

'Are you tired, *querida*? Shall you come home with Mamá now? I can put you to bed next to me.'

'Of course she is not tired!' José's head swung around towards his wife. 'Are you, Lucía?'

'No, Papá, but . . .'

'You must stay and celebrate your coronation!' José said as someone from the crowd handed him a brandy and he gulped it back. '*¡Arriba!*'

'*¡Arriba!*' repeated the crowd.

'Lucía, do you wish to come home with me?' María said gently.

'I . . . think I must stay with Papá.'

'You must, yes. There are many people who want to meet

you, and want us to perform.' José shot a warning glance at his wife.

'Then I will say goodnight, *querida*. I love you,' María whispered as she let go of her child's hand.

'I love you too,' Lucía replied as her mother took hold of Eduardo's arm and walked away.

When she woke the following morning, María stirred and instinctively patted the bed beside her. Thankfully there was a warm body lying next to her and it was snoring like a pig as always. Turning over, she glanced down and saw Lucía, still in her dress, curled up on her pallet, fast asleep.

She crossed herself, hardly able to believe she'd slept through her husband and daughter returning, but she'd been so drained from the journey back and the tension of the day. She smiled as she looked down at Lucía. No doubt today there would be an endless procession of visitors to their door, wanting to find out more about 'La Candela', as La Macarrona had officially named her last night. They'd want to see her dance of course – and she as Lucía's mother could bask in the reflected glory of her talented daughter. 'And I *am* proud,' she whispered, almost to reassure herself she was not jealous, but also because she was filled with fear for her little girl. And her marriage . . .

Eventually, María hauled herself out of bed and dressed, smelling the acrid stench of her own sweat, but knowing there was no time to go and collect more water to wash with. She glanced behind the curtain to the boys' bedroom, and saw that only Eduardo was asleep on the mattress.

María tried not to panic, reckoning that half the families of Sacromonte had relatives who had slept where they'd fallen last night. José's three Catalan cousins lay on the kitchen floor, their boots still on, one still hugging his guitar to him, another with his arms round a brandy bottle. She picked her way carefully over them and went next door to feed the animals and collect kindling for the fire for cooking.

It was a glorious morning, the valley a verdant green under a cornflower-blue sky. The wild lantanas were in full bloom, their pink, yellow and orange flowers burgeoning above the grass, and the air was filled with the heady scent of wild mint and salvia. It was quiet in the village, most of the residents sleeping off last night's exertions. There was still another day of the competition to go, so later the procession would once more make its pilgrimage across the valley to the Alhambra.

'*Buenos días*, Mamá,' said Eduardo, appearing in the kitchen as María stirred the thin maize porridge in the iron pot.

'*Buenos días*. You have seen that neither of your brothers are here?'

'I have. I saw them both at the Alhambra last night, but . . .'

'What, Eduardo?'

'Nothing, Mamá. I'm sure they'll be home when they're hungry.' He took his bowl of porridge and went to sit on the step outside as the bodies stirred on the kitchen floor.

María spent the morning making endless bowls of porridge to relieve her relations' hangovers and collecting water from the base of the hill. By lunchtime, there was still no sign of either of her other sons, and as José got ready to leave, she begged him to ask around.

'Stop your worrying, wife; they are grown men, they can take care of themselves.'

'Felipe is only thirteen; hardly a man, José.'

'Will I wear my dress again today?' Lucía asked as she appeared in the kitchen, and gave her train a triumphant swish. María saw there were smudges of what looked like chocolate all over her daughter's face, and her feet were the same colour as the earthen floor.

'No. Come, I will help you take it off – we do not want it spoilt, do we? And then when everyone has gone, I shall put you and it in the barrel and give you both a good scrub.' María smiled.

'Wear it, *mi princesa*, and everyone will know it is you when they see you again today,' José decreed.

'She is coming back to the Alhambra with you? Surely you are too weary to make the journey again, *querida*?' she added to Lucía.

'Of course she isn't!' José answered on his daughter's behalf. 'Last night she was crowned the new queen by La Macarrona herself! Do you expect her not to bask in the glow of her success, but stay at home with you instead, eh, Lucía?' He turned to the child and winked.

'Can I go, Mamá? Later tonight they announce the winners, you see.'

'Of which you cannot be one,' María muttered. She wiped Lucía's face quickly with a damp cloth and did her best to smooth down her black hair, although there was no time to oil it and restyle it into a neat coil. As soon as she could, Lucía wriggled out of her mother's grasp, her wild black curls flying behind her.

'Come, Lucía, I will saddle the mule and you will ride to

the Alhambra to greet your admirers.' José offered his hand to his daughter and she skipped towards him and took it.

'Please don't bring her back too late,' María called from the cave entrance as the three cousins stumbled past her from the kitchen to follow José.

As she'd expected, María dealt with an influx of visitors throughout the rest of the day. Everyone had heard about the little girl who had the spirit of the *duende* inside her. Even when María said Lucía wasn't at home, some of them poked their noses into the rooms at the back just to make sure she wasn't hiding there. María wanted to die of shame – she had not yet had the time to make the beds, and the sleeping quarters stank of tobacco, sweat and stale alcohol.

'She will be here tomorrow,' she assured them all, 'and yes, she may dance down at the big cave.'

Even Paola ventured up the hill to see her daughter and granddaughter.

'I hear she put on quite a show,' Paola said as she sipped water from a tin mug and wiped her brow. The heat of the day was oppressive.

'She did, yes.'

'Your great-grandmother, the *bruja*, always told me a special child was coming. Perhaps it is Lucía?'

'Perhaps it is.'

'Well, there is time to see if the prophecy is true, for Lucía cannot legally work until she is older. Not that that stops many families around here. I hope it will stop yours.' Paola's brown eyes flared at her daughter.

'José wishes her to become a star, and Lucía wishes it too,' sighed María, her usual guard slipping.

'But you are her mamá! You will say what goes under your

own roof. Honestly, María, I sometimes think you have become as timid as a mouse since you married José. He doesn't beat you, does he?'

'No,' María lied, because occasionally, when he'd drunk too much, he had. 'He is trying to do what he thinks is best for our daughter.'

'And to line his own rotten pockets too,' Paola sniffed. 'Really, I still cannot understand what you saw in him beyond what hung between his thighs. And there was us ready to make you a good match with your father's cousin. Well, you made your own destiny and as I knew you would, you now live to regret it.' She paused to let her words sink in. 'I am here to tell you that you and the family are to come to us tomorrow with Lucía. We have many relatives from Barcelona here for the festival and they wish to meet my famous granddaughter. I am putting on a spread, so at least you will all get fed,' she said, casting a glance at the wretchedly small pile of carrots and a single cabbage – all that was left for supper that night.

'*Sí*, Mamá,' María agreed despondently as her mother rose from the stool.

'One o'clock sharp,' Paola said as she swept out.

María sat where she was. She wondered how a life that had started off full of expectation had somehow disintegrated into this moment. A moment in which she felt she had failed as both a wife and a mother. Tears filled her eyes, but she wiped them away harshly. She had no one to blame but herself.

'*Hola*, María.'

She looked up and saw Ramón, her neighbour, hovering by the door. The two of them had been friends as children –

he'd been a sweet boy, quiet and thoughtful, with a personality that had perhaps evolved from being the youngest of nine far noisier siblings. He'd married a cousin from Seville and the two of them had built their cave home next door. Juliana had died giving birth to her third child two years ago, leaving Ramón a widower with hungry young mouths to feed.

'Come in,' María gestured with a smile.

'I brought you some oranges.' He proffered the basket and María salivated at the sight of the fragrant, gleaming spheres.

'*Gracias*, but how did you get them?' She looked at him with a frown.

'That was what the *payos* paid us in this week,' he mumbled, tipping the fruit into her own basket. 'They said the profits from the harvest were too small for pesetas.' He shrugged. 'But I will not complain. At least the farmer offers me steady and honest work all year round. Although I am a little tired of eating oranges.'

'Then thank you.' She reached into the basket and pulled out the plumpest one. Peeling it open, the bright scent burst from it and she took a bite, the fresh juice exploding in her mouth and dribbling down her chin. 'It seems so unfair that they grow everywhere around here and yet we cannot afford to buy them for ourselves.'

'As we have both learnt, life can be unfair.'

'May I offer you some water? Presently, it is all I have.'

'*Sí*, María, *gracias*.'

'Where are your girls?' she asked him as she handed him a tin mug.

'Off at the competition with their Seville grandparents. It seems everyone has come to Granada. And your family?'

'José and Lucía are there already—'

'I heard from a friend she danced last night,' said Ramón. 'And that she was a sensation.'

'Yes, she was. Eduardo has gone for water, and as for Carlos and Felipe, I haven't seen them.'

'Well, at least we both have a few minutes to sit together and be calm. You look tired, María.'

'Everyone in Sacromonte is tired today, Ramón.'

'No, María, you look tired to your soul.'

She felt his gentle gaze upon her and the look of genuine concern and sympathy brought a lump to her throat.

'What troubles you?'

'I would like to know where my sons are, that they are safe.' She lifted her eyes to meet his. 'When your children are older, you will understand.'

'Even then, I hope they will listen to their papá.'

'For your sake, I hope so too. Well now, I must get on.'

As María made to rise, Ramón reached out a hand to her. 'If there's ever any moment you need my help, please tell me. We have always been friends, *sí*?'

'*Sí. Gracias*, but all is well. And thanks to you, I have freshly pressed orange juice to offer any more visitors who come in search of Lucía.'

'And thanks to you, María, I was able to go out to work after my wife died, knowing my children were in safe hands.'

'We are neighbours, Ramón, we help each other.'

María watched him wander out of her cave and cast her memory back to the little boy he'd once been. He'd seemed to appear wherever she was in the village, and had often asked to accompany her on his guitar when she danced. She'd always refused, because he'd never been very good.

As she began to prepare the oranges, unable to stop herself

from taking an occasional bite into a juicy segment, she pondered whether Ramón had once been in love with her.

'María Amaya Albaycín,' she taunted herself. 'You're a sad old woman clutching onto the past!'

# 12

'José, wake up! We must be at my parents' for lunchtime, and where are the boys? Did you see them up at the Alhambra last night? José!' María raised her hand instinctively, wanting to slap him out of his drunken slumber. The sun showed her it was nearing noon, and she was in a frenzy of concern about Carlos and Felipe. Lowering her hand, she instead shook him, gently at first, but when he did not stir, with more force.

'What is it, woman?!' José grumbled as he came to. 'Can a man not have a decent night's sleep after the greatest triumph of his life?'

'He can, when he tells his wife if he has seen their children in the past two days.'

'Does Lucía not lie safe and sound beside you?' he murmured, holding out a limp arm to indicate the huddled form on the pallet beside the bed.

'I am not talking about Lucía, as you well know,' María continued, taking courage from her mother's words yesterday. 'Where are Carlos and Felipe?'

'I don't know, all right? You are their mamá, it's your job to keep track of them, isn't it?'

María ignored him and turned her attention to Lucía, who

was obviously as deeply asleep as her father had been. She lifted the child from the pallet and carried her into the kitchen.

'Come, Lucía, you must wake up. Your grandparents are expecting all of us in an hour.'

'Mamá?' Lucía hovered between sleep and wakefulness as María sat her on her knee and took a cloth from the basin to clean her filthy face.

'People feeding you chocolate again last night, were they?' she commented as she wiped the cloth briskly over her daughter's cheeks and mouth.

'¡Ay! Yes.' Lucía smiled as her mother proceeded to strip off the flamenco dress, the train of which was now caked in brown dirt. 'All I had to do was dance for them and they gave me coins and chocolate.'

'And today you must dance again for your grandparents. But not in this,' she said as she set her naked daughter on the floor, then rolled up the dress and stuffed it into the wooden chest that she used for dirty laundry. 'Here.' She proffered a clean shift dress, which at least had some delicate embroidery at the neck and hem to distract the eye from the cheapness of the fabric. 'Wear this instead.'

'But, Mamá, I wore that when I was six! It is a baby dress!'

'And see, it still fits you!' María soothed, determined that her daughter, who was almost certainly going to be centre stage after lunch, would not disgrace her. Even if her husband already had, and her sons were nowhere to be found . . .

'Now, I will brush and plait your hair. Sit still whilst I do it, and I will give you a glass of fresh orange juice.'

'Orange juice? Where did you get that from, Mamá?'

'Never you mind.'

Once she had fixed Lucía's hair and sent her outside with

her orange juice, María attended to her own toilette, which consisted of a brief wash in the barrel of water Eduardo had refilled, and donning a fresh white blouse. She rubbed precious almond oil into her long black hair and with no mirror to guide her, she coiled her hair into a bun at the nape of her neck, then carefully slicked down the baby hairs on the sides of her face into two gleaming curls that caressed her cheeks.

'We must talk about what happened last night.' José strode into the kitchen.

'Later, after we have visited my parents for lunch. Here, I have brushed your best waistcoat.' She held it out to him.

'I must tell you that Lucía and I have received . . . offers of work.'

'Which I'm sure you refused because she is underage.'

'Do you really think anyone cares about that? If Lucía can dance in their bars and can bring in the customers, they will find ways around it.'

'And where have these offers come from?'

'Seville, Madrid and Barcelona. They want her, María, and we would be fools to turn them down.'

As José took the waistcoat, putting it over his filthy, smelly shirt, María stopped in her tracks.

'You haven't accepted any of these offers, have you?'

'I . . . we will discuss it later. Where's breakfast?'

María bit her tongue and offered him a bowl of porridge, having hidden the rest of the orange juice away as she knew he'd drink the whole lot down in one. While her husband went to sit on the step outside and smoke a cheroot whilst eating his porridge, María went in search of Eduardo, who was getting dressed.

'Did you see your brothers last night?'

'Early on in the evening, yes.'

'They were watching the competition?'

'They were in the crowd, *sí*.' Eduardo avoided her gaze nervously.

'Then where are they now?'

'I do not know, Mamá. Shall I go and see what I can find out?'

'What is it you're not telling me?' María studied her son.

'Nothing . . .' Eduardo tied a red polka-dot scarf around his neck. 'I will go and make enquiries.'

'Don't be too long, we must be at your grandparents' very soon,' she called after him as he left the cave.

Her mother and father's cave was at the bottom of the hill, which in terms of social position in Sacromonte, meant they had reached the top. It had a wooden front door, small shuttered windows and a concrete floor over which her mother had laid brightly coloured rugs. There was a proper sink in the kitchen, which they could fill from the well nearby, and a separate fire, just for cooking on. The furniture had been made out of local pine by her father, and when María stepped inside, she saw the table was heaving under pans filled with food.

'María, you are here! And my little Lucía too.' Paola swept the child up in her arms. 'Here she is, everyone!' she called as she entered the sitting room next door. María followed her and stared blankly at a sea of faces she did not recognise, but was at least relieved that Paola hadn't yet seemed to notice that her husband and sons were absent.

Lucía was surrounded by her relatives, who ranged in age from ancient to very young, and the cacophony in the hollow room as they greeted her made María's ears ring.

'Of course she will dance for us later, after lunch perhaps,' Paola told them all.

María saw her father sitting in his usual chair and went to greet him. 'How are you, Papá?'

'I am well, *querida*. And as you can see, your mother is in her element.' Pedro winked at her. 'Personally, I will be glad when the whole thing is over and we can get back to normal.'

'How is business, Papá?'

'Good, very good,' he nodded. 'The *payos* like my pots and pans and I am happy. And your boy, Eduardo, one day he will take over from his old grandfather and perhaps move inside the city walls. I have told your mother we have enough to build a small house there ourselves, but she refuses. Here, she is at the top and there we would be at the bottom.' He raised his broad palms towards the ceiling.

'We *gitanos* like staying with our own, Papá, don't we?'

'Yes, but perhaps too much. It is why the *payos* dislike us; they do not know us and our ways, so they fear us. Well.' He smiled gently. 'There it is. Where is José?'

'He is on his way here, Papá.'

'Treating you well, *querida*?'

'Yes,' she lied.

'Good, good. I will tell him he has a son to be proud of. Now, there is someone I wish you to meet. Do you remember your cousin, Rodolfo? You played together as children, and now like you, he has his own, a small boy about Lucía's age. The boy has a gift.' He signalled to a tall man standing nearby. 'Rodolfo! Do you remember your cousin, María?'

'Why, of course I do,' Rodolfo said as he strode over to them. 'You are as lovely as ever,' he added as he greeted her with a kiss on the hand.

'He obviously learnt his fine manners in Barcelona,' Pedro chuckled. 'Give your cousin a hug, *hombre*!'

Rodolfo did so, and as they talked, a small boy, not much taller than Lucía, came up to him and wound his arms around his father's leg. He had clear nut-brown eyes, set deep into his face, and the dark skin of a pureblood. His hair stuck up in strange tufts and María thought how odd he looked.

'I know I'm not handsome, señora, but I am clever,' he said, gazing directly up at her.

María blushed, wondering how he could have known what she was thinking.

'Chilly, don't be rude. This is María, and she is your second cousin.'

'How can she be my cousin when she is so old and sad?' he asked his father.

'Enough,' Rodolfo said as he gave the top of his son's head a gentle swipe. 'Don't listen to him, María, he must learn to keep his thoughts to himself.'

'This is the boy I was telling you about, our little *brujo*,' Pedro explained. 'He told me earlier that I would be bald by the time I was sixty. I feel lucky that I have ten years left of hair!'

'Why are you so sad?' Chilly repeated, continuing to stare at María. 'Who has hurt you?'

'I . . .'

'One of your sons is in trouble, señora, big trouble,' the boy nodded vehemently.

'I said enough, Chilly!' Rodolfo clapped a hand over his son's mouth. 'Now, go and find your mother and ask her for your guitar. You are to play after lunch, so off with you to practise.' Rodolfo smacked him on the bottom to send him on his way. '*Perdón*,' Rodolfo said, sweating with embarrassment. 'He is too young to know what he says.'

María's heart was beating like a *cajón* against her chest. 'Is he usually right?'

Pedro, seeing his daughter's distress, touched his full head of hair. 'In ten years' time we will know!'

'Excuse me, Papá, but I must help Mamá.' She nodded to Rodolfo and left the room, walking swiftly through the kitchen and out through the front door to look for José. There was still no sign of him, so she couldn't tell her husband what the little *brujo* had said.

'What to do . . .' she murmured, searching the path for any sign of José. 'Please God, make him wrong,' she prayed.

*But they're never wrong, María* . . . her inner voice told her.

Returning inside, María was at least kept busy helping her mother serve lunch to the many guests – great bowls of spicy bean and sausage casserole accompanied by egg tortillas and crunchy *patatas a lo pobre*, which on any other day she would have tucked into with pleasure. Today, she could barely swallow. Having made sure Lucía had eaten her fill, in between relatives fussing over her, María once again went outside to search the pathway for her husband. She did not find him, but instead saw Eduardo running towards her.

'What news of your brothers?' she asked, halting her son before he reached the prying eyes in her parents' cave.

'Mamá,' Eduardo panted, bending forwards to catch his breath. 'It is not good news. I thought as much when I saw them up at the Alhambra last night. They were part of a gang who were picking the audience's pockets. Both of them were caught red-handed by the police, but Carlos managed to escape. I went to talk to one of the other boy's fathers, and he told me they are all in the jail. They will be sentenced tomorrow or the day after.'

'And Carlos? Where is he?'

'He must have gone into hiding,' shrugged Eduardo.

'¡*Dios mío!*' María buried her face in her hands. 'My little Felipe! Tell me, what must we do?'

'There is nothing we can do, Mamá. He must serve whatever sentence they give him.'

'But you know how they treat the likes of us in their *payo* jails! They beat *gitanos*, abuse them . . .'

'It was only petty theft, so perhaps the sentence will be short. And maybe it will teach Felipe a lesson.'

'If it doesn't, I will!' María's anguish overflowed into anger. 'Maybe it will also show him that following his big brother around like a shadow is stupid and dangerous. Do you know what the sentence is for such a crime?'

'No, but perhaps we should talk to Grandfather. He has experience with the *payos* and he might know somebody who could help.'

'Your grandfather is a blacksmith, not a *payo* judge! My poor, poor Felipe! He is only thirteen – still a child.'

'Yes. Maybe there is some law that children can't go to adult jail.'

'But what if they take him away from me?! I have heard of that before.' María paced up and down, wringing her hands in despair.

'Mamá, try to calm yourself. I will try and find out when they are being sentenced, then perhaps you could go to court and plead for mercy, say that Felipe was influenced by others—'

'Yes, by his *brother*! Go, quickly, and please try to find your father also.' María watched as Eduardo ran off, then gathered herself as she heard her mother approaching.

'Where have you been, daughter? Where is José?'

'He is coming any minute, Mamá, I promise.'

'I hope so, because everybody waits to see Lucía dance, and of course José must accompany her. Our relations must begin the journey back home soon.' Paola indicated the stretch of grass in front of the cave, which led directly down to the river. There were a number of wagons parked upon it and mules grazed idly between them. A large group of people had also begun to collect around a small makeshift dance floor. María saw more people walking along the path towards them.

'What is this, Mamá?'

'Nothing.' Paola had the grace to blush. 'I merely told some friends and neighbours that Lucía would be dancing here after lunch.'

'You mean you told the entire village you would be holding your own private show,' María muttered. 'Well, it is not possible without José.'

'Perhaps we do not need him. Maybe there is someone here who can stand in his place. I will go and find someone.'

'Mamá, *Abuela* says she wants me to dance but Papá is not here.' Lucía appeared beside her. 'So she wants *him* to accompany me.'

María followed Lucía's tiny pointing finger across the gathering crowd to Chilly, the boy who had earlier made such unsettling predictions. He was holding a guitar that seemed far too big for his body.

'*Him?*' María frowned at her daughter.

'Last night he played at the *Concurso*. He is talented, but I want Papá to play for me.'

'María?' A soft hand grasped her shoulder, and she turned to see the *bruja* Micaela, standing beside her.

'Congratulations on your daughter's success. You must be proud,' she said, as Chilly joined them. Micaela ruffled the boy's head. 'And this one . . . equally talented in his way. He has the gift like me.'

'I know,' mumbled María, hardly daring to look at the boy in case he told her something else she could not bear to hear.

'So, Lucía, I will play for you now, *sí*?' said Chilly.

'No, *gracias*. I will wait for my papá. He is the only one who knows how to play for me,' Lucía replied autocratically.

'Chilly will play many times for you in the future,' stated Micaela. 'And . . .'

María turned to look at the *bruja* and saw her eyes were rolling back in her head as they always did when she listened to the spirits.

'. . . This young man' – Micaela tapped Chilly on the shoulder – 'will one day guide your granddaughter back home.'

'*My* granddaughter?' asked María, confused.

'No – hers.' Micaela pointed directly at Lucía. 'Remember what I said, little *brujo*,' she said to Chilly. 'She will come. Oh, it is so hot! I must find some water.'

Micaela left, and Lucía looked up at her mother in bewilderment.

'I am too young to have a grandchild, Mamá, aren't I?'

'*Sí*, Lucía. Of course you are. So, will you have Chilly play for you or not? The crowd is growing and will get restless.'

'It would be my honour to play for you, señorita.' Chilly smiled, showing the gap where his milk teeth were missing.

'I suppose you must,' Lucía sighed. 'I will dance a *bulerías*, yes, Mamá?'

'I think that will be suitable.'

'You can play one?' Lucía asked Chilly suspiciously.

'I can play anything, señorita. Come.' Chilly grasped Lucía's hand. 'We will do this now, as my family too must make the journey home.'

Surprisingly, Lucía followed him without complaint. The green was now packed with onlookers as the two miniature performers took up their places on the platform. Someone had been found to play the *cajón* and Chilly joined him on a stool as Lucía took centre stage and assumed her opening position.

'¡*Olé!*' she shouted.

'¡*Olé!*' the crowd replied.

Chilly began to play, his eyes never leaving Lucía as he took his lead from her. The pounding of her tiny feet began, and María watched, mesmerised. Whether it was the almost tender accompaniment of the boy, who seemed to pre-empt her every movement with the strings of his guitar, or the confidence Lucía had gained from the adulation she'd received in the past two days, she thought she had never seen her daughter dance better.

The crowd was electrified and yelled encouragement to the young performers.

'¡*Vamos ya! ¡Olé!*' they cried. Lucía ended her dance with such a thundering final stamp, the wooden platform almost splintered beneath her.

María cheered as Lucía took a bow, sweeping a regal hand towards her guitarist in acknowledgement.

'Who is that child playing for our daughter?' said a voice from behind her.

'It is my second cousin, José. He is talented, *sí*?'

José ignored her comment. 'Why is he accompanying Lucía?'

'Because you weren't here to do so,' María stated.

José belched and put a heavy arm on his wife's shoulder to steady himself. She could see and smell that he'd been drinking. He made to move towards the makeshift stage, but María grabbed him by his waistcoat.

'No, José! I need to speak to you urgently. Did Eduardo find you?'

'No, he did not. Let go of me.'

'Not until you listen to me. Let's go somewhere where we can have a private conversation.'

'Can it not wait?'

'No, it can't! We will walk over there.'

The two of them moved to stand together behind one of the nearby wagons.

'What is it that is so important, woman?'

'Your son Felipe is in a cell in the town jail. He and Carlos were caught picking pockets by the police at the *Concurso* last night. Eduardo said three other boys from the village have been caught too. I've been told they'll be sentenced in the next couple of days. Carlos managed to escape, but our poor Felipe . . .'

María gave a guttural sob, and knew she finally had his full attention.

'Nooo . . .' José groaned and put his head in his hands. He looked up at his wife, devastation on his face. 'For all my faults, the one thing I have never done is steal. I believed I had drummed it into my boys too. *Dios mío,* I cannot believe it!'

'What will happen, José, do you know?'

'No, but maybe those who have been in such a situation before could tell us.'

'Yes, perhaps they can. Eduardo has gone to search for Carlos and to find out more about Felipe.'

'This is all Carlos's fault. Wait until I get my hands on him,' José growled. 'He'll have gone to ground in the caves. He's probably more frightened of what I might do when I find him than he is of the police! So, I'm going now to search the village and I won't be back without the little *malparido*.'

'Don't beat him, José. He's probably frightened and—'

'I am his papá and he will get what's coming to him. What he deserves!' he shouted, his body shaking with anger.

María watched her husband stride off, then break into a run as he disappeared up the winding path.

'Wasn't Lucía wonderful!' Paola had found her daughter in the crowd and clasped her hands together as she spoke. 'Our cousins were amazed. You must be very proud.'

'I am, Mamá.'

'You don't look it. You are ashen like a spirit. What is wrong?'

'Nothing. I am tired from the weekend, that is all.'

'Tired? María, you are only thirty-three years old and yet you act like an old woman. Maybe you should see Micaela for a potion to bring the light back into your eyes. Now, come and say goodbye to your cousins before they leave.'

María followed her mother over to the group of carts and wagons that would deliver their relatives back to Barcelona and beyond. Each one congratulated her on Lucía and expressed the hope that she and her family would visit them soon. María nodded and smiled by rote, her throat so tight she could hardly speak.

'Goodbye, señora.' Chilly was tugging at her skirt, beckoning her down to him. 'Don't you worry, help will come. You will not be alone,' he whispered. He patted her arm like a parent would a child's, then climbed up onto a wagon next to his father.

Even though her legs were weak with shock and fatigue, María stood with her parents and Lucía, waving off the wagon train until it was a mere speck in the distance.

She somehow gathered the strength to help her mother clear away the detritus left by the guests while Lucía sat on her grandfather's knee, sucking her thumb and listening to stories of the old days. When she went to collect her daughter to go home, Lucía was sound asleep.

'Too much excitement for the little one, I think.' Pedro smiled as he lifted her into María's arms. 'She told me she'd received many offers to dance in cafés in Barcelona, but I hope you will not be taking them up until she is much older.'

'Of course not, Papá.'

'Are you quite well, *mija*? You don't seem yourself.'

Her father gently brushed a wisp of his daughter's hair back from her face. The tenderness in his gesture made her want to throw herself into his arms and tell him everything, ask for his help and advice, but she knew José would never forgive her if she did. *He* was the head of her family now.

Back at home, Lucía had woken up and went to practise her *zapateado* ostentatiously outside, clearly hoping to attract more praise from any passing villagers. It was obvious that attention was a drug to which Lucía was already addicted.

María kept herself as busy as she could while she waited for José or Eduardo to return home with news of her missing sons. No doubt rumours would be all over the village by now.

As dusk fell, María finally saw José walking along the path. With a sigh of relief, she saw Carlos lagging some distance behind him.

'Get in there.' José shoved his son through the cave entrance. Carlos tripped on the step and fell to the earthen floor. José followed and drew back a foot to kick him.

'No!' María screamed, putting herself between her son and her husband. 'That is not the answer, José, even though he deserves far worse. We need his senses intact to tell us where Felipe is.'

'Oh, I know where our boy is; as Eduardo told you, Felipe is locked up in a cell in the city.' José bent over Carlos and heaved his cowering son to standing. 'And with his little brother in jail, this one was hiding in the stable of his friend Raul, like a frightened goat meant for slaughter. He did not even think to come home and tell his mother and father what had happened to Felipe!'

'Forgive me, forgive me, Mamá, Papá. I was frightened, I didn't know what to do.' Carlos' eyes were those of the child he had once been.

'You were more interested in saving your own sad skin, and I should march you down to the city jail now and hand you over to be sentenced with your brother and the others. It is no less than you deserve, you pathetic coward!'

'No, Papá! I will never be so stupid again. It was the other boys' idea, I swear, and me and Felipe, we thought we could help Mamá to buy some food and perhaps a pretty dress for Lucía.'

'Shut your filthy mouth,' snarled José. 'No more excuses, when we both know all the money you stole would have been tipped down your throat! Never in the history of the Albaycín family has one of us gone to jail. Even when we were starving to death, we may have scraped through the *payo* bins for what food we could find, but none of us has ever sunk so low as you. You are a disgrace to the Albaycín name! I have a good mind to turn you out of this house and set you onto the streets. Now, get out of my sight.'

'Yes, Papá. I'm so sorry, Mamá.'

'You put a foot wrong again, and it will be your own father who turns you in to the police!' José roared as Carlos slunk away and disappeared behind the curtain into his bedroom.

'What is happening, Papá? Why were you shouting at Carlos?' Lucía had appeared in the kitchen.

'It is nothing, *querida*,' María comforted her daughter. 'Why don't you go and visit your little friend Inés next door? Perhaps you could show her and her sisters your dance,' she encouraged as she shooed her out of the cave.

José sank onto a stool, head in his hands. 'Ay, María, I am so ashamed.'

'I know, José, and what will we do if one of the other boys names Carlos when they are questioned by the police?' María asked him.

'That is one thing I shouldn't worry about. Honour amongst *gitanos* will keep him safe. *Dios mío*, that boy has a wildness in him that makes me look like a kitten. Perhaps he needs the love of a good woman to tame him.' José reached out a hand to his wife and gave her a weak smile. '*You* are a good woman, María. Forgive me for not remembering that as often as I should.'

María took José's proffered hand and a rare moment of tenderness passed between them.

'So, what do we do now?' she asked him.

'We wait for Eduardo to come back. One of the other boys' parents went down to the jail this morning, but the guards would not let him in to see his son. The jail is packed with those who had taken advantage of the visitors to the Alhambra. Another gang held a *payo* couple at knifepoint. They ambushed the carriage and stole their money and jewellery.'

'If Felipe is sentenced, how long will he get?'

'It depends on the judge. It will be a busy courtroom tomorrow.'

Eduardo arrived back an hour later with no more news than José had already imparted. He looked haggard and twice his young age, but he was at least relieved that Carlos had been found and was home. Once the children had been fed and were in bed – José had insisted Carlos ate alone by candlelight in his room – María brought her baskets out of the stable and sat down to work.

'There's no need to do that tonight, Mia.'

She looked up at José, surprised that he was using his pet name for her. He had not done so for many months. 'Using my hands soothes my mind. Are you not going out with your friends tonight?'

'No. You and I need to talk about Lucía.'

'I think there's been enough talking today, don't you?'

'This cannot wait.'

María put the basket down and watched her husband

settle himself into his chair in the kitchen. 'Then you'd better tell me.'

'I have had many offers.'

'So you told me.'

'Serious offers, which would bring in good money to this household.'

'And as I said, they are offers that you must turn down.'

'And as *I* said, there are ways around that. It will be me who is employed as a guitarist. Lucía will suddenly appear on the stage, just as she did at the *Concurso*. Everyone is prepared to take the risks to show Lucía's talent off to a wider audience.'

'And to fill their own pockets, while they make my child work illegally and pay you a pittance for both your troubles, no doubt.'

'No, María, my old boss in Barcelona offered to triple my wages if Lucía was with me. That amount would enable you to cook a decent meal for our family every day of the week!'

'Yes, but without you and Lucía here, José. Barcelona is a long way away.'

'Mia, do you not think we should try it? What kind of life do we have here now anyway? Sons who are so desperate for money that they are prepared to steal! Nothing in the pot for you to cook, clothes that are threadbare?' José stood up and started to pace. 'You saw Lucía dance, you know what she can do. She is unique, and we are desperate.'

'Desperate enough to separate this family so that my husband and daughter go away and we are left behind without you?'

'If all goes well, you can move to Barcelona with the boys in a few weeks' time.'

Even though María had not been expecting her husband to suggest she came with them immediately, the fact that it had actually crossed his mind as an option to leave them behind shocked her.

'No, José! Lucía is too young, and that is that. Barcelona is a big city, full of thieves and vagabonds . . . you know it is.'

'Yes, I do, because I know the city well, which is why I will choose it above the other offers from Madrid and Seville. I know people there, Mia. I can keep our daughter safe.'

María saw a light in his eyes, one she hadn't seen for years, and realised that this wasn't just about Lucía, but about him too. He was being given another chance to shine, to attempt to make his own thwarted dreams come true.

María narrowed her eyes, suddenly seeing the truth. 'You've said yes, haven't you?'

'He was leaving today. I had to give him an answer.' José's eyes beseeched her to understand.

Silence fell in the kitchen. Eventually, she gave a deep sigh and looked up at him, tears pooling in her eyes.

'When do you leave?'

'In three days' time.'

'Does Lucía know?'

'She was there, begging me to say yes. The Bar de Manquet is one of the best flamenco cafés in Barcelona. It is a wonderful chance for us . . . for *her*. Surely you must see that?'

'She did not even think to ask her mamá,' María whispered. 'So, what if Felipe goes to jail? Will you leave your son to fester there alone? And Carlos needs the guidance of a father, José.'

'I am sure that for the short time it will take to establish Lucía's reputation in Barcelona, you can be both mother and father. This could be the start of a whole new life for all of us,' he implored.

'So, the decision is made.' María stood up and turned her back on her husband. 'There is nothing more to say.'

He stood up and trailed a hand along her back. 'Come, Mia, let us go to bed. It is a long time since you and I . . .'

*Because you are never here when I fall asleep alone . . .*

Knowing a *gitana* wife must never deny her husband his marital rights, María reluctantly took his hand and followed him into their bedroom. She lay down next to him and felt him pull at the cotton skirts that shielded her most intimate part. As he climbed on top of her and thrust himself into her tender flesh, she merely waited for his moment of release, and the peace and silence that would follow.

It didn't take long before he grunted and rolled over. She lay there, her skirts still bunched above her waist as she stared into the darkness. A single tear rolled down her cheek.

*What have you become, María?* she asked herself.

*Nothing*, was the reply from her weary spirit.

# 13

'A month?' María looked at José and Eduardo in horror. 'Did you not explain to the judge that he is only thirteen? *¡Dios mío!* He's a child, and he will be locked up with the rest of those criminals when all he did was follow his brother!'

'We tried, Mamá,' Eduardo explained, 'but the courtroom was madness – so many men to be sentenced, we could not get near to plead for him. They brought them all on together – the whole gang. The charge was read out, and within a few seconds the judge had pronounced their sentence.'

'That is not justice!' cried María.

'*Gitanos* never receive justice, only punishment,' said José, going to the kitchen cupboard, where he kept a dwindling bottle of anise brandy. 'It could have been worse, the thieves before him received six months.' He pulled the cork from the bottle and took a large swig. 'We are all guilty as charged in *payo* eyes.'

'My poor son,' María said, not caring if tears streamed down her face.

'Let us hope the experience teaches him a lesson. And you,' José barked, as a sheepish Carlos appeared from the bedroom. 'Look what this has done to your mamá.'

'Forgive me,' Carlos pleaded as he held out his arms to embrace María. She turned away from him.

'Can I at least go and visit him?' she asked as she harshly wiped away the tears.

'Yes, I have the times written down here,' replied Eduardo, who was the only one in the family who could read. He handed the piece of paper to his mother. 'I will come with you.'

'What's happened to Felipe?' Lucía appeared through the entrance of the cave. 'Someone just told me that he is in the jail in the city. Is it true?'

'*Sí*, it is true,' said José. 'Felipe did something bad – he stole some money at the *Concurso* – and now he will be punished. You would never steal, would you, *mi princesa*?'

'I will not need to, Papá, because you and I are going to make this family rich with our singing and dancing!'

'What does Lucía mean?' Eduardo turned to his father.

'You'd better tell your sons, José.' María wiped her nose on her apron, as Eduardo and Carlos looked on, confused.

José did so, his excited daughter now perched on his knee.

'And whilst I'm gone, you boys had better look after your mother, or there'll be me to answer to.'

Standing in their miserable little kitchen, for a moment María wished it was *her* who was running away to Barcelona. Word was already out in the village about Felipe, and however talented her daughter might be, nothing could make up for the humiliation she felt as his mother.

When Carlos had slunk back to his bedroom and José had announced he had 'things to see to' before they left, Eduardo sat with his mother on the step outside. He took her hand in his, and she saw how his young skin was already calloused and scarred by the rough work he did at his grandfather's forge.

'I'll look after you, Mamá, while Papá is away.'

María turned to him, cupped his face in her hands, and gave him a weak smile. 'I know you will, my beautiful boy. And I thank God for it.'

'Goodbye for now, Mia.' José took María's hands in his and kissed her fingertips.

'How will I know you have arrived? That you are both safe?' she asked as the family stood next to José's cousin's mule and cart, on which José and Lucía's luggage had been placed, her husband's guitar case taking pride of place.

'I will send a message to you with a traveller coming back this way as soon as I can. Lucía, say goodbye to your mother.'

'*Adiós*, Mamá,' Lucía said dutifully. But as she hugged her tightly, it was obvious to María that her daughter was eager to be on her way.

'It is a pity you were unable to visit your son in jail before you leave,' she said under her breath to José.

'Visiting is not until Friday and I promised my boss Lucía and I would be there by Thursday. It is only a month, María. It will pass quickly and teach him a lesson he will never forget.'

'If he survives it,' María muttered, seeing that José wished to leave in triumph, with no negative thoughts of his jailed son.

'So.' José plucked Lucía out of her mother's embrace as if he was worried María would never let her go, then lifted the child up onto the rough wooden bench at the front of the cart. 'We must be off.' He climbed up next to Diego, his cousin, who took hold of the reins. 'Send news with everyone who is travelling to Barcelona. Tell them to come to the Bar de Manquet and see the new star! *¡Vamos!*'

Diego slapped the reins against the mule's backside, and they began to move off down the path. There were others standing in front of their caves to wave the travellers off, so María did her best to restrain herself from an emotional performance, leaning heavily on the firm arm of Eduardo.

'*Adiós*, Mamá, come and see me dance in Barcelona! I love you!' shouted Lucía as the cart rumbled away.

'I love you too, *querida*!' María waved until they were just specks in the distance.

'Are you all right, Mamá?' Eduardo asked as they walked inside. 'Perhaps you should come with me and spend some time with Grandmother. Today must be difficult for you.'

'They will be back.' María dug deep to say the words. 'And I wish them all the success they deserve.'

'Then I must be off to work. Carlos is coming with me to see if he can beat some metal into a pan.'

María glanced at her middle son as he shrugged in uncomfortable submission. As the two of them left, she consoled herself that at least beating metal was better than beating up a human being in a bare-knuckle fight.

'So,' she said to herself, 'I am alone. What do I do?' She looked around her cave in confusion. Even though she knew that many of her days began like this, with her husband and children absent, the difference today was that three of them would still be missing tonight.

But there was good news too, she told herself firmly. Perhaps Lucía and José *could* make enough money for them all to move to Barcelona, even if it meant leaving the only home she'd ever known. It might give them all the fresh start they needed.

'I do not know how you can bear to show your face in the village, María,' Paola murmured the following Friday as María prepared to go into Granada to visit Felipe in the prison. 'Your son has brought disgrace on both our families. Let us hope your father's *payo* customers do not hear he is our grandson and withdraw their business.'

'I am so very sorry, Mamá,' she sighed, 'but what's done is done and now we must all make the best of it.'

In the centre of Granada, the streets were teeming with the morning rush to the market, and María and Eduardo dodged past carts piled high with figs, lemons and oranges, spreading their fresh scent through the dusty air. They joined the long queue of visitors outside the prison gates and, with the sun pounding down on their heads, waited to be admitted.

Eventually, they were let through, and in stark contrast to the bright sunshine, inside the air was dank and fetid, the smell of unwashed and festering bodies so strong that María had to use a handkerchief to cover her nose. The guard led them down numerous steps, using a candle to light the way.

'Why, it is as if the prisoners are buried alive in here,' whispered María as they followed him along a narrow corridor, the floor beneath them wet with what smelt like sewage.

'Your son is in there,' the guard said to them, pointing to

a big cell. Behind the bars, María could only just make out a mass of bodies, sitting, standing or lying where they could find space.

'Felipe!' she called out. A few of the prisoners roused themselves, then looked away.

'Felipe? Are you in there?'

It took some time for him to appear and push his way through the throng. When she finally grasped his hands through the metal bars, she began to weep.

'How are you holding up, *hermano*?' Eduardo asked, his own voice choked with emotion.

'I'm okay,' Felipe said hoarsely, but he looked far from well. His thin face was as pale as the moon, his long black curls roughly shorn off, leaving scars on his bald head. 'Mamá, don't cry, it's only a month, I can manage.' His lip began to tremble. 'Forgive me, Mamá, I did not know what I was doing, I did not understand. I am so stupid! You must want to thrust a knife through my heart for the shame I have brought on the family.'

'*Querido*, it will be all right, Mamá is here for you, and I forgive you.' She clutched at his hand; it felt clammy despite the bitter cold. 'Are they feeding you? Where are you sleeping? Surely there must be more room . . .' María's voice trailed off as her son shook his head.

'I sleep where there is space and *sí*, they feed us once a day—' He clutched his chest suddenly as a cough rattled through him.

'I will bring you a flask of tonic from Micaela for that cough. Oh my Felipe, I—'

'Please, Mamá, do not cry. I have brought this on myself. I will be home soon, I promise.'

'Is there anything you need, *hermano*?' Eduardo took over, seeing his mother's distress.

'There's a black market here for everything, and it's the strongest men who dole out provisions to the rest of us,' Felipe admitted. 'Anything you can bring . . . some bread and cheese and maybe some warm clothes.' He shivered involuntarily.

'Of course,' Eduardo agreed, as the guard told them their time was up. 'Keep strong, and we will see you next week. God be with you,' he whispered as he led his distraught mother away.

In the days that followed, María took the miserable journey to the prison alone, whenever visiting was permitted. And at every visit, her son seemed weaker.

'It is so cold here at night,' he whispered to her, 'and the blanket you gave me was stolen immediately. I did not have the strength to fight him . . .'

'Felipe, it's only two more weeks, that's all you have left here, and then you can start again, *sí*?'

'*Sí*, Mamá.' He nodded wearily, his tears making tracks down his filthy face. María's heart had clenched as she heard his wheezing breaths.

'Here is the potion for your breathing, Felipe. And here, eat this quickly before anyone else sees it.'

She passed him a small loaf of bread and watched him wolf half of it down, then hide the rest under his thin shirt.

Leaving him when visiting time was over was one of the hardest things María had ever had to endure. She cried all the way home, wishing she had José to talk to. She did not want to burden her other sons.

'I will cope, if only for Felipe,' she told herself as she

arrived back to her silent cave. She hadn't yet had the heart to tell Felipe that his father and little sister had left for Barcelona.

'*¡Hola!*'

María turned round and saw Ramón at the entrance to the cave.

'Am I intruding?'

'No,' María shrugged. 'Everyone is . . . out.'

'I brought you something,' he said, holding out a basket.

'More fresh oranges?' She gave him a weak smile.

'No, just cakes my mother brought round, that we cannot eat.'

María knew that the *magdalenas* in the basket were delicacies that *everyone* could eat until they were bursting, and was touched by the gesture.

'Thank you.'

'How is Felipe?'

'He is . . . struggling,' she said, as she bit into one of the cakes, hoping that the sugar would make her feel less faint.

'I am sure he is. Well, I will leave you, but anything I can do to help, please let me know.'

'I will, thank you,' she said gratefully.

Ramón nodded at her and left the cave.

Every day that went by in that hot and dry July, María stopped *gitano* travellers either when she was in the city, or when they passed through the city walls into Sacromonte. Not one of them had any news from Barcelona. She consulted Micaela when she went to collect Felipe's potions.

'You will see them sooner than you think,' was all she had to offer.

At least, as each day passed, it was one day closer to Felipe coming home.

Finally, the day she'd been dreaming of arrived. María stood in excitement and trepidation with the other mothers outside the jail. The gates opened and a motley, dishevelled line of men trooped out.

'*Mi querido*, Felipe!' María ran to her son and clasped him to her. She could feel he was skin and bones, his clothes hanging like rags off his body and the stench of him bringing bile to her throat. *No matter*, she thought, as she tucked his scrawny arm through hers. *He is free.*

Although she had brought Paca the mule, the long trek home was a struggle. Felipe's deep cough rang through the cobbled streets of Sacromonte as they finally wound their way up the steep hill, and she had to steady him as he could barely sit upright on the mule's back.

When they arrived home, María stripped him of his clothes and gently washed the filth off him with a hot cloth, then wrapped him tightly in blankets in his bed. What was left of his clothes were crawling with lice, and she put them aside to be burnt later.

Throughout her ministrations, Felipe lay on the bed hardly speaking, his eyes closed and his chest heaving.

'Would you like something to eat?' María asked him.

'No, Mamá, I just need to sleep.'

All through that night, the cave echoed with the sound of Felipe's coughing, and when María rose in the morning, she found both Eduardo and Carlos asleep in the kitchen.

'We moved out because of the noise,' said Eduardo, as

María handed him flatbreads for his breakfast. 'Mamá, Felipe is very sick. He has a fever, and that cough . . .' He shook his head in despair.

'I will go and tend to him. You two get off down to the forge.'

María went into the boys' sleeping quarters to find Felipe was burning up. Hurriedly, she went to her herb cupboard and mixed together an infusion of dried willow bark, meadow-sweet and feverfew, then cupped Felipe's head and spooned the liquid between his lips. He vomited it up a few seconds later. She sat with him all day, using a damp cloth to cool his fever, and dribbling water into his mouth, yet still the fever did not abate.

By sunset, María could hear that Felipe was struggling to breathe, his chest heaving with the effort.

'María, is Felipe sick? I heard his coughing through the walls,' came a voice from the kitchen. María peered around the curtain to find Ramón holding two oranges.

'Yes, Ramón, Felipe is very sick.'

'Maybe these will make him better?' He indicated the fruit.

'*Gracias*, but I think it will take more than that. I should fetch Micaela and have her come out to give him a potion, but I dare not leave him and the boys are not yet home from work.' María shook her head. '*Dios mío*, I think his condition is very serious.'

'Do not worry, I will go and get Micaela.'

Before she could stop him, Ramón had disappeared from the kitchen.

Micaela arrived half an hour later, her face a mask of concern.

'Leave me with him, María,' she ordered. 'There is only enough air in here for two of us.'

María did as she was told and tried to concentrate on putting together a thin soup of potatoes and a carrot for her other sons.

Micaela came into the kitchen looking grave.

'What is wrong with him?'

'Felipe has a disease of the lungs. He must have caught it in the dampness of those cells, for it is well advanced. Bring him out here into the kitchen where there is more air.'

'Will he recover?'

Micaela did not answer. 'Here, try to get some poppy tincture down him. At least it will aid his sleep. If he is not improved by morning, you must consider taking him to a *payo* hospital in the city. His lungs are filling with water and they need to be drained.'

'Never! No *gitano* ever comes out of that hospital alive! And look what the *payos* have already done to my poor boy.'

'Then I suggest that you light a candle to the Virgin and pray. I am sorry, *querida*, but there is little more I can do.' She clutched María's hands in hers. 'It has gone too far for my help.'

When Eduardo and Carlos returned from the forge, they carried Felipe through to the kitchen and laid him on his pallet. María shuddered as she saw his pillow was spotted with the blood he had been coughing up. She took a cleaner pillow from her own bed and placed it gently under his head. He barely stirred.

'His skin looks blue, Mamá,' Carlos said nervously, looking at María for reassurance. She had none to give.

'Shall I run down and fetch our grandparents?' Eduardo

asked her. 'They may know what to do.' He paced up and down as his brother lay on the floor, struggling for breath.

'I wish Papá was here,' Carlos added poignantly.

María shooed them outside then knelt next to Felipe.

'Mamá is here, *mi querido*,' she whispered as she bathed his forehead. Shortly after, she called for her boys to bring sacks of straw from the stable to prop their brother up and aid his breathing.

As the night wore on, Felipe's breathing became increasingly ragged; it seemed he did not have the strength left even to cough and clear his lungs temporarily. Standing up, she walked outside to where her other two sons were smoking nervously.

'Eduardo, Carlos, go and fetch your grandparents. They must come now.'

Understanding what she meant, their eyes filled with tears. 'Yes, Mamá.'

She handed them an oil lamp to light their way so they could run as fast as they could, then crouched next to her Felipe.

His eyes fluttered open and focused on her. 'Mamá, I'm frightened,' he whispered.

'I am with you, Felipe. Mamá is here.'

He gave a small smile, mouthed '*Te amo*' and, a few seconds later, he closed his eyes for the last time.

As word was sent to anyone travelling to Barcelona to fetch José and Lucía home, María and her family went into mourning. Felipe's body was laid in the stable after the animals had been moved out, so that relatives and villagers could come and pay their respects. White lilies and bright red pomegranate flowers were set all around, their strong scent adding to that of the incense and candles that burnt beside him. María sat there day and night, often in the company of others who joined her to help ward off the spirits. Micaela cast the traditional spells and charms to protect Felipe's soul so it would fly off unfettered to the heavens. Again and again, María asked forgiveness for all the ways in which she had let her son down. No one touched the body for fear of interfering with the spirits.

Her most constant companion was Carlos, who wept and wailed for his brother. María knew he was terrified of Felipe returning to haunt him for the rest of his days. Twice, he made the pilgrimage up to Sacromonte Abbey at the top of the mountain, to pray for his brother's soul. Perhaps he'd felt that this was a way to get out of sitting hour after hour in the fetid heat of the cave, but María was prepared to believe the best of him.

Life was put on hold for everyone in the family – custom demanded that no one could eat or drink or wash or work until Felipe had been laid to rest.

On the third day, as María felt she might faint from thirst, hunger, shock, and the smell of rotting flesh which permeated the air, Paola sat down beside her and handed her daughter some water.

'You must drink, *mija*, or we will be following your coffin soon.'

'Mamá, you know we are not allowed.'

'I am sure that Felipe would forgive his mother taking some water as she watches over him. Now drink.'

María did so.

'Any word from Barcelona?' Paola asked.

'No.'

'So I beg you to lay Felipe to rest without José. Apart from anything, the smell is terrible . . .' Paola wrinkled her nose. 'It is already attracting flies and will spread disease.'

'Hush, Mamá.' María put her finger to her lips, fearful that Felipe might hear the way his earthly remains were being discussed, as if they were nothing more than a hunk of decaying meat. 'I cannot bury our son without his father. José would never forgive me.'

'I say that it is *you* who should not forgive *him* for leaving when his son was thrown into jail. María, you must bury him tomorrow. And that is that.'

When her mother left, María followed her out of the stinking stable and staggered into the kitchen. Even she knew that she could hold the funeral back no longer.

She allowed herself a small smile as she glanced around the kitchen. It seemed the whole village had come by with a gift of food, brandy or sweetmeats. At least she would have something to offer after the funeral. Lighting a candle, she went to kneel under the faded image of the Blessed Virgin. She asked for forgiveness from her, then turned away and asked the same of the spirits in the Upperworld. Then she walked outside, to find Eduardo and Carlos smoking listlessly.

'Can you put word around the village that we will hold the funeral tomorrow?' she said.

'Yes, Mamá, we will go now. I will take the lower path, and you take the high one, *hermano*,' Eduardo suggested to Carlos.

'Boys . . .' she stopped them as they made to run off. 'Do you think your father will be angry?'

'If he is, then he deserves it,' Eduardo replied tersely. 'He should never have gone away to begin with.'

The funeral procession wove up the hillside, peppered with cypress trees and flowering cacti, accompanied by the heady scent of the lilies that adorned the mules. María walked ahead of the coffin her father had fashioned with help from her sons from remnants of oak in his workshop. A mournful wail went up and María recognised her mother's voice as she began to sing a funeral lament. Though rough with age and emotion, Paola's voice soared as the crowd began to sing along with her. María let the silent tears fall down her face and onto the dry earth below her.

The ceremony was a strange hybrid of a traditional Catholic funeral, side by side with Micaela quietly muttering indecipherable words to protect Felipe's soul and those left behind.

María cast her eyes down the valley and up again to the Alhambra, which had seen so much bloodshed in its thousand-year history. She'd always feared it for some reason, and now she understood why. It had been where her son's death sentence had been given.

# 14

María woke the next morning, feeling as if every last ounce of energy had been sucked from her. She made sure her sons left on time for work. Carlos was the first to rise of the two. If there had been anything good to come out of Felipe's death, it was that the guilt Carlos felt had – at least for the present – reformed him.

After pouring herself some orange juice from the fresh batch Ramón had delivered yesterday evening, María sat on the step and sipped it. Once they'd been a family of six; now they were down to half their number. Somehow, she had to accept that Felipe would never come back, but her husband and daughter . . . She blinked away tears in the strong sunlight, fearing that they too were becoming mere wraiths in her imagination.

'Where are you?' she asked the skies. 'Please, send me word.'

Later that day, she donned her mourning veil, picked up two of her hens' precious eggs and went to Ramón's cave.

'I wish you to write to the employer of my husband in Barcelona,' she told him. Ramón was one of the few *gitanos* who could write, and for the odd gift of food or wood, he would willingly craft a letter. 'Here, I have brought you these.' She held out the eggs.

He put his hands over hers and shook his head. 'María, I could never take any form of payment from you, certainly not at this time.' He went to a cupboard and took out his writing implements, then motioned for María to sit at the kitchen table with him. 'First of all, can this man read?'

'I do not know, but he is a man of the city with a business, so we must assume he can.'

'Then begin.'

'Dear Manager of the Bar de Manquet,' María dictated. 'I believe that you offered a position to Señor José Albaycín as a guitarist some weeks ago when you met him and my daughter Lucía at the competition in Granada. If he is still working at your café, could you please pass on a message to tell him that his wife has urgent news for him . . .'

Ramón looked up at her, sympathy in his eyes, his pen hovering above the sheet of paper.

'No,' she faltered, realising suddenly she was writing to José and Lucía's employer, who would not take kindly to a request from a wife, bidding his employees to return home immediately. 'Thank you, but I must find some way to contact José directly.'

'I understand, María,' he said as she rose. 'Anything else I can do, just ask.'

'I have decided I must go to find Papá and Lucía in Barcelona. I cannot rest until they know what happened to Felipe.'

María eyed her sons over the kitchen table.

'Mamá, I am sure that one of the messengers we sent with the news will find them soon,' Eduardo said.

'But not soon enough. Besides, this is news that only a wife and a mother should impart.' María took a mouthful of the stew the boys had brought up with them from her mother's house. She knew she would need all the strength she could muster.

'But you cannot go alone. We will come with you.' Carlos nudged Eduardo, who nodded uncertainly.

'No. Your grandfather's business has suffered enough recently from your absences. And you must stay here in case I miss your father on the road and he returns to find us gone.'

'Then I will stay here and send Carlos with you,' Eduardo suggested.

'I said no,' María repeated. 'Carlos is lucky to have employment and we need the money he earns.'

'Mamá, this is ridiculous!' Eduardo banged his spoon against his bowl. 'A woman cannot go on a journey such as this unaccompanied. Papá would not allow it.'

'I am the head of the household now, and I say what is allowed!' María snapped back. 'So, I will leave tomorrow at dawn. I will take the train. Ramón says it is very easy. He has told me what to do and where to change.'

'Has some spirit taken hold of your senses, Mamá?' Carlos asked as she stood up and collected the dishes.

'No, quite the opposite, Carlos. I have finally got my senses back.'

Despite her sons' constant protests that at least one of them should accompany her, María rose before dawn the very next day, and packed a bag with water and a little food left over from the funeral. On Ramón's advice, she wrapped a black tablecloth around her to form a cloak and covered her tell-tale *gitana* curls with a black shawl. On the road, she would be taken for a widow – which would at least command respect and ensure security.

Ramón had offered to take her to the station on his cart. He was waiting for her with his mule already harnessed.

'Ready, María?'

'Ready.'

As they set off, the sun was just beginning to climb into the sky, drops of morning dew trapped on the spines of the cacti that they passed along the narrow roads into the city. As they entered the city gate, and made their way through the already busy streets of Granada, María wondered if indeed she had taken leave of her senses. But it was a journey she knew she had to make.

At the bustling station, Ramón tethered the mule and came with her to help her buy a ticket. Then he stood beside her on the crowded platform until the train steamed into the station.

'Remember to leave at Valencia,' he told her, as he helped her into the third-class carriage. 'There is a respectable boarding house called the Casa de Santiago right beside the station, where you can spend the night before continuing on to Barcelona in the morning. It is not expensive, but . . .' He pressed some coins into her hand. '*Vaya con Dios*, María. Be safe.'

Before she could protest, the guard's whistle blew and Ramón left the train.

The day was hot and sunny, and on either side of the tracks lay groves of olive and orange trees. The Sierra Nevada mountains had a light dusting of snow on their peaks, the white shimmering in the pure azure sky.

'Can you believe,' she whispered to herself, feeling suddenly elated, 'that never in my life have I been out of Granada?'

Whatever had possessed her to take this journey, María decided she was glad of it. She was seeing the world for the first time in her life.

She alighted that afternoon in Valencia and spent the night in the boarding house Ramón had suggested, barely sleeping a wink as she kept her bag clutched tightly to her body for fear of thieves.

The next morning, she boarded another train as the sun began to rise above the mountains. Even though her backside ached from the hard seat, and the invented widow's weeds made her skin damp, she felt strangely free. Out of the windows she saw occasional glimpses of the ocean behind the small villages they passed, and she thought she smelt the fresh scent of sea and salt.

As the day wore on, she realised they must be approaching Barcelona, because at each stop, the train became more and more crowded with people speaking Catalan; some words were familiar to her, some not. Late in the afternoon, María finally saw the city skyline emerging on the horizon.

'¡Dios mío, it's enormous!' she breathed. 'How will I ever find you both here?'

To her right, she could see the sea wrapping around a peninsula like a sparkling blue apron, and the inhabitants of this great city had dwellings which stretched out across the plain, protected by a mountain range on one side. On the skyline, church spires soared upwards like daggers to the heavens.

She stepped off the train at the busy station and made her way outside, where the wide road was bustling with trams and automobiles, constantly beeping their horns. María felt like the peasant she was as she saw *payo* women wearing skirts that revealed their ankles and part of their shins, their hair cut short like a boy's, their lips scarlet as though they had used a bright red crayon to colour them in. There were shops built into the lower half of the buildings, which had glass doors and windows displaying life-sized dolls wearing women's clothes.

'What is this place?' she said under her breath as a number of cars behind her hooted.

'*!Oye!* Move out of the way! You're causing a traffic jam!'

The noise and the shouting made her break out into a cold sweat, and feeling faint, she darted to stand in the shade of an impossibly tall building. She asked a passing older man with dark skin, whom she took for one of her own, where she could find the Barrio Chino. The man spoke Catalan, but at least he waved in the direction of the sea, which was where María decided she should head.

A good while later, she was about to give up hope, lost in the endless cobbled backstreets, when she emerged out onto an esplanade, opposite which was the sea. By now, she was panting with thirst – she'd used up all her water some time ago – but was comforted by the sight of some shacks on the beach. She crossed the road and walked onto the white sand, and as she drew closer, heard the low strumming of a flamenco guitar.

She bent down to scoop up a handful of the sand and chuckled as the grains tickled her palm. Further along the beach, she noticed *payo* families having picnics and laughing as their children splashed in the waves. 'How I wish I could do that,' murmured María, realising there was a good chance she would drown if she tried, for she had never learnt to swim.

She turned away from the happy scene and headed for the more familiar shacks and the sound of the music – many of them were little more than sheets of tin and lengths of wood hammered together. Each one had a lopsided chimney poking out of the top, billowing with smoke. As she drew closer, she could smell a strong scent of rotting vegetables and overflowing drains.

She stumbled along the narrow, sandy walkway between the shacks, for the first time in her life feeling privileged to live in her cave. The shacks themselves were barely the size of her kitchen, and as she peered surreptitiously through the open entrances, she saw entire families crouched inside, eating or playing cards on the floor.

Eventually, panting and dizzy with thirst, she sat down where she was and rested her aching head on her knees.

'*Hola*, señora.'

Maria looked up and saw a small, filthy child eyeing her from the entrance to a shack. 'Are you sick?' he said in Catalan.

'No, but do you have some water?' María asked desperately, indicating her tongue and panting to convey what she meant.

'*Sí*, señora, I understand.'

The child disappeared inside and brought out a coffee cup

the size of a doll's. María's heart sank but she gulped down the cool liquid, which tasted like ambrosia on her tongue.

'*Gracias*,' she said, 'do you have some more?'

The boy ran back inside and refilled the tiny cup, which María returned to him again after draining it. He giggled and, as if they were playing a game, proceeded to refill the cup for her several times.

'Where is your family?' María asked, finally feeling revived.

'They are not here, they go to work.' The boy pointed to the great city behind them. 'There is no one here but me. Play *chapas*?'

She smiled and nodded as he took some colourful bottle caps out of his pocket, and together they flicked the caps along the sand to see who could get one the farthest. She suppressed a laugh at the ridiculousness of having arrived in Barcelona and playing *chapas* with a strange boy, just as she had once with her own children.

'Stefano!'

María looked up in surprise to see a large woman dressed in black staring down at her accusingly, as though she was a child snatcher.

'Stefano! Where have you been, I have been looking for you everywhere! Who is this?'

María explained, then begged her pardon.

'He told me there was nobody minding him,' she said as she stood up and brushed the sand from her skirt.

'He is always going missing,' the woman clucked. 'Now get inside, shoo!' She sent the boy packing.

'Where are you from?' To María's relief, the woman spoke in the *gitano* dialect.

'Sacromonte.'

'Ah, Sacromonte!' She pulled two stools from inside and offered one to María. 'Where is your husband? Looking for work in the city?'

'No, he is here already and I have come in search of him.'

'A wandering husband! I know the problem well. I am Teresa, what is your name?'

'María Amaya Albaycín.'

'Amaya you say? Why, I have Amaya cousins!' Teresa slapped her huge thigh. 'Do you know Leonor and Pancho?'

'Yes, they live only two streets from me in Sacromonte. Leonor has just had a baby boy. She has seven children now,' María explained.

'Then you and I must be blood related.' Teresa smiled. 'Welcome! I am sure you are hungry after your long journey. I will bring you a bowl of soup.'

Relieved at her good fortune, and thanking the Blessed Virgin for the vast *gitano* network of relatives that stretched across Spain, María gulped back the thin soup, which tasted strange and salty.

'Where is your husband working?'

'In the Barrio Chino district in the Bar de Manquet.'

'What does he do?'

'He is a guitarist, and my daughter is with him, dancing. Do you know where it is?'

'*Sí.*' Teresa nodded and pointed behind her. 'The Barrio Chino begins just along there, but if you are going at night, mind yourself. The bars are full of drunken dockworkers and sailors. It is not the place for a woman alone.'

'But my husband told me it was the centre of flamenco and very well respected.'

'The *cuadros* that perform there are indeed the best in Spain. My sons go there often, but that does not mean it is a respectable part of town.' Teresa raised her eyebrows. 'My sons visit whenever they have the money to do so. One of them told me there is a woman who dances there who strips off her clothes in search of a flea!'

'Surely not?' María was aghast.

'This is Barcelona, not Sacromonte. Here, anything goes to earn your living.'

Visions of little Lucía being forced to strip off her clothes to find an imaginary flea filled María's head. 'Well, I must go and find them immediately. I have some very sad news to impart.'

'What is that?'

'Our son died recently. I tried to send a message via travellers heading for Barcelona, but I've had no reply.'

Teresa crossed herself and laid a stocky brown hand on María's slender arm. 'I am sorry to hear that. Listen, you stay here with Stefano, and I will find one of my sons to escort you tonight to the Barrio Chino.'

She heaved herself up and María was left in the claustrophobic, sandy alleyway, every bone in her body aching to be back home in the safe environs of Sacromonte.

Any fantasies she'd previously harboured about their Barcelona relatives had been laid to rest. She'd envisaged them in pretty houses, with running water and big kitchens, just like the *payos* in Granada. Instead, it seemed they lived more like rats swarming on a beach, the shifting sand a metaphor for the uncertain path they trod between life and death. And somewhere amongst them were her husband and daughter . . .

Teresa returned shortly with a scrawny young man who sported a neatly oiled moustache.

'This is Joaquin, my youngest son. He has volunteered to take you to the Bar de Manquet tonight. You know the place, *sí*?'

'*Sí*, Mamá. *Hola*, señora.' Joaquin gave María a small bow, sizing up her widow's weeds.

'And you are welcome to stay with me tonight,' Teresa reassured her. 'Although I can only offer you a pallet on the floor.'

'*Gracias*,' she said. 'Do you have anywhere I can wash?'

'At the end of the row.' Teresa pointed.

María walked along the row of shacks and stood in the queue of women waiting to use the public latrines. Inside, it stank worse than her poor son's decaying body, but at least there was a cracked and faded mirror hung on the wall and a barrel of water in which to wash her hands and her face. Avoiding her lips for fear of a drop of it going into her mouth, she splashed the water on her face and removed the smudges of dirt. Discarding her widow's weeds, she shook her hair loose, took a comb to it and stared at her reflection in the mirror.

'You made it here alone, María,' she told herself. 'And now you must find your family.'

By the time she returned to Teresa's shack, various men and women, none of whom María recognised but who were apparently related to her, had gathered outside to welcome her. Someone had brought some anise brandy and someone else a bottle of manzanilla wine to toast the sad passing of her son. As night fell, a guitarist appeared and María realised she was attending an impromptu wake with people she'd never met before. Such was the *gitano* way, and tonight she was glad of it.

'Is it not time to go?' she whispered to Joaquin, who shook his head.

'Nothing happens in the Barrio Chino until late.'

Eventually, he nodded at her and told the assembled party, which had grown in number as the evening wore on, that he would take María to find her husband. As they set off, it crossed María's mind that no one here had said they had seen either José or Lucía.

Unused to alcohol, María regretted the glass of wine she'd taken to be sociable, as her feet struggled over the sand behind Joaquin. She could already hear the thrumming sound of fla-menco coming from the other side of the road, and her stomach somersaulted at the thought of seeing José.

A row of lights in the distance and a constant flow of people indicated where they were headed. Joaquin didn't say much and, unlike his mother's, his Catalan accent was strong. After crossing the road, Joaquin led her into a rabbit warren of cobbled alleyways, each one lined with numerous bars. Chairs were set outside and women in tight-fitting dresses were advertising the food and the music on offer inside. The sound of strumming guitars was even stronger now and María followed him until they came to a small square filled with bars.

'The Bar de Manquet is here,' Joaquin grunted, indicating a café out of which people spilled, the sound of a *cantaor* singing a melancholy song emanating from within. María could see that this was not a sophisticated crowd; those around her were either *gitanos* or common labourers drinking cheap wine and brandy. Yet the throng outside was larger than any other café they'd seen.

'We will go in?' asked Joaquin.

'*Sí*,' nodded María, not wishing to lose him in the crowd.

Inside, the noise was raucous, people sitting at tables and at the bar, with not an inch of space to be had.

'Do you know who the manager here is?' María asked, casting her eyes to the small stage at the back of the café where the *cantaor* was sitting. A couple of girls in flamenco dresses were smoking at the bar and talking to *payo* customers.

'Buy me a drink and I will ask,' Joaquin suggested.

María used her dwindling supply of pesetas to buy Joaquin a brandy. He talked in fast Catalan to the bartender as a roar went up. She turned and saw that a dancer had sashayed onto the stage.

'He says the manager will be back later,' Joaquin shouted into her ear, handing her a glass of water.

'*Sí, gracias.*' María stood on tiptoe to peer over the heads, watching the dancer. Another roar went up as a male dancer swaggered onto the stage.

'*Señores y señoras!*' shouted a man. 'Put your hands together for La Romerita y El Gato!'

The crowd erupted as El Gato placed a hand on his partner's cheek. She smiled at him and they nodded at the guitarist.

A small shiver ran down María's spine as the two of them began to move together. The woman's feet began to tap out a beat, and her arms rose above her head as El Gato swept a hand down her back.

María remembered how she and José had danced together in their youth, and as she watched them, her eyes filled with tears for what had been. No matter that this café was ostensibly unimpressive and the audience basic, the two dancers were amongst the best she had ever seen. For a few minutes, she was transported with the rest of the audience as all their passion and brilliance played out on the stage in front of her. María raised her hands in applause as they took their bow and left the stage to make way for the next performer.

'They were wonderful.' She turned to Joaquin in excitement, but found he was no longer next to her. Panicking, she looked around her and saw him smoking at the bar, chatting to an acquaintance. Her eyes fell on La Romerita, who was enjoying the attentions of admiring male customers, then travelled back to the stage, where another beautiful woman with huge flashing eyes was performing a *zambra*. Like La Romerita before her, María knew the woman was a dancer of brilliance. Then she looked closer, because there was something about her she recognised . . .

'Juana la Faraona!' María muttered. She was a cousin of José's who had left for Barcelona years ago, and had arranged José's first contract at a bar here. If anyone would know where her husband and daughter were, it was this woman. She was family after all.

After Juana had walked off stage to rapturous applause, María took a deep breath and pushed through the crowd to speak to her.

'*Perdón*, Juana, my name is María Amaya Albaycín. I am the wife of José and the mother of Lucía.'

Juana's lovely eyes turned towards her and surveyed her. María had never felt so bedraggled and dowdy as she did next to this exotic creature. In her flamenco heels, Juana towered over her, and despite the sheen of sweat on her smooth skin, a black curl of hair was still placed perfectly in the middle of her forehead.

'*Hola*, María,' she said. 'Drink?' She proffered the bottle of manzanilla that sat on the bar in the dancers' corner.

'No, *gracias*. I have come to find José and Lucía; I have some news for them. José said this was the bar where they were working.'

'They were here, yes, but they left.'

'Do you know where they have gone?'

'To the Villa Rosa. They were offered more money by the manager, Miguel Borrul.'

'How far is it?' María said, feeling her legs go weak with relief.

'Not far, but' – Juana glanced at the clock on the wall – 'I doubt you will find them still there. The child dances earlier in the evening to avoid being caught in a late night police raid.'

'Do you know where they live?'

'*Sí*, three doors away from me.'

María listened as the woman explained where she should go to find them.

'*Gracias*.' María turned and made to leave.

'Why not go tomorrow?' Juana's eyes seemed to signal a warning. 'It is late now and perhaps they're asleep.'

'No, I have come a long way to find them.'

Juana shrugged and offered her a cigarette, which she refused. 'Your daughter is very talented, María; she will go far as long as the fire is not sucked out of her by her father while she is still so young. Good luck,' she called out to her as María made her way towards the door. She looked around for Joaquin, but he had disappeared, so she left the bar.

Even though it was after midnight, the streets were crowded with drunken men who leered at her and shouted filthy expletives. She did her best to follow Juana's instructions – she'd said it was no more than a five-minute walk away – but ended up taking a wrong turn and finding herself down a narrow passageway that led to a dead end. Turning round, a hulking figure of a man walked towards her, blocking her path.

'*Hola*, señorita. How much for *follar*?' He made to grab her, but she ducked out of his way and he fell heavily against the wall.

'*¡Dios mío! ¡Dios mío!* How can José have brought our daughter to live in such a place?!'

The building she was looking for was on the other side of the road, down another narrow passage. Breathing heavily, María rapped on the front door, only to be met with someone shouting at her from another window.

'Go away! We are sleeping in here!'

María tried the door, desperate to get inside, and found it was open.

In the dim flame of the single oil lamp that lit the space, she saw she was standing in a hallway. There was a steep wooden staircase rising up in front of her.

'Juana said the first floor, second door on the left,' María panted, mounting the stairs as quietly as she could. The light from the lamp downstairs barely lit the floor above but she located the right door then knocked timidly. There was no response. Knocking once more, but afraid of waking up the other residents, she turned the handle, which opened easily.

A streetlamp lit the tiny room through the uncurtained windows. And there, on a mattress on the floor, lay the beloved and familiar shape of her sleeping daughter.

María swallowed down the tears of relief at the sight of her. She tiptoed across to the mattress and sank to her knees. 'Lucía, Mamá is here,' she whispered, not wanting to startle the child, but knowing that Lucía slept the sleep of the dead. She stroked her daughter's tangled hair, then laid her arms around her body. Lucía smelt unwashed, the mattress smelt worse, but she didn't care. Somehow in this huge city, amongst the kind of people who made Sacromonte's residents seem as if they had taken holy orders, she had found her daughter.

'Lucía.' María gave her a little shake to encourage her into wakefulness. 'It's Mamá, I am here.'

Finally, Lucía stirred and opened her eyes.

'Mamá?' She studied her then shook her head and closed her eyes once more. 'Am I dreaming?'

'No! It really is me. I have come to find you and Papá.'

Lucía sat bolt upright. 'You are real?'

'*Sí.*' María reached for her daughter's fingers and pressed them against her cheek. 'See?'

'Mamá!' Lucía threw herself into her mother's arms. 'I have missed you so much.'

'And I have missed you, *querida mía*. Which is why I came to find you. You are well?'

'Oh yes, very well,' Lucía nodded. 'We work at the best bar in the whole of Barcelona. Everyone calls it the cathedral of flamenco! Imagine that!'

'And your father? How is he? *Where* is he?' María looked

around the tiny room, which had space to hold little more than Lucía and her mattress.

'Maybe he is still out at the Villa Rosa. He brings me home to bed and then goes back to play again. It is not far.'

'You are left here alone?' María was horrified. 'Anyone could walk in and steal you during the night.'

'No, Mamá, Papá's friend minds me when he is not here. She sleeps next door. She is very nice. And pretty,' Lucía added.

'And where does Papá sleep?'

'Oh,' Lucía hesitated. 'Out there.' She waved at the door uncertainly.

'Well,' María said, trying to swallow the lump in her throat, 'as I have come all this way, I had better go and see if he is back.'

'Oh no, I do not think he will be, Mamá. Please, stay with me here. It is late and you can curl up on my mattress and we can hug.'

María was already on her feet.

'Shh,' she said, 'I'll be back soon.'

Outside the door, María let out a gasp of devastation. Of course Lucía may have got it wrong, but somehow she doubted it. Inwardly preparing herself, she tiptoed to the next door along, and as quietly as she could, turned the handle to push it open. The same streetlight illuminated a brass bed on which her husband and a woman – who looked no older than perhaps eighteen – lay naked on the mattress. José's arm was flung across the woman's taut belly, just above the down of black fur that protected her womanhood.

'José, it's María, your wife. I have come to visit you here in Barcelona.'

She spoke in a normal voice, not caring if every resident in the street shouted at her to be quiet.

It was the girl who opened her eyes first. She sat upright and stared at María, blinking to try and make out her shape in the darkness.

'*Hola*,' María said, striding across to the bed. 'And you are?'

'Dolores,' the woman squeaked, at the same time pulling the thin bed sheet over her naked form.

María almost laughed. It was like a comedy.

'José!' Dolores shook him. 'Wake up! Your wife is here!'

As José stirred, Dolores jumped out of bed and grabbed her night shift. As she reached up to throw it over her head, María glimpsed the full breasts, slim hips and smooth backside before the muslin covered them.

'I will leave you two to talk,' Dolores said, as she tiptoed towards the door and María like a timid fawn.

María let her pass. The girl was little more than a child after all.

'He told me he was a widower,' Dolores said, shrugging before she pulled the door closed behind her.

'So.' María strode over to the bed and stood at the bottom of it, arms folded. 'You are a widower now, eh? Then I must be a spirit come back to haunt you.'

José was wide awake now, staring at María in abject horror.

'What are you doing here?'

'I could ask you the same thing.' María indicated the space next to him on the mattress.

'It is not as it seems, Mia, I swear. The room Lucía and

I have is too small for both of us, so Dolores kindly let me
share . . .'

'Do *not* lie to me any longer, you coward! Do you take me
for an idiot as well as a betrayed wife? I have known about
your other women for years, but like every good *gitana* wife
who has children, I chose to ignore it. I . . .' María caught her
breath as the volcano of anger that she'd kept below the surface for years finally erupted. 'And while you lay with that
child, your daughter slept only next door. How you disrespect
me, you pig!' María spat on him. 'You are filth, and my parents were right from the start. You were never any good!'

José had the sense to stay silent while she continued to
rage at him. Eventually he spoke.

'Forgive me, María. I know I am a weak man, easily led.
But I love you, and I always will.'

'Shut up!' María shook with fury. 'You do not know what
love is. All you care about is yourself. You used Lucía to get
you back here and now my daughter lies alone in a filthy room
in a filthy city because of *your* ambition!'

'You are wrong, María, Lucía loves it here! She is gathering a group of fans that grows every day and learning
flamenco from the very best at the Villa Rosa. No' – José
wagged a finger – 'you cannot blame me for *her* ambition. You
ask her, she'll tell you.' A sneer of a smile crossed his face. 'So,
I am here, you have hunted me down. Now what do you
want?'

*A divorce* . . . was the first thought that came into María's
head. She ignored it because no *gitano* couple could end their
marriage legally, and took a deep breath to calm herself.

'I came to tell you that Felipe died of a disease of his lungs on the seventeenth of July, only a day after he was released from prison.'

María searched José's face to gauge his reaction. And in an instant, as guilt leapt into his bloodshot eyes, she knew he had already heard the news.

'I sent word with as many travellers heading for Barcelona as I could find, asking them to tell you that you and Lucía must return home immediately. But you didn't. And in the end' – María let out a guttural sob – 'our boy's body was stinking and I had to go ahead with the funeral without his Papá and sister present.'

Imparting the news of Felipe's death to the man who had given the seed to create his life immediately dissipated any anger she felt. Instead her sorrow fell out in wrenching sobs, tears of despair streaming down her cheeks. She sank to the floor, her hands over her face, mourning all over again for the loss of her precious boy.

Rough hands came around her shoulders and for a few minutes she clung to them because they were finally there to hold on to.

'Mia, I am so very sorry. Our little Felipe . . . gone . . .'

Through the mist of her emotion, María remembered the look of guilt in José's eyes. She pulled away and faced him.

'You already knew, didn't you?'

'I . . .'

'*¡Dios mío!* No more lies, José. Our son lies in his grave! Did you know?'

'Yes, I did, but not until five days after his death. By then, I knew you would already have buried him.'

María swallowed and took a breath. 'Yet, even if you had missed the funeral, you did not think that perhaps you should

make the journey back to Sacromonte to comfort your grieving wife and children?'

'María, I heard of Felipe's death on the very day we were
due to begin our new contract at the Villa Rosa. You cannot
understand what an honour it is for Lucía and I. If we had left
then, let them down when they were placing so much faith in
us, it would have been the end of the future.'

'Even if you had told them that you had to return home
because your young son had died?' María could hardly voice
her disbelief.

'Yes. You know very well how *gitanos* have a reputation
for being unreliable. They would have thought I was lying.'

'José, they are *gitanos* too, they would have understood.'
María shook her head. 'It was you that didn't.'

'Forgive me, I made a mistake. I was too scared to leave;
after all these years we'd finally won a place in the cathedral
of flamenco. The money it could earn for our family, the fame
it could give Lucía . . .'

'There is no excuse on God's earth, José, and you know it.'
She rose from the floor and looked down at him. 'Maybe I
could have forgiven you your latest infidelity, but I can never
forgive you this. I only hope that your dead son can.'

José shuddered and crossed himself at his wife's words.

'Have you told Lucía?' she asked him.

'No. As I told you, it was our first day at the Villa Rosa,
and I did not wish to unsettle her with such terrible news.'

'So, I will go and sleep with my daughter next door. And
tomorrow morning, I will tell her that her brother is dead.'
María walked towards the door. 'Your friend is welcome to
come back to your bed if she wishes.' María nodded at him
and left the room.

'Felipe is gone?' Lucía's eyes were round with disbelief. 'Where?'

'He has become an angel, Lucía, and grown wings and flown up to be with the Blessed Virgin.'

'Like the ones in the Abbey of Sacromonte?'

'Yes.'

'But they are made of stone, Mamá. Felipe isn't.'

'No, but I am sure that now he is flying around the skies, and perhaps he has already been to watch you dancing at the Villa Rosa.'

'Maybe he is a pigeon, Mamá. We have lots in the plaza outside the Villa Rosa. Or a tree,' she mused. 'Micaela, the *bruja*, says we can be anything on the earth when we return. I wouldn't like to be a tree though, because that would mean I could only wave my arms and not tap my feet.'

María gently combed Lucía's damp hair as the child spoke. She had washed it earlier in a basin of water she'd taken from a fountain in the plaza, before patiently picking out the lice. She sighed, reflecting that it was no wonder that Lucía's image of the afterlife was confused, given the fact that Spanish *gitanos* had been forced hundreds of years ago to convert to the national religion of Catholicism, yet alongside that ran their own instilled *gitano* beliefs and superstitions.

'Whatever he is, Mamá, I hope he's happy,' Lucía added.

'So do I, *querida*.'

'I won't see him again for many years, will I?'

'No, we will all miss him and it's very sad he is no longer with us.'

'Mamá.' Lucía had obviously decided it was time to change the subject. 'Will you come and see me dance tonight at the Villa Rosa?'

'Of course I will, *querida*. But I was talking to Papá last night. I think that perhaps you are a little too young to be here in Barcelona without your mamá.'

'But I have Papá! And you could stay here with us.'

'You do not miss Sacromonte? And Eduardo and Carlos?' María continued to rhythmically comb her daughter's hair.

'Sometimes, yes, but especially you. Papá doesn't cook, you see, and his friend Dolores doesn't either, but they feed me at the café, as many sardines as I want. I love sardines.' Lucía smiled happily. 'And I am learning so much, Mamá. There is a *payo* who dances there, La Tanguerra, and you should see her tango and *bulerías*! And there is another *gitana*, La Chícharra, who strips down to her petticoat when she tries to catch a flea! And Señor Miguel has a daughter who uses castanets! She has been helping me learn how to use them. *Click click* they go.' Lucía mimicked the movement with her small fingers. 'They tap out the beat like your feet. Do you remember Chilly? He lives here too! We are friends now, even though he is strange, and we perform together at the bar sometimes.' Lucía's words tumbled out in a torrent of excitement until she had to pause for breath.

María contemplated what she had just heard. 'So you do not wish to come home to Sacromonte with me?'

'No, Mamá, I want you and Eduardo and Carlos to come here with me and Papá.'

'Eduardo and Carlos both work for your grandfather, Lucía. And besides, Sacromonte is our home.'

Later that afternoon, when José knocked on the door and

said it was time for him and Lucía to leave for the Villa Rosa, María waved them off, saying she'd follow on later. She sat down on the stinking mattress in her daughter's room. She had been so certain that morning that she would gather up her child and take her back to Sacromonte. But now, listening to Lucía's passion and determination, she knew she could not do that. The child had been born to dance, and if María dragged her home, not only would Lucía be inconsolable that her future had been thwarted, but she as a mother would feel guilty for denying her the chance.

Lucía and José returned at five from the café to take an hour's rest before the evening's performance. María was waiting for them at the entrance to the apartment building.

'We should talk,' she said to José as he lingered outside to finish smoking his cheroot, while Lucía skipped up the stairs in front of them.

'What do you wish to say to me?'

María watched as José ground the cheroot out beneath his boot, his normal swagger back in place after the high emotion of last night.

'You have broken your sacred oath to me. From now on, we can no longer live as husband and wife.'

'Please, María, let's not rush into this. It has been a difficult time—'

'That will not get better whilst we are still pretending to be together.'

'You cannot seem to understand that everything I do is for our family, and to further Lucía's great talent.'

'I will not argue any further with you, José,' María sighed. 'I just wish for an end and a new beginning. However, even though every part of me wishes to take Lucía home with me to grow up with her family around her like a normal child, I know that I cannot. She must have her chance. Therefore, I entreat you to take better care of our daughter in future, to protect her as best you can. I must trust you to do this, if nothing else.'

'You can trust me, María, I swear.'

'You are free now, José. But never let Lucía know the truth about us. To her, we will always be husband and wife, and her mother and father.'

'As you wish,' José agreed.

'Now, I will go and spend some time with Lucía before you go to the Villa Rosa. I will come to see her dance, and then I will leave for Sacromonte.' María took a deep breath and stood up on tiptoe to give José a final kiss. 'Thank you for the precious gift of my children.'

Then she turned from him and walked inside to speak to her daughter.

# Tiggy
## Kinnaird Estate, The Highlands, Scotland

January 2008

*Scottish wildcat*
*(Felis silvestris grampia)*
*Also known as the Highland Tiger.*

# 15

My head jerked upwards as I came to. I shifted my weight and felt my back muscles complaining from holding myself upright for so long on the three-legged stool. It was dark now and the air in the room was stale; the fire in the woodburner must have petered out some time ago. Taking my mobile from my jeans pocket, I used the light of the screen to navigate my way to the oil lamp and relight it. I saw Chilly was asleep in his chair, his head lolling to one side. I had no idea at what point both of us had fallen asleep, but I knew that before I'd done so, I'd entered another world; a world full of poverty, desperation and death. Yet the pictures Chilly had conjured up in my mind's eye were full of colour and passion too.

'A world that is part of me . . . of my past,' I whispered. I shook myself slightly, feeling I needed to be grounded, to leave this dreamlike world that I seemed to enter every time I walked through the door of Chilly's cabin. Even if Chilly could afford to exist in it permanently, I couldn't, and just now, I felt I was in danger of being drowned by it. After rekindling the woodburner and collecting more logs for Chilly to use overnight, I made a pot of strong coffee for him and left it next to his chair.

Glancing down at his lined face, I tried to picture him as the young boy he'd been, playing the guitar for Lucía, his cousin . . .

'That means,' I breathed out loud, 'that you are distantly related to me too . . .' I faltered. How could it be that out here in the middle of the Scottish Highlands, I had found a relative? And was his story even true?

'Goodbye, Chilly,' I murmured and bent down to kiss his forehead, but he didn't stir.

Leaving the cabin, I stepped out into the brutal cold and, feeling light-headed from the smoke of the woodburner and Chilly's pipe, I headed back to the cottage.

'And where ha' you been all day?' Cal looked at me accusingly as I walked in and hung my jacket on the hook. 'No' been carousing with our special guest, I hope?'

I'd never been as glad to see his solid, reassuring bulk filling the low-ceilinged room.

'I was with Chilly in his cabin. He, umm, wasn't feeling well today.'

'You and he are tight, tha's for sure. You're a willing victim for his stories,' he chuckled. 'Been filling your head with faerie tales and stories of his past, no doubt?'

'He's an interesting man, I like listening to him,' I said defensively.

'Aye, that he is, but don't start falling for any o' his tales, lassie. He once told me I was a grizzly bear in another life, stalking my prey across the Highlands.' Cal gave a hoot of laughter, yet as he stood there towering over me, it didn't take much of a leap of imagination to believe he *had* once been a bear. And to this day, Cal, the man, was *still* stalking his vulnerable prey . . .

'Come on, Tig, you've got that dreamy look in your eyes. You need to snap out o' it, and I've got just the news to bring you back to reality.'

'What?' I walked towards the kitchen in search of something to eat. I'd had nothing since breakfast.

'Lover Boy requests your presence up at the Lodge at ten tomorrow.'

'Why? What for?'

'Don't ask me. He wants tae take you somewhere special,' Cal said as he stood at the kitchen door whilst I cut a thick slice of bread and spread it with margarine.

'Obviously, I'll say no. I'm employed here to do a job. I can't just go gallivanting off to goodness knows where, just because our precious guest wants me to. Besides, what would the Laird say? Or Beryl?'

'Och, Beryl's all for it. Says it will get him out from under her feet and she'll be able to open the windows in the Great Room to give it a good airing from all that cigar smoke. His Lordship doesn't like the cold, she says.'

'Christ, Cal,' I said, as I swallowed a mouthful of bread. 'I feel like I'm being prostituted! I'm a wildlife consultant here, not an escort service! I'm sorry, but it's a no. I'll go up to the Lodge now and tell Beryl that I have a lot of work to do on . . . erm, investigating European elk. Or something,' I added as I opened the fridge door to see what there was for supper, which wasn't a lot, so I slammed it closed again in frustration.

'Come on, Tig, it's no' like you to get so wound up. He'll be gone soon enough and, let's face it, you're not exactly chock-a-block with things to do around here, are yae?'

'And whose fault is that? I've been here almost a month and I still haven't sat down and had a proper conversation with Charlie to discuss the future. I'm used to being busy, Cal, and I'm absolutely not playing hostess for some weird rich guy who thinks I can just drop everything to be at his beck and call.'

'Tig, what's wrong with you tonight? You're in a real blather. Here.' Cal indicated two bottles of red wine that had appeared on the worktop. 'Beryl sent them down to thank us for our help on New Year's Eve. I'll open one now. Looks to me as if you need a drop o' the hard stuff this evening.'

'There's nothing to go with it for dinner, Cal. I didn't get out to the shops today, because I was with Chilly and . . . oh dear,' I sighed, feeling the tears welling up. 'Sorry, I'm just not myself tonight.'

'I can see that,' Cal said gently as he pulled the cork out of the bottle as easily as a plug from a bath, and reached into a cupboard for two wine glasses. 'Now then.' He proffered me a brimming glass. 'You take that with you, go and have a wee soak while I pull something together for supper.'

'But I've told you there isn't anything and—'

'Shoo . . .' He propelled me to the door of the bathroom. 'In you go.'

By the time I emerged half an hour later, feeling a little calmer, a delicious aroma was drifting from the kitchen.

'Tatties, neeps – that's potatoes and swedes tae you – an' my granny's secret gravy recipe,' Cal said as he plonked two plates down on the table. 'I've added chicken to mine, but I swear there's nothin' animal or dairy in yours.'

'Thanks, Cal,' I said as I gratefully plunged my spoon into the steaming bowl of vegetables, covered with a rich-looking brown sauce. Cal topped up my wine and sat himself down opposite me.

'Actually, this is really good,' I said after a couple of mouthfuls.

'It may surprise you tae know that I did manage tae feed myself before you arrived. So now, who is it that's upset you? Just Zed, or was it Chilly too?'

'Both.'

'Well, you've already explained your feelings about your billionaire thinkin' he can buy your company, so let's move on to the barmy gypsy.'

'You'll just say he's crazy, Cal, which he probably is, and that I'm crazy for believing anything he says, but . . .'

'What?'

'He says he was told when he was younger that one day he would guide me back home. He also says he knows who my grandmother was. And he told me all about her today.'

'Right. An' you believe him?'

'I *think* I do. There were things that he told me that my father told me too in his letter and . . . it's all ridiculous really, but . . . I don't know. I'm probably just confused and emotionally drained. Even if I've always believed in another level – I mean, a spiritual level – even for me, what happened this afternoon was far out. And the thing is, I just don't know whether to trust what he's telling me.'

'I understand.' Cal nodded, motioning for me to continue.

'The bottom line is . . . I'm ashamed to say that I'm having a crisis of faith. I'm always the one who's telling everyone else to trust the universe, to *believe* in a higher power . . . and here I am tonight in a mess because I'm scared that all Chilly told me might only be the vivid imagination of an old and lonely man. Do you see?'

'I do. Well now.' Cal set his tray aside. 'I'll tell you something for nothin'; I may joke about Chilly being as mad as a March hare, but I cannae say he has a malicious bone in his body. My dad told me that in the old days, people round here flocked tae him, with their animals, for his herbal medicines and tae have their own futures told. And I never heard o' him putting anybody wrong. And yes, now he's old, and no one wants him and his ways any more, but he's a good man. An' if I believe anyone has a special gift for seeing and healing, it's him. Plus it's obvious for all tae see how fond he is o' you. He would nae do yae any harm, Tig, really.'

'I know all that, Cal, but what if he *has* lost it in his old age? Maybe he just wants to *believe* that there's some connection between us, that I'm the girl he was told about . . . that I *am* related to him in some way—'

'Sounds tae me like you're almost too scared to believe him. You know what a cynic I am, but even I cannae see any reason why he would put you wrong. Remember, he is a gypsy, and how many thousands of people have trusted tae their skills o' second sight? An' if your daddy told you this too, why do you doubt it?'

'Because I *am* scared,' I whispered truthfully. 'Maybe it's because it's so very personal . . . I mean, my biological family, where I come from . . . it's overwhelming.'

'Mebbe one day you'll tell me what Chilly said about your family, Tiggy, but I definitely think you should go an' see wherever it is for yourself.'

'Yes, but I can't just up and leave my job, can I? What there is of it.' I rolled my eyes at Cal and took another large gulp of wine.

'The Laird'll come good soon enough. You just need tae have patience.'

'Another bizarre thing is that one of the first things Chilly told me was that I'd be leaving soon. I mean, the cats are basically fine now. Charlie'd be much better off employing someone to help you maintain the estate.'

'As a matter o' fact, I have Lochie starting in a couple o' days' time. I called the Laird and he sanctioned it.'

'Cal, that's really good news! Lochie seems like just the kind of person you need.'

'He only agreed 'cos Lochie's bein' subsidised by the government on one o' their trainee programmes, mind you, but I'm happy anyway. Now then, it's obvious you're wrecked. Why don't yae have an early night?'

'You mean get my beauty sleep for Zed? Maybe I should get out my best lingerie and paint my toenails too . . .'

'Aye.' Cal stood up. 'Yae've made your point an' I agree. I'm going tae go across to the Lodge now and tell Beryl that you're busy tomorrow, okay?'

'But then I'll feel bad for Beryl. I mean, it's not her fault, and she seems so stressed at the moment . . .'

'Don't yae worry, lassie, I'll sort it.' Cal was already walking towards the door. 'You get off tae your bed.'

I was relieved that I slept a dreamless sleep and woke up the following morning feeling much calmer. As I fed the cats, I decided I'd have to brave the Lodge at some point, not only to chase up my European elk contact, who hadn't yet replied to my email, but also to look up Sacromonte and Lucía Albaycín on the internet. Only then would I know if Chilly was telling the truth.

'Feeling better this morning?' Cal asked me when I got back.

'I am. Sorry about last night, I wasn't myself, but I'm fine today. Thanks for being so great, Cal.'

'Don't be daft. Now listen, why don't you come out wi' me this morning? I'm off to do a headcount of the deer in the main glen.'

'So you can reduce their number tomorrow?'

'Aye, but there's no harm in you knowing more about where they like to hide themselves, is there? And it'll put you out o' harm's way this morning in case his Lordship won't take no for an answer from Beryl.'

'You told her then?'

'I did that, an' she agreed. So I'm off in ten minutes, and we'll take Chilly's lunch with us too. By the way, turns out it might be me who has tae deal with our guest, rather than you. He caught me as I was leavin' the Lodge last night and asked if I'd organise a gun and some target practice for him while he's here.'

I pondered on the information Cal had imparted as I donned my habitual layers in preparation for going outside. I stood in the courtyard and whistled for Thistle, who lumbered out of the barn and happily hoisted his gangly body onto the back seat of Beryl. Then, armed with binoculars, we drove slowly down into the main glen. Cal stopped every so often and pointed to clumps of trees, under which the stags and hinds were taking shelter in separate groups on opposite sides of the valley.

'They'll be off up tae higher ground to graze soon, so early morning is the best time tae count them,' said Cal, pointing out a small copse that lay just across the frozen burn that snaked through the valley. 'How many over there, Tig?'

I focused my binoculars on the copse where seven stags huddled close together, then I looked again. And again . . .

'Cal, quickly!'

'What?'

'Oh my God! I think there's a white stag, just there, to the left . . .'

Cal shifted his own binoculars to my window.

'Can you see him? He's just between those two, standing apart right at the back . . .'

'I cannae, Tig.' He dropped his binoculars after a while and shook his head at me. 'That's what comes o' staring at snow for too long. It starts to move and take on strange shapes in front of your eyes.'

'No! I'm sure I saw him!'

Without waiting for Cal's response, I heaved open the door and leapt out. Once off the narrow track, the snow was up to my knees, the wooden bridge a treacherous ice rink. Having negotiated it and now only forty metres or so away from the copse, I retrained my binoculars, but the stags must have heard the crunch of my footsteps approaching and had disappeared into the trees.

'Damn it!' I swore under my breath. 'I saw you, I know I did.'

I made my way back to the car and saw Cal sitting with his arms crossed against his chest. He gave me one of his special frowns, which indicated he thought I was being flaky.

'Any sign o' him then?'

'No, the whole herd had vanished.'

'Really?' he said, sarcasm dripping from his voice as we

drove off. 'That's what comes o' spending too much time with our gypsy friend. You'll be seeing unicorns next, you dafty.'

Outside Chilly's cabin a few minutes later, Cal put a hand out to stop me leaving the car.

'Under the circumstances, best if I take his dinner intae him today. You wait here.'

While Cal was gone, I closed my eyes and saw a picture of the white stag in my mind. 'I *did* see him,' I whispered to myself. 'I really did.' Thistle laid his head on my shoulder as if in sympathy, and I patted him absent-mindedly.

Cal was back ten minutes later, and reassured me that Chilly seemed fine and had asked after me. As we drove back home, we heard a thundering noise over our heads and I looked up to see a helicopter skimming low over the glen.

'Wow, I've never seen one fly over here before,' I commented.

'Probably a search an' rescue taking some poor soul to hospital in Inverness. It was a rough ol' night out on the sea, so the shipping forecast said.'

Yet as we arrived back at the cottage, we saw the helicopter sitting in the centre of the lawn in front of the Lodge.

'Must be for his Lordship,' Cal said as we climbed out. 'Perhaps he needs it to take him intae town to buy a bottle o' the best brandy and some more cigars.'

Five minutes later, as Cal and I were warming up with a cup of coffee, there was a knock on our cottage door.

'Well now, I'm guessin' this is trouble,' he muttered as he went to answer it.

'Is Tiggy in?' asked a familiar clipped voice.

'Yes,' said Cal brusquely. 'I'll get her for you. Tig? You have a visitor.' Cal turned towards me with a small shrug. 'I'll be in the sheds.'

'Hello, Tiggy,' said Zed as he stepped inside, while Cal stepped out, despite my frantic eye contact imploring him to stay. 'It seems you're back just in time.'

'For what?'

'A scenic tour of the surrounding area. Then lunch at a little place I know in Aviemore. It is a ski resort only half an hour's helicopter ride away from here.'

'I . . . thanks, but I'm afraid I have to work.'

'Surely you have a lunch hour? You will be back by three, I promise.'

Obviously anything Beryl had said to him about me not being available had fallen on deaf ears.

'Now, you need to get into these.' He handed me a black Chanel carrier bag.

'What's this?' I managed to squeak.

'Just a few things I picked out for you and had sent up here in the helicopter. I realised you might not have your full wardrobe with you. Now, go and change, please, and we can get going.'

Given I was so shocked that I couldn't think of a thing to say, I decided the best thing was to retreat into the bedroom and take a few seconds to regroup in private. Closing the door behind me, I sank onto the bed, the carrier bag between my legs.

Curiosity getting the better of me, I opened it and brought out various parcels, all wrapped beautifully in white tissue paper with a little white camellia stuck to each. The first one I opened contained a cream jumper, similar in style to my holey Aran one, but made of the softest cashmere. In the next parcel was a pair of beautifully tailored black woollen trousers; the third and largest package contained a gorgeous quilted cream ski jacket, and in the last was a black cashmere beanie with matching scarf and mittens.

I couldn't help stroking the jumper and feeling the tug of desire towards such a beautiful thing. A thing that could be mine if . . .

*Tiggy, behave!*

Hating myself for the regret I felt as I re-parcelled the clothes, I took a deep breath and went outside to face Zed – aka my personal version of Richard Gere in that *Pretty Woman* film.

'Thanks for getting this stuff for me, but I'm afraid I can't accept it.'

'Why not?'

A million answers – every single one of which would be beyond rude – came into my head. I managed to desist because I knew Charlie needed Zed's business. I offered him only a lame, 'I just can't.'

'Good.' To my surprise, he clapped his hands together with what seemed like glee. 'You just passed the first test! I can now declare that, without a doubt, you are different from every other woman I have ever met.'

'Really?' I said, anger rising inside me. 'Well, I'm glad I've made you happy by passing a test I didn't even know I was taking. Now, please, can I just get on with my job here?' I turned to walk away, but he stepped forward and gently grasped my arm.

'Tiggy, I see I have made you angry. I am very sorry; in retrospect I can see it was a stupid thing to do. But, well, you cannot imagine what it is like being me.'

'No, I can't,' I agreed with feeling.

'I mean, the women I meet . . . It may sound like first-world problems, but I can never be sure if they like me for me, or for what I can offer them.'

*And I can't be sure if I like you at all . . .*

'Yup, first-world problems,' I said. 'About as first world as they get, actually.'

'I just wanted to make sure that you could not be bought.'

'Right. Well, now you know I can't be, I need to go out.'

'Yes, of course. I will cancel the helicopter – it was a ridiculous idea, but I wanted to fly us both out of Kinnaird so we could get to know each other better. The whole thing was well intentioned. Forgive me.'

'Sure. Thanks for the thought anyway.'

He walked towards the door, then turned round.

'By any chance . . . I mean, as the helicopter is here, and it seems like a waste, would you like to take a trip over the estate? No strings attached, I promise, and I will have you back down by two.'

*I actually* would *love to*, I thought, *it would be amazing to see it from the air. But . . .*

'Er, no thanks, Zed. I'm afraid I really hate helicopters. I had to fly in one when we transferred from La Môle to my father's boat in Saint-Tropez and it just made me feel sick. Now, excuse me, I really do have work to do.'

With that, I walked to the cottage door and opened it for him. Finally taking the hint, and with his head bowed like a naughty schoolboy, Zed left.

# *16*

Opening the front door the following morning, I found a huge bouquet of flowers and an envelope addressed to me on the mat outside. I picked them up and went back inside to open the missive.

I unfolded the sheet of paper from the envelope and studied the beautiful scripted hand, written in ink.

*Kinnaird Lodge*
*5th January 2008*

*My dear Tiggy,*
   *A small token to once again offer my apologies*
*for my crude and thoughtless behaviour of yesterday.*
   *Can we start again, please?*
   *Zed*

'Humph!' I said to Thistle as I walked across to the Lodge.

'Morning, Tiggy,' Beryl said as I entered the kitchen to find her frying bacon. 'Are you well?'

'Yes, thank you. I've come to collect Chilly's food. Oh, and is your office free by any chance? I need to check my emails.'

'Yes, though our current guest normally commandeers it from nine o'clock onwards, so I'd be quick if I were you.'

'Thanks,' I said and made my way along the corridor to the office, shutting the door firmly behind me.

'Right,' I murmured as I went to Google and typed in 'Lucía Albaycín'. The Wheel of Death turned intolerably slowly as the machine did its best to connect me with what might be my past . . .

Finally, it managed to begin downloading, the information unfurling like a modern-day scroll on the screen. I clicked on the first link and saw it was Wikipedia, which surely must mean that Lucía had been famous and therefore what Chilly had told me about her hadn't been a complete fantasy. On the other hand, she could be a horse trainer in South America, but . . .

Just as the site began to download and I caught a tantalising glimpse of a black and white photograph showing her name and half a forehead, I heard the door open behind me. I pressed 'print', then minimised the screen.

'Good morning, Tiggy, you're up bright and early.'

Before I had a chance to turn round, I felt two hands placed gently on my shoulders. I actively shuddered.

'You are shivering?' he asked me.

'Yes. I must be getting a chill,' I lied as I immediately stood up.

'Will you be long? I need to send an urgent email.'

'No, I just have some printing to do, then I'm finished.'

'Then I will go and get some breakfast while I'm waiting.'

Collecting the pages from the printer below the desk, I was gratified to see a grainy photograph of the woman Chilly had told me about, and the banner at the top, which read: 'Lucía Albaycín – Flamenco Dancer'.

Tingling with anticipation, I managed to restrain myself from diving in and reading it immediately. Instead I left the office and scurried out of the back door.

I caught Cal just as he was about to leave and hopped into Beryl beside him.

'What are you doing here?'

'Avoiding Zed and hitching a lift down to Chilly's,' I said, indicating the Tupperware box I was holding. 'I was also wondering, if we happened to be passing by the copse where I thought I saw—'

'Y'know full well where I pass to get to Chilly's,' Cal sighed. 'You're on a road to nowhere with that little fantasy o' yours. If there's a white stag at Kinnaird, I swear that I will run around in the snow naked with only a haggis covering my bits 'n' pieces!'

'I look forward to that,' I said. 'Because I'm telling you now, Cal, I know what I saw.'

'And I'm sure the stag was dancing with the faeries in the glen when you did.' Cal laughed heartily as the back door of Beryl opened and I turned round to see Lochie climbing in.

'Morning, both,' he said as he slammed the door behind him.

'Hello, Lochie, nice to see you again.'

'Hi, Tiggy.' He gave me a warm smile and we set off into the glen.

Cal deigned to stop opposite the copse without being reminded, and I hopped out, understanding he had a lot to do and wasn't impressed by what he saw as my flight of fancy.

I walked across the bridge then trained my binoculars on

the copse, but the deer had already moved up to the higher slopes, and I was too late.

'Anything?' Cal asked me as we drove off.

'No, but could we please come out earlier tomorrow?' I begged him. 'Before they set off up the hill to graze.'

'We can, even if it's only tae convince you that you were seein' things,' he agreed. 'Now, let's get you tae Chilly, 'cos me an' Lochie here have deer to count and fences tae be mended.'

'Maybe it's best if you take in Chilly's food again, Cal. He's less likely to cajole you into staying,' I said, as we drew up near his cabin. 'Tell him I'll see him tomorrow!' I shouted out of the window. 'Send him my love.'

That afternoon, I rooted through the cupboards for ingredients for a curry I'd been promising to make Cal for ages. He'd been patient with me recently and I decided I needed to say thank you. The lack of almost everything I needed had me jumping into the spare Landy to race to Tain and gather supplies.

'Hi, Cal,' I said when he arrived back home that evening. 'Good day?'

'Very good, thanks,' he said. 'Lochie's a gem – much stronger than he looks an' he really knows his stuff too.'

'That's great,' I said, as without further ado he headed for the bathroom. To my surprise I heard the taps running. Normally Cal – being the gentleman he was – would let me use the bath first.

*Maybe he's fallen in deer poo*, I thought as I went back to the kitchen to check on the curry.

When Cal hadn't emerged after fifteen minutes I knocked on the bathroom door and smelt a pleasant waft of aftershave emanating from behind it.

'The curry'll be ready in ten, okay? I told you I'd make it for you and I have,' I called.

The door opened and Cal emerged in his dressing gown, freshly shaved.

'Tig, I'm sure I told yae that it's my night for seeing Caitlin? I'm away tae Dornoch tanite.'

'Oh, of course! I'd completely forgotten. Never mind, curries are even better after twenty-four hours. I'll save you some for tomorrow.'

'Thanks, and sorry about that, Tig.'

'Don't be,' I said, following him as he made for his bedroom to get dressed. 'And you really should bring Caitlin here for supper soon. I'd love to see her again.'

'I will.' He proceeded to shut the bedroom door in my face, then emerged ten minutes later dressed in a checked shirt and clean jeans, looking very un-Cal-like indeed.

'Will you be back tonight?' I asked him, feeling I was clucking round him like a mother hen.

'If the skies stay clear, yes. Bye, Tig,' he said, throwing on his jacket. 'Keep out o' trouble while I'm gone.'

'Hah!' I said to Alice as I fed her. 'Chance would be a fine thing, but I will let Thistle in,' I added, feeling subversive. I opened the front door and called him, feeling an icy blast of air that was already sub-zero.

'Come on, darling!' I called to encourage the dog.

'That is a nice welcome,' said a human voice as Thistle loped forward, followed a moment later by a man.

'Hello, Zed,' I said, my heart sinking. 'Do you need something?'

'Yes. Someone to share this very good bottle of Château-Neuf-du-Pape with on a freezing winter's evening. Something smells good,' he said, sniffing the air. 'Are you expecting company? I saw Cal go out.'

'No, I just decided I fancied a curry,' I responded, unable to think of a single reason – apart from blatant rudeness – not to invite Zed in. 'You're welcome to join me for a drink.'

He stepped over the threshold, but Thistle positioned himself in front of me, his hackles raised, a threatening growl coming from his throat.

'*Scheiße*, control that thing!' Zed muttered, taking a step back.

'Shh, Thistle, it's okay,' I said, laying my hand on the dog's back. 'I don't know what's got into him, he's usually so calm and gentle—'

'He's obviously had no discipline,' said Zed curtly.

'Thistle,' I whispered into his ear as the growling continued, 'if you don't stop, I'll have to leave you outside.'

Feeling horribly disloyal to my canine protector, but fearing complaints to Cal or Charlie about Thistle's behaviour, I coaxed the dog out into the courtyard as Zed entered the cottage. As I closed the door behind us, I thought what an unfortunate trade-off it was. I tried to close my ears to the persistent whines coming from outside.

Zed followed me into the kitchen and I handed him the ancient corkscrew, which was bent and took serious skill to manipulate. I watched him struggle with it, before pouring the ruby liquid into two glasses.

After his usual sniffing and swirling, he took a sip and put

261

his head back, sluicing the wine around his mouth before finally swallowing. 'It is good,' he announced. 'It would probably complement a curry perfectly.'

'Is that a hint? If it is, you can have some, but I'm warning you, it's vegan. Besides, I'm sure Beryl has something delicious waiting for you at the Lodge.'

'It is Beryl's night off so the half-wit serving girl was brought in to heat me up some soup,' was Zed's disparaging reply. 'Even your curry sounds better than that.'

'Er, thanks. Well, no harm in you trying some. And I'm starving.'

'Can I do anything?' he asked.

'The fire probably needs stoking,' I said, and as he wandered out of the kitchen, it crossed my mind that he most likely didn't know how to stoke a fire. He probably had a minion to do it for him.

'So where did you go to university?' I asked him, for want of anything else to say, as we sat down to eat.

'At the Sorbonne in Paris. I only realised a couple of nights ago why your name was familiar to me. I was there with your sister, Maia.'

'Really?'

'Yes. We saw each other for a while actually. Nothing serious, but I do remember her telling me about her five adopted sisters with the strange names. I finished university and she had another year to go, so we lost touch.'

'She's never mentioned your name to me, but then she wouldn't. She's a very private person.'

'So I remember. Sweet girl though. And incredibly beautiful of course.'

'Yes, out of the six of us, she is known for that.'

'And what are you known for?'

'Oh, I'm the flake.' I grinned. 'They call me the "spiritual" sister.'

'You mean you are a witch?'

'If I am, I'm as white as the snow outside. It's part of my problem actually. I don't want to ever hurt anyone's feelings,' I said pointedly.

'Now remind me, am I right in thinking that Electra is one of the D'Aplièse sisters too?'

'She's my baby sister – the youngest. Are you saying you know her as well?'

'Our paths have certainly crossed socially in New York at charity events and such, yes.'

'She does a lot of that kind of thing. Do you?'

'I used to. It was fun, so why not?'

'It's exactly the kind of stuff I hate,' I grimaced. 'Big spaces full of vacuous people air-kissing each other, so they can be photographed and appear in magazines.'

'Hold on, Tiggy.' Zed put up a hand. 'You cannot tar everyone with the same brush.'

'I can, to be honest. Electra is empty and shallow these days and I reckon it's all to do with the celebrity scene she lives in.'

'Maybe it is not about the place, but the company,' Zed suggested.

'As a matter of fact, my life just now is *all* about the place, and not company,' I smiled.

'Well, like you say that you hate celebrity parties, I could not cope with the isolation up here. I fully admit to having a short attention span and the patience of a devil, rather than a saint. Being at Kinnaird is about facing my fears: limited internet, kilometres from the nearest town and no social scene or people, except you, of course, Tiggy. And at least you are excellent company.'

'Thanks, even if you make Kinnaird sound like it's some kind of ordeal. I mean, you're not exactly roughing it, are you? The Lodge is beautiful and there *is* internet, however patchy.'

'You are right,' Zed agreed. 'I am a spoilt brat. Now, tell me how your father is? Maia talked very fondly of him.'

'Sadly, he died last June. We all adored him, and his loss was a big blow.' For once, I actually stopped myself going into my spiel about feeling that he wasn't dead – I simply couldn't imagine Zed having a spiritual bone in his body.

'I am sorry for your loss, Tiggy. My father died recently too,' Zed said quietly. 'Technically it was cancer, but having never had a day's illness in his life, soon after he was given the terminal diagnosis, he took himself off on his yacht and committed suicide.'

'Oh Zed, that's really hard. I'm sorry.'

'It was probably for the best, he was very old – over ninety – and he had certainly lived a good life. He was at his desk in the office in New York to the end.'

'What business did he run?'

'Lightning Communications, the company I have inherited. I had been working for him for years, and I imagined I was well prepared, but it is a totally different ball game when the buck stops at *your* door.'

'What was your dad's name?' I asked.

'Kreeg, and Eszu is our surname. You may have heard of him. He was always in the papers, pictured at some social event or airing his opinions on TV. He was a larger than life character, that is for sure. So, what did your father do?'

'I don't really know. He was always off travelling when we were younger, but he kept his business interests well away from all of us girls. He said that when he was at Atlantis – that's our family home in Geneva – it was our time together.'

'Papa first took me into his office when I was a baby, so my mother told me. And I have barely left since.' Zed offered me a rueful smile. 'Especially in the past few months, there has been much to sort out.'

'I can imagine. Is your mum still alive?'

'Sadly not, even though she was thirty years younger than my father. He always called her his child bride. They divorced when I was in my teens, and there was a court battle over who I should live with. Papa won, as he always did – though why he bothered to fight to have me when all he did was send me off to boarding school, I do not know. Mama died in a skiing accident when she was in her forties. Tragic, really. Forgive me, Tiggy, I have no idea why I am telling you all this, but thank you for listening.' He put a hand on mine. 'And thank you for the dinner, it was unexpectedly good.'

'You're welcome. I like cooking. When I was a child, I used to spend hours in the kitchen with Claudia, our housekeeper. She taught me to make lots of tasty vegetable dishes.'

'"Housekeeper"?' Zed smiled, and I realised I'd given myself away again.

'Please, Zed, can we leave that subject alone?'

'Of course. So, tell me.' He leaned forward. 'What is your dream job?'

'I've always wanted to go to Africa, work with the big game out there,' I said.

'In what capacity?'

'Conservation mainly – that's what I specialised in during my zoology degree. Though I've realised recently that I'm also interested in hands-on caring for the animals too.'

'You mean, as a vet?'

'Perhaps.'

'For my money, conservation is far sexier.'

'I'm not really interested in "sexy", Zed, only in putting my skills to good use,' I said as I stood up to clear the table.

'Well, you are definitely sexy,' he said, standing up too and following me towards the kitchen. He grabbed the bowls from my hands, put them down, then swung me into his arms. 'Can I kiss you?'

Before I had a chance to reply, his lips descended on mine. Shock was addling my brain as I tried to wriggle out of his grasp.

'Evenin' all.' Cal stood in the doorway, the pile of snow on his hat making him resemble the Abominable Snowman. The vicelike grip on my back relaxed immediately. 'Am I interruptin' something?' Cal said innocently.

'No!' I said hurriedly, as I walked over to him. 'Zed was just leaving, weren't you?'

'Well, don't do so on my account. Sorry tae disturb, but I took the spare Landy, it bloody well packed up. I had tae walk a couple o' miles back here. I fancy a hot choccy tae warm me up. Care tae join me?' he asked Zed, as he divested himself of his dripping outerwear.

'No, thank you.' Zed read the signs. 'Right, I will leave then. Thank you for the curry, Tiggy. Goodnight.'

The door slammed shut behind him.

'Oh my God! Thank goodness you came in when you did!'

I said, flopping onto the sofa, shock and relief racing through me.

'Well, I'm glad my ruined evenin' wi' my own lady-love had some advantages,' Cal said wryly, moving to stand in front of the fire. 'I gather that wasn't a welcome advance?'

'No, it definitely wasn't,' I panted, genuinely spooked. 'He just grabbed me!'

'He has the hots for you an' that's for sure.'

'I felt as stalked as any deer during a shoot.'

'Listen, I'm here now tae protect you, Tig. I'm off tae change into some dry clothes, but we'll talk in the morning, okay?'

'Okay, thanks, Cal.'

I didn't sleep a wink that night, having visions of Zed trying to jemmy open my window with a crowbar so he could pounce on me and have his wicked way . . .

'Come on, Tiggy,' I told myself the next morning as I staggered out of bed. 'All he did was try to kiss you, not rape you. He's obviously used to making the first move . . .'

*But what if Cal hadn't come in when he had . . . ?*

'You look rough,' Cal appraised as I met him in the kitchen by the kettle.

'I feel it,' I sighed. 'I want to keep all the curtains shut just so I know he can't be watching me.'

'Yae've got yourself in a right ol' pickle, you femme fatale, you.'

'It's not funny, Cal, really, it isn't. I don't know why, but he frightens me.'

'Well, I'd reckon that if he realises he's on a losin' streak and can't win yae over, the old lizard'll be off back to whatever damp dungeon he crept out o'.'

Venturing out after Cal left, I saw the snow was deep after another big fall last night, so I decided to take Beryl the Land Rover down to visit the cats. If it was this bad up here, it would come up past my knees in the glen. Understandably, the cats weren't coming out to play, so I drove back up to the cottage, lit a fire and took the pages I'd printed off about Lucía Albaycín to the armchair by the fire, partly because I wanted to read what I could about her before I went to visit Chilly today, and also because it provided distraction from thinking about Zed.

Sure enough, the Wikipedia version of Lucía's early life and her rise to fame closely matched what Chilly had told me. And as he couldn't read and had probably never laid eyes on a computer, it was doubtful he'd cribbed any detail. I read up to the point where she'd danced at the Bar de Manquet in Barcelona and decided to go no further. It was better if Chilly told me himself, but at least I knew now that I could check his story was real, and that we *were* family.

'So,' I said to my reflection in the mirror, 'it looks like you *do* have gypsy blood.' And in all sorts of ways, I thought as I went up to the Lodge to collect Chilly's lunch, it explained a lot. On my way to his cabin, I stopped once more by the copse to search for the white stag, but it was deserted, so I continued onwards.

Unusually, when I opened the door to the cabin, Chilly was not in his chair. Instead, he was asleep, and the cabin was freezing. I tiptoed over to the bed, already aware that he was alive, due to the grunts and murmurs emanating from it.

'Chilly? Are you okay?' I said, looking down at him.

He half-opened one eye, glared at me, then used a hand to brush me away. Then he coughed, a cavernous rattling sound that came from deep in his chest. The cough went on and on until it sounded as though he was choking.

'Let's sit you up, Chilly,' I said, panicking. 'It might help.'

He was too busy coughing to stop me, so I put my arms around his shoulders, and heaved him and his pillow up. He was as light and floppy as a rag doll, and when I touched his forehead, I found he was burning up with fever.

*Just like Felipe . . .* I thought.

'Chilly, you're sick. That cough's awful, and I'm going to radio for a doctor now.'

'*No!*' A trembling finger pointed towards the dresser. 'Use herbs; I tell you which and you do boil them,' he rasped.

'Really? I think this is the moment for proper medical help.'

'Do like I tell you, or go!' His eyes, already tinged red from fever, blazed at me. Another coughing fit ensued and I brought him a glass of water and made him sip it.

With Chilly directing me, I took star anise, caraway, thyme and eucalyptus from the dresser, then lit the gas flame and put water and the ingredients into a pot. I left it simmering, then fished out a clean rag from the dresser, dampened it and went to press it against his forehead just as Ma had done when I was a child and so often sick in bed.

'I had asthma really badly when I was small,' I told him. 'I was always getting terrible coughs.'

'Another sickness do come for you,' he muttered, his eyes rolling back in their sockets as they tended to when he was having a moment.

He dozed off and I sat by his bed, contemplating what he'd just said to me and hoping he just meant a cold. It also struck me that it was all very well hearing about my apparently famous grandmother, but who had my *mother* been? And if Lucía Albaycín was such a star when she got older, she must have been quite rich too, so presumably it wasn't financial circumstances that had led to me being given away?

The herbs and spices – which had filled the cabin with an almost antiseptic smell – had turned the water a murky brown colour. I took the pot off the gas burner and poured the concoction into Chilly's tin mug.

'Chilly, it's ready. You need to wake up and drink it.'

He took some rousing, but I managed to put the mug to his lips and he took small sips until the mug was empty.

'Be okay now, Hotchiwitchi.' He smiled, patted my hand and closed his eyes again. I decided that I'd give him an hour to see if his potion had brought down the raging temperature, and if it hadn't, I'd radio Cal to call the doctor.

It was snowing again outside, the flakes obscuring the light from the tiny windows as they piled up on the sill. I wondered yet again how on earth Chilly had survived for all these years here, alone. But then he'd say that he wasn't alone – that the trees, the wind, and the birds talked to him and kept him company.

It was interesting how most people I knew found silence impossible. They drowned it out with music, TV or chat. Yet I loved it, because it allowed you to hear the silence properly, which of course wasn't silence at all, but a cacophony of natural sounds: the birds singing, the leaves on the trees rustling in the breeze, the wind and the rain . . . I closed my eyes and listened, hearing a faint tapping as the snowflakes fell against the windowpane, like fairies trying to gain entry . . .

I must have fallen asleep too, exhausted as I was from last night, because before I knew it, I felt a hand on my arm.

'Fever gone now, Hotchiwitchi. Give me more and you do go.'

The light had grown dim, and as I reached over to check Chilly's forehead, which was now as cool as my own, I saw too that his eyes had cleared and were looking at me with something akin to affection. He coughed, and I heard the continuing deep rattle in his chest.

'I will, yes, but I don't like the sound of that cough, Chilly,' I replied as I got up and went to the dresser. 'It sounds as if you need an inhaler and maybe some antibiotics.'

'Man medicine is poison!' he said for the umpteenth time.

'Man medicine has saved countless lives, Chilly. Look at the age we're all living to these days.'

'Look at me!' Chilly beat his chest weakly, like an ancient Tarzan. 'I do same without any!'

'True, but then we all know that you're special,' I said as I lit the gas flame to warm the smelly potion up.

There was silence from Chilly, which was unusual.

Eventually he spoke. 'You are special too, Hotchiwitchi. You'll see.'

I braved the swirling snow outside, wondering whether I'd actually manage to find my way home or was stuck here for the night, and collected some logs to re-stoke the fire, as well as bringing in the radio pack from the Land Rover. When the brew was ready, I held the cup for Chilly so he could sip it.

He refused my help and held it himself, his grasp shaking a little, but it was obvious that he was much better than he'd been earlier.

'You get home before dark. Bad weather.'

'I'm going to leave my radio pack with you, Chilly. Do you know how to use it?'

'No. Take it away. If my time here is gone, it's gone.'

'Chilly, if you tell me that, I really can't leave you.'

He grinned at the expression on my face then shook his head. 'Hotchiwitchi, not my time yet. But when it is . . .' He grabbed my hand suddenly. 'You will know.'

'Don't say that, Chilly, please. Now, if you're sure, I'd better go before it gets properly dark. I'll be back to see you tomorrow first thing. Whatever you say, I'm leaving the radio pack with you. Just press either button and Cal or me will answer the call at the other end. Promise?'

'Promise.'

There was a real blizzard outside now, and my heart bumped unnaturally as I navigated Beryl through the curtain of snow. I drew the car to a halt, searching for what was road and what was burn, iced over and covered with a snowy topping. I knew if I strayed off course, the frozen water would not be strong enough to take a Land Rover's weight.

'Shit!' As my heart rate crept up, I decided that I'd try to turn round and go back to Chilly's until the blizzard abated, but I realised I couldn't do that now either, because the river might only be a few centimetres away to my left and I could easily back straight into it.

'*And* you left the radio at Chilly's, you stupid woman,' I admonished myself, my teeth now chattering with cold and fear.

Just when I was resigning myself to slowly freezing to death, I saw a pair of bright headlights in the distance. Five minutes later, Zed's brand-new Range Rover appeared next to my car. I was filled with relief and trepidation as the driver climbed out and made his way over to me.

'Thank God!' both Cal and I said together as he heaved open the door.

'Why didn't you radio?' he asked me as he virtually carried me to the warmth of the newer car and turned the heating up full-blast.

'I left it at Chilly's,' I said as Cal did a scary three-point turn and we set off, the wipers at full pelt. 'He was ill.'

'Jesus, Tig! Yae know the first rule here is to always have the radio pack with you! D'you know how worried I've been when you didnae answer?! You could ha' died out here! It's a miracle I found you in this!'

'Sorry,' I said, my frozen hands and feet tingling as warmth began to flood back through them.

'When you didnae come back, I went tae Zed and begged tae borrow his smart new car. I'd reckon this piece o' steel has saved your life tonight.'

'I'll go and thank him tomorrow,' I said. 'And thank *you*, Cal,' I added as he helped me out and into the cottage. 'I'm really, really sorry.'

Later, as Cal piled my bed with blankets, made me a hot toddy and a hot-water bottle, I thought how blessed I was to have him. Never mind spirit guides, I seemed to have my own protector here on earth.

# 17

I was relieved that the only ill effect I suffered from after my night in the blizzard was a chill, which eventually turned into a stinking cough and cold.

'Chilly was right again,' I said to Cal over breakfast a few days later. 'He said I'd be sick. How is he?'

'Och, right as rain now. He was worried about you though.'

'I'm fine, really,' I said, though I still felt drained, probably from all the coughing and sneezing. 'Are you okay?' I asked him. 'You've been a bit quiet in the last couple of days.'

'No, Tig, I'm not. The Laird had promised a visit today and has just cancelled on me again. I had a list as long as my arm of stuff I wanted tae talk to him about, including gettin' a replacement for Beryl.'

'I presume you mean the car, not the housekeeper?' I smiled at him.

'Hah! It's nae a laughin' matter, Tig. If I hadn't found you that night, and wi' Beryl having no heating, you could have died o' hypothermia. Ditto, this cottage; it's freezing too. Caitlin told me I had to ask for proper central heating. Aye, I told her, any budget's been spent on the poncey house tae please her ladyship and the guests. An' it's just not fair on the staff.'

'Cal MacKenzie, Kinnaird Shop Steward,' I commented wryly.

'Afore I go back tae my potholes, I'm calling him and booking a telephone meeting. Charlie's not going tae wriggle out of his responsibilities again.'

'Maybe you could ask him what he wants me to do, while you're at it? I've got no proper work other than to throw in kill to the cats, and let's face it, Lochie could be doing that on a permanent basis.'

'Yes, but I'll nae talk you out of a job, Tig,' he said as he left.

Half an hour later, I lit a fire and settled on the sofa with Thistle; me reading a book, Thistle snoring loudly. I noticed his breathing sounded noisier than usual and that he gave a couple of little coughs in his sleep.

'I hope you haven't caught my cold,' I said, stroking his ears to soothe him.

There was a sharp rap on the door and, immediately, Thistle bounded off the sofa and began to growl.

'Heel,' I ordered him, and he came to me reluctantly. 'Sit!' I said as I opened the door to see Zed standing there.

'Hi,' I said, knowing I had to at least thank him. 'Come in.'

'Is it safe?' he asked, as Thistle continued to emit a low growl.

'I'll get his lead and hold him on that,' I said, not prepared to put him outside after what had happened last time. I reached for where I'd hung the lead on the peg beside the door and fastened it onto his collar. 'Come on, Thistle.' I dragged him across the floor to the sofa.

'First of all,' I said as I sat down, 'thank you so much for letting Cal use the Range Rover to rescue me. And also, for these.' I indicated the new flowers on the windowsill, which had turned up on my doorstep a couple of days ago. 'They really cheered me up.'

'Did they? Then I am happy. So,' he continued as he sat down gingerly in the chair next to the fire, eyeing Thistle warily, 'I hear the Laird is not coming up to Kinnaird today after all? What a shame, I was looking forward to meeting him.'

'So was I,' I said. 'I had lots of things to discuss with him and so did Cal.'

'It must be difficult when you have an absentee boss, I would imagine.'

'Yes, it can be, but Charlie has another job – he's a cardiac surgeon in Inverness. So it's difficult for him too.'

'One thing my father taught me was never to spread yourself too thinly, to concentrate on one thing at a time, and give that all your energy,' Zed murmured.

'Charlie's not got much of a choice just now. He can't just walk away from his patients, can he?'

'What about his employees here? It has been obvious since the moment I arrived that this estate is understaffed, and, without a captain at the tiller, effectively rudderless too. I mean, even though I am physically here at Kinnaird, I spend at least six hours a day – sometimes more – communicating by phone or email with my staff.'

'Charlie can hardly do that in the middle of open heart surgery,' I said, hearing the defensiveness in my voice.

'Agreed. So, he has to decide what he wants to do, and soon. I looked into the estate's accounts a couple of days ago and it is running at a huge loss. In reality, it is bankrupt.'

'How on earth did you look at the accounts?' I asked him, horrified.

'Anything is accessible online, if you know where to look. It is a limited company, registered at Companies House.'

'Oh,' I said, although that still didn't explain *why* he'd looked them up in the first place.

'So, how long is your contract here?'

'Three months, but Charlie said it would almost definitely be extended.'

'Right. Although looking at those accounts and the loan he took out to refurbish the Lodge, I do wonder how he is going to pay his electricity bills, let alone his staff next month. Tiggy' – Zed leant towards me – 'I will come straight to the point. I have a position coming up in my company that I wanted to discuss with you.'

'Oh, well, I'm afraid I know nothing about communications and technology and stuff.'

'I know you don't, and nor do I want you to. That is my department. This particular department – newly created by me – comes under the Lightning Communications global charity fund.'

'And what does that consist of?'

'It is about giving something back to the world from what I have taken out of it. I will be honest and tell you that my father did not have a good track record. Most people in the business community regarded him as a crook – and I am sure that, to become as successful as he did from nothing, takes some subterfuge. But now that I am in charge, I can assure you it has all stopped. I am not my father, Tiggy, and I want to build myself a much more positive media profile. You and our conversations have inspired me; what better way to do that than to start a charitable fund? In short, I want you to run the wildlife charity division for me.'

'I . . . goodness! But—'

'Please hear me out before you speak. My accountant assures me there is plenty of money available – charitable donations are tax deductible, so the budget is very healthy indeed. Millions, in fact, which would be at your disposal to do as you thought best with. You would choose the projects, and of course, you would be the charity's spokesperson, because you would be the only one who would know what she was talking about. And you are very photogenic as well.' He smiled as he made his fingers into a frame and peered through it at me. 'I can just picture the photo on the first presentation slide when we have the launch. You looking up at a giraffe somewhere out in the African savannah.' Zed slapped his thighs. 'Good or not? So . . . what do you think, Tiggy? Does the idea appeal to you?'

*Did the idea appeal to me?! Having millions to spend as I chose around the world, safeguarding the future of rare breeds, protecting vulnerable animals and having a real platform from which to speak out about their suffering. Elephants hunted for their tusks, mink farmed for their fur, tigers shot to become a trophy rug . . .*

'Tiggy? Are you listening?'

I brought myself back to reality, and stared at Zed across the table.

'It sounds amazing. I mean,' I breathed, '*amazing*!'

'Good, I am glad you think that.'

'But why me? I'm just . . . well, the cat-sitter at the moment.'

'Taygete D'Aplièse,' he chuckled, 'I looked you up online as well. I happen to know that you won a major prize for achieving the top marks in Europe for your final zoology dissertation.

There was a photograph of you in the *Tribune de Genève* with your trophy. You were then offered various high-profile positions, and decided on Servion Zoo, before you left after six months and came here to Scotland.'

I felt even more invaded by him, but I also understood why Zed had checked me out. 'Yes, but it doesn't mean I have the kind of experience you'd need for such a major undertaking.'

'One of your problems is that currently you do not realise or utilise your potential. You're twenty-six years old, only eighteen months out of university. I have spent the last few months weeding out the dead wood that my father employed for far too long. All the new people who work for me are young like you and not hampered by their past. The world is changing, Tiggy, and I need people around me who can look to the future, who have the energy, drive and the passion to succeed, just like their boss.'

I looked at him then and wondered if he'd ever thought of becoming an inspirational speaker. He was certainly on the verge of convincing me.

'I know you mentioned your passion for Africa,' he continued. 'It would certainly fit my brief. Big game is sexy – it gets a lot of coverage in the media. Yes, there would be some commuting between there and Manhattan where my headquarters are based, but I will include first-class travel in your package, along with a six-figure salary, accommodation, oh, and a company car – with heating,' he chuckled.

'Oh my God, Zed. I'm seriously overwhelmed. I can't take it in. But still, why me?'

'Please try to remember that your track record at university and at Servion Zoo would place you anyway at the forefront of suitable young candidates. This is not a favour,

Tiggy, however fond I might be of you. It is a serious proposition, although I will expect a lot in return.'

'I'm sure,' I said, trying to cover up any irony in my voice. 'And it's an amazing opportunity,' I agreed, 'but—'

'You need time to think it over.'

'Yes, I do.'

'That is okay, you shall have it,' he said as he stood. 'I think we would work together very well.' Zed made to walk towards me, halting abruptly as Thistle began to growl. 'I will leave you to think about it and when you are ready we can discuss it further.'

'Okay, I will,' I promised. 'And really, thanks for the opportunity.'

'Goodnight, Tiggy.'

'Night, Zed.'

Later, as I lay in bed in my freezing room in the cottage, and despite the massive drawback of Zed being my boss, I couldn't help myself fantasising about the plains of Africa, all that money, and the countless animals I could help to save with it . . .

I was awake very early the next morning and padded into the kitchen, where Cal was ramming a piece of toast into his mouth in readiness to leave.

'Morning, I was just off tae feed your cats. Up tae coming and say hello to them yourself?'

'Yes, my cough seems much better after being stuck inside for the past few days, and I could do with some fresh air. How have they been?'

'As antisocial as usual. We'll take Beryl, as I want tae go on and see where the deer are hidin' in the snow. We have a big shoot here tomorrow, your Lover Boy included. Hopefully it will bring in a few pennies tae put towards a new Beryl. I've finally got a phone call booked with the Laird later today.'

Thistle, who was still coughing, clambered into the back of the car with us, and we set off.

Gratifyingly, the cats came out to say hello to me, almost as though they'd missed my presence.

'You know, I really think it's doubtful they'll breed this year. If ever,' I muttered, as I threw the kill into the enclosures.

'Not like you tae be negative, Tig.'

'I've got to be realistic, Cal. And I really am wondering if there is a job here for me to do,' I said as we got back into Beryl.

'Well now, I'm going tae tell you something that might perk you up.'

'And what would that be?'

'It's your kind o' thing, Tig. You'll laugh when you hear, especially comin' from me.'

'Tell me, then,' I urged him, as he pulled Beryl to a stop in front of the birch copse of his own accord and trained his binoculars on it.

'Well now, that night I came out tae find yae, the blizzard was something else, one o' the worst I've ever seen. I got tae about where we are now, an' I was nervous of driving any further, what with the burn being so close. Even for me, who knows the road like the back o' my hand, I was disorientated. And then – and this is the bit you'll laugh at – the snowflakes on the windscreen seemed to morph together and form a shape. And . . .' Cal took a deep breath. 'I saw a white stag standin' just there.' He pointed through the window. 'It was staring at me – I saw its eyes glinting in the moonlight. Then it turned and began to run along in front of me, stopping tae turn its head back as if it was encouraging me tae follow it. So I did. A few minutes later, I saw the shape o' Beryl, covered in snow, with you inside. The stag stood there for a few seconds, then as I made tae get out, it disappeared into nowhere.' Cal continued to train his binoculars on the copse. 'It was like he was leadin' me to you.'

'Wow,' I breathed, then eyed him. 'You're not teasing me, are you?'

'I only wish I was. Problem is, now I'm as eager as you tae spot the damned thing, otherwise I'll start tae believe in those faeries that live in the glen too.'

Despite his joking, I could sense that the whole experience had really affected him. One part of me was happy that I might just have won over my most challenging convert, and the other was full of wonder and awe that perhaps my mythical creature *had* saved my life.

'I didnae tell you at the time, but if it hadnae been for that stag, or what looked like a stag anyway, I'd never have found you,' Cal admitted. 'Now, let's take a walk over there, shall we? See if your familiar will come out and say hello tae his girl.'

We did so, crouching behind a row of gorse bushes so that the deer wouldn't notice we'd come closer. As it was early, they were still there, packed together under the meagre shelter the trees provided, but fifteen minutes later, we headed back to the relative warmth of the car, having seen nothing except the red deer.

'What d'you say tae staking out the copse at dawn every morning?' Cal suggested.

'You know I'm up for it, Cal. He's there somewhere.'
'Finally, Tig, I'm beginning tae believe you.'

Later that afternoon, I was surprised to hear the rare ping of a text arriving on my phone. I ran to the bathroom where I usually left it propped against the window in the hope of getting a signal, and saw it was a message from Star. The gist of it was that CeCe had been photographed in Thailand with some guy who was wanted for bank fraud and the picture had ended up in the newspapers.

'Shit!' I muttered, wondering what that was all about and feeling guilty for not keeping in touch with my sisters more often. I managed to reply to Star and send CeCe a text asking if she was okay before the signal died again.

In need of distraction, I decided to take Thistle down to Chilly's cabin in Beryl.

Chilly was once again lying on his bed, eyes closed, rather than in his habitual position in the chair beside the wood-burner. Worried that his fever might have returned, or worse, I approached the bed with trepidation. As I did so, his eyes popped open.

'You better now, missy?'

'I am, yes, but Thistle's got a cough. I wondered if you have any herbs I could mix to help him?'

Chilly contemplated Thistle, who had sunk to the floor in front of the woodburner.

'No, Hotchiwitchi, you do cure him yourself. Use your own hands – they have the power in them. I did tell you that before.'

'But I don't know how, Chilly.'

He reached out his own gnarled hands to take mine, his eyes suddenly rolling back in his head.

'You'll be gone soon, but then you will come home.'

'Right then, I must get back,' I said, ignoring what he'd said and feeling unusually irritated by the way he spoke in riddles. I just wanted a cure for Thistle's cough.

'What did he mean by me being "gone"?' I muttered to Thistle as we traipsed back across the ice.

When I arrived home, the snow had begun to fall again, so I lit the fire and laying Thistle down in front of it, I knelt beside him to try and 'use my hands' as Chilly had told me to. I placed them on Thistle's throat and chest, which only succeeded in making him think he was on for a fuss and had him rolling onto his back with his paws in the air. Although I'd been told many times that I had a 'knack' for healing animals, consciously trying to do so was obviously another matter.

When Cal came home, I pleaded with him to let Thistle stay inside.

'He's just not himself, you must have noticed his cough,' I said. 'Can't we let him sleep in the warm for a few nights?'

'He's gettin' on is all, and it's just the time o' year for animals and humans to get the wheezes. An' it'll no' do him any good to be flittin' from warm to cold all the time.'

'I went to see if Chilly had a herbal remedy for him,' I persisted, 'but I came away empty-handed.' I didn't mention my own feeble attempts at treating the dog, or Cal would probably think I'd lost the plot completely. 'Would you mind if I got Fiona to take a look at him?'

Cal went over to scratch Thistle behind the ears for a few

moments, then relented. 'Aye, it cannae do any harm, and he's due a check-up anyway.'

I offered Cal some vegetable soup and sat down opposite him to eat my own.

'Cal, I need some advice.'

'Fire away, though if it's tae do with relationship stuff, I'm not the person tae be talkin' to.'

'Actually, it's got to do with my future career.'

'Then I'm all ears.'

So I told Cal about what Zed had offered me and he whistled when he heard the budget.

'You can imagine how tempting it sounds, especially as things up here at Kinnaird seem to be so . . . uncertain at the moment.'

'True, true, but what about Zed? I cannae help feeling that you'd be walking straight into the lion's den, literally,' he cackled.

'He said I'd be based in Africa a lot of the time.'

'An' the question is, how often would your boss be poppin' over on that private plane he's bound to have on permanent stand-by? On the other hand, Tig, I agree you're wasted here at the moment.'

'I keep thinking about Chilly and what he said to me the first time I met him. He said it again today.'

'Which was?'

'That I wouldn't be at Kinnaird for long; that I'd be leaving soon.'

'Och, don't pay too much attention tae him, Tig. His heart's in the right place, but he's getting frailer by the day.'

'And this from a man who recently told me that snowflakes morphed into a white stag that led you to me!'

285

'I agree, but when you're makin' big decisions, you shouldn't let anything he says affect your judgement.'

'No, but it's hard not to.'

'I think it's time we stopped dancin' around and got tae the heart of the matter. How do you feel about Zed, apart from the fact he's rich as Croesus and has just offered you your dream job?'

'Truthfully? I find him totally creepy.'

'Then tha's not good news, is it, if he's goin' tae be your boss? There'll be nobody tae stop him either, 'cos whatever your official relationship, he's going tae make sure he'll be working closely with you. An' yae've got to be sure you can cope with that if you take the job.'

'Oh God, I know.' I shuddered. 'Why can't life be simple?'

'Well, you asked my opinion and I'm tellin' you straight; that Zed's used tae gettin' what he wants. And just now it's you. Seems to me he'll stop at nothing, even if that means inventing a wildlife charity so he can offer you a job. Now then, I've said it and I'm sorry.' Cal stood up. 'I'm for a hot bath an' my bed. Night, Tig.'

The next morning, with Thistle still coughing, I called Fiona the vet, and she arrived within the hour.

After examining Thistle, she smiled up at me.

'I don't think it's anything serious. Just a minor infection. I'll prescribe him a course of antibiotics and give him a steroid shot to open up his airways, which should do the trick. If it doesn't, call me again then we can get him up to the surgery and run some tests. My instinct is that he'll be fine.'

'Thanks, Fiona,' I said gratefully. 'Talking of instincts, the thing is . . .'

'Yes?' she said, as she administered the injection.

'Well, even though I have no proper training, I've always been quite good at nursing sick animals. I've been thinking that's what I'd like to do more of in the future. Like, use natural methods.'

'You mean, work holistically?'

'Well, yes, but is there such a thing for animals?'

'Absolutely there is. I know a number of vets who combine both medical and alternative treatments in their practice. I've always been interested in taking some courses, but to be honest, I've never had the time. If you did decide to do that, I'd certainly be open to you working alongside me.'

'Oh my goodness, really?'

'Really,' Fiona smiled. 'Anyway,' she said as she repacked her medicine bag, 'that conversation is for another day. I have a sick heifer to run to now.'

After she'd left, I sat with Thistle on my lap, staring into the fire. 'Lions and tigers, or you, sheep and cows.' I said to him as I nuzzled my face into his fur. Even though I could hardly bear to think of turning Zed down, I already knew I had no choice. But before I made the final decision, I needed to email my sister. I didn't want to upset Maia by bringing up a past boyfriend, but if anyone knew the details of a relationship she'd had in the past with Zed, it was Ally. Later, I sneaked into the office and fired off a quick email to her.

**Hello darling Ally,**

**Sorry I've not been in touch very often. There's only one internet computer here which we all have to share, and the**

mobile signal is nearly as bad! I hope you and my little
nephew

(I added 'or niece' even though something told me it was going
to be a boy)

are well and healthy. You'll never guess what there's a
guest staying in our main lodge at the moment called Zed
Eszu. Apparently he knew Maia at uni, and they 'saw' each
other. I don't want to mention this or him to her as it might
be upsetting, but I thought you would know what happened, as you two are so close. He's an unusual man (!) and
seems very keen to get to know me. He's even offered me a
job! The question is, why?

Anyway, got to run now and count some deer, but email
me back as soon as you can with anything you know.

A big hug to you, that little one of yours, and your newly
discovered twin brother (I'd love to meet him soon!)

Tiggy xxx

'So,' I said, as I stood up and made my way back to the
cottage, with Thistle by my side, 'let's see what my big sis has
to say about Zed, shall we?'

# 18

'By the way,' Cal said as we drove back from the birch copse after the fourth day's fruitless dawn vigil looking for the white stag, 'Beryl told me last night that the Laird's wife wants to come up here tae Kinnaird tae stay for a while. Apparently she's irritated that our guest is outstaying his welcome.'

'I think we'd all agree with her on that,' I said with feeling.

'Odd though, as in their whole marriage, she's probably come up here for no more than a few nights. I reckon she designed the Lodge with an eye on livin' in it herself.'

'Well, I'm sure Zed wouldn't mind sharing it with her – Ulrika's probably exactly his type.'

'Aye, if he's intae older women,' Cal said bitchily. 'Yae up for another dawn stakeout tomorrow?'

'Absolutely, we just have to persevere and we *will* see that white stag, Cal, I promise.'

It was another three freezing-cold mornings until we did . . .

At first, I thought I was hallucinating; I'd been staring at the snow for so long and his white coat blended in so perfectly with the snow beneath him, his large antlers the same soft brown as the trees he slowly emerged from. But now he stood alone, away from the other red deer, perhaps only a few metres from me.

'Pegasus.' The name arrived on my tongue as though it had always been there. And then, as if he knew it was his name, he lifted his head and looked straight at me.

A precious five seconds passed, during which I thought I might never breathe again. Pegasus blinked slowly, and I blinked back, a moment of understanding passing between us.

'Jesus!'

Pegasus started, then ran into the copse and disappeared. I groaned in frustration and glared at Cal, who had just lowered his binoculars and was staring at me as though he really *had* just seen Jesus.

'Tig, he's real!' he stage-whispered.

'Yes, and you scared him away,' I scolded him. 'But he'll be back, I know he will.'

'Are you sure you saw him too?'

'Absolutely,' I confirmed.

'Oh my God.' Cal swallowed hard and blinked. I realised he was close to tears. 'We'd better tell the Laird what he has on his land. Ask what he wants us tae do about the stag. It'll need protecting from poachers once word gets out, that's for sure. I couldn't name a price for a white stag's head but it would be just that – priceless.'

'God, Cal,' I shuddered, horrified at the thought. 'Can we not just keep it between ourselves for now?'

'The Laird should know, Tig, it's his land after all – his stag come tae that. An' he wouldnae put any animal in danger, I promise. I need tae ask him if I can build a hide near the copse. We're going tae have to put our Pegasus under twenty-four-hour watch just in case, an' that'll take manpower. The stag's as vulnerable as a newborn baby naked in the snow once others find out about him.'

So Cal put in the call to Charlie, and with the help of Lochie and Ben, the handyman, swiftly erected a simple but effective hide from timber and tarpaulin, which would keep Pegasus's protectors shielded from the freezing wind.

Over the next week, I got into the habit of waking at five every morning and going down with a thermos of coffee to take over from the night shift made up of tried and trusted ex-Kinnaird employees, to wait for Pegasus to arrive. It was as if he could sense me, because like clockwork, he would arrive out of the foggy darkness, and we would watch the sun rise together, the red and purple lights streaking across the sky and dappling his white coat like a painting, before he would retreat once more into the safety of the copse.

Charlie had asked for photos, and it was one snowy dawn in the fourth week of January that we managed to snap pictures of Pegasus before the stag disappeared into the blinding white landscape.

'I'll go and get these pictures developed so at least the Laird won't think we're imagining things. And nor will I,' Cal added with a grin.

I went with him to the tiny local post office that did everything from developing pictures to cutting keys. We had a coffee whilst we waited for the film to be developed, then pounced on the photos, which were still sticky from the machine.

'Aye, he's real enough,' said Cal, flapping the best one of Pegasus at me.

'He is indeed,' I said, my fingers gently tracing the image

of his elegant body as he stood in the snow. 'Remember your promise, Mr MacKenzie,' I teased him.

I added the completed grant applications to the envelope to send off to Charlie and scribbled him a quick note. 'Hope you're okay,' I muttered as I handed over the envelope to the postmaster.

Later at Kinnaird, I was just debating whether to run the Zed gauntlet so I could access my emails in the office – I hadn't yet had a reply to the email I'd sent Ally – when I saw Beryl come out of the house and walk towards me.

'I've just had a call from the Laird. He's just heard that Zara has gone missing from school again. She's done it before and usually turns up here. The Laird is giving her twenty-four hours to arrive at Kinnaird before he calls the police. If I'm out and Zara comes to you, please let me know.'

'Of course I will. You don't seem very worried.'

'If she's not here by this time tomorrow, then I will be,' she sniffed. 'Oh, and Zed told me to tell you he'd like to see you. He thinks you may have been avoiding him.'

'Oh no, I, well, I've just been busy, that's all.'

'Right, well, just passing on the message,' Beryl said. 'And let's hope Zara shows up here soon.'

That evening, Cal went off to see Caitlin after his aborted visit of a few weeks ago, and with Lochie and his dad watching over Pegasus at the hide, I went to bed early. I must have dozed off immediately, for I came to at the sound of somebody tapping on my window. My immediate thought was that Zed had resorted to desperate measures to see me, but as I crept out of bed into the biting cold and twitched back the curtain to peer out surreptitiously, it was Zara's face that appeared within the frosty frame.

'Oh my God, Zara, you must be half frozen! Come in,' I said through the window, then gesticulated towards the front door. 'How on earth did you get here?' I asked her as I opened it.

'I hitched a lift from Tain station up to the entrance, then just walked up the rest of the way. I'm okay, really,' she said as I drew her shivering frame to the chair by the fire.

'You should have called me,' I said as I stoked the fire and reached for Zara's hands to warm them with my own.

'There's no signal, Tiggy, and besides, I don't want anyone else to know that I'm here.' She looked around nervously. 'Where's Cal? In bed?'

'No, he's in Dornoch with Caitlin. Zara, your dad has already called Beryl, so I think I should at least let them both know you're safe.'

'No! *Please*, Tiggy, I just needed some time alone to think. Twenty-four hours is all I'm asking for.'

'I . . .'

'If you won't promise, I'll find somewhere else to hide out.' Zara stood up immediately.

'Okay, okay, I won't say anything for now,' I capitulated. 'Are you sure you're feeling okay?'

'Not really, no.'

'Anything I can help with?' I said as I walked to the kitchen to warm up some milk for cocoa.

Zara followed me and leant against the doorframe. 'Maybe . . . Like, you're the only grown-up I trust, but please, Tiggy, don't say anything. I just need a bit of time to work some stuff out, okay?'

'I'm flattered, Zara, but you hardly know me.'

'Thanks,' she said as she took her cocoa and we went back to sit by the fire.

'So,' I said as Zara cradled her mug, 'I'd guess it's something to do with a boy?'

'Yes, it is. How did you know?'

'Instinct,' I replied with a shrug. 'Is it that Johnnie you mentioned to me at Christmas?'

'Yes!' Tears sprang immediately to Zara's eyes. 'I really thought he liked me, y'know? Even though all the other girls had warned me, he told me I was special and I believed him . . .'

Zara's body seemed to crumple as her shoulders heaved with sobs. I removed the mug from her hands, knelt in front of her and held them with mine.

'I just feel so *stupid* . . .' she continued. 'I'm just as pathetic as all those other girls I used to laugh at when they got used by a boy. Now it's me, and . . .'

'What happened, Zara? Can you tell me?'

'You'll just say I'm stupid. I mean, I knew his reputation, but I didn't listen, because I thought I was different . . . that *we* were different. I . . . loved him, Tiggy, and I thought he loved me too. And that would make it okay.'

'Make what okay, Zara?' I had a pretty good idea what 'it' was, but I had to hear it from her.

'I . . . well, he went on and on about it, said we couldn't be a real couple until we did. So, we . . . *did*. And then . . . and then . . .' Tears welled up once more in her eyes.

'Yes?'

'And then the next morning he sent me a text, dumping

me! Like, the idiot couldn't even say it to my face! He's just what the other girls said he was – only after one thing. Then I heard he'd told all his friends, so when I walked in for tea, everyone was giggling and pointing at me and it was so . . . humiliating, Tiggy. So the next morning – like, earlier today – I had town leave, so I got on a train and came here. And I can't ever go back! *Ever,*' she stressed, just in case I wasn't convinced.

'Oh Zara, how awful for you,' I empathised, seeing that she was still cringing with embarrassment. 'No wonder you ran away. I'm sure I would have done too.'

'Really?' Zara looked up at me.

'Really,' I repeated. 'Listen, you are *so* not the one to blame in all this. It was *him* that did the bad thing, not you.'

'Tiggy, you're so nice, but I did do a bad thing. I lost my virginity to him in the grounds of a Catholic school! The sins of the flesh are beaten into us day and night. If the monks knew, I'd be on a gazillion Hail Marys for the rest of my life! Plus I'd get expelled.'

'It's him who should be expelled,' I muttered darkly. 'Why is it always us women who get the blame in situations like this? You're feeling like a total slapper while your Johnnie is parading around like a . . . stallion at a stud farm!'

Zara looked at me and my vehemence in surprise. 'Too right, Tiggy! You go, girl! And by the way, he's *not* "my" Johnnie. Even if he crawled on his hands and knees all the way to Kinnaird, I'd tell him where to stick his precious . . . stud!'

We both giggled then and I was glad to see Zara a little brighter.

'Zara, have you spoken to your mum about any of this?'

I ventured. 'I'm sure she'd understand, she was your age once too—'

'Oh my God! Never! I can't talk to Mum about anything, let alone sex! All she'd do would go on at me for how I've messed up!'

'Okay, I understand, but I am going to have to let your dad know where you are. Beryl said he was going to call the police if you hadn't turned up here by morning. And you really don't want the hassle that will bring on top of everything else.'

'Then just give me until the morning, please, Tiggy,' she begged me.

'Okay,' I agreed after a long pause. 'You can sleep here on the sofa.'

The next morning, I woke to find Zara gone, a scribbled note on top of the blanket on the sofa.

> *Sorry, Tiggy, just need a bit more time by myself.*
> *Don't worry about me, I'm fine.*
> *Z xx*

'Shit!' I dressed hastily and ran across to Kinnaird Lodge.

'There you are, Beryl,' I said as I found her in the kitchen, my breaths coming in short gasps, my heart hammering.

'What is it, Tiggy, dear?'

I gave Beryl a brief run-down of the situation.

'You're not to blame yourself, Tiggy. You did what you thought was best,' Beryl said supportively, which surprised me.

'Thanks, but I need to contact Charlie, Beryl. Can I use the landline?'

'Of course, dear.'

I rang Charlie's mobile, which went straight to voicemail, so then I tried the home number. Having not expected him to pick up there either – logic told me he was probably at the hospital – it took me a couple of seconds to register the foreign-sounding female voice that answered on the second ring. *Ulrika, of course.* My heart sank like a stone.

She sounded about as happy to hear my voice as I was to hear hers, but given the circumstances, I had no choice but to tell her Zara had turned up at Kinnaird. I had to hold the phone at arm's length for several seconds while she sobbed dramatically – presumably with relief – into the receiver, but eventually she calmed herself.

'I have not slept a wink all night! I'm in no state to drive, but I'll be up there as soon as I can,' she told me before slamming the phone down. I sighed heavily, realising that I hadn't told Ulrika that Zara was currently missing again and only hoping she would reappear before her mother did.

Already dreading the Valkyrie's imminent arrival, I trudged back to the kitchen and relayed the finer points of the conversation to Beryl.

'I hope she thanked you. You've done what you can and now it's up to the Kinnairds to sort out their family affairs.'

As I sipped the strong tea that Beryl placed in front of me, I wondered how a job that I had worried would be too quiet seemed to be turning into a constant drama of Chekhovian proportions.

'While I'm here, is the office free by any chance?' I asked her.

'Yes, his Lordship's taking a call on the landline extension in the Great Room and can't be disturbed.'

'Great, thanks.'

I went into the office and logged into my email account. I'd finally received a response from the European elk man who said he could come up to Kinnaird to look at the terrain, and suggested a date in about a month's time. My heart leapt as I saw I also had an email from Ally.

Dearest Tiggy,

How lovely it was to hear from you, and I'm glad you're settling into your new job. As I look out of my window, the snow is covering everything and the fjord is part frozen – I'm sure it's the same where you are. I'm getting fatter and fatter, and I'm glad I've only got another few weeks to go until the baby makes its entrance into the world. My father Felix visits me every day – (I have hot chocolate and he has aquavit!) – and yesterday, he brought me down a cradle that his father Pip had once slept in. Seeing it really made me realise that the baby is on its way.

Now, Tiggy, on to other matters: you asked me about Zed Eszu and Maia. Well, yes, he did go out with Maia when they were at university and . . . Oh Tiggy, I don't want to betray any confidences, but it all ended very badly. On top of that, my darling Theo met him a couple of times through his sailing, and to be honest, thought he was an arrogant idiot. (Sorry.) I'm pretty sure he knows Electra too . . . he seems to have a thing about the D'Aplièse sisters . . .

I also have to tell you that when I spotted Pa's boat near Delos last summer, I also recognised Kreeg Eszu's yacht moored in the bay next to it. I haven't told you before because I still don't understand if it was a coincidence or something more . . . but Tiggy – between father and son – that is an awful lot of coincidences, isn't it?

You didn't say whether you were actually involved with Zed on a romantic level, but take care, please. I'm not sure he's a very nice person. Maybe you *should* speak to Maia who really knows him well – far better than I ever could.

What a strange year it seems to be for all of us as we get used to living without Pa. Let's confirm the date for that trip to lay a wreath with the rest of the sisters where I last saw Pa's boat moored. I think it would be therapeutic for all of us to be together again and really put Pa to rest.

Hugs and kisses from snowy Norway!

Ally xx

I printed off the email so I could mull over it at my leisure, even though it had only confirmed what I already knew, then stood up from the computer and made a hasty exit before Zed came in search of his breakfast.

Two hours later, I heard a car screech into the courtyard. Ten minutes after that, I was just preparing to take Chilly's lunch down when there was a loud banging on the front door.

I didn't even reach it before Ulrika burst in.

'For God's sake, Tiggy! Beryl told me that Zara turned up here last *night*! Why didn't you call us immediately?'

'Ulrika, I'm so sorry, I—'

'And now apparently she's missing again.' Ulrika cut me short, and I could see that she was shaking with anger. 'I've already left urgent messages for Charlie, but he hasn't called me back yet. Absolutely bloody typical – his daughter goes missing and he is not returning his calls.'

At that moment, Cal appeared through the front door. 'The Land Rover's vanished. Are the keys in the pot?'

'I don't know, I didn't think to check,' I told him.

'You think Zara might have taken it?' Ulrika asked.

'Aye.' Cal went over to the pot on the sideboard. 'The keys have gone,' he confirmed.

'This gets worse!' Ulrika shouted. 'Zara's never even had a proper driving lesson, just driven around the estate! What if she crashes? Or gets stopped by the police. She'll be in all sorts of trouble . . .'

There was another knock on the cottage door, which made us all jump. Cal went to open it.

'So this is where you all are,' said the tall man, Fraser, whom I'd last seen on Christmas Eve outside the Lodge. He ducked his head to step inside.

'For once you might be glad to see me,' he said to Cal, as he gave a tug on the female hand he was holding and Zara stumbled over the threshold. 'I found her on the side of the road, trying to change a tyre on that ancient vehicle she was driving. She hadn't a clue how, of course. I would have done it for her, but I thought it was more important to bring her back first to defrost. She could have died out there if I hadn't found her,' he added.

'Zara, thank heavens you're okay!' The Valkyrie walked towards the pair. 'Thank you so much.' I saw Fraser and Ulrika make eye contact and a glimmer of a smile passed between them before Ulrika's attention moved to her daughter. 'Where have you been, darling? We've been worried sick.' She embraced Zara, whose ramrod posture did not soften in her mother's arms. She glanced at me over her mother's shoulder, her expression beseeching me to help. The problem was, I didn't know how.

'We need to get her into a warm bath quickly,' said Ulrika, rubbing her daughter's arms ineffectually. 'We're not going to find that here, are we? It's an absolute hovel, and of course, we can't even go to the Lodge.'

'You can both come down to my cottage,' suggested Fraser. 'I have central heating and plenty of hot water.'

'Then thank you, we will.'

'Mum, I—'

'Not a word from you, miss!' Ulrika snapped and Zara shut her mouth.

'Right,' said Fraser, 'let's be off then.'

When they'd left – without Zara uttering another word – Cal shut the door behind them and turned to me.

'Well, I don't know about you, but I'm treating myself to a dram from my Christmas whisky stash after all that excitement. Want one?'

'Actually, yes please. I'm definitely feeling shaky. Poor Zara,' I groaned as my heart gave a weird palpitation and I collapsed onto the sofa.

'There you go, Tig.' Cal handed me a glass and we toasted each other before knocking back the whisky. The liquid made my heart bump and bounce, but finally steadied it, and I began to feel calmer.

'Here's to mother and daughter, safely reunited,' Cal said.

'Who exactly *is* Fraser, Cal? I've been meaning to ask you since I saw him at Christmas.'

'He's Beryl's son.'

'Beryl's *son*?' I squeaked. 'Why on earth has she never mentioned that to me?'

'It's . . . complicated, Tig; there's a lot o' bad blood from the past, if you know what I mean, and it's not for me tae tell the story. Suffice to say, she's not pleased tae see him back from Canada, and nor is anyone else at Kinnaird. Lord knows why he's here, but I've an idea.' Cal tapped his nose.

'So Fraser doesn't live with his mother?'

'Och no, not after what he did. Anyway, yae know I'm not one for gossip, so let's just leave it be, shall we? Fraser is back for reasons best known to himself and I for one will hold my breath until he's gone again. Now, I'm off out tae fill in some more potholes. I'll see you later.'

Just as I'd settled down on the sofa for a nap after lunch, still feeling worn out from my cold and the early mornings with Pegasus, there was yet another knock on the door.

'Hi, Charlie, come in,' I said, my heart rate rising again at the unexpected sight of him.

'Hi, Tiggy. Beryl told me Ulrika came to see you earlier to find out where Zara was.'

As he stepped inside and stood there, I noticed the purple shadows under his eyes and the deep contours of his features. He looked as though he'd lost weight since the last time I'd seen him.

'Zara's fine, Charlie. She and Ulrika left to go and get Zara a hot bath.' I then explained about his daughter taking Beryl and having a puncture.

'So, who found her?'

'That man Fraser. He brought her back here to Kinnaird.'

'Right.' Charlie's expression darkened. 'Where are they now? Up at the Lodge?'

'No, they went to Fraser's cottage.'

'I see,' he said after a long pause. 'Then I suppose I'd better go and see them there.'

'I suppose so.' I wanted to add a 'sorry' because I could see the pain he was in, but I didn't feel it was appropriate in the circumstances.

'Thanks for looking after Zara last night,' he said as he retreated back through the door.

'That's okay, I think she just needed to blow off some steam.'

'Okay, thanks, Tiggy,' he said, giving me a tight smile. Then he left.

# 19

I woke up at dawn the next morning with what felt like a hangover – my heart felt jittery and my chest felt tight as I breathed in. 'Stress, Tiggy, that's all,' I told myself as I dressed to go and see Pegasus.

Ignoring the hide and crouching in the bracken closer to the deer, I closed my eyes and remembered once again Chilly's words about the power my hands held. Keeping my eyes closed, I reached out into the air in front of me and tried to focus all my power on calling Pegasus to me.

Beginning to feel foolish, I opened my eyes, and wasn't surprised to see that Pegasus hadn't magically arrived. Yet as I stood up, I heard a familiar exhale of breath just centimetres from me.

'Pegasus!' I whispered, turning round and feeling my lips break into a wide smile. He gave a soft snort in response, then nibbled at the winter bracken for a while, before ambling off to join the rest of the herd.

When I returned to the cottage, I saw Cal in the courtyard talking to a man I didn't recognise. From the looks of things, it was a heated conversation. I headed into the cottage to put the kettle on.

'Who was that?' I asked Cal when he came in.

'Och, Tig. How word has got out, I've no idea,' he sighed.

'About what?'

'Your Pegasus, o' course. That chappie standing outside is from the local newspaper. He's heard rumours—'

'Which you of course denied.'

'O' course I did, but I couldn't order him off the land – he's got the right tae roam on it, like anyone else in Scotland.'

'At least he has no idea where to find Pegasus. It would be like looking for a needle in a haystack.'

'True, but it wouldn't take an expert poacher long to suss out exactly where the stags like to graze. I'd better go up to the house and speak tae Charlie about what tae do. If anyone is going to make an official announcement to the press, it has tae be him. See you later.'

'Sure.' I bit into a piece of toast, my head spinning.

'Tiggy? Are you home?' said a voice through the door an hour later.

'Just what I need,' I mumbled under my breath, lamenting the fact that the cottage seemed to have become the main focus of activity at Kinnaird in the last couple of days. 'Coming,' I called and got up from the sofa to greet Zed.

'Good morning, Tiggy,' he said, flashing me a broad smile. 'I have not seen you for quite a while.'

'No, well, I've been busy. I've had a lot to do on the estate,' I said as brightly as I could.

'I see. Well, I came to ask whether you had thought any more about my offer. You said you required time to consider it, and I have given you that,' he reminded me. 'I am very eager to move forward with the project as soon as possible, and you know I would like it to be you who takes the helm. If it cannot be, then I must find someone else.'

'Of course, I understand, Zed. I'm sorry if I've taken my time, but I genuinely have been busy. And it's a very big decision.'

'Of course.' Then, most uncharacteristically, he yawned. 'Do excuse me, I was hardly able to get a wink of sleep last night. The Laird and his wife came up to see me yesterday evening to ask if they and their daughter could have rooms for the night. The two of them had a very protracted . . . disagreement in their bedroom next door. That daughter of theirs also sounded most distressed. I heard her crying. I gather she had run away from school?'

'Yes, she had, but she'll be okay and—'

'So, Tiggy' – he took a step towards me and I took one back – 'I appreciate it is a major decision for you, but I am afraid I must have your answer by the end of the week at the latest.'

'I'm really sorry, Zed, I honestly have been so busy—'

'I appreciate that, Tiggy, but given what I heard through the walls last night, I would advise you to think about my offer very seriously. From what I heard last night, in my opinion Kinnaird is doomed.' He nodded at me, gave me a brief smile and left.

Cal arrived back only minutes after Zed's departure.

'I spoke to the Laird and he agrees we should keep Pegasus's presence quiet for as long as we can before making any kind of official statement.'

'Do we know who spilled the beans?'

'Lochie said old Arthur in the post office commented on the photos o' the stag when he was last in there,' he said grimly. 'I'm sure nae harm was meant, but it looks like that's how word got out to that local reporter. Yae can imagine that gossip like this spreads like wildfire round these parts. Anyway, I'm off.'

'Keep safe, darling,' I whispered to Pegasus, as I felt a shiver of fear pass through me.

'Bloody hell!' Cal swore uncharacteristically the next morning, as we heard a number of vehicles pull up in the courtyard. A TV cameramen had already climbed out of one of the cars and was filming the picturesque view of the glen.

'Are you in charge here?' one of the men asked Cal as he appeared at the door.

'No,' said Cal, 'but how can I help you?'

'Tim Winter, *Northern Times*. Word has reached us that there might be a white stag on the estate.' The journalist dug into his pocket for a notepad. 'Can you confirm this?'

'I cannae say anything as I'm not the boss, but I'd be doubting you'd see anything of that description here on Kinnaird land. I certainly haven't,' Cal lied smoothly.

'My source was pretty confident that one had been spotted. He said there were photos of the stag. He's emailing them over to me later today.'

'I'll look forward to getting a glimpse of those,' Cal replied, poker-faced. I was impressed with his acting skills, when I knew underneath he must be boiling with anger.

Another reporter stepped forward and introduced himself.

'Ben O'Driscoll, STV North. Perhaps you could tell us where the stags tend to hang out? Then we can go and look for ourselves.'

'Aye, I can do that all right.' Cal nodded affably. 'They're just over there, mid-way up the hill at this time of day.' He indicated the opposite direction to where Pegasus grazed and I stifled a giggle as he gave the journalists a set of complicated instructions.

I watched as they all scurried into their cars and vans and set off.

'At least that's bought us some time, Tig,' Cal breathed as we retreated into the cottage. 'I'm going to radio Lochie and tell him tae move the Landy away from the copse and pile some more snow on the hide. We don't want them given any clues, do we?' Cal said, picking up his radio and pressing the button to get Lochie on the line. 'Hopefully, if they find nothing they'll get bored and go and stalk someone else's dirty underwear. Lochie? Can yae hear me? Good. I need you tae hide the Landy an'. . .'

With a sigh, I left Cal issuing instructions and went into my bedroom to feed Alice.

There was a knock at the cottage door and my stomach turned over as I saw Charlie's pale face through the pane of glass when I went to open it.

'Hi,' I said, as he stepped into the sitting room.

'Hi.' Charlie gave me a tense smile in return. He looked terrible – I hadn't slept all night, and obviously neither had he.

'How are you this morning?' he asked, out of sheer good manners.

'I'm okay. More importantly, how is Zara?'

'Not so good. It all got very heated last night when we told her she had to go back to school. Zara ended up going to her bedroom and locking herself in. She's refusing point-blank to come out. Anyway,' he sighed, 'Zara isn't your problem. Tell me about this white stag . . . it seems the news is well and truly out, if the number of cars and vans roaming the estate is anything to go by. Cal says you've seen him in the flesh too.'

'Yes, I have. He's far more beautiful than in the photos we sent you.'

'And definitely not a figment of your and Cal's imagination?'

'No, Charlie, but now we have to do everything we can to protect him.'

'Well, I can pull in a few fellows and get some more man-power down there, but, Christ!' Charlie ran a hand through his hair. 'What a mess everything is at present.'

He looked so lost, all I wanted to do was to walk over and give him a big hug. And to sit him down with my arms around him and ask him what exactly had happened since I'd last seen him. But I knew I couldn't – it really wasn't my place. So instead I offered him the ultimate cure-all – a cup of tea.

'Thanks but I can't stay, Tiggy. I need to get back to the Lodge and try to coax Zara out of her bedroom. Any advice you could give me? We're still not sure what it is that's happened. She won't say a word. Is it something to do with a boy?'

'Er, well, it's basically a case of hurt pride,' I said carefully, knowing it wasn't my secret to tell. 'Perhaps if you offered her a few days off school to lick her wounds, it might help. I'm sure she'll get bored hanging around at home with nothing to do. She'll miss all her mates and want to know what's going on.'

'Yes, you're probably right.' Charlie looked at me in relief.

'I'll try that strategy. It's just a shame that at such a difficult time in her life, Zara feels she can't confide in her mother.'

'Maybe as she grows up, she will,' I said.

'Sadly, I doubt it. Look, Tiggy,' he said after a pause, 'I'm sorry I haven't been in contact recently. There's been a lot going on. Could I ask you to bear with me for a while longer on the work front? I really don't want to lose you.'

*Although I've felt that I have lost you . . .*

'Of course you can. I just feel like a fraud, feeding a few cats twice a day and getting paid for it,' I said with a shrug.

'Well don't. Filling in those grant application forms for me saved me so much time, I can't tell you. And there may be more to come,' he added lamely.

'I have a meeting booked with the European elk man, but don't worry about that for now, Charlie; you do what you have to and we'll try to keep Pegasus safe up here.'

'Thank you, Tiggy. You're wonderful, you really are.'

I watched him take a step towards me, think better of it, then step back.

'Okay, I'll be in touch soon,' he said. 'Bye now.'

'Bye, Charlie.'

An hour later, still dreamy from Charlie calling me 'wonderful', I saw his battered Range Rover fly past my window, followed closely by Ulrika's far smarter jeep, both on their way out of the estate.

'For God's sake, get a grip!' I told myself firmly. Still, I watched the Range Rover until it was a mere speck on the horizon.

I spent the next two days avoiding Zed yet again as I agonised over his job offer, a task helped by taking my turn in the rota of Pegasus-patrols.

'Right, Tiggy,' I said to myself, 'before you make any decisions, it's time to call your big sister for advice on Zed Eszu.' Then, having stoked up the fire for Cal to return home to, I walked across to the Lodge.

Unfortunately, Zed was standing in the kitchen with Beryl, his arms crossed.

'What's all this I hear about a white stag being seen at Kinnaird?' he asked me.

'I know, crazy, isn't it?' I said.

'Well, there's never much news in January, is there?' Beryl added.

'Normally, there is no smoke without fire, but . . . more importantly I need an answer from you, Tiggy. Perhaps you would join me for lunch here tomorrow and we can discuss it?'

'I . . . yes.' I realised I could put him off no longer.

'Good. Beryl, I have to make a call to New York in fifteen minutes, I will take it on the landline extension and I am not to be disturbed, okay?'

'Of course, sir.'

When we heard the door to the Great Room shut behind Zed, Beryl let out a sigh. 'When is that damned man going to leave?' she muttered.

'Very soon I hope,' I whispered under my breath. 'Beryl, before Zed commandeers the phone, would it be okay if I used the landline to make a quick call to my sister? I really need to speak to her, but she lives in Brazil, so obviously I'll pay for the cost.'

'Don't be silly, Tiggy, I'm sure that with what Zed is paying to stay here, we can grant you a few minutes of a long distance call. Now hurry up, before Zed complains the line is engaged.'

'Thanks, Beryl. I won't be long.'

I walked along the corridor to the office, shut the door behind me and picked up the receiver, pondering what to say to Maia.

The line rang and rang – it was the afternoon in Rio, so I hoped that she wasn't out.

'*Oi,*' said the familiar mellow tones of my eldest sister.

'*Oi,* Maia,' I smiled into the receiver at the sound of her voice. 'It's Tiggy here.'

'Tiggy! How fantastic to hear from you! How are you? Where are you?'

'Still in the middle of nowhere up in the Scottish Highlands, looking after my animals. You?'

'Busy with my English teaching in the favela, and Valentina keeps me on my toes too. How Ma managed to control all us sisters when I have a problem with one six-year-old, I don't know. The child is never tired,' Maia added but I could hear the warmth in her voice. 'How are you?'

'I'm good, yes. It's just that Ally advised me to contact you. About someone called Zed Eszu.'

There was a long pause on the other end of the line.

'Right,' she said eventually.

'Well,' I ploughed on, 'he's offered me a job. And oh, Maia, it's a fantastic opportunity.'

I went on to explain the job spec and how much money Zed was offering me to spend on the charity.

'And that's even without my pay package and all the perks. So, what do you think?'

'Of the job offer? Or Zed?'

'Both, I suppose.'

'Oh Tiggy . . .' I heard Maia sigh deeply. 'I don't know what to say.'

'Whatever it is, Maia, please just say it,' I urged her.

'Before I do, I just want to ask you whether you and Zed . . . Well, are you romantically linked? Or is this a completely professional relationship?'

'It's professional on my side but on his . . . to be truthful, I'm not sure.'

'He's giving you a lot of attention?'

'Yup.'

'Writing you letters, bringing you presents and sending you flowers?'

'Yup.'

'Turning up at your front door uninvited?'

'Yup.'

'In essence, stalking you?'

'Yes. Cal – my housemate – even *calls* him my stalker.'

'Right. So do you think he's offering you this job because you're the right person for it? Or is he using it as bait to get you?'

'That's the point – I just don't know. A bit of both, maybe.'

'Well, Ally might have mentioned that I'm not Zed Eszu's biggest fan, so I'm not sure I can give you an unbiased answer. All I can say is that everything you've just told me that Zed has done, he did to me too. It was as if he'd stop at nothing until he got me – like he was hunting me down. And then when he *did* get me, when I stupidly surrendered, he lost interest soon afterwards.'

'Oh Maia, I'm so sorry. This must be really painful for you to talk about.'

'I'm over it now, but at the time . . . Anyway, it might be different for you. Zed might have changed – matured or something – but actually, now I think back on our early days together, I'm pretty sure he mentioned there could be a translation job for me at his father's company when I finished uni. As it turned out, he hardly said goodbye when he left the Sorbonne a year before I did.'

'Oh God,' I said. 'Ally said that Zed might have a thing for the D'Aplièse sisters. Maybe it's true.'

'Well, it's certainly odd that it was his father's boat which Ally saw moored next to the *Titan* in Greece last summer. And then his son appears up in the remote Scottish Highlands, where you just happen to be working.'

'I'm sure that part is just shitty coincidence, Maia,' I said. 'He seemed very surprised when he met me and put two and two together.'

'Tiggy, do you like Zed? I mean, in *that* way?'

'No. Definitely not. I find him –' I lowered my voice – 'seriously weird. He comes across as really arrogant, although I can't help feeling sorry for him. Remember, he lost his father too at about the same time we lost Pa.'

'And I'm sure he's used that to bond with you, Tiggy. We all know what a soft heart you have. You'd give the Devil the benefit of the doubt, and I wouldn't mind betting Zed picked up on that too.' I heard the edge of bitterness in Maia's voice. 'Sorry, Tiggy, ignore me. The job sounds amazing, and I understand why you'd love to take it. And as far as Zed being your boss is concerned, on a professional level, I can't comment. On a personal level, please watch out. He'll do anything to get what he wants, and from the sound of things right now, that's you.'

'Maia, the bottom line is this: do you think he's a good person at heart?'

There was an agonising pause before Maia replied.

'No, Tiggy, I'm afraid I don't.'

'Okay. Thanks for being honest and I'm so sorry if this has brought back bad memories.'

'Oh, it's fine, Tiggy, really. It was a long time ago. I just . . . don't want you to get hurt the way that I did. Besides, you're the one with the intuition, so it must be your decision.'

'Yes. Anyway, I'd better sign off now as I'm using the boss's landline and our . . . mutual friend wants to call New York.'

'Oh, okay. It's been lovely to speak to you. Keep in touch, won't you?'

I put the receiver down, hoping I hadn't upset her. I could tell that Zed was not just someone who had passed briefly through Maia's life, but someone who had hurt her deeply.

Then, on a whim, and while Zed was elsewhere and the computer free, I went online to look at jobs abroad for zoologists. If I wasn't taking the job with Zed, it may be – what with the uncertain situation at Kinnaird – that I needed to find something else.

A number of what Google thought were suitable positions appeared on the screen and I scrolled through them.

'Assistant professor in Animal Immunology and Landscape Ecology, South Georgia, USA.'

*Not appealing*, I thought, even if I had the experience to become an assistant professor, which I didn't.

'Zoological Field Assistant, specialising in seals and sea-birds, Antarctica.'

*Not on your life, Tiggy, as if Scotland isn't cold enough . . .*

'Conservation officer required on game reserve in Malawi.'

*Now that sounds interesting . . .*

I shot off a quick email and attached my CV, only realising after I'd pressed 'send' that I hadn't changed my address on the CV from Switzerland to Kinnaird, but knowing Ma would immediately send any correspondence on to me in Scotland.

Having given myself at least one positive alternative for the future, I woke early the next morning feeling calmer. After feeding the cats, I paused briefly halfway up the slope from the enclosure, and listened for sounds in the glen. Not even the whisper of a breeze stirred the complete stillness. I'd learnt that the eerie silence often came before a snowstorm. The cats obviously agreed, for none of them had come out to see me. As I trudged the rest of the way to the Lodge to collect Chilly's food, I contemplated what I would tell Zed over today's dreaded lunch. Or in fact, how I would frame the 'no' that I had to give him.

'Me in New York?! Never,' I said to myself. 'You'd hate every moment of it, Tiggy, being in some tiny glass box in the sky. Manhattan's probably the same size as the Kinnaird estate,' I added, 'but chock-a-block with buildings.'

*Zed did say you'd be spending a lot of time travelling . . .*

'No, Tiggy,' I told myself firmly, 'whatever happens, however he tries to convince you, you have to say no. It's just not . . . *right*. And that's all there is to it.'

'Are you ill again, Chilly? Should I call someone?' I asked as I arrived in the cabin to find him once more lying on his bed.

'No worse than I was yesterday, or will be tomorrow.' Chilly's eyes opened as I approached him. 'You is goin', not me.'

'Honestly, Chilly,' I said, 'you do talk some rubbish sometimes.'

'Tell Angelina it was me who guided you home like I promised.'

His eyes closed again, but I went to him and took his hand.

'I'm not going anywhere, Chilly,' I said softly.

'You going home. And after that,' he said with a small sigh, 'so am I.'

Even though I spent the next few minutes begging him to tell me what he meant, he was either feigning sleep or he really was dozing, for he said no more. I kissed him on his forehead, and since it was obvious that he wouldn't respond, I could do no more than leave his lunch by the gas ring for him to warm up later and say a gentle goodbye to him.

'Hello, Beryl,' I greeted her as I walked into the kitchen an hour later.

'You're a little early for lunch. Zed told me he was expecting you at one.'

'He is, but I need to use the computer again first if it's free.'

'As a matter of fact, it is, our guest is on one of his endless foreign calls in the Great Room. Mornings it's China and the

East, afternoons and evenings it's New York and the West. I really don't know why he's here – he hardly ever takes advantage of what's beyond the windows . . . He only goes out to shoot at a target for an hour each day in the copse. To be frank, Tiggy, one way and another, just now I could scream.'

I watched her viciously attack the carrot in front of her with a knife.

'I'm sorry, Beryl. Hopefully he'll leave soon and you'll get the Lodge back, and some fresh air into it,' I added, trying to lighten the conversation.

'And then who'll arrive here the moment it's free? She's back again – I saw them together this morning on my way here, out riding. They were grinning at me, as bold as brass,' she muttered, giving another carrot a brutal chop.

'Who, Beryl?'

'Oh, no one.' Beryl reached into her apron pocket for a tissue and blew her nose. 'Ignore me. It's a depressing time of year, isn't it?'

'Yes. And, Beryl . . . honestly, any time you want to talk, I'm here, I really am.'

'Thank you, dear.'

Shutting the study door behind me, I sat down at the desk and logged into Hotmail. Two emails appeared – one from Charlie and the other from Maia.

I read Charlie's first.

Hi Tiggy, forgive typos as this is written (as usual) in haste. Firstly I realised that I have never apologised about the near miss you had in the snow. If 'Beryl' hadn't been in such a poor state, it might have been avoided. And I'd never have forgiven myself if anything had happened to you. I also apologise for not saying a proper goodbye when I left the other day. You deserve huge thank yous for helping Zara – and also from me on how to handle her. Your advice worked: after getting home, she asked to go back to school. We haven't heard anything untoward from her since, so fingers crossed she's settled down again.

It was good to see you and have a chat – albeit brief – but I look forward to seeing you again soon, when I hope to have some more positive news about the future of the estate.

Take care

Charlie x


I gave myself a small hug of pleasure, at the kiss and the warmth and concern the email contained. Being the sad lonely creature I was, I even printed it off to read again later.

Then I read Maia's email.


Dear Tiggy,

I've been thinking about our conversation a lot since we spoke and I'm worried about you and our weird 'stalker'. Even though the job sounds amazing, please think carefully.

I hummed and hahed about whether to send you the attached, but I think you should see it before you decide. It's from a year ago but . . .

Don't hate me!

Hope to see you in the summer,

Speak soon,

Maia xx

I scrolled down and opened the attachment. And there in front of me was a picture of the man currently waiting for me in the Great Room. He had his arm slung around my sister Electra's shoulder, and the caption read:

*'Zed Eszu and Electra enjoy each other's company at a gallery opening in Manhattan. Seen out and about in the city occasionally in the past eighteen months, one wonders whether they are officially an item or whether they'll keep us guessing.'*

'That confirms it,' I muttered, as I clicked 'print', then folded the sheet and stuck it in the back pocket of my jeans.

Gathering myself together for a second, I took a deep breath and headed for the Great Room.

'Tiggy.' Zed rose and walked towards me from his chair by the fire – the heat in the room was stifling. 'I feel I have not had you to myself for a long time. It is almost as though you have been avoiding me,' he added as he kissed me on both cheeks.

'Not at all, Zed. Everything's just been very busy.'

'With the sighting of the white stag, you mean?'

'I . . . it's only hearsay, Zed.'

'Come along, Tiggy, we all know you have seen him, that Cal took photographs of him, which have somehow made their way into the media's hands. If I was Charlie Kinnaird, I would be singing to the treetops about it. It is a sure-fire way to put the Kinnaird estate on the tourist map. What is he waiting for?'

'Charlie would never do that, Zed, because we must do everything we can to *protect* the stag, and letting hundreds of people onto the estate is hardly the way to do that. Not to mention the threat of poachers. The stag's so rare, he's almost mythical. Please remember that my profession – and my remit here – is all about wildlife conservation.'

'Of course, and wouldn't it be incredible if we could get a shot of you and the stag for the launch of our charity? Forget the giraffe,' Zed chuckled, 'they are two a penny, as they say here in the UK. Next time you go out to see the stag, can I come with you and bring a camera? I believe he has been spotted in the birch copse. I saw the old Range Rover parked there yesterday when I took a ride out in my own to try to spot him.'

'Zed, we have to talk,' I said firmly, horrified that Zed seemed to know where Pegasus was.

'Of course. You will want to know the details of your package. I have my eye on a loft in Chelsea that I think would suit you when you are in Manhattan, and not saving lions in Africa. Now, I have some champagne on ice' – he indicated it, nestled in a silver ice bucket on the drinks cabinet. 'Shall I open it?'

I stared at him in disbelief. He was obviously convinced I was going to take the job.

'No, Zed, because—'

'You have concerns,' he said without missing a beat. 'So I have prepared a file for you that sets out your job specification and, of course, your salary. Here.' He offered me a folder.

'Thank you for going to so much trouble, but I'm afraid I can't take the job, and nothing can change my mind.'

Zed frowned at me. 'Can I ask you why?'

'Because . . .' The many answers I'd prepared flew out of my head as his gaze didn't waver. 'I like it here.'

'Come now, Tiggy, I am sure you can do better than that.'

I saw the glint of steel surface in Zed's eyes.

'I really am a country girl at heart and this feels like home.'

'If you cared to glance at what is in that file, you would see that I have included a first-class flight for you to travel back to anywhere in Europe once a month. You would also see that I envisage you spending at least six months a year in Africa, especially in the beginning, when you are looking for ways to spend the twenty-five million dollars you will have at your disposal.'

*Twenty-five million . . .*

'It all sounds amazing, but I'm only twenty-six, and have zero experience in anything other than animal conservation. There's no way I could do all the business stuff.'

'Which is why you will have an experienced team around you. As I have already said, your sole mandate is to source the projects and to front the whole enterprise. We will get you a stylist, a new wardrobe, a public-speaking coach . . .'

I stood there as Zed continued to tell me how I would be taken and moulded and *owned* by him. And as I thought about this, Zed's face and body began to change, and he morphed into a giant green and horribly venomous lizard, his pointed tongue flicking in and out at me as he spoke . . .

Zed eventually stopped talking, and as he did so, transformed back from reptile to human.

'Er, right. Um, thank you, Zed, really, I'm honoured, but whatever you say to me, it's still a no.'

'And it really is this place – Kinnaird – that holds you here?'

'Yes,' I confirmed. 'I love it.'

'Well then, my decision is made.' Zed slapped his thigh. 'I will buy this estate. I have been thinking about it for the last few days. I'm sure Charlie will agree to sell to me. We all know how desperate he is. He will be only too happy to have it taken off his hands.'

'You want to buy Kinnaird?' I whispered, my voice quivering with horror.

'Why not? It will be tax deductible; we can hold team-building exercises for my staff in the great outdoors, and perhaps use some of the land for an eighteen-hole golf course. I can extend the Lodge into a proper hotel and turn those old barns into retail outlets selling local products. In short, I would bring the whole place into the new millennium. And you, Tiggy, can stay here and help me.'

I was so completely shocked that I opened and closed my mouth like a goldfish.

'So,' Zed continued, smiling, 'whichever way you throw the dice, Tiggy, it looks like you will end up working for me. Now, let us have that champagne.'

'Zed, I'm sorry but I have to go.'

'Why? What is it I have said or done that has offended you?'

'I . . . You've been more than generous, and I really appreciate it, but I can't work for you, Zed, either here or in New York.'

'Why ever not, Tiggy? I thought we were getting on very well?'

'Well, it's just that . . .' I fished in my back pocket for the printout. 'I spoke to my sister Maia about you. And she sent me this.' I proffered the paper to him and watched him unfold it. He looked at the photograph, then up at me.

'It's my sister, Electra,' I prompted.

'I know who it is, Tiggy, I just do not understand your reaction to it.'

'First you date Maia, and then you move on to Electra, and now here you are with me! I'm sorry, but I just think it's . . . weird.'

'Tiggy, please don't be so naive. You must know how the media can take a completely innocent friendship and make it look like the greatest love affair since Burton and Taylor. I told you openly that I knew Maia *and* Electra. And yes, with Maia I had a relationship, but with Electra, only a casual friendship. As you know, she currently has a boyfriend, so I have not seen her for months. Besides, you are all beautiful women who move in similar circles to me. It is as simple as that.'

'I certainly *don't* move in similar circles to you. And I never will. Now, I'm going, and I'd really prefer it if we didn't see each other again.'

'Surely you are not jealous of your two sisters?'

'Of course I'm not!' I almost shouted at him in frustration because he still didn't get it. 'Your fixation with us sisters, it's just . . . creepy. Bye, Zed.'

I walked from the room, half expecting him to follow me and glad that Beryl was there as protection in the kitchen and that Cal would be home for lunch. Once out of the house, I bolted across the courtyard, opened the front door to the cottage and slammed it behind me.

'Shit!' I said as I contemplated moving the sofa against the door as extra protection.

'Where's the fire?' asked Cal, sauntering out of the kitchen, eating a huge slice of meat pie.

'Are you going to be here for the next hour?' I panted.

'I can be, yes. Why?'

'Because I just turned down Zed's job offer. He wasn't very happy, to put it mildly, so then he said he wanted to buy the

Kinnaird estate, so either way I'd end up working for him and
. . . then I showed him a photo of him with one of my sisters
in a magazine, and he dated my other sister too, and . . . God,
Cal, I seriously think he's mad!'

'Whoa, Tig, you've lost me. What was that about him
buying Kinnaird?'

'He just told me he was going to. Oh Cal!' Tears sprang to
my eyes. 'He was talking about putting in a golf course and
retail outlets and . . .'

Cal sank into a chair. 'Surely the Laird would never sell?
Especially not to someone like Zed.'

'We can both guess how broke Charlie and the estate are.
Even if we get the maximum amount of grant money, it's still
going to be touch and go.'

'Jesus,' he breathed, 'that would be the end of an era for
sure. Never mind my dreams of marrying Caitlin and buying
a cottage of our own.'

'The worst thing is, Zed would just be buying the estate as
a plaything – maybe just to spite me.'

'You think you're worth a few million, do yae, Tig?' he teased
me, and I blushed, which lightened the atmosphere a little.

'I didn't mean it like that, but I just feel like he's out to get
me whatever I do.'

'Aye, he does seem tae have a strange fixation on you. And
you say he's been out with two o' your sisters as well?'

'Yes, and Maia didn't have a good word to say about him.
God, Cal, I've just turned down a twenty-five-million-dollar
budget to spend as I wished,' I groaned. 'And – if he buys
Kinnaird I'd have to leave, I really would.'

'I really don't think it'll happen, Tig.' Cal shook his head.
'Mebbe you should speak tae Charlie about it.'

'Maybe,' I shrugged. 'Anyway, I'm going to take myself off to Tain for the afternoon and see Margaret. Then I'm going out to watch over Pegasus tonight. Zed knows where he is. You don't think . . . ?'

'Jesus! An' there's me arranging target practice for him. You sure about going out again later, Tig? There's a blizzard comin' in,' Cal said to me as he studied the benign blue sky through our cottage window, the midday sun sprinkling a glitter topping on the layer of snow that covered the ground all winter. The view was Christmas-card perfect.

'Yes! We just can't take the chance, Cal, you know we can't.'

'I doubt even the Abominable Snowman'll be out tanite,' Cal muttered.

'You promised we'd keep watch,' I entreated him. 'Look, I'll take the radio with me and contact you if there's any trouble.'

'Tig, d'you really think I'm going tae let a wee lassie like you sit alone in a snowstorm while there's a possible poacher with a rifle prowling the estate? Don't be a dafty,' Cal growled at me, his ruddy features showing irritation, then finally compliance. 'No longer than a couple o' hours, mind. After that, I'm dragging you home by the hair. I'll not be responsible for you ending up with hypothermia again. Understand?'

'Thanks, Cal,' I replied with relief. 'I know Pegasus is in danger. I just . . . know it.'

The snow had fallen thickly around us in the dugout and the tarpaulin roof had buckled under its weight. I wondered if it would collapse altogether and we would be buried alive under the sheer weight of snow above us.

'We're leavin' now, Tig,' said Cal. 'I'm numb to my innards an' we'll be struggling tae drive back. The blizzard's eased for a while and we need tae get home while we can.' Cal took a last slurp of lukewarm coffee from the flask then offered it to me. 'Finish that. I'll go an' clear the snow off the windscreen and get the heat going.'

'Okay,' I sighed, knowing there was no point in arguing.

We'd sat in the dugout for over two hours, watching nothing but the snow hurl itself to the ground. Cal left and headed towards Beryl, parked beyond a stone outcrop in the valley behind us. I peered out through the tiny window of the dugout as I sipped the coffee, then turned off the hurricane lamp and crawled outside. I didn't need my torch as the sky had cleared and now twinkled with thousands of stars, the Milky Way clearly visible above me. The moon, which was waxing and within two days of being full, shone down, illuminating the pristine white blanket that covered the ground.

The utter silence that came just after fresh snowfall was as deep as the sparkling carpet that claimed my feet and most of my calves.

*Pegasus.*

I called him silently, then walked slowly towards the trees, begging him to make an appearance so I'd be able to go home and sleep, knowing he was safe for one more night.

He appeared as if from nowhere, a mystical sight as he raised his head to the moon, then turned, his deep brown eyes fixed upon me. He began to walk hesitantly towards me, and I to him.

'Darling, Pegasus,' I whispered, then saw a shadow appear

on the snow from the cluster of trees. The shadow raised a rifle.

'No!' I screamed into the silence. The figure was behind the stag, his gun aimed and ready to fire. 'Stop! Run, Pegasus!'

The stag turned round and saw the danger, but then, rather than bolting away to safety, he began to run towards me. A shot rang out, then two more, and I felt a sudden sharp pain in my side. My heart gave a strange jolt and began to pound so fast that dizziness engulfed me. My knees turned to jelly and I sank onto the snowy blanket beneath me.

There was silence again. I tried to hold on to consciousness, but I couldn't fight the dark any longer, not even for him.

Some time later, I opened my eyes and saw a beloved, familiar face above me.

'Tiggy, sweetheart, you're going to be all right. Stay with me now, won't you?'

'Yes, Pa, of course I will,' I whispered, as he stroked my hair just as he used to when I was sick as a little girl. I closed my eyes once more, knowing that I was safe in his arms.

When I woke up again, I felt someone lifting me from the ground. I searched around for Pa, but all I saw above me were Cal's panicked features as he struggled to carry me to safety. As I turned my head back towards the cluster of trees, I saw the prone body of a white stag, blood-red drops spattering the snow around him.

And I knew he had gone.

# 20

'Morning, Tiggy, how are you feeling?'

I forced my eyes open to see who was speaking to me, because the voice wasn't one I recognised.

'Hello.' A nurse smiled down at me. With huge effort, I dredged up fleeting memories of . . .

'Pegasus,' I whispered, my bottom lip quivering as tears appeared in my eyes.

'Try not tae upset yourself, dear.' The nurse, who had bright red hair and a kind face covered in freckles, put her plump hand on mine. 'You've had a shock and that's for sure, but at least you came out of it in one piece. Now, the registrar will be here to see you shortly. I'll just take your temperature and blood pressure, but I'm afraid I can't offer you any solid food until the registrar says it's allowed.'

'That's fine, I'm not hungry anyway,' I replied as more memories of last night began to download in my brain.

'Then how about a nice cup of tea?'

'Thank you.'

'I'll get one of the health assistants to bring it to you. Open, please,' she added before placing the thermometer under my tongue, then tightening the armband around my upper arm. 'Your temperature's fine, but your blood pressure's still a wee bit high, though it's down from last night. Sure tae be all the drama.' She comforted me with a smile. 'Now then, your friend Cal is waiting outside. Can I send him in?'

'Yes.' The thought of Cal and the way he'd cared for me yet again last night brought further tears to my eyes.

'Morning, Tig,' he said as he strode in a few minutes later. 'It's good tae see you awake. How are yae feelin'?'

'Distraught. Is Pegasus . . .' I bit my lip. 'Gone?'

'He is, Tig, he is. I'm so sorry, I know what he meant tae you. Maybe you've just got tae imagine him like the mythical Pegasus; growin' wings and flyin' up tae the heavens.'

'I'll try,' I said, giving him a weak smile. It wasn't Cal's way to indulge in flights of fancy, so I was grateful for the effort he was making. 'I like that thought, but I just feel responsible. He trusted me, Cal, came out to see me like he normally does and got shot because of it.'

'Tig, you couldnae have done more – none o' us could.'

'You don't understand! I shouted at him to run away, but instead he ran *towards* me. If he hadn't been between me and the poacher, it really *would* be me who's dead now. He saved my life, Cal. Really, he did.'

'Then I for one am grateful tae him. Even though it's a terrible loss for us, as well as the natural world, I'd rather him than you. Has the doc been in tae see you yet?'

'No. But the nurse says he's on his way. I hope he'll remove all these' – I indicated the tubes and the beeping machine I was wired up to – 'so I can come home.'

'There are some who say our health service isn't up tae much, but that helicopter was there in the glen with the paramedics within half an hour of me making the call.'

'That explains all the whirring and clanking,' I said. 'I thought I'd dreamt it.'

'You didn't. I followed by road and I'd doubt there was a bit o' yae that wasn't scanned, X-rayed, or tested last night. The doc said he'd have the results this morning.'

'I honestly can't remember much – just a lot of noises and bright lights. At least I'm not in any pain anywhere.'

'I'm not surprised, with the amount of drugs they pumped intae yae. Now then, I have tae tell you there's a detective waiting to interview you when you're feeling stronger. I've told him everything I know, but, if you remember, I wasn't there tae see the shooting itself.'

'A detective? Why on earth would they want to speak to me?'

'Someone took a potshot at you last night, Tig. As yae just said, they could have killed you.'

'But only by mistake, Cal. We both know he was after Pegasus.'

'Well, for now, they're treating it as suspicious.'

'That's ridiculous, although I do want them to find out who it was who killed him. Poaching's an offence too, and especially such a rare animal.'

'Did you see who it was, Tig?'

'No, did you?'

'I didn't. By the time I arrived, the bastard had vanished.'

We were both silent for a while, thinking about the conversation we'd had yesterday about Zed, but neither of us mustering the courage to voice our thoughts.

'Now, do you want me tae call anyone for you? One of your sisters? Or that lady you call Ma?' Cal asked me.

'God, no, unless the doctor has told you I'm dying.'

'He certainly hasn't done that. He said you were a very lucky lass. Talk o' the devil.'

A man who looked barely older than me had entered through the curtain.

'Hello, Tiggy, I'm Dr Kemp. How are you feeling this morning?'

'Fine, good,' I nodded, my heart immediately giving a bounce as it prepared itself for my health status report. I saw the doctor glance at the monitor, then turn his attention back to me.

'The good news is that the X-rays we did last night both came back clear and confirmed what we thought. The bullet went straight through the side of your ski jacket and put a hole through the three jumpers you were wearing, but only gave you a flesh wound. We didn't even have to stitch you up. You've just got a nice big plaster to cover it.'

'Am I free to go home then?'

'Not quite yet, I'm afraid. When the paramedics helicoptered you in, they reported that your heartbeat was all over the place, and your blood pressure was very high – we initially thought you were having a heart attack. That's why we've got you wired up to a monitor. The ECG we took showed you're experiencing something called arrhythmia – that's when the heart can't manage to keep a steady beat. You are also having bouts of tachycardia, where the heart beats faster than normal. Have you noticed if you've been getting any palpitations or a racing heart recently?'

'I . . . yes, a bit,' I said, knowing I needed to be honest.

'For how long?'

'I can't remember, but I feel perfectly okay, really.'

'It's always a good idea to get things checked out for any underlying condition, Tiggy. And that's what we want to do.'

'I'm sure my heart is absolutely fine, doctor,' I said firmly. 'I had very bad asthma as a child and constantly got bronchitis. I had lots of tests in the hospital and my heart was checked every time.'

'That's reassuring, but the cardiology team want you to have an angiogram just to be on the safe side. A porter will be along shortly to take you. Are you up to sitting in a wheelchair?'

'Yes,' I replied miserably. I hated hospitals, and as the porter pushed me along the corridor ten minutes later, I decided I agreed with Chilly and would definitely opt to fade away in my own habitat.

The angiogram was painless, if unpleasant, and within half an hour I was back in bed with a watery bowl of soup that was the only vaguely vegan thing on the lunch menu.

'What do you think about seeing that detective now, Tig?' encouraged Cal. 'The poor bloke's been hangin' around since the wee hours.'

I agreed and the man was ushered in. He introduced himself as Detective Sergeant McClain, was dressed in plain clothes and had a practical, kindly air about him. He sat down by my bed and took out a notebook.

'Hello, Miss D'Aplièse. Mr MacKenzie has already made a statement and filled me in on what he thinks happened last night. We've taken your jacket and jumpers for forensics. Talk about a near miss. They have the bullet from the stag, but they're searching for the casing at the crime scene. We should be able to identify the exact type of rifle from both of them and that. Now, I'm afraid I need to take a statement from you too as the sole witness of the shooting itself. If at any time you want to stop, please say so. I understand it may well be upsetting for you.'

I took a deep breath, focusing on getting this over with so I could be released and be back in my own bed at Kinnaird by tonight. I took the detective through everything that had happened, with him prompting me for further detail as I went.

'So, you didn't get a look at the shooter?' he clarified.

'Not really. All I saw was his shadow on the snow.'

'You think it was a man?'

'Yes,' I said. 'The shadow was really tall anyway, although I suppose shadows aren't anything to do with the height of a person, are they? It sounds strange, but I think he was wearing an old-fashioned trilby hat. At least that's what it looked like in the shadow. But then I saw Pegasus running towards me . . .'

'Pegasus?'

'The white stag. I called him Pegasus—'

'Tig and the stag had a bond, detective,' Cal put in by way of explanation as tears bubbled in my eyes.

'And now I really wish we hadn't, because Pegasus would still be alive now . . .'

'All right, we can stop here, Miss D'Aplièse, you've been very helpful.'

'Will you be able to charge this man for poaching?' I asked.

'Oh yes, don't you worry. If we catch the barmpot who did this to you and the stag, I'll make sure the CPS have him up on every count we can manage. Sounds to me like that stag took a bullet for you, so we might even get him on attempted murder. I'm warning you, though, the press is on to the story,'

Sergeant McClain sighed. 'Bad news travels fast, especially given the fact that the stag was already on the media radar. There's a couple of reporters hanging about at the hospital entrance. When you're discharged, I suggest you look for a side door. My advice is to say "No comment" in answer to every question, okay?'

'Okay, thanks.'

'Now, I'll just ask you to read through your statement, and if everything is correct, just initial each page and sign at the bottom for me.'

I did so, then handed the pages back to him, trying to stop my hands from trembling. Recounting the story had drained every last ounce of my strength.

'Here's my card if you remember anything else in the next few days. I have your contact details, so now I can leave you in peace to recover. We'll let you know if we find the casing, and our victim support service will be in touch shortly. And please think, Miss D'Aplièse – anything else you remember might mean we can get the idiot charged. In the meantime I hope you recover swiftly, and thanks for your help.'

Once he'd left, I felt my eyelids become heavy. I was just closing them when I heard the curtain being opened again.

'How are you feeling?'

I opened my eyes and saw Dr Kemp, the young registrar, looking down at me.

'Fine.' I did my best to look convincingly alert. 'Can I go home now?'

'Not quite yet, I'm afraid. Mr Kinnaird, the senior consultant in the cardiac department here, is coming down to visit you. The results of the angiogram should be back tomorrow morning. I'm afraid he's going to be some time, as he's in theatre at the moment. He sends his best wishes, by the way,' he added. 'Apparently you know each other.'

'Yes,' I gulped as my heart did another bounce. 'I work for him. I mean, in his other life up on the estate.'

'Right.' The registrar looked confused and I realised he probably knew nothing about Charlie's personal life.

I glanced out of the window and saw the sky was already darkening. 'Will I be able to go home tonight?'

'No, because he'll want the results of the angiogram back and he may want to run some more tests. Just one last thing, Tiggy. Cal here told me that you're not a British citizen, but Swiss.'

'Yes, I am.'

'That's fine, Swiss citizens can be treated on the National Health Service, but I'm afraid you don't seem to be on our system. Have you ever registered with an NHS doctor's practice in the UK?'

'No.'

'Well then, we need your passport, National Insurance number and a couple of forms filled in to sort out your future care. If you don't have it to hand, your National Insurance number will be on your payslips.'

'Right.' I looked at Cal. 'I'm so sorry, but my passport's in my bedside drawer, along with my payslips.'

'Is this urgent, doctor?' Cal asked. 'It's a good three hours' round trip.'

'Reasonably,' said the registrar. 'I'm sure you know what NHS bureaucracy is like. Is there anyone who could bring them here for you?'

'No, I'll have tae go myself. Unless you want Zed as a visitor, Tig,' Cal grimaced at me.

I looked at his weary features, then the clock, that showed me it was already past four in the afternoon. The detective had been with me for over two hours. I made a decision. 'Cal, why don't you go home now and get some sleep? If I'm not going to be out of here until tomorrow, maybe you could come back with the passport and payslips then and hopefully collect me at the same time?'

'Are you sure you're goin' tae be okay alone here for the night?'

'I'll be fine, really. You look worse than I do.'

'Thanks, Tig, and you're right. I need a decent scrub in the tub.'

'I'll be off then,' said the registrar. 'See you tomorrow, Tiggy. Sleep well.'

'I'm so sorry about all this, Cal. It's the last thing you need with so much going on at Kinnaird.'

'The last thing *you* needed was a graze from a bullet. Okay, Tig, I'll get goin'. At least I'll have the pleasure of driving a spanking new Range Rover back. Zed lent me his when he heard you'd been helicoptered off to hospital.'

'That was kind,' I said begrudgingly, remembering what had passed between us yesterday.

'Aye.' Cal frowned, 'Or it could've been guilt. We all know there's a thin line between love and hate and you'd turned him down yesterday. Besides all that, a white stag's head is a helluva trophy to hang on a wall. The ultimate I'd say, especially for a man like Zed. You don't think it was him who shot at you, do yae?'

'Christ, Cal,' I said as my heart bumped again. 'I really don't know.'

'Sorry tae spook you, but from what you've said and I've

seen, he's used to gettin' what he wants. At least I know you're safe in here.'

'I hope so,' I breathed. 'Cal, could you possibly bring back some other stuff for me? My rucksack and bag, which I think I left on my bed, some jeans, a shirt, a jumper . . . and um . . . some clean undies. My clothes are with forensics and I don't fancy leaving here in my hospital gown.'

'Course I will. Now, don't you be gettin' yourself intae any more trouble whilst I'm away, will yae?'

'Look where I am. That's impossible, even for me.'

'Nothing's impossible for you, Tig,' he said and kissed me on the forehead. 'I'll be back in the morning. If you remember anything else yae need, just call Beryl at the Lodge and she'll pass on the message.'

'Thanks, Cal. Just one more question . . .' I steeled myself for the answer. 'Where have they taken Pegasus?'

'As far as I know he was left where he was, because he was part of the crime scene.'

'I'd just . . . really love to say goodbye.'

'I'll find out and let yae know. Bye, Tig.' He waved as he left and I suddenly felt very alone. There was definitely something about Cal that made me feel safe and secure. Not only that, but he made me laugh. The bond we had forged was really something special and I wondered if we'd been related in a previous life . . .

'Hello, Tiggy,' said a different nurse as she walked towards the bed. 'My name's Jane and I need to bother you for your temperature again.' The thermometer was popped into my mouth. 'Aye, that's fine. Not in any pain, are you?' she asked, picking up a red plastic file from the end of the bed.

'No.'

'Good, then hopefully we can take out your intravenous line later on. Now, you have another visitor to see you. Are you up tae it?'

'It depends who it is,' I said, my heart giving another one of its jumps as my imagination conjured up Zed lurking beyond the curtain.

'Her name is Zara and she says she's a close friend o' yours.'

'I'd love to see her, yes.'

Zara's bright face appeared around the curtain a few seconds later.

'Tiggy, you poor, poor thing. And Pegasus . . . oh my God! Why didn't you tell me about him?'

'Sorry, Zara, but he was meant to be a secret.'

'Well, he isn't now. The shooting was on the local radio station in the car. How are you feeling?'

'I'm okay, I just can't wait to get home.'

'Who do you think did it?'

'I honestly don't know, Zara. I just saw a shadow,' I said, reluctant to go over the whole episode again. 'And how are you? Your dad said you were back at school.'

'I am, but we have a weekend exeat. Mum came to collect me – and I asked to come straight here to see you.'

'Is everything okay at school?'

'Yeah, it's okay . . . Johnnie texted me asking if we could meet up – that he was really sorry and stuff. I told him where to stick it,' she giggled.

'Good girl.' I put my palm out and gave her a weak high five.

'So are you really going to get better, Tiggy?'

'Oh, I'll be fine. I should be out tomorrow,' I reassured her, failing to add that her dad was the one keeping me in here. 'How are things at home?'

'Pretty awful. I prefer school to being at home with Mum. Dad's either at the hospital, or shut in his study talking to his lawyer.'

'His lawyer?'

'Something to do with the estate. I dunno.' Zara scratched her nose. 'Whatever, he looks like he's got the weight of the world on his shoulders. Anyway, I'd better go. Mum's waiting for me. We're going up to Kinnaird for the weekend, which will be nice. Mind you, Zed Eszu's really weird – I hope he leaves soon. Bye Tiggy.' She reached towards me and gave me a big hug. 'Thanks for everything, you've been amazing.' She stood up and breezed out.

I lay back and felt the soreness of my side now that the painkillers had worn off. I closed my eyes again as the events of the past two days began to take their toll.

'Hello, Tiggy, how are you feeling?'

I opened my eyes a few minutes later and looked up to see Ulrika drawing up a chair towards the bed.

'I'm okay, thanks for asking.'

I watched as she sat down and leant towards me.

'Good. I'm sorry about the gunman. I hope he's caught soon.'

'So do I.'

'Now, forgive my bad timing, but I wanted a word with you.'

My heart did another trapeze act as I sensed the anger pulsing beneath Ulrika's calm exterior.

'What about?'

'Your influence over my daughter, for one thing. She hangs on every word you say. Please remember I am her mother.'

'Yes, of course. I'm sorry, I—'

'Then there's my husband. It's been obvious from the start that you're out to get your claws into him. Like many others before you . . .'

'That's just not true!' I said, horrified. 'Charlie and I are work colleagues – he's my boss!'

'Don't think I don't know about those early morning walks the two of you took together, your little tête-à-têtes outside over Christmas. Let me tell you now, you're on a road to nowhere. Charlie will never leave me, never.'

'No, Ulrika.' I shook my head, distraught. 'You've got it all wrong.'

'I don't think so. It's obvious to everyone that you're smitten.'

'I'm really not—'

'What I'm asking, Tiggy, is that you leave my family alone. You can think what you like about my marriage and my relationship with my daughter, but you can do it well away from all of us.'

It took a few seconds to grasp what she was suggesting. 'You want me to leave my job? And Kinnaird?'

'Yes. I think it's best all round, don't you?'

Her steely blue eyes bored into me and I lowered my own.

'I'll leave you to think about it. I'm sure you'll see it's the best thing for everyone. Get better soon,' she added tersely, before she stood up and disappeared behind the curtain.

I slumped back on my pillow, feeling another shock ricochet through me. No wonder I had palpitations at the moment, I thought miserably. Too exhausted to even begin to think what

I should do, I closed my eyes, willing myself to go back to sleep, because my heart really *was* racing now. I dozed fitfully, woken periodically by nurses coming to check on me. I was just nodding off for the umpteenth time when I heard a familiar male voice.

'Tiggy? It's Charlie.'

There was just no *way* I could face him now, so I feigned sleep.

'She's obviously out cold and sleep's the best thing for her,' I heard Charlie whispering to the nurse. 'Tell her I came to see her and that I'll visit her as soon as I can tomorrow morning. Her numbers are okay at the moment but any problems overnight, bleep me. The Adenosine I've prescribed should keep things calm. Give it to her when you do the next set of obs.'

'Yes, Dr Kinnaird. Don't worry, I'll take good care of her,' the nurse replied as the curtain closed behind them before their footsteps faded away.

*Why has he prescribed more medication?* I thought. Perhaps it was for the muscle that had taken the brunt of the bullet as it had passed through my jacket. It hurt a little to breathe, but that was probably just the bruising . . .

I dozed off, woken later by the nurse appearing to do my last obs.

'Good job we didn't remove your cannula, because the consultant's prescribed something for you,' she said as she squirted liquid through a syringe she'd attached to it. 'Now, I'll leave yae to rest. Press the call bell if you need anything.'

'I will. Thank you.'

I was woken from a broken sleep by the morning nurse, who wanted to do yet another round of obs.

'You'll be pleased to know everythin's looking much more like it this morning,' she said as she recorded the details. 'A tea trolley will be round shortly,' she added as she left.

I sat up, thinking that I *did* feel better this morning. My heart had stopped jumping around and I felt clear-headed enough to process the conversation with Ulrika last night.

*How could she claim that I was after her husband? How dare she say that I'd tried to influence Zara! I tried to help her! What right has she got to fire me . . . !*

Then I contemplated my options: the first was to tell Charlie what had happened, but I knew I'd be far too embarrassed to recount Ulrika's accusations that I was 'smitten' with him.

*Is this because she might be right . . . ?* my inner voice asked me.

It was no secret to my soul that I had been drawn to Charlie from the first moment I'd met him. I'd loved spending time with him, and yes, I was definitely attracted to him . . .

The simple truth was that Ulrika's radar had spotted it.

'She's right,' I groaned. The tea trolley arrived and as I sipped the tepid, watery substance I was given, I wondered what to do.

I thought about Zed, still up at Kinnaird, and the fact that someone had taken a potshot at me. On top of which, from what both Zed and Zara had told me, the future of the Kinnaird estate was just about as unsteady as my heartbeat . . .

'There may be no job in a week's time anyway,' I muttered to myself. 'Best to get out whilst the going's good.'

'*You is goin*' . . .' Chilly had said . . .

That capped it.

By the time I had drained the cup, I knew I only had one option available. And that was to do as Ulrika had asked and remove myself from Kinnaird. Whilst I waited for Cal to arrive, I laid my plans. When the nurse returned, to unhook the intravenous drips and remove my cannula, I asked her for some paper. I wrote a note to Cal, and penned my official resignation for Charlie. Without an envelope, I folded both notes together and wrote Cal's name on the front in capitals. For now, I hid it under my pillow.

Cal arrived at nine o'clock, looking far fresher. He dumped my rucksack in a corner.

'Morning, Tig. Hope I got everythin' yae asked for. You'll understand I felt a bit funny going through your drawers, tae find your . . . drawers!' he cackled. 'Anyway, how are yae feeling?'

'Heaps better, thanks,' I said brightly. 'I'm sure they'll let me out today. The nurse said my obs were looking good.'

'That's the best news o' all, and, boy, do I need it. Kinnaird's swarming with journalists desperate to get a photo o' our precious Pegasus.'

'Oh God, is he still lying where he . . . fell?'

'No – and here's the odd thing; after the police had removed the bullet from his side, Lochie an' Ben helped the forensics erect a tent over him tae protect the evidence. The lads kept watch all night, but what do yae know? When they went into the tent this morning, the body had disappeared. Gone.' Cal clicked his fingers. 'Like that.'

'Please don't tell me someone has stolen him to make a trophy out of him!' I moaned.

'Unless both the laddies were slipped somethin' in their flask o' coffee and fell asleep so deeply that they didn't hear a large vehicle turning up and a massive stag being dragged out o' the tent, I'd doubt it. And –' Cal waggled a finger at me – 'another strange thing that you'd appreciate: where he'd lain, there'd been blood around him. As the police said this mornin' when they looked inside the tent, not only had the stag disappeared, but the snow where he'd been was pure white.'

'As if he'd never existed . . .' I whispered.

'That's what I thought too. Weird, eh?'

'Everything is weird at the moment,' I said. 'You absolutely swear that you're not just telling me a story to make me feel better, are you?'

'As if I'd do that, Tig. You can ask them when you get back to Kinnaird if yae don't believe me. Beryl sent these by the way.' Cal handed me a Tupperware box full of Millionaire's Shortbread. 'She says you have a likin' for them. She sends her love o' course, as does everyone.'

'Including Zed?'

'I haven't seen him so I cannae say.' Cal shrugged. 'I dropped the keys tae his Range Rover in with Beryl an' made a hasty exit.'

'Everything's gone wrong at Kinnaird since he arrived,' I sighed. 'I just hope he takes the hint and leaves. Cal, would you mind awfully if I sent you off for half an hour to get a cuppa whilst I have a wash and get changed into my clothes? It might make me feel more human.'

'O' course, an' I'll help myself tae a bit o' breakfast at the café too. One way an' another, I didn't get time tae eat before I left.'

'Take your time,' I said as I climbed out of bed. 'Cal?'

'Yes, Tig?'

'Thank you for everything. And . . . I'm really sorry.'

'Don't be a dafty,' he smiled back at me. 'I'll see you in a bit.'

Feeling horribly guilty that I was about to give Cal another shock, but knowing it couldn't be helped, swiftly, I went into action. I pulled the sticky pads attaching me to the ECG machine from my front torso, then I picked up my rucksack and dumped it on the bed to check the contents. Happily, I saw my passport and wallet were present, but my mobile phone was missing. *Never mind*, I thought, *I'll just have to buy a new one when I arrive . . .*

Leaving the note for Cal on the pillow, I carried my rucksack to the nearest loo and shut the door. I dressed hastily in the jeans and hoodie Cal had brought me, swept my hair up and twirled it into a topknot.

Peering round the loo door, I knew I still had to run the gauntlet of the nurses' station a few metres along the corridor. I was relieved to see that at present it was unoccupied. Opening the door wide, I strode out blatantly and exited the ward. I then remembered what the detective had said about the media hanging around and hunted for a side exit from the hospital, which I eventually found.

Once outside, I got into one of the waiting taxis.

'Inverness airport, please,' I told the driver.

'No problem, miss.' He started the engine and we drove off.

At the tiny airport's ticket desk, the attendant asked me where I wanted to go.

'Geneva,' I said, deciding there was nothing I needed more than Ma taking care of me and Claudia cooking my favourite bean stew. Yet, as the woman tapped away on her computer, in my mind's eye I saw the white ceiling of a cave . . .

*Tell Angelina it was me who guided you home . . .*

'Wait a minute,' I said. 'Forgive me for my bad English,' I lied to cover up the fact I was about to look like a complete idiot. 'It's not Geneva I want, I meant Granada . . . in Spain!'

'Right,' sighed the woman. 'Now that's a bit more complicated . . .'

An hour and three-quarters later, the plane bound for London Gatwick accelerated down the runway and I felt a huge pressure release from my chest. As we were about to disappear into the clouds, I looked down below me at the grey city and the snowy landscape beyond it, and blew a small kiss.

'You were right, darling Chilly. And I promise I'll tell them it was you who sent me home.'

# 21

Many hours later, my plane touched down on the runway at Granada airport. Thankfully, I'd slept the whole leg from Gatwick, so I'd had a good three-hour snooze. As I took the steps to the tarmac, the sweetest scent of warmth, citrus, and fertile land assailed my nostrils. Although it was only the beginning of February, I saw the temperature was ten degrees even this late at night, which, after my winter in sub-zero temperatures, felt positively tropical. Once through passport control and baggage, I enquired about a hotel in Sacromonte at the tourist information desk. The woman handed me a card.

'*Gracias*. Er, could you give them a call to see if they have a room?'

'No telephone at hotel, señorita. They will have room. You not worry.'

'Right, thanks.'

I walked to the airport forecourt and headed for a cash machine to extract some euros. That done, I went outside to find a taxi rank.

'Where going, señorita?' the driver asked me.

'Sacromonte, *por favor*, señor,' I said, dredging up the remnants of my schoolgirl Spanish.

'You go to flamenco show?'

'No, to a hotel – Cuevas el Abanico.' I handed him the card the woman at the information desk had given me.

'*Ah, sí, comprendo!*'

We raced off at breakneck speed and I was sad that it was dark and I couldn't see where I was. There was no snow on the ground, that was for sure, I thought as I removed my hoodie in the humid air. It took twenty minutes to get into the city, which seemed to have a thriving centre, judging by the number of people out on the streets, even though it was eleven o'clock at night. Then the taxi took a left along what resembled a narrow alleyway rather than a road, and we began to drive upwards.

'We stop here, you walk, señorita. Go straight.' My driver pointed towards an open gate set into a thick wall. 'Five minutes to hotel.'

'*Muchas gracias*, señor.' I paid him, hoisted my rucksack on my back, and looked at the twisting path ahead of me, lit only by occasional old-fashioned lamps, with a low stone wall hugging one side of it. I listened to the taxi reversing, then disappearing down the hill. With the wound on my side throbbing, I began to walk.

I rounded a corner and there, up above me, on the other side of the valley, soft lighting illuminating its ancient beauty, was the Alhambra.

The sight brought tears to my eyes and I knew, just *knew* that I'd been here before. I stood mesmerised by the ethereal vision – everything else around it was so dark that the palace looked almost as though it was suspended in mid-air.

'Lucía danced there . . .' I muttered, astounded that I was

349

actually seeing what up to now, had only existed in my imagination.

I carried on along the narrow path, which curved around the mountain. Whitewashed stone dwellings fashioned out of the rock behind them lined one side of it, their colourful shutters closed to the night. Very few lights were on in any of them and I only prayed that the lady at the tourist office hadn't made a mistake and that the hotel wasn't closed for the winter.

'If that's the case, I just have to sleep where I fall,' I panted, feeling my heart begin to protest.

Thankfully, just around the next corner, I saw some lights and a small sign proclaiming that it was the hotel I was looking for. I opened the wrought-iron gates and walked through them.

'*Le puedo ayudar?*'

I turned to my left to see a woman sitting at one of the tables on the small terrace, smoking a cigarette and looking at me askance.

'Er, do you have a room?'

'*Sí*, señorita.' She stood up and beckoned me towards the door. 'You are British?' she asked me in English.

'I'm actually Swiss, so I speak French as well.'

'We stick to English, yes? I am Marcella, owner of this hotel.' She smiled at me, the wrinkles on her face deepening further. As she led me into the reception I realised the hotel was built out of a series of whitewashed caves. She drew out a set of keys, and led me through to a room with a number of sofas covered in colourful patterned throws. At the back, Marcella opened the door to another cave, with a sweet little wooden bed set in the centre of it.

'The bathroom.' My hostess pointed to a narrow doorway, protected by a curtain that led to a toilet and a tiny shower.

'This is perfect,' I smiled at her. '*Gracias*.'

I followed her back to the small reception and gave her my passport details in return for the key.

'You are hungry?' she asked me.

'No, thank you. I ate on the plane. If you have a glass of water, that would be wonderful.'

She disappeared off to a small kitchen area and brought me back a glass and a plastic bottle. 'Sleep well,' she said as I walked towards my room.

'*Gracias*.'

Having taken what Ma used to call a 'cat-lick' instead of actually washing, as I didn't want to chance a shower with my wound, I climbed into what proved to be a very comfortable bed. Lying down, I looked up at the ceiling. It was identical to the one I'd seen so often in my mind's eye.

'I'm actually here,' I whispered in awe, before sleep over-took me.

I was amazed to see that it was past ten o'clock in the morn-ing when I checked the time on the fluorescent hands of the alarm clock, which sat on a chest by my bed. Not a wink of daylight penetrated the cave.

I coughed, my throat catching some dust, and the sound echoed around the room. I could only imagine the terrible sound Felipe must have made when he was dying in a cave just like this . . .

Before I did anything else, I took the first aid kit I'd bought at the airport out of my bag. Wincing, I pulled off the plaster covering my wound. It was weeping a little, but not too badly, considering what I'd put it through yesterday. Using some sterile wipes, I cleaned it, patted on antiseptic gel, then covered it in a new plaster. Comforted that it was on its way to healing and I wasn't about to die of septicaemia where I'd been born, I washed the rest of me, then put on the cotton dress I'd bought at duty-free. I threw my hoodie over it and added the pair of pumps I'd also bought on my shopping spree to replace the heavy ski boots I'd been wearing the night that Pegasus died.

'Well, Tiggy,' I chuckled as I looked down at the flowery shift, 'you certainly blend in with your surroundings in this.'

I left my room and walked through to the reception area. The smell of strong, freshly ground coffee was emanating from the little kitchen to the side of reception.

'*Buenos días*, señorita. Did you sleep well?'

'Yes, thank you,' I said, wondering if Marcella – with her long mane of jet-black hair and olive skin – was a gypsy herself.

'I think it is warm enough to take breakfast outside,' she said.

'*Sí.*' I followed her out into bright sunshine and blinked like a mole whilst my eyes adjusted.

'Sit there,' Marcella said. 'I will bring your breakfast out.'

I hardly heard her, because my attention had been caught by what lay beyond the wrought-iron gates that enclosed the front terrace. Walking to them and pushing them open, I crossed the narrow path in front of the hotel and leant over the wall to take in the splendour of both the verdant valley beneath me and the majestic Alhambra above me. In the light of day, I saw how the dusky orange walls rose out of the dark green foliage surrounding it.

'Now I understand what María meant about having the best view in the world,' I breathed. 'I really think it is.'

Over a breakfast of bread and delicious jams, plus a glass of fresh orange juice, I reread the letter Pa Salt had written me.

'You're looking for a blue door,' I murmured to remind myself.

'You tourist? Going to the Alhambra?' Marcella said, topping up my coffee.

'Actually, I've come here to find my family.'

'Here to Sacromonte? Or Granada?'

'Sacromonte. I even know the exact door I must knock on.'

'You're a *gitana*?'

'I think I might be, yes.'

She narrowed her eyes as she looked at me. 'You have some *payo* for sure, but maybe there is some *gitano* blood in you.'

'Do you know of a family called Albaycín?'

'Of course! The Albaycín family were one of the biggest in Sacromonte, in the days when we all lived here.'

'The gyp—*gitanos* don't live here any longer?'

'Some, but most of the caves here are now empty. Many of us moved into modern apartments in the city. They don't live in the old way any more. It is sad but true. Sacromonte is like a ghost town these days.'

'Are you a *gitano*?'

'*Sí*, our family has been here for three hundred years,' she answered proudly.

'How come you've opened this hotel?'

'Because the only visitors we have here now are tourists who come for the flamenco show in Los Tarantos, or to see the museum of how we used to live in the caves up above us. I think to myself that this street has one of the best views in the world. It was too good to waste it.' She smiled. 'Besides, I belong here.'

'Your English is very good. Where did you learn?'

'At school and then university. When my mother and father die, I sell their apartment and use money to buy back my old family home to convert this into what they call boutique hotel.'

'You've done a beautiful job. And you're right about the view – it's incredible. How long have you been open?'

'Only a year. Trade has been slow, but everything takes time and I have many good bookings for summer.'

'Well, I love it here already,' I smiled.

'So where is your family?'

'I was told to look for a blue door on the Cortijo del Aire and ask for someone called Angelina. Have you heard of her?'

'Have I heard of her?' Marcella blinked in disbelief. 'Of course! She is the last *bruja* of Sacromonte. Are you related to her?'

'I think I might be, yes.'

'She is old woman now, but when I was a child, I remember the queues outside her door for herbal remedies and fortune telling. It wasn't just *gitanos* who came, but many *payos* too. Now not so many people come, but if you want to know your future, Angelina can tell you.'

'Does she live close to here?'

'Señorita, she lives next door!'

A shiver ran through me at Marcella's words as her hand indicated the hill to her left.

'Does it have a blue door?'

'*Sí*, it does. Many of my guests go to see Angelina when I tell them of her skills. She help our business and we help hers.'

'I never expected finding her to be this easy.'

'When something is destined, life *can* be easy.' Marcella's brown eyes appraised me. 'Maybe most difficult part of journey was decision to make it in the first place.'

'Yes,' I said, surprised at her intuition. 'It was.' Something ticked in my brain as I looked at her. 'I heard that my ancestor's neighbour was a man named Ramón. Is this his cave?'

'It is!' Marcella clapped her hands together in delight. 'I am the great-great niece of Ramón. My great-great grandmother was his sister! I never meet him of course, but I hear stories of Lucía Albaycín practising her flamenco right here.' Marcella pointed to the path in front of the gates. 'My grandmother remembers it too. Lucía once the most famous flamenco dancer in the world! Have you heard of her?'

'Yes, and if the person I spoke to was right, she was my grandmother.'

'*¡Dios mío!*' Marcella breathed in awe. 'Do you dance? You have same figure as her.'

'I did ballet as a child, but not as a career. I . . . I think I should go and see Angelina, don't you?'

'Wait an hour or so – like most *gitanos*, she is a night person, and does not get up before lunchtime.' Marcella patted my hand. 'I think it very brave of you to come here, señorita. Many *gitanos* of your age want to forget where they come from, because they are ashamed.'

With a raise of her eyebrow, Marcella disappeared inside. I sat where I was in the sunshine, thinking about what Marcella had just told me. It was almost too much to take in. I'd expected to have to hunt Angelina down – if I ever *could* find her – not to find her living next door to where I now sat.

*Maybe your life has been complicated enough recently and you deserved a break, Tiggy . . .*

I stood up and opened the gates again, then turned left and walked a few steps down the winding path. I paused in front of the next-door cave. The door was indeed a vivid blue, and another shiver ran through me.

*Your life began in there . . .* my inner voice told me. I turned to face the view, imagining María and Lucía sitting on the doorstep weaving their baskets, the village a cacophony of continual noise from its residents. Now, there was only the tweeting of birds hidden in the olive groves that cascaded down the hillside below me.

'A ghost town,' I said, feeling sad that the lifeblood had left it, but also careful not to romanticise how it must have been to live in Sacromonte all those years ago without even the basic necessities. Yet, ironically, the modern age had destroyed the vibrant heartbeat of this community.

I sat on the wall, gazing up at the Alhambra. Until the moment Marcella had expressed her surprise that I'd come back in search of my heritage, I'd never considered that it might be shameful to have gypsy blood. Chilly had celebrated the culture he – and apparently I – came from, so I had simply felt honoured to be a part of it. But now I thought about it, it was very different for me; I'd never suffered an ounce of prejudice in my life – accepted everywhere I went simply because of my neutral Western European appearance and Swiss passport. Whereas those who had once lived on this hillside had been banished from within the city, persecuted and never accepted by the wider society in which they lived.

'Why . . . ?' I murmured to myself.

*Because we are different and they don't understand us, so they are scared . . .*

I stood up and walked a little further along the path where I saw a sign for a museum on the wall by a narrow set of steps that led upwards. I began to take the steps, then felt a tight band around my chest. My body was obviously still recovering from the trauma of the shooting, so I walked back slowly to the hotel and sat down in the sun until the pain subsided.

'Angelina's door is open,' Marcella said to me as she arrived back through the gates with a basket full of eggs twenty minutes later. 'That means she's awake. Here.' Marcella took three eggs out of her basket and handed them to me. 'You can take these to her for me,' she encouraged.

'Okay.'

I went to my room, gave my hair a quick brush and took a couple of Ibuprofen to calm the pain in both my side and chest.

'Right.' I picked up the eggs. '*Courage, mon brave,*' I muttered as I kicked the gates open with my foot and walked the few metres downhill to the blue front door. It was open, and given my hands were full, I couldn't announce my presence by knocking.

'Hello? *¿Hola?*' I spoke into the gloom.

A man eventually appeared, sporting the most impressive handlebar moustache I'd ever seen. He had a matching head of thick silver-grey hair. He was well built, and his brown skin – wrinkled heavily by years under the Andalusian sun – encased a pair of chocolate-coloured eyes. He was holding a sweeping brush, which he held out as if he might use it as a weapon.

357

'Is Angelina here?' I asked.

'No readings until seven in the evening,' he said in heavily accented English.

'No, señor, I don't want a reading. I've been sent here to see Angelina. I might be a relative of hers.'

The man looked at me, then shrugged. '*No comprendo*, señorita.' Then he shut the door in my face.

Putting the eggs down carefully on the step, I knocked on the door. 'I have eggs,' I managed in Spanish, adding, 'from Marcella.'

The door was opened again, the man bent down and grabbed the eggs.

'*Gracias*, señorita.'

'Please, can I come in?' I hadn't come all this way to be refused entry by an old man with a broom.

'No, señorita,' he said and tried to shut the door, but I stuck my foot in it.

'Angelina?' I called. 'It's Tiggy. Chilly sent me,' I shouted, as the man won the battle of the door and it slammed once again in my face. Sighing, I walked back to the hotel in search of Marcella.

'She was not there?' Marcella looked confused.

'I think she was, but there was a man there who wouldn't let me in.'

'Ah, Pepe is very protective of Angelina – he is her uncle, after all,' Marcella explained. 'Maybe you try knocking again.'

I didn't even get as far as the gate before Pepe came round the bend towards me. Without a word, he took my hand in his large one, and smiled down at me.

'It is you . . . you are a woman now,' he said, and there were tears burgeoning in his brown eyes.

'I'm sorry, I d-don't—' I stuttered.

'I am Pepe, your *tío*, your great-uncle,' he said, before clasping me in his arms. Then he pulled me down the path back towards the blue front door. '*Perdón*, señorita,' he said, then mumbled something in Spanish. 'I did not realise it was you!'

'You speak English?'

'Of course! I just pretend "*no comprendo*" if tourists come knocking too early,' he chuckled. 'Now, I take you to Angelina, your cousin.'

Standing just inside the doorway was a small woman with a mane of gold hair that was greying at the roots. She was as petite as I was, and dressed in a red and blue patterned kaftan that fell to her feet, which were encased in comfortable leather sandals. Her blue eyes twinkled at me from behind long, black lashes, and her eyeliner had been drawn on as thickly as her eyebrows.

'*Hola*,' I said as I gazed at her.

'*Hola*, Erizo.' She smiled at me, then tears appeared in her eyes. 'You here,' she said in stilted English. 'You come home.' Then she opened her arms to me and I walked into them.

She sobbed on my shoulder, and I didn't know what to do except join her. Then we both wiped our eyes, and I heard Pepe blow his nose loudly behind us. I turned to him, and he joined us for a further embrace. My heart was pounding and I felt dizzy as I looked from my great-uncle to the woman I had been told to find. Eventually, we all extracted ourselves and I was ushered to a small paved area just beyond the cave, which housed a large number of potted plants. I smelt mint, sage, fennel and lavender as Pepe indicated a rickety wooden table and four similarly decrepit chairs. We all sat down, Pepe and Angelina's limbs moving fluidly despite their obvious age.

Angelina reached a hand towards mine and squeezed it.

'My English okay, but speak slowly,' she advised. 'How you find us?'

I explained as clearly as I could about Pa Salt's letter, then my move to Kinnaird and my meeting with Chilly.

Angelina and Pepe both clapped their hands in glee, speaking together in rapid Spanish.

'It has done my heart good to hear that the old ways still worked their magic,' said Angelina.

'So, did you know Chilly?' I asked her.

'No, only by name. Chilly was told he would send you home by Micaela, who look after me as a child. I feel Chilly is old and sick. He is at the end of his days,' Angelina added soberly. '*Sí?*'

'*Sí.*' I whispered, hating that I knew too. I'd realised immediately that there was no shielding my thoughts from this woman. Whatever gift Chilly had was dwarfed by Angelina's. I could feel the electricity around her – her power – already, and it was stirring my own.

'Of course, your blood is diluted by your *payo* forefathers, but' – I felt Angelina scrutinise me – 'I sense you have gift inside you. I will teach you, like Micaela taught me.'

Angelina smiled at me then, and the gaze contained so much warmth it brought a lump to my throat. Everything about her was so . . . *vital*. She paused to study me again, then took my hand into her soft palm and held it.

'You are sick, Erizo. What has happened to you?'

I related the story of the night Pegasus died as succinctly as I could.

I watched Angelina's eyes roll slightly backwards and, still holding my hand, she cocked an ear as though she was listening to something in the distance.

'This creature sent to protect you,' she said. 'He your spirit guide and will take many forms in your lifetime. Do you understand?'

'I think I do, yes.'

'Everything is for a reason, Erizo, nothing happens by chance. Death is not the end, but the beginning . . .' She began to examine my palm closely. 'Pepe,' she said to him, 'I need *la poción*.' She then explained in fast Spanish what it should contain, counting the ingredients off on her fingers. 'Bring it to her.'

Pepe disappeared for a while as Angelina continued to stare at me. '*Pequeño Erizo* . . . little hedgehog . . .'

'That's what Chilly called me!' I gasped. 'Except his word was *hotchiwitchi*,' I smiled.

Pepe returned with a glass of some noxious-looking liquid clasped in his hand.

'Will help heal the wound in your heart and soul,' she said, as Pepe placed it in front of me.

'What is it?' I asked.

'Not important,' said Pepe. 'Angelina says you must drink it.'

'Okay.' I picked up the glass dubiously and hesitated at the strong, strange smell.

'Just drink,' Angelina urged me.

'How long are you staying?' Pepe asked as soon as I'd swallowed the last mouthful of the revolting liquid.

'I haven't even thought about it. I just got on a plane and came here. I didn't expect to find you so easily.'

'Now you are here, you must stay for a while, because Angelina has much to teach you.'

I turned to look at my great-uncle and then to my cousin.

'Did either of you ever meet my mother and father?'

'Of course,' said Pepe. 'We live next door for many years. We here at your birth.' Pepe indicated the outer wall of the cave. 'You born in there.'

'What was my mother's name?'

'Isadora,' Pepe said gravely and Angelina lowered her head.

'Isadora . . .' I said, trying out the name on my tongue.

'Erizo, how much you know about your past?' Angelina asked me.

'Chilly has told me most of what happened before Lucía went to Barcelona. And then about how María went to find her and José there. Will you tell me what happened next, please?' I urged them.

'We will, but first we must go back to where Chilly left off,' said Angelina. 'You must know everything. It will take many hours to tell the story.'

'I have all the time in the world,' I smiled, realising I did.

'You must know where you have come from to see where you are going, Erizo. As long as you have the energy to concentrate, I will begin.' Angelina reached to me and took my pulse. She nodded. 'Okay. Is better.'

'Good,' I replied, thinking that I *did* feel better. My heart had stopped racing and I felt unusually calm.

'Well then, you know Lucía was with her papá, dancing in Barcelona, after her mother left to return to Sacromonte?'

'Yes.'

'Lucía stay away from Sacromonte for over ten years, learning her craft. She dance in many places, but always she and José go back to Barcelona. So I will begin from when Lucía is twenty-one. It would have been, let me see . . . 1933 . . .'

# Lucía
## Barcelona, Spain
### August 1933

*Flamenco fan (abanico)*
*Used in flamenco dancing as well as the secret*
*language of flirtation.*

# 22

'Come, Lucía. It is time to go and dance.'

'I am tired, Papá. Maybe someone else can take my place tonight.'

José looked at his daughter lying on her old mattress in her tiny room, smoking.

'We are all tired, *chiquita*, but the money has to be earned.'

'That is what you have said to me every day of my life. Maybe today is a different day, one where I will *not* work.' Lucía tapped her cigarette and ash fell to the floor. 'Where has it got me, eh, Papá? I have travelled to Cadiz, Seville, on tours right across the provinces, and I have even danced with the great Raquel Meller in Paris, yet still we live in this shitty dump!'

'Now we have our own kitchen,' José reminded her.

'As we never cook anything, what use is it?' Lucía stood up, wandered to the open window and tossed out the cigarette stub.

'I thought you lived to dance, Lucía.'

'I do, Papá, but the bar-owners work me like a common dockhand – sometimes three shows a night to put more money into *their* pockets! Besides, the crowd gets smaller every day because they do not want me any more. I am twenty-one years old – no longer a child – just a woman stuck in a child's body.' Lucía swept her hands down her body to emphasise the point. With her tiny waist, flat chest and slender limbs, she stood at little more than four feet tall.

'That is not true, Lucía. Your public adores you.'

'Papá, the men who come to the café want breasts and hips. I could be taken for a boy.'

'That is part of your charm, what makes La Candela unique! People don't flock to see you for your breasts, but for your footwork and your passion. Now, stop your self-indulgence, get dressed and come to the bar. There is someone I want you to meet.'

'Who? Another impresario who will claim to make me famous?'

'No, Lucía, a famous singer who has recently recorded a record album. I will see you at the bar.'

The door slammed behind José, and Lucía thumped the wall with her fist. She turned back to the open window and gazed out onto the busy, burning streets beneath her. Eleven long years she'd spent here, dancing her heart out . . .

'No family, no life . . .'

She looked down and saw a young couple kissing beneath her window. 'And no boyfriend,' she added as she lit another cigarette. 'Papá wouldn't like that, now would he? You are my boyfriends,' she told her feet – so small that she had to wear children's shoes.

Lucía stripped off her nightdress and donned her white and red flamenco gown, which stank of the sweat that poured off her when she danced. The ruffled white sleeves barely managed to hide the yellow stains, and the train was tattered and filthy, but there was only enough money to take it to the laundry once a week on a Monday, and today was a Saturday. She hated the weekends – her own stench made her feel no better than a common prostitute.

'If only Mamá was here,' she sighed as she stood in front of the cracked mirror, gathered her long raven mane and twirled it up into a coil. She remembered how her mother had once sat here on the mattress beside her, gently combing her hair.

'I miss you, Mamá,' she said, as she rimmed her eyes with kohl and added rouge to her cheeks and lips. 'Perhaps I will tell Papá again that we must return to Granada, because I need a rest, but he will say as always that we do not have the money for such a journey.'

She pouted at her reflection, then shook out her train and struck a pose. 'I look like one of those dolls they sell in souvenir shops! Maybe a rich *payo* would like to adopt me and play with me!'

She left the apartment and walked down the narrow passage and onto the main thoroughfare of the Barrio Chino. Shopkeepers, bartenders and their patrons waved and whistled at her in recognition.

*Which isn't surprising really, as I must have danced in every bar in the place*, she thought.

Still, the attention she drew and the raised glasses from the bars accompanied by voices shouting 'La Candela! *La Reina!*' cheered her up. She was certainly not short of a free drink or company round here.

'*Hola, chiquita*,' she heard someone call from behind her and turned to see Chilly weaving his way through the throng. He was already wearing his black trousers and waistcoat, ready for the performance tonight, his ruffled white shirt partially unbuttoned in the sweltering August heat.

In the past few years, Chilly had become a close friend. He and Lucía were part of José's *cuadro* – her father's troupe of flamenco artists who performed together in the numerous bars of the Barrio Chino. Whilst Chilly and José played the guitar and sang, Juana la Faraona, her father's cousin, danced with Lucía, the older woman's maturity and curves providing a contrast to Lucía's youth and fire. It was Juana who had suggested they brought in another female dancer to their little troupe over a year ago now.

'We do not need another dancer,' Lucía had immediately protested at the suggestion. 'Am I not enough? Do I not bring in many pesetas for you all?'

Despite his daughter's irritation, José had agreed with Juana that another younger and more voluptuous dancer would make them more bookable. Rosalba Ximénez, with her auburn hair and green eyes, was no match for Lucía's passionate *bulerías*, but danced the *alegrías* with sensuality and elegance. Already aware of Lucía's fiery reputation, she had gravitated towards the calmer Chilly, and Lucía's initial jealousy had only grown as she had perceived that Rosalba was slowly taking her childhood friend away from her.

Yet now, Chilly was a grown man, and, ignoring Lucía's sulks, he had married Rosalba a month ago in a weekend-long wedding that had the entire Barrio Chino celebrating their nuptials.

'You look better than yesterday, Lucía,' he said as he caught up with her. 'Did you take the tonic I prepared for you?'

Chilly was the *cuadro*'s resident *brujo*, forever concocting herbal remedies for its members, and Lucía trusted in his skills and his gift for seeing implicitly.

'Yes, Chilly, I did. I think it helped, I feel a little more energy today.'

'Then that is all to the good, although the most basic cure is to stop pushing yourself so hard.' He stared at her in the way that made her feel he was scanning her soul. She averted her eyes and did not answer, so he continued. 'You are on your way to the Bar de Manquet?'

'Yes, I'm meeting Papá there.'

'Then I will accompany you.'

Chilly walked along beside her in the sweltering sunshine. Being a weekend, the bars were already packed with dock-workers and labourers spending their wages on beer and brandy.

'What is wrong, Lucía?' he asked her quietly.

'Nothing,' she said immediately, not wishing her woes to travel back to Rosalba's ears.

'I know there is – I can see your heart is empty.'

'*Sí*, Chilly. You are right,' she capitulated. 'My heart is . . . bored, but most of all lonely.'

'I understand, but . . .' Chilly halted and grasped her hands in his. He looked upwards and Lucía knew he was seeing. 'Someone is coming, oh yes . . . very soon.'

'Pah! You have told me this before.'

'I have, yes, but I swear, Lucía, the moment is upon you. So,' he kissed her on both cheeks as they reached the Bar de Manquet, 'good luck, *chiquita*. You will need it.' He winked at her and strolled off along the street.

The Bar de Manquet was humming as always and Lucía pushed her way through the crowd to a roar of applause, heading for the *cuadro*'s table at the back near the stage. Her father was already seated, his head bent in concentration as he spoke with a man whose back was facing her.

'The usual, Lucía?' asked Jaime, the bartender.

'*Sí, gracias. Hola*, Papá, I have dragged myself here as you can see. *¡Salud!*' She raised the small glass of anise brandy that Jaime handed to her and knocked it back in one.

'Ah, the queen has arrived,' José responded. 'And look who has come to worship at your throne.'

'La Candela! We finally meet.' The man stood up and gave her a small bow. 'I am Agustín Campos.'

The first thing Lucía noticed about him was that he did not tower above her like most men. His diminutive but elegant frame was attired in a crisply cut suit, his black hair neatly combed back from his forehead. His skin was paler than most *gitanos*' and Lucía bet her new castanets there was *payo* blood in him. Although his ears stuck out rather, his mellow butter-scotch eyes were warm.

'*Hola*, Señor Campos. I hear your guitar recordings have become famous all over Spain.'

'Please, call me Meñique, everyone does,' he said.

'Meñique . . .' Lucía said with a smile. '"Little finger"?'

'Yes, I was given the name as a child, and as it seems I have not grown much since, it is still an apt name, don't you think?'

'And as *you* can see, neither have I,' she giggled, enchanted by his honesty and lack of arrogance. Most guitarists – especially successful ones – were insufferable. 'What are you doing here in Barcelona?'

'Making a new recording for the Parlophone Company. And whilst I am here, I felt that I should drop in to the Barrio Chino to see old friends, and perhaps make new ones . . .' he said as he swept his eyes down her body. 'I can see that La Candela burns brightly.'

'No, her light is fading because she is exhausted by performing the same dances to the same crowds. But you, Meñique, are on every gramophone I hear.'

'Let us find another drink.' Meñique snapped his fingers to alert the barman. As José watched his daughter rise out of her earlier dark mood, he sent up a prayer of gratitude.

Esteban Cortes, the owner of the Bar de Manquet, came over to their table, and after greeting Lucía with kisses on both cheeks, turned to Meñique.

'It is time for you to do your magic, *hombre*. Show Barcelona what we have been missing here!'

As Meñique stepped onto the stage, the audience cheered, then grew silent in anticipation. Lucía sat at her table, now nursing a manzanilla wine, and cooled herself with her fan.

She watched as Meñique tuned his guitar, then his long slim fingers struck the first chords of a *guajira*. Lucía smiled inwardly; it was the most showy and complicated style of flamenco song – even her father stumbled when playing it – and only the most confident guitarists took it on.

As the beat of the *cajón* started and Meñique began to sing in a low mellow voice, Lucía could not take her eyes off him, his fingers caressing the strings with huge speed but a light touch. He looked up suddenly and sought her out in the crowd. As their eyes met, she felt her body respond, her heart matching each beat of the music, a trickle of sweat trailing down her neck.

With a flourish, he came to a triumphant stop, a small smile playing on his lips. She found herself smiling back as a clear thought formed in her mind.

*Chilly was right. I will have you, Meñique. You will be mine.*

Later that evening, once the public in the bar had been satisfied, the flamenco artists went upstairs for an improvised *juerga* in a private room.

'*Dios mío*,' said Meñique, entering with Lucía and finding it packed.

'It is payday for us here in the Barrio Chino, and we all gather together to dance and sing for each other,' she explained.

'Look, there is El Peluco.' Meñique pointed to an old man sitting regally in a chair, a guitar over his lap. 'I can hardly believe he is still upright and playing, he drinks so much brandy.'

'I have not met him before, but perhaps he is a guest at the Villa Rosa along the street,' Lucía said with a shrug. 'Now, please get me some brandy.'

Already, El Peluco had taken the floor with his guitar, singing what Lucía recognised as one of the old songs her grandfather had sung when she was young.

'I must introduce you to him, he is a legend,' Meñique murmured in her ear as loud applause greeted the old man and another singer took up his vacant stool. 'El Peluco!' Meñique waved at him.

'Ah, the protégé from Pamplona.' El Peluco returned the wave and came to join him.

'Brandy for you, señor.' Meñique offered him a glass. They toasted, then he turned to Lucía. 'And this is La Candela! Another protégée in the room.'

Lucía felt El Peluco's hooded eyes upon her.

'So, it is you that I hear so much about. Yet, there is hardly anything of you,' El Peluco laughed before he gulped back his brandy, then leant in to Meñique. 'Certainly nothing of a woman. And it takes a woman to dance flamenco. Perhaps she is just a little fraud,' he whispered loudly, before letting out an enormous belch.

Lucía heard him as she'd been meant to. Anger welled up inside her and there was only one way she knew to rid herself of it. Standing where she was, her feet still bare following her performance earlier, they began to beat against the floor. Her arms raised slowly above her head, the backs of her hands touching and forming the shape of a rose, as her mamá had taught her. And all the time she stared into the eyes of the man who had called her a fraud.

As the crowd realised what was happening, a circle opened around Lucía and the *cantaor* was hushed to silence. Meñique and José took up the beat and began to hum some ancient verses of a *soleá* as Lucía's feet pounded the floor. Still staring at the man who had insulted her, she summoned the *duende* and danced only for him.

Finally, Lucía sank to the floor, spent. Then she nodded to her audience, who roared in approval, rose and pulled up the nearest chair so that it was right next to El Peluco. She climbed upon it so she could look him in the eye.

'Never call me a fraud again,' she said, jabbing a finger towards his bulbous nose. 'Okay, señor?'

'Señorita, I swear on my life I never will. You are . . . *magnifica*!'

'What am I?' Lucía jabbed her finger at him again.

El Peluco looked for heavenly guidance before he bowed – 'The queen!'

The room cheered at his reply, then Lucía put out her hand for him to kiss it.

'Now,' she said to Meñique as he helped her down from the chair, 'I can relax.'

Lucía woke the next morning with her habitual headache, caused by too little sleep and far too much brandy. Her fingers searched on the floor beside her mattress for her cigarettes. She lit one and watched the smoke rings rise to the ceiling.

*Something is different . . .* she thought, because even in the fug of her hangover she did not feel the usual depression that another day in this world had dawned.

*Meñique!*

Lucía stretched luxuriously, her cigarette held behind her head, and wondered what it would be like to have those sensitive, famous fingers touch *her*.

Then she sat upright, common sense prevailing. 'Don't be ridiculous,' she told herself. 'Meñique is a star, a heartthrob. He is famous in Spain and can have any woman he wishes with a click of those fingers.'

But maybe he *would* have had her last night, and she'd have surrendered willingly, had it not been for her father hanging around like a protective mother hen at the end of the evening.

'Will I see you tomorrow, Lucía?' he'd asked, as her father had made it clear it was time for them to go home.

'She must dance at three cafés tomorrow night, Meñique,' José had reminded him.

'Then maybe I can come and play for her at the Villa Rosa?'

Meñique's request had hung in the air as José led his daughter away.

That evening, Lucía went to the Villa Rosa where she was due to perform, but there was no sign of Meñique.

'Perhaps it's for the best,' she muttered, disappointment flooding through her as she took the stage. 'My dress smells even more tonight than it did yesterday.'

Later, she and her father trudged along the street to the Bar de Manquet with her usual clutch of ardent admirers following on behind her. There, waiting outside the café, was Meñique.

'*Buenas noches*, señorita, señor. I'm afraid I was delayed earlier, but as I mentioned, I would like to play for Lucía tonight,' he said as the three of them walked inside. 'I have asked the manager and he has agreed, if you are both happy.'

'*Sí*, Papá, I would like it very much,' Lucía urged her father.

'I . . . of course if the management, and my daughter, wish it,' José agreed, but Lucía could see the thunderclouds gathering in his eyes.

That night, Meñique tested her to her limits. Starting deceptively slowly, suddenly he stamped his foot, shouted '*Olé!*' and moved into a series of arpeggios that were almost impossible for even Lucía's feet to keep up with. The audience clapped, cheered and stamped as the two protégés – one of the fingers and one of the feet – tried to win the battle to outshine each other. Lucía transformed into a whirling dervish of heat and passion until Meñique gave a final strum, shook his head, and stood up to bow to Lucía. The crowd erupted as they moved off stage together to drink brandy washed down with plenty of water.

'Do you always have to win?' he whispered in her ear.

'Always.' Lucía flashed her eyes at him.

'Meet me for lunch tomorrow? At the Cafè de l'Òpera, without your chaperone.' Meñique nodded at José, who was holding court further along the bar.

'He never wakes up until three.'

'Good. Now, I must leave. I promised to play at the Villa Rosa.' Meñique took her hand and kissed it. '*Buenas noches*, Lucía.'

He was already waiting for her at an outdoor table when she arrived at the café the next day.

'Forgive me,' Lucía said as she sat down opposite him and lit a cigarette. 'I overslept,' she added with a casual shrug.

In truth, she had spent the past hour trying on every dress, blouse and skirt she owned, all of which were old and out of date by about ten years. In the end, she'd settled for a pair of black practice trousers and a red blouse, with a jaunty red scarf tied around her neck.

'You look captivating,' said Meñique, standing to kiss her on both cheeks.

'Don't lie to me, Meñique. I was born with the body of a

boy and the face of an ugly grandmother, and there is nothing you or I can do about it. But at least I can dance.'

'I assure you that you do not have the body of a boy, Lucía,' Meñique said, his eyes resting briefly on the veiled outline of her small, upright breasts. 'Now, shall we take some sangria as the day is warm? It is very refreshing.'

'It is a *payo* drink,' she said with a frown, 'but if it tastes good, why not?'

Meñique ordered a jug of sangria then poured some into her glass. Lucía took a sip, swirled it around her mouth, then spat it out on the pavement.

'It is so sweet!' Lucía snapped her fingers at a waiter. 'Bring me some black coffee to take the taste away.'

'I am learning that you have a fiery temperament to match the passion of your dancing.'

'*Sí*, it is my spirit that gives me *duende*.'

'You Andalusians – you're all the same. Completely uncontrollable,' Meñique said with a grin.

'And you are a pale Pamplona señor. I hear your mamá is a *payo*?'

'She is, and thanks to her, I went to school and I can read and write.'

'So now that the *payos* pay their pesetas for your *gitano* music, you become one of them?'

'No, Lucía, but I see nothing wrong in sharing our flamenco culture with an audience outside our own community. And you are correct, the *payos* are the ones with the money. The world, and our world of dance, is changing. These –' Meñique gestured to the many *café cantantes* lining the street – 'are becoming outdated. People want a show! Lights, costumes . . . an orchestra on a big stage in a theatre.'

'Do you not think I know this?! I was in Paris four years ago in Raquel Meller's show at the Palais du Paris.'

'I hear it was a big success. So what happened?'

'La Meller did not like the fact that the Los Albaycín Trio – me, La Faraona, and my father – became more of a hit than she was. Can you believe she punched La Faraona on the nose?' Lucía giggled. 'Accused her of deliberately trying to upstage her.'

'That sounds like La Meller. She has an ego bigger than her talent.'

'*Sí*, so we left and worked instead in the cafés of Montmartre, which was far more fun. The lifestyle suited me, but we were earning next to nothing, so we ended up back here. It seems to be the story of my life, Meñique. I get a big chance, and think, yes! This will be it! Then it all falls through my fingers and I am back to where I began.'

'Don't exaggerate, Lucía. You are famous – one could say infamous – in the flamenco world.'

'But not out there . . .' Lucía waved her hand to indicate the vast country laid out behind them. 'Not like you, or La Argentinita.'

'Who is, may I remind you, some years older than you,' Meñique said with a gentle smile.

'She's practically a grandmother, yet she has just been in a new film!'

'One day, *pequeña*, you will be a star of the screen too, I promise.'

'Oh, so I suppose now you can see the future like my friend Chilly?' she snapped.

'No, but I can see your ambition. It burns like a flame inside you. Now, shall we order?'

'My usual,' Lucía announced grandly to the hovering waiter. 'You know, I have been dancing almost as long as La Argentinita, and where has it got me? While she travels around Europe in her furs and her carriages, I sit here and eat sardines with you.'

'*Gracias* for that compliment.' Meñique raised an eyebrow. 'So, what next?'

'Carcellés has arranged for us to tour the provinces.'

'Carcellés? Who is he?'

'Another fat impresario, making money off our hard work,' shrugged Lucía. 'So I will be performing in country bars with farm animals as my audience while La Argentinita lights up stages in front of thousands.'

'Lucía, you are too young to be so bitter,' Meñique chided her. 'Will you go on the tour?'

'I have no choice. If I stay here in the Barrio Chino for much longer, I will die,' she pronounced dramatically, lighting another cigarette. 'You know what else frustrates me?'

'What?'

'Do you remember Vicente Escudero, the dancer? He recommended me to La Argentinita's famous manager, Sol Hurok. *He* wanted to take me to New York! Imagine that!'

'So why didn't you go?'

'Papá said that *gitanos* couldn't cross the water. Can you believe he refused the offer?' Lucía banged the table hard with her fist, rattling the ice in the water glasses. 'I did not speak to him for a month afterwards.'

Beginning to get the measure of Lucía's temperament, Meñique surmised she wasn't exaggerating.

'Well, you told me you are already twenty-one, so you are

technically in charge of your own destiny. Although I think your father was right about New York.'

'Right to be scared of crossing water because of some *gitano* superstition?'

'No, right to let you continue to mature here. The Barrio Chino produces some of the best flamenco dancers in the world. Keep watching and learning, my Lucía. You will blossom with the right teaching and guidance.'

'I don't need a teacher! I improvise every night! Stop treating me like Papá does, when you're little older than I am!'

Their food arrived and Meñique watched Lucía wolf down the sardines in order to light another cigarette as soon as possible. He knew she was sulking about his comments, and it was obvious she was potentially a diva of extraordinary proportions . . . Yet, there was something about her that fascinated him, like no other woman had before. He wanted her.

'You should come to Madrid if you can. There is a wider audience and I live there too . . .' He smiled, moving his hand across the table in her direction. She looked at it in surprise and with a little fear.

His fingers reached her hand and closed over it, and he felt her shudder slightly, then compose herself.

'I . . . where would I dance in Madrid?' she asked, trying to concentrate on the conversation.

'There are many large theatres that have productions with a cast and a full orchestra. I will mention your name to those I know, but in the meantime, my Lucía, try to remember that the goal is not fortune and fame, but the art itself.'

'I will, I already do . . .' Lucía sighed, the touch of his hand on hers feeling like a balm to her soul. She offered him a weak smile. 'I am bad company, *sí*? All I do is sit here and complain.'

'I understand, Lucía. Like me when I play guitar, you give your innermost self every time you perform. I agree that your career has stagnated and that you and your talent deserve to be seen and recognised by the world. I swear I will do what I can to help you. For now, you must be patient and trust me, okay?'

'Okay,' she agreed, as Meñique brought her hand to his lips and kissed it.

For the next month, Lucía and her troupe trudged by wagon through the provinces of Spain; along the coast to the small villages surrounding the great city of Valencia, to Murcia where the Gothic cathedral spanned the skyline. Then further south, where she could see the mountains of the Sierra Nevada glimmering in the distance, a tantalising glimpse of her true home.

She danced night after night for ecstatic but small audiences, then returning with the other musicians and dancers to sit round a fire and drink brandy or wine as they listened to Chilly's mystical stories of the other worlds. Some nights, as she lay in the wagon, Meñique's words of encouragement were all that kept her going.

*I must keep learning*, she thought, so, rather than leaving a bar after her own dance had finished and sitting outside smoking, Lucía remained there and studied Juana la Faraona's flawless technique and grace.

'I am a bundle of fire and spirit, but I must learn to be

feminine,' Lucía muttered to herself as she watched La Faraona's elegant arms, the graceful way she picked up her train and the sensual curve of her lips. 'Then maybe Meñique will love me . . .'

'Papá, Juana said we will be performing in Granada next week,' Lucía said as they walked back to their campsite in Almería after the night's show. 'We must go and visit Mamá and Carlos and Eduardo, *sí*?'

José didn't answer, so Lucía gave him a sharp jab with her finger. 'Papá?'

'I think it is best if you go alone,' he said eventually. 'I am no longer welcome in Sacromonte.'

'What do you mean? Of course you are!' Lucía chided him. 'Your wife and your children and many of our relatives are there. They will be so happy to see us.'

'Lucía, I . . .'

She saw José had stopped where he was in the middle of an orange grove.

'What, Papá?'

'Your mother and I are married in name only. Do you understand?'

Lucía put her hands on her hips. 'How could I not understand, Papá? I have had so many "aunties" over the years, I'd be an *idiota* if I didn't. I thought that you and Mamá had an arrangement.'

'The truth is, your mother did not wish for an "arrangement", Lucía. She hates me, and maybe Carlos and Eduardo do too. They might think I deserted them to take you to Barcelona and give you your chance.'

Lucía looked at her father in horror. 'You are saying this is my fault?'

'Of course not. You were a child, and I had to make a decision.'

Lucía cast her mind back to the last time she had seen her mother in Barcelona, eleven years ago now. She remembered how she had sat, gently combing her hair. Then, after María had seen her dance at the Villa Rosa, they had said goodbye outside. Lucía remembered that her mother had been weeping.

'Whatever happened between the two of you, I must go and see her, Papá.'

'Yes.' José turned from Lucía, and made his way towards the wagon, his shoulders stooped.

A week later, Lucía entered Sacromonte through the city gate. The sky was a perfect blue, the white wisps of smoke coming from the caves that fell down the hillside trailed up in plumes towards it, and the valley was as green and verdant in late summer as she remembered it.

She looked upwards to the Alhambra, remembering the night she'd sneaked like a thief onto the stage at the great *Cante Jondo* competition, and danced in front of an audience of thousands.

'Papá made that happen for me,' she reassured herself as she walked up the dusty, winding paths towards her childhood home. She smiled at an old man smoking a cheroot on his doorstep. He looked disdainfully at her as though she was a common *payo*. As Lucía walked, she thought about her father's newly confessed abandonment of his wife and sons. Despite part of her hating him for lying to her for years, Lucía could not deny what he'd done for her that night at the Alhambra, nor his dedication to her career in the last eleven years.

'Their marital business is none of mine,' she told herself firmly as she glanced upwards to see the smoke emanating from her mother's chimney. When she reached the cave, she let out a small breath of wonder because there was a shiny blue-painted door in the roughly carved entrance, and the cave now boasted two glass windows, with bright red flowers planted in boxes beneath them.

She hesitated nervously at the threshold; presented with its unfamiliar formality, she wondered whether she should knock.

'This is your home,' she told herself and reached for the doorknob to swing the door open.

And there in the kitchen, sitting at the old wooden table, now covered in a pretty lace cloth, was her mother. Apart from the odd streak of grey in her hair, María looked exactly the same. There was a little boy of about ten sitting next to her, all black curls and smiles as her mother tickled him.

María looked up at her uninvited guest, taking a moment to gather her senses before she took a deep breath and stood up, hand over her mouth.

'Lucía? I . . . Is it you?'

'Yes, Mamá, it is me.' Lucía nodded uncertainly. 'And who is that?'

'He is Pepe. Go play with your guitar outside, *querido*,' she told the little boy, who then departed with a smile at Lucía.

'*Dios mío*, what a shock this is!' María said as she opened her arms and went to embrace her daughter. 'My Lucía is returned! Would you like some orange juice? I have just squeezed a fresh batch.'

María moved to what Lucía recognised as a new set of wooden cupboards that ran along one side of the wall. In the centre of them was a cast-iron sink, and a pitcher of water stood next to it.

'*Gracias*,' she said, not only sensing her mother's discomfort but also thinking that her mother seemed to have come up in the world since she'd last been here. The wonderful bright light in the valley shone through the windows into the interior of the cave, which had clearly been recently whitewashed.

'Now, tell me how you are? Why you are here . . . tell me everything!' María laughed in delight as she offered a beautifully carved rocking chair to Lucía to sit down in.

'Our troupe is on tour nearby. Last night we were in Granada, performing at a café in the Plaza de las Pasiegas. There were big crowds.'

'Why did I not hear of this?' María frowned. 'I would have given anything to see you dance, *querida mía*.'

Lucía could perhaps guess why friends and neighbours had not told her that her husband and daughter were visiting the area, but she let it pass.

'I don't know, Mamá, but oh, I am so glad to be here!'

'And I am so glad to see you.'

'Are Eduardo and Carlos home as well?'

'Today is a fiesta and they are out celebrating with the rest of Sacromonte, but if you are staying tonight, you will see them in the morning.'

'I cannot stay so long, Mamá. Tonight we must move on.'

María looked momentarily crestfallen. 'Well, no matter, you are here *now*.' María drew a stool close to her daughter and sat down. 'You have grown, Lucía—'

'Not much, Mamá, but what can I do?' she shrugged.

'I meant that you have grown into a woman. A beautiful woman.'

'Mamá, I know any mother must say that her daughter is beautiful, but I know I am not. It is life. So –' Lucía looked around the room – 'you are well? The cave seems much more comfortable than I remember it.'

'I am well, yes. Although I must tell you that both your grandparents were taken by an outbreak of typhoid in the summer.'

'That is indeed sad news.' In truth, Lucía could hardly remember them.

'But at least before they passed away, your grandfather's business had thrived thanks to your brothers' help. Both of them have been so kind to their mamá. It is Carlos who is responsible for all the new furniture and the kitchen, mind you. Do you remember how as a child he was always whittling pieces of wood?'

Lucía did not, but she nodded.

'Between you and me,' María continued, 'I know that your grandfather had been in despair over Carlos's clumsy metal-work at the forge, but had noticed his passion for woodwork. He gave Carlos some pieces of pine and suggested he try to make a table. So it turns out that your brother is a talented carpenter, and now both *gitanos* and *payos* flock to buy his furniture. Would you believe, he is just about to open a shop in the city as a showroom for his wares? His wife, Susana, will run it for him.'

'I see.' Lucía could hardly keep up with what her mother was telling her. 'And where do they live?'

'They built a home in a cave next door to your grandparents, at the same time as Eduardo and Elena did. They have Cristina and her older brother, Mateo, and I am soon to have a third grandchild—'

'Slow down, Mamá! My head is spinning with all these names!'

'Forgive me, Lucía, it is the shock of seeing you, my tongue is running away with me and—'

'I understand. We are both nervous, Mamá. It has been a long time.' Lucía put her hand out towards her mother's, her face softening. 'It is wonderful to see you, and I am happy that all has gone well with you and my brothers since we left.'

'Not at the beginning. The first few years were very hard indeed. But enough of that.' María smiled brightly. 'Tell me more about you, Lucía.'

'Mamá, first I must tell you that I finally know what happened between you and Papá.' Her earlier resolve that her parents' marriage was none of her business melted away in the moment. 'He admitted he had left you here and taken me against your will.'

'Lucía, we were both at fault.'

'I don't think so, Mamá, and I cannot help but have a deep anger for all the years when I thought you did not care about me, why you did not come to see me. Now I understand.'

'Lucía,' María whispered, her voice breaking. 'I have missed you and prayed for you every day since I left you, believe me. Every year, in the month of your birth, I sent a small parcel to your father to give to you. I hope that you received them?'

'I did not,' Lucía stated flatly. 'Papá never gave me anything like that.'

María could see her daughter's eyes narrowing and her expression darkening, so she hurried on. 'Well, perhaps they were lost on the long journey. Your father did what he thought was right. He did it for you.'

'And for *him*,' Lucía hissed. 'What really happened, Mamá? I only remember a few things about that time, like after the *Concurso* . . . and Papá was shouting at Carlos – he was crying on the floor, right here.' She pointed at the spot. 'Then we left for Barcelona and many weeks later you came. You told me that my brother Felipe was up in heaven with the angels.'

María shut her eyes, as the memories flooded back to her. Haltingly, she told Lucía the tragic circumstances of Felipe's death.

'It was the *payo* jail that killed him, Lucía. He died the day after he was released. So I came to Barcelona to tell you and your father.'

Lucía reached out and took her mother's hands in hers, the deeply tanned skin rough with hard work. Then she bent her head over them and cried. Back here, the loss of her childhood, and her brother, hit her fully.

'Mamá?' came a voice.

Lucía looked up in surprise, wiping the tears from her face. Pepe had come back into the kitchen, clutching his guitar.

'Why are you both crying?' he asked, as he walked forwards.

Lucía looked more closely at Pepe's face, and registered the large dark eyes, the strong planes of his cheekbones and the mass of black hair.

'Is this . . . is h-he . . . ?' she stuttered.

'Yes, Lucía.' María nodded solemnly and brushed her own tears away. 'This is your brother. Pepe, say hello to your *hermana*.'

'*Hola*,' he said shyly, and gave her a grin. Without a doubt, he was the image of José.

'It is nice to meet you, Pepe.' Lucía managed a smile.

'You're smaller than Mamá told me you were. I thought you were my big sister, but I'm taller than you!'

'Yes, you are right, and cheeky too.' Lucía found herself unable to prevent a chuckle.

'If you are here, is Papá with you? Mamá says that he plays the guitar, just like I do,' Pepe said. 'I want to play him a new song I learnt.'

'I . . .' Lucía glanced at her mother. 'I am afraid Papá could not come.'

'Pepe, go feed the chickens, and then we will eat,' María instructed. As Pepe reluctantly went out again, Lucía watched him in wonder.

'How . . . ?' she began.

'After I left you with your father in Barcelona all those years ago, I returned to Granada. It was two months before I realised the sickness wasn't just grief, but a parting gift from your father. Yet Pepe has been my salvation, truly, Lucía. You should hear him play the guitar; one day he will be better than José.'

'Does Papá know?'

'No. I understood when I left Barcelona that I was setting him free.'

'Yes, free to put his *picha* wherever he wanted,' Lucía muttered, feeling a fresh surge of anger at her father.

'Some men can't help themselves, it is as simple as that.'

'Well, he hasn't learnt his lesson yet, Mamá.'

And then they both laughed, because there was little else to do.

'He is not altogether a bad man, Lucía; you above everyone will know that. Is he happy?'

'I don't know. He plays his guitar, he drinks, he—'

'Well.' María cut her daughter short. 'He is who he is, as we all are. And a part of me will always love him.'

Lucía watched her mother sigh, and believed her.

'Don't hate him, please,' María entreated. 'He wanted to give you your chance.'

'And his,' Lucía mumbled, 'but I will try not to hate him. For you.'

'I have some fresh soup ready for lunch. Would you like some?'

'Yes, Mamá.'

Lucía devoured the whole bowl and asked for more, pronouncing it the best food she'd eaten since she'd left her mother's kitchen eleven years ago. María glowed with pleasure as she watched Pepe and Lucía sitting at the table, eating together like a family. Afterwards, the two women went to sit outside.

'Do you remember when you used to try to get me to help you with the baskets?' Lucía asked.

'Yes, and you would always find an excuse after a few minutes and be gone.'

'It's so peaceful here, so beautiful,' Lucía said as she cast her eyes across the valley. 'I'd forgotten. Perhaps I didn't realise what I had.'

'None of us do, *querida*, until it's gone. I've learnt that the secret of happiness is to try to live in the moment.'

'It's a lesson I might find quite difficult to learn, Mamá. I'm always thinking of the future!'

'We are different, you and I: you were always ambitious for your talent in a way I never was. I wanted a home, a family and a husband. Well.' She smiled. 'I managed to get two of those things, at least.'

'Do you still dance? You used to be so good, Mamá.'

'For pleasure, yes, but I am getting old. I am an *abuela* with two grandchildren.'

'Mamá, you can be little older than forty! Many of the dancers in Barcelona are in their fifties and sixties. So you're happy here?' Lucía probed.

'Yes, I believe I am.'

An hour later, as Lucía sat listening to Pepe playing his guitar in the sitting room that María told her had been fashioned out of the old stable, she heard a male voice from the kitchen.

'*Hola, mi amor*, I brought us a treat for our dessert after the stew tonight.'

Lucía heard her mother hush the guest as she walked into the kitchen and saw Ramón, their next-door neighbour, standing with an arm around her mother's shoulder. María blushed and stepped away from him.

'*Hola*, señor, how are you?' Lucía asked.

'I am well, thank you,' Ramón answered stiffly, the colour rising to his cheeks. Lucía wanted to giggle.

'How are your daughters, Ramón?'

'They are well, yes, very well.'

'Two of them are married and we celebrated Magdalena's

engagement only a week ago, didn't we, Ramón?' María encouraged him.

'Yes, yes, we did,' Ramón agreed with a nod.

'How are your oranges?'

'They are well, thank you, Lucía.'

'Ramón now owns a small grove of his own.' María continued to speak for him. 'His parents died within a few months of each other and after their funeral, Ramón found some coins hidden in their chimney. Who knew how long they had been there, but the fact they had never melted after all those years made Ramón believe they were a gift from the Blessed Virgin. So, he bought his orange grove with them.'

'I did.' Ramón looked nervously at Lucía, waiting for her reaction.

'*Gracias*, Ramón, for taking care of my mother while I have been gone. I'm sure you have been a great comfort to her.' Lucía put a placatory hand on his.

'It has been my pleasure, señorita.' Ramón smiled in relief.

When he left, María turned to her daughter, her flapping hands trying to cool the embarrassment flooding her cheeks. 'What must you think of me?'

'I have learnt that life is hard, Mamá. And you have taken solace when it has been offered. There is nothing wrong in that.'

'I . . . we, Ramón and I do not advertise our . . . friendship. Believe me, I would never disrespect your father in public.'

'Mamá, I have seen everything in the Barrio Chino. Nothing – least of all a need for comfort – can shock me.'

'*Gracias*, Lucía.' María took her daughter's hands and squeezed them. 'You have become a lovely young woman.'

'Mamá, I hope I have your sense and Papá's passion. It is

a good mixture, *sí*? Now.' She looked at the sun beginning to dip its nightly curtsey below the Alhambra. 'I must begin the walk back to the city. We leave tonight for Cadiz.'

'Can you not stay a little longer, *querida*?'

'I cannot, Mamá, but now we are reunited, I swear I will visit more often. Perhaps even come and stay for a holiday.'

'Next time, give me notice and I will arrange a party for you to meet all your family. My door is always open and I am always here.'

'Mamá, what do you wish me to tell Papá about . . . his son?'

'If you can bear it, I think it is best if you say nothing for now. One day, I must tell him in person.'

'Of course. *Adiós*, Mamá.' As she hugged her mother, Lucía felt the prickling of tears. Before they could hatch, she left the cave and walked back along the dusty path of her childhood.

# 23

'I have news for you,' said Carcellés as they sat together outside his favourite bar in the Barrio Chino. Lucía looked at the impresario who had organised their tour of the provinces. Carcellés' face was red from too much brandy, and his stomach strained over his tightly belted trousers. The smoke from their cigarettes curled up into the darkening sky.

'What is that?'

Carcellés poured some more brandy into their glasses. 'The Fontalba Theatre in Madrid is organising a tribute to the actress Luisita Esteso. I am putting you on between two other acts. It is time your talent was showcased in the capital.'

Lucía – by now used to Carcellés' extravagant promises, designed to spur her on but which usually amounted to nothing – stared at him in disbelief.

'You are taking me to Madrid?'

'*Sí*, Lucía. You will fit perfectly on the bill. The great Meñique has even offered to play for you. How about that?'

'*¡Dios mío!*' Lucía stood up to embrace Carcellés, knocking the trestle table and spilling their brandy everywhere. 'Why, this is wonderful news!'

'I am glad you are happy, Lucía. It is just one night, and

you will only have five minutes on the programme, but they are *your* five minutes and you must show the people who matter in Madrid what you can do.'

'I will, I promise I will. *Gracias*, señor.'

'Did you hear, Papá?' Lucía burst into José's bedroom. He was alone, lying on his bed, smoking.

'About Madrid? Yes, I have heard. Of course, you will not be paid. You realise that, don't you?'

'Who cares about the money?! I am to perform in front of over a thousand people. Isn't this wonderful news?'

'I hear Meñique is to accompany you.'

'Yes, so there is no need for you to come. Carcellés will be on the train with me and Meñique will take care of me once I am there.'

'That is what I am worried about,' José mumbled morosely as he stubbed his cigarette out into a half-full bottle of beer.

'I'm a big girl now, Papá; remember I am now twenty-one years old. I will be back before you know it.'

Lucía returned to her own room, refusing to let her father's sulk spoil her joy. Removing her flamenco dress, she sank stark naked onto the mattress and lay there with her arms and legs splayed, thinking. Eventually, an idea started to form in her mind.

'Yes!' Lucía jumped off the bed and went to the corner where she piled up her clothes, and began to search through them, knowing exactly what she would wear to make this performance – and her – unforgettable.

'Madrid . . .' she breathed, finding what she was looking for. 'And Meñique!'

'Are you all right, *pequeña*?' Meñique whispered in her ear as, two weeks later, they stood in the wings together at the side of the enormous stage, listening to the rapturous applause for El Botato, who was dancing his famous *farruca* with comedic acrobatic leaps.

'*Sí*, but I am nervous, Meñique. I'm never nervous before I dance.'

'All to the good; the adrenaline will give more depth to your performance.'

'No one has ever heard of me here.' Lucía bit her lip. 'What if they boo me off the stage?'

'Everyone will know your name after this. Now' – he gave her shoulder a gentle push – 'go.'

Lucía walked onto the stage to muted applause, the bright spotlights burning her eyes. She felt hot and itchy underneath the heavy cloak she was wearing. Meñique followed her on seconds later and the audience cheered and clapped.

'Mamá,' she whispered as she took up her opening position, 'I dance this for you.'

Sitting to one side, Meñique watched the tiny figure draw herself up in the centre of the enormous stage. As he began to play the opening bars in preparation to sing, he saw Lucía's chin tip up and her nostrils flare. As the beat increased, she swept off her cloak in one fluid movement and threw it across the stage. The audience gasped in shock when they saw that this tiny woman was wearing high-waisted black trousers and the starched white shirt of a male dancer. Her hair had been pulled back, parted down the middle and slicked down, and her kohl-rimmed eyes issued a challenge to the audience.

Then she began to dance. Any dissenters' whisperings ceased after a few seconds as the fourteen-hundred-strong audience was held spellbound by the child-woman whose miraculous feet managed to somehow tap out so many beats, it was impossible for even experienced hands to keep up. When they realised that Lucía was performing the same *farruca* as El Botato – a dance reserved for men – the audience went wild, whooping and whistling at the strange sight. Meñique was so entranced as she became a whirling dervish of sheer energy, that he almost forgot to come in for the next verse of his song.

*She is so pure . . . the essence of flamenco*, he thought.

By now, the audience were on their feet, clapping along as Lucía's feet beat relentlessly, until Meñique wondered if she might simply fall to the floor and collapse. Where her little body found the energy to keep up the incredible pace for as long as it did, he simply didn't know.

'*¡Olé!*' she shouted as, finally, she gave one last stamp and fell forward into a low bow.

The audience erupted as Lucía took bow after bow. Meñique walked forward to take his own applause next to her.

'You did it, *pequeña*, you did it,' he whispered as he ushered her forward again and again.

'Did I . . . ?' Lucía asked him, as Meñique eventually led her off stage and into the wings, where there was already a crowd ready to greet her.

'You made your perfect Madrid debut.'

'I cannot remember anything.'

Meñique could see she looked dazed as she hung on to his arm for support. He steered her through the crowds towards his dressing room, shutting the door behind them firmly.

'Take some time to steady yourself.' He sat her down in a chair and handed her a measure of brandy.

'*Gracias.*' Lucía swallowed the drink down in one. 'I never remember what I danced afterwards. Was I good?'

Meñique could see that it was a genuine question and that she was not fishing for compliments.

'You were not simply "good", Lucía, you were . . . miraculous!' He gave her a salute.

There was a loud banging on the door, and the sound of voices behind it.

'Is La Candela ready to receive the acclaim of her adoring public?'

'I am.'

She stood up, turning to the mirror and taking a tissue to pat down her sweat-drenched face.

'But just before you do . . .'

Meñique took her in his arms and kissed her.

'What do you mean, Papá is arriving today?' Lucía sat up next to Meñique in his comfortable bed a few days later. 'He is not meant to come until next week! I am doing perfectly well here in Madrid by myself.'

'Lucía, your father has managed your career since you were a little girl. Surely you will not deny him his moment of triumph? Besides, he is your guitarist. He alone knows how to play for you best.'

'No!' Lucía grabbed Meñique's fingers and kissed them. '*These* know how to play for me best. And not just on the guitar . . .'

Meñique felt a stirring as Lucía wriggled her naked body next to him.

'Yes, *pequeña*, but I am already contracted elsewhere for the next two months, as you know.'

'Then cancel,' she said as her hand crept under the sheet. 'I need you to play for me at the Coliseum.'

'Now, now.' Meñique caught her elbows. 'Your star may be rising, but you are not a fully fledged diva yet, so don't act like one. Your father will bring your *cuadro* with him. It is far better you have your own guitarists and singers to support you – those who you know and can trust – rather than having them chosen for you.'

'It has been so good to be free of him,' Lucía complained. 'Being here with you . . . I have felt like a woman, and not a child, which is how Papá treats me.'

'You've certainly been a woman, Lucía.' Meñique reached for her breasts and caressed them, but now it was she who pushed him away.

'Even when Papá comes, can I stay here?'

'When I'm here in Madrid, of course you can, but now you are finally earning some good money with your contract at the Coliseum, you will be able to get an apartment with the rest of the *cuadro*.' Meñique climbed out of bed and began to dress.

'Don't you want me here any longer?'

'I do, but I cannot always be here for you.'

'Your career is more important than me?'

'My career is *as* important as you,' Meñique chided her. 'Now, I must go, I have a meeting about the new recording. I will see you later.'

Lucía threw herself back on the pillows, furious that both

her lover and her father were thwarting her plans. Since her triumph at the Teatro de Fontalba, she'd experienced her first taste of freedom, and she was not inclined to give it up without a fight. Especially considering the new delights she had discovered in the bedroom with Meñique.

'I love him!' she shouted at the empty apartment, slapping her hand down on the mattress. 'Why is he leaving me here alone!'

She clambered out of bed, took her cigarettes and sat on the windowsill to light one. Below her was a wide tree-lined avenue swarming with people and cars. Four floors up, she could only hear the noise if she opened up the window, which she did, to let a plume of smoke filter gently out into the morning sunlight.

'I love it here!' she shouted down to the street. 'And I don't want to leave! How dare Meñique suggest I get another place?!' Throwing her cigarette stub out of the window, she walked naked through the apartment to put some water on to boil for her normal strong coffee. Just like Meñique, the rooms were small, immaculate and organised. 'He even cooks!' she murmured as she took a cup down from a shelf. 'I want him!'

Carrying her coffee into the sitting room, Lucía curled up in a chair to sip it, looking at his guitars neatly lined up along one wall. He was different from any other *gitano* she knew, having a *payo* mother and being brought up in Pamplona in the very north of Spain. His family had lived in a house – a house! – and he had grown up amongst the *payos*. Sometimes, Lucía felt like a wild animal in contrast to his calm sophistication. He did not see the *payos* as the enemy, as she had been taught to, but merely as a different breed.

'I am both, so I must embrace each culture, Lucía. And the

*payos* are the ones who will take both of us on to the success we crave,' he'd said to her one night as she'd ridiculed him for reading a *payo* newspaper. 'They have the power and the money.'

'They killed my brother,' she'd shouted at him. 'How can I ever forgive them for that?'

'*Gitanos* also kill *gitanos*, *payos* kill *payos*,' Meñique had reminded her with a resigned shrug. 'I am sorry for your brother, it is a terrible thing that happened, but prejudice and bitterness get one nowhere in life, Lucía. You must forgive, as the Bible tells us to do.'

'Now you are a priest?!' she'd railed at him. 'Telling me to read the Bible? Are you trying to patronise me? You know I never learnt to read.'

'Then I will teach you.'

'I have no need of it!' She'd brushed off the arm that came around her. 'My body and soul is all I need.'

Yet Lucía knew deep down that Meñique was right. The crowds that were buying tickets in advance to see her perform were not *gitanos*, but *payos*, and it was their money that would pay the big weekly wage she had been offered.

Lucía stood up. 'He treats me just as Papá does!' she shouted to the guitars. 'Like an ignorant little *gitana* who understands nothing. And yet, he takes me three times a night to satisfy his lust! Mamá is right, men are all the same. Well, I'll show him!'

She drew back a foot and kicked out at a guitar. The strings twanged as it fell to one side. She looked at the ordered shelf of books and swiped at them with her hand, sending them tumbling to the floor. After walking back to the bedroom, she dressed for the first time in days in the flamenco gown that Meñique had stripped from her body. Picking up her shoes, she walked to the door of the apartment, opened it and left.

Having found the mess in the apartment when he'd returned home, Meñique sighed and headed for the Coliseum Theatre, where Lucía was due to have a rehearsal that afternoon.

Meñique found José smoking by the stage door, with the rest of the *cuadro* assembled inside.

'Is Lucía in the theatre already?' Meñique asked José.

'No, I thought she was with you,' José answered. 'No one has seen her.'

'*Mierda*,' Meñique swore under his breath. 'I left her in my apartment this morning . . . where would she have gone?'

'You tell me,' said José, barely keeping his anger under control. 'You were meant to be her keeper.'

'As you know, señor, no one can "keep" Lucía, especially if she is in a rage.'

'She opens next week! We arrived here to rehearse! After all this, will she miss her big chance?'

Meñique's brain was turning over the possibilities. 'Come with me, I think I know where she might be.'

Half an hour later, they arrived at the Plaza de Olavide, a hub of cafés and bars. And there in the centre of the plaza was Lucía, in the midst of a crowd that had gathered around her. Two random guitarists had joined her and as Meñique pushed through the mass of bodies, he heard the ping of coins landing on the ground around her. He stood there, arms folded, watching her dance. When she had finished, he and José joined in with the huge applause she received.

He watched her as she went to pick up the coins and indicated to the crowd that her performance was over.

'*Hola*, Lucía,' he said as he walked towards her. 'What are you doing here?'

Lucía finished collecting the coins, then stood up and looked at him, her eyes defiant.

'I was hungry, and I had no money for lunch. So I came here and got some. Now, shall we go to eat?'

Despite Lucía's reluctance to have her father in Madrid, she was at least pleased to see the rest of the *cuadro*.

'Chilly, have you brought my tonic?' she asked him, ignoring Rosalba, who was standing next to him.

'From the look of you, Lucía, I'd say that Madrid is suiting you well,' Chilly replied with a sly smile. 'You are happy?'

'I am never happy, but yes, Madrid has its benefits,' Lucía agreed.

Over the following few days, the *cuadro* found an apartment in the city and José began to hold auditions to extend their troupe of guitarists, singers and dancers. After several long afternoons in the empty theatre, they had found their new members.

Sebastian was a guitar player who bought everyone drinks and cigarettes, although it soon emerged that his fingers were as smooth at picking *payo* pockets as they were on his guitar. He had promised to keep his nose clean, but miraculously, he still had a steady flow of pesetas to share.

Sebastian's brother Mario, known as 'El Tigre', the tiger, was a lithe and masculine individual, who attacked every dance as if it were a bull to be taken down. He had been the only dancer Lucía felt could match her ferocious energy. Two other young female dancers were also engaged, chosen by Lucía simply because they were the plainest.

'So, daughter.' José raised a glass to Lucía after their first run-through with the orchestra. 'Tomorrow, the Albaycín *cuadro* opens at the Coliseum.'

'And so do I,' Lucía whispered as she toasted him.

During the next few months, Lucía's fame spread. Queues formed at the Coliseum box office; everyone wanted to see the enchanting young *gitana* who danced in men's clothes.

Finally, Lucía Amaya Albaycín was becoming a star.

Although she missed the sea and the culture of Barcelona that so suited her *gitana* spirit, Lucía loved Madrid, with its grand white buildings and wide avenues. There was a sense of urgency and passion in the air, what with the daily rallies of the various *payo* political parties, each attempting to drum up support, most of them disgruntled after the Republicans had won the elections that November. Even though Meñique often tried to explain to her what all these men were shouting about, she would laugh and kiss him on the lips to stop him talking.

'I am bored of *payos* fighting each other,' she would say, 'let us watch a *payo* square off against a bull!'

'This place is a pigsty,' Meñique had remarked the first time he'd visited her room in the *cuadro*'s apartment. Sardine bones and other food scraps festered on plates that were piled high in an overflowing sink, and dirty clothes lay where she had dropped them days ago.

'Yes, but it is my pigsty, and it makes me happy,' she'd said, as she kissed him.

At times, Meñique felt as if he was trying to tame a wild animal; at others, he wished to protect the vulnerable little girl Lucía could so easily become. Whichever she was, he was totally entranced by her.

The problem was, so was the whole of Madrid. Now, rather than Meñique, the famous guitarist, being the centre of attention when they were out in the city together, it was Lucía everyone wanted to meet.

'How does it feel to be the most famous *gitana* dancer in the whole of Spain?' he asked her one morning as they lay in bed at his apartment.

'It is what I always expected.' She shrugged nonchalantly, lighting a cigarette. 'I have waited a long time for this.'

'Some have to wait a lifetime and still it never comes, Lucía.'

'I have earned it, every second of it,' she replied fiercely.

'So now you can be happy?'

'Of course not!' Her head lolled back against his shoulder and he smelt the scent of the oil she used to smooth down her hair. 'La Argentinita has captured the world! Me, only Spain. There is much more to do yet.'

'I'm sure there is, *pequeña*,' he sighed.

'Did I tell you that I have been asked to dance in a film? It is some *payo* filmmaker – Luis Buñuel. I hear he is very good. Should I do it?'

'Of course you must! Then your talent will be captured forever for generations to see when you are dead.'

'I will never die,' Lucía retorted. 'I will live forever. Now, *querido*, we must both get dressed and go and meet my new *payo* friends for lunch in one of their fancy restaurants. I am guest of honour! Can you believe it?'

'I can believe anything of you, Lucía, truly,' Meñique said as Lucía pulled him out of bed.

# Madrid

## July 1936, two years later

# 24

'What has happened?' Lucía lit a cigarette and leant back against the pillows, the sunlight spilling across them from the window of her room.

'There has been a coup in Morocco,' Meñique said without looking up from his newspaper. 'There is talk that the uprising will spread here any day soon. Perhaps we should leave Spain while the going is good.'

'What uprising? What is there to rise up against?' Lucía frowned.

He sighed deeply. He had done his best to explain the fraught situation in Spain to her, but Lucía did not have a political bone in her body. Her days were occupied with dancing, smoking, making love and eating her beloved sardines, in that order of importance.

'Franco wants to take over Spain with his armies,' he told her patiently. 'He wishes to turn Spain into a fascist state, just as the Nazis are doing in Germany.'

'I am so bored of these politics, Meñique, who cares?' She yawned and stretched, her little fist bumping into his face.

'*I* care – and you should too, *pequeña* – because it affects everything we do. We should think about going to Portugal early – you are due to perform there very soon anyway. I fear that Madrid will be at the centre of any struggle to come. There could be violence.'

'I cannot go to Portugal when I still have my show at the Coliseum. People have been queuing around the block for tickets. I must not let them down.'

'Well, if nothing changes we shall leave straight after that. Let us hope it will not be too late by then,' muttered Meñique as he got out of bed.

'They will not harm me, I am the darling of Spain,' Lucía called after him. 'Maybe they will crown *me* queen instead!'

Meñique rolled his eyes as he found his shirt and trousers in the rubble of the room. Sadly, he could not disagree about her fame. Not only had she been a roaring success in Madrid, but accepting the title role in the most expensive Spanish film ever produced had cemented her national status as a household name.

'I'm going back to my apartment for some peace and quiet,' he told her as he kissed her. 'I will see you later.' He left Lucía's room and walked along the communal corridor of the apartment, tripping over a cup of day-old coffee that Lucía had left in the middle of the floor. 'Infuriating,' he muttered as he used his handkerchief to mop up the spillage.

Not only did Lucía live in her own private state of chaos, but also with a houseful of ever-changing people – some of them friends or family, others merely acolytes who hung around her. Perhaps it was simply the way she'd been brought up; a large family in Sacromonte, then living for years in the tight-knit community of the Barrio Chino. Lucía seemed to need people around her constantly.

'I am afraid of being alone,' she'd admitted once to him. 'Silence, it scares me.'

Well, it didn't scare him – after two and a half years with Lucía, he relished it.

Entering the stillness of his own apartment, Meñique gave a sigh of relief and wondered for the hundredth time what would become of the two of them. It was obvious that the whole of Spain – and especially Lucía herself – was waiting for him to marry her. Yet he was still to ask. They had separated numerous times after Lucía had erupted at his lack of a proposal. He would walk away from her, relief filling his soul that he was no longer on the roller coaster of his relationship with her, her career and her crazy lifestyle.

'She's impossible!' he'd tell himself, 'no one but a saint can deal with her!'

Then, after a few hours of the peace he'd yearned for, he'd calm down. A few hours after that, he'd begin to long for her until he had to crawl back and beg forgiveness.

'Yes, I will buy you a ring,' he'd say when Lucía stood there with her eyes ablaze, and then they'd make love hungrily, passionately, both relieved that the pain of separation was over. All would be serene until the next time Lucía's patience ran out and they would go round in the same cycle yet again.

Why he could not make that final commitment, Meñique did not know. Equally, why he could never finally walk away was a mystery to him. Was it the raw sexual attraction he experienced when he thought of her? Or the aphrodisiac provided by her sublime talent when he watched her perform? *It was all of her*, was the only conclusion he could reach. *She was simply . . . Lucía.* Sometimes it felt to him as though the two of them were trapped in an eternal *paso doble* from which they could never escape.

'It isn't love, it is addiction,' Meñique murmured as he tried to focus on a melody he was struggling to compose. His concentration was non-existent and this, he thought, was another problem: being with Lucía was a full-time job, which left him little time for pursuing his own career. When she had received the offer to perform in Lisbon, she had not even asked him whether he wanted to go – just assumed that he would.

'Perhaps I should stay behind,' he told his guitar. 'Let her go.' Then he looked out of the window and took in the alarming sight of armed soldiers marching down the street beneath him. If civil war did break out in Spain, it was a dangerous moment to be parted, and besides that, Lucía's rag-tag retinue of dancers and musicians did not have a clue about the real world beyond flamenco. They'd probably end up in jail, or facing a firing squad for saying the wrong thing.

But was that *his* problem? If it was, he had made it so.

Meñique yawned. They hadn't returned until the early hours from the party held after Lucía's sell-out performance last night. He laid his guitar carefully on the table, then stretched out full-length on the couch and closed his eyes. Yet, even though he was exhausted, he could not sleep. He was filled with an impending sense of doom.

'What is all that noise outside?' Lucía asked him as he came into her dressing room at the Coliseum the following evening.

'It's heavy artillery, Lucía.' Meñique listened to the rumbling and felt fear clutch at his heart. 'I fear the uprising has begun.'

'The theatre is still empty, yet it is nearly opening time. I was told tonight was sold out.'

'It isn't safe on the streets, Lucía. The sensible people are staying in their homes. Many of those who did come have already left. We should decide whether to cancel the performance and make our way home while we can. After all, it is our last, and given we are due to leave for Lisbon tomorrow—'

'I have never cancelled a performance in my life and I never will! Even if only the cleaners watch.' Standing there in full stage make-up, her face was even more luminous than usual. 'No *payo* military will stop me dancing!' she insisted.

As she spoke, the sound of a huge explosion from somewhere in the city made the sturdy walls of the theatre shudder. A handful of plaster dust fell on Lucía's jet-black hair, and she grabbed Meñique in panic.

'*¡Ay, Dios mío!* What is happening out there?'

'I believe the Nationalists are attempting to take control of the city. The army garrison is so very close to the theatre . . . really, Lucía, we should leave now and get to Lisbon while we can.'

The rest of the company had begun to appear in the dressing room, terror on their faces.

'Perhaps it is too late to leave, Meñique,' said José, overhearing. 'I just took a look outside, and there are people running everywhere. It's chaos!' He crossed himself out of habit.

Chilly pushed through the anxious throng and grasped Lucía's hands, his features alive with fear. 'Lucía, Rosalba is alone in the apartment. You know she stayed home today because of her ankle sprain! I must go to her, she could be in terrible danger!'

'You cannot go out there.' Sebastian, the guitarist, clasped Chilly's arm to calm him. 'Rosalba is a sensible woman, she will stay where she is in the apartment. You should remain here, then you can go to her in the morning.'

'I have to go to her now! Stay safe tonight and, God willing, we will meet again in this life.' Chilly gave Lucía a brief kiss on each cheek, then swiftly ran from the dressing room.

The *cuadro* stood together, shell-shocked by Chilly's sudden departure.

Meñique cleared his throat. 'We must find shelter. Does anyone know if there is a basement?'

A woman holding a broom had appeared in the doorway of the dressing room, her features taut. Meñique turned to her. 'Señora, can you help us?'

'*Sí*, señor, I will show you the entrance to the cellar. We can take shelter down there.'

'Right,' Meñique said as the rattle of gunfire made the pack in the dressing room start in further fright. 'Everyone, take what you can to make yourselves comfortable, then we shall follow you down, señora.'

After gathering what they could salvage, the woman with the broom led the *cuadro* to the cellar door. From a cupboard along the corridor, she'd produced two boxes of candles and some matches.

'Is everybody here?' Meñique called along the passage.

'Where is Papá?' Lucía said in a panic as her eyes searched for him.

'I am here, *querida*,' a voice replied from the steps that led from the auditorium. José emerged, his arms full of bottles. 'I went to the bar in the foyer for supplies.'

'Hurry now!' Meñique urged him as another blast shook the walls and the lights along the corridor flickered and died. Candles were hastily lit and passed from hand to hand.

'Now we descend into *el infierno*,' José joked, raising a bottle to his mouth as they took the steps downwards.

'How can it be so cold down here when the air is so warm above?' Lucía asked no one in particular as they all made themselves as comfortable as they could in the damp cellar.

'At least we are safe here,' Meñique said.

'What about Chilly?' demanded El Tigre, pacing the floor, unable to keep still. 'He has gone out there – maybe to his death!'

'Chilly is a *brujo*,' said Juana. 'His sixth sense will keep him safe,'

'*Ay*, maybe, but what about us? We shall be trapped down here, the building collapsing on us!' wailed Sebastian.

'And there may not be enough brandy for everyone,' added José, clanking his bottles to the floor.

'This is what it all comes to.' El Tigre shook his head. 'We shall die here and be forgotten.'

'*Never!*' said Lucía, trembling now. 'I shall never be forgotten!'

'Here, señorita, you must stay warm.' The broom lady took off her thin apron and wrapped it like a shawl around Lucía's bare shoulders.

'*Gracias*, señora, but I have a better way to keep warm . . .'

Half of her sentence was drowned out by an explosion that felt as though it came from directly above them. '*Señores y señoras*.' Lucía shouted to be heard as she lifted her arms above her. 'As the *estupidos payos* explode this beautiful city, we *gitanos* will dance!'

Of all the memories Meñique would hold of his Lucía in the future, the hours trapped in the cellar of the Teatro Coliseum while the beginning of Spain's destruction began in earnest were the most vivid.

She roused the terrified *cuadro* to standing, insisting that the men pick up their guitars and that the women dance. As the army garrison was attacked by the Nationalists, the noise of the guns was drowned out by a dozen *gitanos* celebrating their ancient art, a lady with a broom as their only audience.

At four in the morning, the city fell silent, and, fuelled by fear, exhilaration and the alcohol José had brought with him, the *cuadro* sank to the floor and slept.

Meñique woke first, feeling dazed from the effects of too much brandy. It took him some time to work out where he was – it was pitch black – and when he did, he reached around the floor to find the candles that he'd stowed under his jacket last night. Lighting one, he saw everyone was still asleep, Lucía's head lolling against his shoulder. Gently moving her to lie on his jacket, he took the candle, and, disoriented, searched for the steps that led upwards to the door. It took all his courage to push it open, knowing if he couldn't that everyone in the cellar was already the living dead, buried under what rubble remained of the theatre above them.

Thankfully, it opened easily, and he stepped out into the passageway that led to the dressing rooms. All there was to show for the night's violence was some missing plaster from the ceiling. Meñique offered up a prayer of thanks, then walked along the passageway until he came to the stage door. Opening it slowly, he peered outside.

The air was still thick with dust from the endless explosions, and the silence of the usually bustling city was eerie. He looked up and saw that the building opposite was scarred by bullets and grenades, the windows shattered. Meñique stifled a sob. He knew that this was the beginning of the end for his beloved Spain.

He returned to the cellar in a daze and regarded the peacefully sleeping *cuadro*.

'I'm thirsty,' Lucía said as he shook her gently awake. 'Where are we?'

'We are safe, *pequeña*, and that is what is important. I will go upstairs to the bar and see if I can find some water.'

'Don't leave me.' Lucía clung to him, her nails like talons against his skin.

'Then come with me, and help.'

The two of them took the steps up to the theatre, using their candles to find their way through the deserted auditorium and out into the bar.

Lucía piled chocolates on top of the boxes that Meñique had filled with jugs of water.

'All this for free,' she exclaimed, despite the circumstances obviously delighted as she stuffed the expensive confectionery into her mouth.

'You know that you can buy as many chocolates as you want to, don't you?'

'Yes, but that isn't the point,' she shrugged.

Downstairs in the cellar, its inhabitants were waking up,

assessing where they and Spain found themselves this morning.

'We must leave for Lisbon as soon as we can,' Lucía pronounced. 'How can we get there?'

'More to the point, how can we get the papers to *take* us across the border?' asked Meñique.

'And how can I get to the apartment to get the money I've hidden under the floorboards?' grunted José.

In the end, it was decided that Meñique and José would venture out and try to make their way to their apartments to take what they needed, leaving the rest in relative safety.

'I will come with you,' declared Lucía. 'I cannot arrive in Lisbon without my wardrobe.'

'There will be no room for that, Lucía. No, you stay here and behave yourself. No one leaves but me and José, okay?'

'Okay,' the occupants of the cellar chorused.

Meñique and José ventured out into the street, José seeing what Meñique had already witnessed. 'What have they done?' he said in horror as they hurried down a street where a few dazed residents had also ventured out. 'And which side are we on?'

'Our own, José, our own. Now, let's get to that apartment.'

Thanking God that they lived only a couple of streets away, José went to retrieve the *cuadro*'s papers, his sack of pesetas and two of Lucía's dresses, whilst Meñique went to perform a similar salvage exercise at his own apartment.

After gathering what he could, Meñique glanced down from the window and saw that the streets below him were still silent, so on impulse he grabbed the keys to his car then set off in the direction of Chilly and Rosalba's apartment, a ten-minute drive away. He had travelled less than three hundred metres before he spotted the military road block. In anguish that he was unable to ascertain his friends' safety, but mindful that Lucía was waiting for him back at the theatre, he made a swift U-turn and drove the short distance to the Albaycíns' apartment, praying that he would still be able to get through. As he arrived, José stumbled down the stairs with all he could carry and they piled it onto the back seat.

'Hide any valuables in your clothes for safekeeping in case we are stopped.'

José did so, but placed the large sack of pesetas between his legs in the passenger seat. 'Even I cannot fit that in my trousers,' he said, rolling his eyes.

They set off along the street, and had only travelled a few metres before they saw an army truck appear from a side road. A hand was held up, and Meñique brought the car to a halt.

'*Buenos días, compadre.* Where are you heading?' asked a uniformed officer as he descended from the truck and approached the car.

'To the theatre to pick up our family, who were stranded there during the troubles last night,' Meñique explained.

The man peered into the car, his beady eyes fixed on the sack between José's legs.

'Get out of the car now!'

Both occupants did so as the soldier pointed his gun at their chests.

'Hand me the keys. I am taking your car for the use of the military. Now get on with you.'

'But . . . my daughter is Lucía Albaycín!' José cried. 'She must have her dresses to wear for tonight's performance.'

'There will be no performance tonight,' the soldier said. 'A curfew will be in place by sunset.'

'But the car, my mother, she is old and ailing and—'

The soldier jabbed José's chest with the muzzle of his gun. 'Shut up, *gitano*! I have no time to stand and argue. Move on or I will shoot you where you stand.'

'Come, José,' said Meñique. '*Gracias, capitán*, and *viva la republica*.' He put his arm through José's and dragged him away from the car, not daring to look back into the soldier's line of sight until they were safely around the corner. When they were, José sank to his knees and sobbed.

'Everything we had! It is all gone!'

'Nonsense! We escaped with our lives.'

'Twenty thousand pesetas, twenty thousand . . .'

'And you will earn it again, a hundred times over. Now, get up and let us return to the theatre and work out how we leave Spain.'

Everyone crowded around them as they arrived back down in the cellar at the theatre. José was still sobbing inconsolably.

'I should have left it where it was,' he moaned, 'or put it in a bank . . .'

'I wouldn't worry,' El Tigre said. 'By tomorrow, the peseta will be as worthless as a grain of sand on the beach.'

Lucía grabbed Meñique's hand. 'Did you bring my dresses?'

He frowned at her. 'No, but I did try to look for Chilly.'

Lucía looked momentarily chastened. 'Did you find him?'

'It was not possible to reach his apartment. There are too many soldiers on the streets. All we can do for now is plan our own escape and hope Chilly can follow us to Lisbon later.'

'Will the trains be running?' she asked him.

'Even if they were, we have no money to pay for tickets to Portugal.'

'There will be a safe here,' piped up Sebastian. 'It will be in the office, they always are.'

'And how would you know that, señor?' questioned Lucía with a suspicious glance in his direction.

'It is only instinct,' he replied innocently.

'And if there is a safe, how would we know how to get into it?'

'Again, señorita, I think my instinct might guide me.'

Sebastian was despatched upstairs with Broom Lady, whose name was revealed as Fernanda and who knew exactly where the safe was, whilst the others discussed the best way to flee from the stricken capital.

'And what's to become of those who stay?' Lucía shook her head. '¡Ay! Our country is destroying itself. What of Mamá? My brothers and their families?'

'If we manage to find a way to leave, then perhaps we can send for them.'

Fernanda arrived back with a satisfied-looking Sebastian, who pulled a thick wedge of banknotes and a large handful of coins from his pockets.

'Unfortunately, they must have been to the bank yesterday morning, but at least we have plenty for tickets out of here,' Sebastian said.

'The question is where? And how?'

Fernanda muttered something in Lucía's ear.

'She says her brother is a bus driver. He has a set of keys because his shift is in the early morning when no one else is up.'

The entire company stared at Fernanda, who nodded.

'Where does he live?' asked Meñique.

'Just next door,' she replied. 'You want me to tell him to get his bus here?'

'Señora, perhaps it will not be quite as easy as that,' Meñique sighed. 'The city is in chaos and the military may have already taken over the bus station.'

'No, no, señor, the bus is parked around the corner at the stop.'

'Then please, señora, let me accompany you to see if your brother is prepared to drive us to the border.'

'He will require payment,' she said, eyeing the coins and notes now piled on the floor of the basement.

'We have money, as you can see.'

'Then I will take you to him.' She nodded.

Meñique and Fernanda left. Within half an hour, they were back.

'He has agreed,' Meñique announced, 'and he is bringing the bus round to the stage door to collect us all.'

A cheer went up and Fernanda was smothered in hugs and kisses.

'Someone blesses us,' Lucía smiled at Meñique.

'So far, but there is still a long way to go.'

Fernanda signalled to them all from outside the stage door when the bus arrived in front of it. They climbed aboard, their initial exhilaration that a route of escape had been found tempered by the sight of their beleaguered capital city.

'Do you know the way to the border?' Meñique asked Fernanda's brother, whose name was Bernardo.

'Trust me, señor, I could drive it blindfolded.'

'If he only lives next door, then why did his sister not

return to his apartment last night?' Meñique muttered as he sat down next to Lucía.

'Maybe on the night that Madrid came under fire, Fernanda was having the best fun of her life,' she smiled.

The passengers on the bus soon fell silent as Bernardo – who sported a long grey beard and curls beneath his busman's cap – drove steadily, expertly weaving around piles of rubble and the gaping craters that had appeared in the wide roads.

'Madrid brought to its elegant knees by the violence of a few.' Meñique shook his head. 'Even if the socialist part of me agrees that the Nationalists must be defeated, who could have ever imagined this?'

'What does "socialist" mean?' Lucía asked. She had curled herself up, rested her head on his knee and closed her eyes, unable to cope with the scenes around her.

'Well, *pequeña*, it is complicated; there are two sides in this war,' Meñique said, stroking her hair. 'There are the socialists – people like us, who work hard, and want the country to run in a fair way – and then there are the Nationalists, who want the King back in Spain . . .'

'I liked the King – I danced for him once, you know.'

'I know you did, *pequeña*. Well, the Nationalists are being led by a man called Franco, who is good friends with Hitler in Germany, and Mussolini in Italy . . . From what I've heard, Franco wants to control who we worship, how we work, our very lives.'

'I would never let anyone tell me what to do,' Lucía whispered.

'I fear that if he gains control of our army as well as that of Morocco, then even you cannot stand against a man like Francisco Franco,' Meñique sighed. 'Now, go to sleep.'

In Bernardo's capable hands, the bus rumbled on. He obviously knew the city like the back of his hand and Meñique wondered what angel had sent him and his sister to them. They could not have dreamt up a more innocuous form of transport to carry them over the border. Soon, they were free of the city and driving through open countryside. Bernardo avoided the villages and towns, weaving his way through fields and woodland, just in case.

It was dusk when they finally arrived at the small border town of Badajoz. It was crammed with vehicles of all kinds, and the queue for the border control wound like a snake along the main road. There were automobiles and carts laden with the contents of people's houses pulled by tired mules, and many on foot; women carrying their young children, men carrying their most precious possessions.

'What is taking so long?' Lucía demanded impatiently. 'Can they not see we are trying to get through?' She got up and walked to the front of the bus then pressed down on the horn. It blared out into the street, startling those who were walking ahead of them.

'*Pequeña*, please, have some patience, and let us not attract too much attention to ourselves,' Meñique said to Lucía as he pulled her back into her seat.

It was midnight before they pulled up at the border and Bernardo calmly handed over the company's papers to the guard, who had climbed up onto the bus.

'Why are you trying to enter Portugal?' he asked the passengers.

'Why, to dance!' Lucía stood up, sashaying forward.

'I am sorry, señora, but our orders are to let only Portuguese nationals across today.'

'Then I must marry a Portuguese man. Perhaps you, señor?' she smiled up at him.

'We are here because the Lucía Albaycín *cuadro* have a contract to work in Lisbon,' Meñique added hastily, nodding to José, who swiftly produced the contract. The young guard stared down at Lucía, recognition dawning.

'I saw your film,' he said, blushing as he looked at her.

'*Gracias*, señor.' Lucía swept an elegant curtsey.

'So, I will let you through, but the others will have to turn back.'

'But, señor, how can I perform if I do not have my guitar players and my dancers and singers?' Lucía clapped at the *cuadro*. 'Show the señor how we play!'

Grabbing their guitars from beneath their seats, José, Sebastian and Meñique immediately began to play as Juana sang.

'You see?' She turned back to the border guard. 'The Teatro da Trindade in Lisbon waits for us! How can I disappoint that wonderful city? But no.' Lucía shook her head. 'I must return to Spain with my friends. I cannot go without them. Driver, turn around.'

Bernardo started the engine as Lucía started to walk back to her seat.

'Okay, okay, I will let you pass.' The guard wiped the sweat from his brow. 'But I will put you on the records as arriving yesterday, or I will have trouble from my boss.'

'Oh! Señor!' Lucía turned back and gave him a dazzling smile, then reached up to plant a kiss on his cheek. 'You are too kind. We thank you, Portugal thanks you, and you must come to the stage door to collect tickets for the show this week.'

'Can I bring my mother?' the guard asked. 'She loved your film.'

'*¡Sí!* Bring your whole family.'

The young man left the bus, blushing profusely, and Bernardo closed the doors.

'*Drive*, Bernardo!' mumbled Meñique as he saw another border guard wearing a crested cap approaching their new friend as he waved them through. Five or six kilometres beyond the border, Bernardo drove the bus into a field before turning a sharp left and pulling to a halt in front of a small farmhouse. He slumped over the wheel as Fernanda stood up to minister to him.

'Bernardo says he has had enough and can drive no further. We will rest here for the night.'

'Is he sick?' Meñique asked in concern.

'No, he tells me he is too old for all this excitement,' replied Fernanda.

'Where is this?' Lucía sat up and looked around her, slightly dazed.

'The home of our cousin,' confirmed Fernanda.

Everyone climbed off the bus as a sleepy middle-aged man and his wife and children appeared at the front door and stared in surprise at the women, still in their flamenco dresses. Bernardo explained the situation to his cousin, and even though it was now almost one in the morning, soon the entire company was sitting down at the back of the farm to a meal of fresh bread, cheese, and olives recently harvested from the trees.

'It feels like a party, but I know it isn't,' Lucía mumbled to no one in particular. She lit a cigarette as the rest of the company finished eating. José too was quiet, no doubt still struggling to come to terms with the loss of his precious pesetas.

Eventually, the *cuadro* settled onto blankets in an open field around a small fire, Lucía lying in Meñique's arms and gazing up at the bright stars in the black sky above her.

'Out here you can believe that what happened in Madrid last night was just a bad dream,' Lucía sighed. 'Everything is exactly the same.'

'Well, let us pray that we will one day be able to return.'

'If not, we shall simply live on the farm with Fernanda's cousins and I will dance while I harvest the olives. Somehow, we made it here.'

'We did.' Meñique nodded.

'All except Chilly, of course.' Lucía bit her lip. 'Will we see him again?'

'That I cannot say. All we can do is keep him and Rosalba in our prayers.'

'And what do you think will happen to Spain, Meñique?'

'God only knows, *pequeña*.'

'Will it spread through the country? If it does, I must find a way to get Mamá and my brothers out. I cannot leave them behind.'

'Let's just take one day at a time, shall we?' He stroked her hair and kissed the top of it. '*Buenas noches*, Lucía.'

They arrived in Lisbon the following afternoon, bedraggled and exhausted from the long drive.

'We must find somewhere to stay. I cannot go and see Señor Geraldo looking and stinking like a pig,' Lucía pronounced.

'What is the best hotel in Lisbon?' she asked Bernardo, who was a fount of knowledge about everything here, due to his mother being Portuguese.

'The Avenida Palace.'

'Then we shall stay there,' she said.

'Lucía, we have no money,' José reminded her.

'Which is why I must get clean, then go and see the man who has hired us. He must make us a loan against our wages.'

José rolled his eyes, but ten minutes later the bus pulled up in front of a grand hotel, its imposing front doors flanked by two doormen in smart red uniforms.

'Wait here and I will go inside.' Lucía clambered down as Meñique hastily followed her. She marched past the doormen and through the marble-floored lobby to the reception desk.

'I am Lucía Albaycín,' she announced to a startled receptionist. 'Myself and my *cuadro* are here to perform in the Teatro da Trindade, and we need some rooms.'

The woman took one look at the street urchin in her filthy flamenco dress, and immediately called the manager.

'We have gypsies in reception,' she murmured as she led the manager out to the front desk.

The manager strode towards Lucía, ready for trouble, then did a double take and immediately smiled.

'Lucía Albaycín, I presume?'

'*Sí*, señor, I am only glad that someone in this godforsaken country recognises me.'

'It is an honour to have you here. I have seen your film three times,' the manager explained. 'Now, what can I do for you?'

Fifteen minutes later, the company were installed in a set of luxurious rooms. Lucía had been given a suite. She danced around it, stealing apples and oranges from the fruit bowl, along with two ashtrays and a bar of soap from the bathroom, then hiding them in a cupboard to take with her when she left.

'We must eat,' she declared as the rest of the company gathered in her room. 'Order from the menu for me, if you can understand the Portuguese for sardines, and I will take a bath.'

'I hope Geraldo is prepared to give us a loan; these rooms must cost the ransom for King Alfonso,' muttered José as he knocked back brandy from the bottle he'd found in the bar.

When room service arrived, they sat on the floor of the suite and ate hungrily with their fingers. Fernanda and Bernardo – who spoke fluent Portuguese – had been despatched to find Lucía something to wear for her meeting as her flamenco dress soaked in the bathtub.

'How do I look?' she asked Meñique an hour later, twirling in the red-spotted dress that Fernanda had found in the children's department of a local store.

'Lovely.' He smiled and kissed her. 'Shall I come with you?'

'No, it is better I go alone,' she said as she walked towards the door.

With Bernardo as her guard and translator if needed, Lucía found the offices of the impresario. The receptionist insisted he was out, but Lucía marched straight in.

'Geraldo,' she said as she walked towards the man sitting behind an elegant partners' desk. 'I am here!'

The heavily moustached man looked up from his paperwork and studied her. Eventually, recognition dawned, and he waved his anxious receptionist out of the room.

'Señorita Albaycín, how delightful to meet you in person,' he said in passable Spanish.

'And you, señor.'

'Please, sit down, and forgive my bad Spanish. Is this your father?' he asked, indicating Bernardo, who was standing sentry-like next to her.

'No. I brought him to translate, but I see there is no need.' Lucía waved her hand imperiously towards Bernardo. 'Thank you, you can wait outside now. So, where is the theatre I am to perform at?'

'I . . .' He stared at her as though she'd appeared in a dream. 'I must admit, I am surprised to see you here.'

'We would not let you down, señor,' Lucía smiled, sitting in the chair opposite him. 'Why are you surprised?'

'Madrid of course . . . the Nationalist attack . . . I did not think that you were able to come. You were meant to open here last night.'

'I know that, señor, but you can imagine it was a little difficult to leave the country. We are here now, and that is all that matters. We came with the clothes we stood up in. Our money was taken by the military, so I must ask you to make us a loan against our wages for accommodation.'

'Well now' – the impresario mopped his brow – 'when I heard a few days ago what was happening, I, having heard nothing from you, assumed that you would not be coming. So, I have' – he cleared his throat – 'employed another company who were . . . available. They opened last night and were a success, so I hear.'

'Then I am happy for them, señor, but now you will have to un-employ them, sí? We are here, as promised.'

'Señorita, I understand, but you are late and I have . . . well, I have cancelled your contract.'

Lucía frowned at him. 'Señor, perhaps I do not understand

you fully due to the difficulty of translation. Surely you did not say that you have cancelled our contract?'

'I am afraid that I did, Señorita Albaycín. We could not let the theatre stand empty last night. I am sorry you have come such a long way, but the contract stipulated you would arrive in time for the technical rehearsal and you did not.' He stood and went to a filing cabinet, leafed through it, and pulled out a document. 'Here.' He passed it across the desk.

Lucía glanced down at it, the words meaningless on the page. She took a deep breath, as Meñique had taught her to do, before she spoke.

'Señor, do you know who I am?'

'I do, señorita, and it is most unfortunate—'

'It is not "unfortunate"! It is a disaster. Do you know what we have done to get here to Lisbon to perform in your the-atre?!'

'No, señorita, but I can only guess and salute your brav-ery.'

'Señor,' Lucía stood, put her tiny fists on the leather-topped desk and leant forward so her eyes were only centimetres away from his. 'To fulfil our contract, we risked our lives. We had everything we owned taken by the military, and you are sitting there in your big comfortable chair, telling me that our contract is cancelled?!'

'I am sorry, señorita. Please understand that the news from Spain was not good.'

'And please understand, señor, that you leave us penniless, with no work in a strange country!'

He looked at her and shrugged. 'There is nothing I can do.'

Lucía slammed her fists down on the table. 'So be it!' She turned from him with such speed that tendrils of her long hair whipped across his face. She walked towards the door, then paused and turned back.

'You will be sorry for what you have done to me today.' She pointed a finger at him. 'I curse you, señor, I curse you!'

As she left, the impresario shuddered involuntarily and reached for the decanter of brandy that sat on his desk.

Back at the hotel, Sebastian the safecracker was instructed to empty his pockets of all the pesetas he had stolen, minus what they had paid to Bernardo for bringing them here.

'How much for each room?' Meñique asked Lucía.

'The manager didn't say. He believes I am a film star and so rich I do not need to know. Hah!'

Meñique was despatched to find out the prices from the tariff board behind the reception desk. He returned, shaking his head.

'We have enough to cover the cost of one of the smaller rooms. For one night.'

'Then we must find a way to earn the rest,' said Lucía. 'Meñique, will you accompany me downstairs for a drink at the bar?'

'Lucía, we do not have the money to drink in a place like this.'

'Don't worry, we will not be paying. I will just renew my make-up and we shall go.'

Downstairs, the large, elegant bar was packed. Lucía's eyes searched the room as Meñique reluctantly ordered them both a drink and, propped up on barstools, she raised her glass. 'To us, *querido*, and our miraculous escape.' She chinked her glass against his. 'Now, try to relax and look as if you are enjoying yourself,' she added through clenched teeth.

'What are we doing here? We cannot afford this extravagance, Lucía, and . . .'

'The great and good of Lisbon must come to this bar. Someone will know of me and help us.'

As if on cue, a deep male voice rang out behind her. 'Señorita Lucía Albaycín! Is it really you?'

Lucía turned and looked into the eyes of a man who seemed vaguely familiar.

'*Sí*, señor, it is.' Lucía extended her hand to him as regally as any queen. 'Have we met before?'

'No, my name is Manuel Matos and my brother, Antonio Triana, is acquainted with you, I believe.'

'Antonio! Of course, what a wonderful dancer he is. I performed with him once in Barcelona. Why, how is he?'

'I am waiting for news of him from Spain. I believe that things are difficult there.'

'Yes, but as you can see, not so difficult that we haven't arrived safely here.'

'Then your presence amongst us gives me hope for my brother's safety. You are performing here in Lisbon?'

'We were contracted to, yes, but we looked at the venue and found it unsuitable.'

'Really? So, you will move on? To Paris maybe?'

'Perhaps, but myself and the company find Lisbon so very pleasant. And of course the hotel,' Lucía wafted her tiny hand around the bar, 'has been wonderfully accommodating during our stay.'

'I must introduce you to my friends at the Café Arcadio.

There are many there who would love to see you perform before you leave.'

'Well, if we have time, señor, we would love to do so.'

'Then I will take you there tomorrow. Would seven in the evening suit?'

'Can we fit it in?' Her eyes fell on Meñique.

'I am sure we can find space in our busy diary if you wish, señor,' he replied tightly.

'We must, Agustín,' Lucía said firmly, making a point of using his given name, 'as a favour to an old friend. So, we will come at seven, yes?'

'I will let my friends know.'

'Now, you must forgive us, but we have a dinner engagement, señor.' Lucía drained her glass and stood up.

'Of course. Until tomorrow, then,' Manuel said with a bow before Meñique followed Lucía out of the bar.

'Where are we going?' Meñique asked her as they left the hotel and began to walk along the pavement.

'Out for our dinner date of course.' Lucía kept walking until she reached the end of the building, then led Meñique down the alley at the side of the hotel. 'I'm sure there must be a staff entrance we can use to slip back inside and sneak up to our room,' she added.

Meñique grabbed her hand, forced her to a halt, and pinned her to the stone of the wall behind them.

'Lucía Albaycín, you are impossible!'

Then he kissed her.

# 25

The following evening, having used the bathtub in Lucía's suite to wash their stinking costumes, the *cuadro* walked through the streets of Lisbon to the Café Arcadio. The grandeur of Lisbon rivalled that of Madrid, and the Café Arcadio, with its regal art nouveau front, immediately indicated the wealth of its clientele. Manuel was waiting for them outside, wearing an immaculate black dinner suit and bow tie.

'You made it!' he said, embracing Lucía.

'*Sí*, señor, but we cannot stay for long, as we have been asked to dance elsewhere later. May we come inside?'

'Of course, but . . .'

'Is there a problem, señor?' Meñique had picked up on the man's reticence.

'The manager, well, it seems he is not a fan of . . . flamenco.'

'You mean, he doesn't like *gitanos*?' Lucía rounded on him. 'Then I will speak to him.'

Lucía pushed past Manuel and opened the door to the café. Inside, the air was filled with smoke and chatter, which ceased as Lucía made her way through the tables to the bar at the back.

'Where is the manager?' she demanded of a waiter pouring drinks behind it.

'I . . .' The waiter looked on nervously as the rest of the *gitanos* crowded around Lucía. 'I will go and find him.'

'Lucía, don't, there are other places you can dance!' Meñique warned her. 'We will not perform where we are not wanted.'

'Look around, Meñique,' Lucía whispered under her breath, indicating the guests at the tables behind him with a small nod of her head. 'These are rich *payos*, and we need their money.'

The manager emerged, crossing his arms defensively, as if he was ready for a fight.

'Señor, I am Lucía Albaycín, and I have come with my *cuadro* to dance in your café. Señor Matos' – Lucía indicated Manuel – 'tells me you have many customers who are educated in the creative arts and would be appreciative of our craft.'

'That may well be, but no gypsies have ever performed in my café. Besides, I have no money to pay you.'

'You mean, señor, that you do not wish to pay us, for it is obvious from the suit you wear and the way that your customers are dressed that you live well.'

'Señorita Albaycín, the answer is no. Now please, I would ask you and your troupe to leave the café peacefully before I call the police.'

'Señor, by your perfect Spanish I know you are one of us, *sí*?'

'I am from Madrid, yes.'

'And do you know what has happened in our country? And what we have done to be here in Lisbon to perform for you?'

'I have heard about the problems of course, but I did not ask you to come—'

'Then I shall ask the customers themselves whether they wish to see me dance. And tell them how we have been forced into exile from our home country, only to be thrown out by one of our own!' Lucía turned from him and grabbed a chair from a nearby table. Using Meñique's shoulder, she hauled herself up onto it and clapped her hands together in a loud *palmas*. As her feet began to drum on the chair, and her clapping continued, the room fell silent as Lucía stepped onto the table, its occupants quickly swiping their glasses from it before the continual beating of her feet sent them flying.

'*¡Olé!*' she shouted.

'*¡Olé!*' repeated her *cuadro* and the odd member of the audience.

'Now, *señores y señoras*, the manager does not wish us to dance for you. Yet we have come from Spain, risking our lives on the way to escape from our beloved homeland with nothing more than what we stand up in.'

Manuel translated Lucía's words into Portuguese.

'So, will you have me and my friends dance for you?'

She surveyed the audience.

'*Sim!*' came a response from one of the tables.

'*Sim!*' shouted another table, until the whole bar was with her.

'*Gracias.* Then we shall.'

As tables were cleared to make a space for the *cuadro*, the manager pulled Lucía aside.

'I will not pay you, señorita.'

'Tonight we dance for free, señor, but tomorrow' – Lucía

prodded him between his scrawny ribs – 'you will be begging to pay me.'

Meñique watched Lucía devour the bread and meat – the only sustenance the hotel had been able to rustle up at three in the morning. While he was dropping from fatigue, not only after tonight's performance, but from the trauma of the past few days, Lucía seemed unaffected, sitting on the floor and regaling the assembled company with their triumph of tonight.

*How does she do it?* he asked himself. She looked so fragile, yet her body seemed to be able to withstand the punishment she gave it, and her mind and emotions were like a steel trap that closed around anything unfortunate that had happened, allowing her to wake afresh to embrace each new day.

'So! Now we can stay here!' Lucía clapped her hands together like a child. 'And we can buy ourselves some new costumes. We must find some suitable fabric tomorrow, and then a dressmaker.'

'Maybe we can find a cheaper hotel, perhaps an apartment for us all . . .' murmured José.

'Papá, stop your worrying. Yesterday, we could have been thrown in jail by the hotel for taking rooms we have no money to pay for. Tonight we were cheered by hundreds. And word will spread, I promise you.' Lucía went to her father and hugged him. 'Another brandy, Papá?'

'You can celebrate, but I'm off to bed.' Meñique walked over to Lucía and kissed her on the top of her sleek dark hair.

It seemed that Lucía's confidence in winning a place in the hearts of the Portuguese had not been misplaced. Week after week, the crowds outside the Café Arcadio grew, with hundreds clamouring to enter and see the phenomenon that was La Candela. It was almost as if, faced with a new challenge, Lucía doubled the ferocity and passion of her performance. This, as well as the pathos of watching the very essence of the great neighbouring country being brought to its knees by civil war, only fuelled the fervour of the public for flamenco. Yet, as Lucía's public persona reached the great heights she longed for here, her private self became more and more desolate. Every morning, as she lay in bed in the suite, she would have Meñique read out the news from Spain and make him tell her what he heard whispered in the bars of Lisbon.

'They have murdered Lorca – our greatest poet – in Granada,' Meñique said bitterly. 'They will stop at nothing to destroy our country.'

'¡*Dios mío!* They have reached Granada! What will become of Mamá? My brothers?! As I sit here like a queen, maybe they are starving, or even dead! Perhaps I should contact Bernardo, ask him to drive me on his bus back to Granada . . .'

'Lucía, Spain is in chaos. You cannot return,' Meñique told her for the hundredth time.

'But I can't just leave them there! My mother sacrificed everything for her children! Maybe things are different in Pamplona, but in Sacromonte, family is everything.'

439

'Surely your mother is not your responsibility, *pequeña*? She is your father's.'

'You know as well as I do that Papá worships only money and the neck of a brandy bottle. He never took responsibility for Mamá, or for me or my brothers. What can we do for them?' Lucía wrung her sensitive hands as tears appeared in her eyes. 'You have many *payo* friends in high places.'

'They *were* in high places, Lucía, but who knows how far they have fallen by now?'

'Surely you could write to them? Find out how we get papers for my family to travel here? Please, I need your help. And if you won't give it, then I must return to Spain and help them myself.'

'No, it is too dangerous, *pequeña*. Salazar has been supporting Franco in Spain, and there are Nationalist spies everywhere here. If we were even to be caught whispering—'

'Who is this Salazar? How dare he spy on us!' Lucía cried.

'He is the Prime Minister of Portugal, Lucía. Do you not listen to anything I say?'

'Only if it is accompanied by your guitar, *mi amor*,' she replied honestly.

The following Sunday, with no performance that evening to rush back for, and worn down by Lucía's pleading, Meñique borrowed Manuel Matos's car and drove back towards the Spanish border. It had been over a month since he'd arrived in Portugal, and he only hoped he could remember the location of the farmhouse where they had taken refuge on the night they had crossed from Spain. Before Bernardo and Fernanda had left Lisbon, Bernardo had told him they would not be returning to

Spain. Instead, they would sit out the war with their relatives at the farm, who – from what Bernardo had intimated – were his long-time smuggling partners during the Great War.

'Tell him that whatever it costs him to go and to bribe the necessary officials, we will pay,' Lucía had told him.

Some hours later, and after a number of aborted trips down potholed tracks, Meñique arrived in front of a small farmhouse. To his relief, he recognised it.

'Now, I must pray that they are still here,' he said to himself as he stepped out of the car and went to knock on the door. A familiar figure opened it.

'Fernanda! Thank God!' Meñique breathed.

'What is wrong? Is Lucía ill?'

'No, no, it's nothing like that. Is Bernardo at home?'

'Yes, and we are eating cake. Come, señor.'

Meñique sat and listened as Bernardo and his cousin told him of the grim news they had heard from travellers crossing into Portugal from their war-torn homeland.

'It is chaos there. I have not been back since the Nationalists took the border at Badajoz. It is simply too dangerous.'

'Then you may not be able to help us.'

'What is it you need?' Fernanda nudged Bernardo with her elbow. 'Remember, it is only due to our friends from the theatre that we escaped in time.'

'Lucía has said that if I cannot find a way to help her family leave Spain, she will go to find them herself. And we all know that, Lucía being Lucía, it is not an idle threat. She has offered to pay whatever it takes.'

Bernardo looked at Ricardo, his cousin, who shook his head. 'Even for us it is too risky at this time.'

'Surely between the two of you and your connections in

Spain, there must be a way?' entreated Fernanda. 'Think if it was our mamá, Bernardo, you would do anything to help her.'

'Sometimes I think you want me dead, woman,' retorted Bernardo.

'We can get them papers,' Ricardo said, 'but the problem is Granada itself. Between the Civil Guard and the Black Squad, they're murdering citizens in their hundreds. They think nothing of pulling a man out onto the street and shooting him where he stands in front of his children. The city jail is overflowing and no one is safe, señor.'

'How do you know so much about the city?' Meñique eyed him.

'We have a relative who arrived here at the farm from Granada only a week ago.'

'How did he escape if the border is closed?'

'He hid in the backs of trucks and crossed near Faro.'

'Then there is a way,' said Meñique.

'There is always a way, señor,' Ricardo countered, 'but, to be brutal, even if we made it to the city, there is no telling whether we would find Señorita Albaycín's family alive. Her people – the people of Sacromonte – they have even fewer friends than normal civilians, as you know.'

'I do know, señor, but equally, they are used to that. Lucía is convinced her mother is alive and her instincts are normally right. Perhaps you could look into acquiring the papers the family might need to cross the border and think about whether you are prepared to help us.' Meñique pulled out the stack of escudos that Lucía had stolen from her father's hiding place. 'I will wait to hear if you are able to make the trip.' Meñique indicated a card on top of the heap of notes. 'Send me a telegram with your answer.'

'We will do our best, señor,' Bernardo said, eyeing the heavy sack of coins, then glancing at his sister and cousin. 'Goodbye for now.'

Three days later, Meñique received a telegram.

WE WILL GO STOP VISIT US SOON BEFORE WE
LEAVE STOP BERNARDO STOP

Both to the rest of the troupe and in front of her enraptured audiences, Lucía betrayed nothing of her anxiety. But alone with Meñique at night, as the days ticked by and there was no word from Bernardo, she would curl into his embrace like a child in need of protection.

'When will we hear? Every day that passes, I fear the worst.'

'Remember.' Meñique tipped her chin up to him. 'In this difficult life we lead on earth, all we have is hope.'

'Yes, I know and I must believe. *Te amo*, my darling.'

Meñique stroked her hair as she fell asleep in his arms, and thought that perhaps the only current blessing was that Lucía was at her most vulnerable; for the first time since he'd met her, he felt that they shared a secret fear that could not be voiced, and which bonded them. Never before had he felt he possessed her – felt the sense of togetherness that existed now as she lay in his arms. And for that at least, he was grateful.

It was six weeks later on a stormy day in the autumn of 1936 when a porter knocked on the door of their suite.

'Señor, you have . . . guests waiting for you downstairs. The manager suggests they come straight up.' The porter swallowed, looking embarrassed.

'Of course,' Meñique replied, handing the porter a tip for his trouble. 'We are expecting them.'

He closed the door and went to wake Lucía, who was still asleep even though it was past two o'clock in the afternoon. Last night there had been four encores, and they had not returned home until five in the morning.

'*Pequeña*, we have visitors.'

Lucía came to immediately and observed Meñique's expression.

'Is it them?'

'I don't know, he did not give their names, but . . .'

'*Dios mío*, please let it be Mamá, and not Bernardo arrived here to tell us she is dead . . .'

Five minutes later, Lucía had thrown on a pair of trousers and a blouse. She walked into the sitting room just as there was a knock on the door.

'Do you wish to answer it, or shall I?' Meñique asked her.

'You . . . no, me . . . yes.' She nodded, her small hands clenching into fists of anxiety as she walked towards the door.

He watched her cross herself as she took a deep breath and opened it. A few seconds later, he heard a scream of joy as Lucía led a skeletal woman and a young man holding a guitar inside and shut the door firmly behind her.

'Mamá is *here*! She is here! And so is my brother, Pepe!'

'Welcome.' Meñique stood up and walked over to them. 'May I get you some refreshment, Señora Albaycín?'

Meñique saw how María's body shook from the effort of simply remaining on her feet. The boy, who looked far healthier, gave him a shy smile.

'We must order a feast! Mamá tells me she hasn't eaten a proper meal for months,' Lucía said as she led her mother to a chair and helped her into it. 'What would you like to eat, Mamá? Anything you can think of, I can get for you.' Lucía knelt down and took the bird-like hands in her own.

Meñique saw that the woman was dazed, her eyes darting nervously round the luxurious room.

'Anything' – María cleared her throat of its hoarseness – 'anything will do, Lucía. Bread maybe. And water.'

'I will order everything on the menu!' Lucía announced.

'No really, just some bread.'

As Lucía summoned a bellboy, then proceeded to give him a list of everything they wanted, Meñique studied Lucía's mother, and the boy whom he presumed was Lucía's youngest brother. There was no doubt that he was José's son – he was the very image of his father. He clutched his guitar to him as though it were gold, as if it was all that he had left that belonged to him, which it probably was.

María's eyelids drooped as she sat in her chair, drawing down a blind over all the horrors they'd witnessed.

'So, the food is ordered,' said Lucía, advancing back into the room and seeing her mother asleep. 'Pepe, was it a terrible journey?'

'No,' said the boy, 'I have never been in a motor car before, so it was fun.'

'Did you have any problems along the way?' Meñique asked him.

'We were stopped only once. Bernardo, the driver, gave the

*policía* many pesetas and they waved us on.' Pepe smiled. 'They had a gun though, and were ready to shoot.'

'Bernardo or the police?'

'Both,' he said, his eyes huge in his thin face.

'Pepe . . .' Lucía went and knelt by him, whispering so as not to disturb her mother. 'Where are Eduardo and Carlos? Why did they not come with you?'

'I don't know where my brothers are. Carlos went into the city to his furniture shop a few weeks ago and never came back, then Eduardo went to try and find him and he disappeared too.' Pepe shrugged.

'But what about their wives and children? Why have they not come with you?'

'None of them would leave without knowing what had happened to their husbands and fathers.'

Lucía turned and saw María's eyes were now open as she spoke. 'I tried to persuade them, but they refused.'

'Well, perhaps they will follow you when Eduardo and Carlos have been found.'

'If they are ever found.' María sighed deeply. 'Hundreds of men are missing in Granada, Lucía, *payos* and *gitanos* alike.' María put a trembling hand to her heart. 'Three of my sons lost to that city . . .' Her voice trailed off as if she didn't have the energy or the courage to say the words. 'Ramón is gone too. He went out to his orange grove, and did not return . . .'

'*Dios mío,*' Meñique muttered under his breath and crossed himself. Hearing of the tragedy of Spain from someone who had lost and suffered so much brought it home to him like no newspaper report ever could. Lucía was weeping openly.

'Mamá.' She walked to her mother and put her arms

around her thin shoulders. 'At least now you and Pepe are safe.'

'Mamá said she wouldn't come at first,' Pepe said, 'but I said I wouldn't leave her there alone, so she came for me.'

'I could not have Pepe's death on my conscience too,' María sighed. 'He would have perished in Sacromonte. There was no food . . . nothing, Lucía.'

'Well, there is now, Mamá, and it's coming very soon, as much as you can eat.'

'*Gracias*, Lucía, but perhaps there is a bed I could rest on first?'

'You must take mine. Come, I will help you.'

Meñique watched Lucía half carry her mother to the bedroom. He eyed Pepe. 'I could do with a brandy. What about you?'

'No, señor, Mamá forbids alcohol in our house. And I am only thirteen.'

'Forgive me, I guessed older.' Meñique gave Pepe a smile as he poured a shot from the decanter. 'It sounds as if you've been very brave,' he said as he knocked back the brandy.

'Not me, señor. When the Civil Guard came up our street, looking to take young men by force, Mamá hid me in the stable, under the straw. They didn't find me, so they took the mule instead.'

'I see.'

Meñique found himself smiling again. He liked this boy; even though he was so young, his calm demeanour and dry sense of humour had clearly not deserted him during the past few devastating and dangerous months. 'Then you were lucky.'

'Mamá said it was the one good thing about being a *gitano*; the officials had no record of my birth.'

'True, true,' Meñique agreed. 'Do you play a little?' He indicated the guitar the boy was still clutching.

'Yes, señor, but nothing like you – I have heard your recordings. Or Papá. Mamá has told me that he is the best. Is he here? I have never met him, you see, and I would like to.'

'I believe he is in the hotel somewhere, yes, but last night we were playing until very late. He is probably still sleeping,' Meñique replied, desperate to buy some time until he'd spoken to Lucía. Despite José's desertion of his family, it was obvious that María had brought her youngest son up to love and respect his father. The pathos of this alone was enough to bring tears to his eyes. He stood up and poured himself another brandy as there was a knock on the door and room service arrived.

'*¡Dios mío!*' Pepe's eyes widened at the sight of the two trolleys laden with food. 'It is a banquet for the King of Spain!'

Lucía entered the room, her nostrils quivering at the smell of food.

'Mamá is sleeping, so we shall save her something for later. I will go and wake up the rest of the *cuadro* and tell them the wonderful news.'

'Yes, and you must tell your father that his precious son Pepe is here and excited to meet him for the first time.' Meñique's eyes flashed a warning to Lucía, and she read it.

'Of course. I am sure he will be excited to meet you too, Pepe.'

Lucía left the suite and walked along the softly carpeted corridors to her father's room. She did not bother to knock and walked straight in. The room stank of cigarette smoke and alcohol. José was fast asleep, snoring like a snuffling pig.

'Wake up, Papá, I have a surprise for you,' she shouted in

his ear. 'Papá!' Lucía shook him, but he only groaned, so she went to the washbasin, filled a mug with water, then splashed it on his face.

José swore, but came to quickly.

'What is it?' he said as he struggled upright.

'Papá, I need to tell you something.' Lucía sat down on the side of his mattress and took his hands. 'I sent Bernardo with his cousin to rescue Mamá from Granada. And she has arrived! She is right here in my suite! She's sleeping now, but she brings bad news—'

'Stop!' José raised a hand to halt her. 'You say your mother is here in Lisbon?'

'Yes.'

'Why?!'

'Because if she had stayed in Spain, she would be dead! One of us had to do something to save her – Eduardo and Carlos are both missing, along with thousands of others in Granada. I am sorry, Papá, but I used the money that you hide under the floorboards to pay for their rescue.'

José stared at her, doing his best to rid himself of his hangover and begin to take in what his daughter was saying.

'Eduardo and Carlos are dead?'

'We must hope not, but Mamá says they have not been seen for the past few weeks. Listen, Papá, there is something else you must know before I take you to see her.'

'Lucía!' José put his hand up to stop her words. 'Don't you understand that she hates me? I deserted her to go to Barcelona with you. She is likely to attack me with her bare fists if she sees me. Perhaps it is best I stay here.' José pulled the sheet protectively up to his chin.

'No, Papá, she will not "attack" you. She doesn't hate you;

she still loves you, even though I cannot even begin to understand why, but,' Lucía hurried on, 'that is not what I wanted to speak to you about.'

'There is something worse than your mother arriving here in Lisbon?'

Lucía restrained herself from slapping her father's face. Despite what he had done for her, his refusal to accept his familial responsibilities upset and irritated her beyond measure.

'Papá, Pepe is here too.'

'And who is Pepe?'

'Your youngest son. When you left with me to go to Barcelona, Mamá was already pregnant with him.'

José looked at her in total disbelief. 'I think I am still asleep and this is all a bad dream! When your mother came to see me in Barcelona, she did not mention she was pregnant.'

'She didn't know—'

'Or perhaps the child isn't mine.'

The sound of a palm whisking harshly across skin echoed around the room as Lucía lost the last remnants of her control.

'How *dare* you, Papá? To abandon and then to disrespect your wife and the mother of your children like that! You are a disgrace!' Lucía was shaking with anger – even though no *gitano* daughter disrespected her father, enough was enough. '*You . . .*' she said, her finger close to his nose, 'better listen to what I am telling you. Mamá has brought your son up to love and respect his father, even though he has never met you. He knows nothing of the "aunties" that have shared his father's bed, or his love for the brandy bottle, only that his papá is a famous guitarist who must be away from his family to provide for them.'

'*Mierda!* Is she here for money, is that it?'

'Do you not hear a word that I say, or are you just plain stupid?' Lucía was screaming at him now. 'Just because your mind and heart are full of snakes, it does not mean that Mamá's are too. That boy down there believes he will meet a father who will be as excited to see him as he is to see you.'

'You are forgetting one thing, Lucía. No one ever told me I had a son. Is that my fault?'

'Why are you never in the wrong?! Everything in life is always someone *else's* fault, isn't it?' Lucía spat at him. 'You know very well that you deserted your family – you edited my mother from my life, you did not even give me the birthday gifts she sent! I didn't see her for over ten years! And when I did, she made me swear not to tell you about Pepe. Anyway' – she shook her head in despair – 'there is nothing more I can say. You do as you wish, but Mamá and Pepe are here to stay.'

Lucía left the room, feeling the blood sizzling through her veins. She went to the window along the corridor, wrenched it open and took some deep breaths. When she'd calmed down sufficiently to return to her suite, she opened the door to the sound of guitars from within. Meñique was playing with Pepe, both of them lost in a world of their own. The sight calmed her and made her smile. Even if her father could not behave as he should towards his son, then perhaps Meñique could fill the void.

'*Dios mío*,' Meñique breathed as the two of them finished playing. 'Lucía, Pepe has inherited his father's talent! We have a new recruit to our *cuadro*!'

'He is only thirteen, Meñique,' Lucía reminded him.

'And you were even younger when you started dancing, Lucía.'

'*Gracias*, señor.' Pepe looked up shyly at Meñique. 'But I have only played in front of family and neighbours at weddings and fiestas.'

'As all of us once did,' Meñique reassured the boy. 'I will help you, and I'm sure your father will too.'

'Is he awake yet, Lucía?' Pepe asked hopefully.

'Yes, he is getting dressed and will be here to see you very soon. He is excited to meet you too. Perhaps while we wait, you would like to take a bath?' Lucía suggested. The stale smell of Pepe's unwashed body was permeating the room.

'A bath? There is a barrel in here?' Pepe looked around the luxurious suite in confusion.

'There is a room which has a water closet and a bathtub, which you fill from taps.'

'Never!' Pepe's eyes widened in disbelief. 'May I see it?'

'Of course you may.' Lucía offered her hand to him. 'Come with me.'

Meñique watched them go, musing once again on Lucía's many-faceted personality. She was being almost maternal with Pepe, had paid a fortune to rescue her mother and brother . . .

For the next twenty minutes, he wandered distractedly around the sitting room. 'Family is everything,' he sighed, repeating Lucía's words. He wondered then whether the arrival of mother and son would be to the detriment of their tightly knit group. There was a tentative knock at the door of the suite.

'It is I, José,' a voice said from behind it.

'I suppose I'm about to find out,' Meñique murmured as he went to open it. '*Hola*, José. You look smart.'

'I am here to greet the son I didn't know I had,' he said in a hoarse whisper, hovering on the threshold and glancing nervously around the interior of the suite.

'You are, yes.'

'And my wife? Where is she?'

'Still sleeping. The journey has exhausted her. Come in, José. Lucía has taken Pepe to have his first bath.'

'What is he like?'

'He is a fine boy, well brought up by his mother and a talented guitarist.'

'You think he is definitely mine?' José whispered as he sat down, then stood up again and began to pace.

'When you see him you can make that judgement for yourself.'

'My other sons – Eduardo and Carlos . . . Lucía tells me they are missing.' José put a hand to his forehead. 'What a morning of shocks. I think I will take some brandy.'

'Best not,' Meñique advised. 'You will need all your wits about you in the next few hours.'

'Yes, you're right, but . . .'

At that moment, Lucía and the boy emerged from the bathroom. Pepe was dressed in a fresh shirt and trousers.

'He has borrowed some of your clothes, Meñique, although the trousers are too short,' she teased the boy. 'You are tall, like your father. And here he is!' Lucía declared, her eyes fixed on José. 'Papá, come and say hello to the son you've always longed to meet.'

'I . . .' José's eyes travelled up and down the young man, taking him in and realising Lucía had spoken the truth. His eyes filled with tears. 'My son! You look just like me when I was your age. Come here, *hijo*, and let me embrace you.'

'Papá . . .' Pepe walked towards him hesitantly. José

opened his arms and pulled the young man to him, then began to weep openly.

'All these years, I cannot believe it! I cannot.'

Lucía went to Meñique, in need of her own embrace. She was heartened that José's reaction seemed genuine enough.

Then the door to Lucía's bedroom opened, to reveal María. She watched her husband and son, her own tears already brimming in her eyes. Lucía caught her gaze and nodded.

'Look who is here, Papá,' she said.

José turned and saw his wife, her dark eyes huge and fearful in her thin face.

'María.'

'Yes, José. I am sure you have heard that our daughter saved my life and that of our son by rescuing us from Granada.'

'I have.' José walked slowly towards her, his head down like a beaten dog waiting to be reprimanded. He stopped half a metre away and lifted his eyes to hers, struggling to find the right words. The silence seemed to go on endlessly until Meñique broke it.

'I am sure that you both have much to talk about. Why don't we leave you in peace and go and introduce Pepe to the rest of the *cuadro*?'

'Yes!' Lucía jumped on Meñique's suggestion. 'Come, Pepe, you have not yet met your Aunt Juana. She will be amazed to see how tall you are.'

Lucía offered her hand as Pepe's eyes rested determinedly on his parents – the first time in his young life he had seen them together. She took his hand and pulled him towards the door, with Meñique following. 'We will see you later,' she said to her mother and father. 'And then we will celebrate the reunion together.' With a last searing glance at José, she ushered Pepe and Meñique out of the room.

'So, what did he say, Mamá?' whispered Lucía as they sat on the floor of the suite together finishing up the food that Lucía had ordered earlier.

'He said sorry.' María shrugged as she broke off a piece of bread.

'And your reply?'

'I accepted it. What else could I do? Pepe has had enough dreams destroyed – for his sake, I will not destroy another. That is what I told José. And as you know,' María lowered her voice even further, 'I am not innocent of deceit either.'

'No, Mamá, that is wrong. Your husband abandoned you and your children for fourteen years! Ramón was there to help you.'

'*Sí*, Lucía, but I am – and was – a married woman. Perhaps I should have resisted . . .'

'No, he is what kept you alive when Papá and I left. You must not feel guilt.'

'Ramón treated Pepe like a son. He loved him so much – brought him up as if he was his own . . .' María ventured.

'As you did for his girls after they lost their mother, remember?' Lucía gave the floor an exasperated thump. 'Why is it that the bad people never feel guilt or take responsibility for the hurt they have caused? When all the good people who have done nothing wrong continue to punish themselves?'

'Your father isn't a bad man, Lucía, he is just weak.'

'Still you make excuses for his behaviour!'

'No, I just understand who he is. I was not enough for him and that is that.'

Lucía realised it was pointless continuing the conversation. 'So, you are friends?'

'Oh yes.' María nodded. 'Your father asked me whether we could forget the past and start again.'

'And what did you say?'

'I said that we could forget the past, but that I did not have the energy to "start again". There are some things that cannot be reversed, ever.'

'Like what?'

María bit into a small piece of bread and chewed it thoughtfully. 'I will not share his bed again. His understanding of "sharing" is different to mine and, being who he is, I know it won't last, even if he believes it will. I cannot go through that pain again. Do you understand?'

'Yes, Mamá.'

'Try to imagine if it was Meñique who told you he loved you, that you were the only one for him, and then you discovered that he had said the same thing to many others when it suited him.' María made an effort to swallow, her stomach so contracted that any piece of food was an effort to digest.

'I would cut off his *cojones* while he slept in the night,' stated Lucía.

'I'm sure you would, *querida*, but you are not me and I endured that humiliation again and again.'

'Maybe Papá has changed. Men do as they get older. And I swear I have not seen a woman near him since I came to visit you in Sacromonte.'

'Well . . .' María grimaced as the bread went down. 'That is something, I suppose. Don't worry, Lucía, we have agreed that – for Pepe's sake, if for nobody else – we will be reunited. He above everyone must believe in our love.'

'Do you still love him, Mamá?'

'He is the love of my life, and always will be, but that does not mean to say that I can be taken for a fool again. I have grown older and learnt what my heart can tolerate and what it can't. So, I will sleep with Juana.'

'No, Mamá! You will have a room to yourself. I will go down to reception now and arrange it.'

'*Gracias*, Lucía.' María put her hand upon her daughter's. 'I know that it's only natural to want a true reunion between us, but it can't be that way.'

'I understand, Mamá, of course I do. Maybe in the future, *sí*?'

'I have learnt never to say never, *querida mía*.' María smiled weakly. 'For now, I am only happy to be safe, and for Pepe to finally meet his father. I can never thank you enough, Lucía.'

'And tonight, Mamá, for the first time in so many years, you will see me dance!'

'I will, but perhaps I should go and have a rest so I am ready to appreciate it.'

'But I was going to take you out shopping! Buy you a new dress.'

'Tomorrow,' María said weakly as she rose from the table. 'I will have a new dress tomorrow.'

'I am worried that Mamá is ill,' Lucía said to Meñique as soon as they were alone in the suite with the remnants of the feast.

'Lucía, I think you expect too much. Your mother is not ill, she is simply weak from months of starvation, let alone the shock of being here and seeing her husband for the first time in so many years.'

'Well, I hope you are right. We must do all we can to make her strong. I am not sure she looks happy to be here.'

'Lucía . . .' Meñique took a sip of his bitter coffee. 'None of us can know what it is like to make a decision between abandoning two sons that you love to save another. She has come here for Pepe, not for herself.'

'*Sí*, but I hope she is a little glad to be here too. Now, I must go shopping and choose Mamá a dress to wear for tonight. I want her to look beautiful. Will you come with me?'

Meñique agreed as he always did, knowing that his much-needed siesta before the performance tonight would have to be forfeited.

As they left the suite, he also wondered at Lucía's level of emotional maturity and whether her wish to reunite her mother and father was rooted in a desire to absolve her misplaced guilt for creating their separation in the first place.

María listened to the chatter of the elegant drinkers in the Café Arcadio. Even though she could not understand what they said, she knew these *payo*s were very wealthy, from the clothes they wore and the expensive alcohol they drank. Never before had she done anything more than pass a *payo* in the street, yet tonight here she was, sitting in a dress as elegant as any of theirs, with her hair piled up on her head in a fetching style that Juana had fashioned for her.

And they were all here to see her daughter: Lucía Albaycín, the little *gitana* from Sacromonte. To think that she had conquered the hearts and minds of *payos* in another country! It was too much to take in.

'I feel as if I'm in a dream!' Pepe echoed her thoughts as he took a sip of the beer he'd been bought and ventured a look around the café. 'The queue to gain entrance is getting longer. Can we really be here, Mamá, amongst Portuguese *payos*?'

'We can, and all thanks to your sister for rescuing us,' María said.

'And to Papá,' Pepe added. 'He told me he provided the money needed to bribe the officials and obtain our papers.'

'And to him also, of course,' María agreed with a thin smile.

As if on cue, José appeared next to them.

'We begin in five minutes.' His eyes swept over María's body. 'You look beautiful tonight. You have barely changed since you were fifteen years old.'

'*Gracias.*' María lowered her eyes, steeling herself to ignore his comments.

'Now, I must prepare.' José swept a bow.

'But Lucía is not here yet.'

'She is, María, but every night she goes outside to talk with those who cannot get in,' he explained, then strode off to join the other members of the *cuadro* who were gathered at the back of the café.

'Lucía is very famous, *sí*, Mamá?'

'Very,' María confirmed with the same wonder as her son. The rest of the *cuadro* took their places to wild cheering and clapping from the audience. José and Meñique began warming up, and María saw Pepe smile in pleasure.

'Papá is so talented, isn't he? Maybe better than Meñique.'

María looked at her son and observed the utter adoration in his eyes. It made her want to weep again. 'Yes, he is, just like you.'

As Pepe went to take another swig of his beer, María firmly took the bottle out of his hand.

'No, *querido*. Alcohol is bad for the fingers.'

'Really? Then why did I see Papá drinking at lunchtime?'

'Because he has learnt his skills already. Now, watch the show.'

After another few minutes of José and Meñique improvising, José's fingers suddenly halted.

'But where is La Candela?' He looked around the room as the audience held its breath. 'She is not here and we cannot start without her.'

'I am here,' a voice said from the entrance to the café.

The whole audience turned at the sound of Lucía's voice, and began to cheer and clap. She silenced them with a raised hand as she swept through the crowd, the long train of her flamenco dress – the length of which would rival any queen's – following like a serpent behind her. She arrived on stage and expertly flicked her wrist to manoeuvre it into submission.

'*¡Arriba!*'

'*¡Olé!*' cheered the audience in response.

'Now we can begin.' José strummed his guitar with a flourish as Lucía began to move.

Along with everyone else in the room, María sat there transfixed by a creature so full of fire and passion that she could hardly recognise her as her own.

*How you have moved on, querida mía*, she thought as she

460

listened to the audience's ecstatic applause and joined them in a standing ovation. *You are simply magnificent.*

José too seemed to have discovered a whole new level of performance. That evening he matched his daughter beat for beat, seeming to know exactly when he should let her feet take over.

'My sister, she is incredible!' Pepe whispered as Lucía completed her *alegrías* and the entire café stood up demanding an encore.

She used her hands to quieten them.

'*Sí*, I will give you an encore, but only if my special guest joins me on stage first. Come, Pepe,' Lucía beckoned him as all eyes in the café fell upon the boy.

'I can't, Mamá!' Pepe panicked. 'I am not good enough!'

María reached for his guitar, which Lucía had insisted he bring. 'Go, join your sister, Pepe.'

Shaking, Pepe made his way to the stage. Meñique stood up and gallantly offered Pepe his chair. The boy sat down next to his father, who whispered in his ear.

'*Señores y señoras*, may I present José and Pepe – father and son – playing together for the first time!' Lucía announced as she swept herself and her train to the side of the stage.

As Pepe lifted his guitar into position, José reached out to clutch his son's shoulder, then gave him a nod and began to play. After a few seconds, Pepe joined in tentatively, watching his father's fingers and listening to the rhythm. María held her breath as Pepe struggled to conquer his nerves, and finally, as his eyes closed and his shoulders relaxed, María's did too. She watched as José ceased playing suddenly, understanding that Pepe had the confidence to continue alone. Lost in his own world, just like Lucía had always been when she danced,

461

Pepe's fingers moved like fast, agile spiders across the strings. His solo achieved a roar of applause, then Meñique, José and Lucía joined him, bringing the performance to a brilliant crescendo, which had the audience on their feet and yelling for more.

José stood up, pulling his son to his feet and hugging him. Unable to stop them, María let the tears fall freely down her face.

# Lisbon

*August 1938, two years later*

# 26

'I have received an offer for us to perform in Buenos Aires,' José announced as he sat with Lucía and Meñique in their suite.

'Is that not where La Argentinita was born?' Lucía asked her father.

'She was born in Argentina, yes.'

'And where is Argentina? Is it in the United States of America?'

'No, it is in *South* America – Spanish America, if you like.' Meñique rolled his eyes at Lucía's confused geography.

'They speak Spanish there?'

'Yes. We will say no of course,' said José.

'Why?' Lucía narrowed her eyes. 'We have been in Portugal for two years and I have had enough of being an exile in a country that speaks a different language. In Buenos Aires, I will be able to understand what everyone is saying! Papá, I want to go.'

'We will not be going, Lucía,' José stated firmly.

'Why not?!'

'We have to board a ship and spend many days on the water to get there. As you know well, *querida*, no *gitano* can cross the water and live to tell the tale,' José replied solemnly.

'Please, not that old superstition again! Did I die when I crossed the Darro river to leave Sacromonte and walk across the bridge to the Alhambra? There were hundreds of us, Papá, and none of us left the earth.'

*One did* . . . thought María, who was sitting quietly in the background, sewing a ruffle onto Lucía's new flamenco dress.

'The Darro river has welcomed us for hundreds of years. It is a few feet wide where we cross, not an ocean that we must live on for weeks! Besides . . .'

'Besides what, Papá?' asked Lucía.

'We are a success here in Lisbon. We have everything that we want. You are not known in Buenos Aires, Lucía, and we would have to start all over again.'

'Is that not what we have spent our whole lives doing, Papá?'

'La Argentinita is queen there . . .'

'You're afraid of her? I am not! I am bored here, and even though we are earning a lot of money, there are new countries that must see what I can do.' Lucía turned to Meñique. 'Do you agree?' she asked him.

'I think it is an interesting opportunity,' he replied diplomatically.

'It is more than that.' Lucía gave him a defiant stare and stood up. 'It is meant to be. You can telegram that I will be there. It is up to the rest of you if you wish to come with me.'

Lucía swept from the room as her parents and Meñique eyed each other nervously.

'It is madness to leave here when everything is so good,' said José. 'While we are unable to return to our country, we enjoy a good life close by in Portugal.'

'We do, yes,' Meñique agreed, 'but I have been growing

concerned at the wider political situation in Europe. We live a precarious life here, José – I have done my best to protect us from informants, even though Lucía's fame has drawn all eyes upon our little *cuadro*. When will Salazar's *policía* become weary of us *gitanos* and send us back to Spain to be murdered? And when will Adolf Hitler antagonise France and Britain enough for there to be all-out war—'

'*Hombre*, you read too many newspapers, and spend too many nights talking to your *payo compadres*,' José said scornfully. 'There is nothing more dangerous than crossing the oceans; you are trying to seduce us to our deaths!'

'José, with the greatest respect, I am only trying to do what's best for all of us. I have a strong feeling that we should leave Portugal while the going is good and the borders are open.' Meñique turned to María. 'What do you think?'

María smiled gratefully at him. It was not often that she was asked for an opinion. She searched for the right words. 'I think that my daughter's hunger to show her talent off will never be sated. She is still young and wishes to climb taller mountains. As we all did once.' María threw a look at José. '*She* is the one who the public wishes to see, the one who provides our daily bread. And however we may all feel about it, we must satisfy her appetite to conquer new countries.' María shrugged apologetically, then turned her eyes back to her sewing.

'You speak a lot of sense, wife,' José said eventually. 'Do you not think, Agustín?'

'Yes,' he replied, relieved that María agreed, but smarting from her truthful but hurtful comment that it was Lucía the public wanted to see. 'And if we find that I was wrong, then there are ships back to Portugal. Or, if we are lucky, one day to Spain.'

'Then I am out-voted.' José sighed. 'Although I do not know whether the rest of the *cuadro* will follow us.'

'Of course they will.' María's needle paused as she looked up at them. 'They know they are nothing without Lucía.'

*But does she know that she is nothing without us?* Meñique thought.

'*¡Dios mío!* Why did we do this?' Lucía groaned as she leant over the side of the bed to vomit into the bucket Meñique had placed there for her. 'Why does the ocean have so much water?'

'I am sure you will be better soon, *pequeña*.'

'No.' Lucía dragged her body back onto the bed and held onto the sides of the cot as the ship heaved to the right. 'I will die before I reach shore, I am convinced. And the sharks will eat my body and it will be my fault for wanting to come.'

'Well, if you don't eat anything, they won't have a very good supper,' commented Meñique, who was the only one of the *cuadro* who hadn't been seasick since the *Monte Pascoal* had left the port of Lisbon a week earlier. 'Now, I'm going to find a steward to clean up in here. Can I get you anything else?' he said as he opened the door.

'An engagement ring would be wonderful,' she called as the door closed behind him.

'We are dining at the captain's table tonight,' Lucía declared three days later as she pinned her hair up and dabbed some rouge onto her cheeks, which still betrayed the pallor of her previous sickness.

'Are you well enough, *pequeña*?' Meñique asked.

'Of course! The captain has asked especially for me, and I cannot let him down, or he might run this ship aground,' she said, with not a hint of irony. 'Now come.'

Dinner at the captain's table was a pleasant occasion. The captain plied them all with fine wine, and waiters brought out course after course, which only Meñique managed to eat. José sat beside him, talking heatedly to the captain, a great aficionado of flamenco music.

'And you will have heard the news from England?' the captain said. 'The Prime Minister, Mr Chamberlain, has promised "peace for our time" – he is certainly keeping Hitler in line.'

'You see, *hombre*,' José said, slapping Meñique on the shoulder, 'peace! We needn't have ventured onto this wretched sea after all! Oh, how I long for Spain . . .'

'Ah, my friend,' the captain said as he leant over and poured some brandy into José's glass. 'Once you have seen the splendour of Buenos Aires and Argentina, you will never wish to leave.'

'I just went to Mamá's cabin, but it was empty!' Lucía declared exultantly the next day.

'So? She could be anywhere on the ship.'

'Not at six in the morning. So then I walked as quietly as a little kitten along to Papá's cabin. And guess what?'

'Tell me.'

'I push open the door and see them in bed together in each other's arms. Isn't it wonderful?' Lucía performed a quick *zapateado* around their own bed. 'I knew it! I just knew it.'

'Yes, it is good news that they have put their pasts behind them, for now at least.'

'Meñique!' Lucía rounded on him, hands on hips. 'True love is forever, *sí*?'

'Of course. Now, I am off to practise a new song with Pepe.' Before her pronouncement caused him, too, to be violently ill into the bucket that still stood by the bed just in case a further attack of seasickness overtook Lucía, Meñique left the cabin.

As the *Monte Pascal* sailed along the coast of Brazil, the weather at least cheered the spirits of its residents. The *cuadro* came onto the deck, basking in the heat like the sharks they so feared. Now all their energy was focused on preparation for their arrival in Argentina. Even Lucía, out of practice due to her seasickness, deigned to rehearse with them.

'Meñique?' she said the night before they were due to dock in Buenos Aires.

'Yes, *pequeña*?'

'Do you think that we can be a success in Argentina?'

'If anyone can be, it's you, Lucía.'

Her small hand snaked to his. 'Can I be better than La Argentinita?'

'I cannot answer that. This is her homeland.'

'I will be,' Lucía stated with certainty. '*Buenas noches, querido.*' She placed a kiss on his cheek and turned over.

The following morning, the ship made fast to the dock in Buenos Aires. The *cuadro* were on deck, all dressed up for the occasion in their best outfits, their hair slicked down with oil.

'Even if there is no one here to greet us, we will act like we expected there to be,' Lucía whispered to Meñique as they watched the gangplank being lowered. Lucía stood on tiptoe to peer over the side of the ship at the throng of people on the quayside.

'They look and sound like us!' she exclaimed happily.

'Lucía! La Candela!' someone shouted from below them.

'Did someone just call my name?' Lucía turned to Meñique in surprise and delight. She turned back and waved. 'I am here!' she screamed, the sound of gulls acting as her impromptu chorus.

The Albaycín *cuadro* made their way down the gangplank, their cardboard suitcases adorned with bundles of herbs tied on with scarves to ward off bad luck.

'¡*Hola, Buenos Aires!*' Lucía called out in triumph as she stepped onto Argentinian soil for the first time. 'I did not die!' She hugged the rest of her clan. A barrage of flashbulbs went off in their faces as a tall man in a silk suit walked towards them.

'Where is Lucía Albaycín?' he asked.

'I am here.' Lucía pushed her way through the crowd.

'It is you?' The man looked down at the tiny wisp of a woman whose head did not even reach up to his shoulder.

'*Sí*, and who are you?'

'I am Santiago Rodríguez, the impresario who brought you here, señorita.'

'*Bueno*, you pay and we will dance for Buenos Aires!'

A cheer came up from the onlookers.

'How does it feel to be on Argentinian soil?'

'Wonderful! My father, my brother, my mother, even my handbag were sick on the seas!' she said with a smile. 'But we are here now, and safe.'

The flashbulbs went off yet again as Señor Rodríguez encircled Lucía's tiny form and another loud cheer split the air.

'And so,' muttered Meñique, 'a new circus begins . . .'

# Tiggy
## Sacromonte, Granada, Spain

February 2008

*Eurasian brown bear*
*(Ursus arctos arctos)*

# 27

'Now I am sleepy,' Angelina announced, bringing me back from the past. 'No more until after I have rested.'

I looked at Angelina and saw her eyes were closed. She'd been talking for a good hour and a half.

What I wanted to do was to run back to my hotel, grab some paper and a pen and write down everything Angelina had told me so I didn't forget a word of it. Most children had the luxury of their past being attached to their present and their future: they'd been brought up in an environment that they accepted and understood. For me, it felt as though I was having a crash-course in my heritage, which could not be more different from the life I'd led since I'd been taken from here by Pa. Somehow, I had to glue the two Tiggys together into a whole, and I knew that would take some time. Firstly, I just needed to settle into being this new *present* Tiggy I was discovering.

'Time for lunch.' Pepe stood and began to walk towards the entrance to the cave.

'May I help you?' I asked, following him inside and finding myself in an old-fashioned kitchen.

'*Sí*, Erizo. The plates are in there.' He pointed to a carved wooden cabinet, which looked very much like the ones I imagined María's son Carlos had fashioned all those years ago.

I took them out as he'd asked, while he collected food from an ancient fridge that buzzed and whirred.

'Would you mind if I had a quick look around? I'd like to see where I was actually born.'

'*Sí*, just through there.' Pepe indicated the back of the cave. 'Angelina sleeps there now. The light switch is on the left.'

I walked through the kitchen and drew back a threadbare curtain. I fumbled in the pitch-black, found the switch and the room was suddenly illuminated by a single light bulb. I saw an old wrought-iron bed with a colourful crocheted blanket covering it. I looked up at the whitewashed oval ceiling, and let out a sigh of wonder. How could it be that, as a tiny baby, I could remember so vividly being lifted up towards it by those strong, secure arms?

Leaving the bedroom, I felt suddenly dizzy, and asked Pepe for a glass of water.

'Go sit down with Angelina.' Pepe handed me the glass and I did so, moving the chair into the shade of a fragrant bush.

Then he arrived with an overflowing tray and as Angelina stirred, I helped him lay everything out.

'We eat simple food here,' he said briskly, just in case I was about to turn my nose up at the freshly baked bread, dish of olive oil and the bowl of plump tomatoes.

'This is perfect for me. I'm a vegan.'

'What this word mean?' asked Pepe.

'I don't eat meat, fish, milk, eggs, butter or cheese.'

'*¡Dios mío!*' Pepe's eyes swept down my body in surprise. 'No wonder you so scrawny!'

For all its simplicity, I knew I would never forget the taste of the bread, dipped in home-pressed olive oil and the freshest tomatoes I'd ever bitten into. I gazed across the table at Angelina and Pepe, and marvelled at how different they looked, even though they were uncle and niece. If anyone doubted they were related, though, the fluid way they moved and the inflections of their speech marked them out as family. I wondered what I had inherited from them.

'Soon we must arrange for you to meet the rest of your Sacromonte family,' commented Angelina.

'I play my guitar,' Pepe said, snapping his fingers then using them to twirl his handlebar moustache.

'I thought everyone had left here?' I queried.

'They leave Sacromonte, but they are not so far away in the city. We must have a *fiesta*!' Angelina clapped her hands in pleasure. 'Now, I will take a *siesta* and so will you, Erizo, for you need rest. Come back at six o'clock and we will talk some more.'

'And I will prepare more food. We will make you strong, *querida*,' Pepe said.

We gathered the bowls and dishes onto the tray and I carried the water jug and glasses back into the kitchen. Angelina disappeared through the curtain with a wave.

'Sleep, Erizo,' she repeated, so I nodded at Pepe and walked back up to my hotel.

Having slept like the dead, I woke ten minutes before six, splashed my face with cold water to wake me up and hurried back to the blue front door just along the narrow path.

'*Hola*, Erizo.' Angelina was already waiting for me there. She reached for my wrist, holding her fingers upon my pulse, then nodded. 'It is better, but you will take another *poción* before you leave. Come.' She beckoned me forward as she began to walk down the sloping path past her cave.

We walked side by side in the fast-descending dusk. As I looked further up the hill, I could see thin trails of smoke coming from four or five chimneys, and we passed an old woman smoking a cigarette outside her front door, who called out to Angelina. She paused for a chat, and it made me feel a little better to know that Sacromonte was not completely deserted. Then we walked on, eventually arriving in a densely wooded area some way outside the village.

Angelina pointed a finger up to the moon hanging in the sky above us. 'She is a quickening moon. She brings a new dawn, the birth of spring, a time to cleanse the past and begin again.'

'It's odd actually, because I can never sleep when there's a full moon. And if I do drift off, I have really strange dreams,' I said.

'It is same for all us females, especially those with the gift. In *gitano* culture, the sun is the god of men, the moon the goddess of women.'

'Really?'

'*Sí*.' Angelina smiled at my surprise. 'How could it be anything else? Without the sun and the moon, there would be no humanity. They give us our life force. Just as, without both men and women, there would be no more humans. See? We are equally powerful, but each with our own special gifts, our own part to play in the universe. Now, we move on.'

Angelina weaved her way through the trees until we

reached a clearing. I saw it was full of graves, the ground covered in roughly hewn wooden crosses. Angelina led me along the rows until she found what she was looking for.

She pointed to three crosses in turn. 'María, your *bisabuela* – great-grandmother – Lucía, your *abuela* – grandmother – and Isadora, your *madre*.'

Then she waited as I knelt in front of my mother's grave, searching for the date of her death, but only her name was inscribed on the simple cross.

'How did she die?'

'Another time, Erizo. For now, say hello to her.'

'Hello,' I whispered to the mound of grass-covered earth. 'I wish I could have known you.'

'She was too good for the earth,' Angelina sighed. 'Gentle and kind, like you.'

I stayed for a while, thinking I should feel more emotional than I did because this was a seminal moment, but maybe my brain was still processing the information, as all I felt was a strange numbness.

Eventually I stood up and we continued along the line of crosses. I saw the names of the babies María had lost, then those of her three sons, and her grandchildren.

'Eduardo and Carlos, their bodies not here, but Ramón made the crosses in remembrance.'

Angelina swept me along another two or three rows, repeating, 'Amaya, Amaya, Amaya . . .'

The crosses were endless – my whole family on my great-grandmother's side seemed to be buried or remembered here.

We then moved on to the Albaycíns – my great-grandfather José's family – which were equally plentiful. And at last, with the thought of my roots extending back over five hundred years, something stirred in my heart, as I began to feel the unbroken invisible thread that connected us all.

Angelina continued walking through the sea of crosses until we had left the clearing and were in a dense patch of forest.

She was looking down, using her feet to tap the ground. 'Okay,' she nodded, 'first lesson. Lie down, Erizo.'

I turned to look at Angelina and saw she was already kneeling. Then she lay flat on her back on the rich, earthy ground and I followed suit.

'Listen, Erizo.' Angelina cupped one of her ears exaggeratedly, nodding to me.

I watched as Angelina put her small hands behind her head as a pillow, then closed her eyes. I did the same, although I wasn't sure what it was I was meant to be listening to.

'Feel the earth,' she whispered, which didn't help much, but I closed my eyes and breathed slowly in and out, hoping to feel and hear whatever it was I was supposed to. For a long time, I only heard the birds calling goodnight to each other, the buzzing of insects and the rustle of small animals in the undergrowth. I focused on that sound – the sound of nature – and eventually the noise became louder until it was a cacophony in my ears. Then I felt the strangest sensation – it was like a pulse from beneath me, beating softly at first, then stronger and stronger. Finally, the earth's heartbeat became one with my own and I could feel I was in perfect harmony with it . . .

I don't know how long I lay there, but the more I let myself go with the flow rather than being frightened, the more I began to hear, feel and see: the sound of the river far below us felt as if it was pouring its fresh, purifying water over me, then

I saw the gorgeous colours of all the fish that swam through it. I opened my eyes and the tree above me metamorphosed into an old man whose branch-arms waved slowly in the breeze, the long white hair and beard made up of thousands of tiny spider webs scattered along the moss-covered trunk of his body. His twig-hands crossed over the smaller branches as if the tree-man was protecting his children.

And the stars . . . never had I seen so many of them or known them shine so brightly . . . As I stared up, the sky above me began to move and shift until I realised that it was made up of billions of tiny spirits – each with its own energy – and I realised with a shock that in fact, the skies were far more densely populated than the earth . . .

Then I saw what I first thought was a shooting star, but as it hovered above the treetops, I realised it couldn't be one, because, after pausing for a few seconds, it suddenly shot *upwards* and hung directly above me, having found its place in the heavens.

I was immediately transported to Chilly's cabin and saw him lying in his bed, or at least, the body that had once housed him, skin and bones lying discarded like an old set of clothes in his freezing cold cabin. I knew what it meant.

'Our cousin, Chilly . . .' said a voice next to me. I sat up with a start and looked into Angelina's eyes.

'He's dead, Angelina.'

'He just move on to the Upperworld.'

A tear plopped down my cheek and Angelina reached over to wipe it away gently. 'No, no, no. No cry, Erizo.' She pointed upwards. 'Chilly is happy. You feel it. Here.' She put her hand to my heart before pulling me into a hug.

'I saw his soul, his . . . energy fly upwards too,' I told her, still shell-shocked from everything I had seen and felt.

'We send him our love and we pray for his soul now.'

I bent my head like Angelina had, thinking how strange it was that Spanish *gitanos* held such a strong Catholic faith alongside their own spiritual ways. I supposed that – despite their different earthly practices – neither faith contradicted the other because they were both about belief in a higher power; a belief that there was a greater force than us in the universe. Humans had simply interpreted it from their different cultural points of view. *Gitanos* lived amongst nature and therefore the spirits they worshipped were part of that. Hindus saw cows and elephants as sacred, and Christianity celebrated the divine in human form . . .

Angelina indicated we should stand up, and I did so, my senses feeling that they had indeed been washed clean and renewed. As Angelina took my hand in hers and weaved confidently through the trees until we saw the dim lights of the village ahead of us, I experienced a sense of euphoria that I'd somehow managed to feel at one with – and part of – the amazing universe we inhabited. I remembered Pa's words:

'*Keep your feet on the fresh carpet of the earth, but raise your mind to the windows of the universe . . .*'

Back in front of the blue door, Angelina took my pulse again. 'Better and better. I will give you *poción* now and you will be well soon.'

Having drunk the disgusting tonic, with Angelina watching me as I did so, she put a hand to my cheek. 'You are blood of my blood. I am happy. *Buenas noches.*'

Lying in bed in my cave-room at the hotel, my heart felt calmer, as if the steady pulse of the earth's heartbeat had slowed and tamed my own. My mind flew back to the moment I'd seen Chilly's soul leave the earth, and I sent up a silent message to him. The fact that Angelina had felt it too meant that all the times before when I'd had a similar sensation of a soul moving on hadn't been just a figment of my over-active imagination. Which meant that the 'other part' of me was just as real as the sturdy walls of the cave that surrounded me.

And for this alone, I was so very glad I'd decided to take this journey into my past.

# 28

A week on, I felt as though I'd lived another lifetime since I'd arrived in Sacromonte. Angelina hadn't been joking about teaching me all she knew in the time we had. Before we began, she made me swear never to record anything she told me onto a computer: 'Our secret ways must remain secret, so that the wrong people cannot get hold of our magic on that web machine . . .'

So, I had walked down the hill to a little shop on the other side of the city wall that seemed to sell everything from cat food to electronics, and bought a thick notepad and some biros. Already, the notepad was over two-thirds full. How Angelina could remember the endless variations of herbs that went into the different remedies, never mind the exact amount of each, I really didn't know. Then again, I was on a crash-course, whereas she'd been taught from the cradle by Micaela, her *bruja* guide. She also began to teach me how to use my hands for healing.

'Chilly told me I had power in my hands. But animals are my passion. Can it work on them too?' I asked her.

'Of course. All creatures on earth are flesh and blood. It is same.'

Although I became frustrated at times, under her tuition I began to learn how to 'feel' the energy that coursed through every living being and how to let my tingling hands be drawn like a magnet to the source of a problem, then to release any bad energy and disperse it. Angelina encouraged me to practise on Pepe's ancient arthritic cat, but I also found myself stopping in the alleyways of Sacromonte to tend to strays that crossed my path. As I crouched over each animal I only hoped that any passers-by wouldn't think I was trying to sell them on as chicken to a restaurant.

As time went by, I also noticed that my ear was attuning to the Spanish that Pepe and Angelina spoke between them, and I began to recognise more and more words.

'If I spend another week here I'll be fluent – at least in Spanish herbs,' I chuckled to myself as I walked towards the blue door. It was another lovely sunny day, so I knew I'd find Angelina sitting outside, drinking coffee. The usual disgusting-tasting tonic would be waiting for me, because coffee was bad for me, apparently.

'How are you today?' she asked me as I arrived.

'Very well, *gracias*.'

I picked up my potion – it had the strangest aroma of aniseed mixed with sheep dung – and sipped it reluctantly. I knew she would force me to drink it all.

After a couple of hours of tuition and our usual simple lunch, Angelina and Pepe retired for their siestas, and I went back to the hotel to sit on the terrace for a while, working my way through my scribbles whilst everything was still fresh in my mind. Once I'd done that, I too went to take a nap, knowing that Angelina's brain was at its most agile at night, so my own had to be on full alert later to compute and write down the stream of knowledge she shared with me.

But that afternoon I couldn't sleep, and I knew it was because it was time to make contact with the outside world. A week had passed in a flash and people would be worried about me. However much I wanted to remain in my parallel universe, it just wasn't fair, and I needed to tell them I was safe and well.

'Marcella, do you have a telephone I could use to call home?' I asked her.

'Up here?! You are joking! Mobiles have very small signal. There is telephone at the shop just inside city walls. For a fee, the owner let us use it. My fax machine there too, for my bookings. I go every day to get them. In fact, I go now. You come with me?'

'Thanks, Marcella.'

In the little shop, Marcella explained what I needed and I was led to a storeroom at the back and shown an antiquated telephone.

As I was left in private, I pondered which number to call first and decided on Cal's mobile. He rarely answered it, due to the lack of signal, which meant I could leave a message without getting grilled.

I dialled the number and sure enough, it went straight to voicemail.

'Hi, Cal, it's Tiggy. Just to say I'm absolutely fine. Sorry to run out on you but I . . . needed to get away for a bit. I'll be in touch soon, but don't worry about me. I'm really happy where I am. Lots of love to everyone. Bye.'

I put the heavy receiver down, feeling better that I'd made contact. I then picked it up again, thinking I should speak to

Ma – there was no harm in her knowing where I was. I dialled the number and got the Atlantis answering machine. A lump came to my throat as I heard Pa Salt's voice message. And reminded myself to tell Ma she needed to change it.

'Hi, Ma, it's Tiggy. I'm really well and in Spain actually. I needed some warmth after all that cold and it's really helping. I left my mobile behind at Kinnaird but I'll try and call again soon. Really, don't worry about me. Lots of love, bye.'

I put down the receiver, then my hand hovered over it as I felt a compulsion to leave a message on Charlie's mobile too.

'No, Tiggy, he's your ex-employer!' I told myself firmly.

*You want to speak to him, don't you? Because you care about him . . .*

'No, I don't,' I said out loud.

*You do, Tiggy . . .*

Then I sighed. One of the side effects of my recent tuition from Angelina, was that my *in*tuition, aka my inner voice, had sprung to life like a female version of Jiminy Cricket. In fact, these days, it barely shut up, forcing me to face any lie I tried to tell myself.

*Okay*, I answered the voice internally as I paid for the calls and walked out of the shop. Marcella had gone on into the city and I made my way back alone. 'I did . . . I mean I do still care for him,' I said out loud, 'but he's married with a daughter, has a huge and possibly bankrupt estate to manage, and his life's a total mess! So whatever *you* might say, on this one I'm ignoring you!'

I looked up to see two passing women casting me very strange looks.

'I have an invisible friend!' I said loudly in English, before giving them a wave and continuing back up the hill towards Sacromonte.

That evening, Angelina proclaimed me ready to move on to 'university', as she put it. When I arrived, Pepe was just departing to organise my 'fiesta' – planned for a couple of days' time.

'Everyone will be there,' he said to me as he left, and I could sense his excitement. 'It will be like the old days!'

Angelina and I sat together as she began to share some of her most potent magic, involving talismans, charms and protective coins. In the dark cave, lit only by a single guttering candle – she preferred it to the harsh light of a bulb – she showed me sacred objects that had belonged to my ancestors, and as I held them in my tingling hands, she instructed me on how to reach the 'Otherworld' – a world where spirits wandered and whispered in my ear, which was apparently how I 'knew' things.

When it came to curses, at first I said no.

'I thought we were healers – medicine women,' I said. 'Why would we want to hurt anyone?'

Angelina regarded me sombrely. 'Erizo, the world is full of light and dark. And in my lifetime I have seen a lot of darkness.' She closed her eyes, and I knew she was thinking of the past that still haunted her and this beautiful country. 'In times of darkness, you do what you can to survive, to protect those you love and yourself. So, now we go into the forest and I teach you the words of the most powerful curse.'

Fifteen minutes later, she stood me in the middle of the

clearing and made me memorise the words she whispered in Spanish, with a talisman round my neck to protect me. Perhaps it was a good thing that I couldn't understand what they were. I was never to say them out loud, let alone write them down, only go over them in my mind until they were indelibly inked onto my psyche.

'How many times have you used the curse?' I asked as we walked back home.

'Only twice,' she said. 'Once for me, once for someone else who needed my help.'

'What happened to the people you cursed?'

'They died,' she said with a shrug.

'Right,' I breathed, both overwhelmed and appalled by this woman's powers and only hoping the same was not within me, for this was one skill I did not wish to possess.

'So, you have done well, Erizo,' Angelina said two days later. 'And Pepe and I have a surprise for you. Go and see Marcella now.' She shooed me off so she could take her siesta and I walked up to the hotel to find Marcella, who was smiling at me knowingly.

'Come with me, Tiggy,' she said, drawing me into the parts of the cave that were her private rooms. They were decorated with traditional fabrics and blankets, a huge old-fashioned television in one corner.

'There,' she said, pointing to the sofa.

Laid upon it was a beautiful flamenco dress, white with rich purple ruffles trailing down its skirt.

'Try it on,' Marcella said. 'It is my old one from when I

was a child, but it should fit you. We shall make you into a
real *bailaora* – a flamenco dancer – for the fiesta tonight.'

'I'm to wear this?' I said in surprise.

'Of course, it is a fiesta!'

She handed me the pile of soft fabric and ushered me into
the small shower room, where I took off my dress, and slid
the garment over my body. Going out to Marcella so she could
do up the many buttons, I smoothed down the skirt and
adjusted the deep V-neckline.

'Here, Tiggy, look in the mirror.' Marcella turned me to
face it.

I glanced at myself and was shocked at the woman who
looked back me. This Tiggy was brown from the Spanish sun,
eyes sparkling, the dress accentuating my tiny waist and smooth
décolletage.

'*Linda!*' Marcella declared. 'Beautiful! Now, you need
shoes. Angelina has given me these for you – I doubted they
would fit, but now that I have seen your tiny feet, I know she
is right.' She held out a pair of red leather shoes with a slim
buckled band. The sturdy Cuban-shaped heels were only
about five centimetres high – but as I never wore anything but
flats, that was enough for me. I took them from her, and tried
them on, feeling rather like Cinderella. As they slid perfectly
onto my feet, I felt a prickle on the back of my neck.

'Marcella, whose shoes are these?' I asked.

'Why, they are your grandmother Lucía's, of course,' she said.

At nine o'clock that night, Marcella and I walked down the
hill to one of the larger caves, although I would have known

where to find it without her, for the music echoed through the whole of Sacromonte, and it felt as though the very air was alive with it. I patted my hair self-consciously as Marcella pulled me inside the already crowded cave. She had oiled my locks into submission, and had affixed a central curl onto my forehead, just like Lucía's in the pictures I had seen of her.

At my entrance, a sea of people began clapping and cheering, and I was drawn from one person to another by a beaming Angelina and Pepe, who were both dressed in their finest flamenco clothes, like everyone else.

'Erizo, this is your mother's cousin's granddaughter, Pilar – and here are Vicente and Gael . . . Camila . . . Luis . . .'

With my head spinning, I let myself be guided through the crowd, overwhelmed by the genuine warmth of everyone's embraces. Vicente – or was it Gael? – handed me a glass of manzanilla wine, and I saw Pepe at the back of the cave, perched on a chair with his guitar in his lap, next to a man sitting on a box.

'*¡Empezamos!*' he called. 'Let's begin!'

'*¡Olé!*' cried the audience as two young dancers sashayed onto the floor. They began to dance what Angelina told me was a '*chufla bulerías* – a simple dance', but as I watched the women tap their heels and balls of their feet in a fast rhythm, their hands guiding their skirts so the cave was awash with bright colours, their chins tipped proudly in absolute unison, I was in awe of their skill.

And I was a part of this; the *gitano* culture was in my blood and soul. When a young man reached to take my hand, I didn't resist, but let my body relax and be carried along by the rhythm of Pepe's guitar, and what everyone here called the *duende* inside me.

I don't know how long I danced for, but Lucía's shoes seemed to guide me, and I didn't care if I looked stupid as I copied my partner and stamped down on the ancient floor of the cave with the rest of my new family around me. The floor vibrated as every single man, woman and child danced for sheer joy, the beat of the music irresistible.

'*¡Olé!*' Pepe called.

'*¡Olé!*' I shouted with everyone else, then left my partner to go and drink some water.

'Tiggy!'

I felt a firm hand on my shoulder. And was pretty sure that the alcohol I'd drunk combined with all the twirling had made my brain dizzy, for as I turned round I thought how like Charlie Kinnaird the voice sounded.

'Hello, Tiggy,' Charlie said as he grabbed my arm and unceremoniously pulled me through the crowd of stamping, clapping dancers.

'What on earth are you doing?' I shouted, trying to make myself heard above the noise. 'Let me go!'

But he wouldn't, and no matter how much I wriggled and complained, I was attached to him until he chose to let me go.

No one seemed to bat an eyelid at us – what I'd learnt tonight was that *gitanos* were a vociferous and emotional breed, and our behaviour was probably normal to them.

'I'll have to take you outside, I can't hear myself think in here,' Charlie said, taking off his jumper and wrapping it round my bare shoulders.

Once outside, he looked around, spied the wall opposite and led me to it. Only when we reached it did he let go of my arm, then he put his hands around my waist, picked me up and sat me on top of the wall.

'Charlie, what on earth are you doing here?!'

'You have to sit down, Tiggy.' Having let go of my waist, he then grabbed my wrist to feel my pulse.

'Charlie, enough!' I raised my other hand to slap his fingers away.

'Your pulse is racing, Tiggy!'

'Yes, because I've just spent the last hour dancing my feet off,' I retorted. 'Why are you here?'

'Because I and the rest of the world have been trying to get hold of you.'

'What do you mean, "the rest of the world"?' I frowned at him.

'Cal found your mobile in your bedroom and we called everyone in your address book to see if they'd heard from you. They hadn't. It was only when you left the messages for him and Ma that we knew you were in Spain.'

'Sorry, Charlie,' I sighed. 'Can you just slow down, please. What's happened? Has someone been hurt?'

'No, Tiggy, no one else has been hurt,' he said. 'It's you.'

'What do you mean, "me"?'

'I collated and analysed all your test results on the morning you decided to run away from the hospital. Look, Tiggy, in a nutshell, I suspect that you have a serious heart condition called myocarditis. You need immediate medical attention.'

'A serious heart condition?' I said faintly. 'Me?'

'Yes. Or at least, potentially serious, if left untreated.'

'But I feel fine,' I insisted. 'Since I've been here, the heart palpitations seem to have stopped.' I looked him in the eye for the first time. 'Are you saying that you've flown out all this way to tell me?'

'Yes, of course I have. I couldn't get in touch with you so

I had no choice. Seriously, Tiggy, on top of you nearly dying while working on the estate, I couldn't have this on my conscience as well.'

'Well, it wouldn't have been, Charlie. It was me who "ran away" from the hospital, as you put it.'

'Yes, but alongside my professional obligations, I felt a duty as your employer. I had no idea how difficult things were for you at Kinnaird. I understand now why you had to leave.'

I kept quiet, wondering if he was referring to my conversation with his wife.

'Beryl and Cal told me about Zed Eszu's behaviour,' he continued. 'They both agreed that it was him who'd driven you away. I'm so sorry, Tiggy, you should have said something to me. That kind of behaviour is just . . . unacceptable.'

'It's not your fault, really, Charlie.'

'Oh yes it is,' he said. 'I should have been up at Kinnaird running it and then I could have stopped it. It was sexual harassment, plain and simple. If I ever see him again, I swear, I'll wring his neck.'

'No one mentioned to Zed where I'd gone, did they?' I asked him, genuinely nervous.

'Of course not,' Charlie replied. 'I drove straight up to Kinnaird when I heard from Cal what had happened, and told Zed to clear out of my house. He packed his things and disappeared in his Range Rover that afternoon. He's gone, Tiggy, I promise,' he said, sensing my fear and putting a hand on mine, which sent a massive tingle through my body. 'I hope you'll feel that you can come back to Kinnaird now.'

'Thank you.' For now, I was quite happy to let Charlie think that Zed was the only reason I'd left.

'And also, the police have been trying to get in touch with

you about the shooting. They've found the bullet casing and are running forensics on it.'

'Have they found the person who did it?' I asked, thinking of poor Pegasus.

'I couldn't say, but they want to talk to you again at some point. As for your medical problem, I've booked you into the local hospital here in Granada tomorrow. We'll run some more tests to make sure you're fit to fly home.'

I looked up at him in surprise. Even though he was only trying to care for me, he suddenly sounded eerily reminiscent of Zed: i.e. another man trying to control my life.

'Sorry, Charlie, but I feel absolutely fine and I'm definitely not leaving Granada yet.'

'I know you may feel fine at the moment, but your test results showed that you're not. This is serious, Tiggy. It could . . . well, kill you.'

'Charlie, I had loads of tests on my heart as I was growing up. It was fine then, so why shouldn't it be fine now?'

'Okay,' Charlie sighed and leant against the wall next to me. 'Hear me out, will you? Without interrupting. I just want to ask you a couple of questions.'

'Fire away,' I said reluctantly as I heard the beat of the *cajón* and the shouts of '*Olé!*' coming from inside. Tonight of all nights, I really didn't want to be sitting here on a wall outside and discussing an imaginary heart condition.

'When did you first notice the palpitations?'

'Um . . . I've had them on and off for a while, but I suppose they do tend to get worse if I have a bad bout of bronchitis. And I had a bad cold and cough recently.'

'Okay. Now, can you think back a few years to a time you were really sick in bed and had a high fever?'

495

'That's easy. I was seventeen and in my last year at boarding school. I came down with a really high temperature and they put me in the san. The doctor diagnosed strep throat and gave me some antibiotics. I got better eventually, but it took its time. That was years ago, Charlie, and I've been fine since.'

'And did you have any kind of heart scan between then and when you were in the hospital in Inverness?'

'No.'

'Tiggy,' Charlie sighed, 'myocarditis is quite rare and it's not always clear what causes it, but it's usually triggered by a viral infection. Which is probably what you had at seventeen, but it was misdiagnosed as strep throat.'

'Oh, I see,' I said, now all ears.

'Anyway,' Charlie continued, 'the virus, for reasons we don't yet fully understand, causes inflammation of the heart muscle. Other illnesses tend to put extra stress on it, which could be why you started having palpitations after you were ill recently. And the shock of the shooting of course.'

I was silent now, sobering up from the atmosphere and the alcohol and beginning to understand why Charlie was here.

'Could I . . . die?'

'Without the right treatment, then yes. It's serious, Tiggy.'

'And with medication, can it be cured?'

'Perhaps, but there's no straightforward prognosis. Sometimes the heart can heal itself with rest, sometimes it heals with the help of beta-blockers or ACE-inhibitors, and occasionally . . . well, it's not a positive outcome.'

I shivered, partly through fear, but also because now I'd calmed down, the night was chilly.

'Come on, we need to get you in the warm.' He reached

out his hands to help me off the wall, but I hopped off by myself.

'You and all those people look very authentic, by the way,' Charlie commented on my outfit. 'Fancy dress party, was it?'

'No.' This at least brought a smile to my lips. 'Those people inside, they're real gypsies, and more than that – every single one of them is related to me! Now,' – I looked at his startled face – 'even if I do drop dead in the process, I'm afraid I have to go and say goodnight to my new family.'

'Of course. I'll wait here.'

I went inside and watched the entire crowd still stamping, singing and dancing as if tomorrow might never come.

*Which it might not for you, Tiggy.*

I found Angelina sitting beside Pepe, who had set down his guitar and was mopping his face with a large handkerchief.

'I'm going home to bed now. I hope you don't mind, but I'm feeling very tired. *Muchas gracias* for all this.'

They both gave me sweaty hugs and kisses on my cheeks.

'You are now truly one of us, Erizo. Now, go off to your boyfriend,' Angelina said with a grin.

'He's not my boyfriend, he's my boss,' I said firmly.

Angelina raised an eyebrow and shrugged. '*Buenas noches*, Erizo.'

'What is this place?' Charlie asked me as we made our way along the winding path. 'It seemed deserted on the walk from the taxi to check in. Do people still live here?'

'Some, yes, but not many. They used to all live in the caves here until they started moving into modern apartments in the city.'

'It's extraordinary,' he breathed as we took the steps back up the hill. 'It must be virtually unchanged in hundreds of years.' He glanced at me trudging up the steps next to him. 'Take it slowly, please, Tiggy, just until we have you sorted out.'

'Seriously, I feel fine,' I said. 'The air here must have done me good. My heart hardly jumped at all tonight whilst I was dancing,' I added as we reached the top and started to walk along the twisting path that snaked back and forth across the mountain between the rows of caves. 'So how did you eventually find me here?'

'As I said, from your call to Ma, we knew you'd come to Spain, then Cal had a rifle through your drawers looking for clues as to where exactly in Spain you might have gone. He found some Wikipedia pages you'd printed off about a Spanish dancer. They mentioned Granada and Sacromonte, so we reckoned there was a good chance that's where you'd have headed. Wow, Tiggy!' Charlie halted in his tracks as we rounded the bend and there was the Alhambra floating above us in the night sky. 'Isn't that an incredible view?'

'It is.'

'Have you been yet?'

'No, I've been far too busy. Where are you staying?'

'At the only hotel here, according to the information lady at the airport: the Cuevas El Albanico. So we took it.'

'"We"?'

'Yes,' he said as we approached the hotel, 'I didn't feel it was . . . right for me to come alone, so I brought a chaperone along. Come and see,' he said as he ushered me through the gates. 'She may be in bed by now but—'

I'd barely stepped inside as a figure wearing a pair of checked pyjamas ran towards me and threw her arms around me.

'Tiggy! It's so wonderful to see you.'

'And you, Ally,' I said in wonder, as I pulled out of her embrace and studied her. 'Wow, you look amazing.' I took in Ally's sparkling blue eyes, her thick red-gold hair and the big bump in her belly that was straining the buttons of her pyjamas. 'Goodness, you're big! You look as though you're about to burst. Are you sure you should be flying?'

'I'm fine. I've still got about another month to go, but I was going mad sitting at home in Bergen, so Thom, my twin brother, took pity on me and invited me to tag along with him to a concert he was playing in London. I persuaded my doctor it was a good idea for me to get a change of scenery. Then, when Charlie called me and I heard what had happened to you and that he thought you were here, I changed my ticket and came straight to Granada with him.'

'Oh God, Ally, really, I'm fine,' I groaned. 'You should be tucked up safe in Bergen, not running across Europe after me.'

'Tiggy, we were all worried about you. Now, if you'll excuse me, ladies, I'll leave you to chat,' Charlie said, reaching for my pulse again, then nodding. 'It's calmed down now.'

'Has Charlie explained to you how serious your condition is?' Ally asked.

'I have,' said Charlie, 'and even if I have to drag you to that hospital tomorrow, you're going, okay, Tiggy?'

'She'll go,' Ally answered for me.

'Any problems during the night, you know where I am.'

'Yes. Night, Charlie, and thanks,' Ally called after him as he made his way to his room at the back of the hotel. Neither of us said anything until we heard the door close behind him.

'Would you prefer to go straight to bed, Tiggy?'

'No, I'm far too hyped up to sleep and I want to hear all

your news. Let's go and sit in there,' I said, indicating the small sitting room with its leather sofas.

'Not for long, or Doctor Charlie won't be happy,' Ally whispered as I led the way and she eased herself onto one of them.

'So, you were explaining how you found me?'

'Charlie was beside himself when he called me on your mobile. What a lovely guy he is,' Ally smiled. 'And obviously very fond of you.'

'I'm just sorry to put you both to so much trouble.'

'Honestly, Tiggy, as I said, I was grateful for an excuse not to go back to Bergen. You know me – all action,' she smiled. 'Besides, I was really worried about you, we all were. I have to say, you look a lot better than I expected.'

'I'm feeling better too, really. When I arrived here, my heart was bouncy, but it's calmed down a lot since.'

'Good. Charlie also mentioned that your Cal had found some printouts in your drawer about a female flamenco dancer.' Ally indicated my dress. 'I'm guessing that's why you came here? To find your birth family?'

'Yes.'

'Okay, but what was it that made you get out of your hospital bed and leave without telling anyone where you were going?'

'I . . . it's complicated, Ally, but I just needed to get away.'

'I know that feeling,' she said. 'Charlie seemed to think that, quite apart from you getting shot, it was something to do with a white stag and also Zed Eszu.'

'Yes, those things definitely played a part.'

'I hear you spoke to Maia,' said Ally.

'Yup. She confirmed everything I was feeling. I said no to the job, of course.'

'Theo says he's an absolute prick,' she said with a sad smile.

The way Ally talked about the father of her child in the present tense brought a lump to my throat. I gazed at her, feeling the same admiration for my big sister as I had when I was a child. As I had so often been confined on the attic floor due to my regular bouts of illness, I'd spent many hours on the window seat watching Ally speed across Lake Geneva on her Laser. I'd seen her capsize, then haul herself up and out of the water, only to start all over again. I, more than anyone, knew the courage and sheer determination Ally had shown to get where she'd wanted to be. Without a doubt, my strong, capable sister was who I'd aspired to be when I was younger. And her presence here tonight – especially given the fact she shouldn't be here at all with so little time to go until her baby made an appearance – touched me enormously.

'Zed was so weirdly mesmerising, Ally. It's like . . .' I searched for the right words. 'Well, you're the only person in the room. He focuses all his attention on you and it's the same feeling as being a rabbit caught in the headlights. He . . . hypnotises you and won't take no for an answer.'

'I think what you're trying to say is that if he wants something, he's unstoppable in his pursuit of it. And for some reason none of us can understand, he seems to want the D'Aplièse sisters. Maybe it's coincidence, but it's pretty strange that I should see Kreeg Eszu's boat next to Pa's during his private funeral. You're the one with the instincts, Tiggy. What do you think?'

'I don't know, Ally, really.'

'I know that in the past I've teased you about your weird beliefs, but . . .' Ally bit her lip. 'Sometimes I swear I can hear Theo talking to me. Telling me off about something or other, or saying something funny to make me giggle when I'm missing him.'

I watched as my sister's eyes glistened with unshed tears.

'I'm sure he *is* here, Ally,' I said as a sudden tingle ran up my spine, and I felt the hairs on my arms stand on end. I'd always wondered what it meant, and Angelina had explained it was because a spirit was present. So I smiled as I heard Theo ask me a question for Ally.

'He says he wants to know why you're not wearing the eye,' I said.

Ally's face drained of colour as her hand went automatically to her neck.

'I . . . Tiggy, how can you know about that? It was a necklace he bought me just after he proposed. It was only cheap and a few weeks ago, the chain broke and I still haven't got round to getting it fixed . . . oh my God, Tiggy, oh my God.'

Ally looked so terrified that I immediately felt guilty, but I was sitting in the sacred caves of Sacromonte with all the power that they held from centuries of my ancestors, and I couldn't stop what I was hearing.

'He also says he likes the name "Bear".'

'We were once talking about what we'd call our kids, and I said I liked Teddy, and he said . . . he said' – Ally gulped – 'that he preferred "Bear".'

'He loves you, Ally, and he also says . . .' I listened hard as I could feel the energy weakening, 'to be prepared.'

She looked at me in confusion. 'What does that mean?'

'Honestly, Ally, I have no idea, I'm sorry.'

'I . . .' Ally wiped her eyes roughly with the backs of her hands, 'I'm so . . . gobsmacked by what you've just said. My God, Tiggy, what a gift you have. I mean, really, there's no way you could have known those things. Just no way.'

'Something's happened to me here,' I said quietly. 'It's difficult to explain, but apparently I come from a long line of gypsy psychics. I've always felt things, but since I met Angelina, and after what she's taught me, everything has started to make sense.'

'So you have found a relative?' Ally said as she visibly composed herself.

'Oh yes. As Charlie saw earlier, I've actually got scores of them. They were all at the fiesta tonight, but I've been spending the most time with Angelina and her Uncle Pepe – my great-uncle.'

'So . . . this is starting to make sense to me too. You're descended from a line of gypsies, and we all know about their fortune-telling talents.' Ally smiled at me.

'Well, I haven't seen a single crystal ball or a piece of heather so far,' I said, suddenly feeling prickly and defensive. 'Angelina is what they call a *bruja*, in other words, a medicine woman, who knows more about herbs and plants and their healing properties than anyone I've ever met. She's spent her life caring for not only the gypsies but the *payos* – the non-gypsies. She's a force for good, and what she does is real, Ally, I promise you.'

'After what you just said to me about Theo, I'm ready to believe anything,' Ally said with a shudder. 'Anyway, before you freak me out any more, it's time we both went to bed. Help me up, will you?'

Ally reached out a hand and I pulled her upright.

She winced slightly and clasped her belly, then looked up at me. 'Want to feel your niece or nephew kick?'

'I'd love to,' I said as Ally guided my hand just to the left of her belly button. After a few seconds, I felt a sharp thrust into my curved palm. It was the first time I'd ever felt a baby kick and it brought tears to my eyes.

We hugged and then walked along the narrow corridor towards our rooms.

'Night, darling Tiggy. Sleep well.'

'And you, Ally. And I'm really sorry if . . .'

'Shh,' Ally put a finger to her lips. 'Once I've managed to actually process it, what just happened is going to stand out as one of the most special moments of my life. Oh . . .'

'What?'

'You know he said he liked the name "Bear"?'

'Yes.'

'It's not a good name for a girl, is it?'

'No, it isn't,' I said, and gave her a little wink. 'Night, Ally.'

The next day, I staggered out of the blackness of my cave-room and into the bright sunshine. Sitting at one of the tables in the courtyard was the unlikely mix of my boss, my sister, and my newly discovered *gitano* relatives.

'Hello, Sleeping Beauty,' Ally teased me. 'I was just about to come and get you. It's noon already.'

'I'm so sorry, I've never slept in as late as that in my life.'

Angelina muttered something and shrugged her shoulders expressively.

'She says you need your sleep,' said Charlie.

'You speak Spanish?' I asked in surprise.

'I spent my gap year working in Seville. Angelina and I have had a very interesting conversation. She tells me she's a practising doctor of medicine too.'

'She is.'

'She's also told me that she has been treating you for your heart problems since you arrived here.'

'Really?' I looked at Angelina. 'Is this true? 'That stuff you've been making me drink . . .'

'*Sí,*' Angelina shrugged. Then she spoke again in Spanish to Charlie, gesticulating at me, which really irritated me as I couldn't pick up most of what they were saying.

'She said that your "ancestors" came to help you when you went to the woods. And they are helping you still.'

'Did they? Are they? Well, if they are, I'm really happy. Especially if it means I don't have to go to the hospital . . .'

'Sorry, Tiggy, even though I have an open mind when it comes to alternative treatments, we still need to do those tests. And we need to leave now, if you don't mind.'

'Okay,' I sighed, surrendering.

'Marcella has said she will drive us there. I'll be back in a moment.'

Charlie departed to go to his room, whilst Angelina, Ally and I sat in the sun eating warm bread and jam, washed down with another dose of potion.

'This must be good for me,' I said, crossing my eyes exaggeratedly as I sucked the last couple of mouthfuls from the straw. 'Angelina, why didn't you tell me you saw my sickness?'

'Sickness makes fear, and fear becomes a sickness itself. Better you do not know. Then you get better quickly.'

'You certainly look well,' Ally put in. 'I told her and

Charlie what you said to me last night, that you couldn't have known. Honestly, Tiggy.' Ally put her hand on mine. 'I'm still getting over the shock.'

'Oh God.' I blushed to the roots of my hair. 'So Charlie knows all about me too?'

'Yes, but you shouldn't be embarrassed, Tiggy. What you can do is absolutely amazing.'

'*Sí*.' Angelina patted her chest proudly. 'She is of my blood.'

'Right, we'd better go,' said Charlie, reappearing on the terrace.

Marcella sped us down the narrow streets towards the city, and if anything was going to give me a heart attack, her driving certainly could, I thought. Without a care for her tiny Punto, she careered around corners and almost lost one of the wing mirrors squeezing through the tiny alleyways. Charlie, Ally and I all breathed more easily when she drove through the city gates at the bottom of the hill, and we merged into the relative safety of the heavy Granada traffic.

I glanced at my watch and saw it was already nearing one. 'It's going to take us ages to be seen, I'm sure.'

'We won't have to wait,' said Charlie. 'I phoned a friend who knew a friend who works in the cardiac department here. I'm just going to call her to let her know that we're here.'

Five minutes later we climbed out of Marcella's car, giving Ally a hand to extract her from the front seat. As we made our way into the hospital reception I saw a very attractive woman with glossy dark curls approach Charlie. The two of them chatted for a while as Ally and I hung back out of politeness.

'This is Tiggy.' Charlie eventually introduced us in English. 'Meet Rosa, who has very kindly offered to help us jump the queue.'

'*Hola*, Tiggy.' Rosa held out her hand and shook mine. 'Now, we go.'

Rosa and Charlie led the way, still chatting as I walked behind them with Ally, feeling like a child being dragged to a dentist. We went up in a lift and emerged into a small reception area, where Rosa spoke to the woman behind the desk.

'Please, sit,' she said to us. We did so, then I turned to Charlie.

'So, exactly what am I having?'

'You'll have another ECG first, then an echocardiogram, as well as some blood tests. Apart from my professional judgement, Angelina agreed that other tests were a good idea.'

'Is she worried about me?'

'I think the opposite actually. Angelina thinks you're well on the way to being cured, and she wants to prove that to me. Anyway, it certainly won't do any harm.'

A nurse with a clipboard came over and asked me to follow her. I could almost feel the animosity of the other patients who had probably been sitting there for hours and were almost certainly far sicker than I was . . .

Three hours later, having had all the tests and scans, I dressed and went back to sit in the waiting room with Ally.

'Has Charlie left?'

'No. He disappeared with the gorgeous Rosa and hasn't been seen since.' Ally giggled. 'Maybe she's seduced him in the scanner; she certainly looked as though she wanted to eat him.'

'Really?'

'Didn't you notice? It's not surprising, is it? He's a very attractive man.'

'He's quite old, Ally,' I rubbed my nose, just in case I was blushing.

'Old?! Honestly, Tiggy, he's only thirty-eight, and people in their thirties – like me – still have a pulse, you know . . .'

'Sorry, I often forget that there's an age gap of seven years between us. Anyway, there he is, so he's obviously survived the seduction.'

Charlie was holding a large envelope. 'You okay, Tiggy?' he asked me as he sat down.

'Yup, never better.'

'And yes,' Charlie tapped the envelope, 'it seems you are. Better, that is. I'll need to do some more analysis of the scans, but the heart muscle does appear to have recovered somewhat. Your ECG was normal as well, although when you arrive back in Scotland, I'd like to put you on a black box for a couple of days or so, just to make sure it's stabilised.'

'What's a black box?'

'It monitors your heart and gives us an overall picture of how it's functioning.'

'So you definitely think there's been an improvement, Charlie?' Ally cut in. She always liked to get straight to the point.

'Dare I say it, but yes. Of course, this might be something to do with the fact that Tiggy has been resting. Or sometimes the heart begins to heal itself . . .'

'What? Can hearts really mend in ten days?' Ally queried.

'Not normally, no, but—'

'Told you I was feeling better,' I put in smugly.

'Do you think that Angelina's treatments might have had an effect?' Ally asked.

'Something has,' Charlie admitted. 'Although don't get too

cocky, miss,' he added, wagging a finger at me. 'There's still some slight inflammation, but I'm happy to have you fly home tomorrow and then we can monitor you properly for a while.'

'I'm really sorry, Charlie, but I'm not coming back to Scotland. I want to stay in Granada. I have Angelina and Pepe to look after me, it's warm, and I feel more relaxed than I have done for ages. I can always come back to the hospital here and see your Rosa if I have a problem.'

Ally and Charlie shared a look, which reminded me of Ma and old Dr Gerber doing the same when I was a child. Nine times out of ten, that look meant bad news for me.

'Tiggy, we really think you should fly home as soon as possible. I can't stay with you, because of you-know-who –' Ally pointed at her bump – 'but Charlie has told me that what you need is rest.'

'Tiggy, myocarditis is . . .' Charlie searched for the word, 'unpredictable. I want you to take it easy for the time being, instead of wandering through woods at night, speaking to dead people.'

'Don't describe it like that, Charlie,' I reprimanded him. 'I've got better here – even you're saying I have.'

'I don't think Charlie meant it like that, Tiggy.' Ally came to his rescue. 'But neither of us trusts you to rest if you stay here alone.'

'No, we don't, and Beryl has already said she'd be happy to take care of you at the Lodge. She'll have me on speed dial, ready to despatch an air ambulance straight to you in any emergency. So for now, why don't you two head back to the hotel? I'm staying here for a while. Rosa's going to take me to their research lab – it's state of the art apparently.'

'I bet she is,' mumbled Ally under her breath. 'Right, see

you later, Charlie.' She heaved herself up. 'I don't know about you, Tiggy, but I'm starving. Shall we get something to eat in the city before we head upwards?'

With me still smarting that Charlie had abandoned us for the charms of Rosa, we asked for directions and then walked to the bustling Plaza Nueva. With every step I took, I felt the jumbled history of this city, from engravings of Spanish pomegranates, to colourful Moorish tiles. The square was lined with grand sandstone buildings, teeming cafés and shops, and a crowd had formed around a pair of flamenco dancers who were dancing in the bright sun. Up above us, the fortified walls of the Alhambra were flanked by trees, as if they were still guarding this city a thousand years on.

We found a cosy bodega in one of the cobbled alleyways off the square, mismatched chairs and tables squeezed into a tiny room where we could feel the heat from the kitchen. Having chosen from the gorgeous array of tapas dishes, Ally tucked into chorizo and *empanadillas*, whilst I enjoyed *patatas bravas* and roasted artichokes, the only vegan things on the menu.

'So, Tiggy.' Ally eyed me over her cup of coffee. 'I hope you're going to obey doctor's orders and fly back to Scotland tomorrow.'

'No way am I going back to Kinnaird, and that's that.'

'Tiggy, what is it? This is Ally you're talking to. You know I'm like a vault; I won't tell anyone, promise.'

'I . . . the thing is, Ally, there's been nothing going on between me and Charlie but—'

'I thought it might be something like that. I mean, it's been pretty obvious to me from that first phone call how Charlie feels about you.'

'Ally! We're just friends, really. He's my boss . . .'

'Theo was mine. So?' Ally countered.

'And even if Charlie wasn't,' I continued, 'you wouldn't believe how complicated his life is. He's married for starters, to a seriously scary – and very tall – woman.'

'Okay, answer me honestly, Tiggy: have you or haven't you been having an affair with Charlie Kinnaird?'

'No!' I insisted. 'I absolutely haven't, but . . . look, I'll tell you as long as you swear not to say anything to another soul.'

'I don't think anyone in Bergen is interested in your love life, Tiggy.'

'True, but I really don't want Ma or the rest of our sisters to know. The Valkyrie – that's my nickname for Charlie's wife – thinks something's been going on between us too. She came to see me in the hospital and basically told me never to darken her – and Charlie's – door again.'

'Right. Presumably Charlie doesn't know anything about this?'

'No.'

'But you do . . . like him, don't you, Tiggy? I can see you do.'

'Of course I do! So that's why I left, even though I've done nothing I should be ashamed of, I . . . well' – I felt the blush rise to my cheeks – 'I wanted to, Ally. And it isn't right. Charlie's a married man and I'm not going to be a home wrecker. They have a sixteen-year-old daughter too! Besides, look at the way Rosa reacted to him. I don't want to be one of the many women who throw themselves at him. That would be sad, it really would.'

'Tiggy, how many boyfriends have you actually had?'

'Oh, a couple, but not anyone serious.'

'You have had . . . you know?'

'Yes,' I said, lowering my eyes in embarrassment, 'but only a couple of times. I'm afraid I'm one of those old-fashioned girls who equate sex with love.'

'I understand completely, and there's no need to be ashamed of it.'

'Isn't there? I sometimes feel that I'm really pathetic and out of date. All my mates at uni didn't think twice about spending the night with a man they'd just met at a party. And why shouldn't they take their pleasure like a man?'

'Because they're not men?' Ally rolled her eyes. 'I just don't understand the feminists who seem to model themselves on *males*, rather than relying on what I think is our superior set of *female* life skills. I swear, Tiggy, if we use those instead of trying to ape men, we'd be ruling the world within a decade or two. Anyway, I digress. My point was that you're not very experienced with men, are you?'

'No.'

'Well, I'm here to tell you that the one we just left at the hospital two hours ago is not only decent, kind, and incredibly attractive,' Ally winked at me, 'but he's also as keen on you as you are on him. Why else do you think he'd go to all this trouble?'

'Professional reasons, Ally. He told me himself.'

'Rubbish. Charlie came here because he cares about you deeply. I'd say he's almost certainly in love with you . . .'

'Please don't say that, Ally,' I begged her. 'You'll just make me more confused.'

'Sorry, but given what I've been through in the past few months, I've realised that the moment is all we have. Life's too short, Tiggy. And whatever you decide, I just wanted to tell you that the way he feels about you is written all over him, so no wonder his wife was feeling insecure.'

'Then surely it's best I just disappear? It's all too complicated.'

'Life usually is, and certainly to get anything worthwhile. Anyway, the bottom line is, you can't stay here alone. So, if you won't go back to Scotland, then how about Atlantis? Ma would love to have you, and the hospitals in Geneva are second to none. What do you think?'

'I just don't understand why I can't stay here.'

'You're beginning to sound like a sulky toddler,' Ally sighed. 'I appreciate that you trust Angelina to take care of you, but even she couldn't save you from a sudden heart attack. And it's not fair to ask Marcella to mind you either. Besides, the cave hotel is sweet, but given you need to rest, it would be pretty depressing lying in there all day. So, why don't you consider going to Geneva and letting Ma unleash all her pent-up maternal instincts on her patient?'

I looked at Ally, processed what she had just said, and sighed heavily.

'Okay, but I'm only doing it for you, Ally.'

'I don't care who you're doing it for, Tiggy, I just want you to be well.'

'Oh Ally . . .' I found my eyes filling with tears.

'What is it?' Ally reached her hand across the table to me.

'Just that . . . I spent so much of my childhood watching life go on from behind my bedroom window at Atlantis. I really thought those days were over. I have so many ideas . . . plans for the future, all of which involve me being well. And if this thing –' I put a hand over my heart – 'doesn't get better, then I'm not going to be able to do any of them. I'm only twenty-six, for goodness' sake. I'm too young to be an invalid.'

'Well, let's hope you won't be, Tiggy. Surely you can see that ensuring your future health is worth a few weeks' sacrifice? And it might give you some breathing space to think about whether you want to go back to Scotland or not.'

'I'm not going back to Scotland, Ally. I can't.'

'Okay,' she sighed, signalling for the bill, 'but at least we have a plan. So we'll find a travel agent in town to book your flight to Geneva. And after that, we're going to go and visit Granada cathedral, the resting place of my all-time heroine, Queen Isabella the First of Spain.'

'She's buried here?'

'Yes, alongside her beloved husband, Ferdinand. Ready?' she asked me with a smile.

'Ready.'

The woman at the travel agent frowned as she checked her computer screen.

'It is not an easy journey from Granada to Geneva, señorita.'

'How long will it take?' I asked.

'At least twelve hours, maybe more, depending on connecting flights from Barcelona or Madrid.'

'Oh I see, I didn't realise—'

'That's ridiculous, Tiggy,' Ally interjected. 'You're not in a fit state to spend that long travelling.'

'But you came here from London, and you're nearly eight months pregnant!' I protested.

'That's different, Tiggy. Pregnancy isn't an illness – unlike a heart condition,' she reminded me. 'Forget this, I'm going to call Ma. Wait here.' With that she marched out of the shop, all action as usual, and already pulling her mobile from her bag.

I shrugged apologetically at the woman behind the desk and began flicking through travel brochures to hide my embarrassment, while I waited for my sister to return.

Five minutes later, Ally was back with a satisfied smile on her face. 'Ma says she's going to call Georg Hoffman and arrange a private plane to take you directly to Geneva tomorrow evening. She'll text me shortly with the details.'

'But that's ludicrous, Ally! It's not necessary, and besides, I don't have the money for that kind of thing, nowhere near it!'

'Ma insisted – she wants you back there as soon as possible. And don't worry about the cost; just remember, we are all daughters of a very wealthy man, who left everything to us. Occasionally that legacy comes in handy, especially in cases of life or death,' she added grimly. 'Now, I don't want to hear another peep out of you on the subject. Let's get to that cathedral.'

Inside the Royal Chapel, it was cool and dark, and I looked up at the high Gothic arches, wondering if *my* family had lived here as far back as the time of Queen Isabella. Ally took my hand, and together we walked towards the white marble monuments, where Isabella and Ferdinand's outlines were carved into visages of peace. I turned to Ally, who I had expected to be looking at Isabella's image, transfixed, but she was already walking down a staircase. I followed her hastily and we found ourselves in a low-ceilinged crypt underneath the towering cathedral, the air cool and the walls damp. In front of us, behind a wall of glass, were a number of ancient lead coffins.

'There she is, next to Ferdinand for all eternity,' Ally whispered to me. 'There is her daughter, who they called Joanna the Mad, and her husband. Isabella's little grandson is also here . . . he died in her arms when he was only two.'

I gave her hand a squeeze. 'Tell me about her. Now that it turns out I *am* Spanish, I need to catch up on my history.'

'I remember seeing a picture of her in a history book at school and thinking that I looked a little bit like her. Then I read more about her life and I became obsessed. She really was one of the first feminists – she rode into battle alongside her husband, even though she had five kids. She brought huge wealth to Spain, and without her, Christopher Columbus never would have made it to the New World – but when he brought back Native American slaves, she ordered them to be set free. Even if she did start the Spanish Inquisition, but that's another story. Anyway,' Ally said, then winced and held her stomach. 'I think we'd better head back to the hotel so I can lie down. Sorry, it's probably a combination of late pregnancy and sightseeing.'

As we crossed the plaza outside, blinking in the bright sunshine, I heard a gravelly voice shout, 'Erizo!'

I spun around, shocked, and saw an elderly gypsy woman looking straight at me.

'Erizo,' she said again.

'*Sí*,' I breathed. 'How do you know who I am?'

Wordlessly, she held out a bouquet of rosemary, tied together with string, from a basket full of them.

I took it from her with a smile, and gave her five euros.

Then she placed my hand in her rough one and muttered something in Spanish before ambling away.

'What was that about? Did you know her?' Ally asked.

'No,' I said, rubbing the rosemary between my fingers, the fresh herbal scent rising up to my nostrils. 'But somehow she knew *me* . . .'

We returned to Sacromonte as the sun was setting and found Charlie, Pepe and Angelina in the little terrace garden.

'It smells wonderful out here,' Ally commented.

'Are these some of the herbs you use in your work?' Charlie asked Angelina.

'*Sí*,' she answered.

I noticed that Ally was stroking her extended belly tentatively and looking agitated.

'Are you okay, darling?' I whispered.

'I think so. I just . . . need to go to the bathroom.'

As I helped my sister to standing, Angelina looked up at us, her dark eyes narrowing slightly. 'All is good?'

'Yes, I'm just going to help Ally to the bathroom,' I replied.

As we made our way into the interior of the cave, Ally suddenly stopped and winced, one hand on her lower back, the other clutching at her stomach.

At that moment, a sudden gush of clear liquid spattered on the stone floor beneath her legs.

'Ally, oh my God, I think your waters must have broken!' Helping her to a chair in the corner, I shouted frantically for Angelina. She appeared in the kitchen two seconds later, followed by Charlie.

'The baby, it wishes to arrive early. I deliver hundreds of them, no problem, *querida*.' Angelina's eyes were actually alight with excitement. 'And you have the good British doctor here too. What better?' She smiled, and I saw Ally's face relax.

'It's a long time since I delivered a baby, mind you,' Charlie added in hushed tones. 'Should I go and call an ambulance?'

'They cannot get one all the way up here but . . . let us see how many fingers you are, *querida*.'

'The baby isn't due for over a month . . . What if—' Ally was silenced as a contraction took hold of her body and she gripped my hand fiercely.

Angelina rose to her feet and pulled Ally to standing too. She took my sister's face in her palms, staring hard into her pain-soaked eyes. 'No time for fear,' she said firmly. 'You must use energy to help the baby. Now we will take you to my bedroom – more comfortable.' She then proceeded to half carry Ally to the room at the back of the cave.

'So, she is already four fingers!' pronounced Angelina, having shooed us all out so Ally could have some privacy. 'Too late to get her to hospital, but go, Charlie, and call *ambulancia* just in case of the problem. Come with me, Erizo. We get your sister up and we help her walk. Best way to make ready.'

So I did, and in the bedroom where I'd been born, I walked my sister up and down in the limited space until I felt my arm would drop off. Charlie and Angelina kept popping their heads around the curtain – Charlie to take Ally's blood pressure and monitor her and the baby's heartbeat, and Angelina to give her a tonic to keep her strength up and check on the cervical dilation.

'I feel like I want to push!' Ally shouted after what felt like days, but was probably only a couple of hours.

We helped her onto the bed, and I propped her up with

pillows and cushions, while Angelina proceeded to examine her.

'Baby come quickly. This is good, Mister Charlie,' Angelina called to him. 'She nearly fully open. Okay, *querida*, very close now. Ten more minutes and you can push.'

'But I want to *now*!' Ally screamed.

All I could do was sit and hold Ally's hand and stroke her sweat-matted hair as the minutes ticked by.

Angelina checked Ally's cervix again and nodded. 'Okay, now no tears. Take big breath and squeeze your sister's hand. Push on next contraction.'

A few minutes later, with my sister gripping my hand like a vice, Ally let out a huge shriek. A few more pushes and, finally, she delivered her baby into the world.

There were tears, congratulations and broad smiles all round as Angelina raised the squalling infant up from between its mother's legs so that she could have her first glimpse of the tiny miracle she had produced.

'It is boy,' Angelina announced. 'Okay size too.'

Charlie appeared around the curtain and went to Angelina's side to do a quick check of the baby's vital signs. 'From the looks of things, he's perfectly healthy, despite his decision to put in an appearance slightly ahead of schedule.' He gave us all a relieved grin. 'The ambulance is waiting at the city gates.'

Ally's eyes brimmed with tears of joy as she asked to hold her son.

'Ally, we just need to sort out the afterbirth and cut the cord,' Charlie reassured her, walking up to the head of the bed to check her pulse. 'A few minutes only, and he'll be in your arms, I promise.'

However, as he'd been speaking, Angelina had already calmly dealt with the situation, severing the umbilical cord with her own teeth. There were traces of blood still visible on them as she grinned broadly whilst deftly swaddling the infant in a blanket. Somehow it didn't seem macabre or barbaric, just totally natural.

Angelina handed the squirming parcel to Ally. As she did so, the baby opened his mouth as if to cry again, but emitted only a soft noise that sounded more like a gentle growl. Angelina chuckled and murmured something in Spanish.

'She said he thinks he is a baby *oso*,' Charlie translated.

'*Oso*?' queried Ally as she cradled her son.

'It mean "bear",' said Angelina.

'How perfect,' breathed Ally. 'And with all that wild dark hair, he looks a bit like one too.'

Tears welled in my eyes as I observed the poignant scene playing out before me. And yet again, I felt the hairs standing up on my arms and *knew* – even if we couldn't see him – that Theo was present, watching the first few moments of his son's life here on earth.

'Would you like to hold your nephew?' Ally asked me.

'I'd be honoured.' I took the bundle that Ally proffered towards me and on instinct I raised up the miniature human I was cradling in my arms, turning my gaze to the white-washed ceiling of the cave and giving silent thanks to the powers above – whoever and whatever they may be – for the miraculous circle of life.

When Ally had drunk some water and Angelina had cleaned mother and baby up as best as she could, I sat on the bed with my sister.

'I'm so proud of you, darling,' I said. 'And I know Theo is too.'

'Thank you,' she said, tears pooling in her eyes. 'It was actually okay – a lot easier than I thought it would be.'

True to form, my amazingly brave sister had taken the trauma of premature childbirth in her stride.

'As far as I can see, he's perfect. The only thing we can't do is weigh him,' said Charlie. 'I'd reckon he's about three kilos.'

'We can weigh him! We have scales in the kitchen,' said Angelina.

So little Bear was plonked unceremoniously on the big, rusting scales that normally held potatoes or carrots or flour.

'3.1 kilos,' pronounced Angelina. 'Ally, you want to go with *ambulancia* men to hospital?' she said as I watched my sister latch her baby onto her breast.

'No, I think that if you two are happy, then I'd like to stay here, please.'

'Okay. You happy, Mister Charlie?'

'I'm happy, yes,' Charlie confirmed, having examined Ally and pronounced her as well as her baby. 'I'll go and send them away.'

Having made Ally as comfortable as possible, we left her to rest and get to know her little bear. Then we sat outside in the cool evening air and toasted the birth with a glass of manzanilla wine.

'Watch the alcohol, Tiggy,' Charlie cautioned me. 'I'll allow you just this one as it's a special occasion.'

'Thank you, Doctor.' I raised an eyebrow at him.

It was then agreed that Angelina would sleep in Pepe's bed

to watch over Ally, and Pepe would move into Ally's room at the hotel.

'Can you call Thom tomorrow for me? I can't get a signal here. His number is on this,' she added, as she pointed me to her mobile phone by the bed. 'And Ma of course. We'll need to get the little one a passport to get him home – tell Thom my birth certificate is in a box in my file drawer marked "documents".'

'I'll do it first thing. Now,' I kissed mother and baby gently, 'sleep well, both of you.' I was about to leave the room, then I turned to Ally and smiled. 'I think we both know now what Theo meant about being prepared. Night-night, darling.'

On my way back to the hotel, I paused and looked up at the Alhambra. It had stood there for almost a thousand years, solid as the earth it had been built upon. It had watched the trials and tribulations of us humans – from the Moors of a millennium ago, to Ally's beloved Isabella of Spain, to me – and I suddenly thought that Ally was right, and that our lives were so very fleeting compared to anything taken from the earth. In the valley below me, trees had stood there for hundreds of years, and even after they were pulled from the earth, had provided furniture from their sturdy bodies that still remained long after the people that had sat down on them had passed on.

It was a humbling thought and the reality of it belied the power that humans believed they wrought upon the earth. The truth was, the earth was in charge and would outlast each and every one of us. And all I could do was to accept my place in it; that I was a mere snapshot in time, which was fine as long as I used my time here wisely.

*What a lot I have learnt since I've been here*, I thought as I walked into the hotel.

I had been intending to go straight to bed, but my mind was still buzzing with the enormity of the evening's events. So after saying goodnight to Marcella, I made my way out onto the terrace and looked up at the stars.

I don't know how long I stood there, lost in my thoughts, but I jumped when I felt a gentle tap on my shoulder. I turned to find Charlie standing behind me, nursing a glass of brandy in one hand.

'Hello, you,' he said softly. 'You're supposed to be in bed.'

'I just wasn't tired,' I muttered, suddenly aware of how close he was standing to me. 'Wasn't it amazing to be there at the dawn of a life?'

'It *was* amazing. It gives me hope that new beginnings are possible, in all sorts of ways . . .'

Before I could compute what was happening, his head bent towards me. The touch of his lips on mine sent an electric thrill through me, but as the kiss continued and deepened and my body melted against his, warning sirens began clanging in my head.

*He's married! His wife already suspects something . . . Tiggy, what on earth are you doing?!*

I broke away from him abruptly. 'Charlie, this is wrong. Your wife . . . your daughter . . . I . . . I can't do this.'

Charlie collected himself with obvious effort, clearly chagrined by his actions. 'I'm sorry. I shouldn't have done that. But if you'll just stay and talk to me—'

'No! I have to go. Goodnight, Charlie.' And with that, I bolted across the terrace towards the safety of my room.

I woke very early the next morning, the events of yesterday coming back to me as though they had been a dream, but no, I could still feel Charlie's lips on mine . . .

I groaned, and leapt out of bed to dress, trying to cast it from my mind. I went outside to search for a signal, so I could use Ally's mobile to call Thom and Ma. Walking towards the city gates, I took in the smell of the spring flowers that were budding on the cacti and the trees, and with a heavy heart, tried to picture myself in snowy Geneva instead.

When I eventually found a signal, I called Thom, Ally's twin brother. I had to smile at how like Ally he was – all practicality and action.

'Right, I will get on the next flight,' he announced, the joy evident in his voice. 'Little Bear – or *Bjørn*, I should say! – has no passport to fly, so I shall have to come and help Ally arrange one. We'll also have to register the birth as well. I will look up the nearest Norwegian consulate and make the arrangements.'

'Bring some baby clothes too,' I advised him, also telling him the location of Ally's birth certificate. Having given him instructions on how to get to Sacromonte, I called Ma, and I could hear the deep emotion in her voice. After all, in essence, it was her first grandchild.

'I cannot wait to see him and Ally,' she said. 'Please send her all my love and congratulations.'

'I will. And, Ma, are you sure it's still okay that I'm coming home to see you?'

'Of course it is, Tiggy. I would like nothing more than to

care for you. I only hope you are well enough to make the journey.'

'I am, Ma, I promise.'

'You must be at the private jet hub at Granada airport by four thirty. So, I will see you later tonight. Safe journey, *chérie*.'

I walked back along the path in the bright sunshine, still feeling guilty about the private plane, but also thinking how my past and my present seemed to have collided here.

'The old world and the new world,' I murmured as I approached the hotel. The fact that Ally's baby had been born in the same bed as I had made it all the more poignant. And as for Charlie . . .

'Tiggy, can I have a word before I leave?'

*Talk of the devil . . .*

'Yes, of course.' I nodded briskly as I hovered by the iron gates. I saw Marcella eyeing us with interest.

Charlie stood up from where he'd been eating his breakfast. 'Shall we go and sit on the wall? Might as well enjoy the view for the last time.'

He walked through the gates and led me a short way up the narrow path, so we were free from prying eyes.

I hopped up on the wall, my legs dangling like a child's, as he merely sat on it, his feet touching the ground.

'I have to go in ten minutes, but . . .' he sighed. 'It's time I came clean with you, Tiggy.'

'About what?'

'The future. Yours, mine, Kinnaird's . . . It's just not fair on you if I don't. With your instincts, you've probably guessed something was up anyway.'

'Yes, you seemed so enthusiastic at Christmas and then

you left and . . . to be honest, Charlie, I felt you were avoiding me or something.'

'I was, yes, or at least, not you, Tiggy, but the situation. I just didn't know what to say. Put it this way, this is a conversation I've got to have with Cal and the other members of staff when I get back. I was trying to wait to see if there was any other way, but having gone down every possible avenue, I really don't think there is one.'

'You mean, the estate is bankrupt?' I asked him.

'I wouldn't go that far, to be fair.' He gave me a wry smile. 'I mean, there's not any cash in the coffers, but forty-five thousand acres, plus a very nicely refurbished house – even with a loan on it – is worth something.'

'Oh, I'm really sorry, Charlie. Zed told me it was bankrupt.'

'Yes, he mentioned that to me too when he called me to offer to buy it.'

'Oh my God! He told me that he was thinking about it. You haven't said yes, have you? Not that it's any of my business of course,' I added hurriedly.

'No,' Charlie chuckled. 'Even though the offer he made me was healthy. In a way, I wish I could consider offers, but that's the trouble. At the moment, I can't do anything.'

'Why not?'

'It's a very long story. Put simply, my right to inherit the Kinnaird estate has been challenged. Therefore, until it's sorted out in the courts, the estate isn't mine *to* sell.'

'*What?!* But that's ridiculous! You're the rightful heir – the only heir . . .'

'Well, that's what I thought, yes, but it seems I was wrong.' Charlie gazed across the peaceful valley, his eyes moving up to the Alhambra above us. He let out a long sigh and in it, I could hear all the weariness he felt.

'But who's challenged you?' I asked him.

'Would you mind if I don't go into detail? As I said, it's a long story, and I've got to leave for the airport in five minutes. I'm telling you this, because until the situation is sorted out, my hands are tied. I can't do anything other than keep Kinnaird ticking over, which means all the plans we had are on hold. And knowing how long it takes for this kind of thing to even come to court, it could be years before there's a resolution. Please, Tiggy, don't take what I'm saying as a dismissal,' he added hastily, 'there's still a job for you at Kinnaird for as long as you want, and I'd love you to stay on, of course I would, but equally, it's not fair of me to pretend that your job spec will be extended in the near future. I'm aware that you're capable of a lot more than babysitting four wildcats. It's not what you've spent five years of your life training for, is it? What I'm trying to say, Tiggy,' Charlie hurried on, 'is that once we've got you better, even though it pains me to say so, you may want to look for another job. I'd never forgive myself if I was in any way holding you back from what promises to be your brilliant career.'

I looked at his almost perfect profile and it took everything I had not to reach out my hand to his.

'I'm so sorry, Charlie. It sounds like a nightmare.'

'It's not been great, but having said that, I'm not going to feel too sorry for myself. No one's died and myself and my family aren't starving. It's only three hundred years of Kinnaird history after all.' He turned to me and gave me a sad smile. 'Anyway, I'd better be going. Marcella's offered me a lift to the airport. Now, the most important thing of all is that you promise me you'll take some rest when you get to Atlantis. I'll be giving your ma instructions for your care.'

'I promise, Charlie, and please don't worry about me. You've got enough on your plate.'

'I will worry, Tiggy, but whatever happens, I hope you'll be back up to Kinnaird soon, even if it's to say goodbye.'

I watched him stand up and felt tears pricking my eyes at his words. 'I will.'

'I'm really sorry about last night too. Not my usual style. In fact, I haven't kissed a woman other than my wife in the past seventeen years. It was completely inappropriate, and I hope I didn't offend you, especially after all I said about Zed and his behaviour.'

'You really didn't, Charlie,' I said, horrified he thought that his attentions were unwanted when they *so* weren't.

We walked back to the hotel in silence, and he picked up his overnight bag from the terrace.

At that moment Angelina appeared beside us, as if out of nowhere.

'I came to say goodbye, Mister Charlie. Visit again soon and we will talk some more.' She reached up to kiss him on both cheeks.

'I will.'

'*Ay*, you should know that she' – Angelina pointed at me – 'has the answer to your problem. Bye-bye.'

Charlie and I exchanged a puzzled glance as the old woman left the terrace as quickly as she had appeared.

'Right. Well then, keep in touch and let me know how you're feeling, won't you?'

'I will,' I said, as Marcella joined us.

'Ready for the ride of your life, Charlie?' Marcella chuckled.

'I absolutely can't wait,' Charlie said, rolling his eyes at me, as he followed her. 'Bye, Tiggy.'

When they'd left, I poured myself a glass of water and drank thirstily, thinking that perhaps it was no surprise Ulrika was insecure about her husband. It was obvious he had a magnetism that women responded to. Yet he seemed largely unaware of it.

'And perhaps that's part of his charm,' I muttered as I left the hotel to walk down the road and see how the new mother and baby were getting on.

I found Ally sitting in a chair outside Pepe and Angelina's cave with a sleeping Bear in her arms. There were faint shadows beneath her eyes, doubtless from the demands of her first night of feeds, but they were sparkling with happiness and contentment.

'How are you feeling?'

'Tired, but other than that, absolutely wonderful!'

'You *look* wonderful, Ally, I'm so happy for you. By the way, I called Thom and he's busy organising consulate appointments as we speak.'

'Sounds like my brother,' she said with a grin.

'I doubt he'll make it to Sacromonte today. Would you like me to stay another night, in case he doesn't arrive until tomorrow?'

'No, I'm honestly fine, Tiggy. I've got other people here to look after me, don't forget. You go to Atlantis and let Ma fuss over you for a while. Speaking of Ma, did you manage to call her too?'

'Yes, and she was thrilled to hear the news, as you can imagine. She sent her fondest love.'

'Well, tell her I'll bring Bear to see her at Atlantis soon.'

'I will. Now, I think I'd better go and wake up Pepe.'

'You do that. I was about to take a rest anyway, while this little one's sleeping.'

'I'll see you later to say goodbye, darling Ally.'

I went up to the hotel and knocked on Pepe's door.

'What time is it?' Pepe muttered grumpily as he opened it, obviously having just woken up. But as he saw my face, he simply took me into his arms. 'Okay, *querida*, I must go down and prepare breakfast for Angelina, and you and I need some food too . . .'

After Pepe had dressed and we'd walked down to the blue door, he sat me down in the little garden and busied himself in the kitchen. He returned with a tray of warm bread and coffee and Angelina in tow.

'So, you are going home,' she said.

I nodded. 'Yes, in a few hours. But I'll be back as soon as I'm allowed,' I responded quickly. 'I still have so much more to learn from you—'

'*Sí*, and we will still be here when you return. Even if Pepe is old and fat . . . I am strong as an ox,' Angelina winked at me.

'I want to stay here with you two,' I said. 'But Ally and Charlie think it's best I go back to Geneva . . .'

'Sometimes you must trust others to know what is best for you. And for them,' Angelina chuckled. 'Don't deny those who love you a chance to care for you. Understand?'

'Sort of, but I really don't want to leave.'

'I know, because this place is in your heart. You are welcome here any time you wish.'

'Thank you.' I chewed the delicious bread, and tried my best to savour these parting moments with my newfound family. Gathering my courage, I asked them what I knew we had been putting off during my time here in Granada, simply because the outcome had to be a sad one. 'Before I go, can you . . . can you please tell me about my mother and father? I have so many questions, and I can't leave without knowing—'

'Yes, Erizo, of course we must tell you,' Angelina said, and then sighed heavily. 'Not all of it is happy, and perhaps we have been selfish in not telling you before. But Pepe and I do not often like to think of it . . .'

Pepe took her hand in his, and we all sat together quietly for a few moments. Then Pepe seemed to rouse himself, and raised his brown eyes to meet mine.

'So, I will begin, because I was there. It was 1944, and as the world was still destroying itself in a war, Lucía was in South America at the height of her career . . .'

# Lucía

## Mendoza, Argentina

September 1944

*Flamenco dress with train (bata de cola)*
*A dancing dress with a long and voluminous skirt*
*requiring great skill to manoeuvre.*

# 29

Meñique went out onto the terrace, squinting in the bright September sunshine. He leant against the balustrade, looking out over the vineyards that scattered the valley below and, beyond that, the snow-capped peaks of the Andes mountains. Never in his life had he breathed air as pure as this, and even at such a high altitude, the sun warmed his skin pleasantly. He loved it here.

He was ashamed to admit that Lucía's recent misfortune had proved a godsend for him: after years of relentless touring through South America, the *cuadro* had been performing in a packed theatre in Buenos Aires when, during a particularly ferocious *farruca*, Lucía had stamped the stage so hard, her foot had splintered the boards.

Her ankle had been badly sprained, and the doctor warned her there would be no more dancing for good if she didn't give it time to mend. So Lucía had at last been forced to give in and take a break. The rest of the *cuadro* had disbanded for the season, travelling to their own performances across Argentina and Chile.

It was the first time in all his years with Lucía that Meñique had had her all to himself, and it had been bliss.

Perhaps it was the strong painkillers she was taking, or simply the unbelievable stress she placed on her body catching up with her, but Lucía had been as calm as he'd ever known her. If they could stay like this forever, Meñique knew he would marry her tomorrow.

'Telegram, señor.'

Renata, the maid, came out onto the terrace to hand it to him.

'*Gracias.*'

He saw it was addressed to Lucía, who was dozing on her sun lounger. He opened it, simply because she would hand it to him to read anyway.

It was in English, and Meñique sat down at the table and began to decipher it.

ALL TERMS ACCEPTED STOP PASSAGE BOOKED FROM BA TO NY 11 SEPT STOP LOOK FORWARD TO GREETING YOU ALL HERE STOP SOL

'*¡Mierda!*' Meñique swore, his heart pulsing with anger. Standing up, he marched over to Lucía.

'You have a telegram,' he said loudly, watching her jump awake. He threw it towards her and it fluttered to the tiled terrace in the warm breeze.

'I do?' Lucía sat up and reached down for it. Seeing it was in English, she offered it back to him but he refused. 'What does it say?'

'I think you know very well, Lucía.'

'Oh.' She glanced back down at the telegram, searching for a word she could recognise. 'Sol.'

536

'Yes, Sol. Sol Hurok. Apparently you are going to New York.'

'No, *we* are going to New York. As if I would leave you behind! You would be proud of me – I negotiated very well.'

Meñique took time to breathe deeply.

'Did you ever think it might be a good idea to tell me what you were planning?'

'Not until he had accepted my terms. Each time he asked me before, he snubbed you and the *cuadro* and only wanted me. So' – Lucía reached her arms up to him with a big smile – 'now I *can* tell you.'

Given the fact that Lucía could not read what the telegram said, Meñique surmised that the 'terms' had been 'accepted' during a couple of late-night telephone calls when Lucía had thought he was asleep.

Meñique sank slowly onto a chair; after his earlier sense of peace now despairing, for so many reasons that it would take him time to compute them all.

'Aren't you happy, Meñique?' she asked him. 'This has been my dream.' Lucía stood up, now a bundle of nervous energy and excitement. Her little feet started tapping on the terrace. 'Can you imagine? Finally, it is North America! South America is ours, but now we must rob La Argentinita of the true prize!'

'So, this is all about her, is it?' Meñique said, avoiding her gaze.

'It's about nothing and nobody. It's about a new place to show my dancing to the *payos*. And New York *payos* are the richest in the world.' Lucía walked towards him and wrapped her arms around his shoulders. 'Does this not excite you?' she whispered in his ear. 'Señor Hurok said he may be able to hire

Carnegie Hall! Can you imagine that? A handful of Spanish *gitanos* taking the stage of the world's greatest concert hall!'

'I like it here in Mendoza, Lucía. I'd be happy to stay in South America for the rest of my life.'

'But we have seen everything there is to see here, done everything there is to do!' Lucía released him and paced along the wide terrace filled with burgeoning pots of dramatic red blooms, mirroring the colour of the scarf around Lucía's neck. 'We have been to Uruguay, Brazil, Chile, Colombia' – she counted the countries off on her fingers – 'then Ecuador, Venezuela, Mexico, Cuba, Peru—'

'Next time, Lucía, when you make a plan that includes me, I'd ask you to have the decency to tell me.'

'But I was keeping it as a special surprise! I thought you would be as happy as I!' Lucía looked so forlorn that Meñique's anger abated somewhat. She had obviously genuinely thought he would be pleased.

'I have loved being here with you and I just –' he shook his head – 'wonder whether we will ever come to rest anywhere. And have a life together.'

'Maybe we will not rest, but we *do* have a life, and it's exciting, and I will be earning fourteen thousand dollars a week!'

'We do not need more money, Lucía, we have enough already.'

'Nothing is ever enough. We are *gitanos*. Life is a constant search, we can never stay still, you know that.' Lucía surveyed him. 'Maybe you are getting old.'

'Maybe I am just tired of travelling constantly. Maybe I want a home. With you, Lucía . . . And one day, children.'

'We can have all that, but first, let's complete our adventure and go to New York.' Lucía walked towards him then sank to her knees, grabbing his hands. 'I beg you. I must have America. Do not deny me this.'

'*Pequeña* . . .' Meñique took another deep breath. 'Have I ever denied you anything?'

This time, as they set sail for New York, calm seas meant there was no sickness amongst the company, which had grown to sixteen strong during their six years in South America. Lucía had automatically been offered the best suite on the ship and other passengers on board bowed to her or raised their hands in recognition every time she deigned to appear on deck.

'How are you feeling?' María caught Meñique as he leant over the railing, wrapped in a thick coat and a scarf, generously loaned to him by a fellow passenger who had seen him shivering up on deck in the autumnal breeze.

'Sad that we are leaving South America behind us. The warmth, the colour . . .'

'Yes. I understand. I feel it too. But what can we do?'

'Nothing, María.' Meñique reached out and put an arm around her shoulder. Over the years, the two of them had become close, taking comfort and strength from each other when either José or Lucía became difficult.

'I want . . .' Meñique began.

'What do you want?'

'An end and a beginning,' he whispered. 'For the journey to be over. To have a home.'

'*Sí*, I understand. They say the war in Europe will be over

soon. I need to know what has happened to my sons. I wish
to go home too.'

María gave his hand a squeeze before walking away, leaving a solitary figure on the freezing deck.

'You know it is Antonio Triana who recommended me to
Señor Hurok?' Lucía said as she readied herself for dinner at
the captain's table, clipping on heavy diamond earrings and
arranging a fur stole around her shoulders.

'No, you never mentioned it. I thought he partnered La
Argentinita?'

'He does, but I hear that her health is failing. He is looking
for a new partner. And he has chosen me!' Lucía gave a giggle
of delight as she twirled her finger round the black curl that
sat in the centre of her forehead.

Meñique stared at her. 'I thought you preferred to dance
alone?'

'I do, but the last time I danced with Triana in Buenos
Aires, I felt something bigger than myself, *and* he is already
famous in America.'

'Please tell me, Lucía, that we are not travelling all the way
to New York to steal La Argentinita's partner?'

'Of course not, but I can learn from Triana. He is a genius.'

'Really?' Meñique moved to stand behind her and stared
at her reflection in the mirror. 'This from the woman who has
always insisted every dance comes instinctively from her soul.'

'I am older now, and wish to improve further. If Triana can
teach me what it is that made La Argentinita so famous in
America, I will listen. You know how things have changed. It

is not enough just to dance on a stage with an orchestra any more. We need a spectacular show!'

'Isn't that what we have been giving to audiences in South America for all these years?' Meñique said wearily. 'Now, I am hungry. Have you finished or shall I go to the dining room alone?'

Lucía fastened a diamond bracelet on her wrist, then stood up and held out her hand to him. 'I am ready, and hungry for sardines.'

Two days later, the Albaycín *cuadro* arrived in New York. Never had Meñique seen Lucía so full of excitement as she gazed at the impossibly tall skyscrapers that disappeared into the cloudy sky. As they approached a small island at the mouth of a huge river, they passed the very symbol of America, the lady of Liberty clad in her grey-green robes and carrying the torch of freedom.

When they reached Ellis Island, their port of disembarkation, Lucía was all ready for a hero's welcome as she marched down the gangplank, only to be greeted by immigration officials, who insisted the company follow them to a building to fill out the necessary forms.

'I cannot write! Neither can my mother nor my father!' Lucía said in Spanish, looking at the officials in exasperation. 'Surely you know who I am?'

'No, ma'am, we don't,' said one man, after Meñique had reluctantly translated. 'All we know is that you are a Spanish immigrant who needs to fill out the necessary forms before you can enter the United States of America.'

Despite Lucía's protests, they were all refused entry. After contacting Sol Hurok to advise him of the delay, another long boat journey back down to Havana ensued. During the voyage, Meñique and the few others in the *cuadro* who could write spent hours teaching Lucía and the rest of the company to at least sign their names.

When they reached New York again twenty days later, Meñique was heartily glad to see the back of the sea.

This time, the formalities at Ellis Island were completed without a hitch, so the *cuadro* made their way to Manhattan by ferry then piled into several yellow-and-black taxi cabs. As they drove, Meñique was amazed by the huge buildings, the weak winter sunlight reflected in their hundreds of glass windows. Stepping out of the cab, his breath visible in the freezing air, Meñique did his best to hide his misery from Lucía, who was openly delighted at the lavish window displays of mannequins draped in fur and diamonds.

They were to stay at the Waldorf Astoria hotel, where Sol Hurok had booked rooms for the entire *cuadro*. In the lobby, Lucía signed the register with a defiant illegible squiggle. Her father and the others followed suit, as the staff and passing guests looked on in distaste at the noisy, chattering band of gypsies.

A desk clerk handed her the keys to her suite and she swept regally towards the elevators.

As the bellboy pressed the button, Lucía turned round to face the lobby.

'*Hola*, New York! Soon, everyone here will know my name!'

'So, you are to make your American debut at the Beach-comber!' Antonio Triana announced.

'And what is that place?' Lucía looked suspiciously at the slender, dark-eyed man sitting opposite her in the suite. His trousers and waistcoat were clearly expensively tailored and his black hair had been perfectly oiled.

'It is a club – very sophisticated – with many Hollywood film stars often in the audience. I have danced there myself with La Argentinita,' Antonio reassured her.

'So, it is not some shack on a beach?'

'I assure you, Señorita Albaycín, it is not. The tickets to your opening are selling at twenty dollars each! Now, I must leave you but from tomorrow, we will rehearse. Nine a.m. sharp.'

Lucía looked aghast. 'Señor Triana, we never rise until noon!'

'You are in New York, Señorita Albaycín. Here, the rules are different. So, I will see you and the *cuadro* in the foyer at nine tomorrow and take you to our rehearsal room.' With an elegant bow, Antonio left the room.

'Nine o'clock?' Lucía turned to Meñique. 'Why, that is the middle of the night!'

'We must do as he asks. He knows the rules here, Lucía.'

'You are right,' she sighed. 'But tonight, we feast and drink wine!' Lucía declared.

'Are you ready for your New York debut?' Antonio Triana whispered in Lucía's ear as they stood together on the side of the stage two weeks later. She could see the coloured lights flickering through the crack in the curtains, hear the murmur of voices from the exclusive supper club that lay beyond them. The Beachcomber was vibrant at night, and on her way to the stage door earlier she had felt gratified to see a large throng of people vying to get in.

'After all those early morning rehearsals, I have never been more ready,' she declared to Antonio.

'Good, for I must tell you that in the audience tonight are Frank Sinatra, Boris Karloff and Dorothy Lamour.'

'Boris Karloff? The monster man? Why is he here? To frighten me?'

'To see you dance, Lucía,' Antonio smiled. 'I assure you that in real life, he is no monster. He just plays them on the screen very well. Now.' He took her hand. 'Let us give these rich American celebrities a taste of Spain. Good luck, La Candela.' He kissed her fingertips lightly. 'Here we go.'

Meñique watched from his chair at one side of the stage as Lucía appeared, guided to the centre by Antonio. As with all of her debut performances, Lucía was dressed in impeccably cut black satin trousers, a corset that hugged her slim hips and a sharp-shouldered bolero jacket. Antonio bowed to her then left the stage, blowing a kiss towards her. Meñique felt tendrils of jealousy creep up his spine but shrugged them off lest they entered his fingers.

He nodded at Pepe and the three guitarists began to play as Lucía struck the opening pose of a *farruca*, her arms high above her head, her fingers splayed.

'Good luck, my love,' he whispered, knowing Lucía had never had a more sophisticated and demanding audience to enchant.

An hour later, his fingers aching, Meñique played the final

chord and watched Lucía finish her *bulerías*, now dressed in a sumptuous violet flamenco gown. He smiled to himself, knowing that despite Antonio's careful training, Lucía had largely ignored his set routine, and had improvised as she always did.

*That is your magic, mi amor. You are completely unpredictable, and I must try to love you for it.*

Meñique stood with José and Pepe to receive rousing applause. He saw that Frank Sinatra himself was on his feet, and even though Meñique had been so negative about coming to New York, he felt tears welling in his eyes as Lucía took bow after bow.

*How far you have come*, he thought. *And I can only pray it will finally be enough.*

Following rapturous reviews in the press for Lucía's debut, a performance at Carnegie Hall beckoned. She was up at eight o'clock every morning, and never had Meñique seen her so energised. The *cuadro* attended rehearsals all day, Antonio directing them with skill and patience. Meñique was surprised that Lucía took his criticism like a lamb.

'I told you before, I want to improve. I have to learn what they want here in America.'

One night, Meñique found María still sewing costumes in the sitting room of their suite as he wandered from the bedroom to fill up his water glass.

'It is two in the morning, María. Why are you still awake?'

'Why are you?'

'I can't sleep.'

'Neither can I.' María stilled her fingers. 'José is not yet back.'

'Okay. I understand.'

'I don't think you do. I *know* that he is straying again. For the past week, he has not returned here until the early hours, many hours after the rest of you have come back from rehearsals.'

'He told me he is staying behind to practise the new numbers in the show,' Meñique replied truthfully.

'With who?'

'Some of the younger dancers who have joined the *cuadro* here.'

'Exactly. Lola Montes in particular.' María lowered her eyes. 'And Martina. They are very pretty, yes?'

'María, I understand your worry, but you need not fret about Lola. Anyone can see she is in love with Antonio.'

'So that leaves Martina.'

'I really don't think that—'

'I do,' María said firmly. 'Trust me, I know the signs. And I just can't, *can't* go through this again. He promised me, Meñique, when I agreed to take him back. He swore an oath to me on our children's lives. If it is true, I would have to leave, perhaps go home to Spain.'

'You cannot return home, María, all of Europe is still in chaos. And I wonder if your experience of the past is making you oversensitive.'

'I can only hope that you're right, but I am here all day and I cannot see what he does when he is away. Would you be my eyes and ears? You are the only one I can trust.'

'You want me to spy on José?'

'I'm afraid I do. Now, it is time I left for some sleep in my empty bed. Goodnight, Meñique.'

As he watched María's proud, elegant body leave the room, he shook his head in despair.

*Love makes fools of all of us*, he thought.

'They didn't like me!' Lucía threw herself onto the sofa and began to sob loudly, as Meñique kicked himself for not scanning through the *New York Times* review before Lucía had insisted he read it out to her. Yet, the ovations she and their company had received at Carnegie Hall last night had been so enthusiastic, there had not been a doubt in his mind that the review would be positive.

'That is not true,' Meñique insisted as he searched the article to find the positive quotes, of which there were many.

'"*A wonderfully lithe and supple body, keyed to a high nervous pitch but always in control.*"

'"*Speedy, intense and brimming with physical excitement, she makes use of her dynamics entirely legitimately and with admirable artistry.*"

'"*In the alegrías, which she dances superbly, every fibre of her body was sentient of line, mass and dynamics,*"' Meñique translated.

'Yes! But they called it a "mediocre" dance evening, and said that I should not dance to the *Córdoba*. I hated that white lace dress! I know I looked ridiculous.'

'*Pequeña*, all they had to say that was negative was that your style of dance suits a more intimate atmosphere than the

547

Carnegie Hall, so the audience can see you, connect with your passion.'

'So now they insult my size, because I am a tiny dot to the eyes at the top of the theatre! Lola Montes was not insulted over her *bulerías*. Even Papá congratulated her more times than he did me,' she wept.

'The audience loved you, Lucía,' Meñique said wearily. 'And that is all that matters.'

'When we go on tour next week, I will insist that I open the show with the *soleares*. That was Antonio's mistake; I cannot be shaped into anything. I am just me, and I must dance what I feel.' Lucía was upright now and pacing the floor.

'I know, Lucía.' He reached for her. 'You are who you are. And the public loves you for it.'

'You wait and see, when we go on our American tour and play to a real audience! No one will fail to see me and what I bring to their town. Detroit, Chicago, Seattle . . . I will conquer them all!' Lucía shook herself out of his embrace and paced the suite once more. 'I swear, I will put a curse on that newspaper! Now, I am going to see Mamá.'

The door of the suite slammed shut behind her and the whole room shuddered.

They had been in New York for four months now, and while Lucía embraced the electric energy, Meñique felt as if this frenetic city was slowly sapping him of any at all. He suffered from constant colds, the freezing weather making it a rare day when he could escape to wander through the greenery of Central Park, a tame and artificial version of his beloved Mendoza.

Picking up the newspaper again, he read over a line in the last paragraph of the *New York Times* review: five words, but they were words that heartened and uplifted him.

'*Meñique was a definite success . . .*' he mouthed the words to himself.

Just now, he had never needed them more.

A month later, they set off on their tour. Meñique lost track of the days, weeks and months that they spent on trains criss-crossing the country, where the food, the people, the language were all so bland. True to her promise and inspired by the negative review, Lucía danced for her life.

Pepe, too, had blossomed, becoming far more confident in his playing. The two of them often spent late nights poring over *payo* newspapers together, reading news of the war, Meñique helping the young man with his English.

After another successful performance in San Francisco, where Meñique felt as if the interminable fog there was seeping into his very bones, the company took over the majority of the booths in a late-night diner.

'The Soviets are moving closer to Berlin,' Meñique said, skimming the front of a newspaper that had been left on the scarred table.

Pepe sat down beside him and craned his neck to read the article.

'Does that mean the war will soon be over?' he asked. 'I met a sailor at the bar tonight who is preparing to go to Okinawa. Apparently the fighting is fierce in Japan.'

'We can only pray,' Meñique shrugged as they both ordered yet another tasteless hamburger. Meñique glanced at Pepe reading the articles, and thought how genetics had weaved their trickery by giving Pepe the temperament of his mother and the looks of his father. Despite the amount of admiring glances from the female members of the audience, Pepe seemed not to notice. Which was more than Meñique could say about José . . .

María came over to their table. 'Pepe, *querido*, Juana wishes to talk through how many bars you play for the introduction to her *bulerías*.'

'*Sí*, Mamá.' Pepe stood up and left, while María slipped into the booth opposite Meñique.

'Your playing tonight was beautiful.' María smiled. 'You had a longer solo than usual.'

'I had to beg for it,' Meñique replied, lighting a cigarette.

'I didn't know you smoked.'

'I normally don't, it's just another bad habit I've picked up from Lucía. She is smoking two packs a day at least.'

He watched María lean over the back of the red plastic banquette, her eyes searching the diner for her husband. Meñique could see he was sitting next to Martina in a neighbouring booth, an arm resting carelessly on the seat behind her.

'Really, María, since we came on this tour, I swear I have seen nothing beyond talk and drink.'

'Maybe.' María smiled grimly. 'But you do not see everything; there is a catch. Many nights on this long tour I fall asleep alone. José is a rich man now. Famous too, and talented.'

'And you, María, are still a very beautiful woman. José loves you, I'm sure.'

'Not as I love him. Don't try to be kind, Meñique. Can you not see how this tortures me? Being with him, but knowing now for certain I can never be enough.'

'I can, and this tour has felt interminable. It was exciting when we were in South America. There was so much to see, wonderful food to eat and wines to drink. They spoke our language, they understood us – but here –' Meñique gazed miserably out of the window into blackness – 'the best they can offer us is a hotdog.'

'Yes, I miss South America too, but Lucía is happy. She has conquered America. She has beaten La Argentinita at her own game. Maybe now she can slow down and relax a little.'

'No, María.' Meñique shook his head. 'We both know that will never happen. There will be another La Argentinita, another country to conquer . . . Can I tell you a secret?'

'Of course, yes.'

'I have been asked to perform in Mexico as a solo artist at a well-known flamenco café. They saw the reviews in the *New York Times* and the other newspapers.'

'I see. What will you do?'

'I'm not sure. We only have another few weeks of the tour, then who knows what is next? Perhaps I will ask Lucía if she will come with me.'

'What about everyone else in the *cuadro*?'

'They are not invited.' Meñique picked up his glass of beer and took a swig.

'She will not come, Meñique. You know that. She cannot leave everything she knows behind.'

'Well–' he drained the glass – 'it is her choice.'

'And yours,' María countered.

Back in New York, the company was offered a contract to perform at the 46th Street Theatre, but on arrival at the Waldorf Astoria, were told that it was fully booked.

'Fully booked!' Lucía cried as they had been ushered back

across the marble reception hall by hotel staff. '*Ay!* Half these rooms are empty! You should be so lucky to have us here.'

As they stood outside waiting for taxis, a paltry umbrella protecting them from the spring showers, Meñique put an arm around her to calm her down.

'Lucía, they might not be so happy about what you did to their expensive wooden cabinets when we were last here.'

'Well, how else was I supposed to grill my sardines? I needed wood for fire!' she insisted.

The *cuadro* moved into a large, comfortable set of apartments on Manhattan's Fifth Avenue.

'I am pleased to be back here. It feels like home, doesn't it?' she asked Meñique, as she unpacked the contents of her many trunks into heaps on the floor.

'No, it doesn't. I hate New York. It is not my place.'

'But they love you here!'

'Lucía, I need to talk to you.'

'*Sí*, of course. Have you composed something new for our show? I saw you scribbling on the train on the way back.' Lucía posed in front of the mirror in a sumptuous white fur coat she had just unpacked. 'What do you think of this?'

'I think the cost of it could feed the whole of Andalusia for a month, but it looks very nice, *mi amor*. Please–' Meñique knew he was about to burst – 'come and sit down.'

Sensing his tension, Lucía took off the coat and went to sit beside him. 'What is it?'

'I have been offered a contract in a famous flamenco bar in Mexico. As a solo artist.'

'How long will you be away for?'

'Maybe a month, maybe a year, maybe forever . . .'

Meñique stood up and walked to the window, gazing

down at the endless traffic shuttling along Fifth Avenue. He could hear the hooting of horns even up here on the thirtieth floor. 'Lucía, I just . . . I can't do this any more.'

'What can't you do?'

'Trail along behind you. I too have talent, and ability. I must use them both before it's too late.'

'Of course! We will give you more solos in the show. I will speak to Papá and we will change everything, no problem,' she said, lighting a cigarette.

'No, Lucía. I don't think that you understand.'

'What don't I understand? I am telling you that whatever you need I can give you.'

'And I am telling you that what you can give me is no longer what I need. Or want. It isn't just about my musical future, Lucía. It's about *our* future.'

'*Sí*, and it is the future I always look to. You know how long I have wanted to be your wife, and yet, after all these years, you have still not granted me that pleasure. Why will you not marry me?'

'I have thought about this many times.' Meñique turned back towards her. 'And I think I finally have the answer.'

'Which is what? You have another woman?' Lucía's eyes blazed.

'No, but in some ways, I wish I did. Lucía' – he went down on his knees in front of her and grasped her hands – 'do you not see that I want to marry *you*? But I do not want to marry your family, your *cuadro*, or your career.'

'I do not understand,' she admitted. 'You don't like my family? Is that the problem?'

'I think your family are all very good people, but I was and always will be an outsider, even as your husband. Your father runs the finances, he organises the tours . . . he runs your life, but even that wouldn't matter if other things were right. I am thirty-five years of age, and what I want is for you and me to marry, take a small house together in South America, and perhaps one day, go back to our beloved Spain. I wish for us to be able to close the door and know that no one else will walk through it unless we want them to. I want us to have children, bring them up not on the road, but in the proper way, where they are part of a community, as I – and even you for the first ten years – was brought up. I want us to perform *together*, find a venue somewhere where we can walk out of our home in the late afternoon and come back again to sleep in our own bed at night. Lucía, I want you to be my wife properly. I want us to grow our own family. I want us to . . . slow down, enjoy the success we have made before we take off again on another journey of uncertainty. Do you see, *mi amor*?'

Lucía, whose dark eyes had been boring into him as he spoke, turned away. She stood up, then crossed her arms.

'No, I don't see. I think that what you are asking me to do is to leave my family behind, and come with you alone to be your wife.'

'That is part of what I'm asking, yes.'

'How can I ever do that? What would the *cuadro* be without me?'

'There is Martina and Antonio, Juana, Lola, your father, your brother . . .'

'You are telling me that I am not needed?! That they will do well without me?'

'I am not saying that, Lucía, of course I'm not.' He sighed. 'I am trying to explain that sometimes in life, people reach a point where they can go no further down one road and need to cross a bridge in order to move on to another. And that is where I am now.' He walked towards her and put his arms around her. 'Lucía, come with me. Let's start a new life together. And I promise you, that if you say yes, I will take you to the nearest church and marry you tomorrow. We will be husband and wife immediately.'

'Are you blackmailing me? You have said that too often before and it's never happened.' Lucía pushed his arms away. 'I am not that desperate! And what about my career? Will you have me stop dancing?'

'Of course I would not. I already said I wished us to per-form together, just not on the grand scale we have before.'

'You wish to hide me? To force me into semi-retirement?'

'No, Lucía, and I am perfectly happy if you wish to occa-sionally re-form the *cuadro* to perform in big venues. Just not every single day of every single week. As I said, I want a home.'

'This confirms that you are more *payo* than *gitano*! What is wrong with you?'

'Probably a lot,' he said with a shrug. 'We are both who we are, but I beg you, from the bottom of my heart, to think about what I have said to you. I do not yearn for fame and glory in the same way that you do, but equally, my small ego wishes to be recognised separately from the Albaycín clan. Surely you cannot blame me for that?'

'As always, you are blameless, and I am the trouble. The diva! Do you not see that it was *I* that got us to where we are now! Me!' – Lucía pounded her fist upon her chest – 'Me, who rescued Mamá and Pepe from the Civil War, who never gives up, never gives in.'

'I would like to believe I have done something to help also,' Meñique murmured.

'So, you're asking me to choose, *sí*? Between my career and my family, and you.'

'Yes, Lucía, finally, after all these years, I'm asking you to choose. If you love me, you will come with me and we will marry and make a new life together.'

Lucía was unusually silent as she thought about what Meñique had said.

'But you do not love me enough to stay?' she said eventually.

The agonised expression in his eyes was answer enough for her.

# 30

'The war in Europe is over!'

María burst into her daughter's apartment, where Lucía lay curled up on the sofa, shrouded in darkness. She pulled open the curtains and bright light spilled into the room.

'*Querida*, the whole city is celebrating in Times Square. Everyone else in the *cuadro* has gone there – won't you come too?'

There was no response. The plate of food that María had brought her the night before remained untouched, next to an overflowing ashtray.

'Still no word from him?' María asked, walking towards her daughter.

'No.'

'I am sure he will come back.'

'No, he won't, Mamá, not this time. He said he did not love me enough to stay. He wanted me to desert my family, give up my career. How could I do that?' Lucía sat up and downed the cold coffee that had been sitting on the floor for hours, before lighting a cigarette.

'Remember, *querida*, this is your life. Everyone around you would understand if you followed Meñique. Many of us have to do things we don't wish to for love.'

'You mean like you with Papá? And that new whore of his!' Lucía spat. 'I *hate* love, I no longer believe in it.'

María remained silent, reeling from her daughter's revelation. Even though she had known it was true for many months, her daughter's bitter confirmation cut her like a knife.

The two women sat silently, both lost in their own pain.

'I know how much you miss him.' María was the first to speak. 'You have hardly eaten anything since he left.'

'I've had a stomach upset, which has made me feel sick! That is all.'

'You will disappear if you're not careful, *querida*. Don't let him do this to you.'

'He is doing nothing, Mamá! He has made his choice and he has gone. That is the end of it. He chose *himself*, not me, like all men do in the end.'

'At least try to take a mouthful of food.' María spooned up some sardines and offered them to her daughter.

'I cannot. Every time I look at sardines it reminds me of Meñique and that alone makes me want to vomit.'

'Okay, *querida*, I will leave you for now, but I will be here if you need me, I will not go to Times Square with the others,' María said, walking to the door.

She left the room, leaving Lucía alone. Lucía stood up and looked at the lock on the door. She fiddled with the key for a while, then turned it and heard the chunk of steel slip smoothly into the frame.

She took a few steps back, pointing at it as though it was a venomous snake.

'*That* is what he wanted for me! To lock me away from

my family, to close our front door on them and my career. It is good he has gone,' she told the sofa and the two chairs. 'I am better off without him, yes! I am!' Nobody answered back, and she walked round the vast empty room, thinking how peaceful it was not to have the eternal sound of Meñique strumming on his guitar in the background, his *payo* newspapers strewn on the floor and the table.

Unable to settle, she went to the window, peering below to see the jubilant crowds of people streaming down Fifth Avenue to get to Times Square. Traffic was at a standstill. She opened the window and was immediately assaulted by a barrage of horns, shouts and whistles. It seemed that the whole of New York was celebrating beneath her, and she winced as she saw couples embracing and kissing in the street.

She slammed the window shut and tore the curtains closed. Then she squeezed her eyelids together and hugged her arms round her thin frame. The silence in the room was endless and deafening and she could hardly bear it. She fell onto the sofa and pressed her face into the cushion, feeling tears begin to threaten.

'I will not cry! I must not cry over him!' She thumped the cushion with one of her fists, wondering if she had ever felt as desolate as she did now.

*Maybe he will come back. He has before . . .*

*No, he won't, he offered you a choice . . .*

*He loves you . . .*

*He does not love you enough . . .*

*I love him . . .*

'NO!'

Lucía sat up and breathed deeply.

'I have spent my life working to make all this! If it is not enough, then . . .' She shook her head violently.

'I miss him . . .' she whispered. 'I need him, I love him . . .'

Finally giving into her sorrow she buried her face in the sofa cushion and sobbed her heart out.

'What is wrong with her?' José asked his wife as the *cuadro* ate in Lucía's apartment after another sold-out show at the 46th Street Theatre.

María paused, thinking that her husband had not yet asked her why she had moved out of his bedroom.

'You know what is wrong, José. She misses Meñique.'

'So, how can we bring him back?'

'Life is not as simple as that. He has gone for good this time.'

'Nobody goes for good, as you well know, María,' he suggested as he swigged some brandy straight from the bottle.

Before she slapped him hard across his alcohol-ruddy cheeks, or took a knife and stuck it into his treacherous heart, María stood up.

'Sometimes they do, José, and Meñique has been gone for two months. Now,' she said as she rose, 'I am tired and will say goodnight.'

She left the room, knowing it was pointless continuing any kind of conversation with him when he was drunk. He would not even remember what he had said the next morning. María went to her own tiny bedroom and locked the door behind her. Breathing hard in the darkness as she tried to still her beating heart, she walked over to the bed.

'Mamá?' came a voice from under the covers.

'Lucía? What are you doing here?' María reached for the light switch and saw her daughter was curled up in a foetal ball, just as she used to sleep when she was a child on the straw pallet beside her in the cave. 'Are you sick, *querida*?'

'Yes, no . . . Oh Mamá, what am I to do?'

'About Meñique?'

'No, this is *not* about Meñique! He has made his decision and left me because he does not love me enough. And I never want to share the same air with him again.'

'Then what is it?'

'It is . . .' Lucía rolled over, her dark eyes haunted in her thin face. She took a deep breath, sighed as if working up the courage to say the words. 'It is the present he has left me with.'

'What "present"? I do not understand.'

'This!' Lucía pulled back the covers and pointed to her abdomen. To others, the slight curve of her distended belly would have been unnoticeable, but María knew her daughter did not have an ounce of flesh to spare. When she lay down, her stomach was normally concave between her narrow hips.

'*¡Dios mío!*' María crossed herself, then put a hand to her mouth. 'You are with child?'

'*Sí*, I am filled with the spawn of the devil!'

'Don't say that, Lucía. This child is innocent as every baby is, no matter who its parents are and what they have done. How many months?'

'I don't know,' Lucía sighed. 'Often I don't bleed. Maybe three or four . . . I can't remember.'

'Then why did you not say something to him? To us?! My God, Lucía, you should be resting, eating, sleeping . . .'

'I did not know, Mamá.' Lucía pulled herself upright on

the pillows and jabbed a finger at her belly. 'Until this started to look like a half moon two weeks ago.'

'You did not have any sickness? Feeling faint?'

'*Sí*, I did, but it stopped a while ago.'

'You have not been eating, and even your father asked me tonight what was wrong with you . . .' María studied the bump. 'Can I touch it, Lucía? Feel how big the baby is?'

'It is starting to feel as though I have a balloon growing daily down there. I want to rip it out! Oh Mamá, how could this have happened to me?' Lucía wailed as María felt her daughter's stomach.

'There! I just felt it move! It is alive, *gracias a Dios*.'

'Oh yes, it kicks me in the night sometimes.'

'Then it is at least four months! Stand up, Lucía, relax those strong muscles of yours and let me see you from the side.'

Lucía did as she was told, and María looked at her in wonder. 'I am now thinking five months. How you have managed to hide this is a mystery to me.'

'You might have noticed I no longer wear my trousers. I cannot zip them up round my waist, but at least the corset of the dresses pulls my stomach in.'

'No!' María shook her head in horror. 'You must not wear corsets again, Lucía! The little one needs room to grow. And you must stop dancing immediately.'

'Mamá, how can I do that? We have another tour coming up and . . .'

'I will tell your father and he will cancel it tomorrow.'

'No! I keep hoping that if I carry on dancing, the baby will just slip out of me. I'm amazed it has survived so far because I have fed it nothing except cigarettes and coffee—'

'*Enough!*' María crossed herself. 'Do not say these terrible things, Lucía. You will bring a curse upon yourself. A child is the most precious gift we are given!'

'But I don't want the gift! I want to send it back where it came from, I—'

María went to her daughter and put a hand over her mouth to physically stop her talking.

'Lucía, for once in your life, you will listen to me. Whether you are happy about this or not, you must put yourself and the baby first. It is not just the baby that can get sick, it is the mother too. Do you understand?' María released her hand, hoping that putting Lucía in fear for her own life might bring her to her senses.

'You mean I might die giving birth to it?'

'There is a better chance that you won't if you look after yourself now.'

Lucía slowly looked up at her mother, then went into her outstretched arms. 'What will become of us all if I can't dance?' she whispered.

'Having a baby is not a life sentence. A few months and you will be back beating your little feet even faster than you do now!'

'What will we say to Papá?' Lucía sank onto the bed. 'He will be so shocked. It is a disgrace to have a baby without being married.'

'Lucía.' María sat down on the bed next to her daughter and put an arm around her. 'You know as well as I do that doesn't have to be the case. You must tell Meñique what has happened—'

'Never! I will never tell him! And neither must you!' Lucía

pulled out of her mother's embrace and rounded on her. 'You have to promise. Promise me now! Swear on Pepe's life!'

'But I don't understand; you love him, he loves you. He told me himself he wanted children . . .'

'If he had, he would have stayed with me! I curse him, Mamá. I never want to see him again for as long as I live.'

'That is anger and hurt pride talking. If he knew about this –' María indicated Lucía's stomach – 'I am sure he would come back.'

'I do not *want* him back! And I swear,' Lucía stood up, 'if you tell him, I will run away and never return. Do you hear me?'

'I hear you,' María sighed. 'Although I entreat you to think about it. I cannot understand why, when there is a happy solution for everyone, you would ignore it.'

'You may be able to spend your whole life with a man who has disrespected you, but I cannot. I hate him, Mamá, don't you understand that?'

María knew it was fruitless to continue the argument. Just like José, her daughter had a stubborn streak and was too prideful, even in these circumstances, to ask Meñique to return to her.

'So, what is it you want to do? I mean,' María changed the way she phrased the question, 'where do you wish to go to have the baby?'

'I don't know. I must think. Maybe I'll just stay here and hide away in the apartment?'

'If you wish it to be a secret, for now anyway, I think it would be sensible to leave New York.'

'Because the *New York Times* might see my belly as I am

out walking and criticise my morals as well as my dancing?' Lucía replied bitterly.

'If it did get into the papers, I am sure it would not take long for Meñique to hear of it. If you are determined not to tell him, then . . .'

Lucía began to pace slowly. 'Let me think . . . I must think. Where should I go? Where would you go?'

'Back to Spain . . .' The words were out of María's mouth before she could stop them.

'It is a long way away, Mamá,' Lucía smiled, 'but at least they can speak our language.' She walked to the window, placed her small hands on the sill and pressed her nose against the pane.

'Perhaps you should sleep on it and we will talk tomorrow.' María stood, not wishing to sway her daughter with her own selfish wants and needs. 'At least the war is now over and we are free to travel anywhere you choose. Goodnight, *querida.*'

'I have decided, Mamá, and I hope you will agree it is the right thing to do.'

María looked at her daughter, hovering above her as she lay on the floor beside her bed. Lucía was still dressed in the same clothes she'd been wearing last night, her eyes shadowed by deep purple patches.

'I will go wherever you suggest, *querida.*'

'Well, I think it is best if we go home.'

'Home?' María looked at her daughter, trying to gauge

where Lucía thought 'home' was. After all, the child had been travelling since she was ten years old.

'Why, Granada of course! You are right, Mamá. We must go back to Spain. It is also where my heart belongs and always will.' Lucía gazed skywards. 'I want to wake up in the morning and see the Alhambra above me, smell the scent of the olive groves and the flowers and eat your *magdalenas* for breakfast, lunch and supper and grow very, very fat . . .' Lucía chuckled as she gazed down at her tiny bump. 'Is that not what all mamás do?'

As much as her heart leapt in joy, María knew she had to make sure that Lucía was not romanticising her childhood memories.

'*Querida*, you must remember that nothing is the same in Spain. Both the Civil War and Franco's rule after have destroyed much of what it was. I do not know if there are even any of us left up in Sacromonte, or whether your brothers and their families survived. I . . .'

María's voice cracked with emotion.

'*Ay*, Mamá,' Lucía went to her. 'Now the war is ended, surely we must go and find out? I will be there with you. And of course we do not have to live in Sacromonte, but I am sure that we could find a pretty *finca* to rent that is hidden away. No one will be looking for me in Andalusia, will they? Besides, I wish my baby to be born in its homeland.'

'You are sure you do not wish to tell Meñique, Lucía?'

'No, Mamá! Do you not understand?! I wish to travel as far away from him as I can! And he will never think to look in Granada. Maybe I do not wish to dance any more either,' Lucía sighed. 'Maybe that time in my life has left with Meñique. So, I must start afresh. Perhaps being a mother will change me, still my restless feet forever. It changed you, didn't it, Mamá? You hardly danced again after you had my brothers and me.'

'That was for a very different set of reasons, Lucía,' María said, realising now that Lucía's decision was based on nothing more than wanting to run as far as possible from Meñique and what she saw as his betrayal and desertion. 'I was not you, a world-famous dancer who thousands worshipped, just a simple *gitana* who loved to dance for pleasure.'

'I dance for pleasure too, Mamá, and maybe I can teach my baby like you taught me. Maybe I can learn to cook, make *magdalenas* and your sausage stew the way you do. So? We must leave as soon as possible. I do not want to give birth on the water,' Lucía said with a shudder. 'You will tell Papá?'

'*Ay*, Lucía.' María disliked herself for feeling a shiver of pleasure at the thought of her errant husband's distraught face when he heard the news.

'Do not tell him where we are headed – say we will go to Buenos Aires, Colombia . . . anywhere. I do not trust Papá to keep it a secret from Meñique.'

'Well, with your permission, I will tell Pepe. One of the family must know in case they need to contact us.'

'I trust Pepe with my life,' agreed Lucía, then she smiled suddenly. 'Spain, Mamá. Can you believe we are going back?'

'No, Lucía, I cannot.'

Lucía reached out her hand to her mother. 'Whatever we face, we will face together. *Sí?*'

'*Sí.*' María grasped it and squeezed it tightly.

Before leaving New York, Lucía and María went to Blooming-dale's on 59th and Lexington, where they bought a trunkful of toys, material to fashion some clothes for the baby, a Silver Cross perambulator and everything María had never had for her own children. Lucía then insisted they go to the women's department, where they had both been fitted for elegant suits and two tea-dresses. Lucía also bought a wide-brimmed cart-wheel hat with a long ribbon tied around the crown. 'Perfect for the heat of the Andalusian sun!'

She took out wads of dollars from her oversized purse and arranged with the startled cashier to have the purchases packed into trunks and stowed in their cabin aboard their steamer.

'We don't want Papá getting any clues, do we? Now, Mamá, just one last stop on our transformation and we will be ready!'

Still, María had been horrified as Lucía had dragged her into a hair salon and had ordered for them both to have their hair cut and styled into the fashionable victory rolls. As her long raven locks were cut to rest on her shoulders, María crossed herself. Lucía's hair – which fell to beyond her waist – had even more centimetres chopped off.

'I do not want anyone to recognise me on the voyage or in Granada. So we will pretend for a time that we're not *gitanas*, but sophisticated *payos*. *Sí*, Mamá?'

'*Sí*, Lucía, whatever you say,' María sighed.

# 31

María and Lucía arrived in Granada on a gloriously sunny May day, after a week on the ocean. They checked into the Hotel Alhambra Palace under María's maiden name, Lucía hiding her true identity under a pair of oversized sunglasses and her new straw hat. As they walked through the lofty lobby, decorated with colourful Moorish tiles and filled with plush sofas and potted palm trees, María felt as if she had stepped into a different era – one untouched by war and devastation, cushioned in wealth and far removed from reality.

Stepping off the boat into the port of Barcelona had been a shock for her, as she felt the palpable poverty in the air. She and Lucía had taken the train to Granada, and the journey had been rife with delays, as they had had to change carriages several times due to damaged tracks.

María had been relieved to see that Granada's beautiful buildings appeared untouched – from the newsreels she had seen in New York, of Europe devoured in flame and fire, she had expected it to be a smouldering pile of ash. But the opposite was the case – new buildings were being erected, men carrying bricks in the hot sun, their ribs apparent under their tattered shirts. When she had mentioned this to their taxi driver, he had raised a patronising eyebrow.

'They are prisoners, señora, repaying their debts to Franco and their country,' he told her.

Ensconced in the hotel – for once Lucía did not insist on a suite – she was eager not to draw any attention to herself *or* spend any extra cash out of the amount she had had to beg from José before they left. The first sum José had offered them had been enough for Lucía to threaten that she would never have her father control the finances again. José had relented and quadrupled it, but still, Lucía had had to resort to stealing the same amount again on the day they left to board the ship. She also sold two of her precious fur coats, plus some diamond jewellery she'd been given by a rich Argentinian admirer.

'The fact I've had to steal back what is mine and sell my possessions so that Papá's wife, daughter and grandchild can survive makes me want to vomit,' Lucía had spat as they had settled themselves in their cabin on board the ship.

María wondered whether the rift between father and daughter would ever be mended, but as they'd sailed east towards her beloved homeland, neither had she much cared. The freedom and relief she felt as the ship edged ever closer to Spain was overwhelming.

'Whatever Lucía decides, I am never going back to him, *never*,' she told the dolphins that had swum alongside the ship as they crossed the Atlantic.

Despite what she knew she must face there, ironically, María had actually enjoyed the voyage itself. With almost every passenger a returning native, there was a festive atmosphere on board.

And in her new clothes, with her hair styled just like the

other women on board, María had basked in the anonymity of being ordinary. She had even spoken to other guests at the dinners around the beautifully laid large round tables. Yet whilst María began to step out of her normal shell, Lucía retreated into hers. She spent most of her time in her cabin, sleeping or smoking, refusing to join the rest of the guests for dinner, citing seasickness and fear of being recognised. Gradually, her usual high spirits were lost beneath a palpable veil of despondency and despair.

The arrival on Spanish soil had not provided the spur María had hoped it would. Lucía lay on the bed, listlessly smoking one of her endless cigarettes, as María unpacked their trunks in the twin hotel room.

'Now, I am hungry,' María announced. 'Will you come downstairs and have your first taste of a Spanish sardine after all these years?'

'I am not hungry, Mamá,' Lucía said, but María ordered them up to their room anyway. Getting Lucía to eat anything was becoming an impossible task and María worried constantly for both the health of her daughter and the child inside her.

The next morning, María took herself downstairs into the lobby and sought out the concierge.

'Señor, myself and my daughter are newly arrived from New York and wish to rent a *finca* in the countryside. Perhaps you could tell me of a company that deals with such things?'

'I am not sure I know of any, señora. For almost ten years, people have been desperate to leave Granada rather than to find somewhere to rent here.'

'Surely there must be a number of properties that are lying empty?' María – lifted to euphoria by the fact she could for the first time in years converse fluently with a stranger – refused to be brought down.

'*Sí*, I am sure there are many, although what state of repair such places might be in, I do not know.' The concierge studied her more closely, as if mulling something over. 'How many people?'

'Only myself and my daughter. We are both widows, just arrived from New York,' María lied. 'And we have dollars to pay.'

'My condolences, señora. There are many who find themselves in such a position just now. Let me see what I can do.'

'*Gracias*, señor,' she said.

The following day, Alejandro – as he insisted María call him – had news for her.

'I have a possible suggestion for you to look at. I will take you there myself,' he added.

'Will you come and see the *finca* with me?' she asked Lucía, who had hardly moved from her bed since they'd arrived in Granada.

'No, Mamá, you go, I am sure you will choose us something nice.'

So María went with Alejandro and they drove through Granada. The streets were almost empty of other vehicles, as everyone else was on foot, or encouraging emaciated mules to pull their carts. As they went further from the grand hotel, the buildings turned to slums, and where María had once remembered restaurants and flamenco bars, the windows were boarded up and beggars sat in doorways of abandoned buildings, their eyes following Alejandro's car. Three or four kilometres outside town, the road began to cut through the wide verdant plain, burgeoning with olive trees.

'This may not suit you, señora, because it is so isolated and you would need transport to get you into town,' he commented as he turned off onto a dusty track that wound through an orange grove. A few seconds later, they arrived in front of a basic one-storey building, fashioned out of brick, its windows boarded up against intruders.

'This is the Villa Elsa, home of my grandparents, who both perished in the Civil War. My sister and I have tried to sell it, but of course there are no buyers,' Alejandro explained as he led her up the shallow wooden steps onto an overgrown vine-covered terrace that shrouded the front of the house from the glare of the evening sunset.

Inside, the house smelt musty and María saw there was mould growing up the walls. With the windows boarded up, the concierge used a candle to show her into the sitting room, filled with heavy wooden furniture, a kitchen that was small but serviceable, and the three bedrooms placed in the cooling shadow of the foothills of the Sierra Nevada mountains.

'It is probably not suitable for someone who has lived in such a sophisticated place as New York, but—'

'Señor, I believe it is perfect, even if it will take some scrubbing, and I must learn to drive!' she laughed. 'Both are possible.' She nodded as she stepped out onto the terrace, then out of the corner of her eye, caught a familiar shape high above her. She craned her neck far to the left, looked up, and saw the Alhambra sitting far away into the distance. This made the decision for her. 'We'll take it. How much?'

'The *finca* is perfect, Lucía! And because it is in a bad state of repair, and Alejandro is obviously desperate, I have taken it for next to nothing! You must come up and see it tomorrow.'

'Maybe,' Lucía sighed. She was lying huddled in her bed, her face turned towards the wall.

'You can even just see the Alhambra if you look to your left, Lucía,' María confirmed, buoyed by the fact she had managed to find them a home so fast and negotiate a deal all by herself. 'Alejandro treated me with such respect, I don't think he even suspected I was a *gitana*,' she said, glancing proudly at her reflection in the mirror. 'How the tables have turned! A *payo* wanting *our* money!'

'I am happy for you, Mamá.'

'Well, I hope you will also be happy for yourself when you see it. And it cannot be that difficult to learn to drive, can it? There is hardly anyone else driving these days, what with the fuel shortage. Alejandro says he can find me a cheap car through a friend who runs a garage.'

'It sounds as if you have a new admirer.' Lucía swept her eyes over her mother: her dark eyes were sparkling and the summer dress she wore showed off her voluptuous body, the curves sitting in all the right places. There was a new confidence to her that Lucía could only guess came from finally walking away from José. Lucía only wished she could feel the same about parting from Meñique – but then, *he* had left *her* . . .

'Alejandro is a married man with five children, Lucía. He is only grateful to receive some extra income for himself and his sister. He says we may take as many oranges as we can eat before they are harvested. Can you imagine? Our own orange grove?! Now,' María finished counting out the pile of dollars, stacked them together and placed them in her handbag, 'I must take the deposit downstairs to Alejandro before he changes his mind. He says that his friend the cashier will give him a good rate of exchange. Dollars here are like gold dust apparently!' María flashed her daughter a smile and left the room.

Lucía was glad she had gone. Even though she felt mean and selfish, María's high spirits only served to highlight her own non-existent ones.

'What is happening to me?' she whispered as she stared up at a large cobweb in the corner of the ceiling. 'Where have I gone? I have disappeared, like the spider who once made that web . . . there is only a husk left.'

Lucía closed her eyes, tears of self-pity dribbling out of them.

*Where are you, Meñique? Do you think of me as I think of you? Do you miss me . . . ?*

*Forget your pride and tell him what has happened . . . tell him that you didn't realise before that he was more important than anything . . . that you are nothing without him . . .*

Lucía sat up, just as she'd done a thousand times since he'd left. Her hand reached out for the telephone beside her bed, and hovered over the receiver.

*You know where he is, the telephone number of the bar he is playing in . . . Call him and tell him that you need him, that his baby needs him, that you love him . . .* 'Yes, yes, yes!'

Lucía's hand grasped the receiver. All she needed to do was give the number to the switchboard telephonist and within a few minutes, she'd hear his voice and this nightmare would be over.

*He left you!* The devil voice began to stir the hatred she felt towards him like sand in a stormy sea. *He didn't love you enough . . . didn't like you much either . . . he was always criticising your stupidity . . .*

Lucía dropped the receiver into its cradle. 'Never!' she hissed. 'Never will I crawl back to him, beg to be with him. He doesn't want us any more, or he wouldn't have left.'

She sank back onto her pillows, exhausted by the mental merry-go-round that she seemed unable to escape from. 'He has even stolen you two from me,' she said as she looked at her feet, which felt as though they were disconnected completely, a separate entity that had once taken her on a euphoric journey up to the heavens, but now hung on the end of her little legs like a couple of dead sardines. 'I do not even want to dance! He has taken everything from me, everything. And given me you instead,' she said to the bump.

Reaching into the drawers next to her bed, Lucía took out a tablet from the half-empty packet and swallowed it down with a glass of water. The *payo* doctor she'd seen before she'd left New York had prescribed them for her when she said she wasn't sleeping.

Ten minutes later, she slid into blissful unconsciousness.

'Lucía, you must get up!' María entreated her daughter. 'You have been lying in this room for almost two weeks! You are as skinny as our old mule and you look as if you have already joined your ancestors above us! Is that what you want? To die?'

María listened to the rise of her voice. She was at her wits' end with Lucía; nothing she could do or say could stir her daughter from her bed. As she spent her days scrubbing away the years of neglect from their new home, Lucía lay here, inert and more unresponsive by the day. So, it was time to play her final card.

'I am going to the *finca* now, and by the time I get back, I want you out of bed. You have not had a wash since you arrived and the room stinks of your sweat. If you are not up and dressed, then I shall have no choice. I will call Meñique and tell him where we are and what has happened.'

'No! Mamá!' Lucía's eyes shot open and María read the fear and horror in them. 'You wouldn't dare!'

'Oh yes I would! I will not let you lie here any longer. I must protect my precious grandchild.' María picked up her handbag and walked towards the door. 'Remember how much I have already lost, Lucía. I will not see another pointless death occur right under my nose. I will be back by noon. Okay?'

There was no reply so, with that, she slammed the door behind her, glad of the relatively pure air in the corridor. She hadn't been exaggerating when she had told her daughter she stank. Walking towards the lift, she saw her hands were shaking and only hoped that her threat would have the desired effect.

To her relief, when she arrived back just after lunchtime, she found Lucía at least sitting up cross-legged on her bed, wearing a towel.

'I am up and washed as you wished. I had the maid come in to change my sheets, okay?'

'It is a start, yes. Now let us find you some clothes.' As María rooted through Lucía's wardrobe, she realised that part of her was actually disappointed she had not had to carry out her threat. Maybe the best thing that could have happened was for Meñique to know.

'It is hot outside, so wear this.' María laid a cotton dress in Lucía's arms. 'I want you to come with me this afternoon to the *finca* and see where it is that your baby will come into the world. I want you to look up at the Alhambra and remember who you are, Lucía.'

'Do I have a choice?'

'Yes. You can start taking responsibility for yourself, but if you insist on acting like a child, I shall have to treat you as one.'

That afternoon, María put Lucía next to her in the passenger seat of the old Lancia touring car that Alejandro had sourced for her through a friend. Although this had once been an elegant and powerful vehicle, years of neglect had led to copious amounts of rust on its once royal-blue body, and it seemed that the engine was in no better condition, as mother and daughter lurched and stalled their way towards the *finca*.

'If only Papá could see you now,' Lucía uttered a chuckle, as María pressed the brake instead of the clutch and they swerved towards a ditch.

'I don't know why you are laughing.' María feigned irritation as she righted the car back onto the road. 'Your father struggles to keep a mule's nose in the right direction.'

As they bumped down the dusty track, María only prayed that Lucía would approve of what she'd worked so hard on to turn into a home for them both.

'There she is! The Villa Elsa, named after Alejandro's great-grandmother. Isn't she pretty?'

'Not as pretty as my house in Mendoza, but yes, she is,' Lucía added quickly, realising that negativity would no longer wash with her mother.

María gave Lucía the grand tour, proud of the way the

house now smelt fresh, and how all the rooms were filled with soft summer light since the window boards had been taken down.

'This will be the nursery, Lucía,' she said as they stood at the doorway of the small room that lay between her own and Lucía's. 'Just to think how you slept on a straw pallet with me and your father when you were small. How we have moved on, and all thanks to you and your amazing talent. Aren't the rooms a good size?'

Lucía opened her mouth to say the *finca* was hardly the Waldorf Astoria, then shut it immediately, cowed by the threat of the phone call.

'And look,' María continued, opening a door and proudly displaying the toilet and the small bathtub. 'It's all attached to the well, which is filled by the stream that flows down the mountain. Alejandro tells me it has never run dry in forty years. Would you like some orange juice?' she asked Lucía as they reached the kitchen. 'I pressed some this morning.'

'Thank you,' Lucía said. María poured them each a glass and they went out to sit on the shady terrace that fronted the *finca*.

'See?' María pointed to her left, high above them. 'There is the Alhambra in the distance. The night of the *Concurso* was the start of everything for you, *querida*.'

'Yes, it was. For better or worse,' Lucía agreed.

'I am only glad that we bought everything for us and the baby in New York. It is impossible to get anything in Granada unless I buy it on the black market. And the prices . . .' María shook her head as she sipped her orange juice. 'Can you believe the little one will be here within three months?'

'No. I feel that everything in my life has changed in the last few months, Mamá.'

'This is the biggest change of all, Lucía. Having my children is the greatest achievement of my life. I am so proud . . . of you all.'

It was María's turn to stifle a tear.

'Have you . . . made any enquiries yet about Carlos and Eduardo?' Lucía asked tentatively.

'I asked Alejandro where I should start. He told me that . . .' María wavered, having just managed to threaten Lucía out of her depression, she hardly wanted to push her straight back in.

'It's okay, Mamá, I can take it.'

'Alejandro says . . . he says that it is difficult to trace anyone who is missing. There are,' María swallowed, 'a number of mass graves around the city where the Civil Guard dumped the bodies of men, women and children alike at the height of the Civil War. He said there are few records. I was thinking . . .'

'Yes?'

'I was thinking that I would take a walk up to Sacromonte to see if anyone knows anything. In fact, I have thought of it every day since I've been here, but I am frightened of what I might find. Or not find.' María put a hand to her brow. 'At least for all these years, I have been able to believe that one day I will find my cherished sons and grandchildren alive, but here we are, two weeks on in Granada, and I dare not go.'

'I will come with you, Mamá,' Lucía said, putting a hand on María's. 'We will face it together like we promised each other, sí?'

'Gracias, daughter.'

Lucía wondered whether it was this lovely peaceful place that her mother had worked so hard at to turn into their new home that had cheered her spirits. And besides, in all the destruction and devastation that war had wrought on Spain, she was alive, with a new life inside her. Whereas her brothers and their families . . .

'Mamá?'

'*Sí*, Lucía?'

'I am sorry for being . . . difficult since we arrived.'

'You were always difficult, *querida*, but I understand why. You have been grieving.'

'You are right, I have been. For everything I was. But as we said, this is the start of a new life, and I must try and embrace it. When so many others can't.'

María and Lucía moved into the Villa Elsa a few days later. María took out the Singer sewing machine she had brought with her and sat on the terrace at the rough wooden table making curtains and table-coverings out of the pretty flowered cotton she'd brought from New York. Lucía amused herself by taking the old car up and down the dusty path to the road and back, and within a few hours she was a far better driver than her mother would ever be. María also fashioned her some simple maternity dresses from the fabric, and in her big sunhat, with her belly protruding beneath the flowing dresses, and in a city populated by people who looked like her, Lucía started to venture out to collect provisions. And with her mother's home cooking, Lucía suddenly found herself hungry and able to sleep without the aid of pills.

'Mamá?'

'*Sí*, Lucía?' she answered as they sat eating a breakfast of freshly baked bread and trying out the taste of the orange marmalade María had been experimenting with.

'I think that we should go up to Sacromonte before I become too fat to move beyond the terrace. Are you ready?'

'I will never be ready, but yes, you're right,' María nodded. 'We must go.'

'And there's no day like today.' Lucía reached a hand to her mother. 'I will check the petrol.'

Half an hour later, with Lucía's bump pressing against the wheel of the car, she drove them into Granada and up the winding alleys towards Sacromonte. Leaving the car at the city gate, the two women grasped hands and walked through it into a world that had once been everything they knew.

'It doesn't look different,' said Lucía in relief as they walked along the main path. 'Except, look – Chorrojumo's old cave is boarded up. His family must have left.'

'Or been murdered . . .' María said darkly, squeezing her daughter's hand for comfort. 'Look up, Lucía, I can't see any wisps of smoke coming out of the chimneys. The place is deserted.'

'It is high summer, Mamá, no smoke means nothing.'

'It means everything, Lucía. On days when it was too hot to breathe the air, my fire would still burn to cook for my family. Do you hear it?' María whispered as she stopped short.

'Hear what?'

'The silence, Lucía. Sacromonte was never quiet. Day and night you could hear people laughing, arguing, shouting . . .' María gave a sad smile. 'No wonder everyone knew everybody else's business; the caves echoed out all our secrets. There was no privacy here.' María took a deep breath. 'So, first we must head for your grandparents' cave.'

The two women walked down the snaking mountain path until they reached the caves just above the Darro river, where María's parents had once run their successful blacksmith's business. Peering inside, María saw that the pretty home her mother – God rest her soul – had once fashioned was no more. All that was left was the shell itself; the glass windows, colourful curtains, the furniture had all long since disappeared.

'I am happy they did not live to see what became of their beloved Spain,' María said as she stood in what had once been the sitting room but was now a dirty and putrid-smelling empty space, the floor full of rubble, empty packets of cigarettes and discarded beer bottles.

'So.' María swallowed hard. 'Now to your brothers' caves.'

The two women walked a little further up the hill and found both Eduardo and Carlos's once beautiful homes in an identical state to that of María's parents' cave.

'There is nothing left . . .' María wiped away her tears roughly. 'It is as if they were never here,' she whispered, her voice breaking with emotion. 'As if the past never happened. What about Susana, Elena and my beautiful grandchildren?'

'They may have been interned, Mamá. You know many *gitanos* were during the war. Meñique told me it said so in the *payo* papers.'

'Well, we will find nothing more here. Come, Lucía, let us go back. I—'

'Mamá, I know this is hard to bear, but while we are here, surely we must see if we can find someone to talk to who can tell us if they know what happened to Eduardo and Carlos?

There will be someone that does, I swear. So, let us walk up the hill to our family cave, see if anyone is left up there.'

'You are right. If I don't do this now, I will never again find the courage to return.'

'Goodness, did we really walk all this way every day to fetch the water?' Lucía puffed alongside her mother as they trudged up the hill.

'You're pregnant, Lucía, so it's harder for you now.'

'And so were you when you lived here, Mamá, many times!' said Lucía. 'I do not know how you did it.'

'We all do what we need to when there is no alternative,' said María. 'And then when we *do* know something better, we realise how hard our life was. Lucía' – María clutched at her daughter's arm as they rounded the bend and their old cave came into view. 'Look!' María pointed above it. 'There's smoke coming from the chimney. *¡Dios mío!* There is some-one living there! I . . .'

'Steady, Mamá,' Lucía said as her mother's step faltered and her hand went to her mouth in shock. She lowered María gently onto the wall that provided a safety barrier above the olive groves tumbling beneath the cave. 'Sit here a while, take some water. It's very hot today.' Lucía offered a flask from the basket she was carrying and her mother drank long and plentifully.

'Who can it be . . . ? What will we find behind that closed door?'

'Perhaps it is just squatters who have taken over the place and are nothing to do with our family,' Lucía shrugged. 'We must not get our hopes up.'

'I know, I know, but . . .'

'Mamá, do you want to stay here and I will go and find out?'

'No, whoever is in our cave, I must see for myself.' María flapped her fan violently in front of her face. 'Okay, so, we go.'

Only seconds later, they were standing in front of their old front door, the blue paint now cracked and faded.

'Shall I knock, or will you, Mamá?'

'I will.'

María did her best to compose herself, knowing that behind the sturdy piece of timber lay the answers to the questions she had asked herself a thousand times since she'd left Sacromonte. She lifted her hand, which shook violently, to tap against the wood.

'You'll have to knock harder than that, Mamá,' Lucía encouraged. 'Even a dog with his ears pricked wouldn't hear it.'

María knocked harder, holding her breath to listen for footsteps coming towards the door on the other side. There were none.

'Maybe they're out,' shrugged Lucía.

'No, no *gitano* would ever leave a fire burning in a cave that was empty,' said María firmly. 'There's someone in there, I know there is.' She knocked again, and still there was no response, so she went to the small glass-paned windows to try to look through them, but they were covered in the thick lace netting that she herself had sewn and fixed at the windows to prevent prying eyes such as hers.

'*¡Hola!*' she said, tapping on the windowpane. 'It is María Amaya Albaycín. I used to live here. I have come back to find my family. Please let me in! Hello!'

'It is Lucía, her daughter, here too. We mean no harm,' Lucía added plaintively. 'Please open up.'

What Lucía had said obviously did the trick. The heavy

sound of footsteps was heard approaching the door from inside, the latch was pulled up and the door opened by no more than a few centimetres.

One green eye peered from behind the door. Lucía met its gaze.

'Here is Lucía,' she indicated herself, and then, grabbing her mother, pulled María into the line of the eye, 'and my mother. Who are you?'

Finally, the door was opened. And there in front of them was a familiar face – a face now criss-crossed with age, the hair as white as the snow that fell on the Sierra Nevada mountaintops, the body so enormous it filled the doorway.

'¡Dios mío!' the woman whispered in shock as she gazed at them. 'María . . . and little Lucía, whom I helped into the world on the night of Chorrojumo's granddaughter's wedding! I cannot believe it! I just cannot believe it!'

'Micaela?! It is you!' María exclaimed as the village *bruja* opened her arms to embrace both women against her massive bosom.

'Come in, come in . . .' Micaela said, her eyes flickering nervously along the dusty path as she stepped to the side to allow them in. Shutting the door firmly behind her, María saw the pine rocking chairs that Carlos had made for her. The sight of them brought tears to her eyes. And hope spinning up with them.

'Well, of all the people in all the world . . . never did I think I would lay eyes on either of you again,' Micaela chuckled, her laughter echoing around the walls of the cave. 'What are you doing here?'

'We have come partly because of Lucía' – María indicated Lucía's bump – 'and partly to find out what happened to my sons and their families.'

'So.' Micaela placed a hand on the bump. 'You have a girl in there, a treasure, and a fighter. She is very like you, María,' she said as an aside. 'Who is the lucky papá?'

When neither woman answered, Micaela nodded.

'*Ay*, I understand. Well, let us be happy that at least one of a new generation of *gitanas* will arrive soon into this terrible world of ours. So many are lost to us . . .'

'Do you know the fate of my sons, Micaela?' María shook her head and reached instinctively for Lucía's hand.

'I cannot say that I do, María. If I remember, you were still here when both of them disappeared into the city.'

'Yes, I was. And they have not been seen since?'

'No, I am so sorry, María, but few of our menfolk, who either were taken by force or simply never returned from the city, have been sent back to us . . .' Micaela reached for María's other hand.

Lucía watched in fascination as Micaela's eyes rolled back in her head, just as Chilly's had done when he was seeing a vision from the Upperworld. 'They are telling me they are there. They are up there, looking down on us now. They are well and safe.'

'I . . .' María's throat was so dry that she could not swallow. 'I knew it here, of course.' She thumped her heart. 'But still I hoped.'

'What are we human beings without hope?' Micaela sighed. 'There is not a family who remained untouched in Sacromonte, and even Granada itself. Generations wiped out . . . men, women, children . . . murdered for crimes they never committed. *Payo* and *gitano* alike. Well . . . you saw what it was before you left, María. And it only got worse.'

'But . . .' María could hardly speak, her throat still

constricted with emotion. 'What about Eduardo and Carlos's wives and children?'

'After you left, the Civil Guard came up here to clear the rest of the *gitano* community out. María, I am so sorry but Susana and Elena were both taken, and their children . . .'

'No!' María gave a sob. 'So they too are dead? How can I bear it! And I left them here to die as I saved my own skin . . .'

'*No*, Mamá! That is not true!' Lucía interjected. 'You did it to save Pepe, to give at least one of your sons the chance of a life. Remember, you begged both Carlos and Eduardo's wives to come with you.'

'You must not blame yourself, María, you gave them the choice. I remember Elena telling me so just before she was taken,' said Micaela.

'Elena was pregnant . . . She was Eduardo's wife, Lucía. You could not imagine a sweeter girl. Did she have her baby before . . . ?' María could not speak the words.

'*Sí*, she did, María.' For the first time, a smile played on Micaela's full lips. 'And *that* is when the miracle occurred.'

'What do you mean?' Lucía asked.

Micaela sat her bulk down at the table and indicated mother and daughter should do the same.

'In life there is always a balance – even when there is evil all around, there are good, even beautiful, things that happen to provide the natural harmony. Just a few weeks before she was taken, Elena gave birth to her baby girl. I was there with her, helping her, just as I helped your mamá give birth to you, Lucía. And it seems, María, that you are blessed, for not only did you have your Lucía, who is in so many ways special, but your granddaughter, Eduardo's daughter . . . the minute I saw her I knew.'

'Knew what?' asked Lucía.

'That she was the one who had inherited the gift of seeing from your great-grandmother. The spirits in the Upperworld told me she was to be the next *bruja*, and that I was to protect her.'

'Eduardo's daughter had the gift?' María whispered.

'She did. And the prophecy came true: the very morning that she and the rest were taken, Elena had come to me with her baby – she had called her Angelina because she had the face of an angel – and asked me would I take care of her for a couple of hours whilst she went down to the market. I was happy to do this – both Elena and I already knew I would be part of Angelina's future. I strapped the baby to me and we went out into the forest to search for herbs and berries. We were gone for many hours, because already I was beginning to teach Angelina to listen to the rhythm of the universe through the earth, the rivers and the stars. I did not know that while we were there, the Civil Guard had come up to Sacromonte and taken Elena, Susana and their children, as they were on their way into the market.'

Lucía realised she was listening to the old *bruja* as if she was telling one of her tales of the old times. Yet this was reality and . . . Lucía could not even think of where the story might be leading.

'Almost the whole village had been marched away. Only those who were not in their caves when the Civil Guard called managed to escape,' Micaela explained. 'I knew then that the Upperworld had sent me into the forest to protect Angelina. From that moment on, María, I have brought up your granddaughter as my own child.'

There was silence in the cave as both María and Lucía

tried to rationalise what Micaela was telling them. And what it meant.

'I . . . are you telling me that she is alive?' María whispered, hardly daring to ask in case she had heard wrong.

'Oh yes, alive as anything could be. What a clever and beautiful girl you have as a grandchild, María. She already has powers far beyond my own.'

'Then where is she?'

'She is out, foraging in the forest as I have taught her to.'

'I . . . cannot believe it! Out of so much tragedy, Eduardo's daughter survives! It is indeed a miracle, is it not, Lucía?'

'*Ay*, Mamá, it is!'

'There have been many times when I thought we were discovered,' Micaela continued. 'Yet always, Angelina's sixth sense was one step ahead of the Civil Guard. She would tell me when we had to leave the cave and hide in the forest until the "devil men", as she called them, were gone. Never once was she wrong, and I have learnt to trust her instincts better than my own.'

'So you left your own home and moved in here?' María asked.

'It was better that my cave remained empty – it is too near the city gates and I am not someone who can hide herself easily.' Micaela gave a deep chuckle. 'Whereas your cave is far away from the city gates *and* close to the forest, so we could make our escape there easily.'

María looked at the size of the woman and agreed how difficult it would be for Micaela to become invisible. But somehow she had managed it. Managed it to save Eduardo's daughter, Angelina. Her grandchild . . .

'Will she be back soon?' asked Lucía. 'I cannot wait to meet my niece!'

'She will be back after she has conversed with the trees to discover where exactly she can pick the magic herbs she uses to brew her potions. She is like the wind, a spirit who listens to nothing but her own infallible instincts.'

'How can I ever thank you, Micaela? What you have done for me, for this family . . .'

'No. I have done nothing. I was saved because of Angelina. I know it.'

'And now, do people return here to live in Sacromonte?' Lucía asked.

'The community we had once is gone. Dead, or scattered across the world. Sacromonte can never be as it was,' Micaela said darkly.

'Maybe in time,' countered María.

'Now you are here, my work is done.' Micaela shrugged. 'And I am grateful for I was worried what would become of Angelina if I was not here. I was told someone would come for Angelina when I needed them. My heart – it cannot support me much longer, you see.' She roused herself from the table, her face purple with effort. 'Now, I have some soup for lunch. Are you hungry?'

Both María and Lucía accepted Micaela's offer, more for want of something to concentrate on than hunger as they waited for the little miracle child to come home. María told Micaela a little of their life in the past nine years, and that they were now living in an orange grove in the foothills of the Sierra Nevada mountains.

'*Hola, Maestra,*' said a high voice as the front door opened, and a waif-like creature entered the cave with an overflowing basket of what resembled weeds.

María drew in her breath, for this child could not look less *gitana* than if she had been transported from the host of the angels she was named after. With her red-gold hair and blue eyes, Angelina looked *payo* through and through.

The wise, calm eyes stared at the two women sitting at the table. 'You are something to me, aren't you?' she said quietly as she came towards them. 'Are you my family?'

'Yes,' said María, yet again close to tears, 'I am your grandmother, and this is your aunt, Lucía.'

'They told me something special would arrive today,' Angelina nodded, seemingly not at all surprised. 'Is this who I will live with when you travel to the Upperworld, *Maestra*?'

'Yes.' Micaela met María's astonished expression almost smugly. 'I have been telling your grandmother and aunt all about you.'

Angelina placed her basket on the floor, then opened her arms wide to hug María and then Lucía in turn. 'I am glad you have come. The *maestra* was getting worried that her time was running out. Now she can prepare for her journey without fear. Is there soup?' she queried.

'*Sí*,' Micaela began to rise but Angelina used a hand to stop her.

'I can get it. She tries to do everything for me, but I tell her she must rest. Your baby will be a girl, and we will be great friends,' Angelina nodded to Lucía as she scooped some soup into a tin bowl.

'Micaela already told her,' said María. Lucía – for once – was silenced by this extraordinary little girl and María could only continue to stare at her in wonder.

*Eduardo's child . . . she is to be given to me . . .*

Angelina sat at the table and ate her soup, asking a hundred different questions about María and Lucía and the other members of her family.

'I have an uncle as well as an aunt, *sí*?'

'You do, Angelina, and he is called Pepe. Maybe one day he will visit us here.'

'I will know him a long time. The prophecies are coming true, *Maestra*,' she said to Micaela in delight. 'I knew they would not let us down.'

'Does she go to school?' María asked Micaela.

'What do I need with school?' Angelina answered. 'I learn everything I need from the *maestra* and from the forest.'

'Perhaps you should learn to read and write,' Lucía said as she ferreted in her basket for her cigarettes and lit up. 'It is something I wish I had done.'

'Oh, I can do that, Lucía. The *maestra* had a *payo* come here and teach me.' She stared at Lucía inhaling her cigarette. 'You know that it is bad for your heart. It will help kill you. You should stop.'

'I shall do as I wish,' Lucía replied, now irritated by this angel child, who seemed to know the answers to everything.

'Each of our destinies is down to us. Sometimes.' She laughed as she gave Micaela a knowing look. 'When can I come and visit you?' she asked María. 'Your home sounds beautiful.'

'You must come soon,' María said, a wave of weariness overtaking her. There had been so much to take in; this child's sheer vitality and life force was almost overpowering and she was still to process the final confirmation of the loss of her sons and their families. 'Micaela and I will arrange for us to come and collect you and take you there by car.'

'Thank you,' said Angelina politely. 'Now, I must make a potion before the energy in my herbs is gone. It is for the *maestra*'s heart. I will make you one for your baby too,' Angelina declared. She took her basket over to the work surface and wielded a large knife on the chopping board.

Emotional goodbyes were said and arrangements made to collect Angelina in a couple of days' time.

'Thank you for coming, Grandmother, Aunt,' said Angelina as she hugged them. 'It has made me very happy. Goodbye.'

Outside, María and Lucía walked back to the car in silence.

'She is . . . extraordinary,' María whispered, more to herself than her daughter.

'She is, even if I find a nine-year-old child telling me I must stop smoking irritating,' Lucía grimaced as she started the engine. 'Well, at least we know what colour to crochet the baby's blanket,' she added with a throaty chuckle. 'She reminds me of Chilly when he was a boy. He was always precocious. Goodness, I miss him. Another loved one we have almost certainly lost to the stinking Civil War.'

'Should I send a telegram to your father to tell him about the death of his sons and his granddaughter? Surely he should know?'

'Why not? Maybe his newest whore can read it to him,' Lucía drawled, as she steered the car carefully down the narrow cobbled alleys.

'Please,' María sighed. 'There's been enough hatred and

loss in both of our lives for one day. Whatever José is, he is your father and my husband.'

'Do you even know where he is?'

'Pepe sent me a telegram to tell me that they were going on another tour of the States next week.'

'How did you read it, Mamá?'

'Alejandro read it for me,' María admitted. 'He has offered to help me learn to read better.'

'I told you you had a boyfriend,' Lucía giggled, 'which is more than I have – or,' she said, looking down at her stomach, 'will ever have now.'

'You are still young, Lucía! Your life has just begun.'

'No, Mamá. I think it is yours that has, but . . .' Lucía paused for a moment. 'Does Alejandro know yet we are *gitanos*?' Lucía asked her.

'No.'

'Would it change things if he did?'

'I don't know, but perhaps it is safer for you and the baby if he does not.'

'From the sound of things, better for you too.' Lucía smiled wryly. 'Many would say we are betraying our culture, acting like *payos* – living like them too, in a normal house . . .'

'Maybe we are,' María sighed, 'but when I think back to the years up there in Sacromonte, where we were treated no better than dogs, it has been pleasant to live without the prejudice. And we are still who we are inside, Lucía, no matter whether our hair is short or long, the clothes we wear, or where we live. It is . . . easier,' María acknowledged.

'So you do not wish to go back and live in your own cave, Mamá?'

'I can hardly throw Micaela out on the street after all she

has done to take care of Angelina. I think the arrangement suits us all.'

'Yes, Mamá. For now, I think it does.'

# 32

Angelina came down to visit them at the Villa Elsa the following week. Just like Lucía when she had been younger and had visited *payo* houses with her father, Angelina had ooh-ed and aah-ed over the modern conveniences. The inside toilet and bathtub fascinated her the most, and Lucía found her peering down the toilet bowl as she pulled the long chain to flush it.

'Would you like to take a bath?' Lucía asked her. 'The water is very warm.'

'I think I would be too frightened! See how deep it is. I cannot swim and I may drown.'

'I would stay with you to make sure you didn't. And look,' Lucía proffered some bubble bath she'd stolen from her stay at the Waldorf Astoria. 'Now this really is magic.'

The little girl had giggled in surprise and delight as she'd watched the big creamy bubbles appear on top of the water.

'What alchemy makes this?' she said as Lucía had encouraged her to climb in and dab some on her nose.

'American alchemy,' she said. 'Have you ever seen a movie, Angelina?'

'No, what is that?'

'Moving pictures on a screen. I have been in one. Perhaps one day I will show you.'

'Angelina is such an odd mixture,' Lucía commented when she'd arrived back from Sacromonte after dropping the child back at her cave home. 'She has wisdom beyond her years, yet she is a child who has grown up purely in nature, and her innocence is breathtaking.'

'You too grew up in nature, Lucía, in the same cave as Angelina.'

'I was not hidden away from the world, Mamá. I understood it all too well from a very young age. I asked her if she wished to come and stay with us for a while. She refused, saying that she could not leave Micaela alone, that she was too sick, but that she'd also miss her forest home.'

'Well, one day she will have no choice,' said María. 'From what they both say, Micaela does not have long.'

'It is almost as if this was all planned by an invisible hand,' mused Lucía. 'If we had not returned, what would have become of the child?'

'Oh, I am sure she would have survived,' María smiled. 'That is her destiny.'

Lucía stood up from the table where they'd been eating supper, and yawned. 'I am off to my bed, Mamá. I am tired tonight.'

'Sleep well, *querida.*'

'I will, goodnight, Mamá.'

María sat there for a while longer, before she cleared away the dishes, thinking what a change had come over her daughter. It was barely ten o'clock – the time when the old Lucía was only just beginning to come alive in front of an audience of hundreds, sometimes thousands – yet here, Lucía often retired early and slept peacefully through the night. The way Lucía had continued to exert herself over the years was frightening – she'd often worried that her daughter would dance herself to death – but this new Lucía was calm and a pleasure to be with. For now, at least . . .

Three weeks later, as the sun was setting, María saw a forlorn figure walking along the track towards the house.

'Lucía,' María called as she saw the fading light illuminating the small red-gold head, 'Angelina is here.'

María ran down the steps to meet Angelina. When she reached her, she saw the little girl was ready to collapse.

'Please, may I have some water?' she panted as María helped her onto the terrace. 'It has been a very long walk to get here.'

'What has happened?' María said as she sat Angelina in a chair and hurriedly poured her some water from the jug on the table.

'Micaela has gone to the Upperworld, *Abuela*,' she told her grandmother. 'She left this morning at dawn. She had told me to come straight here to you if it happened.'

'You mean . . .'

'Yes,' confirmed Angelina. 'She is no longer here with us on the earth.'

'*Ay! Pequeña*, if only we had known, we could have come

to you. No wonder you are exhausted, it is a very long way to walk.'

'A man offered me a lift on his cart, but then he started asking me strange questions, so I jumped off.' Angelina drank the water thirstily. 'Still, I am here, but we must go back soon because the *maestra* must be buried as soon as possible, or her soul will not settle.'

'Of course, we will go tomorrow morning. Where did she—?'

'I have left her in her bed.'

'Are you sad?' Lucía asked her as she appeared on the terrace.

'Yes, because I will miss her very much, but I know it was her time to go, so I am happy for her. She was no longer comfortable in her body, you see. They wear out and the soul must move on to be free.'

'I am sorry, Angelina.' Lucía put an arm around her. 'But you are safe here with us now.'

'*Gracias*, but you know I must go back to the forest to see my friends and pick my herbs?' Angelina told them, panic in her blue eyes.

'We do. Now, I will get you something to eat.'

'No, I cannot eat until after *Maestra* is in the earth.'

'Tomorrow, we will go early to Sacromonte,' María promised.

'Thank you. I think I would like to sleep now, please.'

'We shall put you in the nursery. There is a small bed in there all ready for you,' María said as the child stood up, her features drawn with extreme fatigue. 'Come with me.'

'Is she settled?' Lucía asked her mother when she returned to the terrace.

'She climbed beneath the blanket and was asleep within twenty seconds. The poor child. She is so calm tonight, but she must be in shock. Micaela is everything she has ever known.'

'She does not seem so,' Lucía commented, 'but then she is the oddest child I've ever met.' Lucía stubbed out a cigarette and lit another. 'What I am thinking is how you and I and Angelina can dig a hole big enough for Micaela to be buried in and carry her to it.'

'You are right,' María agreed, 'we cannot. So, we must find some men who can help us. You see, Lucía, they come in useful for some things, don't they?' she added with a glimmer of a smile.

Angelina woke them both just after dawn, looking rested and bright as a sunflower.

'We must leave,' she said. 'The *maestra* is anxious to begin her journey to the Upperworld.'

As the sun rose over the Alhambra, the three of them approached the cave.

*Dead in the bed where she helped me give birth . . .* María thought, as Angelina opened the front door. The stench of flesh already rotting in the heat was palpable inside. Lucía shook her head.

'Sorry, but I will vomit,' she said as she turned back from the door. 'Angelina, do you know of any families who live here who have young men who might help us bury the *maestra*?'

'*Sí*, Lucía. We will try next door.'

María watched as Angelina walked up the incline to the cave beyond hers.

'Surely that is deserted? Ramón, he was taken by the Civil Guard ten years ago . . .' she said as Angelina rapped on the door, then walked straight in.

'He came back three weeks ago . . . Ramón?' she called to the bedroom beyond the familiar kitchen they were standing in. 'It is I, Angelina, and we need your help.'

There was some grunting from behind the curtain, then an emaciated man with a long grey beard appeared from behind it.

'*¡Dios mío!*' María's hand flew to her mouth as tears appeared spontaneously in her eyes. 'Ramón, is it really you?'

'I . . . María! You are back! How? Why?'

'I thought you were dead! The Civil Guard, they came . . .'

'Yes, and they threw me in their prison and left me to die, but somehow, as you can see, I did not.' He coughed – the rattle so similar to the one María had listened to before Felipe had died. 'Then I was many months in the *payo* hospital, which was not much better than the prison. But you, María, you are more beautiful than ever!'

'Ramón, I cannot believe you are alive. I—'

'Come, let me hold you, *querida*.'

Lucía swallowed a lump in her throat as her mother went into Ramón's fragile, stick-like arms.

'They know each other well?' Angelina turned wide-eyed to Lucía.

'They did once, yes.'

'They love each other,' she decreed. 'This is a beautiful thing, is it not?'

'It is,' Lucía nodded.

Overcome with emotion, Ramón was helped to sit down on a stool before he keeled over.

'Where is the furniture?' María asked.

'Long gone to looters,' Ramón sighed. 'All I have is a straw pallet, but at least I am free and that is worth everything. Now tell me why you are here in my kitchen?'

'Micaela has passed on to the Upperworld and we must bury her. Do you know of any men left here in Sacromonte who can help us?' María asked him.

'I do not know, but we can find out. I just . . . cannot believe you are back, my María.' Ramón looked at her in total rapture.

'Another miracle,' Angelina whispered to Lucía.

The two women, the child, and the man as frail as an eighty-year-old searched the dusty paths of Sacromonte to find help to bury their once-revered *bruja*. Many doors did not open immediately, and the deep level of fear that had descended on this broken community was palpable. Many homes were empty, but once those that were coaxed out of their caves heard what had happened, they were happy to offer their services. The few able-bodied men were despatched with spades to dig Micaela's grave, while the women pooled their meagre resources and prepared food for a gathering after-wards.

One of the women lent her mule to be attached to another neighbour's cart, and after heaving Micaela's earthly remains onto it, they trooped off in a ragged procession to the forest, where they laid their *bruja* to rest.

The gathering afterwards was held in María's cave and an old *gitano*, who used to run one of the illegal drinking caves, brought up some brandy to toast Micaela's passing. Out of perhaps four hundred former residents, now only thirty or so of them were left. María and Lucía received much teasing about their new hairstyles, but beyond the horror and destruction of the past ten years, the flame of the community still flickered. Some of the men had brought their guitars along, and for the first time in years, the sound of flamenco music filled the Sacromonte air.

'Lucía! You must dance for us,' shouted one of the men, his shrunken stomach sending the brandy straight to his head.

'I have a cannonball in my stomach.' Lucía rolled her eyes. 'Maybe Mamá would like to dance? She taught me everything I know.'

'No,' María said, blushing, as other women pushed her forward.

'*Sí! Sí! Sí!*' the crowd chanted, clapping their hands to the beat. María had no choice but to agree and, terrified that her feet and hands would not remember what to do, she performed her first *alegrías por rosas* in twenty years. The rest of the crowd – or at least, those who had the strength to – eventually joined her, little Angelina staring wide-eyed at the spectacle.

'You have never attended a *fiesta*?' Lucía bent down to ask her.

'No, but it is the most beautiful thing I have ever seen,' she said, her eyes shining. 'Lucía, this is not an end, it is a new beginning!'

And as María encouraged Ramón to dance, supporting him as he did so, Lucía rather thought it was.

'Lucía, I have something to ask you.' María appeared by the makeshift hammock that the two of them had tied between two orange trees so Lucía could rest outside in the afternoons.

'What is that, Mamá?'

'I was wondering whether you would mind if I invited Ramón to come and live with us for a while. He is so very sick, and has nothing. He needs someone to care for him.'

'Of course I don't mind. With Angelina moving here, and the new baby on the way, we are starting our own *gitano* community right here,' Lucía chuckled.

'Thank you, *querida*. Even though he is sick now, Angelina believes he can make a full recovery and then he can at least be useful.'

'Useful or not, you want him here, and that is fine. So,' Lucía said innocently, 'will he sleep on the couch in the sitting room?'

'I . . . no. I thought it would be easiest if he—'

'Mamá, I am only teasing you. I know exactly where he will sleep, and that is in your arms. What on earth will Alejandro think when he knows his girlfriend has found another?' Lucía didn't wait for an answer, but climbed out of the hammock to walk up to the house for a glass of water.

'*Dios mío*, it is a sad state of affairs when my mother's love life is more hectic than mine,' she told her baby.

On 7 September, Lucía woke up in the night, feeling sweaty and uncomfortable. She stood up to empty her bladder for the fifth time that night, but before she had taken more than a

couple of steps, she felt warm liquid trickling down the inside of her legs.

'Help! Mamá! I am bleeding!' she screamed into the blackness. Both María and Angelina came running from their different rooms and switched the electric light on.

María looked down at the puddle of clear fluid between her daughter's legs and sighed in relief. 'Lucía, you are not bleeding, your waters have broken. It means your baby is on its way.'

'I am off to the kitchen to prepare a potion,' Angelina said. 'The baby will be here by sunrise,' she announced as she left.

Despite Lucía's high-pitched screams, which echoed around the rooms with enough velocity to frighten off any wolves lurking at the tops of the mountains above them, her stomach muscles, honed from years of dancing, stood her in good stead as her baby began its journey into life. Angelina took over, seeming to know instinctively what Lucía needed; she paced with her, sat her down, stood her up, rubbed her back, all the time whispering words of comfort that her baby was well and would soon be here.

María and Angelina helped her onto the bed when Lucía said she wanted to push and the baby girl came into the world at five o'clock in the morning, just as dawn was breaking.

'Never again!' Lucía panted in relief. 'That is the hardest *bulerías* I ever performed. Where is my baby?'

'She is here,' said Angelina, who had just severed the cord with her teeth, as she had watched Micaela do. 'She is strong and healthy.'

'What will you call her?' María asked as she gazed down at the miracle of a second granddaughter granted to her since she had arrived in Spain.

'Isadora, after the American dancer.'

'That is unusual,' María commented.

'Yes.' Lucía said no more, but as she held her newborn in her arms, her treacherous mind took her spinning back to her thirtieth birthday when Meñique had taken her to an exhibition of photographs of the dancer called Isadora Duncan. She hadn't wanted to go, but once she was there, she was swept away by the pictures, and the story of Duncan's life.

'She was a pioneer – she pushed boundaries, just like you, *pequeña*,' Meñique had said.

'I believe she looks like her grandmother,' said Angelina.

'*¡Gracias a Dios!* Then I am happy because I would want no child to look like me. Hello, baby,' Lucía said, peering down at the little face. 'Yes, you are definitely far prettier than your mamá. I . . .'

As the baby stared up at her, Lucía caught her breath at the tiny features that – even in miniature – were so familiar. But she would never *ever* admit to anyone who the baby really looked like.

Autumn turned to winter, and the strange little family that María and Lucía had collected retreated inside to sit around the small fire in the sitting room. María used it for her cooking, preferring the taste of the food to that produced by the great iron range that stood in the kitchen. Isadora thrived under the care and attention of both María and Angelina, although Lucía had point blank refused to breast feed after the first attempt.

'Why bother when all three of us can take turns feeding

her out of a bottle? Besides, I thought she would rip my poor nipples off with the force of her suckling; it was agony!'

Secretly, María thought that it was much more to do with the fact that Lucía enjoyed her sleep at night, and with other willing hands happy to get up and tend to Isadora, Lucía took advantage of them. The fact that the baby slept with Angelina in the nursery didn't help either. Yet María held her peace as she saw the little girl diligently changing nappies and feeding her bottles. Whilst Lucía sat smoking on the terrace, Angelina would sing Isadora lullabies as she rocked her to sleep. Some women were simply not made for motherhood and Lucía was one of them.

And whilst Angelina tended to Isadora, María used her own tender hands, with the help of Angelina's potions, to care for Ramón, who continued to gather his strength as each day passed. The rattling cough that reminded both of them of the dreadful jail receded and soon Ramón was able to wander in the orange grove, tutting at the lack of care it received.

'Perhaps I should ask Alejandro if he wishes you to tend to the trees?' María suggested to him one chilly evening as they sat in front of the warmth of the fire.

'*Ay*, María, I will do it for free, because it is what I love and know,' shrugged Ramón. 'This house – and you – have saved me. The least I can do is care for the trees that grow on the land.'

There soon began a constant trickle of visitors from Sacromonte, who found their way down the mountainside to drink coffee with María in the *payo* house and to consult the little *bruja* for her seeing and her potions. María was heartened to hear that, slowly, more residents of Sacromonte were returning to the village after years of exile in other countries.

Food was still expensive, with delicacies sold on the black market, but occasionally Angelina would be paid with a bar of chocolate or a bottle of brandy for Ramón, its provenance uncertain.

At Christmas, María made a pilgrimage to the Abbey of Sacromonte and went down on her knees to thank God for the safe delivery of her granddaughters, and her wonderful new life back in her homeland. Yet there was something that told her that this life was a temporary hiatus – a fact that was exacerbated by a sound she had not heard for many months: the continual tapping of Lucía's feet on the tiled terrace outside.

'Mamá,' Lucía announced to María one morning, 'I am ready to go back to dancing now. Pepe has telegrammed to say that the *cuadro* has been offered another season at the 46th Street Theatre. And they will triple the money if I make a return to the stage. Mamá, this is the perfect moment to go back.'

'Surely it is too soon? Your baby is only four months old.'

'If I do not, I will lose everything I have worked for.'

'Lucía, that is not true. You are the most famous flamenco dancer in North and South America. There is no rush, *querida*.'

'The public have a very short memory, and especially now that La Argentinita has passed, every day another new and younger dancer emerges to challenge me for my crown. Besides, I miss it,' she sighed.

'What part of it do you miss?'

'The dancing of course! It is who I am.'

'You are also a mother now,' María reminded her as she

looked down at Isadora sleeping peacefully in her Silver Cross perambulator in the shade.

'Yes, so why can't I be both?'

'You can, of course you can. So, do you want me to make plans for the three of us to travel back to New York?'

'Mamá.' Lucía came to sit in the wicker chair opposite her mother. 'I remember what it was like, to be a child who was always on the road, going with Papá from town to town, sleeping in wagons or fields, to receive no education, have no place that I could call home.'

'I thought you thrived on the life of a traveller, Lucía. You always said that you enjoyed the fact you never knew what the next day would bring.'

'Yes, I did, but I had no choice. Isadora has.' Lucía paused and looked at her mother. 'I know you love it here, Mamá, and how much you love Isadora. So . . .' She paused again before continuing. 'What if you were to stay here with her?'

María did her best not to let out a sigh of relief, and focused on putting the needs of her grandchild first.

'And you will go to New York alone?'

'*Sí*, but I will return as often as I can to see you both.'

'But, Lucía, she is so small, she needs her mother. I am no substitute.'

'Yes, you are, Mamá. You are far more maternal and patient than I will ever be. You know how cross I get when she cries. And besides,' Lucía added, 'money is running short. I must go out and earn some. Or at least see Papá to ask him for some more.'

'How long will you be gone?'

'The contract is for six months and I will earn enough to

*buy* this house,' Lucía laughed, 'and then we will all be safe forever. Just imagine that, Mamá!'

'It would be a very good thing, yes, Lucía,' María agreed, knowing that once Lucía had set her mind to something, nothing in heaven or hell could stop her, so there was no point in arguing any further on Isadora's behalf.

'Whatever you think is best, *querida*.'

'Good. Then that is settled.'

As Lucía stood up, María saw the expression of relief in her daughter's eyes too.

'And how could I ever have expected her to give up her dancing? It is who she is,' María explained to Ramón later that night.

'But she is a mother now, María. And her baby needs her.'

'Your girls did well without one,' María reminded him. 'As long as babies are loved by someone, I'm not sure it matters who it is.'

'And where are my girls now?' Ramón said, his face a picture of misery. 'Lying dead in a mass grave somewhere in the city.'

'With my boys, their wives and my grandchildren,' María added, reaching for his hand.

'Why did we survive, when it was their world to conquer?'

It was a question both of them asked the heavens every day.

'I do not know, and neither of us ever will until it's our turn to go upwards, but at least we can safeguard the next generation.'

'Here are we, weeping for our lost children and grandchildren, while a mother plans to abandon hers.' Ramón shook his head. 'Does Lucía not realise what a gift she has been given?'

María knew he struggled with Lucía and what he saw as her selfishness.

'Everyone has their strengths and weaknesses, and all we can do is accept them for who they are. Besides, Lucía is right; one of us in this household needs to find work before the money runs out.'

'I am hoping that when summer comes I can go back and work as a labourer,' Ramón commented. 'It should be my task to earn the money.'

'Ramón, you know as well as I that there are thousands returning to Spain who are desperate for work. Will you not try to fight to reclaim your own orange grove?' María asked him again. 'It's so unfair, you paid for that grove – it is yours by rights.'

'And what proof do I have, except a sheet of paper from the seller naming the figure I paid for it? It isn't a legal deed, María . . . Me, against Franco's government, who stole it from me originally.' Ramón shook his head and gave a hollow laugh. 'I don't think so.'

'But unless someone starts to fight, then nothing will change.'

'María, I think we have enough battles to fight just to survive. Perhaps you have been away so long you have forgotten who we are; we are *gitanos*, the lowest of the low. No one listens to us.'

'Because we never *speak*!' María shook her head. 'Forgive me, Ramón, but in America it is very different. Look what

Lucía achieved despite being a *gitano*. She was fêted every-where she went.'

'Yes, for her talent, for she is unique and special. Me? I am just a simple labourer.'

'Yes.' María reached for his hand. 'And one that I love with all of my heart.'

'So, you have enough money for the next six months' rent, food, and an extra amount for all the milk Isadora guzzles.' Lucía smiled as she looked down at her baby, kicking on the floor in her napkin, her little limbs naked. Lucía went to her, knelt down and kissed each foot, each hand and both cheeks. 'Ah, my love, *mi pequeña*. Take good care until we meet again.'

'The taxi has arrived, Lucía,' shouted Ramón.

'Then I must go. Goodbye, Ramón, Angelina . . .' Lucía kissed her on both cheeks. 'Bye-bye, Mamá, take care of you and my darling Isadora.'

'I will, and Godspeed on your journey, *querida*. Be safe until we meet again.'

Lucía blew a kiss as her tiny feet clattered across the tiles in her new leather court shoes. With a last wave, she climbed into the taxi and was gone.

Angelina, standing alone on the terrace, found her eyes filled with tears.

*They will never meet again*, she thought silently to herself.

# 33

Over the next few months, even though Lucía's departure was a wrench, without her constant restlessness, the house became a far calmer place. Ramón – always uncomfortable in front of Lucía because of José – relaxed and unleashed all his paternal instincts on baby Isadora.

Through word of mouth, Angelina's stream of visitors began to increase, all wishing to consult the angel child, who had spawned a reputation as being the greatest *bruja* the *gitano* world had seen in a generation. Clients started coming from as far away as Barcelona, and one night Angelina came to sit with María and Ramón.

'I wish to ask your advice,' she said quietly, her hands clasped in her lap. 'Because I am so young and still learning, I do not ask to be paid. People often leave me some goat's milk or eggs, as you know, but I am wondering—'

'Whether you should put down a charge for different treatments and remedies,' Ramón finished for her. 'What do you think, María? After all, we are using our money buying petrol to take the car up to Sacromonte three times a week so that Angelina can forage for her herbs. We should at least cover that cost.'

'Do you know what Micaela charged, *Abuela*?' Angelina asked María.

'Not exactly, no. She never refused to treat a patient if they couldn't afford to pay, but if they could, then yes, she took their money. Especially the wealthy *payos* who came to see her.'

'I don't think *payos* would come to see a child like Angelina and pay,' chuckled Ramón.

'Maybe not yet, no,' María agreed, 'but that was where Micaela made her proper money.'

'Next you'll be suggesting we send Angelina down into the Plaza de las Pasiegas by the cathedral! She can hand out rosemary and a fortune for a few pesetas.' Ramón raised his eyebrows.

'You know,' María commented later that evening, as she took out the box that contained their cash from under the floorboards and opened it, 'even though you joked about putting Angelina in the plaza to catch the rich *payos*, soon it may be necessary. We have only enough money for the next three months.'

'Lucía promised to send some more, didn't she?'

'Yes, but it hasn't arrived. What if it got stolen on its journey? It is a long way from America to Spain, and many hands will have fingered that parcel. How many hungry people are there at the post office in Granada?'

'Lucía is not stupid, *querida*. She would disguise it well. What is it, María? You are not yourself.'

'No,' María sighed. 'I may not be a *bruja*, but I just have a bad feeling, that something is going to go wrong.'

'This is not like you at all.' Ramón frowned, then took her

in his arms. 'Remember what both of us have already survived. Together we can face anything. I promise.'

'I hope so, Ramón, I really do.'

A week later, a car that María did not recognise came sweeping up the drive. It parked in front of the house and a *payo*
woman with a sleek black bob and an oversized pair of sunglasses stepped out.

'*Hola*, señora,' María smiled as the woman climbed up the
steps to the terrace. 'How can I help you?'

'Are you Señora Albaycín?' the woman asked.

'*Sí*, I am. And you are?'

'Señora Velez.'

'Ah! Alejandro's sister. Please, come in. I am very happy to
meet you. Can I get you something to drink?'

'No, señora. I am afraid I have come here because there
have been complaints in the neighbourhood about you and
your family.'

'Complaints?' María looked around at the olive and
orange groves that stood on either side of the *finca*. 'But we
have no neighbours.'

'I have heard that one of your family is using this house as
a place of work.'

'Sorry, señora, what do you mean?'

'She tells fortunes and brews herbs into potions, which she
sells. Is this true?'

'I . . . yes, that is, my ten-year-old granddaughter helps
people if they are sick or need advice. She is a *bruja*, señora.'

'You say this business is run by a child?' The woman took

off her dark sunglasses to show a pair of heavily made-up, hard green eyes.

'Yes, and you are right that recently more have heard of her gifts and have sought her out.'

'Did you know it is illegal for children to work, señora?'

'It isn't work, she does not get paid for doing it—'

'Señora Albaycín, I am sure you can understand my brother and I rented this house out to you in good faith. My brother assured me you and your daughter were respectable women. He did not realise that you kept company with the kind of people who are now visiting. Nor does my brother realise that our home is now housing a business and using child labour at that.'

'Señora, I have told you that my granddaughter does not take money for her services and the people who come here are—'

'*Gitanos*. I suppose we must count ourselves lucky that you have not moved in your entire clan!'

At that moment, Angelina appeared, holding Isadora in her arms.

'*Hola*, señora,' Angelina smiled at the woman. 'How can we help you?'

'Is this the child who tells the fortunes?'

'*Sí*, señora,' Angelina answered. 'Shall I tell you yours?'

'No.' The woman visibly shuddered as Ramón also appeared on the terrace to see who their visitor was.

'And who is *this*?'

'My name is Ramón, señora. And you are welcome to our home.' He smiled, holding out his hand to her.

'For your information, this is *my* home. So he lives here too?'

'Yes, señora,' María confirmed.

'Alejandro did not mention either him or the child. I believe it is just yourself and your daughter named on the lease. So, how many more of you are hidden away inside?'

'Please, it is only who you see. My daughter has travelled back to America and . . .' María followed the woman as she walked inside, opening each door tentatively as if she might be attacked by a savage group of undesirables. Once satisfied there was no one else present, the woman's eyes swept around the kitchen and the sitting room.

'You can see, señora, that I have made your house beautiful,' said María.

The woman flicked an ant off the kitchen table.

'Apart from the fact I have just discovered you have moved further members of your family into our house without permission, and that a minor is working out of it, I have come to tell you that we are putting up the rent from next month. My brother was always a soft touch – and he too realises it is far too low for such a property.'

'How much will you charge, señora?'

The woman named the figure and Ramón and María stared at each other in horror.

'But, señora, that is four times what we are paying now! We cannot afford it and—'

'Perhaps you can have her put her prices up,' the woman glanced at Angelina.

'But we made an agreement—'

'Yes, for *two* people. Now there are four, and besides, I am sure that the *policía* would support us were we to tell them that our beloved grandparents' house had been taken over by *gitano* squatters. So, if you are unable to pay what we wish, you will leave the house by the end of the month, which I should remind you is in three days' time.' The woman turned to walk off the terrace, her sunglasses back in place. 'Oh, and don't think of taking anything from the house. We know exactly what is in it. Goodbye, señora.'

As the woman headed towards her car, Angelina walked down the terrace and pointed at her.

'I curse you, señora,' she muttered under her breath. 'May you rot in the depths of hell!'

'Hush!' said María as the woman looked up at them, turned the engine on, then screeched out of the drive. 'That won't help at all.'

'Must we leave this house?' Angelina asked her.

'Yes, we must.' María took baby Isadora from Angelina's small arms and looked helplessly at Ramón. 'Where on earth should we go?'

'For now, I think we must go back to Sacromonte.'

'Well' – Angelina clapped her hands together – 'at least I will be happy. I will be close to the forest, even though I will miss the bathtub.'

'At least we own it, and no one can claim it back as theirs,' said María. 'I knew something was coming, that this was too good to last.'

'You did.' Ramón stretched out a hand to her. 'Remember we were happy there once before, *querida*. I hope we can be happy again.'

'What if Lucía has sent the money here already and it arrives after we've gone?' María said, panic surging through her.

'We must send a telegram to Pepe to let him know what has happened, and while we are at the post office, ask them to hold any mail that comes for us there. See, María?' Ramón reached for her hand and squeezed it gently. 'There is always a solution to every problem.'

'Why are you so positive?'

'Because there is nothing else to be.'

Three days later, having borrowed a mule to attach to Ramón's cart, he clopped off with all their possessions loaded onto it. María followed behind in the car, which she was hoping she could sell – they wouldn't be needing it up at Sacromonte. Even though María knew that part of being *gitano* was that all homes were temporary, she could not help but mourn the loss of her beloved *finca* and her time as a *payo*.

Ramón did his best to brighten up their cave. He whitewashed all the walls and fashioned a little courtyard to the side where they could sit outside during the long hot days. He even suggested to María that they turn the old storeroom at the back of the stable into a bathroom.

'I cannot provide running water,' he said, as he, María and Angelina stared at the battered tin bathtub and commode he had brought back on his cart from the junkyard in the city, 'but we can make do with these.'

'*Gracias*, Ramón.' Angelina put her arms around him. 'They are just as good.'

In many ways, María thought, as they sat outside together watching the sun set over the Alhambra, their move had proved less painful than she'd feared. Their old home had welcomed them back and it was comforting to be amongst friends.

The telegram had gone off to Pepe and every morning, Ramón went down to the city post office to find out if the package from America had arrived. It hadn't.

'At least we have the money from the car, *querida*, and maybe I can find some work as a labourer soon,' Ramón reminded her.

María looked at him – his skinny body still struggling to recover from the toll the years in prison had taken.

'Let us just hope the package arrives in the next few weeks,' she sighed.

Four months on, there was still no package or word from Pepe. María had taken up her basket-weaving again, but few in the city had money to spare to buy them.

'Can I come with you, *Abuela*?' Angelina asked as María loaded the baskets onto a long stick and prepared to carry them to the central plaza. 'Ramón can mind Isadora for a few hours and you look as if you need some help.'

'Thank you,' María smiled. 'And yes, maybe your pretty face can charm me some customers.'

They set off on the long walk, María glad that summer was here. It had been a particularly wet spring – the mud running in rivulets down the mountain and creating a stink she remembered vividly from her past. Today there was a brilliant July sun and with Angelina chattering beside her, she felt a little more cheerful.

'You're not to worry, *Abuela*, the money will come, I promise,' Angelina smiled at her as they reached the Plaza de las Pasiegas, which lay in front of the great cathedral of Granada.

'Now then.' Angelina looked around her, then pointed towards a spot just by the cathedral steps. 'Mass will finish soon,' she said, having read the board on the front door. 'Many people will come out and perhaps they will like to buy your baskets. Señorita,' she said, approaching a *payo* woman walking across the square, 'my grandmother has made these beautiful baskets with her own hands, are you interested in buying one? They are very strong, you know,' Angelina added.

The woman shook her head, but Angelina followed her. 'Then how about having your fortune told?'

Again, the woman shook her head and began to walk faster.

'But surely you wish to know if your daughter will marry the wealthy man she is courting?' she persisted. 'Or whether your husband will get the promotion at the office he is after?'

At this, the woman paused and turned round to Angelina, shock on her face.

'How did you know that?'

'Señora, for a peseta, I can know much more. Now, let me take your hand and see . . .'

María hung back and watched as Angelina traced the woman's palm with her own small fingers and whispered secrets in her ear, having to stand on tiptoe to do so. After ten minutes or so, the woman nodded, reached into her handbag and took out her purse. She watched as the woman extracted a five-peseta note.

'Do you have change?' she asked Angelina.

'Sadly, señora, I do not, but maybe you would take one of my grandmother's baskets instead?'

The woman seemed dazed and nodded automatically as Angelina skipped over to María to retrieve a basket. '*Gracias*, señora, and I wish you and your family a long and happy life.'

'See?' Angelina said when the woman had gone. She flapped the note as she walked back towards María. 'I told you you were not to worry about money.'

By the time María walked back up the winding alleys to Sacromonte, she had no baskets left to carry. In their place was a bulging pocket in her skirt, full of coins and notes.

'I have never seen anything like it,' María told Ramón that evening as they feasted on the blood sausages María had bought. 'She managed to entice customer after customer to have their fortune told. And she did not even have any rosemary to give them.' María smiled.

'Perhaps it helped that she is a child and looks like a *payo*.' Ramón shrugged.

'Yes, that, but also because with each of them she would tell them a little something about themselves that they all recognised to draw them in.' María shook her head. 'Her gift is frightening, Ramón. It frightened me to watch her. She said she wants to go again next week, but I just don't know whether it is right to use her powers for money. That was what happened with Lucía.'

'And like Lucía, Angelina has a mind of her own. Trust me, that young lady will never do anything she does not wish to do. Besides . . .'

'What?'

'Angelina did what she did today to comfort *you*. She wanted to show you that you are not to worry because she loves you. What is so wrong with that?'

'Because I always feel as though I am reliant on others,' María sighed.

'No, María, we are all reliant on you.' He patted her hand gently. 'Now, time for bed.'

# Isadora

*June 1951, five years later*

# 34

'Are you awake, Isadora?'

'No,' she said, burying her face in the pillow. 'I am asleep.'

'Well, I know you are not because you are talking to me, and if you won't get out of bed, I will just have to tickle you until you do . . .'

Angelina's fingers crept under the blanket and headed for Isadora's middle, which was where she was most ticklish. They moved lightly around her tummy like small spiders, until Isadora started giggling.

'Stop it! Stop it!' she laughed as she threw the covers back and climbed out of her bed. 'Look, I am up! What do you want?'

'For you to come with me into the city before *Abuela* and Ramón wake up.'

'But they say you are not to go and fortune-tell for the *payos*,' Isadora said, rubbing the sleep out of her eyes with her small hands.

'I looked in the money tin and they will also tell us there is nothing for supper if I don't,' Angelina announced. 'Will you come? Please? I always get more customers when you're with me,' she begged.

'All right,' Isadora sighed. 'Do I have to wear that stupid dress? It is too small for me and it scratches.'

'Yes, you do, because you look so sweet in it.' Angelina held up the dress, made of floral cotton with puffed sleeves. Isadora let Angelina remove her nightgown and replace it with the dress.

'This is for babies,' she said sulkily, 'and besides, I have told you, I am a tomboy. Ouch!' she complained as her cousin ran a stiff brush through her long dark curls.

'Afterwards, I promise that I will buy you an ice cream,' Angelina cajoled as she fastened a pink ribbon to one side of Isadora's hair. 'There now, put on your shoes and we will go.'

As they tiptoed past the curtained entrance to their grandmother and Ramón's bedroom, Angelina paused to pour some water from the jug into a flask. As they stepped outside, Isadora felt the heat of the day, even though it was only just past eight o'clock.

'You look pretty in your dress,' Isadora commented as she gazed at her cousin. Secretly she thought Angelina was the most beautiful thing she'd ever seen, and she knew all the boys in Sacromonte did too. With her long gold hair, big blue eyes and skin that never went dark in the sun, Isadora thought she looked like a princess from the book of fairy tales that Ramón had bought her when he taught her to read. 'Will you ever get married? You are nearly sixteen, after all.'

'I will never marry, *pequeña*.' Angelina shook her head firmly. 'It is not in my destiny.'

'How can you say that? All beautiful princesses meet their prince. Even *Abuela* met Ramón,' Isadora giggled.

'I just know,' Angelina shrugged. 'I have much other work

to do, you see. Whereas you' – Angelina caught her hand and swung it high with hers – 'have already met yours.'

'I hope not. All the boys I know are ugly and rude. Are you sure?'

'Yes, I am.'

'How do you know all these things?' Isadora asked her as they passed through the city gate and began to walk down the steep cobbled alleys to the centre.

'I don't know, I just do. And sometimes, I wish I didn't. Especially if it's horrible things.'

'Like monsters, or big long snakes?'

'Yes, those too.' Angelina smiled.

'I wish I had a gift like yours. Then I could see if *Abuela* was going to make me *magdalenas* for tea when I come home from school.'

'Keep up, *pequeña*, and stop dawdling!'

Isadora took her eyes from a green caterpillar that was slowly mounting a stone wall and skipped down the hill towards her cousin.

In the plaza, she stood smiling sweetly as Angelina enticed her first client to have her fortune read. Whatever Angelina said to them about their future, Isadora knew that the conversation between them must remain private, so she would amuse herself by looking along the narrow alleyways that led from the plaza. Her favourite place was the café with the opening to one side that sold ice creams to passing tourists. Every different colour was there and she had tried most of them.

'Today, I will have the green one, with the chocolate bits in it,' she told herself, looking longingly at it. 'Today is so hot,' she said as she wiped her brow and peered round the counter to see if her friend Andrés was at the café today. Andrés was the son of the bad-tempered café owner. He was seven years old – a little over a year older than she was. At weekends and in the school holidays, like her, Andrés came to work with his mamá and papá, but he was always dropping plates and couldn't place the ice cream neatly in the cornets, so his parents shooed him outside into the plaza to play.

They had met along the alleyway next to the café, both of them crouching out of the glare of the midday sun. Andrés had offered her a sip of his lemonade – which had made her mouth all fizzy. And from that moment on, she had loved him – and lemonade – with a passion.

Of course he was a *payo*, so when Angelina said she had already met her prince, she knew Andrés couldn't count. He was so handsome, with his light-coloured hazel eyes and lots of curly brown hair. He was gentle and clever too – he could read and write much better than she could. Unlike other *payos*, he didn't seem suspicious of her at all; in fact, he seemed fascinated by the fact she lived in a cave and had a cousin who could tell the future.

He looked at her sometimes like he wanted to kiss her, his lips near hers, but then he'd blush, wipe his mouth on his hand and suggest they went to kick a football around the plaza.

Isadora hadn't told anyone about her friend. She knew her family hated *payos*, who were only good to take money from for fortunes or baskets. But Andrés was different, and she knew he liked her. He had said that one day he would marry her and they would run their own olive grove together.

'But I don't like olives,' she had said stubbornly, secretly thrilled by his words.

'We can have other things too,' he had said quickly. 'Anything you want.'

'Can we have ice cream every day?'

'Yes, of course.'

'And can we have a kitten or a baby and a bathtub?' she'd asked as she'd kicked the football to him.

'We will get those things and many more. When we get married, we'll have a big fiesta in your cave like the ones you tell me of. We'll dance together, and everyone will eat ice cream.' He'd grinned and kicked the ball back to her.

'You want one, señorita?' said Andrés' father from behind the big freezer that displayed the ice creams.

Isadora emerged from her reverie. '*Sí*, but I have no money, señor.'

'Then go away,' he shouted at her. 'You are putting other customers off.'

Isadora shrugged at him and decided she would not be inviting *him* to any fiesta. Andrés was not at the café yet, but it was still early in the morning.

'She's not putting me off,' said a deep voice from behind her. 'I would like two of those.' The man pointed to the green ice cream.

'*Sí*, señor.'

Isadora turned and saw crowds flooding out of the cathedral. Early morning Mass must have just finished. She saw Enrico, Andrés' father, change his expression and become all smiles for the *payo*. While the two cornets were filled, Isadora looked up at the man, who was very tall and sunburnt, with a pair of deep brown eyes. He looked kind, she thought, and a bit sad.

'Here, señorita,' he said as he handed one of the cornets to her. She looked up at him in surprise.

'For me?' she asked.

'*Sí*,' he nodded.

'*Gracias a Dios*,' she said as she took a lick of the ice cream that was already melting in the sun and dribbling down the cornet. And having identified a potential customer, she smiled up sweetly at him. 'Would you like your fortune told?' she asked him in Spanish.

'*No comprendo. Hablo Ingles*,' he said.

'You like fortune tell?' The words had been taught to her parrot-fashion by Angelina, just in case she got talking to an English-speaking tourist in the plaza.

'You can tell my fortune?' The man looked down at her.

It was Isadora's turn to say she didn't understand. '*Mi prima*, Angelina.' Isadora pointed to the plaza. 'She very good,' she said, as she stretched out her palm and mimed the reading of it.

'Why not?' The man shrugged as he licked his ice cream and indicated that Isadora should lead the way.

Angelina was just finishing with another client and Isadora held back whilst the money was exchanged.

'Here,' she said, when the woman had walked away, 'I have a man for you. His Spanish isn't good,' she whispered quickly.

'*Hola*, señor,' Angelina smiled her brightest smile. 'I see hand?' she asked in English. 'Then I tell you about your daughter.'

'My daughter?'

Seeing the man's shocked face, like all Angelina's clients had when she told them a secret she somehow knew, Isadora walked away and went to finish her ice cream in the shade of an awning across the plaza. She hoped that she would receive a few céntimos in commission from Angelina for bringing the man to her. Perhaps she would buy a present for her grandmother with it. Just as she was thinking this and also feeling sad that Andrés had not yet appeared at the café, a black and white kitten appeared from the alleyway next to her and began to weave its skinny body around her legs.

'Oh! You're so sweet,' Isadora said as she picked the kitten up in her arms and it began to purr. 'Maybe I could take you home as a present for *Abuela*,' she said as she kissed its head. Looking across the plaza, she saw that the man she had taken to Angelina was walking away. She crossed towards her cousin, still holding the kitten.

'Look what I found.' Isadora looked up hopefully, but Angelina's eyes were still following her customer. 'Look!' she demanded. 'Can we take him home, Angelina? *Please*,' she begged.

'No, you know we cannot. We can hardly feed our own mouths, let alone animals. Now, I am too tired and hot for more clients, and we must go home.'

'What about my ice cream?'

'You already had one, didn't you, you naughty girl. That man bought one for you. There is so much sadness in the world . . . *Ay*,' Angelina brushed her hand across her eyes. 'Now, put that kitten back where you found him and we will go.'

Isadora did so, sulking because it was a long hot walk home, she hadn't seen Andrés and, no matter how hard she begged, she was not allowed to have a pet of her own.

'Did you make good money this morning?' she asked Angelina; she was used to her cousin's silences when they returned from her seeing. *Abuela* said it drained her energy, so she would always try to cheer her up on the walk home.

'Yes, that man gave me ten pesetas.'

'Ten pesetas!' Isadora clapped her hands. 'Why aren't you happy?'

'Because even if they are *payos*, I wish I didn't have to take their money, that I could see for them for free.'

'You don't take money from the *gitanos* who come to see you, do you?'

'No, but that is because they have none.' Angelina smiled down at her weakly, then ruffled her head. 'You are a good girl, Isadora. And I am sorry if I am cross sometimes.'

'I understand.' Isadora patted her hand. 'It is a big burden you carry,' she said solemnly, repeating the words she had heard María use three nights ago when one of her neighbours had come to their cave, begging for a potion to save her seventy-year-old mother. Angelina had given it, but when the woman had gone, she had shaken her head. 'She will be dead by morning, and there is nothing I can do.'

'Well, that is kind of you to say, but my gift is also a great privilege. And I should not complain.' She stopped suddenly and hugged Isadora to her. 'I love you, *querida*, and we must spend the time we have been granted together happily.'

A month later, as the heat of June melted into an even hotter July, Isadora came home to find a stranger sitting in her grandmother's kitchen. She looked up at María, who was sitting in her wooden rocking chair, her eyes red-raw from crying.

'What is it? What has happened, *Abuela*?' she said, ignoring the man and walking across the kitchen to clamber into María's lap.

'Ay, Isadora, I . . .' María did her best to compose herself as she put her arms around her granddaughter. 'I am so sorry, *querida*, so sorry . . .'

'What is it? What has happened? You all look so sad.' Isadora stared at the man sitting at the table nursing a glass of Ramón's special brandy. 'Who is he?'

'Well, that is the happy news.' María managed a weak smile. 'This is Pepe, your uncle.'

'Pepe! You mean your son who lives in America?' Isadora's expressive eyes turned back to María. 'My uncle?'

'I do, yes.'

'And he has come here?'

'He has, yes.' María smiled and indicated Pepe.

'But . . .' Isadora put her finger to her mouth as she did when she was thinking. 'Why are you not happy, *Abuela*? You said so often that you miss him and now he is here.'

'I did . . .' María nodded. 'And I am very happy to see him, yes.'

Isadora got down from her grandmother's knee and crossed the kitchen to stand in front of her uncle.

'*Hola*, my name is Isadora, and I am pleased to meet you.' She held out her hand formally.

Pepe chuckled as he offered his in return and she shook it. 'I see my niece has learnt excellent manners.'

'She has, yes. That is Angelina's doing – she takes her sometimes into the city when she is telling the *payos*' fortunes. She speaks a little English too.'

'Well, little one, I am not a *payo*, so come here and give your Uncle Pepe a big hug.'

Isadora allowed herself to be gathered into Pepe's arms. When he kissed her, she could feel his enormous moustache tickle her cheek. 'Look, I have brought you a present all the way from America,' he said as he reached for a box on the floor next to him and handed it to her.

'A present? For me? Look! It's a box wrapped in pretty paper, *Abuela*! Thank you, Uncle Pepe.'

'No, Isadora,' Pepe said smiling. 'You must take off the paper and find what is inside it. That is the present.'

'But the paper is beautiful and I will spoil it if I take it off,' Isadora frowned.

'Here, I will show you.' Pepe took the box and put it on the kitchen table. He began to undo the reams of pink ribbon and then tear open the paper at one end. 'See? You do the rest.'

Isadora did so, and, with Pepe's guidance, removed the lid of the box. She gasped when she saw what was inside.

'It is a doll! And it looks like Angelina! She is so beautiful. Is she really mine?'

'She is, and I hope you will take good care of her. Her name is Gloria,' Pepe said, as Isadora lifted the doll out of the box, transfixed.

'I have seen them in *payo* shops, but they cost many pesetas. Thank you, *Tío*,' she said, holding Gloria to her. 'I promise I will look after her.' She turned to María. 'Maybe you were crying with happiness, *Abuela*?' she said hopefully.

A look passed between Pepe and María.

'We were both sad because Pepe tells me that your mamá, Lucía, has gone up to the heavens to be with the angels.'

'She has gone to the Upperworld?' Isadora asked, as she moved Gloria's arms up and down, then fiddled with the miniature shoe and little sock that slid off her tiny foot.

'Yes.'

'So I will never meet her on earth?'

'No, you won't, Isadora.'

'Well, I would have liked to meet her, but I am sure she is happy where she is. Angelina says that the Upperworld is a very beautiful place. May I go and show Gloria to her now?'

'Of course you may. She is in the courtyard, tending her herbs.'

When Isadora had left the room, Pepe smiled at his mother. 'She is a beautiful child, Mamá. So natural, unlike the kids in America.'

'Yes, she is. And in many ways I am glad that she was too young to remember her mother. Her death will not hurt her so much. You were telling me what happened, Pepe?'

'We were in Baltimore, and yes, Lucía was exhausted and drinking and smoking too much, but no different from normal. She stood on stage as she always did and began her *farruca*. At the end of the dance, she shouted out "*Olé!*", then dropped to the floor. The audience thought this was part of the performance – and so did we, and it was only when she did not get up that we realised something was wrong. An ambulance was called, but she was pronounced dead on arrival at the hospital. They said she'd had a big heart attack. She would have known nothing, Mamá.'

María crossed herself. 'She danced herself to death.'

'*Sí*, Mamá. At least she died doing what she loved.'

'But she was so young! Not even forty yet! And it is so sad she was never able to return to Sacromonte to see her daughter.'

'Yes. Many times I asked her if she would come here, but she always found an excuse. Having seen Isadora, I think I know why. She is the image of her father!'

'I suppose she is, yes,' María agreed. 'And very like him

637

too. Gentle and kind and very, very patient. She follows Angelina around like a puppy.'

'Mamá, do you think we should tell Meñique that he has a daughter?' asked Pepe.

'Lucía always made me promise that I wouldn't, but now she is no longer here . . . What do you think?'

'I heard Meñique is married now, living in Argentina with his wife and two children.'

'You mean he has finally moved on from Lucía?'

'Yes. Is it fair to disrupt his new family with such news, I wonder? But equally, is it fair for Isadora never to know her father?'

'She has had Ramón here, Pepe, and me and Angelina. One thing I must tell you – never did I receive a penny from Lucía after she left. Even though I sent you a telegram saying we had moved and the money should be sent care of the post office.'

'Yes, Mamá, I received the telegram and I swear I was with her when she sent the money to you regularly. None of it ever reached you?'

'No. Even though Ramón has been down to the post office in the city once a week for the past five years. They said that nothing had arrived.'

'Well, then we can assume there is a very rich man at the post office, who is driving around in a fast car. Why did you not tell me if you needed help?'

'I was not going to beg from my family.' María shook her head. 'And we have managed, Pepe, somehow.'

'Mamá.' Pepe stood up and walked over to her. 'I am so sorry. If I had known I would have helped, but I did not. Anyway, now I am back and I can look after you. I brought all my savings here and if we are careful it is enough to keep us fed for many years. And also . . .' Pepe fingered his moustache.

'Yes?'

'I reminded Papá about Isadora before I left. Then I asked him to give me some money for her. After all, Lucía was her mamá, and by rights, all she earned and everything she owned should pass to her daughter.'

'You are right. And did he give it to you?'

'He said it had been a difficult year, that the *cuadro*'s wages had been eaten up by new costumes for the show. He gave me some, but nothing like what Lucía was owed by him.'

'So, he does not change,' María said with a deep sigh.

'No, Mamá, he does not. But before I left, I took the liberty of selling Lucía's furs and all her jewellery. I did not get what I should have done, but at least Isadora now has a good sum for her future. Tomorrow I will go to the bank in town and open her an account. With luck, as Spain's fortunes change for the better, her inheritance should grow. Perhaps we should not tell her, but give it to her on her eighteenth birthday.'

'Yes.' For the first time, María smiled. 'Then at least she will have something to begin her adult life with. Best we forget all about it until then. How long are you staying, Pepe?'

'Well, there is no *cuadro* any more. After Lucía's death, they all went their own ways, and I have had enough of being on the road. So' – he took his mother's hands in his – 'I have come back for good, Mamá.'

'Then that is news that does make me happy! And you can use Ramón's cave as your home.'

'He lives here with you?'

'Yes, he does,' María nodded, no longer wishing to hide

her love for the man who had been everything her husband had not. 'I hope you understand, Pepe.'

'Mamá, I do. I may have idolised my father as a child, but it did not take me long to work out who he really was.'

'Without Ramón, I would not have survived,' María shrugged. 'And what about your father? Where is he?'

'I left him in San Francisco. He likes California because of the weather. He has a job playing at a bar in the town.'

'Is he alone?' María asked, realising it no longer hurt her heart to do so.

'He . . . is not, no. His latest girlfriend is called Juanita, but I am sure she will not last.'

'And neither do I care if she does or doesn't,' María said firmly, finding it was the truth. 'And what about you, Pepe? Do you have a girlfriend?'

'No, Mamá, who would want me?' he chuckled.

'Many women! Look at you. You are handsome, talented, and still young.'

'Maybe I am just not the marrying kind.'

'You wait until the girls here in Sacromonte see you. You will have them queuing up at your door,' María said as she rose. 'Now, I must get on and make our supper. Go and see if Ramón is back with the water yet, will you?'

'Yes, Mamá.'

As Pepe left the cave to walk down the hill, he sighed, wondering whether he should tell the truth to stop his mother trying to marry him off. But there were some things that even a mother who loved her son to the bottom of her soul could never know. The shock of what he was might kill her. He knew it was a secret he'd have to keep to himself for the rest of his life.

News travelled fast around the mountain, and the next day it seemed that every *gitano* left in Granada had come to María's cave to pay their respects for La Candela, the greatest flamenco dancer to have ever been born in Sacromonte, and to attend the burial of the ashes Pepe had brought with him. At dusk, María and Angelina led the pilgrimage to the woods, the women keening and singing the mourning songs as Angelina murmured the spells to guide Lucía to the Upperworld.

Pepe held the carved wooden box that contained Lucía's ashes in one hand, and her daughter's small hand in his other. He looked down at Isadora, who was focusing on the path ahead of them, her eyes dry, her face sombre. He felt his heart splinter at the thought that she would never know her mother, never be held by her, never dance with her . . .

When they reached the clearing in the woods, everyone grew hushed. In the row of crosses where generations of Albaycíns had come to rest, a small plot had been prepared next to Lucía's brothers. As Angelina intoned a prayer, Pepe and María gently settled the box into the ground and used their hands to cover it with the rich brown earth, María's tears mixing with it.

Pepe stood and crossed himself as he looked down at Lucía's grave. *My dearest sister*, he thought, *you saved my life in more ways than you knew.* As he walked back to Isadora and lifted her into his arms for the long walk back to the caves, he offered a silent prayer to the heavens. *I swear to you, Lucía, I will care for your daughter until the day I die.*

# Tiggy
## Sacromonte, Granada, Spain

February 2008

*White stag*
*(Cervus elaphus)*
*A red deer stag with the leucistic genetic pattern,*
*causing a reduction of pigment in hair and skin.*
*The rarest of creatures, they are considered*
*messengers from the Otherworld in British folklore.*

# *35*

Pepe yawned and blew his nose. 'I think I speak enough now,' he finished with a nod. 'Angelina will take over, okay?'

We watched as Pepe stood up and left the terrace.

'Poor Lucía,' I said, dragging myself quite literally out of the 'Otherworld' I'd been in for the past hour. 'She was so young.'

'Yes, she was, but also selfish. She live just to dance. Like many truly great artists, they do not make best wives or mothers,' said Angelina.

'I think I can guess the secret Pepe wanted to keep from his mother,' I said quietly.

'Yes, I see it instant I meet him. Nowadays, is fine to be who you are – to like men, women, or sometimes both – but back then it was not. Especially in the *gitano* community. Poor Pepe, he was born in the wrong century.'

'So, he stayed on with you, María, Ramón and my mother in Sacromonte, yes?'

'He did. He make his living as a guitar player. Somehow we all manage. It was poor life, but not unhappy one. And you already hear that Pepe brought with him some money from America. Also, thanks to Pepe, Isadora receive inheritance from her mother when she was eighteen years old. It is what helped the family to prosper.'

'What do you mean?'

'I mean she use the money to help her husband grow a business. Your father, Erizo.'

'Who was he and what was he like?' I asked her eagerly.

'You already hear his name. He is Andrés, the boy she met as a child, his parents own the ice-cream café in the plaza. Of course, they did not want their son marrying a *gitana*, but Andrés, he did not care and when they marry, he move up here. Ramón, María, Pepe and I made Ramón's old cave our home and make bigger so that Isadora can grow a family with Andrés in her own. Isadora used her money to help Andrés and Ramón set up in business. After Pepe tell him of the portable drink carts he see on the streets of New York, Andrés decide to buy orange grove. Ramón grow and press the oranges, Andrés sell the juice in the city. Your father and Pepe design a refrigeration contraption that harness to side of his moped that held the fresh juice. With this, he make not a fortune, but enough, selling the juice in the plaza. There were enough wealthy *payos* left, and more tourists coming to make it possible. After a while, he make two more machine and in summer he employ others to sell both the orange juice and the Coca-Cola drink that had become so popular. Andrés was, how you say, the entrepreneur.'

'So, when did my parents marry?'

'When your mother was eighteen.'

'But that means . . .' – I did the calculations in my head – 'that they didn't have me for almost twenty years! Why did they leave it so long?'

'"They" did not, *querida*. More than anything they dreamt

of a family, and there was no couple who deserved one more. Such love between them . . .' Angelina sighed. 'I try to help of course, but it seem your poor mother could not become pregnant and they give up long before you arrive. Then, as is sometimes the way, once they stop trying and relax, you decide to come.'

'But if they were happily married, why on earth did I end up being given to Pa Salt?'

'*Ay*, Erizo, remember that even though the Civil War was finished long before, Franco had taken Spain to a very bad place. The years that followed were, for many, nearly as bad as time before. The whole country had money troubles, and again our community was hit hardest. But it would not have mattered if . . .'

'What, Angelina?'

I saw tears appear in the old woman's eyes. She tried to gather herself together and I prepared myself to finally hear what had happened.

'I have seen the bad times in my life, but the tragedy of your mother and father was the worst, I think. Yes' – she nodded – 'the worst.'

'I understand, but you must tell me what happened, Angelina.'

'Well, first I tell you that I have never seen such joy in a human as the day my beloved Isadora come to tell me she is with child. And then your father arrive on his old moped, his arms filled with flowers for her. I never see a man so happy. But I tell your mother she is old and she must rest. Andrés too treat her like precious china doll – he work overtime so he could put away extra money for when you arrive. Every week that went by whilst you are still in her belly is a miracle to them both – after losing so many babies, you can imagine.'

Angelina nodded sadly. 'And then, one evening, when the weather was very bad and the roads washed with too many rain, your father, he did not come home. Pepe went down to police that night and is tell that, yes, a man had been found dead in a ditch, his moped on top of him. It was Andrés . . . the contraption he attach for selling the orange juice was heavy and the police said it made the moped unstable in the bad weather. I . . .'

I watched Angelina pull out a large pink handkerchief and blow her nose. I clenched my hands together, trying not to cry.

Angelina shook her head and shuddered. 'All those years they try for you, but he never live to see you born. Your mother take Andrés' death very hard; she could not eat or drink, although I tell her she must for baby's sake. You arrive a month early – and even though you must believe I try everything to save your mother, there was nothing I could do. I could not stop the bleeding, Erizo, and when the *ambulancia* men that Pepe call arrive, they could not either. She die the day after you were born.'

'I see.' There wasn't anything more to say. We both sat in silence for a while, me thinking again how cruel life could be.

'Why them?' I whispered, more to myself than Angelina. 'After all those years of trying, surely they deserved to have some time with their baby? I mean, *me*?'

'Yes. It is terrible story, and you understand how it break my heart to tell it. Yet, maybe their lives are both short, and you are not allowed privilege of meeting and being cared for by them, but I meet so many people who live a long time, and never find the love your parents did. Be comforted by this, *querida*, that you could not have been more wanted. Many times I feel your mother around me. I feel her happiness – she always so happy, that was her gift. I . . . adored her, yes, I did.' Angelina blew her nose hard on the handkerchief then shook her head. 'Pepe, I think her death, it break his heart forever. That is why he left us just now – he cannot even bear to talk about it.'

'So.' I pulled myself together, knowing my time here was running out and I needed to know everything before I left. 'How did I end up with Pa Salt?'

'He came to visit me for a reading just after your mother die. You were there, just a few days old. He hear of your story, and offer to adopt you. You must understand, Erizo, me and Pepe, we were old and poor. We cannot give you life you deserve.'

'You trusted him?'

'Oh yes, I trusted him,' Angelina reassured me. 'I consult with Upperworld and they tell me yes, this is right. Your father is – was – a very special man. He would give you life we could not. But I make him promise me that he send you back when you were older. And look!' she smiled weakly. 'He kept his promise to me.'

'What about María? Was she still alive when I was born?'

'Ramón died the year before María. They both lived long enough to see Isadora marry your father, but sadly not long enough to see you born, Erizo.'

'Had my mother named me before she died?'

'Not properly, no, but . . . when you were born we all say you look like the hedgehog, with your hair that stuck up. She – and we – call you "Erizo" while you were still with us.'

'And then I became "Tiggy", nicknamed after a fictional hedgehog.' I pondered the coincidence, if that's what it was. 'You know my proper name is "Taygete"?'

'Yes, your father tells us he will name you after one of Seven Sisters. I . . . did he find more of you?'

'One more, yes. My sister Electra arrived a year after me.'

'And the Seventh Sister?'

'No, he said he didn't find her. There are just six of us.'

'I am surprised,' she said.

'Why?'

'I . . .' Angelina opened her mouth to say something, but then shut it again. She shrugged. 'Sometimes the messages, they are confused. Now, Erizo, would you like to see a picture of your mamá and papá?'

'Yes, please.'

I watched her rummage in the capacious pocket of her kaftan. She drew out a colour print.

As she handed it to me, I felt the hairs on the back of my neck prickle. I stared in wonder at the image.

'This is them on their wedding day?' I murmured.

'*Sí*. It was the year 1963.'

The couple in the photograph were gazing at each other, the love and adoration shining out from their innocent young faces. The colours had faded to pale imitations over the years, but I saw that the man had tightly curled brown hair and warm light-brown eyes, and the woman . . .

'You can see you look like her,' Angelina ventured.

And yes, I *could* see. Her hair was darker than mine, but the shape of her eyes and the planes of her face were very familiar.

'*Mi madre*,' I whispered. '*Te amo*.'

It was past two o'clock already, and I had to be at the airport for four thirty. I had so much to think about but it wasn't for now. Leaving Angelina dozing in the sun, I went to collect my rucksack from the hotel, then I walked back to the blue door and pulled aside the curtain to bid farewell to her and the most recent arrival to our family. Bear was suckling at Ally's breast.

'I've come to say goodbye, darling Ally. Take care of yourself and the little one, won't you? And thank you so much for coming here to find me.' I kissed them both.

'No, thank *you* and your wonderful relatives for being here with *me*. What a present I'm taking home,' Ally smiled. 'I'll see you at Atlantis very soon, I hope?'

'I'm sure you will.'

'Are you okay?' she asked me. 'You're very pale.'

'Angelina just told me about my mother and father. And how they died.'

'Oh Tiggy.' Ally stretched out her hand to me. 'I'm so sorry.'

'Well, I suppose it helps that I never knew them. To be honest, I just feel a bit numb.'

'I'm sure. Well, one day, if you want to, I'll tell you all about my birth family and you can tell me about yours. But for now, darling Tiggy, go back to Atlantis and get strong.'

'I will. Bye, Ally. Bye, Bear.'

In the courtyard garden, I woke Angelina and told her I was leaving.

'Come back soon, Erizo, won't you? And bring that nice Mister Charlie with you,' she said as she winked at me and I blushed.

Pepe appeared from inside the cave, holding a stack of CDs.

'Here, Erizo,' he said, handing them to me, 'although you not meet your *abuelo* Meñique, you can listen to the music he made. You listen, and you feel the *duende* here.' He put a hand over his heart and smiled at me, the corners of his brown eyes crinkling. '*Vaya con Dios* – be safe, *querida*.'

Both Angelina and Pepe hugged me and kissed me on my cheeks, which were running with tears.

Marcella was waiting for me by her Punto to drive to the airport. 'Ready, Tiggy?'

I gave one last wave and a smile to my family. 'Ready,' I nodded.

Later that evening, I flew home to Atlantis in the private plane Ma had arranged, my head still full of my past, but also my present. Things being how they were, I decided I wouldn't even contemplate the future. When Ma met me at the dock and Christian handed me off the speedboat into her warm, comforting embrace, I remembered what Angelina had said about those who loved us wanting to be given a chance to care for us. I was here for a few weeks to rest and that was that.

So, I surrendered to the comforting cocoon that constituted convalescence at Atlantis. My bed sat in the middle of the room to take advantage of the wonderful view of Lake Geneva. I lay like a princess in my airy attic retreat, and found that – both mentally and physically – I was far more tired than I'd imagined. When I reflected on the drama of the past few weeks, it probably wasn't that surprising, so I listened to my body and gave in to its demands. Often, to the sound of Meñique's soothing voice and guitar music on my old portable CD player, I'd find myself dropping off after lunch, coming to an hour or so later. Claudia, our wonderful housekeeper, insisted on bringing me up breakfast, lunch and dinner, plus a night-time mug of hot oat milk and homemade cookies.

But by the end of the first week I was becoming restless. 'Please, Claudia, won't you let me come downstairs for supper tonight?' I begged as she delivered yet another tray of food. 'You must be worn out climbing the stairs ten times a day! And I really am feeling stronger . . .'

'*Nein, liebling.* You must stay in bed and rest.'

It was obvious that Charlie had been in contact with Ma, and both my carers irritatingly insisted on following his advice to the hilt and beyond – I'd been forbidden to leave my bedroom and I'd even had to physically prevent Ma escorting me into my bathroom when I'd first arrived. But as the next week passed and it was obvious I was fighting a losing battle, I capitulated and began to think how I could use the time I had wisely. Angelina always said that everything happened for a reason, and as I pulled all my notes I'd taken in Sacromonte from my rucksack and began to commit them to memory, I decided she'd been right. The process made me ponder how exactly I was meant to use my newfound skills. Was I meant to change my career path completely and set up shop as a full-time herbalist-cum-spiritualist like my ancestors? These days, to practise that kind of thing professionally – whether it was prescribing powerful herbal remedies or laying hands on injured bodies, human or animal – involved having qualifications that showed you knew what you were talking about. Ten days with an ancient Spanish gypsy would not cut the mustard in today's bureaucratic world. The *brujas* of the past had treated customers who trusted completely in their gifts; they'd had no need for certificates to confirm the practitioner's talents.

I spent many hours staring out of the window at the mountains on the other side of the lake and wondering how I could incorporate what I'd learnt into my work. And the more I thought about it, the more I realised that Chilly might have had a point when he'd declared that I'd chosen the wrong path. Animal conservation was great, but I knew for certain now that I wanted to use my skills on the animals themselves.

'Your power *is* in your hands, Tiggy,' I murmured, staring at them earnestly.

I then thought about Fiona, the way her man-made medicine had seen Thistle recover within a couple of days. And Charlie and Angelina, using both modern and holistic methods to care for me and Ally, and I wondered if there was a way I could combine the two . . .

'Oh, I don't know,' I sighed, frustrated that everything had been so straightforward when I was working for Margaret. Animals, fresh Highland air, and busy from dawn to dusk. I went online to have a look at courses that could possibly qualify me in the 'normal' world to practise on animals. And to my surprise, found a number of holistic ones, including one in Reiki. *And*, as Fiona had mentioned, there was a list of alternative veterinary practitioners working in such a way.

'Would I really want to go back to uni to retrain as a vet for all those years?' I asked myself as I chewed the end of my biro. 'No!' I shook my head in frustration. 'I'd be an old lady by the time I came out, and besides, I don't want to cut them up and study the inner workings of their lymphatic system. There has to be another way . . .'

As I grew physically stronger, I found myself wide awake at night. So, after Ma had been in to take my blood pressure and say goodnight, and I'd heard her walk softly down the corridor to her suite of rooms, I gave her half an hour to fall asleep before I rose from the bed and began to prowl around the house. The first time I'd felt the urge to do this, I thought that it was simply because I had cabin fever, but as I got up night after night to resume my nocturnal ramblings, it struck me that I was searching for something – or more accurately, someone . . .

I felt Pa's presence in this house so strongly it was as if he had just stood up from his desk to go to the kitchen for a glass of water, or to climb the stairs to his bed.

I found myself rifling through his desk drawers for any evidence of him being here recently, or any clues I might find to explain the enigma of my beloved father.

'Who were you?' I asked as I picked up a small icon painted with an image of the Madonna and wondered if Pa had been religious. He'd certainly taken us all to church when we were small, but had allowed us to choose whether we wanted to attend as we grew up.

I then noticed a forlorn bunch of herbs held together by a fraying length of string. I took it carefully from the shelf, seeing in my mind's eye the gypsy who had accosted me in the plaza in Granada and had somehow known my nickname.

'Did you get this when you were there?' I whispered to the air, closing my eyes and asking my spirit guide for an answer. The problem was, I didn't know if Pa *was* one now, or not.

'If you are up there, please speak to me,' I whispered. But no answer came.

'Ma, I'm begging you, I can't stay in this bed any longer! Please – it's a beautiful day.' I pointed at the weak March sun melting the frost on the window pane. 'After so many days inside, I'm sure Charlie would approve of me getting some fresh air.'

'I don't know,' Ma sighed. 'Besides the risk of you catching a chill, there's all those stairs to get back up to bed.'

'If you really insist, I'll let Christian carry me back upstairs,' I suggested.

'I'm afraid Christian isn't here today but . . .' I could see Ma was mulling something over. 'I will talk with Claudia and Charlie, *chérie*. Oh, I almost forgot, you have a letter.'

'Thanks.'

Ma left the room and I opened the slim envelope, noting it had come from overseas.

*26th February 2008*
*Majete Wildlife Reserve*
*Chikhwawa, Malawi*

*Dear Ms D'Aplièse,*

*Thank you for your application for the position of Conservation Officer at the Majete Wildlife Reserve. We subsequently emailed you an invitation to attend for interview in London at 13.00 on Friday, 7th March, but we have received no response. Please inform us by the latest Wednesday, 5th March, if you*

*are still interested in the position and let us know*
*whether you will be attending the interview, the*
*details of which can be found in the attached docu-*
*ment.*
> *Sincerely yours,*
> *Kitwell Ngwira*
> *Majete Park Manager*

I gulped and climbed out of bed to pull my ancient uni laptop out of my drawer. I'd completely forgotten about the email I'd fired off in frustration, and I'd had no reason or inclination to check my emails since I'd arrived back home.

Not only did I find two emails asking me to attend the interview in a week's time, but also emails from Maia, Star and CeCe, and three from Charlie.

Putting off opening Charlie's messages, I opened those from my sisters first. CeCe's email was the most surprising of all of them.

**Hi Tiggy**

**Ally told me you got hurt and were home at Atlantis. I hope you get well soon. I know you always Hated being ill. Maybe you hard I moved to Australia. I love it hear and am painting again. Im living with my Granpha and my friend Chrissy. Theirs lots of animals hear if you want to come and visit.**

> **Lots of Love**
> **CeCe xx**

'Wow, CeCe,' I murmured to myself, 'you did it, you found your home.'

I took a deep breath and turned to Charlie's emails. Each one was a couple of short gentle lines asking me how I was, the last requesting my permission to book me in for various scans and tests at Inverness hospital in mid March, after my sojourn at Atlantis.

In other words, Charlie presumed I would be returning to Scotland.

'It really is best you don't go back, Tiggy,' I told myself. 'I'm sure Cal wouldn't mind adopting Alice, and packing up your bits and pieces to send them on . . .'

So, not wanting to appear rude and ungrateful for all he had done for me, I typed him a quick reply before I changed my mind.

**Dear Charlie,**

**Thanks for your emails. I'm doing well and resting lots. Thanks for suggesting you book me in for the tests, but it's probably easier if I have them here in Geneva. As you know, the medical care here is excellent.**

**Hope all is well with you,**

**Tiggy**

'God,' I murmured as I pressed 'send', hating myself for sounding so cold and formal, but anything else was a road to nowhere and – for Zara's sake if no one else's – I would not be a home wrecker.

'Right, Tiggy,' Ma said as she appeared back in my room. 'I have just spoken to Charlie and he thinks it a good idea for you to take a walk outside.'

'Oh.' I winced again at the email I'd just sent. 'Good.'

'But he is not yet happy to let you climb all those stairs. So, Claudia and I have decided you must use the lift.'

'The lift? I didn't know there was one!'

'Your father had it put in not long before he . . . left us, as he was struggling to mount the stairs himself,' Ma explained. 'So, *chérie*, let us wrap you up in some warm clothes and I shall take you downstairs.'

Once I was bundled up to Ma's satisfaction, I followed her along the corridor, fascinated to see where this lift was. I headed for the stairs that led down to the next floor where Pa's bedroom was, but Ma stopped me.

'The lift is here, *chérie*.'

She took out a silver key from her skirt pocket and moved towards the wall along the corridor. She inserted it into a lock on a wall panel, turned it, then tugged at the small latch underneath the lock. The panel slid back to reveal a teakwood door, then she pressed a shiny brass button to the side of it, which set off a whirring noise.

'I can't believe I never noticed this was here in the summer,' I said as we waited for the lift to arrive. 'And why did Pa have it come up to the attic floor when his bedroom is on the floor beneath?'

'He wanted to be able to access every floor in the house. Before last spring, it was an old service hatch,' Ma replied as the lift announced its presence with a soft clunk and she pulled the door open.

Ma and I were both slim, but it was still a squeeze inside. Like the outer door, the interior was fashioned from polished wood. It reminded me of the type of lift one saw in grand old hotels.

Ma closed the door and reached for one of the brass

buttons. As the lift started to descend, I noticed that there were four buttons inside, yet to my knowledge, there were only three floors in the house.

'Where does that one go, Ma?' I indicated the last button.

'Down to the cellar. It's where your father stored his wine.'

'I didn't even know we had a cellar here. I'm amazed me and my sisters didn't find it when we were exploring. How do you get to it?'

'By the lift of course,' Ma said as it came smoothly to a halt. We emerged out of another similar wall panel, tucked away along the back corridor that led to the kitchen.

'Now, Tiggy, I will take my coat and boots from the cloakroom and we shall go outside.'

As Ma left me, I walked through to the entrance hall, puzzling over what it was she'd said in the lift that had rung the warning bell of a lie. Opening the wide front door, I breathed in the glorious smell of pure, fresh air to try and boost my brain.

It must have worked, because I suddenly thought that, surely, if the lift was the only way to access the cellar, it must have been there long before last spring, when Ma had said Pa had put it in, or how else would Pa have got down to his wine cellar before that . . . ?

Ma joined me and we stepped out into the bracing but gloriously crisp afternoon. I decided not to mention the lift conundrum, for now at least.

'It's odd,' I said as we walked along the path that led to the lake, 'even though the terrain and climate is similar to Kinnaird, it smells so different here.'

'Do you think you will return to Scotland once you are fully better?' Ma asked.

'I don't think so. The job isn't what I thought it would be.'

'I thought you were very happy there, *chérie*. Is it the shooting that has scared you?'

'No, that was just bad luck. I'm sure the poacher was aiming at Pegasus, not me. As a matter of fact, Ma, that letter you gave me was from a wildlife reserve in Malawi, inviting me to London next week to interview for the position of Conservation Officer.'

'Malawi? London next week?' Ma eyed me nervously. 'You are not thinking of going, I hope?'

'I would like to attend the interview, yes. Africa's a long-time dream for me, Ma, you know it is.'

'Tiggy, you are recovering from a serious heart condition. To go off to Africa is just . . . well, that is sheer madness! What would Charlie say?'

'Charlie's not my keeper, Ma.'

'He is your doctor, Tiggy, and you must listen to him.'

'Actually, I've just written to him to say that I'm going to transfer my care to Geneva. It's far easier than flying to Scotland.'

'Yet you will consider flying to London, then possibly Malawi?!' Ma narrowed her eyes. 'Tiggy, what is going on?'

'Nothing, Ma. Anyway, we'll discuss it later. How's Maia?'

Ma took the hint. 'She is very well. It is so wonderful that she has found happiness. I am hoping that there might be wedding bells soon.'

'She's going to marry Floriano?'

'She doesn't say for definite, but it is my feeling she is eager to make babies of her own while she is still young enough to do so.'

'Wow, Ma, the next generation . . .'

'Speaking of which, I heard this morning that Ally is intending to visit in a couple of weeks with little Bear. I cannot wait. She hopes that you will still be in residence,' she added pointedly.

'Well, even if I go to London for the interview, I'll try to be back to see them both. And if I'm not, at least you won't miss me with a baby to coo over. Gosh, it seems like only a day ago that I was a little girl myself, sick in bed here with Electra screaming the house down!' I smiled.

'Well, let us hope you are now on the road to recovery. It is growing cold, Tiggy. We should go inside.'

'Up to bed with you now,' Ma said as we walked into the house. 'I shall bring you some tea.'

'Actually, as I have the lift, I'd like to sit in the kitchen with you and Claudia for a while. I get lonely upstairs,' I added plaintively.

'*D'accord*,' Ma agreed. 'Give me your coat and I will hang it with mine.'

I did so, then wandered along the corridor to the airy kitchen – my favourite room as a child. When I'd been ill, it had been a great treat to be allowed downstairs and have Claudia mind me, and help her with the cooking whilst Ma ran errands.

'You know, Claudia, if a perfumer could bottle the smell of your kitchen, then I would buy it,' I told her as I went to give her a peck on the cheek. She turned from a pan of delicious-smelling soup she was stirring, her wrinkled skin creasing in pleasure at my words.

'Then it would need to be a range of many different scents, because it smells different many times a day.' Claudia filled up the kettle and switched it on.

'Haven't you noticed, Claudia? I'm downstairs. I've just been for a walk with Ma.'

'I have, and I am glad of it. I agree that you need fresh air. Marina, like most Parisians, seems to be terrified of it.'

I was used to Claudia's derogatory comments about the French – being German herself and of a certain age, the enmity was de rigueur.

'Do you find it . . . difficult working here without Pa?' I asked her.

'Of course I do, Tiggy, we all do. The house has lost its soul . . . I . . .'

It was the first time I'd ever seen Claudia on the verge of tears. Even though I'd forged a closer relationship with her than any of my sisters, I had never seen her display such emotion before.

'I just wish things were different,' she continued as she indicated I should sit down at the table before placing two scones and a little pot of jam in front of me.

'You mean, you wish Pa Salt was still alive?'

'Yes, of course that is what I mean.' As Ma appeared in the kitchen, I watched Claudia's normal brusque manner wrap around her like a cloak. 'Tea?'

Fifteen minutes later, Ma insisted I returned upstairs for a rest. As I watched Ma extract the key for the lift from the key box next to the kitchen door, I felt like a prisoner being escorted back to her cell. I stood behind her in the hallway as she unlocked the panel and slid it back. I carefully noted the technique she used to pull it open.

'Why did Pa decide to hide the lift, Ma?' I asked her as we rose upwards.

'Don't ask me, *chérie*. Maybe he didn't want you girls

sailing up and down in it all the time,' she replied. 'Or maybe it was pride. Perhaps he didn't want you girls to know how sick he was.'

'So the heart attack was not unexpected?'

'I . . . no, it wasn't, and it just shows how serious any form of heart condition can be,' she added pointedly as we arrived on the attic floor. 'Rest now, Tiggy, then I might consider you coming back downstairs again for supper.'

She left me at my bedroom door and I went to sit on the window seat to collect my thoughts. Even though I'd seen many spectacular sunsets at Atlantis, they never ceased to thrill me, as they set the mountains on fire with red-gold light. What was different now was the silence inside; in the past, the sound of music would be blaring out from one of my sisters' rooms, there would be laughing or squabbling – the humming of the speedboat edging towards the dock, or the lawnmower gliding across the lawn.

Now, even though both Ma and Claudia were in the house, it felt as if Atlantis had been abandoned – as though all the energy my sisters and Pa had provided had disappeared, leaving only the ghost of past memories behind. It was depressing and terribly sad, and I wondered how Ma and Claudia dealt with the emptiness on a daily basis. What purpose did they both serve now anyway? Claudia with only Ma to cook for, keeping a house to which us sisters seldom came, and Ma with her large empty nest. Atlantis had been their life; what stood in front of them now must feel like a gaping void.

'I don't like being here without my sisters and Pa . . .' I muttered, climbing off the window seat and realising how much better I must now be. Two and a half weeks here had shown me that I'd outgrown my childhood home.

'I want to get back to my life,' I murmured to myself. 'Or more accurately, I need to *find* a life.'

Opening my laptop, I took out the letter from the wildlife reserve in Malawi. I reread it, and then, without thinking about it further, replied by email that I would indeed be attending the interview in London.

Feeling relieved I'd done something – anything – to move my life forwards, I then turned my attention back to Atlantis. Later tonight, I had something planned . . .

Irritatingly, it was past midnight before I heard Ma's door close. I waited a good twenty minutes, keeping myself awake by reciting some of the ingredients to Angelina's remedies and also by reminding myself of the words of the forbidden curse. I had no idea why my brain was determined that I should not forget them, but it prompted me every day to repeat them.

Finally, putting on my old pair of Uggs and a thick woollen jumper, I took the torch that Ma always left on the bedside table. Leaving my bedroom, I tiptoed along the corridor, then switched on the torch to make my way down the stairs to the ground floor. I went to the key box in the kitchen, extracted the one Ma had used to unlock the lift, then located the panel in the corridor. Having managed to unlock and open it, I shone the torch on the lift door. It was a gamble that Ma wouldn't hear the clanking and whirring from her suite on the top floor, but at least she was at the furthest end of the corridor.

I pressed the call button and the lift arrived. I stepped inside and shone my torch on the brass buttons. Pressing the bottom one, I felt the lift give a slight lurch as it headed downwards, coming to a halt only a few seconds later. I pulled open the door to see nothing but complete blackness. Switching my torch back on, I took a step forward, but as my foot touched the concrete below me, the space was suddenly flooded with light.

I looked around and saw that Ma had been telling the truth about what it contained. The room was more modern basement than damp cellar; low-ceilinged but spacious – perhaps the size of what must be the kitchen above it. The walls were lined with wine racks heaving with bottles and I thought how odd it was that Pa, who only drank wine on high days and holidays, should keep such a vast collection. I wandered round the room, brushing the dust off some of the older bottles and feeling relieved and disappointed at the same time. Whatever it was I'd expected to find, it didn't seem to be here.

Then my eyes moved to a moth fluttering near one of the spotlights set into the ceiling. As my gaze travelled back down from the ceiling, I noticed a break in one of the walls below it, which disappeared behind a wine rack. I walked towards the rack.

'There's no way you can move this, Tiggy,' I murmured, but I did remove the two middle rows of bottles, then shone my torch through to the wall beyond, illuminating a panel exactly like the one that so successfully hid the lift. I then extracted the row of bottles beneath and saw a small round keyhole set into the wall.

My heart began to beat faster as I took the lift key and reached through the rack to see if it would fit. It did, and I heard it turn with a metallic click. Clasping the latch, I tried to tug it forward and sideways as I'd done with the panel upstairs and it gave immediately. Sadly, the wine rack was wedged too close to allow any further movement.

'Damn it!' I exclaimed, and my words echoed around the basement. By now, fatigue was setting in and it took my last shred of energy to lock the panel back into place and put the wine bottles back where I'd found them.

'Not that I should be worrying about doing what I want in a house I part-own,' I comforted myself as I panted my way back to the lift. As I reached it, I saw that the door was surrounded by a steel frame and that there was another pair of doors that I hadn't noticed before, because they were currently concealed within the steel surround. There was a button that I'd bet closed them set into the wall just beyond.

'Wow, this is like a bank vault or something,' I muttered, tempted to press the button, but then realising that if the steel doors did close, I might be trapped down here with no way of contacting the outside world.

Ten minutes later, after climbing wearily into bed, I lay there plotting how on earth I could investigate further.

# *36*

Ma came into my room the next morning carrying the breakfast tray.

'*Bon matin, chérie*,' she said as I sat upright and she placed the tray across my knees. 'How did you sleep?'

Perhaps it was only my imagination, but I was sure I saw a hint of suspicion in her vivid green eyes.

'I'm feeling very well, thank you. Is it Claudia's day off today?'

'In fact, she has taken three days off to visit a relative of hers. So it will be just you and me. As I confessed to CeCe when I was staying with her in London, my cooking is very poor, but Claudia has left your special food in the freezer so all I have to do is defrost it.'

'No problem, Ma, and if the worst comes to the worst, I can make us both a nut roast,' I smiled.

'I hope it won't come to that,' said Ma, wrinkling her nose. Like many Parisians, she was a food snob and considered any plate of food without meat to be a travesty. 'Once you have finished your breakfast, I shall take your blood pressure. You look a little pale today, *chérie*.' She studied me and I did my best not to blush under her gaze. 'Did you not sleep?'

'I slept fine, Ma, really. Actually, I was wondering if you could contact Dr Gerber and ask him to recommend a cardiologist here in Geneva.'

'Ah Tiggy, Dr Gerber died a few months ago, but I will contact the practice, yes. Are you sure you do not wish to stay under Charlie's care?'

'Yes, I am. I'd like to see whoever the surgery recommends here as soon as possible. I'm going to attend that interview in London and I'd obviously need a clean bill of health if I was offered the job.'

'You know how I feel about that, Tiggy, but you are a grown woman, not a child. So, yes, I will make enquiries for you. Now, please eat your breakfast and I will be back up later.'

As I ate, I thought about the basement and its impenetrable steel doors and decided I just needed to ask Ma straight out when she returned. Then I heard the landline ring, and a couple of minutes later, Ma appeared again and held out the receiver to me.

'It's for you. The caller says she's a friend of yours.'

'Thanks.' I took it and said, 'Hello?'

'Hi, Tiggy, it's Zara. How are you?'

'Hi, Zara, how nice to hear from you,' I smiled. 'I'm much better, thanks. Are you okay?'

'I'm good. I'm at Geneva airport.'

'*What?!*'

'Can you tell me how to get to your house on the lake?'

'I . . . Zara, how did you get the number?'

'I looked it up on Dad's mobile.'

'Right. Do your mum and dad know where you are?'

'Er . . . I'll explain everything when I see you.'

'Hold on a moment . . . She's in Geneva,' I mouthed to Ma. 'Where's Christian?'

'He's just dropped Claudia at the airport, so he should still be close by,' she said.

Having told Zara to wait by the information desk in Arrivals, Christian was duly called and told to collect her from there.

'What is she doing here, Tiggy? Do her parents know?' asked Ma.

'I doubt it. She's a past mistress at running away.'

'Well, we must call Charlie immediately.'

'Could you do it for me, Ma?'

'I can but . . . surely you will want to speak to Charlie yourself?'

'Tell him I'll get Zara to call him when she's arrived.'

'*D'accord*, but . . . Charlie has been so kind to you, Tiggy. Why do you not wish to speak to him?'

'I just . . . don't.'

'I see.' Ma gave up. 'Well, if she is staying, then I shall put her in Ally's room down the corridor from you, *chérie*.'

'Thank you.'

'Is this child troubled, Tiggy?'

'Zara's absolutely delightful, but she has a difficult family situation, yes.'

'Well, I hope her arrival will not upset your recovery. She is her parents' responsibility, not yours. So, I will call her father.' With that, Ma turned on her elegant heel and left the room.

'Tiggy . . . !' Zara appeared in my bedroom and walked over to me to give me a hug. 'How are you feeling?' she asked me, sitting down on my bed.

'I'm completely fine, Zara, but Ma insists on me staying up here most of the time.'

'It's only for your own good, Tiggy. We all need you well.'

'I am well,' I said, hearing the hint of petulance in my voice, 'but more to the point, what on earth are you doing here? Ma's called your dad to say you're with us and he said you were to phone him the moment you arrived.'

'I'm amazed he noticed I'd gone, to be honest. I've been at home for study leave and I've hardly seen him.'

'What about your mum?'

'That's what's really weird; she's up at Kinnaird, Tiggy. Like, of her own accord. I don't know what's going on,' Zara sighed, 'but something is. You know Mum's always hated the place, and now suddenly she's telling Dad she's going to take the estate in hand because he's too busy to do it.'

'Then that's good, isn't it? It means you can spend more time there too.'

'Yeah, it would, if I'd been invited,' Zara snarled. 'Mum said I couldn't go up there with her, that I had to stay at home and catch up on all the work I missed when I wasn't at school.'

'I can understand that, Zara. You would be distracted up at Kinnaird.'

'I s'pose so.' Zara looked out of the window at Lake Geneva. 'Wow, Tiggy, this place is like a fairy-tale castle. It's so beautiful, and your ma is really sweet. Christian said he'd teach me to drive the speedboat if I wanted. He's really fit, isn't he, Tiggy, even if he's old.'

'I suppose he is, yes.' I smiled at her comment. 'He's been here all my life as far as I can remember, so I haven't really noticed.'

'Mind you, your sister Electra called him as we were driving here. He's not gonna look at me while he's got a world-famous supermodel on speed dial, is he?' said Zara with a nonchalant shrug.

'Electra called Christian?' I was amazed – I hadn't heard from my sister in months.

'Yeah, what's she like?'

'Electra's a force of nature,' I said and left it at that. We all made it a rule never to discuss our famous sibling with 'outsiders'. 'Now, why don't I show you the room you're staying in and you can freshen up from your journey?'

'Okay.'

I led Zara down the sisters' corridor to Ally's door.

'It must have been really cool to be one of six girls up here,' commented Zara as we entered the room. 'Like being at a fun boarding school all the time. I bet you always had someone to play with,' she said wistfully. 'You couldn't ever have been lonely.'

'I was ill quite a bit as a child, so I spent a lot of time by myself, but you're right, it was nice to have my sisters around. Now, you need to phone your dad.'

'Okay,' Zara said, and I could see her eyes were filled with trepidation.

We walked downstairs together and I led Zara into the kitchen.

'*Chérie*, what are you doing? You know you are not meant
to—'

'Really, Ma,' I said, 'I'm feeling perfectly well, I promise.
And I'm eating lunch down here with you both after Zara's
phoned her dad.' I picked up the handset and gave it to her.

'Thanks,' Zara said and wandered out of the kitchen as she
tapped in the number.

'I hope I can trust her to call him,' I said to Ma, who was
crouched beside the oven, peering anxiously at whatever was
inside.

'How long does a nut roast take to heat up, Tiggy?'

'Don't worry, I'll see to it, Ma.'

'*Merci*,' Ma said in relief as Zara arrived back in the
kitchen.

'I got Dad's voicemail, so I left him a message saying I was
here with you and I was fine.'

'Are you happy for the nut roast too, Zara?' Ma asked as
she set the table.

'Very, thank you. Since I met Tiggy, I've tried not to eat any
meat, though I just can't help craving a bacon sandwich every
now and then.'

'Don't worry, I think we all do that.' I smiled at her. 'I've
no idea why in my case, because I really didn't like pork when
I did eat meat. Right, Ma, can I peel some vegetables to go
with it?'

Eventually, we sat down for lunch and Zara bombarded
Ma with questions about Atlantis and all my sisters. I watched
Ma begin to relax as she indulged in favourite memories of us
when we were younger.

'I wish I could have been in your nursery,' Zara sighed as

I went to collect the lemon tart Claudia had left for dessert and poured Ma's usual post-lunch espresso.

'Some pudding, Zara?' I asked her.

'No, thanks,' she replied. 'Just popping to the loo.'

'Tiggy,' Ma said when Zara had left the room, 'even though she is a sweet girl, this is not what you need at the moment. You are always collecting waifs and strays—'

'They find me, Ma. It works both ways. Besides, I like Zara. Now, I want a bit of fresh air before it gets dark,' I said as Zara reappeared. 'Want to come with me?'

'I'd love to.' Zara nodded and we left before Ma could lodge a complaint.

'It's so peaceful here,' Zara said as we walked across the lawns. The tips of the grass were already covered with tiny droplets of water that would soon harden to a sharp night frost.

'It wasn't like this when I was growing up, not with five sisters,' I cautioned. 'Someone was always shouting at someone. Now, this is Pa's special garden. It's a pity it's March and we only have snowdrops and winter pansies, but in the summer, all the roses around this arbour come into full bloom.' I sat down on the bench as Zara wandered around, ending up at the armillary sphere which lay in the centre of the garden. She beckoned me over to explain it and the inscriptions.

'So there's a missing sister? Wow, Tiggy, don't you want to find her?'

'I don't even know if she exists. If she did, I'm sure Pa would have done so.'

'Unless she didn't want to be found,' she said as she joined me on the bench. 'I'd have loved a brother or a sister,' she added wistfully.

As it was growing dark and cold, we soon went back inside to find Ma in the hall, holding the telephone out to Zara. 'Your father is on the line, *chérie*,' she said. Whilst Zara spoke to her dad, I pushed open the door to the drawing room, a place I'd always particularly associated with Christmas. Three comfortable sofas were arranged in a U-shape around the log fire, which was always set to be lit. I put a match to the logs and they caught immediately, the wood tinder-dry after weeks inside the house.

'What a beautiful view this room has,' Zara said as she came in and sat down in front of the growing fire with me.

'What did your dad say?'

'He says I've got to go home. He's booking me a flight for tomorrow and then picking me up from the airport at Inverness so I don't run away again.'

'Well, that's probably the best thing. But I think you should speak to him about what's been going on at home, with your mum away and him at the hospital all the time.'

'Please come with me,' Zara begged, her blue eyes imploring me. 'I'm so worried about Dad. He looks terrible, Tiggy – like he hasn't slept in months. And he refuses to go up to Kinnaird. He trusts you. He needs you—'

'Zara, I—'

'*Please*, Tiggy, come with me. I need you too, you're the only person I can really talk to.'

I stood up to poke the fire, so I could avoid Zara's pleading eyes. My contrary inner voice was telling me that it *would* be a good idea to return to Kinnaird; at least to pick up all of my things, say goodbye to Cal and Thistle and Beryl. And besides,

I did have to be in the UK next week anyway for that interview . . .

'Okay,' I surrendered, 'I'll come.'

As Zara squealed in delight and gave me a hug, I hated myself for the flutter of excitement that ran through me at the thought of seeing Charlie again.

# 37

'What a surprise,' Zara commented as we walked out of Arrivals at Inverness airport. She looked up at me from her mobile. 'Dad's sent me a text, he's not here after all – he's had to go up to Kinnaird, and we're to get a taxi.'

'Okay,' I said and duly followed Zara outside to the taxi rank.

As we drove the hour and a half up to Kinnaird, I saw that the first signs of spring were emerging. The burns we passed were heavy with melting snow from the mountains as the temperature rose. The loch appeared blue under the clear sunny sky, and the first daffodils were beginning to sprout along its edges in an unruly fashion. As the taxi climbed the steep drive to the Lodge, the first patches of green lawn were revealed by the melting snow.

Zara insisted on carrying my rucksack to the cottage, where Cal was already standing in the doorway waiting for me.

'Hello, stranger,' he said, enveloping me in his great big arms. He was interrupted moments later by a blur of grey fur launching itself towards us. Thistle stood up on his hind legs, effortlessly placing his front paws on my shoulders, then soaking my face with ecstatic licks.

'He's pleased tae see you back, and no mistake,' Cal chuckled. 'But I'm thinkin' that we should be tagging you an' Zara so we know where you are when you stray. How are yae, Tig?' he asked as Thistle, having satisfied himself that I was real, bounded off to greet Zara.

'Much better, thanks. Sorry for causing you so much bother, Cal.'

'Aye, you did, and I'll no' be denying it. The Laird was beside himself when you did your disappearin' act, but all's well that ends well. And that's not what I can say about the things going down here since you've been gone. Stuff has really been kickin' off, Tig.' He lowered his voice so that Zara, who was now playing with Thistle in the courtyard, couldn't hear. 'Has Charlie mentioned anything tae you?'

'He did in Spain, yes. Something about a legal challenge.'

'And that's just fer starters,' he whispered as Zara walked towards the cottage door.

'Right, let's go and see the wildcats before it gets dark,' I smiled at her. 'How are they, Cal?'

'Oh, they're in grand fettle, the lot o' them. Still as antisocial as ever, but I did my best.'

True to form, the cats showed their displeasure at my absence by refusing to appear. Zara, however, eventually found Posy sitting in her favourite box and I tried to entice her out.

'They really aren't very rewarding to care for, are they?' Zara said as we arrived at the back door of the Lodge. She opened it and we could clearly hear the sound of a woman sobbing inside.

'No, they're not. Is that your mum?' I said, already on the balls of my feet, ready to take flight.

'No, it isn't,' said Zara, stepping inside and beckoning at me urgently to come with her.

'Really, I should be getting back to the cottage—'

'*Please*, Tiggy, let's find out who it is.'

I followed reluctantly a good few paces behind Zara as she turned along the corridor into the kitchen.

'Oh Beryl, what is it?' I heard her ask as I loitered unseen outside the door.

'Nothing, my dear, nothing.'

'But you're obviously really upset about something. Tiggy's here too, aren't you?' Zara called out to me, so I stepped into the kitchen.

'I've just had a bad cold that's made my eyes water, that's all. Hello, Tiggy.'

'Hello, Beryl.' I could see her struggling to compose herself.

'Now, Zara' – she wiped her eyes – 'perhaps you can go and find me some eggs from the pantry?'

'Okay.' Zara took the hint and shot me a confused glance before leaving the kitchen.

'Beryl, what is it? What's happened?'

'Oh Tiggy, what a mess, what a mess . . . I should never have told him, and then he wouldn't have come back and I wouldn't have put the poor Laird in this situation. I rue the day I ever gave birth to him! He's a bad lot through and through. I've only come up here to hand in my notice. I'll be packing my things and leaving as soon as I can.' She handed me an envelope. 'Could you make sure the Laird gets this? He's probably expecting it anyway.'

'I honestly don't know what you're talking about, Beryl,' I

679

said as I followed her along the corridor to the boot room, where she put on the sturdy snow shoes and the thick parka, hat and gloves she used to walk home.

'Sadly, you'll know soon enough!'

'I . . . don't you think you should stay and speak to Charlie? Whatever it is, he'll be lost without you here.'

'After what's happened, he'll be only too glad to see the back of me, Tiggy, and that's a fact. I've ruined the Kinnaird family, and there's no two ways about it.' With a last agonised look at me, she left through the back door.

'Wow, she's really upset, isn't she, Tiggy?' Zara said, appearing beside me with the eggs as the door closed behind Beryl.

'Yes, she is. She's said she's leaving.'

'Well, she can't. Kinnaird without Beryl is like, well, Dad without his stethoscope.' Zara shrugged. 'This is her house really and it always has been. Well,' she looked down at the eggs, 'looks like I'll be making supper for me and Dad tonight, unless Mum turns up of course . . .'

As we walked back into the kitchen, we heard the sitting room door open and we peered out to see Charlie ushering a man in a tweed suit along the corridor.

'Thank you for coming at such short notice, James. At least I now know the options,' we heard Charlie say as they passed the door.

'Well now, it's not a good situation you're in, but we'll find a solution, I'm sure. Good day to you, m'Laird.'

We heard the front door close, then a huge sigh from Charlie before he walked back down the corridor towards us. Zara jumped out from behind the kitchen door.

'Hi, Dad! We're here. Who was that man?' she asked him.

'My solicitor, Zara. Oh, hello, Tiggy,' he said, complete surprise on his face as he noticed me lurking behind her. 'I didn't know you were coming.'

'What's going on here, Dad? We've just seen Beryl, who was in floods of tears. She says she's leaving.'

'Oh God, where is she now? I'll go and speak to her.'

I could not only see but hear Charlie's exhaustion.

'You can't, because she's just left,' said Zara.

'And she gave me this, I'm afraid.' I picked up the envelope and handed it to him.

'I can guess what that is,' he said, taking it from me.

'Dad, come on, are you going to share or what? I mean, forget Beryl for a second, where's Mum?'

'I . . .' Charlie glanced at his daughter, then at me, and shook his head in despair.

'Dad, stop treating me like I'm two years old, I'm a grown woman now and I want to know what's going on!'

'Okay then,' he nodded. 'How about we go into the Great Room and sit down? I could do with a whisky, for sure.'

'Why don't you and Zara go?' I suggested. 'I need to head back to the cottage anyway.'

'Please stay, Tiggy,' Zara implored me. 'You're okay with that, aren't you, Dad?'

'Yes.' Charlie gave me a weak smile. 'You've been amazing, Tiggy, and yes, perhaps you should hear this too, as it concerns your future as well.'

In the Great Room, Zara and I settled ourselves onto the sofa, while Charlie poured himself two fingers of whisky from the bottle in the drinks cabinet. He sat down in the chair next to the fire and took a hefty gulp.

'Right, you've asked to be treated like a grown-up, Zara,

so that's exactly what I'm going to do. I'll get the big one over with first. I'm so sorry to tell you, darling, but your mum wants a divorce.'

'Okay.' Zara nodded calmly. 'Well, that's not a shock, Dad. I'd have had to be deaf and blind to think you guys were happy together.'

'I'm so sorry for that, Zara.'

'Where is Mum?'

'She's staying . . . elsewhere.'

'Dad, I asked where she was. "Elsewhere" isn't good enough. She told me she was up here at Kinnaird. Is she?'

'She's staying with Fraser at his cottage just beyond the main gates. He's the man who found you on the roadside with a puncture, when you were trying to run away last time.'

'Oh, him!' Zara rolled her eyes. 'I know Mum mentioned she'd been out riding with him a couple of times – she said he was teaching her.'

'Maybe he was, Zara. So, that's where she is.'

'And Fraser is like, her new boyfriend?'

'Yes.'

'Dad,' Zara said as she stood up and walked over to him, 'I'm so sorry.' She put her arms around him and hugged him.

'Don't you be sorry, Zara. This situation is not of your making. It's your mum and me who have the problem.'

'She told me once when she was really upset that you only married her because she was pregnant. Is that true?'

'I won't lie, Zara – that's the reason we married quickly, but I don't regret a day of it.' He reached out his hand to his daughter and squeezed hers. 'I got you, and that made it all worthwhile.'

I could see Charlie was close to tears, and I wondered if I should just slip out of the room and leave them to it.

'Well, if it makes you feel better, I've been wishing for years that you two *would* divorce. And if you were only staying with Mum because of me, then you shouldn't have done. Even if it hurts right now, Dad, you'll be much happier apart, I'm sure.'

'You know what, Zara?' Charlie's eyes glistened as he gave her a weak smile. 'You're incredible.'

'I'm my father's daughter,' she said with a shrug. 'So, now let's go back to Beryl and why *she* wants to leave.'

'I might have to get another whisky before I can tell you that.'

'I'll get it,' I said, jumping up and taking Charlie's glass to refill it. 'Are you absolutely sure you don't want me to go?' I asked him as I handed back the glass.

'No, Tiggy, because this is the bit that affects you, and every other employee at Kinnaird. I mentioned it to you in Spain, but I want you to know exactly why the future is so uncertain.'

'What is it, Dad?' urged Zara. 'Just get on and say it!'

'Right, here goes: when I was a little boy, my best mate was Fraser – he's Beryl's son, Zara.'

'Blimey!' Zara's face was the epitome of shock. 'Then no wonder she's feeling bad, what with Mum running off with him and stuff.'

'Yes, I'm sure she is, but I'm afraid there's more.' Charlie hesitated for a few seconds before continuing. 'Anyway, you know how few kids live on or near the estate, so, because we were the same age, as I said just now Fraser and I were insep-arable. We did everything together; my father even offered to pay for Fraser to come with me to boarding school when I was ten.' Charlie shook his head. 'I thought he was being kind but—'

'That's all very nice, Dad,' Zara cut in. 'But what actually happened?'

'Fraser and I had a big fight when we were at Edinburgh Uni together. He stole Jessie, my girlfriend – or in fact, at the time she was my fiancée. The two of them left university and went off to Canada where Jessie was from. And subsequently, I met and married your mum. I can honestly say I edited Fraser from my mind for years, so when he turned up out of the blue this Christmas, I was completely taken aback.'

'I remember,' I muttered to myself.

'And now . . . he's done it again and stolen Mum,' said Zara. 'What a bastard! I know you said he was your friend, but he sounds like he just wanted everything you had.'

'I think you're right,' Charlie sighed, 'he did. And being the idiot I was, I was always happy to give it to him. The real problem was that nobody had ever told me the truth about Fraser, although looking back, it was pretty obvious.'

'What was the truth, Dad?'

I watched Charlie pause uncertainly, a pulse beating in his temple.

'Come on, Dad, I can take it. It can't get much worse,' Zara encouraged him.

'I'm afraid it can, darling. Okay . . . well, my dad – your grandfather – wasn't very happy with your granny. The bottom line is, he and Beryl, well, they were lovers for years.'

'Grandpa and Beryl?!'

'Yes. Dad met her years before he met my mum, but Beryl didn't come from the kind of family that my father's parents felt was suitable for the bride of the Laird. So he married Mum, but Beryl soon followed him up to Kinnaird. And here's the punchline, Zara: the upshot was, that Beryl got pregnant and had Fraser a couple of months before my mum gave birth to me.'

There was silence in the room as we took in what Charlie was saying.

'Oh my God, Dad!' It was Zara who eventually broke the silence. 'So you and Fraser are really brothers?'

'Half-brothers, yes. And now I know, I realise I must have been living under a rock for most of my life. If you look at the photos of my dad – Fraser, with his height and love of shooting and whisky, takes after him in every way. Probably everyone saw it except me. What a complete dunce I've been.'

'God, Dad, that's really rough. I'm so sorry.' Zara gave him another tight hug.

'Has Fraser always known he was your half-brother?' I asked Charlie.

'No, he said his mum – Beryl – gave him that news just before he and Jessie eloped to Canada. She told me recently that she thought it might stop him doing such a terrible thing to me, but it obviously didn't. It wouldn't have stopped my father either. He did exactly as he pleased for his whole life too.'

'But what about Granny, Dad? Did she know about Beryl's affair with her husband?'

'I don't know, Zara. Remember, she died in a riding accident when I was seven. Very convenient for Dad,' Charlie sighed. 'It's no wonder Beryl has always felt territorial about this house. The chances are, she became the mistress here in all but name once Mum had died and I'd been packed off to boarding school with Fraser.'

'Do you hate your dad?' Zara asked. 'Like, for doing that to your mum? I would. I mean, I hate Mum now for doing this to you.'

'No, Zara, I don't hate him. Dad was who he was, just like Fraser. But to be honest, I'm not sure I ever loved him, or him me. You don't get to choose your relatives after all.' Charlie cast a sad glance in my direction.

'What about Beryl and what she did?'

'I think she *did* love my dad. And the fact she was here to take care of him as he got older made my life a lot easier. More than anyone, she was, and still is, heartbroken at his loss. She's all alone now.'

'Well, the good news is, that you're *not*, 'cos I'm here, Dad, and I love you loads,' Zara said fiercely. 'I'll look after you, promise.'

I wanted to hug Zara for being so mature – in so many ways, *she* was the real victim of this situation.

'Thanks, darling.' Charlie kissed his daughter's shiny head, obviously moved. 'But I'm afraid that there's even worse.'

'Worse than what you've just told me?' Zara rolled her eyes. 'Jesus! Bring it on then, Dad, while you're on a roll.'

'So,' Charlie continued, a quiver in his voice, 'at first I couldn't work out why Fraser had suddenly come back here at Christmas, but of course he was actually here to see if he'd been left anything in the will.'

'And had he?' Zara asked.

'Well, Dad didn't get round to making one, so on paper, there was nothing. Although I found out recently from the family solicitor that years ago Dad had signed over the deeds to the cottage Fraser is living in now. It was probably organised to assuage Dad's guilty conscience, because he would never be able to legally acknowledge Fraser. Everyone assumed that the estate would automatically pass to me as his heir. Or at least . . .' Charlie took a deep breath. 'They *did.*'

'What do you mean?' Zara frowned.

*God, no* . . . I thought. Given what Charlie had told me in Spain, I reckoned I had an idea of what was coming.

'The problem is, Zara, I mentioned earlier that Fraser is my father's eldest son, and given my dad didn't make a will leaving the estate to me, by rights he has a legal claim on Kinnaird.'

Zara swore heavily under her breath as I grabbed a lungful of my own.

'So what will happen now?' Zara's elfin features showed her horror.

'Well, remember he came up here to the Lodge to see me just before New Year?'

'Yeah, I heard all that shouting and then you said we were going home to Inverness and I was really piss— fed up,' Zara recalled. 'I came to the cottage and complained to you, Tiggy.'

'That's right, yes,' Charlie confirmed. 'Fraser told me that day he'd taken legal advice, and that he intended to go to court to claim what he felt was his rightful share of the estate.'

'*No!*' Zara stood up and began to pace the room. 'You just can't let this happen, Dad. You can't! Fraser hasn't even been *here* for the last God knows how many years!'

'Like father like son . . .' Charlie sighed. 'In so many ways, he's the natural heir. I—'

'Stop it, Dad! You can't just roll over and let this happen!

Kinnaird's yours – *ours*! And just because he shares some DNA with you doesn't mean anything.'

'In a court of law, I'm afraid it does, Zara. In fact, I've just had a letter from Fraser's counsel asking me to provide a sample of saliva and a hair follicle, but there's little doubt from what Beryl told me, that Fraser will be confirmed as my half-brother.'

'But Fraser's a bastard! Like, in every way,' Zara raged, standing up and pacing the room. 'You're the true heir, 'cos Grandpa and Granny were married!'

'You're right that several decades back, an illegitimate heir wouldn't even have been countenanced, but in today's world, that's not how it works. I promise you, I've taken the best legal advice there is, been down every avenue I can think of, but facts are facts. Fraser is my elder brother, the son of my father, the Laird, and – illegitimate or not – stands to inherit at least half the estate. If that happened, Kinnaird would prob- ably have to be sold so the assets could be split, because, sadly, sharing Kinnaird with Fraser is not an option. I'd just have to walk away. I'm so sorry, Zara. I know what Kinnaird means to you, but at the moment, I can't see a way out.'

'Does Mum know?' Zara said eventually.

'Yes, she was there the day he told me.'

'*Oh my God!*' Zara shouted. 'What really gets me is that Mum is obviously on *his* side! I mean' – she was off pacing again – 'she knows what Kinnaird means to me! Like, she's getting off with a man who could end up cutting her own daughter out of her inheritance!'

'To be fair to your mum, she did say that Fraser had agreed that if they had no children, he was prepared to name you in his will as the heir.'

'Oh my *God*, Dad!' Zara said again. 'How can you be so calm?'

I watched as Zara exploded once more at the unfairness of it all. Even though my own blood was boiling at the injustice, I kept silent. This was not a moment to add my own thoughts to the proceedings.

'. . . Besides which, Mum is still young enough to have kids if she stays with Fraser. That offer is just pathetic. Pathetic!' Zara shouted, angry tears beginning to course down her cheeks.

'Zara, you asked to be treated like an adult, and that's what I'm doing,' Charlie said gently. 'I understand how upset you are, but it's just the way it is.'

'Well, Dad, grow some balls, will you? Fight!' Zara kicked the back of a chair hard. 'I need some air, I'm going outside.'

We watched her march to the door, open it and slam it shut behind her.

'The trouble is, I've been fighting since January and it's got me absolutely nowhere.' Charlie shook his head. 'At the end of the day, this will come down to a judge's decision, but it's highly unlikely that Fraser will walk away empty-handed.'

'Should I go after Zara?' I asked him.

'No, she just needs some time to cool off. She may not like it, but she's definitely inherited her mother's temper.' Charlie gave a grimace. 'What a bloody awful mess.'

'Yes, it is,' I agreed.

'The sad thing is that Kinnaird was essentially destroyed many years before I came into the world. What it actually needs is millions poured into it now to save its beauty for future generations. And whoever wins, neither I nor Fraser have the funds to do what's necessary.'

'But what about all the grants you've applied for, Charlie?'

'Tiggy, I don't want to sound patronising, but whatever I'd get is a drop in the ocean. As a matter of fact, I spoke to someone from the Scottish National Trust a couple of weeks ago. And if by some miracle, I did manage to hold on to Kinnaird, that might just be the way forward.'

'How?'

'Well, I could "gift" it to the nation – in other words, give it to them for nothing, in return for my family remaining on the estate – i.e. here in the Lodge – in perpetuity. It's quite common for those in my situation to do that. Anyway, it's really not worth thinking about just now – it could be months if not years before the case grinds its way to court.'

'I'm so sorry, Charlie, I really am. And especially about Ulrika. You must be devastated, under the circumstances.'

'I know how bad it seems and why Zara hates her mother just now, but she – and you – don't know the whole story. The truth is that I should never have married her in the first place. I was on the rebound from Jessie, and Ulrika was very beautiful and very keen, and yes, a lot of it had to do with lust. When that died and Ulrika saw that while she'd married a laird of the land, in reality I was just an ordinary man earning my living as a doctor, she was very . . .' Charlie searched for the word. 'Disappointed.'

'I understand.' I nodded, thinking how loyal he was, even though I'd had to suppress a shudder when he'd talked about lusting after his wife.

'We married each other for the wrong reasons, and it's as simple as that,' Charlie continued. 'It's interesting, because even though I should be giving Fraser a good beating for stealing my wife, the irony is that I'm actually relieved. Really,

Tiggy, I hope they'll be happy together, I honestly do. I've been waiting for years for her to find someone else.'

'You would never have divorced her?'

'No. That either makes me a coward, or a father who wanted to at least try and give his daughter a stable upbringing. The worst thing about it all is that I know I've failed on that score.'

'You did what you thought was right, Charlie, and no one can do more than that.'

'I also know my own faults, Tiggy. When Zara told me to grow some balls, she had a point. I prefer a simple life, with no drama. Sadly, I've managed to get the opposite, in my personal life at least.'

'Well, I think it takes enormous strength to do the job you do every day, Charlie.'

'Anyway,' he sighed, 'none of this is your problem, Tiggy, and I'm really sorry you've become so embroiled in it all.'

'Please don't apologise. From what you've said, none of this is your fault at all. I'm going to go and see if I can find Zara.' I stood up and so did he.

He walked towards me and reached for my hand. 'Thank you for being here for her.'

At that moment, the door to the Great Room opened and there stood Ulrika, with Fraser lurking behind her.

'So sorry to interrupt your little love nest, Charlie,' Ulrika said, as she strode over to us. Charlie immediately dropped my hand.

'Tiggy is my friend, Ulrika, as I've said over and over again. What do you want?'

'I hear Zara's up here at Kinnaird. I want to see her. Where is she?'

'She went out to get some air.'

'You've told her then?'

'Yes.'

'I thought we'd agreed we'd speak to her together?'

'We did, yes, but I'm afraid she'd realised something was up and demanded to know what.'

'Why didn't you call me?' Ulrika's lovely blue eyes flared with anger. 'I could have been here in ten minutes, as you well know! Don't lie to me, Charlie – you wanted to make sure you got your side of the story in first so she'd feel sorry for you!'

'Who do I feel sorry for?'

We all jumped as Zara's wan face appeared at the Great Room door. She crossed her arms belligerently. 'Hello, Mum, hello, Fraser. How nice to see you.'

'Zara, darling, I'm so, so sorry.' Ulrika crossed to her daughter and tried to take her in her arms, but Zara resisted.

'Leave me alone, Mum! I can't believe you've brought *him* with you.'

'Hah, that's just perfect,' Ulrika snarled, pointing to me, 'when *she* is standing there, holding your father's hand, as bold as brass, in *my* house. You do know, Zara, that she and your father have been having an affair for months, don't you?'

'Don't be ridiculous, Ulrika,' Charlie snapped. He moved in front of me protectively. 'Tiggy's done nothing wrong. In fact, both of us should be grateful to her for being there for Zara during all this.'

'Yes, I'm sure she's an angel and I don't expect you to admit what you've done,' Ulrika spat. 'It's always me that's the bad guy. Well, this time I just won't have it!'

'I should go,' I muttered, feeling my cheeks heating up.

'No, Tiggy, I want you to stay,' said Zara, walking across

to me and taking my hand. 'Even if Dad and you have been shagging like rabbits forever, I don't really care!'

I opened my mouth to protest, but then shut it again as Charlie did the protesting for me.

'Oh for God's sake! For the last time, Tiggy and I have not been having an affair. Now could we please get out of the nursery and act like the grown-ups we are?'

'He's lying, Zara,' Ulrika sighed, 'but whatever. She's obviously turned you against me, and after all I've done for you, I . . .' She turned to Fraser, who was yet to add anything to the conversation, and buried her face in his chest. 'I just want my little girl back,' she wailed.

'Yeah, right, Mum. The problem is, that your little girl disappeared years ago. I'm an adult now, remember?'

'Okay, okay,' Charlie intervened. 'Can we all calm down, please. Zara, I'm sure your mum does want to talk to you and explain. Why don't the rest of us leave you alone for a while?'

'I'm not talking to Mum with *him* around.' Zara indicated the silent bulk of Fraser.

'I'll leave you to it then.' Fraser nodded at Charlie, dropped his hands from Ulrika's shoulders and, putting on his hat, turned towards the door. 'I'll be outside waiting for you in the car, okay?'

At that moment, a shaft of sunlight hit him, creating a shadow along the floor. And I saw the very specific shape of his hat outlined on the new carpet that Ulrika had recently had laid.

*Oh my God* . . . I muttered internally, staggering a little in shock as Charlie propelled me towards the door.

'Don't leave the house, will you?' Zara asked us.

'We'll be in the kitchen, okay?' Charlie replied.

'Okay.'

I watched Fraser march out along the corridor, slamming the back door behind him, then I followed Charlie into the kitchen and shut the door firmly.

I only realised I'd been holding my breath for ages as I let it out and took in some deep gulps of air.

'You okay, Tiggy? You look like you've seen a ghost.' Charlie switched the kettle on then turned to me as I sat down heavily on a chair, panting.

'Maybe I have.'

'What is it?'

'It's him, Fraser. Oh my God!' I shook my head. 'It's *him*!'

'Sorry, Tiggy, I'm not following you.'

'That hat, the one I described to the police as a trilby, it was *him*!' I repeated.

'I'm really sorry, but you're making no sense. Just try and tell me calmly what you mean.'

'I'm trying to tell you, Charlie, that it was Fraser I saw that night out in the glen. It was him who shot Pegasus and nearly killed me!'

'But . . . how can you be sure?'

'I already told you – it's that hat he was wearing just now. I saw his shadow on the carpet and it was exactly the same as his shadow on the snow. I'm one hundred per cent positive, Charlie.'

'It's a Canadian Mountie hat – and yes, I suppose it is a similar shape to a trilby. Well, it wouldn't surprise me,' he said, as he came over to place a cup of tea in my shaking hand, then thought better of it and put it next to me on the centre unit. 'Are you sure you're okay, Tiggy?'

'Yes! But what are we going to do? I mean, you know I'm

a liberal, but I'm absolutely not prepared to let him get away with killing Pegasus! The detective I saw at the hospital said whoever did it could have killed me too, that he might not only be charged for poaching a rare breed, but possibly attempted murder too.'

'Then let's phone the police immediately.' Charlie made to stand, but I put an arm out to stop him.

'Wait a bit, while we think about what's best. I mean, if the police do interview him, Fraser's bound to deny it, and Ulrika will probably give him an alibi, knowing her. Can you remember where she was the night I was shot?'

'I have a feeling she was back up at Kinnaird . . . yes, she was, because the next day she had to drive all the way down to North Yorkshire to pick up Zara for her exeat weekend. No wonder she was suddenly keen to be up here all the time.' Charlie raised an eyebrow.

'Damn,' I swore. 'Well, given the circumstances, she's bound to lie to protect him. Still, I know the police have got the bullet that went through me, and the casing, which they can trace to a gun—'

'Which is probably sitting in Fraser's barn as we speak.'

'Fraser could go to prison for this,' I said.

'Or not, actually, if he gets an alibi from Ulrika, plus a shit-hot defence team. Let me tell you, these things can go either way,' Charlie warned. 'I've been called in to testify in a couple of murder trials when it's been obvious to me that the victim died of more than natural causes, but the defendant has walked away scot-free.'

'Oh,' I said, feeling deflated. 'But surely, it wouldn't help his claim on Kinnaird if the judge knew he was being prosecuted for shooting a rare breed on the very estate he wants to own?'

'Sorry, Tiggy, but I'm afraid it wouldn't work like that. Shooting a rare breed wouldn't be considered material evidence in the court case, although I agree, it wouldn't help put him in a good light.'

There was a pause in the conversation as we both caught our breath.

'Charlie,' I said eventually. 'I'm just thinking . . .'

'What?'

'Well, I'm wondering if there's any way we could use the fact that I now know it was Fraser who took a potshot at me to help you?'

Charlie stared at me. 'You mean, blackmail him?'

'Umm, yes, I suppose I do. What about if I told him I recognised him as the man who shot at me and Pegasus that night? That I was going to call the police immediately? Unless . . . because he *is* family, and you didn't want a scandal, I was prepared *not* to go to the police as long as he gave up his claim to Kinnaird, left the country and went back into whichever hole he crawled out of. The question is, how do you think he'd react? Would he brazen it out or would he jump on the next plane back to Canada with Ulrika in tow?'

'Who knows? The thing about bullies – and let's face it, that's exactly what Fraser is – is that underneath, they're all cowards at heart. But, Tiggy, this is too much to ask – surely you want to see him in jail for what he put you through?'

'I lived, didn't I? It's Pegasus's death I want to avenge, and if what I know can save Kinnaird from being destroyed by the man who murdered him, I'd say that's good enough for me – *and* him.'

'A lot depends on whether he's held on to that gun or not,' mused Charlie.

'Does Cal know where his cottage is?'

'Of course he does. Why?'

I peered out of the kitchen window and craned my neck to see whether Fraser's car was still sitting in the rear courtyard with him in it. It was.

'While Fraser's here, why don't you phone Cal, Charlie, and get him down to Fraser's cottage. Tell him to check in the barn for—'

'Yes, the rifle.' Charlie was already on his feet heading for the office and the phone.

'And tell him to call if he finds it,' I added as a plan began to formulate in my head.

'Okay.' Charlie was back in the kitchen a minute later. 'Cal's been despatched and he'll call here on the landline to let me know if Fraser's hunting rifle is there. Thank God there's a half-decent mobile signal near that cottage. Tiggy.' Charlie took my hands in his. 'Do you want to sleep on this? Maybe it's better you let the police handle it—'

'No time like the present, is there, whilst we've got Fraser in captivity? I need to do this now before I lose my nerve, and before he gets wind of the fact I've recognised him and does a runner. As soon as Cal lets us know, you need to call Fraser in here. You don't have a tape recorder handy, do you?' I asked randomly.

'I have my dictaphone in the car, I use it for my secretary to type letters – why?'

'Just in case he confesses,' I said, thinking back to every rubbish detective novel I'd read in my teenage years. 'Then we'd have proof.'

'Probably not admissible in court, but yes, I see where you're headed. I'll go and get it – my car's out at the front – you man the phone.'

We gave each other a childish grin as he left, because, despite the seriousness of the situation, it had a surreal edge to it. And perhaps most surreal of all, I suddenly recalled Angelina's parting words about me to Charlie in Granada:

'*She has the answer to your problem . . .*'

I could only hope that her prediction proved to be correct.

The phone rang in the office a few seconds later, and I dashed to answer it.

'It's Cal, Tig. I'm here in Fraser's barn and I'm holdin' the hunting rifle in my hands now.'

'Jesus, Cal! I hope you're wearing gloves, or they might find your fingerprints on it!'

'Charlie already told me tae do that. What the hell is goin' on up there?'

'I'll tell you later, but stay exactly where you are until we call you, okay?'

'Okay. Bye then.'

I put the landline down as I heard the Great Room door slam shut. I peered out of the office and saw Zara marching down the corridor towards me, shouting expletives at her mother who was obviously still inside the room.

'Zara!' I hissed as I ran to her and dragged her into the kitchen. 'Listen to me! I don't care how you feel about your mum, but there's a chance me and your dad can save Kinnaird if you go back in now and keep her talking.'

'Are you joking, Tiggy? I *hate* her – I never want to breathe the same air as her! Agh . . . !'

'Zara.' Charlie entered with dictaphone in hand. 'Get back

698

into the Great Room with your mother *now*! Do you hear me? And you will stay in there and keep her talking until I say you can come out!'

'Okay, Dad,' Zara nodded, chastened by her father's uncharacteristic aggression.

'Well, she did tell me to grow some balls,' Charlie shrugged as we watched Zara turn tail and head back to the Great Room.

'Right,' I said. 'Hide that dictaphone somewhere quickly and then,' I gulped, 'go and call him in.'

'Okay,' said Charlie, turning the dictaphone on and stashing it behind the bread bin. 'Are you sure you're up for this, Tiggy?'

'Yes, as long as you're with me.'

'Always.' He smiled, then left to go and get Fraser.

My heart was really banging now, so I looked up to the heavens and asked Pegasus to be with me as I gave the performance of my life. To save Kinnaird, Zara, and my beloved Charlie . . .

I heard the back door open and then close as Charlie and Fraser made their way to the kitchen.

'I'm afraid there is nothing you could say or do that would make me change my mind,' Fraser was saying as they walked in. 'I want what's mine by rights, and that's all there is to it.' Then he noticed me sitting at the centre unit and threw a disdainful glance in my direction. 'What's *she* doing here?'

'Tiggy just wanted a word with you, Fraser.'

'Really? Well, say what you have to, then.'

I watched him sit down opposite me; the fact that he was so sure of himself – that he didn't even bother to take off his hat in front of his victim – fuelled me with the anger I needed to say what I had to.

'It's about the night that Pegasus was shot,' I said, deciding this was no time to beat about the bush. 'I told the police that I'd seen my attacker's shadow in the snow and that he was wearing an unusual hat, shaped like a trilby. When I saw your shadow on the Great Room carpet earlier, I realised it was you that shot Pegasus and almost killed me.'

'What?!' Fraser stood up immediately. 'Jesus, Charlie, I can't believe that you two have sunk so low. I'm leaving now.'

'Okay,' I said calmly. 'That's fine. Cal's down at your cottage with the hunting rifle we think you used to shoot at me and Pegasus. The police already told me they have the bullet, plus the casing, and all they need to do is match them up to your rifle. We'll call them and get them to meet you there, shall we?'

'I . . . you're talking bullshit and you know it. Ulrika was with me that night – just go and ask her.'

'We're not interested really, are we, Charlie?' I said lightly. 'It's up to the police to ask you and Ulrika questions. Go and phone them, Charlie. Bye then, Fraser,' I said as I stood up and took my tea cup to the sink to wash it out, giving myself a chance to breathe and for Fraser to think. I saw Charlie move towards the kitchen door.

'We both know it was you, Fraser,' I commented quietly as I put the cup on the drainer. 'And come to think of it, I'm suddenly remembering the rifle being aimed at me that night. I'm sure the police would be very interested to hear about it. They did say it could be classed as attempted murder. If the stag hadn't been between us, it could have been me that was killed.'

'Okay, okay, let's talk,' Fraser said. Charlie paused, one hand on the doorknob. 'What is it you want?' Fraser asked me.

'Justice of course, for Pegasus and for me,' I said as I turned round to him slowly and was pleased to see he'd had the grace to take off his hat. 'But I also want it for Charlie. You're only after a piece of the estate because it's his, not because you love it. It would probably have to be sold to give you your share and then the hundreds of years of Kinnaird history would go down the drain. I think that would be a real shame, don't you?'

'You little bitch . . . !' Fraser muttered as I watched Charlie approach him.

'Enough, Fraser!'

'It's okay, Charlie, he can call me what he wants,' I said evenly. 'Especially as it's all on tape anyway. And he's already admitted it was him.'

'I've done no such thing!'

'I think you have,' I shrugged. 'Anyway, Fraser, it's really up to you. Charlie and you share the same blood after all, and whatever you've done to him, he wouldn't like to see his half-brother put away in prison, would you, Charlie?'

'Of course not, no, Tiggy.' Charlie nodded in agreement.

'So, Fraser, I'm prepared *not* to tell the police that it was you who shot at Pegasus and me that night, if you're prepared to give up your claim to the Kinnaird estate and leave the country.'

'This is out and out blackmail!' Fraser raged, but he stayed where he was.

'Yes, I'm morally corrupt,' I said, 'but what can I do? So, what's it to be? The choice is yours.'

Both Charlie and I watched as a gamut of emotion, ranging from rage to fear, passed across Fraser's cold blue eyes. Eventually, he stood up.

'You'll be sorry you did this for him,' Fraser shouted, stabbing one of his fingers towards me. 'He's pathetic – just ask his wife, or my ex-wife, for that matter. They'll tell you.' He walked towards the door.

'I take it you've decided to leave the country?'

'I'll need a few hours to sort my shit out. You'll grant me that, will you?'

'We will. Oh and Cal will keep hold of that rifle of yours just in case you change your mind. Okay?'

Fraser looked round the kitchen, his entire body shaking with anger. Then he threw us both a look of such hatred, I shuddered. The man was pure evil and, for the first time, I felt glad I knew the words of the curse.

Without another word, Fraser turned on his heel and left the room.

Charlie and I listened as his footsteps retreated towards the back door, and we watched surreptitiously through the kitchen window as he climbed into his jeep, then, with a screech of tyres, exited the courtyard.

'I'll call Cal and tell him to get the hell away from the barn with the rifle. I'll send him up to Lochie's parents' croft for now, just in case Fraser decides to hunt him down. He'll never find him up there,' Charlie called as he headed for the office.

Ulrika appeared in the kitchen a few seconds later, Zara trailing behind her, rolling her eyes.

'Did I just see Fraser's car leave?' Ulrika asked.

'Yes,' I muttered.

'But he was meant to be waiting for me!'

I sat down heavily on a chair, as all the adrenaline, or whatever it was that had got me through the past fifteen minutes, drained out of me.

'Are you okay, Tiggy? You've gone a funny colour,' Zara said, walking over to me, as Charlie reappeared and gave me a thumbs-up sign. Ulrika stood there uncertainly.

'So have you and Zara had a chat?' asked Charlie. 'We have,' Ulrika nodded. 'She agrees it's all for the best.'

'Yeah, right,' said Zara, then mouthed, 'What the hell is going on?!' from behind her mother.

'And you're absolutely sure a divorce is what you want, Ulrika?' Charlie's eyes bored into his wife's.

'Absolutely. No turning back now.' Ulrika glanced at me. 'He's all yours if you want him. Right, I'm off. Fraser and I are going out to dinner tonight.'

'Have a nice time,' I called after her as she left the kitchen and headed for her jeep.

The phone rang, and Charlie went to answer it.

Zara waited until we heard the back door and the office door close, before she turned on me.

'Perhaps you can tell me now what on earth is happening? I, like, had to pretend it was okay that my mum is literally helping that idiot boyfriend of hers steal my inheritance from under my nose! And agree to spend half the hols in his manky cottage when all I want to do is to punch his lights out!'

'Don't be too hard on your mum, Zara. You know how love can make you blind, don't you?' I said.

'What? How come you're on her side now?'

'I'm not, Zara, but . . . let's wait until your dad's back and we'll tell you what's just happened. For now, would you make me a cup of really sugary tea?'

When Charlie returned, he walked over to me to put his fingers to my wrist.

'That was Cal again. He's up at the croft, safe and sound. Now, it's hardly surprising, but your pulse is racing. Bed for you, miss,' he said, putting an arm around my waist and helping me up from the chair.

I didn't resist. I felt totally exhausted.

'Will someone tell me what on earth is going on?!' Zara complained.

'I will when I've put Tiggy to bed, yes. But put it this way, Zara, it looks like this extraordinary woman has just saved your inheritance.'

# 38

I woke the next morning to soft light coming in through the windows, glanced at the alarm clock and saw it was twenty past eight. I'd obviously slept right through the night. I came to slowly, my mind gradually pulling together the threads of what had happened yesterday.

'Was that really you?' I murmured as I visualised myself standing in the kitchen, cool as a cucumber, telling Fraser I knew it was him who had shot at me. Where I'd found the courage to face him down, I just didn't know, because I was the least combative person I knew.

Having woken myself up by splashing my face in cold water, I heard a soft tapping on my door.

'Come in,' I said as I climbed back into bed.

Charlie entered the bedroom with a breakfast tray, piled with a pot of tea, toast, and a blood pressure monitor. He was also wearing his stethoscope round his neck.

'How are you feeling, Tiggy? I popped in a couple of times in the night to feel your pulse, but I want to check your blood pressure now and listen to your heart.'

'Really, I'm fine, Charlie. I slept well.'

'Well, I didn't,' he said as he put the tray down on the bed.

'I just want to apologise now for putting you through that ordeal last night; it was totally selfish of me. All that stress was absolutely the last thing you needed.'

'Honestly, I feel okay,' I said as Charlie hooked his stethoscope into his ears and listened to my heart and my chest, then checked my blood pressure. 'Now, tell me, did you have your tests in Geneva before you left?'

'No, I flew back here with Zara but . . .'

'No buts, I'll book you in at Inverness for them tomorrow. Surprisingly though, your obs are all normal,' Charlie said as he removed the monitor from my arm and poured me some tea.

'Well, I have just spent the best part of three weeks in bed resting. And besides, last night was like an out-of-body experience. I can't really remember what I said. It was as if someone else was saying the words I needed to say for me.'

'Well, it *was* you, and you were magnificent. Really, Tiggy, I can never thank you enough. You're not regretting it, are you? Thinking you should call the police?'

'No, why should I, if it's got rid of Fraser? Being unable to take Kinnaird away from you is just as bad a punishment for him as going to prison. He has gone, hasn't he?' I said, my heart giving a tiny lurch.

'He has, yes, but I had Ulrika up here at seven this morning. She was hysterical – wanted to know what I'd said that had made Fraser pick up his stuff and take off in the early hours without her.'

'He didn't take her with him?'

'No. In fact, he told her it was over and he was going back to Canada by himself. She obviously presumed I'd dished some dirt on her which had put him off. I'm amazed you didn't hear the shouting.'

'I didn't, no. Is she still here?' I asked him nervously.

'No, she drove off at top speed, saying she'd see me in court. Kinnaird's not out of the woods yet,' Charlie sighed. 'I'm sure Ulrika will demand her pound of flesh in the divorce proceedings.'

'Oh, I hadn't thought about that.'

'No, well, I'll just have to find a way to pay her off – maybe sell a few hundred acres to the neighbouring estate – they've been after some Kinnaird land for years, and, thanks to you, Tiggy, at least we'd get to keep the bulk of it. Now, eat your breakfast.'

'Thank you for this.' I smiled at him, glad to see that, even though he looked like he hadn't slept, his eyes had lost the sheen of hopelessness and were a vivid blue. 'What did Zara say when you told her what we'd done?' I asked as I ate the toast.

'The words she used are not repeatable in polite company . . . but in *other* words, she was ecstatic,' he nodded.

'Did she say anything more about you and Ulrika divorcing? I know she was brave last night, but the news must have affected her.'

'If she is sad about it, then she's doing a very good job of not showing it, Tiggy, really. And maybe seeing us separately *will* be healthier for her. She's always been a Daddy's girl right from when she was a baby and Ulrika probably thinks I've promoted it – whispered poison into Zara's ear – which I absolutely haven't. I've always wanted them to get on well, but they simply never did. Mind you, Zara's already making noises about moving up here to Kinnaird with me. Lochie's told her all about the college he went to. Maybe I *should* think about it,' Charlie said. 'I mean, just because all my Kinnaird ancestors and I went to boarding school, it doesn't necessarily mean it's right for Zara, does it? Besides, I'm going to need all the help I can get if I'm going to try and save Kinnaird for her.'

'You're moving up here?' I said, wondering if I had the wrong end of the stick.

'Yes, Tiggy, I am. After I'd put you to bed last night, I did a lot of thinking and the good news is, with the aid of some whisky, I grant you, everything came into sharp focus.'

'Such as what?'

'For starters, Kinnaird's in my blood, and that's the way it is. Maybe it's only when you're about to lose something that you realise how much it means to you. So at least I can thank Fraser for that. I've decided that I'm going to take a sabbatical from the hospital for a year. That will give me a chance to really focus on the estate and to work out exactly what can be done to restore it. And also to see if it's right for me to be here full-time. I owe my ancestors – and Zara – that at least, and I can always go back to medicine if it doesn't work out. Or even maybe do as we once told each other we'd dreamt of and disappear off to Africa.' Charlie smiled.

'Er, talking of that,' I confessed, feeling guilty for some reason, 'I have an interview next week for the job of Conservation Officer on a reserve in Malawi.'

'Malawi in Africa?'

'Yes.'

'Oh. Right.' I saw the concern and a touch of panic in his eyes. 'I see. Well,' he swallowed, 'I did tell you that your future at Kinnaird was uncertain, and far be it from me to dissuade you. But I have to say, I'd honestly be very concerned about your health, because I doubt there's a decent hospital nearby. Besides . . .'

'What?'

'Well, I was obviously hoping you'd stay on here and help me at Kinnaird.'

A pregnant silence, full of the things we both wanted to say but didn't know how to, hung between us. I sipped my tea and looked out of the window, feeling horribly uncomfortable. I watched as Charlie stood up and paced, hands deep in his pockets.

'Last night, when you and I were plotting what I shall now call "Frasergate", I thought that . . . well, that we were a team. And it felt really fantastic, Tiggy.'

'It did, yes,' I admitted.

'And . . . I know it's early days, and even if you've managed to rescue Kinnaird for me, it's still got to be turned into something that's viable and sustainable in the future, which just may not be possible. Plus the fact that I have what I'm sure will be a very messy divorce on the cards, but I was hoping that you'd . . . well, be with me.'

'As an employee?' I clarified, knowing I was being disingenuous, but needing him to actually say the words.

'Yes, that of course, but no, I mean . . . *with* me.'

Charlie walked back to the bed and sat down on it. He snaked his hand towards mine – his long elegant fingers begging to be accepted. I watched my palm open of its own accord and take them and hold them tightly. We smiled shyly at each other, not needing any words because we both *knew*.

*For better, for worse, for richer, for poorer, in sickness and in health . . .*

Charlie moved the breakfast tray from my knees, then reached out his arms and drew me to him. I laid my head against his chest as he stroked my hair.

'I want to look after you for the rest of your life,' he whispered. 'I want us to build Kinnaird together, become a family – a happy family. I've wanted it from the first moment I saw you in the hospital. I've dreamt about it for months, but I could never see a way that it could happen. Yet now there is a way.'

'I've dreamt about it too.' I blushed as he tipped my chin up so he could look into my eyes.

'Have you really? That amazes me. I'm quite a bit older than you, with a load of baggage that's going to take a long time to sort out . . . it's not going to be easy, Tiggy, and the last thing I'd ever want you to do is to resent me like Ulrika does.'

'I'm not Ulrika,' I said quickly. 'I'm me, and I don't do resentment.'

'No, you do magic . . . you *are* magic,' he said as his eyes filled with tears. 'God, I'm pathetic – look at me! I'm crying. Will you stay?'

'I . . .'

However much I wanted to say yes, I knew I owed it to myself to take some time to think it all over. Because this dear, dear man had been through enough, and if I agreed, then it had to be forever.

'Give me a few hours, will you?' I asked him. 'There's someone I need to see first.'

'Of course. Can I ask who?'

'No, because if I told you, you'd think I was mad.'

'I think you're mad already, Tiggy.' Charlie kissed me on the forehead. 'And I still love you,' he added with a grin.

*He loves me . . .*

'Okay, then maybe you can tell me where you buried Chilly?'

'Of course.' Charlie nodded, trying not to let a smile escape his lips. 'In our family graveyard naturally – he *was* family, after all. It's at the back of the chapel.' He stood up. 'I'll see you later – I'm going over to Beryl's cottage to tell her what has happened and beg her to come back.'

'Hello, darling Chilly,' I said, as I crouched down and looked at the simple cross, which replicated those in the graveyard at Sacromonte. It only had his forename on it, as nobody here would know Chilly's surname or date of birth. 'I'm so sorry I wasn't here to say goodbye properly, but thank you for stopping in on your way up that night.'

I patted the snow covering the grave with my gloved hand, then stood and turned my eyes skywards, because that's where he really was. 'You told me that I'd leave Kinnaird the first day I saw you. Well, I'm back now, and Charlie's asked me to stay. It would mean giving up my dreams of going to Africa but . . . could you ask the others up there what they think?'

There wasn't an answer, and neither had I really expected one, because – despite what I could already see would be numerous difficulties in the future – I already knew. And every atom of me was tingling with happiness and certainty.

'Tell Angelina I'll be back to see her soon with Mister

Charlie,' I called as I walked past the graves of three hundred years of Kinnairds to the Land Rover.

*This is where you'll lie one day, hotchiwitchi,* a voice in my head said as I climbed in. I giggled, because it was such a Chilly thing to say and the fact that I *would* lie here one day meant that – however long I had on this earth – Charlie and I were forever. Which was all I needed to know.

'So, the hero of the hour returns,' Cal said as I wandered into the cottage, still feeling emotional from the past few hours and my visit to Chilly. 'How are you feeling, Tig?'

'I'm a bit dazed, to be honest,' I admitted as I went to sit down on the sofa.

'Zara popped down and filled me in. It sounds like you played a blinder. And because o' you, we're all saved. The news is going round that the Laird is getting divorced tae boot. Is that true?'

'I can neither confirm nor deny,' I replied blithely.

'Well, it's about time those two went their separate ways. Now then,' he said, drawing himself up to his full height and staring down at me, 'I need tae show you something else that'll rock your world. Are you up tae it, Tig?'

'It's nothing bad, is it?'

'No, not at all. It's a blinkin' miracle! Coming?'

'Yes, as long as it's good,' I said, even though I was now dog-tired from emotional and mental stress.

A few minutes later, we drove down the hill towards the barn where the pregnant heifers were housed.

'This way.' Cal indicated another small barn to the left. He took a key from his jacket pocket and unlocked the padlock. 'Ready?' he asked me.

'Ready.'

Cal opened the door and I followed him inside. There was a soft rustling from the corner, and in the light coming from the doorway I saw a skinny female deer lying on a bed of straw. I could tell she was very weak by the way she was desperately trying to stand, but failing.

'What's happened to her?' I whispered.

'I found her last night in the birch copse, Tig. She was distressed and on her knees, with a swollen belly that told me she was in labour. Me an' Lochie managed to get her in the back of Beryl and then in here,' Cal whispered back. 'The wee one's nae in good shape either – arrived in the early hours, probably before its due-date, but last time I checked it was still alive. Mum's struggling now though,' he sighed.

We looked at her and saw she had sunk back onto the straw, no longer capable of movement.

'Go and see her baby,' Cal urged me.

'Have you called Fiona?'

'No, you'll see why in a moment,' he said, pushing me gently towards the hind.

Whispering words of comfort both out loud and inside my head, I approached her gradually, a few centimetres at a time. I stopped at the edge of the straw bed, then slowly knelt down.

'Hello,' I whispered. 'My name's Tiggy, and I'm here to help you.'

I sat there, my knees feeling the damp and cold of the barn floor, but never removing my eyes from hers.

*Trust me, I am your friend . . .* my inner voice told the hind over and over again.

Eventually, it was the hind who dropped her beautiful liquid eyes from mine as her thin body finally relaxed and I edged nearer.

'Look in the straw beside her,' Cal whispered from behind me. 'Here's a torch.'

He held it out to me and I shone it down into the gloom, making out a skinny pair of legs that were protruding from between its mother's. I ran the light along its body as it lay prone and ominously still. Then I gave a gasp of astonishment, and, wondering if it was a trick of the light, I swept the torch beam down its body once more.

'Oh my God!' I whispered as I turned to look at Cal.

'I know, Tig. I told you it was a miracle.'

Tears came unbidden to my eyes as I shuffled myself onto the straw. I peered over the hind's prone body to take a closer look at her calf.

'It's white, Cal, pure white! I . . .'

Cal nodded and I could see his eyes were brimming with emotion too. 'Problem is, Tig, Mum may be done for and the calf's hardly stirred since he was born. He needs the suckle.'

'Let me try and get closer,' I said as I shuffled forward a little further to allow me to place my hand under the hind's nose, so she could smell me. I stayed there for as long as I could, then lifted my hand and rested it on the back of her neck. At my touch, she looked up at me and I read all the fear and pain she felt. And knew that her time on this earth was running out.

I moved into a more comfortable position to take another look at the calf, lying next to its exhausted mother. I laid my hand against the soft fur of his flank, then began to stroke him gently, my hand moving along his body as I examined him.

Carefully picking up one of his back legs to check on the bones, I saw that, even though he was weak, he had no physical impediments.

'How is he?' Cal asked.

'Just perfect, but very fragile. I don't know whether he'll make it, but . . .'

*You have to save him, Tiggy . . .* said my inner voice.

'Okay, I'm going to try.' I closed my eyes, then asked for the help I needed.

As Angelina had taught me, I imagined all the life-giving energy from the universe flowing into my hands as I swept them up and down the calf's body. I repeated this process perhaps five or six times, drawing the bad energy out of him and shaking it away into the ether. I couldn't say how long I sat there, but when I came to, I found his eyes were open and he was gazing up at me with interest.

'Hello,' I said.

In response, the calf stretched out his legs away from his mother, so that his head rested against my knees.

'Aren't you a handsome boy,' I said as I bent over to plant a kiss on his newly minted white coat.

I saw his mother struggle to lift her head from the straw. She opened her huge shy eyes again and stared at me.

'You're beautiful too,' I murmured, looking at her long eyelashes, and the white star in the centre of her forehead. 'Pegasus chose you especially, didn't he?'

I put my other hand on her head and one of her skinny legs lifted towards me, as if she was trying to touch me. I could see that she had little strength – or time – left.

'Don't worry,' I whispered as I stroked her head, then leant down to kiss it. 'You'll be safe where you're going and you mustn't worry about your little one. I swear I'll make sure he's taken care of.'

It seemed to me that a tear formed in one of the hind's eyes, before she lay back down on the straw and closed them for the last time.

My own tears dripped all over her orphaned son's warm coat, the parallel of my own birth being played out in animal form not lost on me. I sat in that barn with the baby stag resting against my knee, and together we mourned the mothers we'd both lost before we'd ever known them.

'You okay, Tig?' Cal said eventually.

'Yes. Sad that the mother's gone, but I think her calf will survive. Look!'

The stag was nuzzling at my hand, obviously in search of milk.

'Shit, Tig,' Cal sighed. 'It means we're going tae have tae hand rear him.'

'Do you have any bottles up in the sheds?'

'I'll go an' get a couple and some milk, though he'll probably reject it. I'll bring the portable gas heater down as well. You're going tae catch your death down here.'

'Thanks, Cal,' I said, although it was only when he mentioned it that I realised I was shivering, but that was probably more to do with emotion than cold.

'What will we do with you?' I whispered to try and calm the baby stag, who was fully awake now and frantic with hunger. 'Perhaps we could paint you brown so no one but us would know . . .'

Cal arrived back twenty minutes later, by which time I was very pleased to see the gas heater. I saw Lochie and Zara were with him and I waved them over to look at Pegasus's son.

'I found these two smoking outside the Lodge,' Cal said, throwing Zara a stern glance. 'Thought they'd like to say hello.'

'Oh Tiggy,' Zara breathed, coming over to me. 'He's adorable.'

'I cannae believe it, Tiggy,' Lochie said as he knelt down next to Zara. 'Who woulda thought it? Can I touch him?'

'Yes, he needs to get used to being handled by humans if he's going to survive,' I said, and watched as Lochie and Zara gingerly stroked the newborn.

'Cal says you breathed life back intae him, Tiggy. You have a way with animals, like Mum,' Lochie commented as he rested a hand tentatively on the pale fur.

'Here's the bottle, Tig,' Cal said, handing it to me before pushing the heater across the uneven floor towards us.

Very gently, I eased the teat of the bottle between the calf's lips, but he refused to unclamp his jaw. Then I tried squirting a little warm milk on his gums, praying he would accept it.

'Come on, darling,' I whispered, 'you need to drink, get strong for your mum and dad.'

After a number of further attempts, to our collective relief, he opened his mouth and finally began to suckle.

'He thinks you're his mum, Tig.' Cal smiled, as the calf finished the bottle and began to nudge my hand for more. 'The question is, what are we going tae do with our orphan now? You for one can't spend the night in here. I'll no' be responsible for you suffering further illness, but no one can get wind o' his birth, or his sweet little head'll be on a plinth before you can say "venison"!'

'You could take him up tae mine,' Lochie suggested. 'My

mum would be happy tae have a new pet, especially one as special as he is.'

Cal and I looked at each other, seeing the dawning light of a possible solution.

'Are you sure, Lochie?' I asked him. 'I mean, I'd be up every day, but it's a full-time job, hand-rearing a young calf.'

'I'll help too,' Zara butted in.

''T'would be nae bother, Tiggy,' Lochie reassured me. 'Between us all, I'm sure we can care for him. Our croft is out o' the way o' prying eyes, so he'd be safe with us.'

'It's the right thing tae do, Tig,' Cal said. 'This time we're no' taking any chances. Now, why don't we carry the young 'un to Beryl, and Lochie can drive you up to the croft? The sooner we get him out o' here, the better.'

I stood up and carried the calf – its long skinny legs hanging over the cradle I'd made with my arms – to the car. As Cal helped me up into the passenger seat and Zara climbed into the back, Lochie got behind the wheel.

'I'll stay here and see tae his mum,' Cal said.

'Please don't skin and blood her,' I begged him.

'Course I won't, Tig. I'll bury her over in the forest by the Lodge and mark it wi' a couple o' twigs.'

'Thanks.'

I held tightly to my precious cargo as we set off along the bumpy track. At the entrance to the estate, we turned left towards the chapel and continued for another few kilometres up onto the fells. Eventually, a low grey stone farmhouse came into view, smoke billowing from its chimney, the surrounding land full of woolly white dots, still visible in the encroaching dusk.

'It'll be lambing time soon,' Lochie commented as he

brought Beryl to a halt, then walked round to open the passenger door to help me and the calf out. I stood there for a few seconds with my precious cargo and looked up to see the pale sliver of a new moon welcoming the newborn to the world. Then Zara and I followed Lochie into a low-ceilinged kitchen.

Fiona was standing at the range, stirring a large saucepan of soup.

'Hello Tiggy, Zara.' She greeted us with a smile. 'What a surprise! How lovely to see you both! And what have you got there?' She came over for a closer look.

'He's something very special, Mum, and you and Dad have to swear yae won't say a word to anyone,' Lochie said.

'As if you have to ask.' Fiona raised an eyebrow at her son as she looked down at the calf. 'Oh my goodness, Tiggy, is he really what I think he is?'

'Yes. Here, take him for a cuddle.'

'I'd love to,' Fiona said, obviously overwhelmed. I handed the gangly bundle over carefully, and stood back to watch how the calf would react to a new pair of arms. Yet, as Fiona embraced him, and whispered endearments to him softly, he hardly stirred. I breathed a sigh of relief as every instinct told me that Fiona was the perfect stand-in mother and the croft itself the perfect hiding place.

'Lochie, take that pot off the heat and put the kettle on,' Fiona directed her son, as she beckoned me and Zara to the well-worn kitchen table and indicated I should sit down next to her. 'I presume his mother is dead?'

'Sadly, yes. It was natural causes, though.'

'Lochie told me you got shot when you were trying to save the white stag from a poacher.'

'Yes.'

'Is this . . . ? I mean, it must be the dead stag's son – the leucistic gene is usually inherited.'

'I think we have to assume so, yes. Cal says he was born this morning. I've managed to feed him a bottle, but he's obviously still weak.'

'But he seems very alert, which is a good sign. I'll check him over, if you don't mind.'

'I'd love you to. He wasn't alert when I first saw him,' I said as Fiona retrieved her medical bag from the floor by the back door and took out her stethoscope.

'Cal said Tiggy put her hands on the calf and breathed life back into him,' Zara commented as Fiona listened to the calf's heart.

'Yes, I've heard you have healing hands, Tiggy. Do you?' Fiona asked.

'Cal says she does, yes,' Lochie answered his mum.

'Lochie, why don't you take Zara out to the barn to see the new kittens? Give this little one a bit of space,' Fiona suggested.

'Okay.'

As Lochie led Zara out of the back door, Fiona continued to examine the calf.

'Fancy coming to work with me? I think I mentioned it when we last met. I'm a great believer in holistic medicine operating in tandem with the traditional.'

'Oh my God, I'd love to, Fiona, but I don't have any official training or qualifications.'

'Well, qualifications can be arranged; it's having the gift in the first place that matters.'

'Are you serious?' I said incredulously.

720

'Absolutely,' she confirmed. 'Let's arrange a time to discuss it, preferably over a large glass of wine. There.' Fiona put her medical equipment away in her bag. 'He's in fine fettle. Now, can you hold on to him whilst I stir the soup? Lochie's dad will be in at any second expecting his supper.'

I decided then that Fiona McDougal was the woman I aspired to be one day: wife, mother, homemaker, full-time vet and lovely, lovely human being.

'You know, the mythological Pegasus was actually an orphan raised by Athena and the Muses . . .'

'Then I think we should name him after his father,' I whispered into his fur, my maternal urges stirring in a way that almost frightened me.

'Will you stay for supper, Tiggy? Then we can talk about Pegasus's care,' Fiona asked, as a man who reminded me of Cal, with his stocky build and weather-beaten face, came through the door.

'Hello, darling,' Fiona smiled as he kissed her before taking off his jacket. 'Can you go and call Lochie and Zara in from the barn? They're with the kittens.'

'O' course, but who is this? And . . .' he walked over to take a closer look at Pegasus, '*that*?'

'Hamish, this is Tiggy, who works at Kinnaird as the Laird's wildlife consultant.'

'Hello, Tiggy, nice tae meet you.' Hamish smiled at me and I saw the warmth in his eyes.

'And "that",' Fiona continued, 'is Pegasus, born this morning. He's going to be staying up here with us for a while, out of harm's way. Now, love, could you go and find those kids before the soup goes cold?' Fiona added as she doled it out into bowls.

Five minutes later, we were all seated around the old oak table in the kitchen, drinking the delicious vegetable soup, mopped up with thick chunks of warm white bread.

'So you're another veggie like my wife?' asked Hamish.

'Oh, I'm much worse – I'm a vegan,' I answered with a grin.

A sudden tiny mewling sound came from Zara's direction, and the table's attention turned towards her.

'I couldn't leave him in the barn.' Zara had the grace to blush as she opened her jacket and plucked out a ginger kitten, striped like a tiny tiger and looking just as fierce. 'Mum hates cats, but now Dad's moving to Kinnaird, we can have one – or even two – at the Lodge. Isn't he gorgeous?' she said, stroking his head.

'He is, Zara, but not at the supper table,' Fiona said firmly. 'Now put him down on the floor. He can go and say hello to Pegasus.'

Zara did so and we all watched as the kitten leapt around the kitchen on its tiny legs before venturing towards the range, in front of which Pegasus lay fast asleep on a blanket.

'That is adorable,' said Zara, as the kitten sniffed around the calf, then purred as he nestled against the soft white fur. 'One day, my home will be like this,' she declared, turning to Lochie, who smiled devotedly at her.

*She looks so pretty tonight*, I thought, *simply because she's sparkling with happiness.*

'So the Laird's moving up here permanently?' Fiona questioned Zara.

'Yes, and hopefully, so am I, as long as Dad doesn't change his mind. We're going to visit the North Highland College in Dornoch next week to see what courses they offer – I'm really interested in Wildlife Management. If I go it means I can live up at Kinnaird with Dad.'

'It's right that the Laird is coming up here to take the helm,' Hamish nodded in agreement.

'What about your mum, Zara?' Fiona asked. 'Is she happy about the move?'

'Mum and Dad are getting a divorce.' Zara shrugged. 'So it's none of her business.'

'Right. And you're okay about that?'

'God, yes! I should start a campaign for kids like me who live in an unhappy marriage. Trust me, parents should never stay together for us. Anyway, the great news is that I'll be seventeen in a few days' time, and I've already applied for my driving test. If I pass, I can drive up and help take care of Pegasus when you're at work, Fiona. Until then, you'll bring me up here, won't you, Lochie?' she asked shyly, and I knew from the look in her eyes that Johnnie North was totally forgotten.

'Any time,' he replied eagerly.

'Now, the most important thing is that none of us ever mention a word about our newborn.' Fiona indicated Pegasus, who had woken up and was watching the kitten as he danced around the kitchen, chasing imaginary flies.

'We can work out a rota for his feeding,' I suggested. 'It's not fair on you doing the night shift, Fiona.'

'I'll do those,' Lochie offered.

'And I'll come up during the day when you're at work,' I chipped in. 'Are you sure you don't mind having him up here?'

'Not at all.' Hamish cocked his head at the calf. 'He can go out on the fell at the back with the lambs when they're born. They're the same colour,' he added with a grin.

'It's his future that I'm worried about,' I said. 'He should be re-wilded as soon as possible, but we're signing his death sentence if we do that. Look what happened to his daddy.'

'I know, Tiggy, and it may be that he needs to stay here for the rest of his life,' said Fiona. 'We'll just have to play it by ear. We have plenty of woodland nearby – we could maybe introduce some other calves so he isn't alone, and Cal could help Lochie fence it off . . .'

'Cal could fence what off?'

We all jumped as the back door opened, and I saw Cal's bulk filling the frame.

'Evening all.' He stepped inside, closely followed by Charlie. 'Me and the Laird were feelin' left out down at Kinnaird, so we came up tae join the party.'

'Come in out of the cold, please, the pair of you,' urged Fiona.

'Sorry to arrive unannounced, but Cal has told me about the new arrival. I wanted to see him,' said Charlie. 'Where is he?'

'Welcome, Laird.' Hamish stood up to shake his hand. 'It's an honour tae have yae here.'

'He's down here, Dad,' said Zara, sweeping up the ginger kitten before he escaped out of the open door. 'His name is the same as his dad's: Pegasus. He's a miracle.'

Charlie walked over to the range and bent down towards the calf, who I could see was wriggling about trying to work out how to stand.

'Hello,' Charlie whispered as he put out a hand to stroke him. Pegasus immediately nuzzled it and I knew he was hungry.

'I'll warm a bottle on the range,' I said as I stood up.

'Here's a saucepan, Tiggy,' Fiona offered, bringing one down from the rack and handing it to me. 'Right, kids, can you clear the table?'

'And I'm going tae open something special tae celebrate,' announced Hamish, leaving the kitchen.

'He *is* a miracle,' Charlie breathed, looking up at me. 'Is he healthy?'

'Very,' Fiona told him, 'and from what you said, Cal, that's thanks to Tiggy and her magic hands. I might have to poach her from you sometimes and have her work with me. Look, he's almost up!' Fiona pointed. 'Can you help him, Charlie?'

We all watched as Charlie put his hands gently round the calf's middle and lifted him to standing.

His legs collapsed the first time, but finally, on the fourth try, they understood what they needed to do and bore his weight. And Pegasus's son took his first tentative steps, before collapsing onto Charlie's knee.

We all cheered as Hamish arrived back in the kitchen with a bottle of whisky.

'Goodness, are you really opening that after all these years?' Fiona teased him.

'Aye, that I am.' Hamish opened the seal and poured the liquid into seven glasses, which he handed round. 'The old Laird gave me this years ago after I'd helped him wi' digging the newborn lambs out after a snowfall . . . I'd say this was the perfect moment tae drink it. Tae new beginnings.'

'New beginnings,' we toasted.

After knocking back his whisky, Cal reached into his coat pocket and pulled out a round object, about the size of a large grapefruit, wrapped in muslin.

'What on earth is that?' I asked, as he thumped it down on the table and all eyes in the room fell upon it.

''Tis a haggis, lassie. But I reckon I'll be needin' another dram before what comes next.' He held out his glass to Hamish, who obliged with a hefty refill.

'I once promised Tig that if a white stag was seen on the estate, I'd run around naked wi' only a haggis coverin' my bits 'n' pieces. An' I'm nothing if not a man o' my word,' he explained for the benefit of the assembled company as his stout fingers moved to his shirt buttons.

'Cal, I don't think that's a promise I'm going to hold you to.' I stopped him as we all laughed. 'Besides, I think you've already done enough for both Pegasuses, don't you?'

'I think this one is hungry.' Charlie indicated the calf, who was squirming in his lap, searching for milk.

'Take him next door into the sitting room where it's quieter,' Fiona suggested as I removed the bottle from the hot water and tested it on the back of my hand.

'Thanks.' I made to take Pegasus from Charlie.

'I'll carry him through,' he said. When we reached the sitting room, he settled Pegasus on my knee and the calf suckled eagerly on the teat.

Charlie stood watching me; I saw his eyes were misty, as were mine.

'Did you see Beryl?' I asked, breaking the silence.

'Yes. After a lot of tears and endless apologies on her part, I managed to persuade her to come back.'

'Thank goodness! She's the only one who knows how to work those ovens.'

'Actually, we both agreed they should go and we'd get a range put back in.' Charlie raised an eyebrow. 'Ditto those industrial lights, and that monolith of a centre unit. I kept the original pine table in the barn, so that's being reinstated too.'

'The kitchen's definitely the heart of a house, as we've just seen,' I agreed.

'I also had a word with Cal on our way up here. I was thinking about it before Fraser appeared on the scene at Christmas, but after all Cal's family's years of service, it's about time he had his own patch of land. So as a wedding present, I've told Cal I'm giving him and Caitlin a hundred acres, just near the entrance to the estate. There's an old bothy on it – that's a cottage to you, Tiggy – which has been empty for years. With a bit of work, it could make him and Caitlin a decent home.'

'That's so lovely of you, Charlie, I bet he was thrilled.'

'He was, but it's nothing less than he deserves. I also told him I was going to sell off some land to my neighbours, which, as well as funding the divorce, will pay for some extra staff, plus a new "Beryl".'

'Wow, you have been busy,' I said with a smile.

'Yes, I needed to be, to stop me thinking about what you've been thinking.'

'Right.'

'I mean, if you need some more time . . .'

'I don't, Charlie.'

'So, will you stay, or are you running away to Africa and your lions and tigers?'

I looked down at Pegasus, who had guzzled the whole bottle and was dozing contentedly. Then up at Charlie.

'I think I have enough wildlife to conserve here, don't you?'

'You mean, you'll stay?'

'Yes. Though I'd like to see those lions and tigers one day.'

'So would I.' He reached out his hand to me for the second time that day and I took it without hesitation.

I watched as he kissed it tenderly, then he moved his lips to mine.

'I'm so happy, Tiggy. Truly.'

'I am too.'

'It won't be easy—'

'I know.'

'But together, we can at least give it a shot though, can't we? I mean, the estate, the animals, us . . . ?'

'Yes.'

'Right then.' Charlie stood and pulled me and Pegasus gently to standing. 'Time to go.'

'Where?'

'Back to Kinnaird of course,' he smiled. 'We've got work to do.'

# Electra

## New York

### February 2008

## The Sun

# 39

I looked up and saw snow was falling and settling on the windowsill above me. Maybe that would help dull the sound of the continuous Manhattan traffic below my apartment. Even though the rental guy had said it had triple glazing, nothing stopped the humming of stationary engines, interspersed by the beeping horns of irritable drivers thirty-three floors beneath me.

'Shut the hell up!' I moaned, realising I was focusing on the sound, which only made it louder. I took a deep swig from the bottle, but knowing the vodka wouldn't help drown it out, I dragged myself up from the kitchen floor and staggered into the living room to turn on some music. 'Born in the USA' blared out of the hidden speakers.

'Hey, I'm happy you know where you were born, mister,' I shouted to Bruce, as me and the vodka bottle swayed across the room to the music. ''Cos I sure don't!'

Despite the music playing at full volume, the horns were still blaring in my ears, and I double-checked the china bowl I hid my special medicine in. Apart from a light dusting around the edges, which, with a moistened finger, I wiped onto my gums, there was nothing left.

Ted, my supplier, had been meant to arrive an hour ago with some more, but so far he was a no-show. It would be easy to take the elevator down to the lobby and slip Bill, the concierge, a hundred-dollar note like I knew other residents of my building did. And as if by magic, ten minutes later, a 'package' would arrive for me by hand at my apartment door. But however desperate I was, I knew I couldn't take the risk. One whisper leaked to the press and I'd be headlines all over the world. Especially as I was brand ambassador for a 'natural' cosmetic product they were marketing to teen girls, and had recently done a feature for *Elle* outlining my 'healthy' living regime.

'Natural? Yeah, right . . .' I muttered as I wobbled towards the phone to check with Bill that my visitor hadn't arrived yet. At the shoot, the make-up artist had told me it was all a con – that the basic ingredients might be sourced from nature, but the chemicals they had to use to replace the animal fats in the lipstick made the product as toxic as hell.

'Why is everything a lie?' I shook my head piteously, the swaying motion comforting me and making me dizzy at the same time, so I sank onto the floor where I was. 'Life is just a pile of them. Even love . . .'

I cried then, big wet tears plopping out of my eyes and dripping from my nose, wondering for the thousandth time why Mitch had dumped me only three weeks after asking me to marry him. Okay, fine, the proposal had been in bed, but I'd believed him. I'd said yes, 'YES!' When he'd left for LA the next day, I'd even been stupid enough to lie in bed thinking which designer I'd ask to make my dress, and of possible venues. I fancied Italy – some big palazzo in the Tuscan hills. Then . . . silence. Even though I'd texted and emailed him, left voicemails asking him to call me, I'd heard nothing. Okay, so he was playing the Hollywood Bowl, but, Christ, could he not spare the time to call his fiancée . . . ?!

I'd finally got a message – a message! – from him, saying it was probably time to cool things off, 'baby', adding that we were both busy people and now was not the time to get serious. Maybe in a few months, when his world tour was over . . .

'Jesus!' I screamed, hurling the empty vodka bottle across the room. 'Why does everybody let me down?'

Maybe he thought that 'cos I was Electra, I could just stroll out onto the sidewalk and hook up with another guy. In theory, I could, but that so wasn't the point. I'd fallen in love with him, like, head over heels in love. He could not have been more perfect for me; fifteen years older but super-fit and a global rock superstar, used to being in the spotlight. He was past partying, preferring to hang out at his beach house in Malibu. He could even cook – liked to cook – didn't do alcohol or drugs, and was a real good influence on me. I'd loved his calmness and no-nonsense approach – I was bored with getting away with murder. I'd even cut down my own chemical intake and not even missed it, and had decided I was prepared to move to California to be with him.

'He looked after me,' I moaned, 'knew how to handle me . . .'

*Yeah, he was a father figure, a replacement for Pa Salt . . .*

'Shut up!' I told the voice in my head, because in all sorts of ways, that idea was messed up. Besides, I hadn't felt a thing when Pa had died – like, nothing. Given my sisters were all over the place with grief, I'd felt like a freak. I'd tried vodka, which had made me cry like it always did, but it hadn't succeeded in generating any real emotion. All that was there when I thought about his passing was a numbness.

'And maybe some guilt,' I whispered as I stood shakily upright and pulled another full vodka bottle out of the kitchen cupboard, checking the time and seeing it was past eleven now.

Picking up my mobile I dialled Ted again, but as I did so, the concierge rang to say my 'guest' was here.

'Send him right up,' I said, relief pouring through me. I went to find the dollars I'd need to greet him at the door to do the swap and waited impatiently in the apartment lobby.

'Hi, doll,' said a guy who wasn't Ted as I opened the door. 'Ted sent me. He's busy tonight.'

I was pissed that Ted had sent someone else who may or may not be trustworthy, but I was so desperate I wasn't gonna tell him he'd got the wrong apartment.

'Thanks. Bye.' I was just about to shut the door in his face when he put his hand out to stop it.

'Hey, you havin' trouble sleepin'?' he asked me.

'Sometimes, why?'

'I just got some great prescription tabs that will knock you out and send you off with the angels.'

Now this was interesting. My doctor here in New York had refused to prescribe any more Valium or sleeping tablets. I'd been using vodka as a substitute, especially since Mitch had dumped me.

'What are they?'

'Got them from a qualified doc. They're the real deal.' He whipped the packet from his pocket and showed me.

'How much?'

He named the price for a blister pack of Temazepam. It

was outrageous, but who cared? The one thing I had was money to burn.

When he'd left, I went into the living room and, my fingers shaking in anticipation, did a line.

'Never take drugs or ride motorbikes,' had been Pa Salt's mantra when we were young. I'd done both and plenty more I knew he wouldn't approve of since. Just as I was collapsing on the sofa feeling calmer, my cell phone rang. Out of instinct, I picked it up to see if it was Mitch, because maybe he'd changed his mind and was begging me to come back . . .

It was Zed Eszu. I waited a bit until the cell phone told me I had a voicemail, then listened to it.

'Hi, it's me. I'm back in town and wondered if you wanted to come to the ballet tomorrow night. I have a couple of tickets for Maria Kowroski in the premiere of *The Blue Neck-lace* . . .'

Even if it was the hottest ticket in town just now, I wasn't in the mood for two hours of bendy bodies and a gaggle of media outside asking me why I hadn't been at any of Mitch's sell-out concerts. I knew Zed used me to up his own media profile and, occasionally, it had suited me to go with him. He also happened to be very good in the sack – even though he wasn't my type, there was some kind of weird sexual alchemy between us, but our occasional sleepovers had stopped when I'd met Mitch last summer.

That at least had pleased Pa, who had called me up when a photo of me and Zed at the Met Ball had hit the front pages last year.

'Electra, I don't wish to interfere in your life, but, please, stay away from that man. He's . . . dangerous. Not what he seems. I—'

'Too right you shouldn't interfere,' I'd said, my hackles rising as they did every time Pa had tried to tell me I should do this or that. My sisters hung on every word he said, I thought he was a control freak.

Even though Zed, like the rest of the world, had known that me and Mitch were together, he had still persisted with his calls and I'd ignored them all. Up to now . . .

'Maybe I *should* go out tomorrow night with him,' I muttered as I did another line, thinking that the sleeping pills would knock me out later when I was coming down. 'Get my face on the front pages – that would show Mitch.'

I lit a cigarette, the hit from the coke taking hold and making me feel more like the kick-ass Electra I usually was. I turned the music up loud again, took another swig from the bottle and danced towards my walk-in wardrobe in the bedroom. Rummaging through the endless racks, I decided I had nothing stunning enough to wear. I'd call Amy, my PA, in the morning and get her to have Chanel bike me over something from their new season's collection – I was due on the runway in a month's time for their show in Paris.

Texting Zed back to say that yes, I could make it, I decided I would also call Imelda, my publicist, and have her alert the media to my appearance at the theatre tomorrow night. I hadn't been out for a while, even cancelling a couple of work assignments, unable to bear anyone mentioning Mitch's name to me. The thought of the life we could have had – that I'd dreamt of since the moment I'd met him – gone forever, had torn me apart. I had enjoyed the kick that he was even more famous than me, that he didn't need me to boost his profile – he'd had more famous models and actresses than he could notch up on the widest bedpost – I'd truly trusted that he wanted me for me.

I'd looked up to him . . . I'd loved him.

'Screw him! Nobody dumps Electra!' I shouted to my four tastefully painted beige walls bearing priceless canvas guests covered in bright-painted squiggles, but which looked to me as though someone had puked all over them.

Feeling that awful sensation of a downer starting to seep into the pit of my stomach, I took off my top and sweatpants and walked into the living room naked to retrieve the Temazepam the guy had left me before the feeling spread further. I took two and washed them down with some vodka, then lay down on my bed.

'I just need to sleep now,' I begged the ceiling, something I hadn't done naturally since Mitch had said goodbye. I lay there, but the ceiling spun uncomfortably and closing my eyes only made it worse.

'Just get through tonight, and tomorrow you'll be back to yourself,' I whispered, feeling the onset of more tears. Why did nothing work on me any more? Two Temazepam plus the vodka should be enough to knock out a polar bear.

'Have you ever thought of rehab?' my therapist had asked last time I'd seen her. I hadn't replied, just stood up and walked out of her office, outraged at the suggestion. I'd fired her then and there via her receptionist. I knew no one except Mitch who was clean – coke and alcohol was how we all made it through . . .

I only just made it to the bathroom before I vomited, cursing the guy who had given me the Temazepam. It was obviously made of chalk dust and Christ knew what else and I should never have trusted him. After vomiting again, I must have passed out, 'cos I had a weird dream that Pa was there holding my hand and stroking my forehead.

'I'm here, my darling, Pa's here,' said his familiar voice, 'we're going to get you the help you need, I promise . . .'

'Yes, I need help,' I whimpered. 'Help me, Pa. I'm so alone . . .'

I slept again, feeling comforted, but then I was jolted awake by another bout of sickness. I didn't make it to the toilet bowl this time – I was just too exhausted to reach it. I tried to sit up, looking around for Pa, but I was all alone again, and I knew he had gone.

# Bibliography

Munya Andrews, *The Seven Sisters of the Pleiades* (Spinifex Press, 2004)

Antony Beevor, *The Battle for Spain: The Spanish Civil War 1936–1939* (Phoenix, 2006)

Wayne H. Bowen, *Spain during World War II* (University of Missouri Press, 2006)

Anne Dublin, *Dynamic Women Dancers* (Second Story Press, 2009)

John Fletcher, *Deer* (Reaktion Books, 2014)

Bernard Leblon, *Gypsies and Flamenco,* trans. by Sinéad né Shuinéar (University of Hertfordshire Press, 1994)

Patrick Jasper Lee, *We Borrow the Earth: An Intimate Portrait of the Gypsy Folk Tradition and Culture* (Ravine Press, 2000)

Paul Preston, *The Spanish Holocaust: Inquisition and Extermination in Twentieth-Century Spain* (HarperPress, 2013)

Paco Sevilla, *Queen of the Gypsies: The Life and Legend of Carmen Amaya* (Sevilla Press, 1999)

Rita Vega de Triana, *Antonio Triana and the Spanish Dance: A Personal Recollection* (Harwood Academic Publishers, 1993)

G. Kenneth Whitehead, *Deer and their Management in the Deer Parks of Great Britain and Ireland* (Country Life Limited, 1950)

# Author's Note

Whenever I sit down to write the acknowledgements for a book, it's a few months after I have finished the manuscript and I always feel as if the story simply wrote itself. Maybe it's a little like childbirth – for me, anyway, the pain of the actual process has all been forgotten due to the wonderful wholeness of the end product, be it babies or books. But of course, each book is nine months of very hard graft, partly due to the enormous amount of research needed to make it as factually correct as possible. However, each book is also a work of fiction based on fact, and very occasionally I have to use artistic license to fit around the plot. For example, in *The Moon Sister*, the 2008 full moon Tiggy sees when she ventures into the forest with Angelina actually happened three weeks later in real life. And it's important to remember it *is* 2008 when Tiggy's story takes place; so many huge changes occurred over the following ten years due to technological advances, and especially this year, for women's equality.

Researching the rich *gitano* culture was also a challenge, due to the fact that very little is actually written down; the many mysteries of it are spread by word of mouth rather than the pen, and I am indebted to Oscar González for guiding me round Sacromonte. Also, to Sarah Douglas, Innes MacNeill, Ryan Munro and Julie Rutherford who made me so welcome at the extraordinary Alladale Estate in Scotland, on which Kinnaird is based. Both research trips were equally amazing and enlightening; as with all the sisters' stories, I feel I have personally trodden the paths Tiggy takes in the story. Thanks also to Dr Mark Westwood and Rebecca Westwood, a Reiki Master, whose wonderful holistic veterinary practice provided inspiration for parts of Tiggy's story.

The past year, due to ill health, has been my most challenging yet, and this book could not have been written without the back-up of my incredible team, both editorially and domestically: Ella Micheler, my research assistant, and Susan Moss, my copy-editor and best friend forever, have worked above and beyond to get this book out on time to the publishers. Olivia Riley, who coordinates all things admin, and Jacquelyn Heslop, have also been there for me personally and professionally and I am forever grateful for all their love and support.

My publishers around the world, particularly Jeremy Trevathan, Claudia Negele, Georg Reuchlein, Nana Vaz de Castro and Annalisa Lottini, who, apart from being fantastic publishers, have offered me friendship and belief in myself, as both a writer and a human being. My mother, Janet, my sister, Georgia, also Tracy Allebach-Dugan, Thila Bartolomru, Fernando Mercadante, Loen Fragoso, Julia Brahm, Bibi Marino, Tracy Blackwell, Stefano Guisler, Kathleen Doonan, Cathal Dineen, Tracy Rees, MJ Rose, Dan Booker, Ricky Burns, Juliette Hohnen and Tarquin Gorst – you have all been there for me in so many different ways.

To all the staff of The Royal Marsden Hospital, where I

have spent much of the past year, and where parts of this book were written, particularly Asif Chaudry and his team, John Williams and his lovely girls, Joyce Twene-Dove and all the nurses who have cared for me so brilliantly. Believe it or not, I miss you all!

Finally, to my husband and agent, Stephen, and my children, Harry, Isabella, Leonora and Kit. We have all been on a frightening and eventful journey this year and each and every one of you has been there to give me the courage and strength to get through. I am so proud of you all and I honestly don't know what I would do without you.

And to all my fantastic readers; if I have learnt one thing from the past year, it is that the moment *is* truly all we have. Try, if you can, to relish it, in whatever circumstances you find yourself, and never give up hope – it is the fundamental flame that keeps us human beings alive.

Lucinda Riley
June 2018

To discover the inspiration behind the series, including Greek mythology, the Pleiades star cluster and armillary spheres, please see Lucinda's website http://lucindariley.co.uk/.

Also on the website is information on the real stories, places and people featured in this book: Alladale, a Highland estate; Carmen Amaya; The Caves of Sacromonte; Spanish gypsies and flamenco; and white stags.